End of Empire
M'TK Sewer Rat
Birth of Nation

Delinda McCann

ISBN: 978-1-938586-84-2 Paperback
ISBN: 978-1-938586-85-9 Kindle

M'TK SEWER RAT

END OF EMPIRE

BOOK ONE

Delinda McCann

M'TK SEWER RAT

BIRTH OF NATION

BOOK TWO

Delinda McCann

All characters appearing in this work are fictitious. Any resemblance to real persons, living or dead, is purely coincidental.

Cover and Graphic Design by Writers Cramp Publishing

PLAYERS

Jake Jaconovich, The M'TK Sewer Rat

Leah – Jake's wife. A woman from the north who grew up very poor

Mama – Jake's mama. Mary Anne Spencer Jaconovich

Papa – Jake's papa. Jacob Jaconovich

Uncle John – **John D'NO**. Mama's great uncle, head of the D'NO family

Aunt Luella – Uncle John's wife

Cousin John – Jake's cousin

Cousin Petral - Jake's cousin

Cousin Nicki - Jake's cousin

Cousin Micki - Jake's cousin – younger than Jake, John, Nicki and Petral

Cousin Margaret – Jake's cousin and Micki's older sister.

Lars M'TG – Margaret's husband

Mr. Wu – Jake's first employer and martial arts teacher – crime boss

Mr. Apkouta – Papa's friend, honest man and champion of the people

Mr. Philippe Rouseff – Jake's mentor, owner of the railroads and shopping centers, and head of business for one of the most powerful southern families, enemy of the Vanderholms and Fortenacs, friends with Papa

Rosalie Rouseff – Philippe Rouseff's wife, friend of Mama

Fiona – Jake's first girlfriend

Andrew Corbain– Jake's best friend from college

Johan Puloski– Jake's college roommate, a music major

Nickoli – Another roommate

Hab Vanderholm – Jake's classmate, first president under the first constitution.

Professor Ingleman – Teaches procedural law at the university and mentors students

Leon Fortenac – Emperor's cousin and an evil person

Judge Gannon – An honest judge living in the capital

Judge Stimson - An elderly honest judge living in Mercid near Jake's city

Leah – Jake's wife, a woman from the north who grew up very poor

Young Jacob Jaconovich – Jake's son

Elizabeth Jaconovich – Jake's daughter

Mary Ann Margaret Jaconovich – Jake's youngest daughter

Mr. and Mrs. Chang – parents of a young girl and Jake's hired help

Christian Van Gelen – Jake's first friend in the prosecutor's office

Allison – Office manager in Jake's office, married to Christian

Leroy Spinoza-Carter – Attorney in the prosecutor's office

Jeffrey Farley – Attorney in the prosecutor's office and Jake's friend

Mrs. Shirley – Jake and Leah's housekeeper, she has two birth children and is fostering her sister's three orphaned children

Mr. LaBarge – a professional assassin

End of Empire

Birth of Nation

End of Empire

Chapter 1 Wulfton

In my earliest memories the sky was yellow. I could see a sliver of it from our window. I lived with my parents in the industrial area of the city. The borough was called Wulfton. Both of my parents worked in the factories. I stayed with an old woman while they worked. I called her Nanna, but I didn't think she was my real grandmother.

Nanna lived in a one-room apartment just like ours. Her apartment was one floor down near the toilet. We didn't have a toilet on our floor. Mama said that was good because she didn't like the smell. Several children stayed with Nanna.

I don't remember much about Wulfton because I was young. I remember when my sister was born. I stayed with Nanna the day she was born. Mama stayed home for some time because of the new baby.

I remember looking at my sister. She was bald and wrinkled. I said to Mama, "Not pretty. Will a man love her like Papa an you?"

Mama laughed, picked me up, and hugged me. "All babies look like that. She will grow up to be very beautiful and smart and she can have her pick of the men."

My sister didn't grow up. She got a cough. I got it too. I remember being sick. I remember staying on my pallet on the floor all day long. I remember when my sister stopped coughing. I remember how Mama cried. Most of all I remember my Papa. Big tears ran down his face and he blamed himself, using words I'd never heard before for not keeping his family safe.

"How do you keep us safe from the sickness?" Mama asked. "It is everywhere. You cannot see it but it is here, everywhere.

"You are wise." Papa looked around him. He looked out our window at the small piece of yellow sky. "Yes it is everywhere around us. We can smell it. It makes the sky yellow."

I knew I could ask Papa questions. "I thought you said God made the sky."

My Papa picked me up. I thought he was a big man. He was very strong. "Son, God made the sky blue. Men have turned it yellow. It is a sick sky. They have made even the sky sick."

I could tell he was angry, but he acted gentle with me and treated Mama like precious piece of glass.

Mama went back to work, but she did not laugh so much when Papa said silly things to her. Once he brought her flowers.

She smiled then. "I am foolish to cry so long over what I don't have. I have my son and a husband who loves me. Maybe my husband loves me enough to give me another baby."

I didn't understand this conversation, but I recognized something between Papa and Mama that shut me out. I knew they loved each other. I think, by watching my parents, I learned that the love between a man and a woman is God's greatest gift. I learned a great deal about that love that year.

I remember Mama giggling when she said she was too big for her dress. I asked. "Did you eat too much food?"

Papa laughed.

"No, I love your Papa that is why I am too big for my clothes, but I will get small again."

Mama did get small again. She got very small. I remember her crying and crying.

I remember Papa swearing again. "I vow that we will move out of this place of death. I will write a letter to your uncle. We will go to the coast although I do not know how to fish. As soon as you are well enough, we will go."

I remember Mama and Papa writing the letter. For the letter Papa needed to go to a store and buy paper, and a pencil, and a stamp. These were new words for me. I wanted to touch the paper, but Mama said I must not get it dirty. Together Papa and Mama sat down at our table and used the pencil to write the letter to Mama's uncle telling him that Mama was very sick and they were coming to stay with him. Papa walked all the way to the M'TK railway station to learn when the train left, and when we would get to the coast.

Papa was good with reading and writing, but not so good with numbers. Mama had studied bookkeeping. She told Papa what day we would be to the coast. Papa brought home a piece of paper called the *Schedule of Fares*. They argued over how we would travel. Papa wanted the best for Mama. She said we did not need a private compartment. Papa's voice sounded stern when he answered. "We have that much money. You will need the quiet and the rest." Together they counted out the money for a private compartment.

The day came for us to leave the only home I knew. Papa woke me while it was still night. He wrapped all our belongings in my blanket and tied the blanket around his body and over his shoulder. He helped Mama down the stairs.

When we got to the street, we started walking with Mama holding my hand. We did not go more than a dozen steps before Papa stopped and took my hand from Mama. "Jake, hold on to me here. He wrapped my fingers around his belt. "Whatever happens, do not let go unless I tell you to."

I nodded. Papa seldom talked so stern to me. I felt a little insulted that he would think I might let go when he had told me to hold on to him. He then turned to Mama and picked her up in his arms.

"Come on son." We set off walking again.

I remember that trip. I know now that we walked five kilometers from Wulfton to the train station at M'TK. Papa carried Mama every step of the way. It seemed to me that Papa walked terribly fast and I needed almost to run to keep up. My legs burned and I wanted to cry. Every so often I would get so tired I fell behind a step. I could see Mama's face by the light of the street lamps on the corners. She had her eyes shut tight. Her mouth formed a thin white line. She looked pale, and sweat ran off of her face staining Papa's shirt. I quickened my steps again. I thought maybe death was coming for my Mama, and Papa was running away from it. I tried to run too.

It seemed to me that we walked a long way before Papa let me sit on a bench and rest. We sat at a place called *The Trolley Stop*. No trolleys came. It was too early for the trolley. My legs still hurt when Papa picked up Mama and started walking again. My neck and shoulder hurt from reaching up to hold Papa's belt. I wanted to sit down and cry. I was tired, but I was afraid to stop. Death might catch us.

When we got to the train station, Papa set Mama down so she could stand beside him. We looked around. For the first time in my life, I saw rich people. I knew they were different because they dressed funny. They wore shoes. Mama, Papa, and I wore sandals. Nanna wore sandals. Everybody I knew wore sandals.

The men at the station looked all stuffed into matching coats and pants. I saw a woman who wore a dress with flowers on it. "Look Mama! Look at the pretty woman with flowers."

Mama grabbed my hand and whispered. "Jake honey, do not point. Yes, I see her dress is very pretty."

The woman turned to us and smiled. "Your son is a charmer. He could grow up to be an important man. Too bad you are northerners." She turned her back. I decided I didn't like her even if she smiled at us.

Papa and Mama looked around us. Papa put his hand in the middle of Mama's back and told her, "Look, there is an empty bench. You can sit down."

"Only the rich are sitting. What if I'm asked to leave?"

Papa's voice took on his stern tone. "Tell anybody who troubles you that your are paying full fare for a private compartment and you will sit."

Mama grabbed Papa's sleeve and almost whispered. "Sweetheart, listen to the station master. He just charged those people twice as much for a boxcar as is listed on the *Schedule of Fares*."

"What are the fares again?"

Mama whispered the fares to Papa.

He assured her. "I'll remember. I will watch and see how much he charges others." Papa winked at Mama and told her to sit down.

I stood by the bench beside Mama while Papa stood in line to buy our tickets. I could hear bits and pieces of the stationmaster's talk. I noticed some people did not know how to count money and just put all they had on the counter. I remembered the numbers that Mama told Papa. I knew the stationmaster did not charge everybody the same.

A rich family came into the station. They had three children with them. I saw a girl about my age and smiled at her. She smiled back. She stood close to me so I said, "Hello, you are very pretty."

"Jacob Jaconovich! Do not talk to everyone you see." Mama sounded shocked and surprised.

People around us laughed. The little girl looked at me and smiled. She let go of her Mama's hand to come talk to me.

The lady in the flowered dress said, "Yup, that one is a charmer."

The pretty little girl asked, "How old are you? I'm five."

I didn't know what the question meant. I could clearly see there was only one of her and thought she was strange to be telling me she was five.

I tried for honesty. "I'm sorry I can't talk to you. Mama says I'm not supposed to talk to everybody I see." This produced more laughter from the adults who were listening to me.

Papa's polite voice caught my attention. "Please sir, you may go ahead of me." I wondered why Papa let the rich man ahead of him in line. I watched to see what Papa was doing. He was almost to the front of the line.

I whispered to her, "Mama can I watch Papa?"

"All right dear, but no talking."

The lady in the flowered dress commented. "Oh, I want to hear what comes out of his mouth next."

I went to stand by my Papa. I held onto his belt like he told me to earlier.

The rich man in front of us finished paying for his ticket and moved on. Papa stepped up to the ticket window. "Two adults, one child, private compartment." He put his money on the counter top.

"That is not enough."

"It is what the *Schedule of Fares* states for two adults and one child in a private compartment."

"It is not enough."

Papa leaned toward the ticket master and spoke quietly. I heard a sharp undertone in his speech. His voice grew quiet, but he was angry. "I've been standing in this line for twenty minutes. I've seen fifteen people pay for their tickets. I can tell you, and them, how much each person paid for their fare. I can tell you, and them, how much the *Schedule of Fares* says they should have paid." Papa was quiet then and looked at the man.

The stationmaster looked around. He licked his lips. He looked down at the counter. "Oh I didn't see that you had this many bills. They stuck together. That is correct." He handed Papa the tickets.

Papa took the tickets and carefully read them. "You did not fill in our compartment number."

"You can read."

Papa nodded.

The stationmaster took the tickets back and wrote a number on them.

Papa looked at him again.

The stationmaster stuttered a little. "You won't have any trouble. Those are good."

I remember how excited I felt to be on the train. I had never seen a train before. Now I was going to ride on one.

We did not have any trouble getting on the train and finding our compartment. Papa said we were near the rich man who was in line before us, so we followed him and his family. The pretty little girl kept smiling at me. I winked at her and she giggled.

Mama said to Papa. "He is your son. I can't do anything about that." Papa laughed and patted me on the head.

We entered our own little room on the train and Papa slid a wooden door with a window in it closed. Mama sat down and patted the seat across from her for me to sit. She explained. "Jake, you are four. The little girl wanted to know how old you are. You are four years old."

I asked Mama. "How old are you?"

"I am thirty-two."

"How old is Papa?"

"He is thirty-two also."

"Wow, that is a lot isn't it?"

My parents laughed. It was a good sound.

I had a seat all to myself where I could look out the window. The train left the station. I felt okay at first, but we started moving faster and faster and it scared me. Papa sat beside me on the soft, brown, velvet seat. He put his arm around me and explained how we were safe inside the car.

Mama's seat reclined almost like a bed. She went to sleep. Papa watched her more than the passing suburbs.

"Look, Papa. Look. The sky is blue." I'd seen a blue sky for the first time in my four years. I yawned.

I think I slept for several hours on the train to the coast. I woke up once and asked where we were.

Papa answered, "We're in the mountains."

"What are mountains?"

Mama was awake and sitting up. She smiled and said, "Jake, look out the window."

I saw steep hillsides across a ravine. I had to stare a long time before I could actually make out that we were on a steep hill with a river below us. More mountains were across the river from us. At one point the mountain across from us came really close. I thought it might just keep coming closer until the train ran into it.

Mama sounded excited as she looked out the window. "Look honey, there is a waterfall coming up."

We all looked out the window and watched the waterfall. Next we saw a lake. I thought my head might explode from all the new things we were seeing.

A lady came by selling food. Papa bought a sandwich and two oranges. He showed Mama and me how to peel and eat the oranges. Mama laughed when she bit into her orange and juice ran down her chin. We all giggled and laughed.

We arrived at the train station on the coast just at sunset. I almost threw up when I got my first smell of rotting fish. I heard someone calling names. Finally I heard one I recognized, "Jaconovich." I knew that was my Papa. Suddenly, a big man with a beard appeared beside us. He hugged Mama.

"Why are you hugging my Mama? Papa won't like that." Everybody laughed at my words.

"This is your boy then?" The big man picked me up and swung me onto his shoulders. "You may call me Uncle John. I can hug your Mama because I knew her before your Papa took her away from us. Follow me. My boat is down here." Papa picked Mama up again and carried her to the boat.

I was excited when I asked, "Are we going on your boat?" A boat was another thing I'd heard about but I'd never seen one.

Papa lifted Mama over the side of the boat that sat rocking on the water beside us. "It's awful dark. Is it safe to travel by water after dark?"

Uncle John swung me down off of his shoulders and into the boat. He assured Papa, "I know this coast. We are safer now than in the daylight."

I looked around me. The back of the boat was full of rough brown nets. Looking forward I could see the boat had a downstairs and an upstairs. I was amazed. "Wow, this is as big as a train car."

Mama started downstairs and said, "Jake, come below with me."

Uncle John winked at Mama and said, "I'll need Jake's help on the bridge to drive the boat."

I didn't believe that he would let me drive, but he did after we got out into the open ocean. I liked the motion of the boat. I was surprised when Papa started throwing up over the side.

Uncle John laughed and promised he would get used to it. I don't think Papa ever got used to the motion of a boat.

I fell asleep again on our way to Uncle John's house. When I woke up, I found myself in a room all by myself. I wondered where Papa and Mama were. I went looking for Mama in the most fantastic place I had ever been. Halls ran in all directions. I found stairs everywhere. I found a round window with a little seat under it at the end of one hall. I climbed up on the window seat and looked out at a mountainside. I opened a door and found the toilet. The bathroom had a round window in the wall. Finally, from a hall window I saw my Mama sitting outside. I called her.

She came and hugged me. "There you are my little sleepyhead. It is almost time for lunch." She kissed me on the top of my head.

By the end of the day, I'd met my great-aunt Luella and Mama's cousins and even more cousins. I learned that some of my cousins went to school. "What is school?"

One of the cousins a little older than me explained in disgusted tones. "That is where we learn to read and write and do math."

"Oh. I want to learn that too. Papa and Mama can read. Papa told the man at the train station what was what. The ticket man didn't think Papa knew how to read and count money, but he did. The ticket man couldn't cheat my papa 'cause Papa can read."

My cousins were a little surprised at what I didn't know about living in the country. They started calling me a baby.

I got tired of being teased for what I didn't know. I finally asked a few questions that put a stop to the teasing. "Have you been to the city? Have you been in a candy store?" They did not know what a candy store was.

I explained. "The candy store was downstairs on the street. They sell sweet things. Papa took me in. He bought Mama a whole, big box of chocolate candies. He gave me a penny. I got to choose what I wanted. I got a piece of black licorice, a piece of candied orange and a piece of chocolate with a nut in the center. Sometimes Nanna took us all downstairs and each of us got one piece of sugared ginger."

They didn't believe me.

I went to Mama. "Mama they don't believe me that the candy store was downstairs."

Mama called my cousins to her and asked them what happened. They wailed about my story about the candy store. She smiled. "Yes it is as Jake says. We lived over the candy store. There are many wonderful things in the city. There are many wonderful things in the country, too. Each place is different. It is important for you all to learn about different things and respect what is different."

I eventually learned to get along with my cousins. My ignorance about reading and writing was still a marvel to them.

I finally got frustrated with being teased for something I couldn't help. I nearly cried when I burst out, "Well, if somebody would teach me, I might know how to read. It all looks pretty mixed up to me now." That is when Mama started teaching me to read and to count.

I also learned about seasons. We did not have seasons in Wulfton. We had days when I could go for a walk and times when Nanna said the weather was too nasty. In the country we had seasons. In the spring, I was given the job of weeding the garden. I didn't want to weed the garden. I wanted to go to school and to read.

My aunt explained. "Your Mama needs to eat fresh vegetables if she is going to get well. The vegetables, she needs, will not grow if they have weeds."

"I better learn to weed then." I wanted to act grown up and help Mama and Papa, but I also wanted to learn. I'd seen in the train station that people who did not know how to read got cheated. Finally, I solved my dilemma by learning to count weeds. Every morning I went out and weeded in the garden. My aunt hoed them up and I picked them out so they would not take root and need to be hoed tomorrow. My aunt helped me with my numbers as I carefully made my weeds into little piles and counted my piles.

One night at dinner, Aunt Luella made an announcement. "I talked to the first form teacher about Jake. I think he should go to school."

"But he's just a baby." Mama picked me up and hugged me.

"Mama, I want to go to school."

Uncle John intervened. "Let him try. If he can keep up with the other students then I guess he is old enough for school."

The next morning I carried my lunch in a basket, and went down to the dock to take the boat into the village for school. I was extremely thankful that I did not have to weed the garden that day. When I got home, the weeds were lying on the ground waiting for me to pick them up and compost them.

We ate well at my uncle's house. We had fish every night. Sometimes we had shrimp and squid. Mama got well. Papa did not get used to the motion of the boat. He could barely eat. Often my uncle sent Papa out into the cove to tend the shrimp traps and gather mussels. Sometimes he took me.

The cove was surrounded on three sides by mountains. The water was often a mysterious dark green. It had a narrow opening into the ocean that was not very big. A dangerous shoal guarded the opening. I thought the dangerous shoal must be some sort of sea monster that grabbed boats and ate bad people. I never saw the dangerous shoal, but sometimes the water rippled over the spot where it lived. Uncle John did not take the boats out when the dangerous shoal churned the water.

I liked helping Papa with the shrimp traps. I especially liked pulling mussels off of the sheer rock wall at one end of the cove. Papa seemed eager to catch shrimp and pick mussels. The rowboat in the cove did not make him as sick as the big boat with its diesel engines, but Papa was not well.

I had started the second form at school when Papa said he was going back to the city to look for work.

Mama sounded anxious. "Are we going back to Wulfton?"

"No, it is unhealthy. We will live somewhere else even if I have to walk five kilometers each way to work."

Papa did get a job in the city. He came back and told Mama. "We will live in M'TK."

"Oh no!"

"It is not that bad. The sky is blue. Plants grow in the vacant lots. There are even trees and I found us an apartment with a bedroom, and a closet where Jake can have his own bed." Papa sounded happy.

I didn't want to move back to the city. "Can I still go to school in the city?"

Mama's Aunt Luella comforted me. "Yes, your teacher here will tell the teachers there about how well you do. You can go to school." I also knew that there would not be a garden to weed.

"Will we be able to get Mama the kind of food she needs?"

Mama laughed. "I am well now."

Papa sounded proud. "We will have more money than we did in Wulfton. I have found a good job at a warehouse that is owned by the railroad."

We left my uncle's house to go into the village to catch the train before the sun came up. I stayed awake on the return trip to the city. This time, I knew the names of the things we passed.

Chapter 2 M'TK Apartment

Papa had leased an apartment on the second floor of a tenement that faced the boardwalk running beside the railroad tracks. The toilets were located on the first and third floors. We had running water in the hall, a hotplate in the kitchen and even a small refrigerator. Mama declared the place a palace.

Our window faced the railroad. We could watch the trains going past as they shook our whole building. Mama and Papa's bedroom didn't have a window, but I could see the sky through the cracks in the outside wall. Sunlight filtered in through the cracks causing the dust motes dance like fire-fairies.

My bedroom had once been a hallway. It was just over a meter wide. Papa found lumber from old packing crates at the dump and made me a bed by running boards crosswise of the hall about four feet off of the floor. Two pieces of plywood over the slats completed my bed. It was about one and a half meters long. Our apartment was, as Mama said, a palace. I had my own space that I didn't share with anybody, and I didn't have to weed anything to get it.

Our four-story tenement was tucked between two identical buildings. The steep stairway ran from the front of the building straight to the back of the building. Each floor had a landing and a narrow hall with a rail beside the stair well. Neighbors met in the halls and talked across the stairwell. Children sat on the landings and played games.

M'TK, even at that time, was the worst of the slums. The railroad formed one side of the borough. The northern side of the borough merged into scrubland that bordered the river. Gangs and homeless people lived in the scrub. The dump sat across the tracks from the borough.

Crime happened everywhere. I soon learned two rival gangs fought for control of the area. The smell of drunkenness scented the air and I soon became aware of children my own age, who were too drunk to play with me. I always needed to step over or detour around people who were sleeping off a drunken stupor on the boardwalk. I found the human smells worse than the smell of rotting fish. Rats ran everywhere.

The crime, drinking and rats were negative features of M'TK. The dump was a paradise. You could find most anything you wanted at the M'TK dump. My parents immediately pronounced the dump off limits when I asked if all dead people were taken there. "I saw three of them today, but I found a box of oranges that are mostly good."

Mama found a job doing bookkeeping for the railroad. Papa worked in the warehouse. On his day off he would sometimes go to the dump and bring home broken lamps, or burned out appliances and spend the day repairing them. He would sell these items to a shop on his way to work the next day.

Mama hated the rats. Rats ran everywhere. If we left a piece of food out for even a minute, a rat would be on it. There was no way to keep them out of the apartment.

On my way to school one morning, I met up with another boy who was walking the same direction. He was carrying a box that jumped and wiggled in his hand.

Curious I asked, "What is in the box?"

"A rat."

"What are you going to do with him?"

"Sell him to Mr. Wu for his restaurant. He pays me a penny."

"Where is Mr. Wu's restaurant?" I followed my new friend to Mr. Wu's and watched the negotiation.

I stood just inside the screen door and looked around the dark kitchen. I saw a big stove. Vegetables were spread across a huge table in the middle of the kitchen. The outside wall was covered in shelves containing mysterious looking jars and bottles. I couldn't read the labels on the jars. To my left hung a bright red curtain across a doorway. I stared and stared at the gold dragons on the curtain.

Mr. Wu wore a business suit like the rich men wore. He was not nearly so big as my papa. His dark eyes seemed to peer into my soul when he looked at me. Something about him terrified me, but I felt safe at the same time--like the terror was around us, but he was calm and safe.

I summoned the courage to speak. "Mr. Wu, do you want more than one rat a day?"

"I'll take all of them I can get."

"May I bring you some in a week or so?"

He laughed and asked, "Why will it would take you so long to catch a rat in M'TK?" He laughed as if he thought he said something funny.

I smiled and laughed. Then I had to run to get to school on time.

I slid into my seat just as the whistle blew.

My teacher scowled. "Jake Jaconovich, why are you late?"

"I stopped to apply for a job." I felt quite proud of myself feeling that I sounded very grown up.

My teacher turned livid. "Jake Jaconovich, come here. I am not going to punish you for being late. Hold out your hand."

I knew what it meant when the teacher told a student to hold out their hand. I had never been punished in school before. I held out my hand.

She raised her ruler and brought it down, *slap*, across my hand. "This is for talking about a job at your age." She raised the ruler again and brought it down, *slap*, across my hand. "This is in case you ever think of quitting school before you finish university." Again the ruler went up and came down across my stinging hand. "This is so you will remember that you are supposed to stay in school. Do you understand?"

"Yes Ma'am." I didn't understand, but I thought I knew the right thing to say.

"What is it that you understand?"

I had to think about this one. "I understand that you want me to stay in school. I want to stay in school as long as I can."

She smiled at me then. "Good boy. You have potential. Stay in school. Stay away from alcohol. And, stay away from girls until you finish school."

She was a teacher so I figured she knew what she was talking about, but I didn't intend for my new job to interfere with school.

When I got home from school, I wrote a letter to Uncle John. I explained about the rats and Mr. Wu. I told him that I remembered his two broken shrimp traps. I figured if I put one inside the other they would work for catching rats. I didn't hear from Uncle John for days.

A week after I mailed my letter, I heard a commotion on the stairs that didn't sound like the usual noises of people fighting or being drunk or delirious. I went out and looked down the stairs. I smiled when I saw Uncle John carrying the shrimp traps. He also brought us fish for our dinner. Mama made a fish stew with rice.

Uncle John laughed all through dinner over my plan to sell rats to Mr. Wu.

He seemed to think it was very funny that the Chinese restaurant sold rat meat. I thought this was just country ignorance of city ways and politely laughed at his jokes. Mama declared that if I got rid of a few rats, she would be happy.

Papa leaned back in his chair and declared with great gravity, "Well, I guess that settles it son. If it will make your mama happy you may sell rats to Mr. Wu and the rich people will come and buy dinner from him."

My parents seemed to think this was very funny. Looking back, I doubt that any rich people bought food from Mr. Wu. I think most of his customers were middle class. I saw my teacher in his restaurant once. I saw some of the storeowners eating there.

The next day after school, I came straight home and set up my trap. Earlier, Mama told me that if I set it in the hall, the rats would run out of our apartment to get into the trap. I used some left over fish as bait. I waited five minutes or so and the trap was full. I had to knock a couple rats off of the outside. It was heavy when it was full, but I almost ran the six blocks up to Mr. Wu's restaurant to deliver them. I was out of breath. "Mr. Wu? Do you really want these?"

"What is that contraption?"

"What? Oh the trap. It is really two shrimp traps stuck together. Mama's uncle brought them to me yesterday. Where do you want them?" Mr. Wu stared at me for a long time before he answered. He poked the trap a couple times with his toe.

"Son, if I pay you for these rats, what are you going to do with the money?"

"I don't know. I could buy books or ride the train to visit Uncle John and my cousins." Then a memory flashed through my mind. "My Mama likes flowers. I once saw a woman with pretty flowers on her dress. What I want most is to buy my Mama a dress with flowers."

"The rats go into this tank." He showed me a large, glass, fish tank. Together we emptied the rats into the tank. He gave me twelve pennies.

"I think I have time to bring you more tonight. Do you want more?" He looked at me closely then nodded. When I came back with the next cage of rats, another man let me in and pointed to the tank. He gave me ten pennies.

I got home just as Mama was coming in. We walked up the stairs together. I started looking at rats as pennies. Mama still hated them.

I did not buy a dress for Mama first. My first purchase was a teddy bear. I thought it looked cute and cuddly and I'd never had such a toy, but was not the reason for my purchase. "Mama, I want to hide my money in the bear. Can you help fix him so I can get pennies in and out."

We spent the evening with Mama opening a seam, taking out some sawdust stuffing and making a fold at the seam so the money would not fall out easily.

Papa approved of my choice of hiding place. Because of the crime, everybody hid their money, what little they had. I knew my parents had several places they hid money. Nobody used a bank. Nobody had enough money to put into a bank.

I had been taking rats to Mr. Wu for about two weeks when Mrs. Wu came to the door to let me in. "You. Tomorrow when you come, you bring one dollar. Bring one dollar like I tell you." She looked so fierce and beautiful that I was afraid to disobey her.

The next day I took a dollar out of the bear and delivered my first load of rats to Mr. Wu. Again, Mrs. Wu met me. "Leave them here. You come with me. Did you bring your dollar?" I nodded, terrified. "Come."

I followed Mrs. Wu out to a car. "Get in."

I'd never been in a car before. I got into the car, wondering if I was about to end up in a barbeque at another of Mr. Wu's restaurants. Mrs. Wu got in and drove the car. I looked out the window trying not to stare at Mrs. Wu or at the clever things in the car. I recognized my school as we drove past. We stopped at a magnificent building.

"Get out."

I obeyed. Mrs. Wu got out. I followed her into the building.

Mrs. Wu walked briskly up to a tall desk. I was afraid not to follow her. Our footsteps sounded loud in the huge room. I couldn't believe my eyes. The huge room was filled with books. Row upon row of shelves full of books filled the big room. Mrs. Wu told the lady at the desk, "This is Jake Jaconovich. He wants to apply for a library card."

The woman behind the tall desk looked at me and gave us some cards to write on. Mrs. Wu helped me fill in the information. Our apartment didn't have an address.

Mrs. Wu told me to use the address for the restaurant. "Now if you do not return your books on time I will know, and I will come after you and those books."

I nodded. She took me over to a corner of the library and showed me the children's books. I could take home five books to read.

"Can I take home a book about flowers for my Mama?"

"You will have to put back one of your books."

I put back one book, planning to get it later. She helped me find a book on geraniums." Then, Mrs. Wu drove me all the way home to our apartment.

Mama and Papa worried a little when they saw the books. "Where did you get this many books?" Papa sounded stern.

"At the library." I explained the whole story.

"And they let you bring home all these books. Are you sure you are not supposed to read them there?"

"Yes, I took the books to the desk and showed the lady my card, and she stamped the book here to show when I have to bring it back." My parents looked at the return date." That night I sat and read one story out loud to my parents.

Papa leaned back in his chair and looked at me. "I don't think a duck could really do all those things in the story. What do you think this is really about?" Papa was very good at asking that question. Even after I became president, I would complain about this or that to Papa and he would say, "What do you think this is really about?"

My library card became one of our family's greatest treasures. Mama worked half days on Saturday. On Saturday afternoon, she and I would ride the trolley to the library and get new books. It was our time together. Sometimes, on Wednesdays I would return our books and get five new ones. I always got four for me and one for my parents. After I went to bed I would hear them reading out loud to each other.

Chapter 3 M'TK Slum Life

M'TK was not an easy place to grow up. I was six the first time I got beat up. As I crossed the alley, on my way to sell my rats to Mr. Wu, three big boys stopped me on the boardwalk beside the train tracks. "Give us your money."

"I don't have any money."

"Yes you do."

"No. I really don't."

"Give it to me now, or I'll kick your face in."

"I don't have any money." I started screaming my answer, hoping someone would come to help me, but in M'TK nobody would come. The biggest boy took a swing at me, and I ducked.

"Give us the money Mr. Wu gives you."

"I give my money to Mama. Mr. Wu hasn't given me any today. See, the cage is full of rats. I give him the rats and then he gives me the money."

"Bastard."

At this point, the biggest boy kicked me. I partially blocked the kick with my trap full of rats. While I was busy with the first boy, the second one hit me in the nose and broke my nose. I'd never felt such pain, and I couldn't get away. I started swinging my trap in an arc around me. The door flew open on the trap so as I swung it, angry rats flew out in every direction.

When the bigger boys started getting hit with scared rats, they ran away. I set my cage down and closed the door. I only had two rats left. I started crying with rage, and pain, and disappointment over my lost income.

Now, the citizens of M'TK showed their faces. They came out of doorways and shops laughing and clapping because I had chased off the bigger boys.

I ran to Wu's. The cook, who spoke only Chinese, opened the screen door for me. He started yelling in Chinese when he saw me. Both Mr. and Mrs. Wu were kind to me. Mr. Wu went across the street to get the Chinese doctor. Mrs. Wu put ice on my nose. Then she burned a stick under my nose and told me to breathe in. I could barely breathe.

The Chinese doctor stuffed my nose full of cotton then he straightened it and rubbed a cream on it. The cream made it stop hurting. In fact, for several hours I could not feel my nose at all. I told my story in bits and pieces to the adults. Mr. Wu took me home in his car. We got there just as Mama got home. Mr. Wu said he would come back later and talk to Mama after Papa came home.

Mama took me in and fussed over me. I didn't feel very well, so she let me go to my bed and read a book. I didn't eat much dinner because my nose was still packed with cotton, and my mouth would not work quite right. I went back to my bed to read some more.

Mr. and Mrs. Wu came at seven. I fell asleep shortly after they arrived. I stayed awake long enough to hear Mr. Wu tell Papa and Mama that I was a good boy, and he wanted to teach me how to keep myself safe. Papa said he didn't want any favors from anybody. I fell asleep while they were talking about classes for me and how much they would cost.

The next day when I took my rats to Mr. Wu's I noticed a Chinese man standing in the street a block away. After I passed him, he turned and followed me. I thought he might be one of Mr. Wu's men and was there to protect me. Nobody bothered me. After I delivered my second load of rats, the cook told me to go up the stairs behind the red curtain with the dragons on it. He said this in Chinese, but I had picked up enough of the language to know what he meant.

Upstairs at Wu's restaurant was the most wonderful place I'd ever seen, other than the library. It was a gym of sorts with mats on the floor and pictures of warriors on the wall. I found other students there. They were all Chinese boys--most of them were older than me.

Mr. Wu gave me a kimono, and the lessons began. Learning how to move my body was not as easy as learning to read. Some days I hated the exercises as much as I hated weeding.

Every night after I delivered my rats, I stayed and worked-out in Mr. Wu's gym. Sometimes we had fun. Mr. Wu and his friend had a competition going to see who could throw or knock the other down. I enjoyed watching them spar. On those days, other students and I watched as both men told us what to watch for and the names of their moves.

After I had been doing nothing but moving and exercising and watching for about three months, Mr. Wu told me to spar with another student. Nobody was more surprised than I was when I threw the other student within seconds. The next time we sparred, he threw me. I hit the mat hard enough that the wind was knocked out of me. Our third attempt was a draw.

Mr. Wu asked us what we learned from our exercise.

I told him, "I learned that if I do exactly as you told me, I can throw my opponent, but if he knows what I can do, it is not so easy.'

My opponent's answer confused me. "I learned that, just because he is little and not Chinese, he can still beat me."

Mr. Wu laughed and told my partner that he had learned a valuable lesson.

I learned more than self-defense in Mr. Wu's school. I learned self-discipline. I learned about racial prejudice. I learned to speak, read and write Chinese. Learning Chinese was easier than learning self-defense.

I did not like getting thrown or kicked about. I disliked the potential for hurting others almost as I much as I hated getting hurt.

Mr. Wu kept saying, "Jake you are holding back. Show him what you can do. Show him how he needs to protect himself." I had been studying only about six months when I learned that I could do what I needed to when the need arose.

One evening, I came home from Mr. Wu's a little later than usual. I hurried because I liked to get home when Mama did. I knew I was late and she would be in the apartment alone. When I entered the building, I heard sounds of a scuffle on the second floor. Suddenly, I heard Mama scream. I felt as if a bucket of ice water had poured over me. I knew nothing except that Mama screamed. I ran up the stairs as fast as my short legs allowed. A strange man stood there, holding Mama. In my mind I knew that the knife he held was my biggest problem., I could smell a combination of urine, unwashed body, and alcohol emanating from him. He looked greasy and dirty.

He turned when I yelled. He sneered in the face of my outrage. "What? Who are you?"

I called him names that I heard on the street, a butt-fucker, ball-less, cock-less, a coward, a little girl. I didn't know what the all the names meant. I knew they were very bad.

"Shut up brat and go away. Can't you see I'm having fun?"

I knew we were in serious trouble. "You don't have enough cock to have fun. No woman wants you. That is why you have to use a knife. I suppose you pick on little boys too?" I wasn't sure he heard me over my mother's screams.

"Jake no! Run away!" Mama cried and tried to hold the knife away from her throat. She writhed back and forth to twist out of his grasp.

He leered down her neckline.

"You like little boys too? Coward." I watched his face. His pupils dilated and he squinted. I'd found the word that got to him. I discovered power in that word. Something in my mind knew I could overpower him with one word. "Coward. Afraid to pick on someone who can fight back—coward--has to pick on women--coward, dirty, filthy, cock-less coward."

The man threw Mama against the wall. He turned and lunged at me.

I held an image of Mr. Wu in my head. My feet moved as they'd been trained. They moved as Mr. Wu moved. The man lunged at me with his knife, but I wasn't there. As I had been taught, I became the otter. I moved into the man and slid underneath him. I rolled him over the top of me with almost no effort on my part. He fell head first down the stairs.

I reached for my mama. I looked down the stairs to see the man sprawled on the floor two flights below us. Bile rose up in the back of my throat as I witnessed the law of M'TK. Nobody had come to help Mama. Now when her assailant was helplessly sprawled on the floor, people came out of their doors and swarmed over the body like rats. I suppose they were looking for money or anything valuable. Mama covered my eyes and took me into our apartment.

By the time Papa got home, he had heard the story at least fifty times. "Jake killed a man who attacked his Mama."

He told us that he responded at least fifty times, "No it must be an accident. Jake is still a baby. He is only seven. He is still a baby."

I don't think I killed the man. I'm not sure he died. I never really thought about it. It was just how life was.

That night, Papa and Mama discussed what to do. They finally agreed that Mama would look for a job where she could take the trolley home or perhaps find something up the rail line from where she could take the train. This was when they started talking about moving up the rail line to the next village called, Mercid. They talked about it for years, but didn't move there until I was a rich man and could buy them a retirement apartment. We stayed in M'TK for the rest of my childhood.

The Saturday after the attack on Mama, I took my money out of my bear. When Mama was ready to go to the library, I said I had a surprise for her.

I'd asked Mrs. Wu where I could find a dress with flowers for Mama. She stroked my head, "Your mama is a lucky woman."

"I know. She has Papa."

Mrs. Wu laughed and wrote the names and addresses of two places on a piece of paper for me.

I knew the city well enough that I was able to take Mama directly to the first store. I had no idea of how to go about buying a dress for Mama. She owned one for work so I guessed she knew how to buy one. She didn't. Her good dress, as we called it, was given to her at some charity. The clerk acted rude. She had a shop full of dresses, but she said she didn't have what we wanted.

I took Mama's hand. "Come on, Mama. Mrs. Wu gave me the name of another place. We will go there." Out of the corner of my eye I watched the sales clerk when I mentioned Mrs. Wu. She paled slightly. Good, I didn't like her being rude to Mama.

In the next store, we found the dress. It didn't look like what I imagined, but when Mama saw it, her face lit up like I'd been imagining for months. I felt so proud of myself when I paid for that dress.

Many years later, when I was packing up Mama and Papa's things after they died, I found that dress. I have it still, locked away among my things. It reminds me of how much my Mama loved me.

I was a happy child. Papa and Mama loved each other and me. They gave me everything I needed. What does anyone need beyond some simple food, shelter, something to cover their nakedness and the knowledge that they are thoroughly, completely, unconditionally loved? I had all I needed plus a library card. I even had a light over my bed. I spent hours and hours in my bed every night, reading until Papa turned out the light and said, "Good night, son."

Chapter 4 Kaylee

The same pattern of school, catching rats, and visiting the library continued until I was ten. I didn't understand at the time, but rival gangs were putting pressure on Mr. Wu. This resulted in more violence and crime in M'TK. The worst crime happened in my own building.

My best friend lived in our building. Her name was Kaylee. Her mama died about six months after we moved into the building. I remember when Kaylee's mama died. She worked hard every day taking care of the sick. One morning she got up and was sick. By nighttime she was dead. After her mama died, Kaylee started spending more and more time with my family. She told me that just looking at my mama made her feel less lonely.

Kaylee was two years older than me, but we were in the same classes at school. We walked through M'TK together on our way to school. We sat together in classes and passed notes back and forth. We ate lunch together. We were always on the same team when we played games at school.

We spent hours and hours on the stairs in our building reading together. We took turns reading my books from the library. Of all the children in M'TK, she was the only one who could talk to me about books. We sat on the stairs and talked and talked. We talked like Mama and Papa talked. We never ran out of things to say to each other.

Kaylee told me her mama had come from a mountain village. She was a healer and knew all about herbs and roots. Kaylee wanted to go to school to be a nurse when she grew up. She told me about wanting to go to her mama's village and learn from the healers there too. We talked about where she could learn to be a nurse. We talked about how good it would be to know about the herbs and roots. We planned our futures.

Sometimes Kaylee came to the library with Mama and me. When I was nine, I took Kaylee to the library and bought a library card for her. After that, we could both check out the same book and read it and talk about it.

Mama liked Kaylee. She often invited her to dinner. When I brought Chinese food home, I always invited Kaylee to come to dinner. She and I would sit together on my chair at the table with Mama and Papa. Papa liked to call her Popkin, which means *little sweetheart* in our language. Kaylee was the only friend I wanted to come into my precious time with my parents.

When I was ten, Kaylee started coming to school every Monday morning, terribly beaten up. I asked her if she needed help, but I had no idea what to do. I noticed when she started getting fat. Kaylee was my best friend, so I noticed. Finally, it became obvious that this twelve-year-old girl was pregnant. The beatings continued.

One night after dinner when I was in my bed reading, I could hear Mama and Papa talking. "We must do something more to help her."

I wondered if they were talking about Kaylee.

Papa grumbled, "I had a word with her father. He told me to mind my own business. I don't know what more we can do."

Mama whispered urgently, "Can we send her to The Cove? They will take her. I know they will."

"Isn't it wrong for us to try to send her away? She belongs to her father."

"She deserves to be loved. We love her. He is just using her. That is not love." Mama's voice held an undercurrent of steel. "I don't care what that nasty drunk says or thinks. She is a decent girl. She is smart. Her mama was a good woman. I don't care about her papa, but I would do this out of respect for her mama."

Papa didn't say anything for a minute or so. "We can take money out of our savings and get her a ticket for carriage. Her papa won't think to look for her so far away from here. When should we do this?"

"I don't know. I hate to send her away. Jake will miss her, but she is not safe here. She is just a child." Mama started to cry.

"There…there, we will all miss her, but she cannot go through this every week. When school lets out at the end of the term, I will get her a ticket. We will write to Uncle John before then to make sure they will take her."

Again, I wondered if they could really be talking about Kaylee. I didn't know anybody else who needed help. My stomach turned over at the thought of not seeing Kaylee every day, but my heart hurt when I saw her bruises or even thought about them. I could not bring myself to think about what else happened to her. I decided that if Mama and Papa were talking about someone else, I could buy Kaylee a ticket north.

I talked to Kaylee about running away from her papa. "I will miss you, but

I love you. I hate seeing you get hurt every week."

She hugged me. Her pregnant body distressed me. "Do you really love me?"

I nodded.

"You are the only person who has ever loved me. I'll do whatever you say."

"Good, I'll send you north." I didn't want to be separated from her. She didn't want to leave me. Like Mama and Papa, we decided to wait until the end of the school term.

One morning a week before the end of our sixth form, Kaylee did not come to school. When I got home from school, I asked others if they'd seen her. Someone told me that Kaylee had died in the night. I don't remember who told me. I don't remember the words. I remember being sick over the news. I know I told my parents when they came home, but I don't remember my words.

Both Mama and Papa cried over Kaylee's death. Papa swore a bit, which I found comforting. Their grief helped me some, but nothing could replace Kaylee.

I suddenly had a big hole in my life. I had never suffered such a hurt before. I remembered Mama crying when my sister died. I thought I knew how Mama felt then. Mostly, I felt stunned. I couldn't think. I think I went about my routine, but I don't remember anything about the end of that school year.

I remember Papa tried to comfort me by telling me, "For people like Kaylee, death is a blessing." I remember that one Sunday. Papa decided, we should go to the cathedral and light a candle for Kaylee's soul.

I loved Mass. I'd never been before. Mama said I was baptized, but I was just a baby. I loved the big beautiful cathedral. I loved the music and the smells. The priest gave a talk about Jesus loving all people even the poor. He said that people who treat the poor badly will go to hell. That day, the idea of bad people going to hell comforted me.

After Mass, Papa showed me how to buy a small candle. I lit the candle and read the prayer on the card that came with the candle. I liked that prayer. Nobody asked for the card back, so I put it in my pocket and took it home with me.

The following Saturday, when I went to the library, I checked out a Bible.

It was a big book with tiny print. I asked the librarian if it took me longer than a week to read the whole thing, could I check it out again. She knew me and treated me with respect. She put bookmarks in the Bible at some of the stories I might like to read first. I checked it out twice.

The third time I brought the Bible back to the library, the librarian took it in the back and ripped some pages out. She took the date card out. She came back and handed me the Bible saying, "Jake Jaconovich, nobody but you checks this out. I think you will be a great man someday. I want you to have this and read it every day."

I owned a book

I think I needed that book that year. I was only ten, but I started the seventh form. The first time I entered my seventh form classroom, I saw the other students were dressed alike. The boys wore blue pants, white shirts, and a blue and white sweater. The boys wore a blue tie. The girls were dressed the same except for wearing blue skirts and a blue scarf around their neck. I wondered what that was about. It didn't take long for me to find out. I sat down in my favorite place in the second row.

"Young man, who are you?"

"Jake Jaconovich, ma'am."

"Why are you dressed like a sewer rat?" This struck me as funny. I had seen how rats looked dressed in Mr. Wu's kitchen, but I controlled the urge to laugh.

"Ma'am I was unaware that I needed to dress different, and I do not know where the other students bought their clothes."

"Get out! Get out of my class and don't come back until you are dressed properly."

"Yes Ma'am, can you tell me where to buy the proper clothes?"

"Get out!" She screeched.

I got up and walked out. One of the other boys, Kato, handed me a piece of paper with the name of a store on it. I didn't know Kato very well, but I thought of him as a friend. When we were in the fifth form, our teacher asked me to help him learn fractions. I enjoyed helping him understand. I made up games. We'd laughed and giggled over our lessons. He learned his fractions. I helped him then and now he helped me. That is how friendship works.

Outside the classroom, I ran. I decided that today was no time to be frugal. I had tokens for the trolley. I took the trolley to the M'TK station and ran the block home. I opened my teddy bear and took out a handful of money. I'd been changing my pennies and dimes into paper.

I found Papa's money bag that he hangs around his neck when we must take money out in public. I stuffed my money in Papa's money bag and ran back to the station to catch the next trolley back to the city. The trolley driver told me how to transfer and where to find the store.

At the store, I immediately asked for help. "Please, I was told to come here and buy clothes for school. I'm in a hurry because I don't want to miss more school than I have to."

The clerk looked me over. "You are too young to need a uniform."

"No sir, I am in the seventh form, and all the other students are dressed alike and my teacher called me a sewer rat and made me leave class for not having the right clothes."

"You don't talk like a sewer rat, but you sure look like one."

I grinned at the man. "Please sir, that can be changed if you will show me where to buy the clothes."

He laughed at me then and took me to pick out the clothes. He got me dressed up proper along with some admonitions about washing myself. He wrapped my old clothes in paper. I carried them and wore my new clothes.

Three hours after being kicked out of class, I came back in dressed the same as the other students. I quietly took my place.

The teacher sneered. "I didn't expect you to be back here. How did you steal those clothes?"

I hated being called a thief. It reflected poorly on my parents. "I paid for them. I have the receipt. What page are we on in the lesson?" I could see the teacher was angry, so I kept my eyes down. I didn't like having attention drawn to me.

My time in that woman's classroom was miserable. I normally loved school. That year for the first time, I felt something like dread about going to school. Every time Mrs. Teacher asked me a question, her tone told me that she believed I didn't know the answer. I always did. I made certain that woman did not have any reason to kick me out of class again.

Some of the other students followed the teacher's lead in picking on me. Some students were friends who'd known me since second form. A few times they tried sticking up for me. They got in trouble for that.

I told them, "It is best to let her have her way. I don't like it. I can live with it. I tell myself that she has more schooling than I do, but she is a small person and has not learned to accept others as they are."

She was the first to call me "The M'TK Sewer Rat." I didn't mind. I'd come to look upon rats as an endless source of wealth.

Before this, teachers had always praised me for my schoolwork. I turned in perfect papers. Mrs. Teacher wrote things on them saying she was surprised or accusing me of cheating. Everything I did in that room was wrong, according to her.

I began to wonder if my uniform contained some sort of poison. As soon as I got to school, I started to itch. Angry red welts broke out on my upper arms and around my middle. As soon as I left school, they would start to fade away. By the time Mama got home, they were gone.

Four months after Kaylee died, I got up one morning and could not face going to school. I wanted to stay in bed and sleep. I slept until noon. When I woke up, I realized that I needed to get out of that classroom. I would not drop out of school, so the only way to go was up. I got dressed and went to the school. Instead of going to class, I found my way to the director's office.

I didn't think he knew me. "I'm Jake Jaconovich."

"I know who you are. You work for Mr. Wu."

I smiled and nodded. "Sir, I came to see you because I want to know if there is some way I can be promoted to the eighth form now."

"You can take a test. You have to be able to pass your foreign language test."

We had been studying English. It was required after the fourth form. I didn't think I could pass English. "Can I take the language test in Chinese?"

The man reared back startled and his eyebrows shot up. "Yes. I would have to get a copy of the Chinese test from the head office."

"Good. How soon can I take the test?"

"Why do you want to be promoted? You are already smaller than the other boys. In the eighth form you will be even smaller."

"I cannot help my size. I know the lessons we are studying. I want to work on something more challenging." I was making this up as I went along and trying to talk like the people in the books I read.

The director laughed. "Now, Mr. Jaconovich, tell me the truth. Why do you want to be promoted?"

"I told you the truth. I know the material. I have read all of my books. I have personal reasons for wanting to be promoted. I want to take the test, but I will not tell you anything that concerns others."

"Come along lad. Let's see what you can do." He took me into a little office and gave me the test to take. It was easy enough. After about ninety minutes, Mr. Director came back in with another test written in Chinese. I'd finished the first test. He sat down and watched me as I started on the second test.

"Is there something else you wanted, sir?"

"Yes, after you finish your test, I want to talk to you."

I continued working in Chinese. He continued to watch me. He looked over the first test that I had written. It didn't take me long to do the test in Chinese. I only had one problem. The test was multiple-choice with an answer sheet. I was afraid I would not mark my answers in the correct box for each question, so I went over each question twice before marking my answer.

I finished the test before the end of the school day. "Can I be promoted now?"

"Yes, you are awful eager to get out of that classroom aren't you?"

"Yes sir."

"Do you really think you can keep up in the eighth form when you will be coming in late?"

"I may have to work harder, but I will keep up."

Mr. Director took me to my new classroom and introduced me to a young male teacher. I looked around the classroom and recognized some of the other students. I didn't see anybody from my neighborhood. Good. I missed Kaylee. I didn't feel like sitting in school with anybody just now. I sat with my new class for the rest of the day.

After school let out, I went back to my seventh form class to turn in my books. Mrs. Teacher sounded angry when she saw me. "You can't come back in here after skipping class all day."

"I am turning in my books."

She smiled and lifted her chin triumphantly. "Good. Your sort shouldn't be in our schools."

"I am turning in my seventh form books because Mr. Director gave me a test and promoted me to the eighth form."

Suddenly, an idea born out of my grief and rage, formed inside my mind. I figured that Mrs. Teacher couldn't do much to me now, so I said the words that flowed into my mind. "I don't know what sort you imagine me to be. I live in this city. My parents work here. Yes, I live in M'TK. I've seen horrors that you can't begin to imagine. Those horrors need to stop. I intend to do my best to see that happen."

I paused for breath. "The first step to ending the horror is to see that every child gets an education. Any teacher who stands in the way of a child getting an education is every bit as bad as the lowest scum who commit the atrocities of M'TK."

I had worked myself into a fury. Thoughts came together in my head and flowed out of my mouth to form sentences, much like the great men in my books spoke. For the first time, I knew the power of speaking clearly and with passion.

Chapter 5 Fights

As I said, I didn't like to fight. I took my self-defense classes. I exercised, but I never liked the sparring. I would defend myself, but I did not want to hurt the other students. People pretty much left me alone on the streets. Nobody attacked me again when I had a trap full of angry rats.

I was lucky for a child my age in M'TK. I was still in school. I lived with my parents, both of them. This in itself was unusual in M'TK. I had a job and plenty to keep me busy. I never thought about it at the time, but I also had the protection of one of the most powerful crime bosses in the city, Mr. Wu, yet even his protection was not enough to protect me from all the angry, punk kids. I often had to run away. Sometimes I spent precious money to take the trolley just to avoid trouble.

As the gang tensions in M'TK increased, I had more trouble with others wanting to beat me up. The first time I had trouble at school occurred a few months after I entered the eighth form. The boys had been teasing me about my size. They called me a baby. I laughed it off, agreeing that I was much younger than them. The first lesson I learned from Mr. Wu was the importance of self-control and avoiding a fight.

I made friends easily enough with most of the students. Still, there are bullies in every crowd. After lunch-break one day, three of them jumped me. I didn't hurt them. They were surprised to find themselves suddenly on the ground with the wind knocked out of them. They really did not know how to fight.

News of the scuffle traveled faster than I did. When I walked into class, Mr. Teacher glared at me and asked, "Jake Jaconovich, have you been fighting?"

"Huh? What? Do I look like I have been fighting? Do I have dirt on me someplace?" I looked at my pants and hands.

Mr. Teacher tried to pretend he didn't laugh and I sat down. Rumors of the fight continued to fly for days. I insisted that I had not been fighting. Those who saw the incident thought this was a big joke.

A few weeks after the fight at school, three men attacked me on my way home from Mr. Wu's. I tried to talk myself out of this, but one man grabbed me from behind. I calmly stepped back into him and under him. I grabbed onto him and curled into a ball, just like I'd learned in class. He flew over my back. As luck would have it, the second attacker lunged for me just as the first rolled over my back. Flying feet connected with lunging face. I heard the trolley coming up the street. The third man tried to grab me, but I wasn't where he expected me to be. I tripped him. He hit his head on the lamppost before he landed face down in the gutter.

I ran and jumped on the trolley as it was leaving the stop. I looked back. The three men were still lying on the sidewalk. Again, the human rats of M'TK were swarming over the bodies to pick their pockets.

Sometimes Mr. Wu would send food from his restaurant home with me after school. I carried it in the little brown boxes that he used for take-out customers. One night, on my way home, two young men demanded that I give them my boxes. I tried to tell them that I did not have food in the boxes.

"You liar. Give them to us."

I didn't want trouble, so I quickly agreed. "Okay, I'm going to set them right here. This is not food it is bait." I sat the boxes down and ran.

Earlier, I'd told Mr. Wu that I had trouble finding rotting food to bait my traps. He told his cook to give me something. The cook took two, take-out boxes and filled them with the rat cleanings in the garbage can. This was what I was carrying that night.

The story of the men stealing my rat bait was told around M'TK for days. The men took the boxes and started to eat until they found a foot in one box and a tail in another. Then they got very sick, lying on the sidewalk and vomiting. Nobody wanted to know what I was carrying in the take-out boxes after that.

After the three men attacked me on my way home from Mr. Wu's, I didn't have any more real trouble for months. Once some boys tried to get me to fight, but I told them I did not want to fight. They called me names.

I calmly replied, "Fine you can call me names all you want. I am not going to fight you. I hate getting hurt and I hate hurting others almost as much."

They called me more names and said I was a coward. All the time they were calling me names I was watching them. I was also walking sideways toward the trolley station. There were guards at the trolley stops in M'TK.

Once I reached the station, I greeted the guard by name and the boys ran away.

I was twelve when I got in my last fight in M'TK. I was coming home from my martial arts class. I was tired. I hurt from the sparring. I had lived six years in M'TK. I knew the sounds. I knew enough to watch behind me as I walked.

The street suddenly grew quieter. I saw a shadow in a darker shadow and knew that a man was tying to hide himself in the darkness. I heard the click of a knife as it fell from the sheath on his arm into his hand. He lunged quickly. I responded quick enough. His blade did not hit its mark, but it did cut my skin. I did not feel the pain. I knew I was being attacked. I knew I needed to be quick. Again, as in all the other times, I stepped into my opponent grabbing the arm with the knife in both of my hands. I pulled down with my hands while I pushed my head up into the man's armpit. I did not let go. I continued moving behind the man and turning my whole body with his arm firmly held in both of my hands. Time seemed to move slowly as I spun behind the man. I'm certain that not more than a second passed as I made my move.

I heard a pop and the man screamed. His arm hung uselessly at his side. He made another lunge for me. Again, I sidestepped and tripped him as I hit him as hard as I could on the back. He fell hard, unable to catch himself with his dislocated arm.

I turned and ran. I got home before Mama, so I patched up my side as best I could and shaking, got into my bed.

Chapter 6 Papa

O n June twelfth, when I was twelve, Papa got hurt at work. He told me that some of the other workers had carried him home on a door. We found him lying on the floor of our apartment when Mama and I got home.

I took one look at him and told Mama to take care of him. I was thankful to find the trolley at the M'TK station. I paid a token to ride six blocks to the Chinese doctor. He was out so I waited. I was ready to write him a note when he returned. I told him my Papa needed him. He drove us back to the train station and parked there.

Back at our apartment, he examined Papa. He told me in Chinese, "He has blood in the flesh around the place where he got hit. We must chase the blood back where it belongs. See how the Chi is blocked. We must restore the flow of energy past the blockage. I will give you medicines. He must lie flat for five days. In five days, I will come look at him again.

Mama and I tended Papa when we were home. We gave the neighbor woman a penny for every time she came and gave him water or put more medicine on his back.

I had paid the doctor from my savings. We still had money from my job and Mama's, but that would not be enough for us to live on. We would have to spend some of Mama and Papa's savings.

On Sunday, I went to the Cathedral. I lit a candle for Papa and said the prayer on the little card.

The doctor did return in five days. He instructed Papa to get up and walk back and forth across the apartment one hundred times then lie down and rest for one hour then get up and walk again. He would come back in five days.

School let out at the end of the second five days. Papa could not leave the apartment, but he could sit up a little. I stayed with him when Mama left for work.

He called me away from my reading. "Jake, I could be working fixing things if I had something to work on. Can you go to the dump and find things for me to fix?"

I made six trips that first day bringing things that I thought Papa could work on. I filled half of the main room of our apartment with things for Papa to fix. Our only furniture was a table and three chairs. That took up most of the floor space. The rest I filled with things for Papa to fix.

The second morning I was home alone with Papa, he handed me a lamp and told me to take it back to the dump. "I cannot fix this one."

"Why not?"

"Because it has the wrong kind of screws. See, these screws have a cross. I need screws that have a straight slot."

"Why?"

"Because my screwdriver will not fit in the cross." He showed me a toaster. "I never fix these because the screws are too small."

"Papa, if you had a screw driver that had a cross, could you fix this?"

"Yes."

"Where would I buy a screwdriver with a cross?"

"I don't know. I think such a thing would be very expensive."

"I think the stationmaster might know where I can buy such a thing. I will ask him. If he doesn't know, I will ask Mr. Wu. Somebody must know." The stationmaster did know where to buy a screwdriver. I got thirty dollars out of my bear and took the trolley to the hardware store.

The hardware store was full of things I had never seen before. I wanted to look and ask questions. A clerk asked me what I wanted.

"I need a screwdriver with a cross on the end."

He showed me where the screwdrivers were kept.

They had hundreds of screwdrivers. I asked, "Do you have a very small screwdriver too?"

He showed me all different sizes of screwdrivers. I had no idea there were that many screwdrivers in the whole world. They were all different sizes.

The clerk helped me. "If you need more than one size, you might consider buying a set." He showed me a set of four.

I began to see what I was looking at. "What is this set?" I saw eight screwdrivers four with crosses and four straight. "What are these things?"

"Pliers for pinching things, and these are wire cutters."

"I'll take this set." This was one of the proudest moments of my life. I'd bought Mama her pretty dress with flowers, and now I was buying Papa a set of screwdrivers with pliers and wire cutters.

I started shouting before I got into the apartment. "Papa! Papa, look what I found in the hardware store. They have all sorts of things there." I unwrapped the package with the set of screwdrivers.

Papa turned pale. "Jake did you pay for these?"

"Of course, see how the clerk wrapped them up."

"They must have cost a fortune."

"They did not cost as much as Mama's dress."

Papa's eyes filled with tears when he kissed me on the forehead. "No man ever had a better son."

"No son ever had a better Papa."

"I do not give you the things you deserve."

"You love my Mama and give me everything I need."

Papa laughed. "Yes, I love your Mama." He sat and ran his fingers over each of his new tools. "Jake I want you to learn something now. You work for Mr. Wu. It makes you proud to work and earn money. I am the same as you. I am proud to work. The worst part of lying on this floor has been knowing that I may never be able to work lifting heavy things again. My son, you gave me tools. I can work fixing things. You gave me more than tools. You gave me back my pride. Remember this lesson when you are a great man. When you give a man a job, you are giving him his pride."

On Saturday, Mama came home from work at noon. "Jake did you buy the things you need for Boys Club Camp?"

"No, I thought I should stay home because Papa is hurt."

"No, you are going to Boys Camp. Come, bring your list and we will go buy your things."

"I should stay home and help Papa."

Papa almost shouted. "No! You have helped me more than you will ever know. You are going to go to camp and have fun with other boys your age. Your Mama and I will miss you, but we will be like when we were courting." Mama and Papa smiled at each other. I felt left out, but I stopped feeling guilty about camp.

"I'll get my money."

Mama stopped me. "No. Papa and I will pay for your things for camp."

I didn't protest. I really wanted to go to camp. I'd wanted to go before when the other boys in my form had joined Boys Club and went to camp. I was too young. I had to wait two years. I joined Boys Club when I turned twelve. The other boys were behind me in school, but I didn't care. I wanted to go to camp.

We bought the things I needed. I got a uniform to wear. I got a flashlight, a whistle and a pocketknife. I hardly knew what to do with so many things. Then I got a backpack to carry it all in. I was going to camp.

Finally, the doctor gave Papa permission to use the stairs, so when the day arrived for me to go to camp, he walked with me to the train station. He explained, "I will sit and read the newspaper there and visit with the stationmaster."

Papa met my Boys Club leader at the station. They talked for a minute then the leader went to buy the train tickets. Our leader ordered our train tickets. "Twelve children and one adult for the box car."

Papa spoke up. "No! You cannot take children in the boxcar. They can ride in the coach."

"I do not have money to pay for coach. They can ride in the boxcar."

Papa turned to the ticket seller. "Mr. Stationmaster, give these boys and their leader tickets for coach. I will not have my son and his friends riding in the boxcar. I will pay the difference."

I think the stationmaster was a little afraid of Papa just then. Everybody seemed afraid of him when he spoke so stern.

The stationmaster sounded respectful when he spoke to my papa. "Mr. Jaconovich, you don't have to pay for the boys tickets. I will give them a group rate. They can ride in coach. Their leader can ride free if he promises to keep the boys in order."

I was proud of my Papa for getting us good seats. Riding in coach meant that we had seats and could look out the window. We had more fun than I ever imagined. Two other boys had ridden the train before. The rest had never been to the country.

We had fun looking out the windows. The three of us who had been out of the city were kept busy naming the things we saw and telling about them. If we didn't know what we were looking at, we just made up silly answers to our friends' questions. I laughed so much my sides hurt. I thought I understood why Mama and Papa wanted me to come on this trip.

I loved everything about Boys Club Camp. We hiked and fished. We swam in the river. We had a campfire at night. I learned to play football.

Some boys teased me at first because I did not know how to play. When I figured out that the football was the same as someone trying to attack me, I could handle the ball all right.

When I got back from camp, I noticed that I did not have so much trouble on the streets as before. I grew up in M'TK. I could read the street the same as I could read a book. Some people acted afraid when I walked by. Some women and girls asked me to let them walk with me when I went to the trolley.

I asked Mr. Wu why people had changed.

Mr. Wu explained. Doctor Liu told me that your father would never walk again. Everybody knows that you went to the cathedral and lit a candle when he was hurt. Doctor Liu tells us your papa got better immediately. Powerful spirits guard you Jake Jaconovich. They are afraid of the spirits not you."

I laughed. "I am just a boy."

"Remember that. Remember that you are just a boy and be careful. Watch behind you. You have a reputation. This is not a good thing. They call you the M'TK Sewer Rat. You are powerful because you are humble. If you become full of pride, they will defeat you." Mr. Wu was a wise man. I recognized his wisdom, even as a child, or perhaps because I was a child.

In Boys Club, the other boys had talked about catechism. They told me that the priest was teaching them about God so they could join the church. Catechism class was on Sunday, so I asked my parents if I could go. They consented. I entered the catechism class. I was two weeks behind the other students. The priest said he didn't think I would catch up in class.

The boys who knew me laughed. "He is in the ninth form. He will catch up."

After class, the priest took me aside and talked to me about confession. I shrugged. My conscience was clear.

"I think you might be the one they call The M'TK Sewer Rat. Is this not true?"

"Oh that is true. I catch rats. My boss gives them chloroform. Is it wrong to kill rats? Our building is much better without them."

"I heard it is not rats that you kill but men."

"I have killed no one."

"Why do they say you have?"

"I don't know. I don't know why anyone would say such a thing. I do not like to hurt people. I live in M'TK. Is this a sin? Is it a sin to be poor? Jesus said the poor are blessed."

"How do you know what Jesus said?"

"I own a Bible. I read it every day with my parents."

"Where can I find your parents?"

The priest did visit my parents.

They promised that I was a good boy and had never hurt anybody.

Mama sounded indignant. "Ask anybody in M'TK--they know he does not like to fight. Men call him names to get him to fight, but he runs away."

The priest asked, "Why do I hear that people are afraid of him?"

I spoke up. "Oh, I know the answer to that question." Everybody looked surprised at my sudden outburst. "It is not me they are afraid of. It is God."

I explained about lighting the candle for Papa and then Papa got well. I saw that my explanation pleased the priest. I was not sure if I believed it myself. I worried that I had not told the truth to the priest. I had told him what Mr. Wu told me.

Later I told my parents that I did not believe all I told the priest. "It was only what Mr. Wu told me."

Papa pulled me to him for a hug. Then he explained. "Son, the priest thinks he knows all about God. For this reason, your answer pleased him. I think no man really knows the mind of God. Does God protect you? I don't know. Perhaps God does protect you by letting people fear you. Did you really light a candle for me?"

I nodded.

He kissed me on my forehead. "I am a very wealthy man."

Papa did not get all the way well. He limped. He could not lift heavy things. He was no longer the man who could work in a warehouse. He could not carry his wife across the room. I remembered how he carried her five kilometers from Wulfton to the M'TK Station. He fixed things that I brought him from the dump, but he did not make much money fixing things. He helped me by setting my rat-trap before I got home from school. He cooked dinner for Mama and kept the apartment neat.

Once, at the dump I found a wheeled chair with no seat, and took it home for Papa to fix. He took a seat from a broken chair and put it on the wheeled chair. He did not sell this. He took it downstairs and knocked on Mr. Pickett's door.

I didn't often see Mr. Pickett. He had been a soldier and lost his legs fighting. He lived on a small pension. Papa gave Mr. Picket the wheeled chair. From that day forward Mr. Picket appointed himself the guard of our building and the sidewalk in front of the building. He sat in his wheeled chair with his blanket on his lap. Under the blanket he kept his service revolver. I heard him fire it once after I had gone to bed. Papa went into the hall to check to see if Mr. Pickett was okay. He was.

One night in October, Mr. and Mrs. Wu came to our house. They were carrying large books that I knew to be business ledgers. Mama sometimes brought books like these home from work.

After bowing to my parents, Mr. Wu asked for Mama's help. "Mrs. Jacob, I know that you are an honest woman. You are smart. These are the books from some of my businesses. Can you look at them and see if I am being cheated?"

"I am not the best person to do what you want. I will be slow. I may not know if something is wrong."

"You are an honest woman. You will know if something is wrong."

Mama worked late every night adding and adding the numbers in the books. Every night for a week, after dinner, she spread the books out across the table and worked on those numbers. Papa did not like her working so long. One night, their voices woke me up.

"My love, it is midnight. Come to bed like a decent woman." Papa implored her.

"Jacob Jaconovich, when I get in bed with you, I am not a decent woman."

"You are my wife, and I think you are more than decent. I think you are perfect."

"I think you are getting well."

"I'll show you how good I am."

"I should work on the books." Mama turned out the light. I lay awake for several minutes grinning into the dark. Mama loved Papa well enough. I thought maybe the spirit of my parents' love guarded me in M'TK.

When Mr. and Mrs. Wu came back to get the books, she had a report for them. She showed them where money spent did not match what was sold and what was still on hand to sell. "I am afraid that you are right. These people are cheating you."

Mr. Wu shook his head. "This is a bad sign. It means my power is not what it once was. I fear for M'TK. Things are not what they once were. We may all have to flee. Remember this and plan how you will leave."

After the Wu's left, Papa looked grim. "I think we need to make a plan to leave. We will try to go north by train." They made a plan as best they could. The year closed with more reports of violence in M'TK. The dump caught fire or maybe someone set it on fire. Papa could not get things to fix.

Every day, Papa went to the train station and read the newspapers. He talked to the stationmaster. He reminded the stationmaster that he had worked for the railroad people and was loyal to the railroad. Little by little, the stationmaster let Papa do some of the jobs around the station. He would not let Papa sell tickets, but he let him show passengers to their cars. Papa picked up the mail and sorted it.

One day, Papa came home after Mama got home. We heard him almost running up the stairs and calling to us. "I got a job! I am working for the railroad again."

He kissed Mama and swung her in a circle." We all laughed.

He sounded excited as he explained. "I will not make as much as I once did. It is a start. I will be moving the rail cars around on the side tracks and fixing things at the station."

While we ate, he told us how he got the job. "They were supposed to have four carriage cars ready to put on the passenger train when it came through. The stationmaster got the gerry out to move them to the right track. It broke down crosswise of the tracks with trains due from both directions. That gerry was smack in their path."

Papa remembered to eat a bite of his dinner. "The stationmaster did not know what to do. He tried to run away. I told him that I would help, but he had to tell Mr. Supervisor that I had helped him, and they should hire me because he did not have time and the knowledge to fix things when they break.

"Not much was broken. First I changed the signals and switched the southbound train onto a different track before it got to town.

"Next, I looked at the gerry. I thought I could fix it too. Mr. Supervisor arrived before I got the gerry fixed. I told him to hold the passenger train a few minutes and I would have the carriage cars ready to put on. I got the gerry fixed and moved the cars into position. The northbound passenger train left the station only a few minutes late.

"Mr. Supervisor watched me fix the Gerry and move the cars. He told me that the captain of the southbound freight had told him we had a problem.

"Mr. Stationmaster stood by listening, so I tried to make him look like a hero. I explained. Mr. Stationmaster knew I had worked for the railroad before I got hurt. He also knew I am good at fixing things, so when the gerry broke he called me to help him."

Papa's grin reminded me of a dolphin as he told his story. "I told Mr. Supervisor, I think I did a good job here. I prevented two trains from wrecking and got the carriage cars where they needed to be despite the broken gerry. I want to work for the railroad doing maintenance. I showed him other things that needed fixing. I'd been looking things over long enough that I knew what I was saying was true. He hired me. Mr. Stationmaster is happy to have help. I have a job."

Papa's job did not pay much. He worried and fussed. Mama tried to comfort him. "We still have money from what Mr. Wu pays Jake. I have my job. Jake has his job. We will be fine. You will make more money soon. Soon we will have more money and a better place to live. You'll see. The river is bringing us better times." This was the first time that I heard my parents talk about life as being a river that carries us where we should be.

Chapter 7 M'TK Burns

The violence in M'TK continued to get worse. I started riding the trolley instead of walking to school. If things looked bad, I would even throw an old shirt over my trap full of rats and take the trolley to Mr. Wu's to deliver them. Mr. Wu fussed and worked us harder in our lessons. He yelled at me, "Jake, defend yourself like you mean it. You are not a baby anymore. Throw him! Take him down!"

In January, the dump caught fire again. Sometimes, the flames shot higher in the air than the buildings in M'TK. Some said that this gang or that set fire to the dump. In school, my teacher said that the dump caught fire because it made a gas that caught fire. I went to the library and asked the librarian for a book about it. Perhaps my teacher was right. Perhaps the gas was there and somebody set it on fire, perhaps it didn't need anybody to set it on fire. Some days the dump just seemed to explode. We felt anxious all the time.

Toward the end of the third week of February, people on the street started talking about rumors of riots near Wulfton. My friends at school said the riots might spread to M'TK. I laughed to my friends. "What others call riots would be a quiet night in M'TK."

On Thursday, I went home as usual, got my rats and took the trolley to Mr. Wu's. I found a note written in Chinese stuck to the door. "Flee, the army will burn M'TK tonight. Mrs. Wu went to get your Mama from her work."

I dumped the rats and ran back home. I did not realize it at the time, but I yelled the message on my way. "Run! Flee! The army is coming to burn M'TK."

When I entered my building, I shouted the news to Mr. Picket. I found Mama in our apartment. She'd spread hers and Papa's blanket on the floor and was throwing things into it. I grabbed my blanket and started filling it. My teddy bear went in first, then my books. We talked as we worked. We realized Papa did not know. I had what I needed. I rolled all my things up in my blanket the way I'd watched Mama do with hers. Mama had four geraniums that she kept on the windowsill. She grabbed my rat-trap and laid the geraniums inside.

We ran out of the building with our bundles and the geraniums in my trap.

We ran to the train station. Papa and the stationmaster were in the office. We told them our story.

Papa jumped up and looked outside. The stationmaster went to the safe and opened it. I saw him stuffing money into bags.

Papa turned around. "What are you doing?"

"I'm getting out of here."

"You are not taking more that what is yours."

"Who is to stop me? Not a cripple."

I wanted to help. I stood beside Papa. "Do as my papa says." I didn't know how to look menacing. I knew I looked like a little boy. I took the most ridiculous pose I could think of and hoped the stationmaster had heard about my reputation.

The man looked from me to Papa. Papa's look was enough to frighten anybody. The man grabbed one bag of money and ran. We never saw him again. I wondered if he got caught between the riots and the fire.

Papa threw the rest of the money into the safe and locked it.

"Wait here." He ran out the door. I saw him grab a man twice his size by the front of his shirt. The man was the hairiest person I'd ever seen. He was huge and had hair on his arms and hands as well as his face and head. Papa gestured toward four boxcars that sat on a siding. He shoved the mountain of hairy humanity toward our apartment, and ran off across the tracks toward the gerry.

The man turned and ran bellowing for people to get out. "Get out of the buildings. Get out of M'TK." People started swarming out of the buildings.

Papa brought the gerry to the station. "Come with me." He put Mama on the floor of the gerry. He told me to watch everything he did. We came to a switch. Papa showed me how to move the switch. He ran the gerry past the switch, and I moved it back again. We had to move three more switches to get the gerry to the boxcars. I saw people swarming across the tracks toward the boxcars. Papa ran the gerry up to the boxcars then he took Mama and me to the first car and helped us in, telling us to sit in a corner. From where I sat, I could see the big man and another man who looked skinny by comparison, lifting Mr. Picket in his wheelchair into our boxcar. More and more people kept coming until we were packed in like rats in a cage.

Papa bellowed above all the noise. "Close 'em up. We can't hold more.

Close 'em up."

The doors were pulled closed and the dark filled the boxcar. I felt Mama's arms around me. She put her head on mine.

"Don't worry Mama. Papa will get us out of here."

"I know. I just don't like being separated from him when it is so dark."

The door to our car rolled back a few inches. We had a little light. I could hear Papa's voice still bellowing and swearing saying, "Push men. We'll be okay if we can get her rolling." Nothing happened.

One man screamed, "We're trapped." and flung open the door. He jumped. Within seconds, our car lurched.

Papa's voice held a note of triumph. "Yes. Yes. Keep it up men. We're moving. We'll be okay once we get her rolling." Papa was right. We were moving. We moved slow, but we were moving. Two men walked beside us shouting that we were moving. The men in the car helped them climb on. This was the slowest train ride I'd ever taken. I saw the tops of buildings through the partially open door, as we went past. Finally, I saw a tree, then more trees. I thought Papa would take us to Mercid. Instead, he took us to a siding that ran fifteen miles into the countryside.

After we had ridden for two hours, the siding ended at a lake in woods. About half of the people piled off of the train right away. The other half of them were afraid of the woods until Papa told them it was safe to come out. The railroad ran through a valley between two ridges. We found a small stream that came from the lake.

Papa selected a place for us to camp. I picked up some sticks and started clearing a spot for a fire. Papa asked what I was doing. I explained what I had learned about making a campfire at Boys Club Camp. Some men laughed at me. I was used to people laughing. I knew what I was doing. Within a half hour, I had a small fire burning. We didn't need it for anything, but it seemed to comfort Mama.

The big hairy man who had carried Mr. Picket to the train said, "Mr. Jaconovich, may I take your son to the top of that ridge to see what is happening? I will see that no harm comes to him."

I wanted to see what was happening. "Please, Papa, I have my flashlight. I like the woods."

Papa nodded. The climb to the top of the ridge was easy. The trees grew far enough apart that I could see the stars coming out to the west. I thought I saw an orange glow in the east.

We reached the top of the ridge with about fifty other people. I heard one man swear. We watched in horror as the buildings of M'TK caught fire and burst into flames. We could not see all that was happening. We would hear an explosion then a ball of fire rose into the air. Another building would go up in flames. Time after time we heard the explosion, saw the ball of fire go up, then saw another tall inferno of flames reaching higher than the rising moon as another building burned.

I stood on the ridge numb with shock. Our homes were being burned. I wondered who did not get out. I thought of the crippled. Perhaps others helped them. I thought of the drunks and opium addicts. Nobody would help them. They had long since been beyond help. I turned my back on the flames of my city.

The scene before me could not have been more beautiful. A lake stretched out below us. I knew it was there because it reflected the starlight. The rising moon sent a shaft of light across the lake. I thought then that I wanted to live in this place for the rest of my life. I turned back to look at my past. The flames still licked at the night sky. I could smell the oily smoke from M'TK.

I heard a voice say, "Maybe it needed to burn. Hellish, rat-infested place."

I thought of the rats. Each rat was worth a penny to me. I laughed to myself thinking that I would be a very wealthy man indeed if I had a penny for every rat in M'TK. I wondered how much money I had hidden away in Mr. Bear. I started calculating, twenty-five rats a day five days a week and fifty rats a day on the weekend. That made an easy two dollars a week. Two dollars a week for fifty-two weeks made one hundred four dollars a year. I had been selling rats for six and a half years. I made six hundred twenty-four dollars in six years and another fifty-four dollars in the last six months. That made six hundred seventy-eight dollars. I'd spent some on Mama's dress, Papa's tools, my school clothes, Papa's doctor, and what else? I ran the numbers over and over in my head before I began to believe that I was carrying over six hundred dollars in Mr. Bear. I shuddered remembering that I'd left my bundle with Papa. He didn't know what was in there.

I whispered into the smoky night, "I think I will go back to my parents now." I turned and started down the ridge. The big man came with me. I wondered if he thought I needed protection. I figured if I could survive the last two years in M'TK, I could survive anything. When I found our small campfire, Mama was sitting on my bundle.

"Jake do you have your books in here?"

"Yes, I have my school books and library books. I will get a fine if I do not return my books on time." People around me laughed at my concern for my library books when we were faced with the horror of the burning of M'TK.

"Do you have your Bible?"

I nodded.

"Can you read us the story about when David camped out?"

I found my Bible and began to read the story. It was a good story about a different time. The hero won in the end. I read about David's adventures until my voice got tired. When I finished, I realized at least one hundred people were listening to me read.

We slept by my little fire. When we were unwrapping our blankets, I whispered to Mama. "I have over six-hundred dollars in Mr. Bear."

"Use him for your pillow." I used my books for my pillow and slept with my arms tightly around Mr. Bear.

We laid my blanket on the ground. Mama, Papa and I slept on my blanket with their blanket over us. We had all our worldly goods tucked into bed around us. Mama slept with her arm around me, and Papa slept with his arm around her.

Chapter 8 The Stationmaster's Son

We stayed in the woods for two days waiting for the fires to burn down. On Sunday, Papa announced that he would take the boxcars back to town. He told the people with us, "I will take you partway, but I'll get in trouble if I get caught with all of you on the train. I'll let you off before we come into M'TK. Mr. Pickett can ride with me all the way to the station."

Some of the men had already walked back to town. We got back on the train and Papa took everybody to the edge of the woods. He let them off about five kilometers out of town.

When we pulled into the train station at M'TK, we saw that the brick station hadn't burned. The windows were completely black with smoke. Everything smelled of smoke. We recognized the supervisor of the railroad standing there with some men I'd never seen before. Mama leaned to Papa and whispered, "It is Mr. Rouseff, the owner!"

Papa wore his railroad uniform. He approached the men and nodded respectfully.

Mr. Supervisor sounded slightly surprised and very curious when he asked, "Where have you been?"

Papa's voice sounded respectful but firm. "I heard the emperor's army was coming to burn M'TK. I decided to take the boxcars and gerry out to the woods to keep them safe."

Mr. Rouseff the owner of all the railroads in the country growled, "The station is locked. Can you open it?"

Papa nodded, pulled the keys from his inside coat pocket and opened the station for the bosses. A wave of hot rancid air rushed out to meet us. Papa explained, "I left the money in the safe. I hope it is okay. I thought it would be safer here than with me. I was afraid of bandits." Papa opened the safe. It was still hot so he used the old stationmaster's gloves to protect his hands. The money sat in the bags where we left it.

I heard a tone of respect in Mr. Rouseff's voice when he spoke to my papa. He laughed a little when Papa handed him the bags of money. "Mr. Jaconovich, you're a hero." He paused and looked around him. He shook his head and spoke to Papa again. "We expected everything here to be gone and our employees killed. We lost all our buildings. How can we thank you for what you saved?"

"Give me the stationmaster's job. Let me live here with my family. Let my cousin live with me. He can watch the station when I am working on the machinery."

I wondered who Papa's cousin was.

Mr. Rouseff told Mr. Supervisor that Papa must be the new stationmaster at M'TK. The men showed Papa what land belonged to the railroad. He was supposed to keep squatters from moving in.

Papa ventured in a hesitant tone, "I think some of the other employees managed to escape. If they come back can they have their old jobs?"

Mr. Rouseff gave Papa a curious look and nodded. "Send us anybody who can work. We will try to find housing for them."

Papa asked. "Can one of you help me with my cousin? He lost his legs fighting insurgents. He is in a wheelchair." Mr. Rouseff, himself, helped lift Mr. Picket in his chair off of the train. I noticed he looked around inside the boxcar. I watched as he sniffed and picked up a small piece of paper. He gave Papa another curious look.

When the other bosses left to go to their cars, Mr. Rouseff turned and reached out to shake hands with Papa. "Mr. Jaconovich, people I thought were my friends, Emperor Vanderholm and his supporters, betrayed me. I will never forget those who were loyal to me. Thank you for *all* you have done here."

I shuddered at the loathing and venom I heard in Mr. Rouseff's voice when he said, "Emperor Vanderholm."

I can still feel my surprise at that moment when one of the most powerful men in the country reached out to shake my papa's hand. I was so proud of Papa. I heard Mama gasp beside me at the gesture.

I cannot remember ever being as hungry as I was that night. We had eaten nothing but crackers and water for three days. I stood outside the station and looked at the desolation around me. Everything looked black covered over with a white layer of drifting soot. Some heaps of rubble still smoked and others still glowed a dull red. There was no place to buy food.

"Papa, I am going looking for something we can eat."

Papa gave me some money then put my bear and Mama's coffee pot in the station safe and locked it up.

I almost ran to Mr. Wu's. His restaurant still stood, but the windows were smoky, and nobody was there. This part of town had not burned, but everybody was gone. I walked on toward the city. It was late on Sunday. All the businesses were closed.

I must have walked almost four kilometers from M'TK to the University District before I found a restaurant that was open. The university seemed untouched by the tragedy in M'TK. I saw students going about their business. The grass and trees on the campus were green. The students were from the elite families. I knew enough to go to the backdoor of the restaurant and ask for a dinner for four to take home.

The man who owned the restaurant was a northerner. He said he had some fish stew. I bought two cartons of fish stew and took them home. Outside of the University District, I did not see another person on my way to the restaurant or on my way home. I tried not to think about how many bodies lay mixed with the ashes around me.

We ate our dinner in the stationmaster's office. When we finished eating, I wanted nothing more than to go to sleep. Papa made a bed for Mr. Picket in the office. Mama took me upstairs. The windows were black with smoke making the upstairs apartment so dark we couldn't see. We opened the window for light. Upstairs had a kitchen, a whole room just for sitting in, and two bedrooms. It had another room with a toilet and a shower. Mama turned the shower on. Water came out. She giggled and called to Papa. "This is a palace. Oh my love, we live in a palace." She ran downstairs to kiss Papa.

I flushed the toilet and watched as the water swirled down the drain.

Mama came back upstairs dragging Papa by the hand. She carried her geraniums that were still in my trap. They looked dead, wilted and hanging over the edges of their pots. Mama put them in our kitchen sink and turned water on them. The air still stank of smoke, and I tried not to think about what else I could smell.

Papa decided that he and Mama would take the room facing the tracks. It had a big bed in it. The smaller room faced the street and had a small bed. I had my own bedroom with a real bed.

Early Monday morning, I left for school. Mama wrote me a note telling my teacher why I was absent on Friday. "Jake Jaconovich missed school on

Friday because our home burned. We stayed out of town for the day." I was afraid I might get kicked out of school for missing a day.

M'TK was still deserted. I walked eight blocks before I started seeing people. One woman screamed and ran inside. I heard her screaming, "It is the M'TK sewer rat! It is his ghost." People came out of that building to look. I kept looking for the trolley. Everybody seemed to be looking at me as I looked for the nearest trolley.

When I finally got on a trolley, I greeted the driver by his name. He stared at me with an open mouth then started to laugh. I tried to put my token in the fare meter. He said, "Today, you ride free. If you are alive, there is hope for all of us." I didn't know what he meant.

The other students turned and stared at me when I entered the school. I knew my clothes smelled of smoke. I thought they looked at me because I smelled funny. I felt very embarrassed and just wanted to get to class and slide into my favorite place in the second row.

The teacher entered the room and started to take roll. When he came to my name, he skipped over it. "I am here, sir. I have a note from Mama telling you why I was absent Friday. It really could not be helped, sir." I held out the piece of paper from Mama. He read it.

He started to laugh. "Jake Jaconovich, you lead a charmed life. I did not think anything survived that inferno."

"No sir, but I was not there."

Perhaps the people of M'TK were right when they said that spirits protected me. This was the first of many times when I survived because I was not where people expected me to be.

I got home to find about fifty of the people who had ridden the train with us. The railroad hired them to clean the station so the trains could stop there. In our apartment, Mama was fussing because the workers had nothing to eat. They didn't have anyplace to live yet. The railroad was bringing in more boxcars for the people to live in until they could find houses. She said, "I can cook on the stove, but the people don't have anything to eat out of."

We talked to Mr. Pickett about the problem. He said, "Jake, do you think there are brown boxes at Mr. Wu's?"

"It is locked up. We can't get in."

"Push me up there in my chair. Mrs. Jacob, you start fixing these people something to eat."

I pushed Mr. Pickett in his chair Mr. Wu's. "See, it is locked."

Mr. Picket rolled himself closer to the door. I watched him fumble at the lock with a bunch of small sticks that he kept on a ring. The door opened.

I pushed Mr. Pickett into the restaurant. I saw the till open. It was empty. I noticed napkins fallen on the floor and pans left in the sink. Mr. Picket looked for the brown boxes while I went upstairs to our gym.

Everything sat just as I last saw it. I fingered my kimono. I forgot how much I hated getting thrown and knocked down. I loved this place. I reverently left everything as it was.

I went back downstairs and reached down the boxes for Mr. Pickett. I wrote a note in Chinese saying how many boxes I'd taken. I promised to pay for them if the Wu's would come to the station. I put the note in the till and closed it. I locked the door securely behind me when we left.

On the sidewalk outside Mr. Wu's restaurant we looked down on the city spread out in three directions around us. I knew that M'TK meant knoll or mound, but I never realized until I stood looking around us that there was a slight hill there.

Without the tall buildings of M'TK blocking the view, we could see around us for blocks and blocks. I searched for familiar landmarks in the bleak, empty desert that had once been M'TK. Everything we could see was black and covered in ash. A few surviving chimneys or standing timbers marked the graves of what had once been building some of them still smoldered. This borough had once been full of noise and people. Now, it sat as silent as death.

From where I stood I could now see the rail lines flowing in and out of the city. For the first time I saw the line that went east after it left the M'TK station following the same path as the northbound train until it made a graceful curve eastward and jumped the river on its trestle going on to places I'd never been.

I'd never seen the river before. Now that no buildings and trees hid the view, the river edged the black desolation like a silver funeral ribbon.

I looked back at the station, the lone building among the desolation. It sat hunkered down beside the tracks. The red brick building looked as black and as desolate as its surroundings. A timber from the building closest to the station rested against the slate roof of the waiting room.

My eye traced a line that must have been the trolley tracks buried under the ash. Mr. Picket sighed and recalled me to our mission. "Mr. Jake, we better get these boxes back to your mama. It does no good to dwell on what is gone."

Mama made fish stew with a fish head. I filled the boxes with the stew and carried them downstairs. Mr. Pickett handed out the boxes of stew. Everybody said it was the best fish stew they'd ever eaten. I agreed. Nobody made fish stew like my Mama. She said it was because she used dill.

Before I went to bed that night, Mama told me to take a shower. I'd never taken a shower before. I didn't know what to do. She'd brought me a bar of soap and a towel. "Papa is an important man now. You must act like the son of an important man." She told me how to shower.

I showered and used the towel to dry myself. When I lifted my blanket to roll up in it, I discovered Mama had tucked the end under the mattress. She came into my room and showed me how to sleep between sheets. I wondered how Mama came to know so much. I tried to remember when we stayed at The Cove. I didn't remember showers and sheets. Perhaps they had them and I didn't notice. I realized how much I didn't know just before I fell asleep.

Within a week after we returned, Mama learned that the office where she worked before was closed. The railroad had moved their offices to Mercid. Mama said. "I can take the train to work in Mercid."

I stared. "Wouldn't that cost too much?"

"No son, we can ride the train free now because I am the stationmaster." Papa sounded proud.

Mama said, "So you see I can go to work for free."

Papa sounded stern. "No, I don't want you to go out to work anymore. You can stay here and help me with the station."

Just then I thought of something wonderful. "If we can ride the train for free, does that mean we can we go visit Mama's Uncle John?"

My parents smiled at me.

For about six weeks, we all four worked hard run the station. Mr. Picket rolled himself around making notes of everything he saw that needed cleaning and fixing. He said that because he had been in the army, he knew how things should look.

I helped Papa fix the switches that had been damaged by the fire. Every time he picked up one of his screwdrivers he smiled at me.

Two weeks after the fire, Mama took me to the store to buy new school clothes. When we were done, she still had some money left. She giggled and asked me to come with her to the women's store. Mama bought a pair of trousers. "I want to plant a garden. I am going to wear pants so I can bend down." She giggled all the way home over what Papa would say. I don't know what Papa said. I saw him pat her on the behind more than once when she wore her pants.

About eight weeks after the fire, I came home from school and asked Papa for advice. "Papa, after school today, some boys were kicking a football around. It got away from them and would have rolled into the street, but I kicked it back. They asked me to play with them for a few minutes. I played with them until the trolley came. They asked me to join their football team. They play games against other schools. I told them I didn't think I could because I didn't have a uniform. They wanted me to ask you anyway."

Papa squeezed my shoulder. "Son, I think you can be a great man someday. For that, you will need to know the things that rich boys know. I will give you the money for your uniform and anything else you need. I want you to be the man I know you can be."

I learned the rules of football easily. My moves were unconventional. I used the things I learned from Mr. Wu to move the ball where I wanted to go. I had fun. I enjoyed the competition where nobody got hurt.

Chapter 9 M'TK Market

M ama's geraniums survived. We called it a miracle. Mama called it a sign of better times. She started dividing them as they recovered. Where she started with four, she now had sixteen big plants blooming in baskets at the windows and a big pot by the station entrance.

Papa and some men from the railroad had built a new waiting room for the station. The new addition looked fresh and bright. The station had been scrubbed to remove the smoke from the fire. The platform had been rebuilt in places and the rest was scrubbed clean. Everything around our home looked clean and tidy. Pretty curtains hung at our windows. I felt proud of my Mama for making the station so pretty.

Large sections of M'TK had been fenced off by the railroad to keep out squatters. The fenced off areas had gates with big locks on them. Mama kept looking at the vacant land and watching the sun and talking about drainage. Finally, she decided where she wanted her garden. Papa did not have a key to get inside the fence where she wanted to plant, but Mr. Pickett had his little sticks on the ring. He opened the gate just south of the station.

Mama hired two men. First, she made them clean up the burnt lumber and broken glass. They carried crate after crate of burned wood and broken glass to the dump. On the weekend, I carried two heavy crates of wood and broken pottery to the dump. After my second trip to the dump, I got frustrated with our slow progress. I didn't like the dirty, heavy work. I remembered something I saw at the hardware store when I bought Papa's screwdrivers.

I took some of my money and went to the hardware store. I got a wheelbarrow. Then I remembered Mama's aunt hoeing the garden. I bought a shovel, a hoe and a rake. I wheeled everything home in the wheelbarrow. The workers laughed and cheered when they saw me coming back to the station with the wheelbarrow. We used it to clean up debris from the fire. Papa used it to haul wire and parts to where he worked doing maintenance.

One day, Mr. Rouseff came through the station. He saw how we were cleaning up the debris. He laughed, pounded Papa on the back and paid him for hiring workers.

Mama's face glowed when she told Mr. Rouseff. "I want to plant things in there. It will make the station look pretty. People tell me they like to come here now because the station looks so pretty. If we can get people from Mercid to come to see the flowers, the railroad will make more money on fares." Mr. Rouseff laughed at Mama's words. I thought he was going to tell her she could not plant a garden.

"Mrs. Jaconovich what else to you need? I can get you some dirt to fill this in."

"Good dirt would help. I can get seeds and some plants from my aunt."

I thought Mr. Rouseff was more funning than serious when he grumbled. "I don't want weeds in here."

Mama looked down her nose at the taller man and sparred right back. "I know how to keep weeds out of a garden."

Three days later, the freight train left a car with dirt from the river valley in it for Mama's garden. We hauled dirt. Mama's hired workers hauled dirt. Someone from the railroad brought us another wheelbarrow. Before school, I ran out and moved dirt. After football practice I came home and shoveled dirt by the light that came from the station. We moved that whole train car of dirt to where Mama told us she would plant things. She made sure we didn't waste any of that good river-bottom dirt on her pathways.

When the garden was ready to plant, Mama announced that it was time to leave Mr. Pickett in charge of the station, and visit her aunt to get seeds for planting. She wrote Uncle John a letter telling him when we would be there.

Papa had a thousand instructions for Mr. Pickett.

Mr. Pickett's voice sounded ragged when he said, "Mr. Jaconovich, you saved my life. You made me a man again. I will take care of this station for you better than you do yourself."

Most of the people who went out into the country on the boxcars remembered Papa. Some people had moved away. They sent him letters and little gifts. Most of the people returned to work for the railroad. They would come on their day off just to visit. Sometimes they would help Papa around the station. They promised to help Mr. Picket if he needed it.

Mr. Apkouta, the big, hairy man who had taken me up to the ridge the night M'TK burned came to see us often. He was one of the men who helped at the station. He helped haul dirt. He always called papa, Mr. Jaconovich. He promised to come by the station before and after he got off from work. "I'll have my missus cook something up for Mr. Picket's dinner."

This time, Mama was well and happy for our trip north. I watched out the window captivated by scene after scene as my country rolled past the windows. I wanted to memorize the sight of tidy farms marching into the distance with their new crops a bright green. Occasionally a silver river wound past the fields. I saw birds I'd never seen before. Once I saw a deer.

The farmlands dwindled into forests full of filtered light. I watched the light and thought that surely God must walk in the forests. The rivers and streams churned and sparkled as they fell down the hillsides. The mountains still had some snow on them. They sparkled blue and white in the sun. I sat silent for hours drinking it all in. I could not imagine any place more beautiful. I'd read about other places being beautiful, but I had only read about them. This was my home. I fell in love with it. Finally, I said to my parents, "We are blessed to live in such a beautiful country."

Uncle John met us at the train. I was excited to go for a boat ride. Poor Papa turned a little green the moment he got into the boat. Mama sat beside him and rubbed his wrists. Uncle John took me up to the bridge and started teaching me how to drive the boat. I loved the boat and the water.

We spent two days with Mama's family. I talked and talked to my cousins. They wanted to know everything about the city. They told me that they had girlfriends. They talked for hours about their girlfriends, which reminded me of Kaylee, but didn't say anything. We went outside and played football. I went out fishing on the boat in the morning. I loved the magic of putting out a net and pulling it back in full of fish.

I learned how to have fun with my cousins. They laughed at the same things I found funny. They liked sports. We climbed to the top of a ridge and stood looking out to sea. We talked about the foreign countries on the other side of the ocean. They wondered about the girls on the other side of the ocean.

Four generations of the family lived in the big house in the cove with all its different levels and floors. As the family grew, they built more rooms onto the house. I loved the unexpected stairs and windows in odd places. Our life in the city seemed a little less rich because I did not have family there. I tried to imagine what it would be like to have family in the city. I decided it would be just like having all the friends who had fled the fire with us come over every chance they could. I guessed I had family in the city after all.

Mama got seeds from Aunt Luella. They went around the yard digging up bits of all the plants. Mama got cuttings of some. She carried a large bag full of plants when we got back on the train. I carried a heavy, long canvas bag full of fish we'd caught.

When we got home, I took the fish straight to the closest restaurant. The owner bought all my fish for the price Uncle John told to me ask. The restaurant owner exclaimed over their freshness and asked me. "Can you bring me more? I can't get fish this fresh in the city."

I wrote to Uncle John and told him that I was able to sell all the fish easily. "The restaurant owner says he will buy more, if I can bring them. If I leave here on Saturday morning, can you bring me fish to the train? I will bring them back here to sell on Sunday morning. I can give you the money for the fish when I come back the next week."

Uncle John wrote back immediately. He would meet me at the train Saturday night. Now, I had a job. Mama worried about me working all the time I was not in school. I reminded her that all I did was ride the train and I could study on the way. Mama didn't like for me to be away from home over night. She fussed and worried so much that I made one small change in my business plan. I went to all the restaurants within walking distance and told them I would have fresh fish to sell when the train came in on Sunday morning. I asked them to meet me at the station.

I rode the train north to the coast. My cousin met me with about fifty kilos of fish wrapped in two long canvas bags. I gave him the money from the last fish I sold.

He gave me back a third of the money. "We can't sell the fish for that much here. This will really help us. Uncle John says he wants you to get enough money to make this worth your time."

"It is easy enough to do. I just ride the train." When I got home, I saw my customers waiting by tables near Mama's garden.

Mama told me. "Put the fish here so the men can see how beautiful they are." I put the fish out on the table. Mama told our customers how fresh they were and showed them how to tell when a fish was fresh. She pointed out that they were not bruised. She demanded more money than her uncle asked. She knew how much fish cost in the city. She sold all the fish within fifteen minutes after I got home. The M'TK market was born.

For a year, I spent my weekends riding the train to the coast, getting fish from whichever cousin came to meet me, and riding home. For several months, one of my second or third cousins, Nicki, who was only two years older, would meet me at the train. He would get on and ride with me to the M'TK station. Between us, we carried about a hundred kilos of fish, shrimp, squid and mussels. He would stay with us until the next morning then take the train home.

I loved having my cousin with me. He acted curious about every thing. I showed him how to get a library card. He laughed over being able to take books home. "We can't get any books to read at home." Later he said. "No wonder you like to read. You can get so many books so easy."

Nicki liked to buy candy to take home to the younger cousins. I sent some to Aunt Luella. We found a bookstore where we could actually buy books. I bought one about gardens for our aunt. We bought our lunch from street vendors and sat on benches in the park near city hall. We talked about everything.

Nicki was taking a class on government in school. He asked. "What do you think of our government?"

"Not much. I mean I don't think about them. They burned M'TK you know."

"They've burned a lot of places."

"Have they burned on the coast?

"No. They can't bring enough troops in by sea to have a purge."

"Why not?"

Nicki grinned at me. "Because the independent fishermen won't let them. We know the coast and how to hide. They've run too many boats aground trying to catch us." He stopped grinning. "Still the ruling families own the canneries and some big fishing boats. Occasionally they give us trouble when we want to buy fuel. Mostly, the people in the coves avoid the government and the ruling families."

"Mr. Rouseff says that it was the Fortenac and Vanderholm families who wanted M'TK burned because he wouldn't run his trains to the steel mills. He says the emperor ordered the burning to please his wife who is a Fortenac. The trains ran over three children who worked for Fortenac. Mr. Rouseff doesn't believe children should work in factories. He doesn't want them near his trains."

"Uncle John says, the Rouseffs are one of the most powerful ruling families. Do you really know Mr. Rouseff?"

"Papa and Mama know him. He treats Papa with respect. Papa thinks Mr. Rouseff is fair and honest. Mr. Rouseff is very angry with the Vanderholms and Fortenacs." I didn't tell Nicki that Papa said Mr. Rouseff was angry with the emperor.

"Uncle John is angry with the Fortenacs. He says they are over fishing the fishing grounds. Then they waste tons of fish by not processing it soon enough. He says by the time some of the fish gets processed it is half rotten. Sometimes they throw the rotting fish out. Sometimes they can it."

"Mama says that she thinks the country is changing. She says that if a man like Mr. Rouseff will talk to a man like Papa, then the country will change. My parents want me to go to the university."

"Do you want to go?"

"Yes." When they

"You would. I remember how you wanted to go to school when you were too young and the minute you turned five, Aunt Luella talked to the teacher and we had to baby sit you on the boat to school."

"I never gave you any trouble. I didn't need a baby-sitter."

"You know, you didn't. But, you sure wanted to go to school."

Nicki and I toured the city, visiting places I would never go if he was not so curious. I showed Nicki the cathedral. We went to Wulfton and looked at the yellow sky. We walked around the university campus until some students told us to go home.

One week, Uncle John told me not to come. He would bring the fish down to us. Mama was so excited to have her uncle and aunt visit. She cleaned the whole station. I had to give up my bedroom. I slept on a window seat Papa had built in our sitting room. I liked the window seat so I didn't mind losing my bedroom.

When Aunt Luella and Uncle John arrived, the customers crowded around Mama's tables waiting to buy fish. Aunt and Uncle watched as Mama and I put the fish out on the tables. Uncle John laughed when he saw Mama selling fish. All the fish were sold within minutes. He picked Mama up and danced her in circles. He pounded Papa and me on the back. "You have saved us. We cannot sell the fish for enough to the suppliers in the north. They don't pay me enough at the canneries to take the boat out and still make any money. This will work. Jake, can you go to more restaurants and tell them that we will have fish here on Saturday and Sunday? I want you to find the customers. I will get those fish down here."

Every Saturday and Sunday morning a cousin or Aunt and Uncle would arrive with a load of fish. The customers came. One Saturday morning the bakery owner came with bread to sell. He set up his table next to Mama's fish table. He sold almost all his bread. He had some sweet rolls with raisins in them left. Cousin Petral who brought the fish down, bought the rest of his bread. The market grew slowly at first. Mama's garden started producing more than we could eat. Mama sold vegetables.

One day, a farmer came to Papa. "I can't sell my produce to the suppliers for enough to cover my costs. Can I set up a table and see if I can sell some here?"

Papa thought for a minute. "This land belongs to the railroad. My wife can sell fish because I work here. I guess I can treat you the same as I do Mr. Baker. If you are willing to pay the railroad some of what you make for the use of their land, I can let you set up a table."

The market continued to grow. The railroad made a good income from the venders. Farmers and craftsmen got a good price for their goods. The businesses owned by the elite families complained. They ran ads on the radio and television about unhealthy food at the market. They sent the police to shut down the market, but the railroad security would not let them near it. The market was on private land. Once, the elite sent hired thugs to overturn the tables and knock down the booths. They did not send enough thugs. The vendors attacked back and beat up the men sent to destroy their business.

The M'TK open-air market became a small city in itself. Sometimes I sensed that it had taken on a life of its own. It became a living thing. The people changed, but the smells, the noise and the sense of community remained the same.

Mr. Rouseff visited often and laughed and talked about opening more markets. "I need to diversify. The government is starting to build more highways. The Vanderholms and their bootlickers, the Fortenacs, want to put me out of business. I'll show them." Mr. Rouseff both frightened and fascinated me.

Mama had magic in her fingers. One day, coming home on the trolley, I looked at my home and saw that her sixteen geraniums were now about two hundred geraniums. Bright red geraniums spilled out of window boxes and big pots by the station doors. She had them in her garden. Big baskets of geraniums hung from the eaves of the station. The garden overflowed with flowers. The station looked magnificent.

People started coming from Mercid to shop at the M'TK market. Mama sold geraniums. Sometimes she just gave them away saying. "These geraniums survived the M'TK fire. They are a sign that better times are coming."

When school was about to start for a new term, Mama took my old uniform out to a table. It sold immediately. Next she sold the clothes we bought for Boys Club Camp.

Papa started teasing Mama that he was afraid to take off his pants for fear she would sell them before he could put them back on.

Mama giggled. "Oh it seems to me that you are eager enough to get your pants off."

I am not sure which of my parents was more pleased with the market. Papa was so proud of Mama. He liked to tell me how wonderful she was. "I always knew she was special. Just look at her. See what she has done. She has made our home beautiful. She is helping her family and at the same time she helps all our neighbors." He sighed. I looked at how happy Papa was and thought that someday I would find someone to love as Papa loved Mama.

Chapter 10 Bookkeeper and Chief Stationmaster

M r. Pickett helped Mama with the market. He rolled his wheelchair up and down the sidewalk tending Mama's tables and making certain that vendors paid a fair share for their tables. We didn't know how we could possibly get along without Mr. Pickett. We never thought that including him in our prosperity would some day cause us to lose him. Papa paid him a wage for helping with the station. When Mama and Papa went away for a few hours or when they traveled north to visit her family, they paid him extra. We made the garden paths wide enough so he could roll his chair in the garden. Mama paid him for weeding and harvesting.

One day Mr. Pickett made an announcement at breakfast. "I hired a lawyer to help me find my children. The letter I got yesterday was from my daughter. She sounds happy to hear from me. She says she is coming to see me next week."

"I will have Jake's room ready for her. Is there anything else we can do to make her comfortable?" Mama should have told the woman she could not enter the station. Papa should not have let her off of the train.

Mr. Pickett's daughter, a woman in her late twenties arrived with her ten year-old son. She got off of the train, came into the station, and threw herself on her papa. She cried and kissed him. She scolded him for not writing sooner. She scolded and cried for the full two days she stayed with us. She thanked Mama and Papa for taking care of her papa.

Papa looked sad and grunted. "He is a good worker. He has earned his way."

Mr. Picket smiled at his daughter and called her, "Kitten." They talked about when she was little. He asked about his son. She told him her brother was a sergeant in the army. He asked questions about her husband and his grandchildren. He kept saying, "Imagine me, a grandfather, and I didn't even know."

Mama smiled at Mr. Picket and his daughter, but her eyes looked sad. Papa looked at them and went out to check the switches. Mr. Picket looked at his daughter and grandson and his eyes grew bright with pride and tears.

On the third morning, before Mr. Picket got on the train to go home with his daughter he said to Papa, "Mr. Jaconovich, thank you. I was a sorry mess full of self-pity when I met you. I've learned self-respect. I will miss you and the missus and that boy of yours, but I want to be with my family. I want to see my grandchildren."

Papa squeezed Mr. Picket on the shoulder. "If you need anything, let us know."

Mama kissed him on the cheek. "Please write. I will worry if you don't write."

When Mr. Picket shook my hand as if I were a grown man, I said, "I will miss you, sir. Please write and tell my mama that you are well and happy."

He did write. His letters comforted us for our loss. He told us about his grandchildren. He told us his daughter took in boarders. Her husband was happy to have her papa there during the day when he was gone. Mr. Pickett said he helped with the cooking and was making a garden. Papa quickly learned how much he had needed Mr. Picket's help.

"I have to do something. I can't go out to check on equipment because someone will come in wanting a ticket. I am so busy with the ticket sales, I can't keep up with the maintenance." Mama tried to help, but she was busy with the market and her garden. Sometimes Papa needed to run outside for a few minutes and Mama would be in the garden.

The situation grew worse. Somebody complained that the stationmasters were cheating customers. This complaint did not include M'TK. Papa did not cheat the customers. All of the stations had to be audited. This meant that a man had to come and watch how we did business. The auditor had to talk to the customers.

When the man arrived at the M'TK station, Mama met him with the station's books. When Papa took over the job of stationmaster she started keeping books. She showed the man that we had turned over to the railroad the right amount of money for every ticket sold. Every ticket had a number on it. She recorded the numbers and wrote down the amount of money beside the number. The man talked to the customers. They assured him that Mr. Jaconovich would never cheat. I noticed that the day the auditor came most of our friends who Papa had rescued from the fire, were in the station. They talked to the investigator.

When the investigator had gone away again, Mr. Rouseff came to talk to Mama. I wanted to see Mr. Rouseff so I watched and listened from the corner of the room while I pretended to repair a signal light. "Mrs. Jacob, you've done a good job here. Can you show the other stationmasters how to keep records like yours?"

Mama tried to sound respectful, but I could tell she didn't understand what Mr. Rouseff really wanted. "I was trained to be a bookkeeper. I can try to show others, but if they do not understand why the records need to be accurate, they will not learn."

His tone when he answered her told me that he expected to be obeyed. "They will learn."

"Would the other stationmasters come here? Where would they eat and sleep?"

"No, I want you to visit the other stations. You can stay in a hotel."

Mama looked at Papa. "No. I cannot be away from Jacob. No. I will not be separated from him." I thought she was going to cry. I knew my mama. I recognized a horror under her insistence which I did not understand until I'd spent more time in The Cove.

Mr. Rouseff looked at Papa. He looked at our beautiful station. "Good. Mr. Jaconovich, you can go with her. Make a list of everything you do here and give that to the other stationmasters. Look over the other stations and tell us what needs repaired."

Mama and Papa hesitated because they did not like the idea of someone they didn't know staying in their home to take care of the station. I could see they were excited at the idea of traveling. I wanted to help. "It would only be while I am in school. I'll take care of things when I am home." They still were not comforted.

They debated this for two days. They would make more money. They would get to see the country, but strangers would be in their home. "We cannot leave Jacob with strangers."

Mama asked, "Should we write to Uncle John and see if Ulally and Arvie can come stay with him?"

"Ulally would be afraid to leave The Cove. She is a little…well." Papa kissed Mama acknowledging that Aunt Ulally was different.

On the third day, Mr. Apkouta came into the station to visit Papa just as I got home from school. Papa asked, "Why are you not at work?"

"I got fired." Mr. Apkouta looked sick when he said this.

"What for?"

"My wife is sick. I took time to take care of her before I left so I was late."

Papa bit the inside of his cheek. He put down the paper he was holding, then picked it up again and twisted it. "I am sorry to hear about your wife. Can you come work for me?"

"Mr. Jaconovich! You do not have to give me a job."

Papa's voice rose and he started talking faster. "I'm not giving you a job. I am begging you to help me. My wife and I have been asked to travel to the other stations. We don't want to leave strangers to run the station. Jake will be here. We don't like leaving our son with people we don't know. You will not make as much money here as in the warehouse, but you can bring your wife with you. We will all take care of her."

Mr. Apkouta went home and got his wife.

The Apkoutas got my room. I finally moved down to Mr. Pickett's room. I liked it. It was little more than a closet, actually it was a small storage room with a window in one end. Mr. Apkouta and I built a bed across the whole closet about four feet off of the floor. We built shelves and hooks underneath. I had a window and a light. I found some sports posters in a store near my school. I bought two and hung them in my room. The station had a toilet and washroom downstairs. I had my own bathroom when most people in the city had to share one bathroom with all the people living on two floors of their building.

I missed Mama and Papa when they were traveling. I didn't mind it so much when there were gone during the week, when I was in school, but a few times they were gone on the weekend and I missed them more. Aunt and Uncle came twice when Mama and Papa were gone. It helped to have them nearby. They took me out to eat in a restaurant. I made sure that we went to one that bought fish from us. I had fun telling them about selling rats to Mr. Wu for his restaurant. They were still horrified about that.

Chapter 11 Fiona

I was sixteen and in the fourteenth form when my football team had a game in the capital. We were excited to visit the capital. The girl's team went with us. We would take the train up during the day, play our game, stay in a hotel, and come back in the morning.

I was wild to see the capital. I had a list of cathedrals and parks I wanted to see. We were scheduled to tour The Compound, where the emperor lived and worked. We went on the tour before the game.

At The Compound, we toured the museum, the grand salon, the dining room and ballroom. I was impressed with the gleaming woodwork. Some walls had huge murals painted on them. Some of the rooms were painted in pastel colors with gilt on the trim. We got to see the emperor's office. His desk was made out of beautiful wood from another country. It was huge and smooth as glass. As we were coming down the main staircase in the newest wing, I made a joke to the girl next to me. "This is not bad. I think I'll live here someday."

Our coach heard me. "Jake Jaconovich, you will never live here. Only people who come from the finest families can live here. You are a nobody."

I was embarrassed, angry and a little belligerent. In my heart I knew I loved my little room at the station, but I entertained a little fantasy about what it would be like having a wife and beautiful children and living in the magnificent Compound.

We won our football game. We were wild with excitement. Everybody wanted to go out. I had no idea what *out* meant. We were allowed to do anything we wanted. We decided to go dancing. We walked down the city street and entered the first club we came to.

There was no charge to get in, but we had to buy a drink. I had no idea what to order in a fancy place like this. I watched our team captain and ordered what he ordered. We found a very small table. The other team members asked the girls to dance. I watched, and tasted my drink. It made me cough so hard I slopped some on my hand. While I was drying my hand with a napkin, I remembered my teacher slapping that hand with a ruler. I remembered her telling me to stay away from alcohol. I remembered the image in my mind of the drunks in M'TK. I didn't touch my drink again.

After the first dance, the girl I talked to on the stairs at The Compound asked me to dance with her. She surprised me because she was two years older than me. Her name was Fiona. We talked a little while we danced.

"Are you going to university?"

"Yes."

"What are you going to study?"

"Law."

"You have to be smart to study law."

"More than being smart you have to have a passion for rule of law."

Fiona giggled and jiggled.

I forgot what we were talking about.

She reminded me. "Do you want to be emperor?"

"Our teacher is right. Someone like me cannot be emperor. I will get my degree in law and work for one of the big industries, maybe the railroad."

"If you were emperor what would you do?"

"Give everybody equal rights, install elections, establish a parliament, abolish child labor." I shut up because Fiona had just bumped into me.

I don't know why she put up with me. I'd never danced with a girl outside of our dance class. Fiona wore a sexy red dress that emphasized her womanliness. I really wanted to stare at her breasts. They were so round and soft and jiggly. I became totally tongue-tied. When I returned to our table our team captain laughed at me. "I drank your drink because you danced with my girl."

"I got the better end of that deal." I grinned at him.

The whole party danced a few more times. I danced a fast dance with Fiona. I liked the way she jiggled. I liked how soft she felt when her body bumped against mine. I'd met Fiona.

We decided to move on to another club. Again we had to buy drinks to get in. I tried for beer because it was cheap. I didn't like it any better than the whisky at the first club. The girls were drinking champagne. I set my beer down and claimed Fiona for a dance. I made certain that we bumped into each other a lot during that dance. She giggled when we did. She was so beautiful. I was certain I'd found someone to love. I noticed the other boys drinking my beer when they thought I wasn't looking. I didn't care. I'd met Fiona.

The group started getting rowdy when we went to the next club. I didn't like spending so much money. I finally set my worries aside saying my parents wanted me to make friends. I was in the capital doing what young people do when they are in the capital. I'd met Fiona.

I left my wine on the table and concentrated all my efforts on getting Fiona to dance with me again. She seemed to want to lean on me. I was definitely proud of myself. Our team had won the game. We were celebrating, and Fiona was now my girlfriend. I didn't pay attention to how much anybody else was drinking. I was not spending any more money on anything other than Fiona. She wanted another champagne. I bought her the champagne. I tasted it. It was foul. I wanted to taste Fiona.

I whispered in her ear. "Let's go back to the hotel." I was thinking of all her lush curves and how they would feel in my hands. She nodded. I was not sure I was going to be able to find our hotel when all I could see was my beautiful Fiona.

We stood up to leave. Gordy got sick on the floor. The rest of the team and the girls were getting loud and vulgar. I saw two large men coming toward our table. I had to practically drag Fiona toward the door. She acted silly and staggered when she walked. I should not have bought that last champagne for my darling Fiona.

The rest of the team and the girls were thrown out on the street just after Fiona and I left. They were in bad shape. They were my teammates. I couldn't leave them on the sidewalk. Gordy was not the only one puking by now. Two of the others were sober enough to help me get the rest of the team down the street six blocks to the hotel. I left Fiona for a few minutes and she sat down on the sidewalk then toppled over sound asleep. I picked her up in my arms and carried her back to the hotel. I wasn't so sure about Fiona. I carried her to her room, dumped her on the bed and told the one girl who could still stand on her own to take care of the others.

The next morning I faced the challenge of getting the team up, out of the bathroom and onto the train. The coach was worthless--dead drunk. We left him in his hotel room. Gordy looked green but had stopped with the dry heaves. My teammates kept quiet on the way home. Fiona sat next to me and held onto my arm with both her hands, put her soft head on my shoulder and went back to sleep. She really was sweet, and so soft. I resolved not to buy her any more champagne.

From this point on, everyone acknowledged that Fiona was my girlfriend. We spent all our free time together at school. We kissed on the fire escape. I helped her with her homework. She adored me. I felt ten feet tall with the sweet curvy Fiona on my arm. She was *on my arm*. She *clung* to my arm. This habit made me a little nervous in a crowd, were I might need both arms to protect us at any time. Still, Fiona was my girlfriend.

I finished my fourteenth form at school a month after I turned seventeen. I had my application for university. My grades were perfect. My test scores were excellent. I was from the north. I needed a recommendation from someone in one of the elite families. I was horrified when I learned this. I had no connections to such a person. My parents and their friends were as far removed from the elite as life is from death. I didn't know what to do. I'd not seen Mr. Rouseff for months. I couldn't ask Papa's boss for a recommendation.

A few days before I graduated, the director of the school called to me in the hall as soon as I arrived at school. "Jake Jaconovich?"

I turned to see who was calling. "Yes, Mr. Director."

He motioned me to the side of the hall away from the crowd and asked in a soft voice. "Have you filled out your university application yet?"

"I have it all done except for the recommendation. I don't know anyone who will give me a recommendation."

He nodded. "Come with me, I want to talk to you."

I followed the director to his office. I'd never been here before. I was surprised that it was really rather shabby yet comfortable. The director motioned for me to sit in a leather armchair. He took his place on the other side of his scarred wood desk. I tried not to stare at the stacks of professional magazines and papers that covered every surface. I waited for Mr. Director to speak.

"Jake, you are an excellent student. What is more important, you have good character. I would not do this for anybody, but I can write you the recommendation you need. Don't tell the other students I've done this. I can get a few of you into university. My credibility will be worthless if I recommend too many students or if the students I recommend fail."

"I will not fail."

"I know you won't." He reached into his drawer and pulled out a letter he had already written. He signed it and handed it to me. "Good luck to you son."

"Thank you. I will do my best."

I had everything I needed to go to University. I knew I had enough money for my first year tucked away in Mr. Bear. I had the grades, the test scores, and the recommendation. I could have kissed Mr. Director.

Fiona was not going to be at college. We talked about what she could do as I walked her home after school. "Can you take a business course? That is what Mama did. She is teaching the other stationmasters how to keep books. She has always had good jobs."

"Mmm, Jake," Fiona stopped right there on the sidewalk and turned to face me. She ran her hand up my chest and behind my neck. I checked to see if we were safe. I didn't like being completely exposed on the sidewalk.

She almost lisped. "Why do you talk about me working when you are going to be the big important man and take care of me?"

I laughed. "Because, my love, I am nothing but a student now. I don't have money for a wife. I am very much afraid my wife will have to help support us for several years."

"Can't you ask your Papa for money for both of us?"

I was horrified. "No." I knew my voice was stern.

She pouted. "Oh, I've made my darling Jakey cross."

"Fiona, once a man is married he does not ask his Papa for money. I would feel ashamed to ask Papa for money."

"Of course darling. You are so manly, I cannot think of anything you could do to be less than a man." She pressed all those soft curves up against me. I held her in my arms, but the little cloud of Fiona's imperfections just grew a little bigger and darker.

I took Fiona home to meet my family. Mama fixed a fancy dinner for us. The station looked as beautiful as it always does. Fiona praised everything she saw. She offered to help Mama with the meal and told us all how she cooked at home.

"Oh if you like to cook, take a look at this new cookbook I got from the library." Mama showed Fiona a fat book with a picture of a roast chicken on front.

"What is this?"

"It's a book of recipes."

"I've never heard of such a thing." Fiona set the book aside. "My mama taught me how to cook everything."

I was distressed over Fiona's tone of voice.

Mrs. Apkouta picked up the book. "Does this have recipes for lamb? My parents live in the mountains. They send us lamb in the spring. I'd like some new ideas for fixing lamb. They sent me a big chunk last month because I sent Xanthia a dress so she could work in an office. I was so tired of lamb by the time we finished it." She thumbed through the book.

Fiona looked around us, "Jakey the flowers at the windows are beautiful. When we have our own house we should have flowers at the windows just like this. They make this apartment feel like a grand house."

"Mama started all those geraniums from one plant."

"Oh yes, lets buy dozens and dozens of them for our house." Fiona smiled at my parents. "Jakey has promised that when we are married he will buy me a big house. I want to have lots and lots flowers like you do.

Mama and Mrs. Apkouta busied themselves with serving the meal. Papa grunted and Mr. Apkouta started a discussion about fixing the gerry.

The dinner tasted delicious. We ate silently for a few minutes. Mrs. Apkouta started a discussion. "I see in the paper where the emperor is talking about building a highway to run the entire length of the country from Oceana to Portlandia."

Mama commented, "That will be a challenge through the mountains."

Papa asked, "I wonder if this is another move against Rouseff?"

Mr. Apkouta scowled and thought for a minute before he commented, "Most modern countries have both highways and trains."

"I'd hate to see highways replace the trains." Papa sighed.

"Oh I loved the train when we went to the capital." Fiona announced. "Everybody was so hung over from the night before that we could sleep all the way home on the train. Isn't that right Jakey?"

I mumbled, "They behaved like a bunch of fools."

I noticed both Mr. and Mrs. Apkouta shift in their chairs.

Again we ate in silence. I was uncomfortable and thought I should try to start a conversation. "Oh, I finished reading Les Miserables. The story was well told. It made me uncomfortable."

"I'm surprised the school has such a book on their reading list." Papa looked sad.

I wanted to know what the others thought of the book. "Why? Do you think the people here would resort to a revolution?"

Mrs. Apkouta answered. "I thought that the book could incite riots among our people. Rioting never gets us anywhere."

Mr. Apkouta spoke sternly, "Jake, you are going to go to university. I don't think it is a good idea for you to say more than what you just have about such a book. Between us we know that the people have good reason to rebel. That is why the old families go on purges. You will need to be careful when you are at university." Mr. Apkouta sounded genuinely concerned for my safety.

I agreed with him. "I think I may have to walk a fine line between what I've read and what I think. I was surprised that we were assigned the book to read."

The conversation flowed around the topic of the French Revolution and our confusion over the book being on our reading list at school.

I thought Fiona might join the conversation. Surely she had read the book too. Finally Fiona spoke up. "Jakey your mama has such beautiful knives and forks. I want some just like this when we are married."

The Apkoutas looked at each other out of the corners of their eyes.

Mama smoothed over the awkward change of subject. "Thank you. I think they are beautiful too. I got them at the house wares store on fourth."

Papa signed and patted Mama's hand. He looked sad. "We have many blessings."

"Jakey you'll have to take me there."

I nodded then addressed the group. "When I was little, people on the street called me The M'TK Sewer Rat…"

"Oh how horrid." Fiona looked about to cry on my behalf.

I rushed to assure her. "No, that is okay. It sounds low but I was proud of the name. I wonder now why I am still proud of the name."

Mr. Apkouta got a coughing fit and hid his face behind his napkin. Papa seemed to shake a couple times. Mrs. Apkouta turned away from the table to offer her husband water. Mama smiled happily.

Papa cleared his throat. "It was a name you earned through honest hard work and behaving respectably. A name earned through respectable means will be an honor. It is when you are being a fool that you will not like the names you are called."

The Apkoutas looked grave.

Mama patted my hand.

This was a new thought for me. I wondered why Papa thought I was being a fool. Surely, there was nothing wrong with Fiona. I felt a little silly when she called me Jakey, but she called me that because she loved me.

I walked Fiona home after dinner. She lived over a car repair shop on Doh Creek Road. Gangs sometimes hung out along the creek. I didn't like for her to walk alone.

I tried for a couple kisses in the shadows of awnings. She didn't want to kiss me. "I understand now, sweetheart, some of the things you have been trying to tell me. We cannot live with your parents. It wouldn't be right. I may have to get a job just until you are able to support us."

I kissed her on top of her head. "Just until then, dear." I thought Fiona was acting more sensible and realistic.

The next weekend, Aunt Luella and Uncle John came down with the fish to work the market.

At dinner Uncle John told us his worries about the fishing season. "Nicki, has been conscripted. I don't know what I will do."

I jumped at the opportunity I saw opening up. "I don't start university until September. I've finished school for now. I don't know how to drive your boat, but I am willing to help." I looked to Papa for permission.

Papa nodded his consent.

Uncle John grinned. "All right, young man, pack up your things and come back with us."

"You keep my boy safe." Mama sounded anxious.

"He'll be safer on my boat in the middle of the ocean than in M'TK."

Mr. Apkouta snorted. I knew there was something in of this conversation I was missing. Everybody seemed particularly merry at dinner.

In the morning I took the train north to work on Uncle's fishing boat. I sent Fiona a letter before I left, telling her where I was going and assuring her that this job meant that we could get married sooner. I made certain to write my address clearly so Fiona would know where to write to me.

Chapter 12 Fisherman

We left early in the morning mists to go out fishing. I wanted to whine that the sun wasn't quite up yet. The fishing boat, the M'NO, was a little over ten meters long. It was powered by two diesel engines. We had four bunks in the bow. The bridge was up four steps at midship Living quarters went forward down three steps. Living quarters consisted of the bunks, a tiny galley and the head.

We had a hold midship for the water and fuel tanks. We had some storage for food and anything we wanted out of sight. The back of the boat was half full of fishing nets and the winches for pulling the nets in. We had tall booms for troll fishing, but we usually used the nets.

There were four of us on the boat, Uncle John, Cousin John, Cousin Petral and myself. Uncle started immediately to teach me how to drive the boat and how to navigate the entrance to the cove.

I loved everything about being on a boat from the minute we left the dock. I liked how the motion of the boat communicated to my senses that I was free from the laws of land. It is a totally different perspective for seeing the world. Viewed from the entrance to the cove the house rambling across the hillside, looked like a painting on a wall.

Uncle John lectured me as I watched him handle the gears and throttles. "Our family has lived in this cove for hundreds of years. It is a good place. We have the mountains at our back and the shoal guarding the cove. We have lived free from the government for centuries. The government doesn't even know some members of the family exist. I should never have sent Nicki away to secondary school. It is good that you will be in university before you are old enough to be conscripted."

Uncle John could read the sea like I could read the street. He could see where the currents ran. He knew where the fish would be. We put out our nets. He was right. He knew where the fish would be. The boat was riding low in the water when we pulled in the nets full of fish at mid-day. I noticed my cousins didn't talk. I wanted to ask questions about everything. Uncle answered me patiently.

"He hasn't changed since he was four has he." Petral surprised me with this memory when I answered another of my questions.

I laughed. "What do you mean?"

"You were always asking questions. You never shut up. You shamed the rest of us by thinking up things we never thought to ask about." Petral and Cousin John shook their heads and chuckled at the memory.

I questioned. "How do you learn if you don't ask questions?"

"Never mind them Jake. They never learned half of the things you are asking about. It won't hurt them to learn the answers." Uncle John sounded amused.

I thought we would be home by dinner time. It got late. The setting sun finally told me we were headed north. I was hungry and wanted my dinner.

"Are we going to get dinner tonight?"

The others looked at each other. They didn't tell me when we would eat. About an hour later, Cousin John put up a flag for the country just north of ours. Cousin Petral draped a piece of canvas over our name on the back of the boat. We pulled into the dock in a small cove. I was certain we were no longer in our own country. I knew that I didn't have a passport with me. I kept my mouth firmly shut.

A man came down to meet us. He and Uncle talked quietly. The man left. I saw more men coming down the dock with handcarts. We unloaded our catch into the handcarts. Uncle went with it into the village. I watched everything. I listened to the sounds. I may not be able to read the sea. I could read the street. All was well. Finally, Uncle John came back with a cart load of goods and a hot dinner for us. We untied the boat and left the small harbor.

Petral broke the silence. "He can keep quiet."

Cousin John grunted. "I was afraid he was going to start asking everybody his questions."

I tried to explain. "M'TK was not an easy place to grow up. I learned to survive."

My cousins looked at each other.

Uncle grunted. "I thought so."

We didn't get home for five days. We unloaded the supplies we picked up in the village in another small cove. They gave us a load of shrimp that we sold back in the village where we bought the supplies. We got another boatload of fish that we took farther up the coast. We anchored in a small cove this time. Uncle told us to load the fish into canvas bags. My cousins rowed ashore with the first load of fish, then one rowed back for Uncle John and more fish.

Uncle John gave me instructions. "Jake stay with the boat. If anyone other than us comes into this cove, get the boat out of here. Stay away for twenty-four hours then come back. If we do not show up on the beach within thirty minutes, head for home. Bring the boat into the village there. Someone from the family will be waiting for you."

"Yeah, thanks."

Uncle John laughed at my lack of enthusiasm.

They were gone for six hours. Nobody came into the cove. In the middle of the night Uncle John and my cousins came aboard carrying fish sacks full of lamb. In the morning, Uncle started the engines and headed for home. We stopped and fished for a couple hours and caught a respectable number of fish. We stopped in the port at Midville, sold some fish and refueled. Cousin Victor met us in Norville to take fifty kilos of fish south on the train to sell in the M'TK Market. Uncle complained about the catch to anyone who would listen.

We stayed home for two days. I had a letter from Fiona. I reread that letter several times every day. I carried it on the boat with me. My Fiona loved me.

"Dearest jakey darling, How could you be so crewl as to run off without giving me enuf kisses to last until you return? I miss! Kiss! miss!, kiss! miss! you so much. I think about kissing you all the time. I love you so much. I think about when we are married and you will not go away. We will live in a big house. I will be so prowd of you. I need to kiss you. When we are married we can spend all day in bed kissing and kissing and more. (yes, you know what I mean!!!!!! Oh shocking!!!) I have not gone nowhere since you've been gone. Well I did visit some of Mama's friends but they are old so they don't cownt. I havn't done nothing! I want you to come back. I no you are working hard so we can get maried so I will wate for you to come back. I don't like you being gone but I am wateing like a good girl. I don't want to talk to nobody or go nowhere without you...so you see my darling Jakey I am very upset at being separated from you. Love and kisses and hugs Fiona"

No, my Fiona was not going to work where she needed to write. I thought about her soft curves and sighed. I remembered Papa's words. Was I being a fool over Fiona?"

When we left again, I brought all my books on board. My cousins laughed at how I had wanted to go to school when I was just a baby and wondered that I still wanted to go to school.

I replied to their teasing. "I thought you liked school well enough."

"It was boring." Petral sounded angry. "My second form teacher acted like she was better than we were."

I nodded. "Yeah, I had one like that in the seventh form so I went to the director and got promoted to the eighth form." I looked at Cousin John.

Cousin John sounded as angry as Petral. "In school all you do is talk about stuff. It isn't the same as doing stuff. I don't want to read about life. I want to live."

I wondered if they'd had too many teachers like my seventh form teacher or if the lure of being outdoors was greater than the ideas in books. I wondered at the angry undertones I heard. I decided to end the discussion. "At least I won't be bored out of my mind while waiting for the fish to find us."

This trip out was the same as the last. We visited other coves and villages, picking up cargo or selling fish. Occasionally, Uncle's behavior told me that what we were doing was not completely legal. I saw no harm in it. Uncle made money and people in the villages had fish to process or sell. People in the remote coves were able to trade for goods they couldn't buy in their isolated coves. I never once thought of myself as a smuggler. I never thought about taxes and duties.

The weeks passed. I'd read all the books I'd brought with me. I read all the books in the house in The Cove. When we stopped in the village to refuel, I went looking for books. There were no libraries or bookstores. I was shocked that these people were so poor that they did not have even a small library. I wrote home asking my parents to send me books. I mailed my letter to Fiona.

"Dearest, I was thankful to hear from you. Believe me I think about you all the time. I long to see my beautiful Fiona and hold her in my arms. I am confident that the day will come when we will not be separated. Until that day comes, I am confident that you love me. Any separation we bear now will result in our appreciation of the other growing sharper from knowing how painful it is to be separated.

I am making enough money to pay for another year at the university.

I'm afraid it will be very expensive. I must finish my schooling. That is our greatest hope for a prosperous future.

You may not recognize me when I return for the sun is bleaching my hair and turning my skin quite dark. I love being outside though.

The work is hard. We may move a thousand kilos of fish several times a day. First, we haul the fish out of the sea. When we get the fish to port, we load the slippery devils onto handcarts. We roll the handcarts to the suppliers' scales and load the fish onto the scales. From the scales, we load them into the suppliers' crates to be processed.

Sometimes we buy supplies while we are in port. Then we have a heavy load of supplies to load onto the boat. One of the supplies we load is food. My aunt sends a great deal of food with us. You would not believe how much water we bring onto the boat. The ocean surrounds us, but we cannot drink salt water. Every time we go ashore we refill our water supply. It is usually Cousin Jake who refills the water tanks. My cousins have more important things to do. I think they like to go into town to look at girls. I do not need to do that. I look inside my memories of you and see the most beautiful woman on earth. I love You, Jake

In mid July, we were making our way up the coast. This had been a good trip out. We met up with a boat from farther south. They had fresh crab. We couldn't get crab in our waters. We took the crab north to the nearest northern village in our country. We sold the crab. Uncle took the money from the crab and some of the other money we had with us and had it changed into big bills at the bank. He was carrying five thousand dollars. We needed to walk about five blocks from the bank to the dock where we left the boat.

I felt uncomfortable carrying so much money in a strange village. The hairs on the back of my neck stood up. I told my cousins to walk in front of Uncle, and I would follow behind. I walked close behind Uncle and looked around me.

The village was bigger than most that we visited. Like all the others it perched on a hillside running from the mountains to the sea. The cannery occupied one side of the bay. A swarm of battered houses ran along three streets from the cannery to the one street in the village. The main street had shops or offices on each side. I didn't like the fact that there were walkways and alleys between all the buildings.

I saw a few people on the street when we started. We walked a block. The street grew deserted. I stepped closer to Uncle. "Trouble!" My cousins heard me and immediately picked up our pace. Suddenly, men came out of the shadows beside the buildings and walkways. They quickly surrounded us.

I whispered. "Keep moving forward." We kept walking. The men surrounding us moved along with us for a few steps.

"Why don't you hand us the money you are carrying?" The leader was in a bad position for me to talk to. He was facing my cousins.

"What money?" Cousin John tried to sound ignorant. We came to a halt.

"The money you got at the bank."

I figured the teller tipped these men off that we had money. I remembered my first lessons from my days in Mr. Wu's gym. First, avoid the fight. The second rule demanded honor. It is honorable to warn your opponent that he will get hurt. I said. "I don't want to hurt you. Go on home before you get hurt."

The leader of the group sneered. "Aw the pretty boy doesn't want to get hurt."

"No, I don't. I don't want to hurt you either." I had my back up against my Uncle's back.

The leader sneered. "Hey look, we have a pretty boy here who doesn't want to get hurt. Why don't you just hand over the money if you don't want to get hurt."

I tried again. "What about you? Do you like getting hurt? Have you ever had your nose broken or your arm dislocated? It hurts. A dislocated arm means you may never be able to work." I was watching the men around us. My cousins, Uncle and I were standing back to back. They had us outnumbered by three men.

Uncle sounded commanding when he spoke. "Okay guys, you've had your fun go on home and forget about us."

I saw the light reflect off of the blade of a knife on my left. My first kick knocked the knife flying. My second kick broke the owner's nose. I'd exposed my back and one man made the mistake of trying to grab me from behind. I was stronger now than I when I was twelve. I tried to remember all the moves. I hadn't practiced. I broke into a sweat thinking that I had forgotten. I thought of Mr. Wu. I could almost smell his gym. My body remembered. I could hear Mr. Wu's voice inside my head, teaching me. The second man hit the wall of the building beside us and didn't get up. I flipped the third man into the street. The fourth one ran.

The fifth man grabbed Cousin John and held a knife to his throat. "Give me your money or I slit his throat."

Petral spoke up. "Sorry about this cousin. You've been a pain in the ass this whole trip." We started moving forward again.

"I'm warning you. I'll cut his throat."

Petral shrugged. "We know. We just don't care that much."

I tried. "You know blood stinks. You get blood on you, your woman won't like it."

Uncle John growled, "I don't think he has a woman."

"Ah. Is that why he called me pretty? You like pretty boys do you? Is that how you like it? You know what? I bet you don't have a lover cause you're a coward. Yep, a coward who attacks unarmed men. You think your knife makes you a man. It makes you a coward. So what we have here, cousins, is a virgin coward. Women don't want him and he can't even get another man."

I watched the man's eyes. I found the word that triggered a reaction, virgin. "Yep a virgin. He's a virgin unless he owns sheep. No? A cowardly virgin it is."

That did it. The man threw Cousin John aside to get at me in his rage. I am still a short man. I did not have my full growth then. My assailant was bigger than me. He came at me with the knife. I stepped inside, grabbed his arm and kept moving under his shoulder. His arm came out of its socket. The pain distracted him so I simply pushed him down. I spun around and faced the remaining two men. One ran. The other stood frozen outnumbered four to one.

I was panting a little. "Go on. Go on home. I don't like hurting people." Our last stupid assailant made a lunge for me with his knife. I was tired. I did not want to try dislocating his shoulder. I sidestepped the knife, then kicked his feet out from under him. He fell hard on the sidewalk.

I gasped to my cousins. "Let's get out of here."

We ran. Nobody tried to follow us. I saw the men on the ground behind us trying to get up. One made it to his feet, but he made no attempt to follow us. We cast off while Uncle was starting the engines. We made it out of the harbor with no problems.

Uncle made one terse remark. "I think we'll head for home, boys."

We didn't say anything for several minutes. Eventually Cousin John snorted. "You could have left one of them for us."

I chuckled. "Nah, I'm out of shape for that sort of thing. I needed the practice."

We were silent for another hour or so.

"Jake?" Cousin Petral interrupted my thoughts of Fiona.

"Um?"

"Where did you learn to fight?'

"A man in M'TK, Mr. Wu taught a martial arts class. I haven't really had any classes since I turned thirteen."

"You did okay."

"Yeah, for a while there I was afraid I'd forgotten some moves, but they came back." We were silent for several minutes more.

"Jake?" Petral spoke again.

"Um?"

"Thanks."

"'s okay."

Cousin John finally spoke up. "Hey, I'm sorry if I teased you about going to school and asking questions and things. Man! You do not look like someone who could fight like that."

I laughed. "If I ever run up against someone who does not underestimate me because of my appearance, I will be in trouble. Those men back there were not expecting any of us to have training. They had no idea how to defend themselves against someone trained."

My cousins took turns asking questions. "Why did you get training?"

I thought of the hours in Mr. Wu's upstairs gym. "I was six when I started." I told them the story about Mr. Wu and the rats and the classes. They asked about the fights I'd been in. Finally, they reached the end of their questions for tonight. I sat and watched the stars while Uncle took us home.

We got home in the middle of the day. I had a letter from Fiona. I'd been mailing letters to her every week. This was the second one I'd received from her.

Darling Jakey thank you for your nice long letters. I sleep with them pressed to my heart every night. I would much rather press you to my heart. I miss you. I miss your kisses. You sound so busy. Do you reely miss me? It sownds like you are so busy you must forget about me. I never do nothing here. All I do is think about kissing you and how you are working so hard so we can have a big howse some day. Mama has company over almost every day. I do not like that. It makes me miss you even more. They try to cheer me up but I am still so sad. Frends want me to go dancing but I am not going to go. I wood look at them acting all happy and I wood be even more sad from missing you. I love you. – Fiona

Along with my letter from Fiona, I had a package from Mama waiting for me. I opened the package and found six brand new books. Mama sent a note.

Son, I took the list of classes you registered for to the university bookstore. The clerk there helped me pick out the right books for your classes. I hope this helps you get started. Do not worry about the money. Papa and I are so proud of you, we want to pay for your schooling.

Papa and I have been spending most of our time away from home at the stations in the capital. When we are not working, we visit museums and gardens. I went on a special tour of The Compound Gardens. They were my favorite.

We have also visited the stores. Papa and I bought new clothes for work because we are teachers now. I have a pretty green dress suit. Papa has a real suit with a vest and tie. We both look so fancy. We dressed up in our new clothes and went out to eat in a fancy restaurant. You have a wonderful man for your papa.

All my love,

Mama

We went back out to sea again. This time we went south to catch migrating fish off of the mouth of a river. We had to stay in international waters. The fishing would not be as good here as it would be closer in. My cousins wanted to go closer in. Uncle refused, saying, "We will get enough fish out here. I guess if the fish get past us, they belong to the people who live along the river." We got enough fish. We took them back to our country to sell. I thought we might sell them in the southern port cities but Uncle John refused to put in there. We went further up the coast and sold our fish there.

Uncle explained. "People from the south look down on us because we work for our living. We will not sell them fresh fish. Because they hate us, we will have no dealings with them."

I thought he was too harsh. My cousins called him old fashioned.

Uncle John sat silent for about twenty minutes. Then he explained. "I think we could put in at the southern ports. I think we could sell our fish. I do not think they would let us take the boat and leave again. The boat is too valuable. They would want it."

We made more trips south to fish and back north again to sell them. We spent a few days between trips at home. In mid-August, we returned after six days at sea. We had been less successful this trip. Uncle John said the fishing season was about over. We would go out again, then it would be time to stay in the cove and harvest shrimp and mussels. It was almost time for me to go home. When we got to the house there was another letter from Fiona.

"Mama says I must rite to you myself. I am being maried tomarow. My new husband is 34. He has a nice house. I will not have to wate to be rich. He is rich now. I don't want to have to work. Fiona

I was never so shocked or surprised. I am certain no thoughts ran through my head for a full five minutes. Nobody said anything. They looked at me and looked away. I handed the letter to Uncle John. He read it and shook his head. "Son when you are ready to talk. I'll be here."

I did not talk for days. I took out her other letters to me. I reread them. I thought and thought.

When we took the boat out again, I knew my cousins refrained from saying anything for fear of distressing me more. We hauled in more fish. We went back to the little cove where we anchored and took the fish ashore by rowboat. This time Uncle John stayed with the boat. We hauled the fish ashore and tied up the rowboat high up on the shingle beach. Each of us hoisted a twenty-five-kilo bag of fish over each shoulder and started walking.

We started walking uphill. After the first kilometer or so, I wondered if I was going to keep up. I was carrying fifty kilos of fish. They felt like a hundred kilos by the time I had walked for twenty minutes. We continued to climb. My neck muscles hurt. After thirty minutes, I felt beyond pain. I wondered how I was going to manage to hold my head up. After forty minutes, we were still climbing. When I picked up one foot, I was unsure whether it would go forward or back. We walked on. None of us said anything. After about fifty minutes of climbing I wondered if I was going to survive. I began to hear a new sound, like the wind. It almost had a growl in it. I labored on. I became aware that part of the wind was my own labored breath. I heard my cousins laboring beside me. At the end of an hour of climbing and carrying the fish, I'd had enough.

"Are either of you going to call a halt to this insanity or are we all going to kill ourselves from stubbornness?" We stopped in the middle of the trail and eased our fish bags off of our shoulders. Oh, my neck and shoulders hurt! I started to laugh. My cousins started laughing. None of us knew what was so funny. At that moment I realized something. "You know I think I'm over Fiona. I think I've had another narrow escape by not being where someone expected me to be." We laughed some more.

We stopped at a little farm about four kilometers inland. The farmer hitched his old horse to a wagon. We loaded the fish on the wagon and walked alongside it all the way to the village.

We got a good price for the fish. The people did not speak our language. I wondered if they were one of our isolated mountain communities or if we were over the border. They did not have access to a fresh fish market here. They were happy to buy what we had to sell. They paid us with fruit and lamb.

That was our last stop. When we got back to the M'NO we turned home for the last time. My career as a fisherman was over. I had to get home and get ready for my first year at university.

Chapter 13 University

When I got home, I had a notice waiting for me saying I needed to pay my tuition and fees in two days. "Papa, can I have Thursday morning off. I need to go to the university and pay my fees."

"Mr. Apkouta will watch the station. Mama and I will come with you. I will pay for your schooling."

"Papa, I've saved enough money for school."

"I have money now. Mama and I agree that we want to do this. You have been a good son. It makes me proud to be able to pay for your university."

On Thursday morning, Mama and Papa dressed in their fine new clothes and went with me to the university. Signs told us where to go. I did not see any other parents there with their children. My parents looked so happy and proud to be there. They gave me confidence that I would not fail. This was good because I was terrified. I was entering the world of the elite. What did I know?

We waited in line to be served. Finally, I talked to the cashier and showed her my registration papers. Papa and Mama stood on each side of me. The cashier showed us my bill. I knew Mama was quickly making certain it was accurate. She nodded to Papa. He took crisp new bills out of a wallet and handed them to the cashier. She spoke very respectfully to my parents and blushed when Papa smiled at her. When we walked away, Papa started laughing. "She had no idea that we are from the north. You remember this son. See how she didn't try to cheat us? She acted real respectful. She thought we were from the south. When you are here, I want you to act respectable. You do not need to advertise that we are from the north. I don't want you to have trouble. I don't want the man who gave you the recommendation to get in trouble."

I laughed. "I suppose this will be somewhat like surviving in M'TK. I will be careful." I thought about the situation. I remembered the teachers who gave me trouble in school. I would be careful.

My Papa is very wise. I had no idea what kind of trouble Papa expected until I went to my history class on the second day of classes. The teacher took roll. He came to my name. "Jaconovich. What kind of name is that?"

"I don't understand what you are asking, sir." I wondered where this was going and thought nothing good would come of that question.

"What family do you belong to?"

I thought that I was about to be expelled. I didn't know what to say. "Are you asking me which of the southern families I am associated with?" My fear caused me to speak slowly and carefully.

"Yes."

I was angry at being asked this question. I did not know how to answer. I thought quickly. I'd met Mr. Rouseff the owner of the railroad several times. Mama and Papa knew him. "Rouseff."

The teacher did not bother me anymore. He asked two other students what their family affiliation was. I was afraid they might get expelled, but they had correct answers.

After class, the other students nearly exploded when we reached the hall. "Imagine him having the nerve to ask us who our family is!"

"Who does he think he is questioning our right to be here?" I kept quiet. Another boy slapped me on the back.

"I guess you told him, proper." He laughed. "The tone of your voice when you said Rouseff put him in his place."

One of the girls appeared to be on the verge of tears. "I can't believe he would ask such a question. I was so embarrassed. I'm going to tell my papa."

I smiled at the girl who threatened to tell her papa and decided this discussion had gone on long enough. "Don't bother your papa with such a petty problem. The teacher was rude, insulting really. I figure part of being in university is to learn to deal with such problems on our own."

"Well you sure dealt with it. He won't bother you again. The way you said Rouseff." The other students laughed. I was still uncomfortable and just shrugged.

I had signed up for a martial arts class. I looked forward eagerly to getting more training. I'd purchased a new kimono at the university bookstore. My first day of class not much happened. The teacher talked about theory and history of the martial arts. Most of this material was new to me. As a child, I'd just thought of it as a way to survive in M'TK. I took notes.

The second day of martial arts class we got to put on our kimonos and do some exercises. It felt good to do the exercises again. The teacher lectured on the different levels of skill, called san. I loved learning new material about my skill. We exercised and took notes for a full week before we got to spar in class. I still didn't like throwing another student down. I had no intention of allowing anyone to throw me down. I practiced with different partners for about twenty minutes.

Professor Stodola barked at me. "Jaconovich!"

"Yes sir."

"You have training. What level are you?"

"Um, I'm no level sir. I did take lessons when I was little, but it was mostly just a bunch of kids fooling around with our teacher."

"Who was your teacher?"

I wondered how to handle this one. I decided on honesty and hoping for the best.

"His name was Wu, sir."

"Where did you meet this Wu?"

I did not want to explain that my teacher was one of the biggest crime bosses in the city. "Um...uh...he...was...um...cook."

"Well, your cook seems to have been a reasonably good teacher. Come here." Great. I was going to have to spar with the teacher. We took our positions.

I hit the mat hard before I knew what was happening. I still did not like getting thrown. I remembered something and started to laugh. I got up off of the mat. "Thank you sir. I've always suspected that I'm not all that good at this. I'm okay against someone without any training, but I can improve."

"You have a great deal of room for improvement. Go help Mr. Spencer with the movement we are practicing. He seems incapable of learning the simplest exercise." This became the pattern for my martial arts class for the rest of the term. The teacher lectured. I sparred with the other students and won. The teacher sparred with me and threw me down. Then, he sent me off to help the students who had more trouble.

We had practical tests for the mid-term. The students sparred with each other for the exam. My teacher brought in an older student to spar with me. Luckily, my partner underestimated me. I threw him easily. The teacher interrupted the exam to yell at my sparring partner. He undertook the task of testing me on the moves we learned in class. Much to my surprise, Professor Stodola ended up on the mat.

My other classes went equally well. I liked chemistry. My pre-law class was easy or maybe I was so excited to be in pre-law that I paid extra attention. I reread all the books Mama sent me in the summer. I passed my exams easily.

One teacher continued to vex me. The history teacher continuously voiced his bigotry toward the northerners. One day he and I got into an argument.

"Sir, I disagree with your statements about all northerners. This city is located in a northern province. The capital is located in a northern province. I look around me and I see decent people who just want to go about their business."

The teacher countered, "Business is the problem. We southerners do not dirty our hands with business and politics. You may see northerners on the street, but they are not working. They are lazy."

"That is a second issue. I wish to discuss your statement about northerners being lazy. Many northern families work for the railroad. They work hard. When M'TK was burned, they worked hard to clean up the mess, often without promise of payment. Their work means profits for the Rouseff family. I believe in treating them with respect when I meet them, and when I am among my classmates." The room grew deathly still.

The teacher sneered, "Oh is this the policy of the Rouseff family to wallow with the filthy workers in the mud.'

"I do not speak for the Rouseff family. I speak for myself. I ride the trains all the time. I come into contact with the workers. They do their jobs well. They work hard. I cannot imagine anyone complaining about most of the people I have encountered. I find that when I treat people with respect no matter where they are from, they respond to me with respect. I do not like you talking about the railroad employees as lazy, corrupt, or even filthy."

"Oh the boss's son is standing up for the workers." The teacher smirked and looked at the class as if I was a joke.

"Yes, I guess I am the boss's son. I admit that the money for my clothes and schooling comes from the labor of other people. I will not belittle those who make life easy for me." I heard sounds of shock, disapproval, and hesitant approval from the other students.

A girl behind me spoke up. "I agree with Mr. Jaconovich. I don't work either, but I have everything I need because of the work of others. My mama taught me to treat the servants with respect. She says that we leave them in charge of our house and all our possessions. If they respect us, they will take good care of our possessions. If they hate us, they will rob us and run away before we know that anything is missing."

I continued, "Exactly, if the railroad is to make money, we cannot have employees who cheat us or don't take care of the equipment. It is in our best interest to treat employees with respect. You as a teacher do not have that obligation. You should realize that your students come from a different perspective. Your comments are inaccurate and offensive."

"You are young and naïve." The teacher returned to his lecture.

In the halls, after class, the students debated the validity of the teacher's comments. I saw them struggle to question their bigotry.

One student took me aside. "Jake, thanks. My mama is from the north. She is a fine person. It embarrasses me to have the teacher talk like that."

I had a sudden insight. I don't know where it came from. "Every elite family in this country has members who are from the north. We hurt ourselves when we look down on others. My guess is that our teacher has a parent from the north. Why should he care otherwise?"

Others overheard me and laughed.

I continued. "Well think about it. How much time do you spend thinking about the inferiority of northerners. The topic has never entered my head."

"I think you are right. If he were secure in his position, he would have less to say. My family never talks as he does. It does not enter into our conversation."

"But he is a teacher, surely he knows what is right."

I responded again to the others. "What he considers to be right may not be in our best interest. It is in our best interest to gain the loyalty of those who work for us." At this point, I realized that I had gotten carried away with my role-playing. I decided to shut up

Among all the pleasures of university, there were some horrors. The first-year receptions were hideous. On Friday after classes, the first-year students were required to attend semi-formal receptions hosted by the president and trustees of the university. Their wives were the instigators of these affairs.

About two weeks before the first reception, Mama and Papa took me to the capital with them on the train. We went to a big department store, Sharif's. The clerk outfitted me with a complete wardrobe for attending the receptions.

He insisted that I must wear undergarments under my suit. This seemed like an unnecessary expenditure to me, but the clerk and Mama insisted.

I found a group of friends to go with me to our first reception. We had two girls in our group. They were terrified. I tried to be comforting. "Come take my arm and we will act very polite and grown-up." I offered my arm to the most terrified of the two girls. "That is very good. Now think of your great-aunt and do what she does."

Both girls broke into giggles. I was hoping that others would look at the girls and not notice me other than to see that I was behaving properly. The event turned out to be ghastly. I remember thinking the house where the reception was held was very elegant. For the life of me, I cannot remember one detail about any of the homes where we went for receptions. My friends and I made it through the reception line okay. Some of our group tried eating the sandwiches. I stood quietly talking to the girls.

I analyzed the situation. "Okay, so far so good. Now how long do we have to stay here?"

The girl on my arm, Candice whispered. "At least twenty minutes."

"We don't have to speak to anyone, do we?"

"Jake!" Mr. Rouseff sounded surprised to see me. I bet he was.

"Oh, hello sir. It is a pleasure to see you."

"You are looking good."

"Thank you sir." My mind froze, then I blurted out the first thing that ran through it. "Um…I have to be here because I am a first-year student. You could be doing something fun. Why are you here?" I instantly cursed my tendency to blurt out the first question that pops into my mind. I did not want to draw more attention to myself.

Mr. Rouseff laughed out loud. "You are right. These are damn boring affairs. I attend to keep my wife happy. You are the first person I've seen worth talking to. Who is this young lady?"

"Thank you for the compliment sir." I introduced, Candice. She whispered her acknowledgement.

"I didn't realize you were old enough for university. What are you studying?" Mr. Rouseff made no attempt to move away.

"I intend to study law. Right now, I am taking general courses. I do have my pre-law class."

He looked at me narrowly. "Law is good. You can work for us when you get out of school. You used to play football as I recall. Are you playing for the university?"

"To be honest, the thought did not occur to me. I loved playing in secondary school. I'm not sure I play well enough for the university team. I think I will look into it."

"Jake, you are your father's son. I think you will do everything well enough."

"Thank you sir." I saw my history teacher coming toward me. One thought took over my mind, "Oh shit. Oh shit. Oh shit." He came right up to me.

"Jake, Mr. Rouseff." We both nodded to my teacher. "I wonder, Mr. Rouseff if you are aware of what young Jake has been saying in class."

Horror threatened to overwhelm me. "Sir, surely you are not going to bore him with the musing of a first-year student."

"Oh but I am most curious about this idea that the Rouseff family treats their employees with so much respect that the employees are all honest and respectable themselves."

I watched Papa's boss turn red as he grew angry. "Yes, we treat our employees fairly. What are the students learning in your classroom that you seem to treat this as joke?" The poor girl on my arm looked about to pee her knickers at this menacing outburst.

I probably should have kept my mouth shut. "I do not think the Rouseff employees have anything to complain about. He disagreed with me about how the working classes should be treated. I thought they should be treated as you do sir. He does not think they should be treated so well. He disagreed with me that employees will work better when they are treated with respect."

Mr. Rouseff's good humor instantly returned. He laughed out loud again. "Son, finish your schooling. Do not anger your teacher by sticking up for us. I expect you in my office ready to represent us in the law in five years."

"I do not think it will take me five years to qualify for the law. Do I get a year vacation?"

"No, you'll go boating with your cousins and come back so brown you look like a heathen."

"How did you know about that?"

"Oh your papa told me where you were and why. You had a narrow escape. I hope you learned from it. It looks like maybe you did." He smiled at the young woman beside me. "Ah, I think I can escape now. Jake thanks for entertaining me. Give my regards to your parents." He turned and left. I stood rooted to the spot. A thousand thoughts ran through my head.

The other students joined me. Our teacher did not want to leave us. I couldn't think. I decided to try the same question I asked Mr. Rouseff on my teacher. "Sir, we have to attend these receptions because we are first-year students. Why are you here."

"Oh I believe these are very beneficial events. I like meeting my students in a less structured setting. I'm very pleased to have made the acquaintance of your family. So you spent some time boating with your cousins."

"Yes, I finished secondary school in March. My cousins are out of school so we spent a few months traveling up and down the coast in their boat." This produced a short discussion of boats.

"Did you go as far north as the fishing villages?"

"Yes."

"What did you think of the conditions—the smell?"

"The smell in the villages that process fish is enough to make me gag. I went looking for some new books to read. I could not find bookstores or libraries. I learned that the catch in the north is decreasing. I wonder, without books if the people who fish and work in the processing plants will be able to learn another trade. Most places we visited were very beautiful. We have a very beautiful country. We should be very proud of it." Our teacher excused himself and walked away.

One of my friends whispered just loud enough for our group to hear. "I don't know why he tries to talk to you Jake. He always comes off looking like a pompous ass."

"I don't mean to put him down. He is obsessed with the whole class thing. I just don't care about it much." Another question popped into my head. "Look at it this way. We are at university to prepare us to be leaders in this country. How can we lead or run our businesses if we dismiss most of the people we work with? At what point does our behavior mean that we make less money because our workers are too weak, or they cheat us or..."

"You are asking revolutionary questions young man." Another man joined us.

"Times change sir. If business is going to keep up and prosper we must keep up with the changes in technology and changing social customs."

"Are you studying business?"

"No. Law."

The stranger looked eager for a debate. "We don't know what direction those changes are going to go. How do you propose that we be prepared?"

One of the hostesses nearly caused me to jump out of my skin when she came up behind me and demanded. "What are you discussing here? This is supposed to be a polite reception. You are not supposed to discuss business and politics."

"Yes, Ma'am." I was embarrassed at being corrected and relieved for an excuse to end the discussion.

The man who had been talking to us didn't sound pleased. "Damn. First time one of these things gets a bit interesting, she comes along and ruins it. I guess you are all supposed to learn that receptions are damned boring. I'm getting myself another drink." The stranger wandered off.

I tried to dry the palms of my hands without anyone noticing. "Are our twenty-minutes up yet? I had no idea these things would be this sticky."

My friend Nickoli asked, "Why are you complaining? You can talk to everyone with ease."

I chose to be honest. "No. No, I am terrified out of my mind. I should be keeping my mouth shut." We'd formed a little huddle and were whispering to each other.

"Students, students break this up. You are supposed to mingle." Another one of the women interrupted us. I looked up and saw the man who had just left us had gotten himself a drink. He looked as us, laughed and winked.

I compulsively asked yet another question. "I wonder if most of the men here think this is ghastly?" The other students laughed. I continued. "Um… right… how do we mingle? I mean I am not going up to someone I don't know and introduce myself. That would be rude don't you think? What is it? Do older people approach younger?"

"Yes." The shy girl clinging to my arm finally spoke. I thought she recited what she had read in a book. "We may slowly walk the length of the room and back. We may walk in groups of two. We must keep our chin up and back straight. Fix a pleasant smile on your face. Do not speak to someone older unless they speak to you first."

Her knowledge impressed me. "Wow, where did you learn all that?"

"Poise school."

I concluded, "Actually, I am not supposed to be speaking first because I am surely the youngest. I am only seventeen." The girl giggled. We all stood up straight, lifted our chins and proceeded to walk up and down the room in a leisurely manner. I was thankful for the girl who seemed to know the correct behavior. We finished our twenty minutes and made our escape. We all went to a bar near the campus to recover. I discovered that I could order a Coke. It tasted way too sweet, but I liked it better than beer.

As the year progressed I collected a group of friends around me. Both of the girls who went to the first reception with me, Candice and Lena, were part of my circle of friends. Lena soon became engaged to Nickoli, one of the boys in the group. Candice the girl who knew how to behave at the reception was a good friend for all of us.

I never dated college girls because they were from the south. I suspected that I could get into a great deal of trouble for dating southern girls if people realized I was from the north. When I needed a girl companion for an event, I often asked Candice to accompany me. Since, I did not have a car, I would meet her wherever we needed to be.

We liked to think of ourselves as very modern and daring for having liberal views on equality between the southerners and northerners. Most members of the group confessed to having a grandmother, aunt, uncle or cousin who came from the north. I never confessed to not having a singled blessed relative from the south.

Mr. Rouseff spoke to me on two other occasions when we met. He seemed to like me. Nobody suspected that I was the son of a laborer. I kept my mouth shut because I did not want to get the director at my secondary school in trouble. I did not want to reflect poorly on Mr. Rouseff. Mostly, I liked being treated with respect. I did not want to get kicked out of school.

About mid-year, I joined a group of boys who played football on an informal basis everyday after classes. Part of my schooling was to learn to get along with the elite class. I played football. I went to receptions. I went to bars. I flirted with the girls. Sometimes on Friday or Saturday night I met friends and we went dancing. Sometimes we went to watch the school football or Rugby games.

Papa insisted that my schooling must be like any other job. He expected me to work at it twelve to sixteen hours a day. I got up at six, showered and dressed and left for school by seven. I took the trolley home for dinner, then went to my little storeroom to study. I usually fell asleep over my books. I'd wake up when Papa turned out my light and said, "Go to sleep son."

I took the martial arts class all my first year. I found it easy for me. By the end of the year, I could throw my teacher as often as he threw me. He started encouraging me to participate in competitions. He insisted that I could earn my levels of san. I did not want to compete. I thought of the fights I had been in. Most of those fights, I won because nobody knew what I could do. I was a northerner pretending my family was from the south. I decided to treasure my skills, but keep them to myself.

At the end of my first year, I won a prize for having the highest scores of all the first-year students. The prize was half the cost of my schooling for my second year. Mama and Papa were very proud.

I discussed my finances with my parents. "The thing with this prize is that it means I have plenty of money for the next two years. I want to take classes this quarter."

"Of course you should take classes this quarter. It is your job to go to school."

"I thought I might be needed to help Uncle John fish."

"No. Your job is to go to school. That is what will help all of us the most."

"Ah, Uncle John can manage without me this year when I do not have a silly girlfriend hanging on my arm."

Papa laughed. "Uncle John would be happy to have your help. He tells us that you were a great help. I hope you are not still unhappy over the silly girlfriend."

"No, she was not right for me. Sometimes when she irritated me, I dismissed the problems because I thought she loved me."

"Perhaps she did love you son. A girl like that will look out for herself first. She found a rich man, I hear. She made a poor choice in choosing him over you. She will always make poor choices. Some day you will find the right woman to love."

Chapter 14 University Year Two

Ifound my second year of university, more interesting than the first. I had more self-confidence. The classes were more challenging. I took two law courses along with economics and psychology. I also took English. It was required. I found it to be my most challenging class until I discovered English literature. Perhaps it was not so much literature as it was novels. I became enthralled with westerns from the United States, and, of course James Bond. What impressionable, romantic, young man did not imagine himself as James Bond.

The first movie I ever saw was *From Russia With Love*. We went to see it shown in English as part of our English class. I discovered that the university had a theater that played foreign language films on Friday and Saturday night. More often than not, the film would break half way through. Sometimes they would get it fixed while we waited. Often they could not fix it or a reel was missing.

My favorite book in the English language was *To Kill a Mockingbird*. We read it for English class. We debated in English whether or not Atticus should have tried to get an acquittal for a black man. I carried the discussion over to my law classes. It was a heated discussion. Many students felt that the black man should have been punished because he kissed the girl. Others argued that he did not kiss the girl. She kissed him. The first group countered that he should not put himself in a position to get kissed by a white girl.

I surprised myself when called upon to give my opinion. "A laborer should not put himself in a position to be alone with a woman. That was wrong of him. Her father committed the bigger crime by not taking care of her. In the end, the man spent some time in jail." I thought a while longer. "I guess that I have to conclude that he did not commit the crime he was accused of so he should have been acquitted."

Another student argued. "But what about justice? He should be punished for something."

I countered. "People should not be punished for crimes they do not commit."

The discussion ran around the room with each student having a different comment or insight. "But what if he had been a northerner?"

"Should northerners be punished for crimes they do not commit?"

One of the students, Hab Vanderholm was older than the rest of us. I'd heard that he was related to the emperor. He hung out with the few Fortenac students. He almost sneered at the rest of us and used a very superior tone. "Well somebody has to be punished for crimes."

A friend, Nickoli countered. "Shouldn't it be the people who commit the crimes?"

Vanderholm condescended to explain his position. "Okay, say one of the students here robs a store. Should he be punished or should a northern laborer be punished in his place?" This question galled me. I was horrified that a law student could even ask the question.

The answers from the other students were worse. "Well the student should not be punished because we are from the elite. We should know better, but sometimes people do things because they are drunk or maybe the student spent all his money on girls or gaming and didn't want to ask his papa for more money. Circumstances need to be taken into consideration."

Nickoli countered, "Justice is not served by punishing the innocent."

Vanderholm sneered again. "But what happens to justice if nobody is punished for the crime? It is best to punish a northerner for that crime." He sat back in his seat as if he'd said the final word on the subject and nobody should dare to argue with him.

One of Vanderholm's friends concurred, "Somebody has to be punished and the student had his reasons."

Finally, I'd had enough and spoke up. "I am deadly certain of the answer to this question." The other students seemed surprised at my tone of voice. My friends later said, that even they were frightened by the look on my face. "An innocent person no matter where they are from should not be punished for a crime they did not commit. That is justice. Many crimes do go unpunished. It is more just for a crime to go unpunished than for an innocent man to be punished." I took a deep breath. "As for university students who break the law because they have been foolish with their money. Somebody should punish them, if not their fathers, then the justice system."

Vanderholm sneered. "Yeah, you can say that. I bet your Papa gives you everything you want."

I took a deep breath and tried to calm myself. "Yes, my Papa gives me everything I want and everything I think I might want…well…except for my first girlfriend. Papa sent me off to visit my cousins when he met her." I tried to sound pitiful. The other students laughed.

Another boy whined, "So you see you don't know how it is for those of us who have strict parents."

I heard my voice soften as I spoke of Papa. "My Papa gives me everything I want because I have always been responsible with my own money. I do not spend all I have foolishly. I get good grades. I earn Papa's trust by being trustworthy."

Vanderholm still seemed to be having a difficult time with the concept of justice. "But still if nobody is punished how is justice served?"

I remembered to breathe before I answered the question. "By punishing the guilty when they are caught and trusting God to deal with the ones who don't get caught. Punishing the innocent is never just."

A student I knew had Fortenac relatives argued, "Even if they are no-good northerners?"

Again I told myself to breathe. "Those no-good northerners may have family they are supporting. They may have an employer who depends on them to be at work."

Hab dismissed my statement carelessly, "Oh we can always find more people to work."

I argued. "It costs us money if they miss one day. If we have to find someone new, it will take time for that person to learn the job. The real problem with your position is that it really is unjust to punish the innocent."

I went home early that day in disgust. I'd failed to change the minds of those who could not see the injustice of punishing the innocent.

The next day in my law class, my professor walked past me and dropped a small white envelope on my desk. He put his hand on my shoulder and squeezed. I wondered what this meant. The envelope contained an invitation to a small gathering of men at his house. The teacher lectured for the whole class period. I was thankful to be spared the opinions of my classmates.

On Sunday afternoon, I went to the gathering at my teacher's house. I did not like being singled out, but I dare not refuse. The house was one of the large elegant brick and timber houses on the far side of the university. As I walked up the street I could see that the gardens behind the houses ran down to the riverbank.

My teacher, Professor Ingleman, met me at the door. "Jake, come in, come in. I am glad you can make it. Don't look so scared. My wife went to visit her mama. We can relax and be comfortable. He took me into a sitting room and introduced me to the group. There were a few third and forth year students there and one other second-year student. This was when I met my dear friend Andrew.

Andrew was a science major so I'd never attended a class with him. I'd seen him at the receptions and thought perhaps I'd seen him at the foreign films. I sat next to him and resolved to keep my mouth shut. Unfortunately, I was not going to be allowed to do that.

Professor Ingleman introduced me and added, "This is the student I told you about—the one I'd like to see in the prosecutor's office." I gulped.

"What do you think, young man? Do you want to work for the prosecutor?"

"Um..uh…Mr. Rouseff is expecting me to work for him."

"You would be wasted working for him. Let him hire one of his worthless nephews."

I chuckled. "I think sir, you may have hit on why he wants to hire me."

The others laughed.

Professor Ingleman's voice held a note of pride and excitement. "See, it is as I said, he can think in a stressful situation and turn a discussion easily with humor or talk of something that interests others. No, no, son. We need you in the prosecutor's office."

"Why?"

"For all the reasons we've heard you support in the past. You believe in equality before the law. This country has got to change. We do not want to see it descend into endless civil war like many other emerging nations. We need to establish a government run on rule of law and equal rights."

My whole body screamed, "Yes!" I kept my mouth shut.

"We want to see the country advance in technology. We want to see our natural resources used correctly. It will take establishing equal property rights and rule of law in order to bring about equality. The prosecutor's office is key to establishing rule of law."

I voiced my concerns. "Other students disagree with my position on equality before the law. They may have more family influence to bear in the practice of law or the activities of the prosecutors office."

"We are not saying it will be easy. It won't. We want you to train for the position."

"I'll consider it." I did not reveal that I intended to discuss this group with Papa. The discussion turned to other topics. I heard the name of the director of my secondary school mentioned with respect. I wondered how much they knew about me. I occasionally made comments on the general discussion when called upon. The rest of the time I kept my mouth shut. I remembered my cousins teasing me about the questions I asked and talking about how I never shut up. I smiled.

"What do you find amusing?" Andrew whispered to me.

I whispered back, "My cousins tease me about never keeping quiet. They would be amazed to see me now." I smiled at Andrew.

"Let's go out after we get out of here."

I nodded. The talk lasted three hours. Much of it I did not fully understand. Much of it sounded lofty and unrealistic. Most of it centered on social justice. I understood that part. I realized how much I did not know. I had an image of myself when I was six with my rat-trap. I realized that I was back at the beginning and these men were asking me to catch much bigger rats.

Finally, Andrew and I escaped as the other men leisurely left the meeting. I burst out with, "What was that all about?"

Andrew explained all he knew. He'd been to other meetings earlier. "I think they are planning to eventually form a new political party. Right now they are trying to get people they consider to be enlightened into key positions. They are interested in me because I am good in physics. I fear that they may want me to build a nuclear bomb."

"No!"

"They have not hinted at any such thing. They have hinted at nuclear power plants among other things. They invite other students in the sciences. You and I may be the youngest."

"I am not yet nineteen, so I would think so."

"Ah, is that why you still live with your parents?"

"How did you know that?"

"Some of the other boys mentioned it."

"I never considered living elsewhere. I have my own bedroom and my own bathroom. I live very well where I am. Why should I want to move?"

"So you can hang out with the guys and do what you want."

I laughed. "I hang out with the other students as much as I like. I go home to excellent food, clean sheets and interesting conversation. My parents travel around the country so I sometimes join them in other cities. Papa does not place any restrictions on me. I have learned that if he does not like what I am doing, he may send me off to visit family and they keep me so entertained I forget about what I wanted to do here."

Andrew laughed. "I wish my papa were so lenient."

"I get good grades. I am obedient. My papa has no reason to be strict. I should add that I would never want to make my mama worry or be unhappy. She has a way…"

Andrew laughed. "Oh yes, it is really our mama's that make us feel lower than snails if we misbehave."

I enjoyed Andrew's company. We walked toward a park then walked the perimeter of the park several times. I told him about my reservations. "My concern is about the nature of this group. Do you think they are part of some revolutionary group? Will it bring shame down upon our families if we are known to associate with them?"

"I don't know. I've been to three meetings now. This one was fairly typical. They are encouraging students to be in key positions. The other students seem to have high integrity. I have not been uncomfortable in the meetings. Far from it, I can voice my opinion that modernizing the country is vital to our survival. They smile at me. I think they are committed to helping the country through peaceful means."

"I am committed to helping the people of my country in whatever way I can, but I do not want to be involved in something that leads to civil war."

"I think civil war is what they are trying to prevent."

"Do you think civil war is possible?"

Andrew sighed. "Yes, I cannot see how much longer the northerners are going to put up with the senseless oppression from the south. I apologize if I offend you. I know you respect your family and this is good. The fact remains that the inequality has erupted into violence in the past. It will again unless things change to give the northerners equal rights."

"I am not blind. I know the north has grievances. I also know that most just want to go about the business of caring for their families. The rest seem to drown their grievances in alcohol."

"You are hard on them."

"I have stepped over the bodies on the sidewalk. I agree in equality. I agree in social justice and equal rights. I hate to think of the northerners getting to the point where they start a civil war."

"Jake Jaconovich, have you ever considered that it may not be the north who starts it?" We walked on, silent for a long time.

Finally, I said, "I do not see why the south would attack the north. The south has all the power and privileges. I can see why the north might resort to violence. Why would the south?"

"For the same reason it has resorted to violence periodically for the past three hundred and fifty years; to keep the north down. Don't you read between the lines of your history texts? The wool rebellion—who got killed? The cannery rebellion—who got killed? You must know something about the burning of M'TK—who got killed?"

"It was my thirteenth birthday. I watched the slum burn. My father was put in charge of much of the rebuilding. I know the army burned the buildings. It was partially a move against the Rouseff family and partly against the rival gangs in the area." I smiled.

"What do you think to smile about? That was mass murder."

"I know that some people died. I can offer you some comfort. The people were warned ahead of time. One of the crime bosses learned of the attack, hours before it happened. People fled. My papa was put in charge of the rebuilding because he loaded over four hundred people, mostly families with children into boxcars and removed them from danger. Yes, people died. I am sure they did. Still I believe most escaped. Perhaps those who were too drunk or strung out on opium to leave had an escape from the hell of their constant craving. I've thought long about it, I thought about the people who died. I've thought about those who lost their homes and jobs. I've never thought about it as an act of anything more than gang warfare."

"When it is the emperor's army doing the burning and killing it is not gang warfare."

I chuckled. "I guess when I was thirteen, I thought of the government as just another gang, another set of crime bosses."

Andrew laughed a long time. "I think you got to the point of our discussions when you were only thirteen. The northerners are gaining ground. More youth are staying in school. Some northern youth are going to university in other countries and coming home to teach or practice in their field. Fewer parents will send their children to work in the factories. The south will not put up with this for long. They will attack again and kill masses of people."

Out of this whole discussion, I grasped onto the idea of students studying abroad. I learned that I could complete my schooling in another country if I got kicked out of school here.

Andrew continued. "Anyway, the point of the discussions seems to be that if we are going to be a modern country, our government needs to be more than another set of crime bosses."

I wanted to go home and discuss this with Papa. I was glad Papa and Mama were home. We sat down to dinner with the Apkoutas. I brought up the topic of the meeting I had attended. "My problem is that I feel as if I cannot turn down an invitation from a professor. I do not want to do anything that will get me expelled. I don't want to be part of a revolutionary group either. Andrew thinks that the group is trying to divert another massacre such as the burning of M'TK or the wool rebellion or cannery rebellion."

"Or the barge rebellion, or the workers rebellion." Papa spoke. He and Mama looked grim. Papa looked unbearably sad as he continued. "Your friend is right. Every twenty years, or so, the armies of the south come through and slaughter whole villages of young men. They claim to be putting down this rebellion or that rebellion. My father and brothers were killed on their way home from work in the worker's rebellion. They were not rebels they were honest men going about their business. I had a sister Virginia. I have not seen her since the day our family was cremated in an open pit along with several hundred other men. I put her on the train to go stay with Mama's parents in an eastern province." Papa rubbed his hands over his face. "Be very careful son. Talk to Mr. Rouseff. Do not tell him any names, but tell him you run into people who talk about averting another slaughter and ask him how dangerous it is to associate with such people."

Papa's advice for me to visit Mr. Rouseff did not surprise me as much as it would have five years earlier. Mr. Rouseff respected Papa a great deal for his knowledge and dedication to his job. I knew Papa considered Mr. Rouseff to be an honest man. My parents had visited the Rouseff's in their home more than once.

I commented, "Andrew thought the burning of M'TK was the same as the other rebellions."

"No, the burning of M'TK does not come close to being the same as the *rebellions*. It was bad, but nowhere near as bad as those. It is not the north that rebels. It is the south that slaughters those they see as different."

"Then you think the men in this meeting have reasons to want to create a different social order."

Papa sighed, "I will go to the cathedral and light a candle for them. You make an appointment to see Rouseff. I don't want you in danger."

I did call Mr. Rouseff and made an appointment to have dinner with him a few nights later. His invitation sounded genuine. "My wife has gone south to visit her family. Come join me for dinner. We can talk without interruption."

The Rouseff's lived in a neighborhood of large houses surrounding a private park. Like the houses along the river, these were made of brick and timber. The inside was paneled in a beautiful variety of woods. Thick oriental carpets covered the tile floors.

I arrived in good time for dinner. When we were seated at one end of the dining table, Mr. Rouseff dismissed the servants saying we could serve ourselves. The servants left the room, closing the double sliding doors behind them. "Now, Mr. Jake, what is this weighty matter you wish to discuss with me?"

I explained about the group of professors and students inviting me to an informal meeting. "The other students say the goal is to place students who favor equality and justice in positions of influence. My law professor thinks I should be in the prosecutors office."

"What? He wants to take my attorney away from me?"

I chuckled and nodded.

He leaned back in his chair. "You would be an excellent choice for the prosecutor's office. I am torn between wanting a competent attorney for my business and knowing what you could do for the country in the prosecutor's office. Have you considered politics?"

"No. I do not have the background for politics."

"Who is to say you don't. My papa is dead. If I tell people your grandpapa was my papa's dearest cousin, who is to say no?"

"That would not be honest sir. Surely there is someone who would know the truth."

"Perhaps, perhaps not. You may or may not be related to my family. You may be related to the Spinozas. I'd hate to think of you related to the

Vanderholms or the Papadakos families. The Vanderholms have been the worst for purging the north of undesirables. They are the most radical of the southern families. The truth is that everybody in this country is related. Men from the south marry women from the north. Too often the men of the north have been killed leaving their women with no choice but to marry the men who killed their fathers and brothers. As for me, I want to run my business as best I can and retire with enough money to enjoy my later years. I want to sit in the sun with my wife beside me."

I was having trouble keeping my pasta on my fork but Mr. Rouseff did not seem to notice. I tried watching how he managed, but he was more intent on talking.

He continued, "I've learned that trained adult workers are best for my business. I do not want children near my trains. I refused to serve Fortenac steel because I made a rule that nobody under the age of eighteen can come near my trains. We ran over three children one year. My train captains are good men. They were devastated over the accidents. I suspect that part of the burning of M'TK came from their influence with the government. They wanted to get back at me." He chuckled. "They hurt us yes, but most of my employees fled in time thanks to you and Mr. Wu." He shook his head. "I never got to thank Mr. Wu for tipping us off. He was a decent man in his own way—much better than those who think they are so high and mighty."

I was getting an earful. I was not sure this was answering my questions. "So, as far as I can figure out, some people think it is getting close to time for another one of the Vanderholmes' purges. They think they can divert this through several means."

Mr. Rouseff agreed with my professors. "That is my guess. I think we may have ten to fifteen years before they get into a position to attack. They need to build roads in order to get their troops to where they want to be. They will have to be very careful if they think they are going to ride on my railroad. They could slowly amass troops. Your Mama has made it much more difficult for them to do so. Her simple system of writing down every ticket that is sold, the starting point and the destination will help us pick up unusual movement."

"Why are you siding with the northerners?"

"It…well… when the government came to burn M'TK, Mr. Wu warned us. Your father saved many people and my equipment. I can see well enough who my true friends are. I know who is honorable and who is not." He paused and took a drink of his wine. "Perhaps it is also that my grandmother was from the north. "

"Perhaps we are cousins then. I have a missing aunt."

"Ah, so you see, it is not so far fetched for you to say you are related to my family. We are just a little unclear about where the connections are. Jake, I am proud to let people think I have family members as fine as you are."

I think I blushed. I nodded.

Mr. Rouseff continued. "I value honesty and hard work. I've learned that my business depends on my skilled workers. The stations that are kept in good repair have fewer delays. Trains that run on time attract more passengers and freight. I do not take this lightly." We ate in silence for a couple minutes. Mr. Rouseff struggled with his pasta. I felt less awkward.

He started a new topic for discussion. "I have been thinking about your schooling. I can see you being part of a much bigger game than I thought originally." He paused, took another sip of wine and leaned back in his chair. "For now, I think we need to be very careful about who you are, especially since others have noticed your social stand. Be cordial with this group of men. Get to know them when you have time. Get involved with sports. You do not look like a young man who has led an idle life. Let people surmise that you got your build through recreation not carrying ten pounds of rats in a cage through M'TK."

I laughed at this. "I did bulk up some when I was carrying fish for my uncle. It became nothing for me to throw a twenty to thirty kilo sack of fish over each shoulder and walk or run a kilometer or two." We laughed a little over my description.

Ever since the night I threw my daughters over my shoulders and ran with them, I have thanked God over and over and over for the ease with which I could carry a heavy weight over each shoulder.

Mr. Rouseff shocked me with his next idea. "I think we need to make one more change. I have a rental house near the university. It is divided into flats. I want you to find three more classmates and move into a flat at the beginning of next term. I do not want someone to follow you home and ask questions about you living at the station. Your parents are seldom there anyway. I am planning to visit the United States. I want them to come with me."

"I shall miss them. I am happy where I am. I like the people at the station."

"Jake, whether we intended it or not, whether you like it or not, you have become involved in something much bigger than yourself. It is a huge gamble. Nothing may come of any of this. You may graduate and come to work for me. If things look bad for the north, I can move most of my people south. It may be these new friends of yours intend to do as they say. They may also be working for the wrong people from our perspective. Be nice to them. Do not give anything away. Oftentimes I think you can be too busy to go to their meetings. Tell them you have a social engagement in the capital and go stay with your parents."

I was sobered by these instructions. "You think they could be agents for those who oppose equality for the north."

"For now, it is safest to keep that possibility open. Whine a little and say that I want you to work for me. Do not commit. Watch your back. If you sense any trouble come to my house." This sounded like good advice.

"I am glad I talked to you sir. I wondered if I was being foolish to be wary. I think the other students are earnestly sincere. I know Andrew is sincere in his beliefs. He thinks the professors may be playing straight with us, but he has his doubts."

"Jake you have hit on the reason things need to change. You are right to be wary. It is a fact of life in this country. I thought I could trust the other big families. I thought I was friends with Vanderholm. They, he betrayed me. I thought Mr. Wu was nothing more than a crime boss and a thorn in my side. He proved to be a friend. You were a friend. I heard the story of you running down the street yelling at the top of your lungs for people to flee. Your papa was my friend. He saved my equipment and the lives of the most vulnerable people in M'TK. I've learned lessons that I wish I never learned. I will stand by those who stood by me."

I went home and told Papa everything Mr. Rouseff had told me. Mama cried over the news that I should move into my own place.

Papa took her hand, "Sweetheart, we've known this day would come. Our son is a man and needs to lead a man's life. That does not include hanging on his mama's hem."

"But, I would much rather hang on my mama's hem."

Papa smiled. "Perhaps we have kept you home too long and spoiled you if you do not want to move out."

"I have too many comforts here."

Mama tried to reassure me. "I'm sure your new flat will have many comforts."

Chapter 15 Leaving Home

My new flat did not have many comforts. First, it had one bathroom that I shared with Andy and two friends from my first year, Johan and Nickoli. It did not have Mama to cook for us. We did not have anyone to shop for us. After four days of these discomforts I was at my wits end.

"Look at this will you? My clothes have not been washed. How am I supposed to get my clothes washed? I've never thought about this in my whole life."

Andrew laughed at me. "Aw does Jake want to go home to his mama?"

"Yes. Jakey wants to go home to his mama, and clean clothes, and edible food. Do you realize it is my turn to cook tonight? Do you know I've never cooked? I've watched others cook. I might be able to make something Chinese. Perhaps I'll pretend to shop for food at the M'TK market and get Mrs. Apkouta to cook it for us."

Johan whined, "Please do. I'm getting hungry. Last night was inedible. Do you suppose we can get some girls to come over for a dinner party and get them to cook?"

"No! I've been told no girls in the apartment. We get it on good terms, but there are some rules. I think I will see if I can beg and plead to get one of the cooks I know to cook for us."

I was successful with getting Mrs. Apkouta to cook. I helped out at the station and she cooked a nice dinner for us. I bundled the food up and took it back to the apartment where we feasted and plotted on how many other places we could get someone to cook.

The next morning, I was faced with the same problems as the day before. "Where am I going to get clean clothes? I solved the problem of dinner last night. Can one of you tell me where to get my clothes cleaned?"

Andrew patiently explained. "It is called a laundry, Jake."

"What is a laundry?"

They laughed at me. "You are a baby. It is no wonder you got kicked out of your house full of servants."

"And my own bathroom. Please do not forget that I had a toilet and sink all to myself."

"Oh the hardships he has to endure."

"Okay where is this laundry place?"

Andrew took me to the laundry. A Chinese family owned the laundry. I read their name and advertisement written in Chinese on their window. When I entered the laundry, I heard one of the young women say, "Oh look, we have college boys for customers."

The other girl said, "I do not think the one with the blue eyes is a boy. He looks like a man to me." They giggled.

I replied in Chinese as fluent as theirs, "Thank you for the compliment. This man needs his clothes washed. How will I know I am getting my own clothes back?" The girls were shocked and giggled and blushed some more. The first girl explained how the laundry process worked. When I protested that I could not wait so long for my clean shirts, she told me to go buy more shirts.

"You should have at least five sir, so you do not have to come here so often."

"Perhaps I shall keep just two so that I can come and talk to you every day." They giggled some more.

I didn't get to visit the laundry every day. Andrew took me to the department store.

The clerk recognized me when I came in. "Mr. Jake, how may I help you today?"

Andrew took charge. "He needs more of everything. His mama has kicked him out of the nest and insists that he learn to take care of his own clothing."

The clerk laughed. "Come with me gentlemen. It is always a pleasure to dress Mr. Jake."

"I am at university now. It seems I need more clothes than I want. They are becoming a burden to me."

Andrew remained unsympathetic. "Shut up Jake." He smiled at the clerk and boasted, "Today I taught him how to take his clothes to the laundry. He needs something to wear while they are being washed."

The clerk laughed and seemed to be having a merry time as he and Andrew plotted to keep me respectfully clothed. They examined styles and talked about fabric. The clerk insisted that my new jacket could not have more than two buttons.

"I can't buy all these clothes. I did not bring that much money with me. I do not need these undershorts. Nobody sees them."

"Yes you do." Both the clerk and Andrew spoke together. I could see they were bonding.

The clerk smiled at me. "Mr. Jake, you do not need to pay me today. Your family has always been good customers. You can pay me what you have with you and pay the rest anytime you stop buy."

"I don't like to owe money."

Andrew blew out his breath, exasperated. "Jake stop whining and get the clothes. Everybody knows you will pay for them as soon as you get the opportunity to stop by."

"I suppose I can get the money and bring it back this afternoon."

Andrew sighed and rolled his eyes. "I am rooming with this now. He can get quite tedious."

The clerk laughed at everything Andrew said. "It looks as if we can trust you to keep him properly clothed. Do not blame his poor mother for the state of his wardrobe. She tried her best, the dear woman."

"I cannot help the fact that I outgrew clothes as soon as she bought them. I may outgrow these. Perhaps we should put them back in case I'm not done growing."

The clerk turned to Andrew, "Are you studying law too?"

"No, I am in physics. I'm not sure what I will do with that degree."

"It sounds impressive. The country needs more development in the sciences. We are behind the rest of the world." My new clothes were bundled up for me to take home whether I wanted them or not.

The stories of the hardship I suffered moving into an apartment became fodder for campus jokes. I found the jokes embarrassing because they made me sound like a spoiled rich kid who grew up tripping over servants instead of tripping over dead-drunk bodies on the streets of M'TK. I knew my education and to a lesser extent my safety depended on people believing I was a member of the elite. I felt the charade betrayed the true depth of all my parents had given me.

Before my parents left for the United States with "Cousin Philippe" as I was now to call him, Mrs. Philippe held a dinner party for some of my friends.

I was supposed to find some girls to invite, especially any from the Spinoza family who were considered appropriate for me to marry. Fortunately, Candice had a cousin who married a Spinoza. Lena and Candice promised to find three more girls to fill out my guest list.

The girls gave us long lectures on how we were to behave. I arrived at the Rouseff residence in good time to greet my guests. Candice drove the other girls. The boys came on the trolley. The idea that Candice had a car was a novelty to all of us. This curiosity furnished us with a topic of conversation for five minutes before we ran out of ideas.

My parents came to this party. Mama entered looking stunning in a dinner dress. "Mama, I didn't know you were coming. You look wonderful." I gave her a hug then hugged Papa.

Papa tried to sound stern, but his voice was full of approval. "Now young man stop hanging on your mama's hem and introduce us to your friends."

"It is a very pretty hem." I made the introductions. Mama enquired what the others were studying. The conversation picked up as the Rouseffs and my parents made an effort to draw the students into conversation.

One of my friends commented on unfair treatment from one of the teachers. Papa asked his favorite question. "What do you think that is really about?"

"Um…I…uh…I don't really know sir. I worked hard on my paper. It… it was good. It should have scored higher. I read some of the other students' papers that did not seem to me to be half so good. They scored higher."

We continued to discuss the mystery of the low grade. One of the girls came up with the best answer we could find. "Professor is really a disappointed Papadakos. He wanted to be in politics, but he failed several attempts to get elected in our province. He was running against a Fortenac. He may suspect that you are either a revolutionary or a Fortenac."

"Well, I am a Fortenac on my mother's side. I do not agree with the family business practices." Here he turned to Mr. Rouseff. "I am well aware sir, that you refused to supply train service to the Fortenacs until they stopped using children to load your trains. This topic was discussed in my home. Papa and Mama agreed that you were within your rights and that your position was morally superior. I was not brought up to believe that oppressing the work force is a moral option." From here the conversation turned uncomfortably revolutionary. I learned that my peers did not agree with the way much of the country was run.

I enjoyed my dinner with my parents. Mama looked so beautiful. I wanted to stare at her. Papa did spend much of his meal admiring her. He kissed her fingers more than once. The other students noticed. One of the girls commented on it in English class. "Oh Jake, I enjoyed dinner with your family. It was the best dinner party I've ever attended."

"Thank you. Mrs. Philippe will be pleased to know that the party was a success."

"I think it is sweet that your parents obviously love each other very much."

"I think it is my greatest blessing." I smiled. The class continued to discuss the dinner.

Candice's friend answered the other students' questions. "The adults talked to us as equals. Jake's papa was very courteous. He acted genuinely interested in us. Didn't he?" This last was to my friend who wrote the paper that got a poor grade.

"He was interested. I understand Jake better now. Did he ask you what you thought something was really about, often?"

I laughed. "Yes, even as a very tiny boy I could not read a children's story without Papa saying, 'I don't think a duck could really do all those things. What do you think this is really about?' It was a challenge. When I was just enchanted with making out the words on a page, he wanted me to think about it."

My friend continued. "I learned a great deal from that one question. I know where to be careful now." We nodded.

I had one more social engagement with Cousin Philippe before he left. I got another invitation to attend another student/faculty party. I mentioned the invitation to Cousin Philippe. "Yes, accept this invitation. Say you are bringing a friend. I will go with you."

I was well aware that the rest of the group would be shocked when I walked in with Cousin Philippe. I introduced him.

He sounded jovial as he took the offered chair. "So you are the people who are trying to take my attorney away from me." Mr. Rouseff settled himself for a comfy chat. "I do not like the idea of losing him from my business. I like even less the idea that he may be placed in a position of danger. I do agree that the prosecutor's office would be a good place for him to make some changes in this country. I'll be honest and say that I am not blind to the injustice. I'd like to see some changes."

The rest of the group made some restless murmurs.

Cousin Philippe continued, "The prosecutor's office would be a higher calling for him. He will not make as much money there. That does not seem to be important to him."

I elaborated. "I see the injustice. If I can change some of that, I'd like to. I will not place myself, my parents or any of the Rouseff family in danger."

Professor Ingleman tried to explain. "That is not what we are asking. We are well aware that for any of us to become noticed for our attempts to bring about rule of law and social justice will place innocent people at risk. Our concept is to work together as a group to bring small changes over a period of twenty years. At the end of that time, we hope to have enough strength in rule of law to prevent any future purges."

"Ah"

Another professor tried to sound sympathetic. "Mr. Rouseff, you were the brunt of this last purge, the burning of M'TK. You must have lost thousands of employees."

Cousin Philippe laughed. "Do not be outraged on my behalf. Very few people died in that fire. Thanks in part to Jake here and to his parents." I watched Mr. Rouseff debate with himself in the silence that followed his surprising statement. "I guess I shall tell you the story. For a number of years, Mr. Wu operated his crime syndicate out of M'TK. I did not bother him. He kept order. Yes, there was a great deal of alcoholism in M'TK. There was a great deal of poverty. My father, before me, refused to evict the poorest of the poor. I followed his policies. Mr. Wu's protection was the piece that made the whole mismatched community of railroad employees, gangs, the sick and the disabled hold together. A couple years before the burning, we noticed a change in the type of crime. More of my workers were beaten--a few were killed. Mr. Wu warned me then that he was losing power because of rival gangs with outside support. I moved more of my offices to the south. Since the burning, I have found that the outside support probably came down from the emperor."

Mr. Rouseff paused, sipped the glass of wine Professor Ingleman handed him and continued into the silence. "On the day of the fire, Mrs. Wu came to my offices and told us that the army planned to burn M'TK. We immediately began an evacuation." Cousin Philippe turned to me. "The second part of the alarm occurred when young Jake here went to Wu's gym for his private martial arts lesson."

Professor Stodola, my martial arts teacher was sitting across the room from us. He whistled then laughed. "Jake! That was the Wu you studied under? It was a wonder I was able to throw you that first time."

"I did not study with him after I turned thirteen. I turned thirteen the day of the fire. I have not seen Mr. Wu since."

Mr. Rouseff continued his story. "Wu left a note for Jake, telling him about the plan to burn M'TK. Jake ran off to meet his parents at the station. Along the way he yelled at people to flee. They knew he was part of my family. They thought he was official. They ran. At the station, Cousin Jacob loaded all the weakest people into rail cars and ran them out of town to safety. I have no idea how many people were left in M'TK when it burned. We found remains of twelve during the clean-up. We should have found signs of more but we did not. Most of my workers returned to work within two weeks." The others in the room sat in silence.

"Praise God."

Cousin Philippe chuckled. "I figure Mr. Wu gets about as much of our praise. He did not need to warn us."

I watched my martial arts teacher out of the corner of my eye. He was staring at me and pulling at his lower lip. Finally, he spoke. "This explains a few things to me. Jake I agree now that competing in martial arts is not the best idea for you. You have an outstanding foundation. You need more exercise and practice." He addressed the room. "I think it would be a good thing for him to be my teaching assistant. I can keep an eye on him. He can practice the skills he needs to keep himself safe." The other men grunted their agreement.

Rouseff was not finished. "Another thing, his parents and I will be out of the country for about three weeks. We are going to the United States. Jake is very capable in many ways, but he needs to concentrate on school without worrying over which Vanderholm is out to wipe out all the Rouseffs this week."

The men laughed at Mr. Rouseff's tone but shifted anxiously in their seats.

"You know how it is. I don't want him near any Vanderholms," He paused then added, "or Fortenacs for that matter."

"We do not have any members of the Vanderholms on the university staff. They tend to think academia is beneath them. The Fortenacs prefer the university in the capital."

"Do you think they will ever learn that they are surrounded by northerners when they are here?" Andrew was gaining confidence in speaking out in meetings.

"Oh they know. That is why they periodically commit genocide." The conversation turned general. The teachers seemed to forget that Mr. Rouseff was still present. He made our excuses after another twenty minutes. We left. I went back to my apartment to study and wait for Andy to get home from the meeting.

I nearly pounced on him when he came through the door. "Well, what happened after we left?"

"Yes. Yes, they had much to say about you after you left. Let a fellow get his coat off will you."

I tried to wait patiently. Andrew fussed at his buttons. When he held his coat up in front of himself and examined it closely, I knocked it out of his hands. "Well?"

"Jake that was my coat."

"Well?"

"Okay, they speculated some over whether or not Rouseff could be trusted. There was some surprise over you being in M'TK before it burned. I passed that off by saying that your family has several homes in the city and that we had dined with your parents in a very elegant home. That satisfied everyone except the martial arts professor. He is much taken with the idea that you studied under this Mr. Wu. Who is he?"

"One of the more successful crime bosses in the city. In some ways he was decent enough, like warning people about the burning."

"There was a discussion on the possibility that most people escaped."

"I think the only people left behind were those too drunk or strung out on opium to move. I watched the people being loaded onto the trains. It was, as Cousin Philippe said. They helped the weak. One man was in a wheel chair. They carried him in his chair. I think most people got out."

"Why were you there that day?"

"I had lessons with Mr. Wu everyday after school. What else did they say?"

"They think there is something about you that bears watching. They trust you. The martial arts thing seemed to be a big point with a couple professors. They thought you might have reasons for not wanting to compete."

I snorted, "Yes, the biggest reason is that I don't like to get hurt. I don't like hurting others. Andy, I've been called a mama's boy all my life. You've met my parents. I don't mind being a mama's boy. I'm not a fighter. That was the reason they wanted me to take the classes. I enjoyed it. I loved being in Mr. Wu's gym and the exercises. He used to get mad at me because I was not more aggressive in my fighting. I can defend myself nicely if I have to."

'They speculated on whether or not you can defend yourself. Your martial arts professor thought you could and vowed to make certain that you can. They may be thinking of something more for you than the prosecutor's office. They debated allowing you to go to work for your cousin and keeping you hidden. Jake, I very much suspect that you are their secret weapon."

"I wonder what that means? They are most likely to be disappointed because I am good at some things, but I'm not aggressive. I don't want to break the law. I am not a revolutionary."

"That is the sticking point isn't it? Are they revolutionaries. Are we just pawns in some power game they want to play?"

"Ah, you see it too. Good. Let's go find some dinner then watch girls." We went back out.

I did become Professor Stodola's teaching assistant. The thing I liked most about it was that the university paid me a little money. Professor Stodola also had private classes for young boys. I loved helping with the little boys. He paid me for that too.

One night after working with Professor's private students, I came in and asked Andy a question. "Well Andy, what do you think? Shall I disappoint everybody who has high hopes for me and take up teaching as a career? I love working with the little smolts."

"I don't think they would be disappointed. They'd find some other way to twist your choices around to fit their purposes

"They do seem manipulative. I think I am beginning to see a carnivorous gleam in their eyes when they look at me."

Andrew laughed. "Yeah, I noticed that too. I think for our next invitation we will be obligated to visit my family that weekend."

"Thank you for the invitation. We also have our camping trip that we must take."

"Are you really thinking of buying property?"

"I am determined to buy property and build a house on it. I've been out there a couple times at sunset. It is magnificent. I'd like to build a house right on top of the ridge with windows on both the east and west so I could sit in my sitting room and look both ways. That will not be possible because of the problems of getting water up to the top of the ridge." Andy shook his head over my idiosyncrasies.

Chapter 16 Camping with Flatmates

We decided to take our camping trip a few weeks after my parents returned from the United States. One evening, when my parents brought a dinner over to my apartment, Mama warned my friends about the camping trip. "You will have to take proper bedding and food. Jake will lead you out into the forest with nothing more than a blanket to wrap up in."

Papa added to Mama's comments. "My Dear, he would certainly take more than a blanket. He would take several pounds of books to read by the firelight."

Mama sighed. "If he remembered to bring matches to start the fire."

My friends laughed and assured my parents, "We will bring a few luxuries." They outfitted us with more than a few luxuries. They wanted to bring a tent.

I rolled my eyes over the tent idea and argued with them. "It never rains this time of year. There is no harm in sleeping on the ground."

"What about hammocks? Are there trees?"

"There are plenty of trees if you must sleep up off of the ground." I later admitted that I liked the hammock.

Finally, we were ready for our weekend camping trip. We arrived at M'TK station after classes on Friday. I planned to take the Gerry out to the site. Mr. Apkouta met us. "Jake you can't all fit on the Gerry with your equipment."

"I told them not to bring so much."

Mr. Apkouta had already thought out the problem. "Help me move one of the old trolley cars to the train tracks and you can drive out there in style. Mr. Apkouta and I went out and lifted a spare trolley off of its tracks. It was a very small one and would not go very fast. It would serve our needs.

"Come on guys help us roll this onto the rail line." We all got together and pushed the small car around the station and over to the railroad tracks. It had to be lifted again to set it onto the tracks properly. I was quite pleased with our work. My friends held their sides and moaned after getting the trolley onto the train tracks.

The others didn't know much about the workings of trolleys and trains. Johan asked, "Can the trolley really run on the rail tracks?"

"Sure."

He asked again, "Can the train run on the trolley tracks?"

"Well," I paused and thought a second. "Yeah."

Nickoli joined the discussion. "Why don't we ever see trains running through town?"

"You are half dead from moving this small trolley to the rail tracks. How would you propose to move the big engines from the rail to the trolley tracks?"

Mr. Apkouta looked at us. "You know, if we built a switch with a cross connection, we could run rail cars on the trolley tracks. That might allow us to move heavy supplies from Wulfton directly to M'TK." He wandered off to think.

I was too excited about our camping trip to consider what we had just come up with. None of us could have guessed the role the cross connection would play in bringing about the changes our professors wanted.

I took charge of the trolley. "Okay, guys, look sharp. We have to run this thing across all these tracks to a spur that runs out to the country. Watch me closely when I switch the tracks so you can switch them back for me."

Finally, we switched onto the siding out to the country. I had clear track in front of me. I opened up our little engine. We had a splash speeding through the forest. It took us only a half hour to reach the lake. We were disappointed that the ride had not lasted longer.

Once we climbed to the top of the hill where Mr. Apkouta and I stood watching the city burn, I ran back and forth trying to find exactly the best spot for seeing the city and the sunset. Finally I settled on a spot just before sunset.

Suddenly, the sun shone sideways on the city. We got quiet and watched as the sun went down. The city turned gold. It was magnificent. The show lasted about a half hour as the setting sun turned the city gold then as it got darker the lights came on. The final view of the city was of the golden tops of the cathedrals still reflecting the sun and the velvet darkness twinkling with thousands of lights. We turned to the west and watched as the last rays of light slid out of the sky in a burst of purple. Then the stars began to light the sky.

Johan grumbled. "Great now we have to set up camp in the dark."

Nickoli suggested. "Maybe we should sleep in the trolley."

"It will be more fun to sleep under the stars." I promised.

Andrew was practical as always. "Not if a bird shits on you."

"Uh could we go back to the trolley?" Nickoli actually sounded uneasy about sleeping outside.

"Didn't one of you insist on bringing a light?" I started piling twigs for a fire. "I think our eyes will adjust and we won't need it in another minute."

Andrew was no help. He stood in the dark and observed. "I think seeing in the dark is another one of Jake's strange secret talents."

"Do you suppose he has x-ray vision? You know like superman." Johan could be counted on to be fanciful.

"That wouldn't be too bad for looking at what girls have under their clothing."

I chided Nickoli, "Hey don't mention that. I'm trying to get a fire going here and if I start thinking about girls I'll give up and you'll never get any light." My plea was in vain. We spent the next hour or so talking about girls. This was not an unusual activity for us.

All weekend, we amused ourselves in the woods. We swam in the lake and hiked the entire length and width of the ridge. We experimented with cooking on the campfire. We were no worse on the open fire than at our apartment so we did not starve.

Late on Sunday afternoon, we got back on the trolley and sped back into the city. Our ride through the forest with the late afternoon sun slanting through the trees was glorious. Johan was taking an opera class so he entertained us with songs that matched the rhythm of our speeding trolley.

I'd planned our return for when there were no trains due in. The station looked deserted. We were tired as we unloaded our gear from the trolley. My friends grumbled about carrying their gear across the tracks to the station, but I knew the trolley would be in the way closer in.

Johan suddenly sounded enthusiastic. "I've got an idea. Let's call Candice and see if she will come get us with her car so we don't have to lug this stuff back on the trolley."

I wondered if Johan just wanted to see Candice. I approved, if that was his choice.

Andy grunted, "Good idea."

I agreed with Andy and Johan. "Okay guys wait here. I'll use the phone in the station. I need to tell Mr. Apkouta that we are back. I'll only be a minute. They are most likely eating dinner. I won't bother them."

"You just want to be the one to talk to Candice." Johan set his gear down and started to follow me.

"Okay, okay you can be the one to call Candice. I just don't want anyone disturbing the Apkoutas, like to beg for food."

"But, she is a good cook." Andrew and Nickoli followed. The station door was locked. I assumed the Apkoutas were upstairs eating. I quickly slid my key in and opened the door to discover that someone was disturbing the Apkoutas during their dinner time.

Three intruders filled the small office in the station. Mr. Apkouta stood bleeding profusely from a wound on his head. One man stood next to Mr. Apkouta with a nightstick thrust up under his chin.

The second man appeared unarmed and half-turned when I entered.

The worst part of the tableau before me was the gun the third man held to Mrs. Apkouta's head while his other arm held her around her fragile neck holding her body against his.

I felt more than saw Johan and Nickoli flatten themselves against the outside of the station. I knew Andrew had slipped silently away to get help. The scene before me froze.

"Oh no, oh no," I put my hands up in the air. "Take it easy. I'm innocent. What is going on here?" I could smell the tension and unwashed bodies of the intruders.

Mr. Apkouta's voice broke. "He wants me to open the safe."

"Well open it."

"I can't. I don't have a key." I thought that mountain of fierce humanity that I called Mr. Apkouta was going to cry.

"Okay, take it easy here." The slightest slip and the man would shoot Mrs. Apkouta in the head. I thought quickly. "I can open it. My papa is the stationmaster I have a key. Just let me open the safe. I will move very slowly and open the safe for you. Can you let the woman go?"

The third man nodded toward the safe. I wondered if he was the boss.

I spoke softly and soothing. "I don't want any trouble. I am going to open the safe now. You do not want to hurt that woman. Let her go. Let her go upstairs. She is just a woman. She will not hurt you." I saw something in the man's eyes. The pupils dilated ever so slightly. I tried again. "She's just a little bitty thing, a women. She never hurts anyone. Let her go. I am reaching for my keys." I broke into a sweat knowing that my keys were still dangling in the lock to the door. "See how I unlocked this door? I will open the safe. Please let that little tiny woman go. She is weak. She won't hurt anybody."

I got my keys from the door handle. I saw Nickoli and Johan were still pressed against the wall of the building.

I watched the eyes of the gunman. I wished I knew what he was reacting to so I could push it. Was he reluctant to hurt a woman? Did he hate women? His eyes rolled from side to side and a muscle in his cheek twitched when I said the word, woman. "She is such a tiny woman. She can't hurt a big guy like you. Please let her go. See now I have the keys for the safe." I held the keys up high where they could be seen.

I spared a second to glance at the other men inside the station to see what they were doing. They were sweating, yet they seemed transfixed by the tension between the man with the gun and myself. I noticed that their suits were worn and ill fitting. The way their jackets fit told me that these men would not be a challenge in a fight. No, my problem was the gun at Mrs. Apkoutas head.

Mrs. Apkouta was turning grey. I saw beads of sweat on her upper lip and forehead.

I kept talking slow and steady. "Okay, I have the keys in my hand. See, I am doing what you asked. I will open the safe. Please let the woman go. She has never hurt anybody. You do not want to hurt an innocent little woman. I need to move closer to the safe. I am going to slowly move closer to the safe then I will have to kneel down and put the key in the lock. You can let the woman go. I am cooperating."

The man was not cooperating.

Finally, Mrs. Apkouta, herself, gave me the break I needed. She convulsed then vomited on the arm that held her.

The gunman reflexively jerked the arm holding Mrs. Apkouta away from the vomit.

She dropped to the floor, twisting her body away from me as she went down.

The gun discharged into the wall as I kicked it out of the man's hand. The man with the nightstick swung wildly in my direction. I danced away from the nightstick.

The third man who hadn't done much so far grabbed me from behind. My attention was focused more on the nightstick. My body knew what it was doing. I stepped back into the man behind me and rolled him over my back and into the gunman who was attempting to charge into me. Both men landed on the floor. The thug with the nightstick was still on his feet. He made a lunge to grab me. I remembered something from my distant past. I danced away from the man, spun, and brought my leg up under his hips. The momentum of his lunge, my spin and kick lifted the man off his feet and flipped him over. I heard a popping sound as he landed on the edge of the desk on his back. His feet folded under him.

Mr. Apkouta had grabbed his wife out of the middle of the room and thrust her into the storage room where she sat sobbing on the floor. He picked up the gunman by the back of his shirt and pants and threw him headfirst out the door. He swung around on the other two thugs and tossed them after the gunman. Mr. Apkouta uttered a string of swear words that I found quite comforting.

"Take care of your wife and call Rouseff." I commanded. I was panting despite the fact that I hadn't really exercised enough to make me breathe heavy.

I tried to control my breathing. "I think Andy went for help." I brushed my sleeve. "I will interrogate the suspects."

Mr. Apkouta looked wild with his head bleeding and the veins standing out on his neck. His lip curled and his nose flared making me afraid he would kill the attackers. I knew he needed me to appear calm when I was torn between kicking the shit out of the thugs and holding Mrs. Apkouta in my arms. I knew we needed to question the thugs.

Mr. Apkouta snarled, "I will check on my wife then, I am going to cut off their balls for touching her."

I strolled outside and spoke to the intruders. "Okay you heard the man. You are going to lose your balls. No. No don't try to get up that is another bad choice."

The gunman tried to get to his knees.

Nickoli looked gleeful when he pounced on the gunman landing with his butt firmly in the middle of the gunman's back. The thug fell back onto the platform with the wind knocked out of him. Nickoli snarled, "Listen you bastard, that woman you frightened has saved me from starvation more than once. If you move so much as a muscle I will make you hurt so bad you'll beg for death."

Johan paced back and forth waiting to see who moved next. The man who had mostly been and observer was smart enough not to move. The third man who had been brave enough with the nightstick couldn't move.

Johan grinned at Nickoli. "Ah are you referring to that little experiment we had in biology class where if you stick a knife in a nerve here," He nudged the man under Nickoli with his toe. "it will cause his whole body to spasm. Or, we could do the experiment when we hit the nerve that makes him poop his pants."

Nickoli waved his hand in front of his face. "I think we are too late for that one."

I thought my roommates were slightly crazy. I spoke to the thugs. Maybe I was slightly crazy too. I was thinking of myself as an important prosecutor. "Now tell me what you are doing here. The safe does not have enough money to make this worthwhile on Sunday afternoon."

The bodies remained mute.

"I have the feeling that you three guys did not get the idea to come rob the station on a Sunday afternoon all by yourselves. You are the ones with your balls on the line. Tell me who sent you and I might let you keep some of your cherished parts. Why are you here? What do you want?"

The one who I suspected had a broken back lay on his side and stared into space. I didn't expect anything out of him.

I continued, "The station does not have much money on Sunday afternoon. Who sent you and what did they want?"

The one with the broken back whispered. "No. Not money. Books. We were supposed to get some books from the safe."

"Thank you sir. For that piece of information I will let Johan here call you an ambulance. I doubt that you will ever have sex again, but we will get you medical help. Can either of you share any information before I stretch you out across the tracks and let the six-o'clock train cut your legs off."

The man with apparently the most brains confessed, "I don't know anything. He said I could have money if I came and helped fight off the big guy. The big man was supposed to open the safe. Only nobody could find the key."

"Mr. Apkouta doesn't have a key. Who hired you?"

"I don't know who the boss is. He hired me." The informant nodded toward the gunman.

"Your operation has not gone well. You did not have good information, I think. So you hired you? Who betrayed you?"

The gunman finally spoke. "He'll kill me."

"He already did try to kill you. Who wants you dead?"

"I don't know. Bernard. Bernard is all the information I have. I was told to come at this time and make the stationmaster open the safe. Then I was supposed to bring his missus and the books back to Bernard."

I felt as if a bucket of ice water was dumped over my head. I saw black spots dancing before my eyes and I broke out in a sweat. I remembered my breathing exercise. I tried to breathe for myself, and my mama's safety. "Why? Why would you need the stationmaster's wife? Are you sure those were your instructions?"

"Yes, the wife was important. She made the books. She is supposed to tell Bernard what they mean."

Andrew interrupted this little chat followed closely by Mr. Rouseff sprinting across the platform toward us. "Jake what's going on here?"

I told Mr. Rouseff everything that I knew. I finished with, "We called for medical help for that one. I think his back is broken."

I was thankful to have Mr. Rouseff take charge. "Boys, I want you out of here. Get your gear and get in my car. Jake, here are the keys. Go to my house." He turned to our assistant stationmaster who still looked grey and shaken. "Mr. Apkouta, put these two men in a boxcar and lock them up."

We ran to do as we were told. My feet moved. My brain kept saying, "Mama? Where is Mama? Where is Mama?"

I didn't know how to drive so Johan took the key and got behind the wheel. He remembered how to get to Rouseff's house. Mama and Papa arrived in a taxi at the same time we did. Papa left again immediately.

We went into the house with Mama. "Jake what is it? You are out of breath and shaking. Have you been fighting?"

I knew I was still slightly breathless. I just wanted to cling to Mama to keep her safe. "No. No fighting. Someone tried to rob the books from the station. They were supposed to abduct you too."

Mama was not letting go of her first thought. "That sounds serious. Why did you say you were not fighting?"

Nickoli was not sick and having trouble breathing like me. He was still high from his part in the adventure. "I saw the whole thing through the window Mrs. Jaconovich. Jake mostly did some fancy talking. There was a bit where things got lively. I would not call that fighting."

Johan agreed. "Yes, I saw it. Fighting implies that one side defends themselves or attacks someone."

Nickoli added his bit. "No, that was not fighting. What was that?"

Johan suggested. "Mr. Apkouta threw some men out of the station."

Nickoli sounded confused. "Yeah, I got that part. What was the part before that when it got noisy and all the bad guys fell down?"

"Jake, I think that you have not told me the whole truth." Mama sounded more worried than disapproving.

"I don't know the whole truth. A man held a gun on Mrs. Apkouta. She vomited on him. He let go of her and she dropped to the floor. I kicked the gun out of the man's hand. That was the point at which as Nickoli said, all the men fell down."

Mama gave me her look. I felt better. I smiled at my Mama then picked her up into a hug.

Mama was not appeased yet. "I still want to scold you for not giving me a straight answer."

"The thing is Mrs. Jaconovich that I still wouldn't call that a fight. It was over in less than thirty seconds. Nobody even touched Jake. That is for sure."

Mama and Mrs. Philippe discussed what the incident could mean. Mrs. Philippe remembered to feed us. We'd just finished eating when Papa and Mr. Rouseff returned. They asked me to come into the study with them.

Before I got settled I asked, "What did you learn?"

"They were apparently after the ledgers and your mama." Papa sat down heavily in one of the big leather armchairs. "Have you mentioned those ledgers or your mama's work to anyone?"

I shook my head. I wasn't really listening. I was thinking.

"First, I think Mama needs to go stay with Uncle John." I glanced at Mr. Rouseff. "Papa should to go too."

Papa nodded. He looked sick and grey.

I added, "I cannot think of anytime I've mentioned Mama's work. I don't talk about Mama and Papa if I don't have to. I told Fiona that Mama trained as a bookkeeper. I may have told Candice that Mama is educated."

Mr. Rouseff looked grim. "What about the others in your student/faculty group?"

"They all think that Mama is a very elegant woman who lives in a fancy house with so many servants we trip over them."

Cousin Philippe took charge of the situation. "Jake, go back to your apartment. You and your friends did not see or hear anything. Do you know what I mean?"

I nodded. I also knew I should watch my back.

Chapter 17 University Sleuths

W ithin two weeks after the attack, I knew that I was being followed. I figured one person came from railroad security. I suspected the person who sent the thugs to the station hired at least one of my shadows.

I went out of my way to annoy my followers. I went to the Cathedral almost daily. I lit candles and prayed while the entourage waited looking bored. Foreign films became another of my frequent activities during this time. I attended receptions and dinner parties. I strived to be a very boring student, but my shadows did not give up.

Early one Saturday morning, Andy came out of our bedroom to find me hiding behind the curtain and looking out the window. He crept up behind me and looked out the window. "Jake, what are you looking at?"

"See the man dressed in brown by the sycamore tree?"

"Which one is a sycamore?"

"The one with the big leaves and grey trunk."

"Okay what about him?"

I asked Andy. "What do you think?"

Andy thought for a couple minutes. "Is he watching our house?"

"Yes."

Johan joined us. "Who is watching our house?"

Andy sounded superior. "The man by the sycamore."

"What is a sycamore?"

I didn't wait for Andrew to explain. "So is the man in the blue car, but he is from the railroad."

Nickoli looked over our shoulders and yawned. "Why are they watching us?"

"That is what I want to know. Shall we capture him?"

"Sure."

What idiots we were! My roommates did not hesitate to join this mad plan. The plan was simple. Andrew and Johan left and started through the park. After they walked past the waiting man, Nickoli and I came running out calling to them to wait for us.

The plan came off flawlessly. The man stepped partly behind the tree as Nickoli and I came running out of the apartment. When we approached the tree, Nickoli suddenly ran around the other side and pushed the man into my path. I kicked his feet out from under him and all four of us pounced on him.

I assumed my future prosecutor role while I held the captive face down on the ground with my knee in his back. "Okay, who are you and why have you been following me for weeks?"

"I don't know what you mean. I'm not following you."

I looked at my friends. "Okay this one is not railroad security." I turned back to the weasel we'd captured. "I've been watching you all week. Who sent you?"

"I don't know." He squirmed as if trying to get up and got Johan's knee in his back for his efforts. "I don't know anything."

"Shall we take him back to the apartment and hold him hostage until he talks?" Johan sounded surprisingly ghoulish. Perhaps he had spent too much time with the opera.

"I'm not sure we want to put up with him that long. I am tired of being followed." Now that we had my shadow, I wasn't sure what to do with him.

"Jake, I'll take this from here. I'm tired of following you." The newcomer startled me. However, I suspected he worked for the railroad.

"Hi, I figured you worked for the family. We pay better." I grinned at the new arrival. "What are you going to do with him?"

"Lock him up in a warehouse until he tells us what we want to know."

"I want to know what he is up to. It is me he is following."

The man nodded. "I will give Mr. Rouseff a full report."

I studied the man standing over us. He had an athletic build. His clothing was new and fit well. His jacket fit loosely as if it might conceal a shoulder holster. "I think you work for us, but I am not sure. I hate to turn my prey over to someone I am not sure of."

I thought for a few minutes, trying to decide whether or not to turn the weasley man over to the one I thought was from the railroad. My roommates and I discussed a plan. I fully intended to turn the weasel over to Rouseff, but I wanted to think about the man who claimed to be from security. My friends' suggestions amused me.

"We can hold him hostage and cut off a toe for every day that he doesn't talk."

I protested. "Johan that opera class is a bad influence on you."

Andy argued, "We can just tie him up and leave him on our floor until he talks."

Nickoli added that he thought the man would talk after a day or so of eating our cooking.

Johan protested that feeding him our cooking was worse than the toe severing idea we'd condemned him for.

A familiar voice sounded reassuring. "Jake it is okay. I'll take this from here."

I felt surprised and relieved in an instant. "Cousin Philippe how did you know to come here?"

Cousin Philippe patted Blue-Car-Man on the shoulder. "We supply our security with car phones."

"Okay, you can have Weasel." I stood up taking my knee out of Weasel's back. "I've taken him to the cathedral almost every day for two weeks and he hasn't grown a soul. I'll give you any of the others I catch."

"There are more?"

"It's silly. I can't go anywhere without three to five people trailing me."

"Jake, take care. I'll deal with this."

My roommates and I speculated about the man following me until Mr. Rouseff invited me to dinner about two weeks later. Before dinner, he took me into his study and told me the story.

"We think your man…"

"Weasel?"

Mr. Rouseff laughed. "He does have a weasel look to him." Mr. Rouseff laughed again. "We think he is from the Vanderholms. We've had ledgers stolen from other stations. I can only assume that they have realized that they are not going to be able to move an army on the trains if they want to. They know now that we have a system for tracking how many people go where. I am adding enough security to keep track of who goes where."

"Why do they care?"

"Because they need to use the railroad if they are going to attack competitors. They are pushing the government to build highways, but parts of the country are so rugged that roads will not reach them for years. Barges can move large numbers of troops, but they are too slow. In the past they used the railroad. I won't allow that. I think they have joined forces with the Fortenacs to destroy us."

He settled back in his chair and was silent for a few minutes. "Jake you may have chosen the wrong family to side with. Perhaps you need to find a nice Spinoza girl to marry. Join her family."

I asked the question that had been foremost in my mind for weeks. "How long do you think Mama needs to stay with Uncle John?"

"I expect your parents back in a couple weeks. Your Papa is devising plans to thwart the Vanderholms. I understand they killed his family."

I nodded. We stood up to go to dinner.

Mr. Rouseff continued his explanations. "I learned that you have had a crowd behind you. Most of the people have been locals watching to see that you are safe. Half of them were watching Weasel."

We laughed.

After this discussion, the Vanderholms had a long spate of bad luck. They were into shipping. Their flagship had an explosion in the engine room and sank. There were rumors that the explosion occurred after the propellers fouled in a fishing net from a small fishing boat. The drag on the propellers caused something in the engine to overheat. I couldn't wait to talk to my cousins.

Maybe all those candles I lit while I was being followed did some good. The Vanderholms lost another ship at sea. The weather turned unseasonably dry. Their grain dried up in their fields. They couldn't find men to work on their ships. Rumors circulated that the ships were unsafe because of poor maintenance.

Cousin Philippe put a further strain on the work force of the country. He started massive development projects on railroad land. He sold or leased large sections of land. He broke ground for the M'TK mall. This was a shopping mall based on the ones he'd seen in the United States. He needed workers. He had the mall, another rail line, a bridge and several housing developments under construction. He pulled over one hundred sixty-thousand workers from all over the country. The Vanderholms had to pay better or go without workers. They could not hire enough help. Mr. Rouseff took to laughing and saying, "Don't mess with me."

In my third year classes, I needed a practicum project. I drew up the legal papers for the sale and leasing of Mr. Rouseff's land. One project he started that was near to my heart was the development of Rouseff Lake and my ridge behind it. I worked with hiring the surveyors. We went over and over the details. I insisted on buying two lots that backed up to the ridge. Most of the ridge was to be public lands. I convinced Mr. Rouseff to sell me that part of the ridge behind my lots. "I like a little more protection at my back."

I worked one whole term for the Rouseff developments. The next term I worked part time as an intern in the prosecutor's office. For the prosecutor, I worked both as a public defender and a prosecutor. Most of the clients I represented were poor people from the city. They were charged with drunkenness, petty theft, assault, and the usual crimes the poor in any city commit.

I had one case as a prosecutor that interested me. A man was charged with assault for beating his daughter. I was expected to reprimand him to use caution in punishing his child and let him go. I visited the child in the hospital. She had both arms broken. Most of her ribs were broken. Her neck was bruised. Her shoulder was dislocated. She was just a tiny little child. I looked at the tube in her arm and the one that went up her nose and down her throat to help her breath. Another tube ran from under the covers to a urine bag under the bed.

The father's public defender was old and drunk. I knew I could handle him easily. The judge presented a bigger problem. He was accustomed to letting offenders like this man off with a light sentence. I pulled the man's assault record. I argued that the man was a menace to all society. I told the judge. "We will just go through this again and again with this man. Put him in prison and leave him there so we do not waste our court time on him again next month. The man went to prison for ten years. At the time, the prison conditions were barbaric. For this man, I smiled every time I thought of him in that hellhole. He died there. My only regret was that he did not live long enough to serve his full sentence before he died.

I graduated first in my class. I gave a speech at graduation. The crowd cheered and clapped as I talked about a future based on mutual respect and cooperation. The Rouseffs hosted a large party. People on the street stopped me and gave me cards and notes wishing me well. I thought perhaps I had convinced the professors that I was from the elite. I had the strong feeling that the people of the city knew that I was the M'TK Sewer Rat. My people love stories of the common man who tricks the powerful. The people of the city seemed to think my charade was a great joke.

I got another invitation to a student/faculty meeting. I went intending to say goodbye to this group. They acted enthusiastic and rowdy when I arrived. Professor Ingleman explained the party atmosphere to me. "Jake, you are going into politics."

"Um…no…I don't think so. I am going to work in the prosecutor's office as you requested. I will work part-time for my cousins so I will have enough money to live on. I will find a nice woman to marry and raise children and stay out of trouble.

Professor Stodola sobered as he studied me. "Jake that is how everyone in this country wants to live, except for a few among the power elite. You cannot live that way. If you manage to live the life you want, your children will have to face these same issues. We need to have a country with a strong government, independent of the elite families."

I settled back in my chair and thought. I ran my fingers through my hair. "Okay, you have been trustworthy so far. I will confide in you. I've taken my exams for the law. I will be qualified. You cannot kick me out of school."

I took a great breath and a great risk. "I have not led a life of privilege. My father is a laborer. I do not have one blessed relative among the elite. Mr. Rouseff claims us out of love and respect, but my family is solidly, historically from the north. I cannot hold public office."

The room grew absolutely quiet. Professor Stodola started to shake. Then I thought I heard him giggle, much like a schoolgirl. Finally, he broke into a full belly laugh. Tears began to run out of his eyes. He eventually regained control enough to ask a question. "Jake Jaconovich, tell me that you are not the one they call the M'TK Sewer Rat."

I grinned. "I am."

Most of the teachers still sat in shocked silence. They had not heard the name.

"Actually, I am rather proud of the title."

Professor Stodola had tears in his eyes. "I should say! What a joke!" His voice sounded full of emotion. "Men, this man will be the president of this country some day and we will have justice."

The others smiled happily.

"But I'm from the north. And, we have an emperor not a president."

Professor Ingleman sounded confident. "Things will change Jake. I don't know how, but things will change."

The oldest professor scolded. "Jake, you have not been listening to us. We are determined to unite this country. We will stop the purges." The speaker paused. "Your cousin seems to have crippled the Vanderholms for the time being. This is giving us time. Keep up your friendship with Rouseff. Work for him part-time. Do a good job. The time will come when you can enter politics."

I was the one to be stunned. "You still want me?"

Professor Uzara said, "Yes, that is what we want: the best men to serve this country no matter where they are from."

I went home in a state of shock. I considered their talk of politics nonsense. I went to work for Mr. Rouseff and the prosecutor's office processing petty criminals. I saved my money to build a house. I looked for a woman to marry. I still spent a great deal of time with the Rouseff family.

Chapter 18 Early Career

I spent most of my first week in the prosecutor's office processing prostitutes. I grumbled to everybody in the office. "Why are the police arresting these women? They take up court time. They just go back to work. What else are they supposed to do?"

My supervisor answered, "The laws are on the books. We arrest them because they spread disease. We can't just let them practice without punishment."

I persisted. "Well, we could. Arresting them does no good."

My supervisors laughed at me. "The good women of the city would never allow us to just let them practice."

I whined, "I think sometimes they have fun in jail. They certainly laugh when they see me. Let someone else handle these cases. I do not believe in harassing the poor when they are trying to support themselves."

My usual procedure involved requesting that they be sentenced to a medical exam at the court's expense. I recommend a small fine, and job counseling.

The drunks were the same situation. They were happy to have someplace warm and dry to sleep off their drunk. Being arrested made no impression on them. Most of them did not have any money to pay a fine.

I tried to come up with an alternative to our current system. "Can we set up an overnight detention program so we do not have to process these cases through court? This is ridiculous. I spend all day Monday and half of Tuesday processing drunks and prostitutes. Can we give them a citation and send them on their way without their case appearing in court?"

I whined incessantly about the nuisance cases for a year before I was allowed to make some changes. After that we held the prostitutes in an old office building instead of jails. In the morning we gave them a citation and told them to stay off of the streets. We stored the drunks on a different floor of the building. Occasionally someone broke out of the low security building. Mostly, they seemed happy for a good meal and warm place to sleep. It freed up almost half of my week. I was able to spend time and money prosecuting what I called real crime.

For Mr. Rouseff, I continued to draw up legal contracts for land sales and purchases. The railroad workers formed a union. Mr. Rouseff grumbled about this. "What will they demand? I should break this right now. I'll hire workers from someplace else."

I tried to reassure him. "When you give your workers good conditions your profits increase. My advice is to wait and see how this plays out."

"Surely they will not be reasonable."

"My advice as your attorney and a friend is to wait and see what they want."

The workers formed their union. They held meetings. Nothing changed. Just getting organized took them well over a year. The newspapers went ballistic with the story. On my walk to work one morning I read the headlines at the newsstands, "*Rouseff to Purge Railroad Workers!*" and "*Weak Rouseff Sells Out to Working Scum*" and "*Rouseff Must Break Union Now or Face Destruction of Our Nation.*"

Mr. Rouseff wrung his hands and asked me at least a thousand times, "Are you sure we should not break this up now?"

"I am certain. Your policy has been to treat your workers fairly. Continue with that policy. I think this will be okay." I worried and sweated wondering what kind of advice I was giving.

Finally, the union bosses wanted to meet with Mr. Rouseff. He invited me to the meeting. Papa came as someone the workers trusted. Three men from the union arrived.

The men were differing styles of muscular. I was surprised that they had probably been laborers when they were young. Now, they appeared to be in their fifties. I looked closer and revised my estimate of their ages downward. Their skin looked fifty. Their eyes appeared closer to forty. They wore identical black suits, a brand sold at the local department store.

The tallest, heaviest of the three served as spokesperson. "The workers want a contract."

We nodded. Silence ensued.

I prompted them. "Uh…what do you want in the contract?"

The leader answered, "The workers want to be guaranteed their jobs. They want us to represent them. They want a set salary."

The other two men flanking their leader nodded solemnly.

I nodded encouragingly. "That sounds very fair. Do you have a copy of the contract they want?"

The three men looked at each other. The leader explained again, "The workers want to be guaranteed their jobs. They want us to represent them. They want a set salary."

Mr. Rouseff was letting me do the talking. I said, "I am an attorney. I think contracts are a good idea."

My audience shifted in their seats and looked at each other. The leader made sounds, "Um…uh." His comrades grunted.

I took over the discussion. "We know how many trained workers we need. We can guarantee that many job slots. We know how much we pay for each position and for experience. We can guarantee those wages. The contract must also specify that people will show up for work, prepared to work. We can give leave for family emergencies, if a wife or child is sick."

The union leaders nodded their heads intently. They made eye contact with me and grunted appropriately at my remarks.

I continued. "It would be a conflict of interest for me to draw up the contract. I want you to find an attorney who knows about contract law and have that person draw up a contract. We will look it over and make suggestions or changes to suit the needs of the railroad. Next, you present the contract to your workers and have them vote on it."

The men nodded. I wondered if they were relieved to have their next step outlined for them. They stood to leave.

Mr. Rouseff sounded gruff. "You might also mention to your workers that we treated you fairly and with respect. I want to run an honest business. I intend to treat my employees fairly. You make it real clear that we are being fair with you."

We all stood. We shook hands. The union leaders looked bemused as they shuffled out the door.

I sat down and held my head. "They're babes. They have no idea what they are doing. They are as bad as I was when I first learned I must find a laundry to do my shirts." We sat shaking our heads.

Papa finally summed up the situation. "We could come out of this looking real good. It depends on what the attorney comes up with."

We had no trouble with the attorney they eventually found. When he phoned me, he sounded a little stunned from talking to the union leaders.

"These folks have no real idea what unions do. The company can do whatever it wants with them."

I sighed. "The company wants to treat the workers fairly. We want them to be able to support their families. We want their children to be able to stay in school. We want them to be healthy."

"Well then, what do they think they need a union for?"

"We are not opposed to having a contract."

"I can see your point."

I explained what we had to build a contract on. "We have written job descriptions for each position. We have codified the skill requirements for each position. It would be good for us to communicate that to the workers. We have a pay scale that we think is fair. Perhaps others see areas where it needs adjusting. I'm sure we can negotiate some details."

"Why didn't you put a stop to this?"

"We see potential benefits to both sides. Mr. Rouseff took a team of employees to the United States a couple years ago. They think we can have that same standard of living."

"We are not a rich country."

"We do not manage well. One thing you might talk to the workers about is health care. If they are going to organize and pay dues, they can buy some benefits like immunizations for the children. I confess that I am not much more knowledgeable about unions than the union bosses. My mama suggested the immunizations."

He said, "I'm glad I talked to you. I admit, some of the headlines in the newspapers had me worried about taking on the union as a client."

I laughed. "I saw one headline in one news shop that read, *'Jaconovich Will Betray the Business Class.'* I might have been upset if I had not received the assurance at another newsstand, within a half a block, reading, *'Incompetent Jaconovich is Front for Rouseff's Plan to Crush the Union.'*"

He laughed. "I read, *'Union Vows to Destroy Industry'* and *"Unionization: Conspiracy to Overthrow Government."*"

"Ah yes, the conspiracies, *'Rouseff Sells Nation to US Union Bosses.'*" We both laughed.

For the next year as we worked out the details of the contract, we continued to share the best headlines we'd seen. This became a standing joke between the union leaders, their attorney, and us.

I continued processing petty crime in the prosecutor's office. I began to think that my time could be spent more productively than sorting out who started a drunken brawl and fining the participants. We had a few riots that led to arrests. These produced mountains of paperwork and little else.

The mountains of paperwork may be the basis for my dislike of any form of rioting. I understand civil disobedience. I have even participated in it. I did not make paperwork for some poor civil servant! I tried to find a way around the paperwork. My favorite suggestion for processing rioters was to let everybody go and burn their paperwork in the courtyard. My supervisors wouldn't let me do that. I had to process each rioter who got arrested. I complained bitterly. "There has to be a better way for dealing with petty offenses than for one man to spend forty-eight hours a week processing paperwork."

I learned that I could save some court time by bundling cases. "Your honor, I have here the paperwork on twenty-two men arrested for brawling. The facts are essentially the same. They were arrested at the scene. I have informed them that they must pay a fine. Can you please sign off on these sir?" He'd sign the papers.

"What's next?"

"Eighteen women picked up for prostitution and taken to the holding center. They paid their fines." He would sign that batch of papers.

"Next?"

"Five, where the defendants plead innocent to rioting saying they were on their way home from work. I am not charging them."

"You don't want to spend more time on their paperwork."

"Do you?"

"Let me sign those."

By Friday morning I would clear my desk, ready for another onslaught of weekend revelries. I used to grumble that we had too many police in the city or that they were not doing what needed to be done. I had an acquaintance who worked in the morgue. His client's cases seldom made it to our office. Selling sex was a punishable offence in the city. Murder was not.

Chapter 19 Vacation at The Cove

It took a little over two years from the beginning of talk about unions until we had a signed contract. I explained it to Mr. Rouseff. "We set the wage scale for two years. We've set rules for conduct on the job. We have made it clear that we will fire people who show up drunk. We can fire them for fighting and refusing to follow orders. The union contract will give the railroad workers prestige in the community so we can hire the best people available."

When the contract was signed Mr. Rouseff asked me, "What are you going to do to celebrate?"

"I have requested a week leave from processing drunks and prostitutes and plan to visit my cousins in the north."

"Ah, you are going boating again. Wear a hat. Do not come back so brown we don't recognize you."

I left work early enough on Friday to catch the evening train north. I stopped at the station and spent some time with Mama and Papa. The Apkoutas moved out shortly after the attack on Mrs. Apkouta. Mama and Papa were living alone at the station.

"It is strange for us to sit down to dinner just the two of us." They looked at each other and smiled.

"Perhaps I should move back into the spare bedroom. I don't like my apartment."

"Oh no young man, you are not moving back in and having your Mama wait on you hand and foot."

Mama reached up and brushed the hair off of my forehead. "Jake you need a haircut. You need to look like the big important man that you are."

"Mama, I am a low level civil servant."

"You negotiated an important union contract."

I changed the subject. "Have you found a part-time person to stay here at night?"

"No, I will look at the applicants. You should clean your things out of your downstairs room."

"I didn't know I had anything down there. I'll take care of that now."

I barely fit in my old room. I pulled down my old faded sports posters. I dropped a thumbtack down the crack between the bed and the wall. I moved the boards for the bed aside. I uncovered a treasure trove of bits of paper, cookie crumbs, several tacks, a pencil, and eraser, eraser dust and the little sticks Mr. Pickett used to open locks. I remembered that at one time, they'd hung on the wall by the door. I had no idea how they ended up in the bed. Most of the stuff I emptied into the waste. The pencil, tacks, and eraser I put away in the desk. In a corner, I found one of the small socks I was forced to wear at Boys Club Camp. I pushed Mr. Pickett's sticks into my pocket and took the posters and sock upstairs.

Mama pounced on the sock. She pressed it flat with her fingers. "It is hard to remember that you were this small. You did not want to go to camp. I remember you did not want to go to camp." Mama's mood struck me as unusual.

"It is time for me to catch the train. I'll be back in a week to fine more prostitutes and drunks." I kissed Mama on top of her head and ran downstairs to catch my train.

Riding the train had become a bit ridiculous. The train crew would hardly let me move by myself.

"I will take your bag Mr. Jaconovich."

"Let me get the steps, sir."

"I will get your door." I felt embarrassed. I thought having a contract and a union would make the workers less dependant on the bosses. I hoped they realized the company had been fair. An attendant brought me a small basket of nuts and fruit. Perhaps they did know we had been fair.

My cousins met me at the train but did not seem as enthusiastic to see me as usual.

"What's wrong?"

Cousin John almost moaned. "Trouble with the canneries. Uncle John will tell you."

"You act as if it is serious."

"It is. We cannot get fuel for the boat."

"Ouch, why is that?"

Petral rolled his eyes as he untied the boat. "Uncle John will explain it at great length."

"Endlessly." Cousin John sighed.

"I'm concerned. You know, anything I can do to help, I will."

Uncle John met me on the dock when I arrived. "Come in, come in. It is good to see you lad."

As soon as I set foot on the dock I asked, "What is this I hear about not being able to fuel the boat?"

"Oh come in and let us look at you before we start moaning and groaning with all our troubles." They did get me into the house. I think I got my bag set down before the story started.

"The cannery won't let us tie up at the fuel dock in Midville."

I didn't know the legalities of ownership in this province. "Who owns the dock?"

"The provincial government built the dock. It seems they gave it to the cannery company because the government did not want to maintain it."

"Who owns the cannery?"

"The Fortenacs" Uncle John almost snarled out the name.

"Well that is one good reason to fight this."

"There is more." Petral moaned.

Uncle John choked and could barely get out his next words. "They're claiming a lean against our shrimp boat."

"What? You bought that outright."

"They claim we owe them port fees for it." Uncle John looked grey as I pried the details out of him.

I thought about the five months I'd spent fishing. "I remember paying port fees. I remember keeping the receipts. Do you still have all your receipts?"

Aunt Luella snorted, "Your mama would kill us or at least look at us if we lost a receipt!"

"Okay that problem is easy enough to deal with. Where is the shrimp boat anyway?" The family looked at each other.

Uncle John's voice was so full of anger, I was afraid he would make himself sick. "They locked it up when we went in to refuel."

"What? What makes them think they have the right to lock up your boat? How do you lock up a boat? Bring me all the paperwork you have from these people."

Uncle John reached a basket of papers down off of a shelf and set it beside me. I started sorting papers. I looked up and saw the family sitting silently around the room staring at me. Even some of the littlest school children were sitting cross-legged on the floor staring at me. "What are you looking at?"

"You dress funny." One of the littlest ones said.

Her mama gasped. "Marianne!"

"Well he does."

"You are right. I am glad you noticed. Noticing things that look unusual is very important." I wanted to pick that little cousin up and hold her on my lap and read her stories.

I looked over two or three more papers. "Why didn't you write me about this sooner."

"We didn't think you could do anything about it. Even you cannot kick in one of the Fortenac's faces." I chuckled at the memory. I laughed outright at the next letter I picked up. It was gibberish. It looked impressive enough. The paper was very fine. The letter concerned the confiscation of the Ona Elsee, the shrimp boat. I read and started laughing as I read.

Finally I addressed my family. "Well, the first order of business is to go get that shrimp boat."

"It is locked up." Petral snarled.

"How is it locked?"

"With a chain that would take us all night to saw through and a padlock too big for cutters." I'd never seen Petral get so angry.

I grinned like a shark. "Oh good. That's great. Do you have a lock like it? Can you get me a lock like it? Do you have any locks?" This last question was not as foolish as it may sound to a city person. Mama's family lived in a cove with mountains behind the house and rocks at the mouth of the cove. They never locked anything at the house—still don't as far as I know.

"I have a lock." One of the smaller boys got up and ran out of the room.

"He doesn't want just any lock." His young cousin shouted after him.

"Well actually, I do. I want as many different locks as you can find for me." When all the locks in the house were assembled before me we had a reasonable collection of styles.

I pulled Mr. Pickett's lock picks out of my pocket. "Okay kids, I am going to practice opening locks with these little sticks. While I do, I'll tell you a story."

"What kind of story?"

"A true story, the very best kind. Now, all good stories start with, 'Once upon a time.' Once upon a time, my papa, Uncle Jacob, was hurt in an accident and could not work."

I told about bringing him the wheeled chair to fix. I sat and played with the locks and the sticks as I told my story. "So Mr. Apkouta and another man lifted Mr. Pickett and his wheeled chair onto the train."

By the time I got to the part about, "He went away with his daughter, but he left these little sticks hanging on the wall of his bedroom," I'd opened all except one jewelry box and a diary. I'd opened the biggest padlock three times.

I glanced up to see Cousin John's and Petral's eyes dance as they watched me. "Now," I said to the children, "it is a good thing to help other people. Good things come back to you when you do. We must also be humble when we help other people, because sometimes we get help in ways we do not understand. I do not know why these sticks were in the bed I took apart yesterday evening. For that matter, why did Papa tell me to clean things out of that room when I haven't lived there for years? There is a mystery in much that happens in life. Sometimes we call that mystery God. It is good to recognize the mystery and to love God and love other people."

A small diary was the last item to open. It was giving me trouble. "I will leave this closed because it might contain secrets. The lock does not want me to look at other people's secrets." I grinned at my cousins. "I think we can go get that boat tonight."

"Ahoy! The wind is up! Hit the oars Jake." John and Petral were now grown men. They'd jumped to their feet and were dancing around the room, acting very silly. The smaller children got up and danced and clapped with excitement.

Uncle John worried. "Are you certain you will not get in trouble for taking the boat?"

"There will be a risk in going after it, but I have not seen any papers that give them more rights than any other thief. They are just fancier thieves. I assume we are going in tonight."

Loading four grown men in the five-meter rowboat was tight. Petral and John had agreed to take our cousin Micki. He was only sixteen. He made himself a nice bed in the bow out of boat cushions and fell asleep. We woke him up to switch positions twice during the row down. Micki acted so excited

I thought he was going to fall overboard. He was as strong as any man and better at rowing than me, which was good because the tide was flowing against us.

We rowed south for almost two hours before we put into shore near a creek. A small sandbar hid the rowboat from the open water. Petral told Micki, "Stay with the boat. Stay out of sight. If anyone comes into the cove…um what should he do?"

I snorted. "Tell the truth. His cousins went into town to see some women and left him with the boat."

"If that story got back to my wife, I'd be sleeping in the shed for a month, or more."

I laughed at Petral. "Your wife knows what you are doing and the story won't get back."

We followed a narrow, heavily overgrown, rabbit-trail up the hill.

Petral sounded disgusted. "Ugh, shit, where did these trees come from?"

John whined back at him. "Are you sure this is the right path?"

"No, I'm not sure it is the right path. You are the one who headed this way."

I had a horrible feeling. "Have either of you done this before?"

"Yeah."

"Sure."

I eyed their backs suspiciously "How long ago?"

"You don't want to know."

I tried again. "Can you beat down the brush so it doesn't hit me in the face?"

They were not about to baby me. "Take care of it yourself."

"You know, we will want to find our way back. It will be dark. It would help if we had a better trail returning."

Cousin John made a rude noise. "Do they teach you to think of these things in your fancy university?"

"No. It is trailing behind you two that causes me to think of these things." We continued to beat our way through the underbrush up the side of a small ridge.

From the top of the ridge we could see the village of Midville. We found a civilized trail coming down the ridge. We ran into some fierce looking cattle. We stepped in some cattle droppings.

The trail took us through the cemetery and churchyard. Cousin John moaned, "Oh joy, we are going to have to walk back through the cemetery after dark.

I caught both cousins by the back of their shirts. "Hold up."

"What now?" Both cousins whined at me at once.

"Look at you two." I pulled twigs out of their hair. "I doubt I look much better."

"Yeah, you have a nasty scratch on your face. Looks like it bled." Petral sounded cheerful.

"Well, we need to get cleaned up a little if we are not going to attract too much attention." We picked at each other's hair and brushed off our jackets. We wiped our shoes on the grass as best we could. We decided to split up in town in order to cover the most territory.

They assigned me the high street. I think this was to keep me out of trouble. I went to the town hall and looked over the village. I stood on the steps and shuddered. It was obvious that we would be totally exposed coming into the harbor.

"May I help you sir?" A man in a suit stood behind me locking the town hall door.

"Oh, hello. My name is Jake Jaconovich. I'm an attorney from the south. I was hoping to look for court records on the sale of the dock to the Fortenacs."

"We are closed."

"So I see. I can come back tomorrow. Do you work here?"

"I don't have time to stand here talking to strangers."

"Certainly, have a pleasant evening sir. It is beautiful here." I put my hands in my pockets and stared out to sea a few more minutes before I made my way to the pub.

I entered alone and ordered a beer and some fish. I introduced myself to a couple fishermen using the story of being an attorney and sat at a table.

A young man approached me. "I'm Lars M'TG. What did you say your name was?"

"Jake Jaconovich."

"Related to the D'NOs?"

I nodded. M'TG sat down. "Fortenac's a thief. I don't see where he has the right to lock up our boats."

Several men nodded and made noises agreeing with M'TG. I noticed the men huddling into groups, looking at me and talking among themselves.

"Can you tell me anything about the province selling the dock to Fortenac?"

"Fortenac," The grizzled old fisherman seated at the next table, spat when he said the name, "stole the dock the same as he steals everything else."

"I heard the government didn't want to pay for upkeep and transferred it to him." The bartender added this information as he set my beer and fish in front of me and walked away before I could pay him.

I watched the room. About twenty fishermen and five women were seated around the room. There were no children.

M'TG seemed sensible and informed me, "My uncle is certain Fortenac didn't pay for the dock."

Another fisherman corrected him. "Fortenac stole the dock." I noticed more spitting around the room at the name Fortenac.

Another man spoke up. "My brother in-law has a cousin who works for Fortenac. He says the provincial government owed Fortenac some money and Fortenac took the dock as payment 'cause the government don't have no money."

I worried about the men huddled in the corner whispering among themselves.

When John and Petral entered, I left my beer on the table and we went out immediately. The pub behind us remained silent for a few minutes, then I heard laughter. I wondered what that meant.

We scrambled our way back over the ridge behind the church. When we reached the shore, we couldn't see the rowboat.

"Are we in the right place?" I whispered because of the way sound carries on water, especially at night.

"Micki?" Nothing.

"I'm sure we came down the same trail." Petral sounded confident.

"Micki?" John tried more urgently.

"Do you suppose he ran into trouble? Micki!" I was concerned. I didn't trust all the men in the pub.

"I'll work my way right you go left. Micki? Oh shit." I heard splashing. The tide had come in much higher than when we left the boat.

"Micki!!" Both John and Petral whisper-shouted together.

"Huh? What? Are you back already?"

"Were you sleeping?" Petral sounded disgusted.

"Yeah, you woke me up."

"We can't see a thing. Where are you? Show us the light." A flashlight flicked on and off two meters in front of us.

"Can you bring the boat in closer?" We heard oarlocks rattling. Finally, I saw the bow of the boat in front of us.

As we rowed toward the point at the head of the harbor, Cousin John informed Micki and me, "The dock where the *Ona Elsee* is moored is locked and guarded at the landward end."

When we rounded the point into the harbor, voices drifted to us over the water. I could hear a group of young people singing a folk song. Their voices drifted across the glassy bay crystal clear and beautiful. I could make out the words. We looked at each other knowing every noise we made could be heard equally clear in the village.

Micki rolled over on his stomach with his eyes over the bow. I slid down off of my seat keeping below the gunwales.

My cousins slipped the oars out of locks and used them to paddle a few strokes. The momentum carried us closer to the Ona Elsee. When we were two hundred meters out, the boat rocked, then lurched forward. The cousins quietly put their oars down. Micki had gone overboard and was swimming soundlessly toward the Ona Elsee with our bowline over his shoulder.

I soon began to admire Micki a great deal. The water was not warm. He was pulling a rowboat with three full-grown men in it without making a sound. Finally we drifted into the shadow of the Ona Elsee. Micki slid soundlessly like a sea otter over her back end.

We maneuvered the rowboat behind the Ona Elsee so the bow of another boat hid us from view. I slipped onto the dock and crawled forward almost on my belly to where the boat was chained to the dock. The noise from the pub grew louder. I found the lock and pulled out my picks, terrified that I might drop them in the water. The lock seemed to work easier than I expected. The first trip was easy. The second trip required that I try pick after pick before it would budge. I heard a crash from the direction of the pub. Someone started yelling drunkenly. I was thankful for the noise. The third trip sprung on the fourth try and the lock dropped open.

I loosened the chain on the Ona Elsee and looked toward the town. Drunks came spilling out of the pub. The guard at the head of the dock was watching the crowd from the pub. I crawled and slithered to the boat in front of Uncle

John's. I knew which picks worked last time. I tried them first hoping the same manufacturer had similar lock combinations. Five minutes later, I silently dropped the padlock on the next boat into the water. I crawled forward.

The noise in town was turning into a riot with men throwing things and yelling. I unlocked another boat.

Unlocking the boat closest to shore would be risky, but the rioting in the village grew louder. Women started screaming. I heard drunken laughter. The guard turned his back toward the dock. I unlocked the boat closest to shore.

While watching the guard, I scuttled backward on the dock to the boat chained up behind the Ona Elsee. Damn. It had a different lock. I started sweating. Cousin John tugged at my pants to get me to get into the rowboat. I shook him off. I heard a clatter of pans and swearing in the street. I kept trying. I noticed the guard turn and look at the boats chained to the dock. He turned back toward the crowd and left his post. The last lock opened. I slipped the lock into the sea and slid into the waiting rowboat.

Micki had successfully untied our ropes, but the chain on the bow made a loud grating sound as the boat drifted away from the dock. Micki dropped over the edge of the Ona Elsee onto the dock and gently eased the chain off of the dock. We would just have to drag it until we were clear enough to work on the boat. He jumped on her bow as she floated free of the dock. With the sound of the riot in town covering our noises we worked our way to the bow of the boat. I grabbed the chain to use as a towrope. My cousins slipped their oars in the locks and put their backs into rowing the boat out of the harbor. I heard cheering in the town.

I was glad the cousins were rowing. I shook all over from the fright of crawling around on the dock, afraid the guard would see me or I would drop my picks in the sea. The tide changed. It started going out again and taking us with it. I was profoundly thankful for the help. We didn't speak until we were around the point at the head of the harbor. "Does Micki have some way to get warm?"

"He can take care of himself." I heard pride in Petral's voice.

"He knows enough to strip and roll up in a blanket." John grunted.

Petral snorted, "The slacker is probably sound asleep again."

We grinned at each other. Micki was all right.

We rowed north forever. We took turns two men rowing, one resting. Even with my gloves on, I could feel a blister growing in my hand. "Do you think the people in the pub knew what we were doing?" I asked.

"Yeah." John chuckled. "They're all right. Those singers were probably watching for us and ran to the pub. Everybody has been waiting for something to happen."

I worried, "I hope the other boat owners get their boats out before Fortenac discovers they are unlocked."

"Yeah they probably had crews on the way before we got the Ona Elsee out of the harbor." John started to huff as he rowed.

We rowed in silence a while longer. Finally, Petral pulled out the big light and shown it toward shore "We're too far out."

We changed course. When the mountains on shore started blacking out the stars, we checked our position again.

"Shit." Both cousins swore at once.

"What is the problem?" I asked.

John explained. "We are rowing against a back current. We are still way south of where we want to be."

I was naïve. "I thought we must be almost home. We've been rowing so long."

Petral explained, "Yeah, well, we're towing the Ona Elsee against the current. We went too far out to sea."

We heard an engine. The noise seemed to surround us growing louder. The cousins grunted and put more effort into rowing.

"What is that boat?" I could see a long, low boat speeding along the horizon.

"The owner of the boat tied in front of ours." Petral grunted as he put his back into his rowing

"Good. I hope he doesn't have any trouble." I grinned I wanted to get back at Fortenac any way I could for burning M'TK

John asked for about the hundredth time. "Jake are you sure this will not get us in trouble with the law?"

I thought for a few minutes. "The papers I read were nothing more than legal-sounding nonsense. It was in legal form but this was not a court order. There was no seal and signature. The paper was fancy extortion."

"Ooo, listen to the fancy lawyer talk."

Suddenly the sea became choppy, Cousin John asked, "Is this the rip?"

I was not sure what he was talking about. We had been rowing through low swells. We crossed a line in the water and it suddenly started swirling and churning around us. We rowed for five minutes. Conditions got nastier.

"Yeah it is the rip." Petral sounded excited that water was slopping at us from all directions. We changed course sharply toward shore. I rowed with John while Petral shone the light on the cliffs above us. A wall of granite came straight down to the waters edge. I could not see any sign of a break or a beach. We rowed closer.

This did not look good to me. "Are there rocks under the water?"

"Not here." Petral said as he played his light across the water and cliffs. "We'll negotiate a shoal getting into Rocky Bay. That won't be a problem except for rowing against the tide and keeping the Ona Elsee from getting scraped up on the rock walls. Where is that damn opening?"

"Listen." I heard the sound of an engine. The cousins grunted, satisfied.

Petral sounded relieved. "There, there it is."

John ordered. "Let's hit it from the north side."

"You just want me to row more." I complained knowing that my oar was the one to turn the boat if we came in from the north.

"Jake stop whining." Petral scoffed.

"Want me to take a turn on the oars?" Micki surprised us in the dark as he sat down on the bow of the Ona Elsee. "Is that M'TG, I hear?"

"Yeah, he went south a while ago."

"Good." I could hear the grin in Micki's voice.

"Micki, stay where you are and keep her from scraping on the walls. What should we do with Jake?" John took charge.

Petral decided. "Put him on with Micki to keep her off of the rocks."

"I'm not too tired to row." I wanted to do my part.

"You are not that good at rowing." I had no idea that there was any skill beyond the basics involved so they must have been right.

Petral grumbled. "This is going to be hellish without engines. How're the Ona's engines."

Micki said. "The engines look okay. All the wires and fuel line are cut."

"Damn." Petral spat.

John's instructions sounded easier than the actual operation. "Okay Jake we're gonna let the Ona Elsee slide alongside us. Your job will be to take a position in the stern on the port side. If she tries to swing into the rock wall, keep her from hitting."

The tide was pushing against a stronger current making both boats heave and roll as we brought the rowboat alongside the Ona Elsee. I'd never moved from the rowboat to the bigger boat in such rough water. I got slopped to the waist with the churning water as I made the transfer to the Ona Elsee.

"Okay, here we go." John ordered. Both cousins strained at the oars. They communicated in little grunts and swear words. The boat rocked in the inky blackness that grew darker. I realized that we were in a crack between the tall granite walls."

"Okay Jake, this is where we have fun." Micki sounded gleeful. "The channel runs south for about seventy-five meters then turns hard starboard. Our job is to keep the boat from hitting the wall at the turn. Without engines we have no control."

"Which position is easier? Yours or mine? I can take the position requiring more muscle."

"It is about the same. The bow might be slightly easier to turn. The stern may swing around fast. You'll have to be fast to kick us off of the wall." Our cousins in the rowboat just laughed.

"Don't worry about him Micki." John chuckled. "Jake, think of the wall as three big men armed with guns and knives."

I teased back. "Oh? I thought you said this would be hard."

The wall was more like eight big men armed with guns and knives. Micki was hard pressed to keep the bow off of the wall. I sprang forward and delivered a good kick to the wall. The boat swung around and threatened to dash her stern against the rock. I vaulted to the back and rolled into position to kick the wall again before the boat crashed into it.

The Ona Elsee was low and flat across the back to make dragging in the shrimp nets easier. I'd rolled onto my back on the nets with my butt hanging almost over the water. The first impact jarred my ankles, buckled my knees and hips and sent shock waves up my body. The nets scraped my shoulders as my body slid across them. The stern of the Ona Elsee, lightly bumped the rock wall. My feet told me that using them both together was not the best idea. I needed to use smaller more rapid kicks against the wall. Soon the wild, uncontrolled swinging settled into a gentle rhythm. I had the feeling that I was walking the Ona Elsee through the cut.

From the bow I heard Micki whining again. "Would you guys like me to start some coffee?"

"Micki, what the hell?" Petral was puffing out of breath.

"I don't have anything to do. I'm bored."

"Don't get smart, kid. Keep the bow off of the rocks." John growled.

"You are holding it out far enough and Jake is dancing with the wall in the back."

I didn't have strength to protest that my job was not as easy as it looked to Micki. My stomach muscles were starting to hurt from the strain and my shoulders were scratched raw where I braced them against the nets to give me some leverage. If I shoved too hard with one foot, the boat would start swinging again. I needed to keep it smooth and steady. It was taking a great deal of muscle and control. I was sweating. I remembered to be thankful that I had been soaked to mid waist earlier. The cold wet clothing actually felt good. It took us twelve minutes to negotiate the cut at a walking pace. I thought it took hours.

Rocky Bay was a small, almost round harbor no more than a kilometer across. The walls went straight up from the water. My cousins edged the boat along the rock wall where mooring rings had been set in the stone. We tied up there. The sound of a motor and swearing echoed off of the rock walls as another boat came through the cut into the bay. I wanted nothing more than to curl up and sleep.

Micki had been sleeping. Now, he wanted to party. He turned on the boat's lights and stood on the back of the boat welcoming the next boat into the bay with gleeful shouts and waves. I didn't know these people. I was wet. Now, that I wasn't exercising, I was cold. I found the forward bunk, stripped and went to sleep to the sounds of celebration.

"Jake, hey Jake, wake up." Cousin Petral's voice broke into my dead sleep. I felt the toe of his shoe poking me.

"Mnf,"

"Come on, wake up."

"What?"

We're getting a ride home with M'TG to bring the M'NO back to tow the Ona home."

"Oh sure, let me get my pants on and I'll be ready to go with you." I lay there thinking how much I didn't want to pull on cold, wet pants.

"We need you to stay here with Micki and talk to the other boat owners."

"I want my breakfast with my family, a hot shower and dry clothes."

Petral refused to be sympathetic. "You've gotten soft and citified."

I heard a shout, and they left me alone to try to struggle into wet pants. Topside, in the dawn light, I saw my cousins pulling away in the sleek motorboat I'd seen on the horizon the night before. I looked around at the other boats in the bay. A lot of swearing came from the open hatches on the other boats. I found Micki on the bow, fishing.

"Are there fish in here?"

"Yeah, there are some big whitefish that feed on small animals on the rocks. I don't have the right gear to catch them, but maybe I can get one to take a hook.

"What should I do?"

"Boil some water, and see what else you can find to eat."

I found some dried fruit and tea. I had the water ready to boil in a large pot. All of a sudden, the boat started bobbing. I looked up at Micki. He was in danger of being drug off of the boat by whatever was on the other end of his line.

I headed forward before he called.

"Jake! Jake, I got a big one!" The fish on the line was pulling Micki toward the edge of the bow while he tried to brace himself.

"Give it some more line!"

"No way! Help me haul this in."

I wedged myself onto the bow as best I could, then wrapped one leg around Micki.

Micki was fishing with little more than a heavy line on a spool. "Here you take the reel. I'll work the ratchet."

I took the reel and immediately felt the pull of the fish. I was not in danger of being pulled off of the boat, but I felt the strain across my shoulders. Micki worked at a lever he called a ratchet.

It took both of us the best part of an hour to haul the fish to the surface. I stared at the monstrous, whiskered, slimy beast. "How the hell are we supposed to get that on board and why would we want to?"

Micki instructed, "Hold it and I'll get a net. It is probably less than fifty kilos. We can get it onboard."

"Why?"

"To eat."

I wondered, "Who will do the eating?

"We will."

"Are you sure?" I looked at the large ugly sea monster hanging just below the surface of the water and thought it could just as easily eat me. I heard shouts and calls from the other men. They'd come out of their holds to watch Micki and me haul the leviathan on board. Micki arrived on the bow with a net and dropped it into the water. I walked the fish into the waiting net. It took us another ten minutes to haul the monster in the net on board. I dropped onto my back breathing heavily. I looked up and saw the winch for the shrimp nets mocking me from overhead. "Is there some reason we did not winch that aboard?"

"Yeah, no power. The engines power the winch." Micki sat beside our fish breathing heavily. He pulled his knees up to his chest and rested his head on them. Our fish flopped and wobbled in it's net. Micki draped shrimp net over it. We sat breathing for a few minutes.

Micki sounded as if he was looking deep into his brain when he spoke. "You know. That is a design flaw—not having separate power for the winch. I can almost see how to fix that. I'll think on it."

I had an idea that Micki saying he would think on something was a powerful statement. I finally, rolled onto my stomach and pushed myself up. "If we are going to eat this thing, maybe we should clean it."

"Yeah, it is easy to clean. Start the water boiling."

"Do we boil this?"

"Yeah, it's too strong otherwise." Micki got a knife and set about cleaning the fish. It was mostly meat. As soon as the water boiled we added salt and two big pieces of fish. The sun had finally climbed above our cliffs by the time the fish was ready to eat.

"Not bad." It tasted delicious.

We spent the next hour eating our breakfast, and cooking the rest of the fish. Micki asked me question after question about the city and more specifically about university. He took the Ona Elsee's tender and delivered cooked fish to the other boats. I noticed the other men asked him questions about their engines or this part or that. I wanted to lie in the sun and go back to sleep. I remembered Mr. Rouseff's warnings about not getting too brown. Southerners were supposed to be sickly pale. I snorted. Micki came back aboard. It was my turn to ask questions? "Are you good with engines?"

"Yeah."

"You like working on them?"

"Not so much as knowing how they work and thinking about ways to make them work better."

"You still in school?"

"Yeah, Uncle John doesn't like it. He's afraid I'll get conscripted."

"You like school? How do you do?"

"I'm due to graduate at the end of two terms. My scores are perfect." He sounded proud.

"What would you study if you went to university?"

"Engineering." The quickness of his answer made me smile.

"Well, I guess when you finish school here, you better come to the city and live with me, or Mama and Papa and go to university."

He grinned from head to toe. "I'd love that, but I can't get in because I am not from the south."

I looked at him. "I got in. I will give you a recommendation, or get one from someone else."

"I don't have any money."

"I figure the family can help with that." I liked watching Micki smile. I smiled to myself. "You know, I think I might like having a roommate."

Micki asked, "What about living with your papa and mama?"

"They might let you live with them for a year, but they kicked me out at the end of a year."

We were silent a few minutes.

I broke the silence. "I can get you into university because I graduated from there. It is not all that easy to stay there." I outlined the problems of hiding the fact that you are from the north. I told him how Mr. Rouseff stuck up for me. "I have a few friends who really are from elite families. They will help as best they can. You will have to be careful. I...I...did not like pretending that my parents were from the south, pretending that this whole family is not part of my life. For four years, you will have to pretend you are someone else."

Micki looked serious then nodded once. I had the feeling I would soon have a roommate. I smiled. I napped for another half hour.

"Jake, wake up. Uncle John is here."

I woke up but saw no sign of the fishing boat. "Where is he?"

"Almost to the cut."

"How can you tell?"

"I hear the engines."

I wondered if this young cousin could tell one boat from another by the sounds of the engines. I remembered how I'd been able to distinguish the trains in M'TK, by the sounds of their engines.

He nudged my foot where I sprawled on the nets. "Come on, I want to set up a pump to move fuel from here to the fishing boat."

"Ah yes, the fuel problem. I'd almost forgotten that we have that little vexation to deal with."

"Do you have a plan?"

"Well not completely. Fortenac controls the fuel. If step one is to avoid contact with Fortenac, we must get fuel elsewhere."

"There isn't any place close enough."

I said, "First, I will need to get cleaned up. Then, we will go to the train station and I will think.

Micki sounded like a pouty adolescent when the M'NO pulled along side. "It's about time you got here. We've been bored."

I joined Micki and helped with the lines as we tied the boats together. I added my story, "We were bored when we were not fighting off sea monsters. Would you like some leftover sea monster for lunch?"

Men hailed Uncle John from the other boats. They asked Uncle John how long they needed to hide their boats. Where they going to get arrested? They rowed over to the M'NO in their tenders. I held a meeting there on the fishing boat in the middle of Rocky Bay.

"Yes, Mr. Fortenac may try to take legal action." I told them. "I think I might have fun representing you. The letter he sent Uncle John was legally what we call extortion. It is a crime. If I were the local prosecutor, I would happily prosecute him for it. I will certainly talk to the local prosecutor about that possibility."

"He's more likely to have us put in jail that to go to jail himself." Grumbled the owner of the boat that had been chained up behind the Ona Elsee.

"That is the reality. I advise keeping your boats well away from his influence."

"Our boats aren't any good without fuel. We have to go to his dock to refuel." This man reminded me of the M'TG I'd met the night before.

I summarized. "We are working on that problem too. Mr. Fortenac may seem very powerful to you. He is powerful. His power is limited. His power comes from money. I am thinking about how to cut off his income."

"Those are pretty words. I'm not seeing any action." This complaint came from a scrawny looking fisherman who appeared to be about seventy.

"I've been here a little over twenty-four hours. You have your boats back. You have an attorney to represent you if Fortenac makes trouble. I just really have not had time to get to the rest of the problem. Give me a couple days okay?"

Uncle John laughed. "He looks fancy but don't go judging a man by his looks. As he said, you have your boats back."

We arrived back at The Cove about three. The whole family came out to wave and cheer at the return of the Ona Elsee. She was an expensive boat. They had worked and saved a long time to buy her. The thought of losing her must have made them heartsick.

Uncle John bellowed orders about tying up the boats and transferring fuel. "Get this boy into a shower and his fancy clothes. He has to be at the train station by four." This produced a general outcry while I assured everyone that I was just going to the station to practice being a lawyer.

I didn't get much of a shower with someone on the outside yelling at me to hurry up because they almost had the boat refueled. We made a merry party when we went back to the boat. Aunt Luella decided to visit the village. My cousins and their wives decided to come. Micki had managed to transfer the fuel and get mostly cleaned up enough to come.

We pulled into the harbor in Norville, the village closest to The Cove. I asked, "Who owns this dock?"

"The province." Uncle John answered.

I nodded to a second dock closer to the rail station. "Who owns that dock?"

"The railroad."

"Tie up there."

"We are not supposed to tie up there." Uncle John sounded shocked.

"You are with me. You are Mama's family. It is okay." I liked the layout. The railroad dock was not convenient to the village. It ran along a rock and concrete pier. I noted the structural stability. Once I was ashore on the pier I found that my guess was right--a rail line ran out onto the pier. I grinned. "Somebody find me a crew of men to clean these rails. We will pay them union wages for this work."

Micki asked. "Do you have an idea?"

"I don't want to promise anything until I've talked to Mr. Rouseff and Papa."

When I got to the station nobody was there. Most of the family went off to shop and hire help cleaning the rails. Uncle John entered the station with me. I called Mr. Rouseff first.

"Cousin Philippe? It's Jake. How would you like to make life a little less pleasant for the Fortenacs?"

My boss's voice chuckled on the other end of the line. "Sounds like fun. What do you have in mind?"

I explained about Fortenac refusing to sell fuel to small fishermen. "That is just half of the problem. The other half of the problem is marketing. Most of the catch is still being canned. It makes me weep to see all that beautiful seafood being ruined by canning. Can we get the catch from the independent fishermen to market fresh? I know we've been bringing it to the M'TK market for years. We are still selling out within minutes. Can we expand the market?"

Mr. Rouseff started laughing on the other end of the phone. "Call your papa and tell him what you need. I can get a tank of diesel up there fairly quickly. The problem will come if the Vanderholms refuse to sell diesel to me."

"You have some in reserve. Can you buy more before they know what you are doing?"

"I intend to try. I'll send everything that is empty to the south and one full car north." We chatted about some common things. He warned me not to come back brown and we hung up.

I turned to Uncle John. "You will be able to fuel your boat in a couple days. We need those tracks cleared. I better call Papa." Once again, I explained about the fuel.

Papa understood what I needed immediately. "I'll start sending supplies up on the next train. I'll send up some security and someone to assess the tracks on the pier. There is another line that runs between villages. We never use it because everybody prefers to use boats. If some people cannot take their boats into some harbors, maybe you can use the rail line to get around.

"I may need to get into some courthouses. Can you send my trolley? It will be fun to give the cousins rides."

The owner of the speedboat from last night came into the station. He shook hands very respectfully with Uncle John.

I told Papa about the second half of my plan. "I talked to Rouseff about shipping the catch south while it is fresh. Canning everything is really criminal anyway." Three more men entered the station, all carrying papers.

Papa said, "I know what you need. I've looked over the idea of shipping from there before. We have the equipment for fueling."

I hung up and turned to the men in the station. "Now gentlemen, I am Jake Jaconovich. I am an attorney. My mama…"

The man who owned the speedboat interrupted me. "We know who your mama is. We are not too happy with your Papa for taking her away from us."

I grinned. "I think she went eagerly enough. They are well suited to each other. Now, what do you have for paperwork?"

I sat down at the stationmaster's desk and looked over the papers. All of the men had the letter about confiscating the boats. "Is this all you have?"

They nodded.

"I need to be absolutely certain that none of you have received any other letters about confiscating the boats."

"No, this is the only one."

I spoke firmly when I explained. "This is a piece of garbage. It has not been presented to a court. It is important for you to keep this letter and keep it safe. I may want to press charges against Mr. Fortenac for extortion and thievery."

The owner of the speedboat narrowed his eyes and studied me before he spoke. "You seem confident of what you are saying."

"I am confident that this piece of paper is meaningless and that the Fortenacs, with a few rare exceptions, are crooks."

The men relaxed, shuffled their feet, smiled and nudged one another with satisfaction.

I went on to explain, "I just talked to Papa. He is sending up fuel. You need to use the railroad dock for fueling. It may also be the safest place to tie up. I've done enough fishing with Uncle John to know how it is done." I didn't want to come out and accuse the men of smuggling, but I wanted them to understand that I was making their job easier. "I want to start sending more fresh fish south. You know Mama started the market in M'TK. We've been selling fresh fish there for years. Mr. Rouseff is expanding markets at other stations. Now seems like a good time to expand our markets for fresh food."

"Does your mama know what you are doing?" M'TG asked.

"I assume Papa has told her by now."

"If it is okay with her, we will go along with it. We don't want trouble with Fortenac." M'TG spoke for the others.

It was my turn to ask questions. "Who are the judges here? Are they bought and paid for by Fortenac? Are they fair?"

"Fortenac owns the courts." Uncle John sounded grim.

"That may give us some trouble. If he thinks the Rouseff family is behind you, he may decide not to pressure you. Mr. Rouseff is very popular right now. The Fortenacs may not want to anger him." I think we all knew that justice was not always just. "If you have any legal trouble, tell people to talk to me. Say that I am your attorney." I smiled at the prospect of actually practicing law. I had no idea that I would spend the next year practicing real law as a prosecutor.

My family seemed a little subdued when we were ready to return home. I was excited over solving their problems in a manner that made money for the railroad. Micki immediately went below and threw himself down on a bunk. I looked at the rest of the family. "What's wrong?"

Cousin Petral sighed, "Bad news, a young girl in the next village over, Midville, was raped and murdered. We all know her family. Micki goes to school with her."

Old feelings welled up inside me. I felt sick inside. "Do they have any idea who did this?"

"Not yet. You can depend on it being someone beyond the reach of the law—the son of a cannery owner, the captain of a company fishing boat." Petral's wife sounded bitter.

For the rest of the trip home, I watched the water and remained silent in respect for my family's grief.

The tank car arrived at the station two days later. Papa sent a crew with it to get it positioned on the pier. He sent guards and a maintenance crew. The switch to open the line to the pier was broken. I had planned to have four men move it by hand, but Micki looked over the controls and rewired them to work correctly.

I wondered how long it would take fishermen to hear that they could fuel at our dock. By the time the tank car was locked into position on the pier, the boats were lined up to fuel.

The men didn't say much when I showed them the refrigerator car we had waiting for their fish. I explained that we would buy anything edible that they wanted to bring us. They nodded. They fueled their boats and left. When I returned that night from another project, the refrigerator car was gone and another one was being moved into position. The stationmaster said the first car was about as full as it could get when it pulled out. The fishermen had made good money selling fish, shrimp, and squid.

We had crews cleaning the line that ran to the other villages. After four days, The foreman of the crew told me I could get my trolley through to the next village.

Uncle John's voice cracked as he asked me, "Are you taking that car down the coast?"

"I thought I'd try it today."

"Can you take Micki and some of the others with you?"

"Sure."

Uncle John sounded so sad that I assumed this must have something to do with the girl who had died. I was right. Her parents were having a Mass for her.

My first trip along the coast in the trolley was sad. The rumor spread that the trolley could take people to the next village. They were afraid to go by boat because Fortenac was still yelling about confiscating any boat that came into the harbor. The stationmaster had run the trolley down the line twice before I got there.

This was the same small car my roommates and I had taken camping. I liked it, so Papa had taken extra good care of it. Maintenance workers painted it pretty and the brass shone. I thought I saw Mama's hand in the geranium red paint on the trim.

I took twenty-eight people on that little trolley. I went to the courthouse while they went to Mass. I wanted to see if I could find any record of the provincially-owned dock being sold to Fortenac.

I immediately noticed another attorney there looking for records with his secretary. I thought she was the most beautiful woman I had ever seen. I tried not to stare. She had long fair hair and all the right curves despite having small bones and a slender appearance. She had an elegance about the way she moved that held me enthralled. I was in luck. Her boss gave her more ledgers to hold than such a delicate creature could manage. She dropped several. Her boss scowled at her.

I bounded up from the table where I worked. "Here let me help with those. They are heavy. Would you like me to put them on this table?" I made certain to place the beautiful lady's books where I could look at her.

She smiled at me and thanked me for helping her.

I forgot where I was and what I was doing. I sat down at my table with my records and tried to see if the woman was wearing a wedding ring. She wasn't! She spoke to her boss. Her voice sounded cultured with just the slightest undertone of a northern lilt. I sighed.

My legal search proved significant in that I could find no evidence that Fortenac had any legal right to prevent people from using the provincial dock. Enforcing their right to use the dock would be another problem.

I got back to the station late. My trolley made three trips bringing people home from the Mass. I felt comforted that it had been helpful. We were quiet as we untied the boat and chugged out of the harbor.

My head was full of the beautiful woman at the courthouse. I made an announcement. "I just figured out why I am not married." I captured everybody's attention with this revelation. "I prefer northern women. People have been telling me to find a nice Spinoza woman and get married. Sometimes they tell me a Rouseff woman will do. I've met dozens of girls at university. They did not excite me. They are too bland. Their voices are harsh. I like northern women. They look more feminine and healthy. Their voices are like music."

My cousins' wives kissed me on the cheek for the compliment.

Petral told me, "You're slow if you just figured out that north coast women are the best."

We lamented that my vacation was almost over. I'd wasted it on legal work and stealing boats instead of looking for a wife. Everybody volunteered to look around for me.

I wanted to take another trolley trip, just for fun. I made my announcement when we were all gathered at the dinner table. "I'd like to take all the children on a trolley ride to the end of the line tomorrow. We can pack a lunch and they can fly through the forest on the trolley. You have all had so much trouble, you need to let the little ones just have some fun."

"I don't like for the girls to be out of The Cove just now." Uncle John seldom growled at me like that.

"Micki will come with us. I can have some of the railroad guards come too. I don't think I could leave the guards behind anyway."

Aunt Luella sounded hesitant. "I don't know. We've had so much trouble. You wouldn't want to take Marianne too?"

I heard a little squeak out of Marianne. She was bouncing with excitement.

"Of course Marianne must come too. All the children need a treat. The children have had enough of your worries. We will go out and be merry."

"I am not sure it will be safe." Uncle John had one idea in his head.

Finally, Cousin John said, "They will be with Jake. I can't imagine any place safer." He grinned at me. "Thanks Jake, I'd offer to come with you, but I think I will stay home with my wife."

Everyone laughed knowing what he had in mind.

The day of our trolley ride dawned warm and clear. It might even get hot later in the day. We had agreed that eight children would come with me in addition to Micki who was too old to be called a child. I had argued that his sister, Margaret, who was almost eighteen should come too. Her Mama refused to let her come. Margaret looked disappointed but declared herself happy to stay at home. I let the matter rest until morning when I approached her again.

"I really wish you would help me with this. I have no idea what Micki and I will do if one of the little girls needs to use a rest room." This thought had not occurred to the others. Margaret was quickly packed up and sent with us. I thought she was way too young to be so serious.

When we pulled into the railroad dock, I saw another boat there before us fueling. Two railroad workers rushed down to meet us. They called me Mr. Jaconovich and helped the girls out of the boat. The girls giggled at hearing Cousin Jake addressed so formally. Micki made certain that the boat was tied correctly, but no, the railroad workers insisted Mr. Jaconovich's cousin must not do the work himself. As we walked the length of the pier I noticed Micki shaking his head and muttering.

I nudged him with my elbow. "Get used to it. When you graduate from university, people will treat you like a big important man too." The girls giggled. The girls giggled at everything I said all day.

Micki laughed at the girls. "They think you are a big hero."

"God, they needed to get out." I was genuinely distressed over how serious the children acted.

"Yeah, sometimes Uncle John gets to acting afraid of everything outside our cove. I think we've been prisoners for months. He fusses and carries on over the possibility of me being conscripted. Nicki says it wasn't so bad. He got to travel and meet new people. He tells me he learned more about why things are the way they are here. He told me that he intends to have a talk with the others about the outside world. He thinks it's good for the children to get away from the fear."

"Micki, I am part of this family. The situation with the shrimp boat should not have gone on as long as it did. Someone should have written to me. If there is any more trouble of any kind, I want you to go to the train station and call me. Make sure the other fishermen know that I am their attorney." I thought only of needing to read more legal documents and be reassuring. I had no idea where this statement would lead.

Our outing was everything I hoped it would be. All the children were wild with excitement from the moment the trolley started moving.

"Keep your hands inside the windows!" I was driving the trolley and did not pay too much attention to the kids other than watching to see that they stayed inside the car while we were traveling. Micki asked questions about the mechanics of the car and looked at all my gauges and levers.

I enjoyed spending time with the children. They exclaimed over every new wonder, every leaf on the trees, even over rocks. These children knew The Cove and the sea. Land was a novelty for them. They ate our lunch before mid-morning.

The ride to the farthest village, Soville, was spectacular. The rail line followed a small stream between cliffs. Sometimes the ravine narrowed so there was only room for the stream and the trolley. I liked it best when the ravine opened out and we traveled through a tunnel of forest. Once I stopped the trolley just below a waterfall so the children could get a look.

I let the children off to explore the little village at the end of the line. It was not much of a village. It had a cannery, a church, the town hall, a school, a company store and a few offices.

I was bored with the little town within five minutes. Then, I saw her again. I saw the beautiful, elegant woman with the stunning hair. I thought she might have just left a little house on a side street. She looked sad. My brain froze. I couldn't think of anything to say to her. She walked within half a block of me and I stood kicking myself for not thinking of some excuse to approach her.

On our way home, we stopped longer in Midville. I learned that the harbor was not as deep here. The town spread out across a gentle sloping hillside. The mountains rose up steeply on either side of the village, but it sat snug in a broad valley between the mountains.

I had not really looked around, when I came to do the records research and survey the village before getting the Ona Elsee. The village had a number of shops, the pub and a restaurant. The girls were amazed at the pretty things in the shops. I saw a little museum, but I thought we should visit the restaurant first.

The children loved the restaurant. I ordered a fish steak. The children wanted sandwiches. The sandwiches were a rare treat for them. I suggested that Micki order some fish with rice. The food was really ordinary, but to these children who had seldom left The Cove except to take the boat to Norville for school, it was wildly exotic.

On the way home the children started singing. My heart swelled to hear the old folk songs. I fell in love with my country again as I heard those precious clear voices rejoicing at the world around them.

By the time we got to the boat, the children were ready for a nap. They went below and went to sleep, even Micki. I took the boat home by myself. I negotiated the entrance to the cove while Micki slept. I had pulled into the dock and called for someone to help me with the lines before anybody on board woke up.

I left for home before sunrise the next morning. Nicki took me into the station.

I admonished him again, "Remember you can always phone me from the station or call Papa at the M'TK station. The fishermen may have more legal trouble. Tell them that I am their attorney. I don't think they will have much trouble when the Fortenacs figure out that they know how to get legal representation." Niki put me on the train and waved me off.

Chapter 20 Prosecutor Jaconovich

I dreaded going back to sorting out drunks and prostitutes on Monday morning. I felt grumpy. I didn't like my office. I didn't like my clothes. I didn't like my job. I thought I would be happier moving north and living in The Cove and marrying the lovely, elegant, blond woman.

I found a whole line of prostitutes waiting in the holding room for me to approve their fines. I regarded them with resignation. I confess, I snarled. "Why on earth can't you women practice your trade outside the city limits so we don't have to go through this every damn week?"

Ilsette, one of the older women I saw at least twice a month furrowed her brow until her make-up cracked. "What difference would that make?"

I explained. "There are no ordinances about prostitution outside the city."

A bleached blond who called herself Cordelia snorted. "There are no hotels either."

I knew Cordelia had two nephews and a grandmother she was supporting. She was thin and usually had a cough. She was too frail to do heavy work. She could not make enough money at any other work, to keep her family fed and housed.

"Well then find a damn tent. I am tired of doing this every week."

The following Monday I entered the holding room. It held about two-thirds fewer women. I asked. "Where are your other sisters?"

Ilse answered, "They went outside the city limits."

"Well what are you doing here? Go get a health check and stop practicing inside the city limits." Prosecutor Jake Jaconovich had just solved the city's problem with prostitution. I cared nothing for the red light district that grew up outside the city. I did not get praised for reducing city revenue by the amount the girls were paying in fines.

I'd been back in the city for about two weeks when I passed a newsstand and saw a headline, "*Leon Fortenac arrested for the murder/rape of fisherman's daughter.*" I picked up a copy of the paper and stared at the headline feeling a very old, sick feeling in my stomach. I dropped the paper in disgust.

When I walked into our office Darlene our clerk greeted me with the news. "Did you hear Leon Fortenac has been charged with murder? I can't imagine that he can really be convicted."

I shook my head to agree with her and continued to my desk.

Darlene called to my retreating back, "Oh and you have a message from somebody named Micki. He was breathing so hard that at first I though it was a pervert, but then he asked for you."

Jeffrey Farley our senior prosecutor met me at my desk with his morning coffee. "This is a sad business about Fortenac."

I didn't know how to take his meaning. "A child died."

Jeffrey surprised me. "And, the man who killed her will most likely go free. Today, I feel disgusted with my own sex and heritage."

I nodded. A call from Papa interrupted Jeffrey. Papa had called me at work to tell me the news.

I got off the phone with Papa and Darlene put through a call from Micki.

"Jake? Is that really you?"

"Yeah."

"Jake, it's ugly here." Micki's voice was high pitched and strained. "What they are saying. She was a nice girl. Jake…" I heard Micki gasping for breath. "They are saying things that aren't true. They are calling her names." I thought I heard Micki sob.

I tried to use a reassuring tone of voice. "This happens often. Slandering the girl and her family usually keeps families from pursuing legal course. In this case the prosecutor's office will have to act, even if they just go through the motions."

"Will they convict him? Will he go to jail?"

"Micki, I don't know. It will be a tough case from the prosecutors position."

"But, he admits he did it. Doesn't that make a difference?"

I rubbed the back of my neck and wished I could hug Micki. "The power someone like that has behind him may be too great. In a situation like this, the Fortenacs may well be more powerful than the government."

"I bet you could get him convicted." The lust for vengeance in Micki's voice traveled the phone lines and touched a deep memory.

"I'd would do my best, but he is very strong. The elite families stick together."

The next day, I had lunch with the attorney for the union and Mr. Rouseff. Mr. Rouseff reported he had been slowly building markets near the stations in most villages and towns.

"Your mama wrote out recipes for fresh fish that we are giving out when people buy fish. With the fish sales, we are picking up more farmers who want to sell at our markets. The same thing that worked here is working in other villages. In the capital, we are not able to keep the restaurants supplied with all they want." Mr. Rouseff sounded very happy. His plan for shifting from an emphasis on transportation to shopping centers was working.

Micki called again in the afternoon.

I answered. "How are you doing?"

His voice shook somewhere between outrage and tears. "They are talking of not prosecuting."

"Why?"

"The prosecutor is Fortenac's brother in-law."

I grunted. "He will have to recuse himself in that case."

"What was that word?" Micki's voice was high pitched and strained.

"*Recuse*, it means to disqualify himself. I could not act as a prosecutor against someone in my family. I would either wring their neck for getting me into the position or I might not do my best job to get them convicted. He must recuse himself."

"Does that mean Fortenac will go free?"

"No it means the court will have to appoint another prosecutor."

"Could you do it?" I didn't really understand the intensity in Micki until he asked this question.

I sighed. "Yes, theoretically, but your court will most probably assign someone closer. Any attorney can serve as a prosecutor if the court will allow. You have a couple other attorneys up there. One of them will probably be assigned to prosecute Fortenac. But, they may not try very hard."

"What was that word again?"

"Recuse." I spelled it out.

Micki spelled the word back to me and repeated his understanding of the term. "It means the prosecutor must disqualify himself because Fortenac is his brother in-law."

"Do you want to study law? Specifically it means disqualify himself. The reason he would recuse himself is because he would have a conflict of interest in prosecuting his brother in-law."

"He would have a what?"

"A conflict of interest. Are you writing this down?"

"Yeah."

"Why?"

"Because everybody is upset. They think Fortenac will be set free."

I rubbed my face. "Son, they may be right."

The next afternoon I was almost waiting for Micki to call. I answered the phone. "What's happening?"

Micki sounded as if he was controlling his emotions better. "The people are demonstrating outside the courthouse. They have signs telling the prosecutor to recuse himself."

"Is that the word they are using on the signs?"

"Yeah."

"Micki, don't get yourself into trouble."

"What do you think the prosecutor will do?"

"He knows now that the protestors have spoken to an attorney. If he wants to keep his license the easiest thing for him to do is recuse himself. He ends up looking honorable and doesn't have to deal with the mess. If he does not step down, he will have to leave town and may lose his license."

Micki didn't call for two days. Papa told me that Uncle John had confined him to The Cove. School was closed due to the demonstrations.

During my lunch break on the third day, I went to the cathedral and lit a candle for Micki's friend. I remembered when Papa brought me here the first time. I lit another candle and said the prayer on the little card they gave me that first time.

In the past, I'd always seen the cathedral as beautiful. Today I wondered if anyplace could be beautiful in a country where little girls are dishonored and murdered and the men who do such deeds are allowed to walk free. The cathedral disgusted me.

I went back to my desk at the city prosecutor's office. I had a couple picked up for fighting to process and a case of theft. Micki didn't call after school. I thought school must still be out.

"Jaconovich." I looked up at my supervisor.

"Yes sir." I stood.

"You have connections in the north."

"Um…yes."

"I hear you have private clients in some fishing village in the north."

"Ah, yes. They have a contract with Rouseff to ship their fresh fish. I worked out the details on that."

"I hear you agreed to represent them."

"If they have problems with the canneries or the company boats, yes. The railroad considers them part of our shift to a market based industry."

"Well, I just got the word that we are to send you north to prosecute Leon Fortenac for rape and murder."

I broke into a sweat and sat down. I knew an uncontrollable urge to shake Micki. I put my head down on my desk. "Oh God. Oh my God. I have never failed at anything I've tried before now." I look up at my supervisor. "How… how on earth did this happen?"

"From what I hear, the people in the villages have been rioting over the case. The local prosecutor recused himself on the grounds that the accused is his brother in-law."

"Well he had to, didn't he?"

"Yeah, well, he said the girl's family had an attorney."

I shook my head.

"The judge apparently asked the girl's parents if they had any suggestions for someone to prosecute the case and they named you."

"Well shit." I moaned. "Those people don't know what an attorney is. They have no idea what a prosecutor is. They just know my name. What do you suggest sir?"

"You could recuse yourself saying it is too far to travel."

I shook my head.

"You have a conflict of interest?"

I gulped for air. "Other than hating men who hurt little girls, no. Well my cousin went to school with the girl. I've never met her family. I know nothing about them."

My boss leaned one hip on my desk. "It will not hurt your career if you lose, everyone knows you cannot win this case. It is a fact of life that he can rape and murder a northern girl without consequences."

I poked at the papers on my desk. "You think I should take the case?"

"Yes"

"Why?"

He looked away. "The people are asking for you. The courts try to honor those requests. As your supervisor, I will not stand in their way. I recommend that you honor the request."

"Thank you for your advice sir." I remembered my sense of disgust in the cathedral. I knew I had no choice but to take the case. "I guess I am about to fail for the first time in my life. It will be a novel experience to learn what it is like when my best is not good enough."

My boss squeezed my shoulder.

Chapter 21 Fortenac Case

I took the night train north to the Norville station where we'd left my trolley. I let myself into the one room train station. The room had a desk and a bench. I left my bag with my change of clothes at the station and took the trolley through the beautiful forest to the picturesque village that sloped gently to the sea.

I went to the courthouse and introduced myself to the information clerk and asked for contact information for the judge and defense attorney. She asked everybody in the office what she should do to answer my question. I finally got the information for the judge and the recused prosecutor. My first day on the case, I accomplished absolutely nothing.

Tired and discouraged, I returned to the damp train station intending to sleep there. I noticed the M'NO tied up at the pier. I didn't see any of the family until I opened the station door.

Micki pounced on me and gave me a hug. "Mrs. Trevvor told me you were here. Why didn't you tell us when you would be here? No worry, Aunt Luella had a room made up for you two days ago." Micki grabbed my bag and pulled me by the sleeve toward the waiting boat.

"Micki I shouldn't stay with the family. There might be trouble." I was too tired and discouraged to protest further.

Micki tossed my bag aboard. "Take the helm and I'll cast off. We won't want to keep Aunt waiting dinner."

When we reached the shoal, Micki surprised me by sounding the horn in a series of long loud blasts that brought every member of the family pouring out of the house and running to the dock. I waved from the bridge.

As the M'NO glided into her slip, at least a dozen hands grabbed her and the lines. Cousin John tried to help me out of the boat. Aunt hugged me and cried. "Oh my baby."

Uncle John grabbed me away from his wife and hugged me, "Welcome home son."

The children danced around the rest of the family as we walked up to the house in mass. Petral's wife started to ask me a question. Uncle John interrupted, "No, no there will be time enough for questions later. Let the man get into the house and eat his dinner."

I approved of Uncle John's priorities.

Petral laughed, "Uh, yeah, Sweetie, Jake pouts something fierce if he thinks he is not going to get his dinner."

Something that had been knotted up in my stomach relaxed and I realized I could eat dinner.

My second day on the case, I actually talked to the judge. He was a physically fit man in his fifties. His robust coloring was not the fashion for a southern man. I wondered if he liked fishing or perhaps hiking in the mountains. He greeted me cordially. "Mr. Prosecutor, come in, come in. Here make yourself comfortable. Can I have my secretary bring you something?"

I stood by the offered chair waiting for the older man to sit. "No thank you, Sir."

"I am happy that you came so quickly. The atmosphere in the villages is tense. I am worried about violence erupting at any time. Now, tell me about yourself. I admit that I was surprised the fishermen had an attorney."

I smiled and explained about Rouseff's contract with the fishermen.

"Do you have experience in criminal law?"

I snorted, "If you call fining drunks and prostitutes criminal law, yes. I am working on my certificate in criminal law." I handed the judge a copy of my qualifications.

After the judge asked me a dozen questions he summarized his thoughts. "Well, we have to make the motions of going through this case. The girl was just a fisherman's daughter so we won't get a conviction. Don't get too worked up over this." His words sounded callous, but I watched his eyes. His eyes held great sadness.

"Sir, I intend to prosecute this case competently. If it is as you say...if the man is indeed innocent of wrong-doing then he should be freed without a shadow on his reputation."

The judge smiled at me. I knew I'd said what he wanted to hear.

I continued. "Sir, there are several procedural steps we can take. My first concern is the influence of the local people. Are they likely to make life uncomfortable for you or the other officers of the court?"

"That is a distinct possibility."

"I will think about whether or not to move the case south."

The judge beamed at me. I suspected that he wanted out of the case. I thought I might have a better chance of conviction in my city. I asked, "What is your relationship to Fortenac?"

The judge's eyes slid away from mine. He cleared his throat. "We have no formal relationship. I…uh…we…uh, I see him socially. I have Fortenac cousins on Mama's side. Um, he…well…he could, that is his family could see that I am replaced."

I continued to express my concerns. "One of my first priorities must be to proceed in a manner that will not endanger the court." I knew my approval with the judge was soaring.

He sighed. "Thank you. We will not convict Fortenac, but I confess the local barbarians frighten me."

"I will do what I can."

We smiled at each other.

I asked, "Where is the accused now?"

"He is in jail."

This news took me by surprise. "What? I assumed house arrest."

"We've been afraid of the fishermen."

"I see. How far have you gotten with the process?"

He held out his hands palms up in a gesture of helplessness. "We didn't have a prosecutor."

I got down to business. "I am ready to set a court date for formal charges and to set bail. We will need to take into account that the prisoner may not be safe from the girl's family."

The judge and I worked out a schedule for formalizing the charges the following day. I proceeded to the next step. "I should meet Mr. Fortenac's attorney."

"He doesn't have one."

"Of course he has one. He has dozens on his staff. I've met some of them. I even went to law school with one. Do you mean to tell me that none of them are in the village?"

The judge shrugged. "They do not think he needs an attorney."

"What about the brother in-law? Since he is not prosecuting, can he come to court so that we have all the correct proceedings? A man's reputation is at stake. Your safety is at stake. I am convinced that we cannot get a conviction based on what I know now. I am determined that our procedures will be flawless so that you and I do not suffer from the misunderstandings of others."

The judge smiled. "I admit that I did not expect the fishermen to come up with someone who understands the position of the court."

I smiled. "They know my name and that I am an attorney. I suspect some of them do not like me. I've certainly heard enough grumbling from them. I understand the potential for misplaced violence. My first step is to seriously consider the safest venue for the trial. You did a good job in acquiescing to the fishermen's request to hire me. It shows good faith on your part. I want to have a cordial working relationship with the court on this case." I stood. "I won't take any more of your time today. I'll see you tomorrow. If you or Mr. Fortenac's attorney need to contact me, I'll be at the train station." We shook hands and I left.

The next day, I made certain I had my paperwork ready before I left the station. Today's procedure was not much different from processing the prostitutes. I met the other attorney. He was an older man closer to sixty than fifty. His face was puffy. I wondered if he could withstand the stress of a trial. Again I expressed my concern for the safety of the members of the court. I wanted him to be a little afraid of the fishermen so that he would be willing to work with me. I talked to him about my plan for following the details of correct procedure so that the court would not be censured for poor work.

The defense attorney studied me for a few minutes before he spoke. "I admit I've been between the mountain and the sea here. I live in this town. I have a comfortable home, and a wife. The rest of his family refuses to believe that an attorney is necessary. They don't know these fishermen. They don't live here." He rubbed his hands over his face and studied me through squinted eyes. "Yes, I think you have the correct approach. You and I shall do our best and leave the rest of the problem in the hands of the judge. The Fortenac family will not understand. They called me and told me to call it self-defense and let him go." The attorney looked away from me then he met my eyes, "His family does not understand the need for legal proceedings. They had Emperor Vanderholm call Judge Sylvia demanding Fortenac's release." The man sighed again. "We've been trying to explain about the fishermen and the rioting."

I nodded; surprised that Emperor Vanderholm had called the judge. I wondered about the close relationship between the Fortenacs and Vanderholms.

"Like you, the local judge has to live here. Would you agree to a change of venue, if I think the need arises?"

The attorney nodded.

I saw Leon Fortenac for the first time the next day in court. He came alone with his attorney. I found him a presentable man, slightly older than myself. We formally charged him with one count of rape and one count of murder. He plead, "Not guilty." We sent him back to the jail to wait for his bail proceedings. I took the night train home.

When I returned to the city, I had a message from Professor Ingleman inviting me to a student/faculty meeting at his house. I had not heard from him for several years. I picked up Andy at his home and we went to the meeting.

The professors stood, shook my hand and expressed their approval of me for taking the Fortenac case.

"Don't get excited. I haven't done anything yet."

Professor Stodola beamed at me. "You got him charged."

"He will probably get off."

Professor Ingleman stroked his new goatee and asked. "Do you think he is guilty?"

I snapped back. "He admits that he raped her and he killed her because she was fighting him. He is pleading innocent because she is the daughter of a northern fisherman."

Professor Ingleman used his classroom voice when he asked, "He admits his actions led to her death?"

"Yes,"

Professor Ingleman addressed the gathering, "Okay how is Jake going to get a conviction?" They sat and thought for several minutes.

The history of law professor suggested, "Can he get the name and gender of the victim sealed so that the court won't know it was a northern girl?"

The physics professor asked, "Is there any chance the judge will be impartial?"

I shrugged. "I don't think so. I've heard that Fortenac owns him. I was told Emperor Vanderholm has urged him to let Fortenac go. When I talked to him he agreed to follow procedure mostly to placate the fishermen. He stated that he knew we couldn't get a conviction. Well, he more than hinted that he was afraid he'd lose his job if he convicted Fortenac."

"How did you manage to get Fortenac charged?"

"The judge is afraid of violence from the fishermen. I was able to convince both the judge and the defense attorney that in order to clear Fortenac's name we have to follow court procedure in every detail. We don't want a mistrial. To keep the locals from rioting and burning the judge's house we need to be meticulous."

Professor Stodola snorted, "Good for you. You've gotten more than most would so far."

"Yes, you are good at the details. You will work the details." Professor Ingleman was staring at the wall in deep thought. "Can any of you think of anything in case law that might allow Jake to seal the name of the perpetrator?"

They sat and stared at the table. The law professors slowly shook their heads.

I added, "I think I can get the judge to request a change of venue if I can find a judge who might convict." This comment produced a discussion of judges who might be not be owned by the old families. We came up with one possibility in the city and one in the capital.

I placed my hands flat on the table in front of me as I voiced my next step in the case, "Okay, I will talk to both judges and outline my game plan for following procedure and mention the safety of the court issues in the north. I'll see if either of them will be amenable to a change of venue. I am not sure it is necessary yet."

Professor Ingleman clapped me on the shoulder, "You know procedure. Follow procedure. That is your best hope for winning."

My History of Law Professor said, "I'll do some research on this. I'll look for any obscure ruling that might give you leverage."

I spent the next few days talking to the judges and getting their opinions on change of venue. I liked the judge in the capital best. He said, "I don't see why you think you will lose this case just because the man is Leon Fortenac. I would have to hear the details of the case. Don't come to me with your prejudices."

"Sir, you encourage me. I don't have all the details yet. I haven't talked to anybody concerned with the case. My first concern was for the safety of the court. The local judge had some valid concerns. There has been some rioting."

"So people are threatening the judge to return a guilty verdict."

"Not yet. They protested that the local prosecutor recuse himself because he is the defendant's brother in-law. He is now the defense attorney of record. I decided to deal with the threat of violence by adhering strictly to proper procedure. The locals are quiet now that the man has been charged."

"If this case appears in my court, you damn well better have followed every procedure to the last detail."

"I intend to. I intend to keep this case as clean as I can. I don't deny that the press is pressuring the government to intervene and let him go."

The judge sat and stared at me. "You'll do. If you think you need a change of venue, I'll take the case."

"Thank you sir. For now, I will try to work with what I have."

I spent the next two months interviewing people and slowly assembling the story of Alice's murder. Alice had worked for the local printing shop. Her boss asked her to deliver a stationary order to Fortenac's office late in the day.

I questioned the shop owner. "Why so late. Was the order late getting done?"

"No the order was ready earlier. His office was closed. He came in special to receive the order."

As I listened to the shop owner's testimony I thought, "Oh shit. This could be premeditated." I went back over the whole process with the stationary order and who did what when.

"Sir, I will need for you to make a deposition. That is a statement under oath telling the court exactly what you told me."

The shopkeeper's eyes filled and his nose turned red. He scratched at the back of his hand. "I'm not going to get in trouble for sending her up there am I?"

"No it is very important for the court to know that she did not volunteer to go there. Part of Mr. Fortenac's defense will be that she went there to seduce him. We need to make it clear that she was delivering an order that he placed with you. Do not talk to anyone about this until after you make your deposition."

I scheduled three people to make depositions at the office of the prosecuting attorney in Soville. I grumped about having to travel to another village to do the deposition.

When I arrived in Soville, I walked into the court recorder's office to be greeted by the beautiful, elegant lady I'd seen trying to hold too many ledgers in the courthouse. I forgot I was grumpy. I instantly decided to take a deposition from everybody I saw.

Her blue eyes met mine, and her lashes dropped. "Can I help you?"

I netted in my thoughts and remembered why I was there. "We have an appointment with the court recorder to take some depositions."

A delicate flush painted her porcelain cheeks. "Oh…I…Of course, you must be Prosecutor Jaconovich. The recorder will be ready in a moment. Can I bring you some coffee or tea?"

I looked at my witnesses. They shook their heads. "No thank you miss…"

"Leah." She offered to shake hands

I smiled.

Her elegant melodic voice delighted me. I tried to think of something to say. My words sounded stilted to my ears. "I am afraid we may be disrupting your routine for several weeks while we make certain that the procedural details are meticulously met."

She looked at me and lowered those eyelashes again. "I understand. Anybody can say anything. If you do not do a good job we will not have justice."

We spent the afternoon on the depositions. The court recorder promised to have the papers ready for me in a day or two. "Make it two days and I'll come pick them up."

I did return, often. I talked to Leah every chance I got. I learned that Leah's mother was very ill and not expected to live. Leah seemed devoted to her mama. Her papa had died years earlier.

"Do you have anyone to help you with your Mama?"

Those eyelashes fluttered as she looked at the floor. "I…I…have a…a…a brother. He works. He's not much help."

I wanted to take her hand and tell her that I would help her.

Once, Leah volunteered to bring the finished depositions into Midville to meet me. I took her to lunch.

Once our orders were taken, I searched my brain for something to talk about. "Um," Her eyes fluttered up to mine. I swallowed. I blurted out the first thing that came to my mind. "Uh, you live here in the villages. Do you hear any rumors of riots or violence over the trial." Mentally I swore at my stupidity and kicked myself under the table for not finding a better topic.

She smiled and suddenly seemed less shy. Her eyes met mine and rested on my face. "There is always talk of rioting over this or that. The people do riot. I'm surprised they hasn't been more talk of rioting." She blushed. "The only reason the fishermen did not capture Leon and take him twenty miles out to sea and leave him there is that they trust you."

I knew the urge to sweat over my responsibility. I forgot all responsibility again as soon as I looked at her eyes and her hair. She usually wore her hair in a knot on the back of her head. Today, it was pulled up high on her head and wrapped in some sort of knot with a braid coming out of it. My eyes followed the braid to where it ended curled on her right breast. I jerked my eyes back to her face. Our waiter rescued me by bringing our food. During our meal, she told me about the local happenings in the villages.

After lunch I returned her to the boat she was riding on. I was certain that I was on my way to being in love. I'd never seen the sky and the ocean so blue. I was even fond of this dumpy little village that stank of rotting fish.

My romance, as the family called it, was one of our most popular topics of discussion. "Is she talking about how strong and successful you are? Does she talk about wanting a big house?"

"No, not at all. She talks to me about her mother and the case. She is concerned that I may need to move the venue south. She worries about violence."

"Does she cling to your arm so you can't defend yourself?"

"No, not at all. She has not made any move to touch me. I've only touched her to help her onto her boat." I sighed. "In fact, I am not getting much encouragement. I get the impression that she is very dedicated to taking care of her mama. She smiles at me, and talks to me. She has taken over the job of delivering the finished depositions to me. That is all she has done that I can call encouragement." I sighed some more.

I talked to Leon Fortenac in his home. "Mr. Fortenac I need to be certain that I understand the details of your statement."

"I don't have time for this. She was just a fisherman's whore."

His attorney helped me out. "Damn-it Leon, the people in this village are ready to tear you limb from limb. They bombed one of our warehouses the other night. They can bomb this house any day. You will never escape from them unless we go through this and see you acquitted in court. The prosecutor is doing an excellent job of keeping the people from rioting and burning down the cannery or this house. We are doing our best to get you out of this mess."

Leon slouched. "I guess." I could smell the drink on his breath from six feet away.

He denied asking that Alice deliver the stationary. He got himself another drink. He did not recall ordering any stationary. He finally lost patience with me. "Listen I told you she was a fisherman's whore. What more do you need to know?"

I took a few deep breaths to keep my professional objectivity instead of throwing Leon across the room. "Mr. Fortenac, I know this is tedious. I am trying to do the best job possible to see that when you walk out of court, this case is completely resolved. I have talked to your brother in-law. We agree that the facts of the case will speak for themselves. We need to be certain that due process is followed so that nobody has further recourse to hassle you through the law on this case."

He sniffed at me. "I have better things to do."

I tried for humble to hide my loathing. "I know that sir. We all feel that way and will be glad when it is over. Your business is in this village. If you want to continue to do business, we need to get this cleared up."

My sticking point on this case was that the court was going to rule that Mr. Fortenac was innocent on the grounds that the girl was the daughter of a fisherman. As far as I knew she was. I researched case law. I found case after case that had not made it this far, for the simple reason that the woman was from the north and the man was a member of the elite families. Always the court ruled the same. I had a good case that he planned to rape the girl. Perhaps he intended to kill her as well. We were on rougher seas if she died because she fought him. The autopsy suggested some of her wounds, the disfigurement, did not come from fighting her assailant. I spent fifteen minutes vomiting after I read the autopsy report.

I stopped sleeping. I had a good case. Yet everything I read told me I was going to lose. I made another trip north. I had talked to the girl's family. I would talk to more of her family. One of her cousins and her younger sisters told me that I needed to talk to their grandmother. I went back to the village and found the grandmother. She lived in a reasonably large, well-kept house in a nice part of town. The view from the front porch and sitting room was magnificent.

Mrs. D'SnG welcomed me graciously. "Mr. Prosecutor, you are here about our tragedy."

"Yes, Mrs. D'SnG." The woman had large bones. She might have been beautiful when she was young. Her skin was dark and course as if she had worked on a boat herself. Her dress appeared expensive. The chair she directed me to certainly spoke of more money than I would expect the mother of a fisherman to own. The fact that a manservant set a silver and china tea service in front of her convinced me that Mrs. D'SnG was a bit out of the ordinary. Her voice sounded cultured as she commanded me to have some tea.

I accepted the tea. "Now, Mrs. D'SnG, tell me about your granddaughter."

"What do you want to know?"

"I am not certain myself. Your other granddaughters thought you might be able to help me understand this tragedy."

When, Mrs. D'SnG started talking she became fretful. "I disapproved of her working you know. She should not have been working. But, you know how kids are these days. They don't listen to their parents. They think I am old-fashioned because I think the girls need to be guarded. I insist that the boys go to school. The village children just run wild. The girls are not taught how to be poised and charming. It is no wonder he thought Alice was loose." Her words brought up memories of those horrible first-year receptions. I noted how she held her cup and how she sat. I listened to her voice. Her voice was cultured, but without the soft lilt of Mama's voice or Leah's.

"Mrs. D'SnG, you are not from the north."

Her chin went up slightly. Her mouth puckered and her eyebrows arched.

I grinned. "Oh don't try to intimidate me with that look. I am not a first year university student to be intimidated by the grande dames of society. You probably went to poise school."

Her back straightened ever so slightly. "Well it is good to know somebody recognizes a woman of breeding."

"Mrs. D'SnG, what family are you from?"

"Uzara."

"Ah, I see it. I thought you reminded me of somebody. My roommate dated a Uzara girl for a year. Yes, she resembled you. Something about the eyes and the chin."

The old woman smiled.

"Yes, and the smile. You can't know how glad I am to meet you. I am going to need to get a deposition from you."

She seemed to sit even straighter. "So you know my cousins?"

"Oh yes, Woody Uzara was in my law classes. He is practicing in

Portlandia, I think. Are the Uzara's into shipping?"

She nodded slightly. "We do imports, mostly quality products for the fine families. I met Mr. D'SnG when Papa was here importing furniture from Europe." She laughed, "Mr. D'SnG was a rogue and I loved him almost as much as I loved running off with him and shocking my whole stuffy lot of relatives. He took me to sea with him. Of course, he entered Papa's import business and was very successful."

"Ah, so did Alice's father join the family import trade or does he fish?"

The woman gave me the puckered-mouth, arched-brow, grand-dame look. "Her father is in charge of all of our northern operations."

I nodded and refrained from yelling at her to inquire why nobody had told me this before. Had I thought to ask? I hadn't. I felt as if a bucket of ice water had been dumped over me. I'd forgotten to ask Mr. D'SnG's occupation. He had been gone on business much of the past couple months. I'd assumed he was at sea. Perhaps someone had said he was at sea. Alice's mother was a local woman. I'd met all her family.

I was shaking when I stood up. "Mrs. D'SnG, I need to go to my office now. Can I pick you up tomorrow for a trolley ride so you can make a deposition."

"What do I have to say?" She asked.

"This will just be a formal statement that you are Alice's grandmother. Do you have any identification? I could also use a copy of your marriage license."

"Mama never let me ride the trolleys. What did you say your family is again?"

"Rouseff."

She looked almost coy. "I always thought the Rouseff men were boring but you seem a bit livelier than the others."

"My papa is a bit like you. He married a northern girl. Mama is a D'NO."

She laughed, "You'll do. You come get me for your trolley ride." I wanted to warn the old woman not to talk about our conversation. I decided I would do better not to draw her attention to the significance of it.

Next, I went to the judge's house. He allowed me into his study. "Sir, thank you for seeing me. I need to change the venue to the capital."

He nodded and sighed as he settled into his chair. "Why?"

"I am getting close to presenting the case. You know how we think this will come out. I've talked to the girl's family. I've talked to others around town. I am concerned for the safety of the court." I'd said the magic words. I could get my change of venue. I continued, "I confess I've always thought it would come to this. Also, the defense attorney told me a Fortenac warehouse was bombed in Soville. He said it was bad."

The judge nodded and sighed again. "Burned to the ground before the fireboat got there. Did he tell you a truck from the cannery was bombed last night? The people are likely to riot any day now." He picked at the upholstery on his chair. "I would like to be away from the case."

"Sir, I would consider visiting your family if I were you. I spoke to Judge Gannon in the capital. He is willing to take the case. I will call him this afternoon. He may want to talk to you about your understanding of the safety of the court."

The judge winked at me. "I would have moved the case south weeks ago, but you seemed intent on dragging half of three villages in for depositions just so you can flirt with the elegant Leah."

"Ah, people noticed that?" I tried not to grin too much. We ended the conversation on a cordial note and I prepared to return to the train station in the trolley.

As soon as I got back to the station I called Judge Gannon and told him about the bombings and the tension in the villages. He agreed to the change of venue. "I expect you to bring in a good clean case."

"I expect that I will sir. I talked to the defense attorney last week and he seemed comfortable with his preparation."

"Has he cooperated with you?"

"I think he has shared everything he has with me. I have certainly shared everything he has asked for with him. He has sat in on every deposition I took." The judge had a few more instructions on how to fill out the change of venue form. "Thank you sir. If I get right on this now, I can have it to your office first thing in the morning."

Micki picked me up at the station and took me home to dinner at The Cove.

The women at The Cove fussed over me and gave me a good dinner. I went off to bed early. "Oh I won't be here for dinner tomorrow. I have another deposition to take tomorrow. I am going to take the evening train home. I can do the rest of the work on the case from there."

"You are almost done then?" Petral's wife had been upset over the case. She was a third or fourth cousin to Alice D'SnG

I nodded.

"Is there hope?" Micki's mama asked.

I kissed her on the top of her head. "There is always hope."

Micki started dancing. "Jake's done it! I knew you could do it! You figured out how to win the case."

"Micki, calm down! I've had a breakthrough. Things do not look as bad as I thought at first. I will contact some of my classmates for help. Please don't say anything to anyone here." Everyone nodded solemnly.

Mrs. D'SnG, met me well prepared for the open trolley. She had two man-servants and a fur robe with her. She looked so old and frail, I was thankful for her servants.

When I reached the court recorder's office, I asked after my beautiful Leah. The court recorder almost whispered. "Her mother passed away yesterday. She is taking the week off."

"I am sorry for her. I assume this was not unexpected."

Mrs. D'SnG gave me her look. "Ah, you are figuring out why I ran off with a northerner, too much inbreeding in the south. Makes 'em weak." Her chuckle sounded almost bawdy.

The defense attorney seemed a little confused as to why I brought this old woman in. I asked for her maiden name. I asked her how her granddaughter had been raised. Her answers sounded very respectable. I watched for a reaction from the defense attorney when the name Uzara came up. He did not seem to catch the significance of the name.

I returned Mrs. D'SnG to her home.

Mrs. D'SnG sounded sad when she said goodbye at her front door. "Thank you son. Thank you for trying so hard that you would listen to the ramblings of an old woman. I don't know if it will do any good."

"There is one more thing that would help ma'am. Both the Uzara family and the D'SnG family will be allowed to make a formal statement to the court. I intend to call Woody when I get back to the city. Can you find an attorney to speak for the D'SnGs?"

She gave me the same hopeful look Micki's mother had earlier. "I will write to my family at once."

When I got home, I wrote a very proper letter of condolence to the elegant Leah. Next I called Woody. He was expecting my call. "I heard some rumor from Papa. What is going on?"

"Your great Aunt Violet D'SnG's granddaughter Alice was raped and brutally murdered by Leon Fortenac. His defense is that she did not have any family connections of importance."

Woody stammered. "What?"

"I'll send you a copy of the autopsy report. I'll warn you, it is ugly." I could hear Woody breathing on the other end of the phone so I continued. "The D'SnGs plan to make a statement on her behalf. I think it would help if the Uzaras made a statement also."

"Jake, thanks for calling me. I think we will want to make a statement. Has the man actually admitted that he murdered the girl?"

"I can send you copies of most of the testimony. I'll make up a whole packet and send it down by train tonight."

"Yeah, thanks."

I put together a bundle of photocopies of the depositions and autopsy reports. I asked Mrs. Apkouta to hand carry the package south.

A few days later, Woody called. "Jake, I went over the case with some of the other family attorneys. We are experts in import law not criminal cases. How do we present our statement?"

"First, you need to make a written Statement of Outrage. Emphasize that you consider this an attack on your family. I know this sounds archaic. It is."

"We have very little influence compared to the Fortenacs."

"Which may be why this man thinks he can kill young girls without consequences. I will present your letter to the judge with the rest of the case. The judge will review the papers to see if he has everything he needs and that we have followed correct procedure. He will set a date for us to appear in the courtroom and present our final summations to him. On the day we appear before the judge, it would help if someone from your family can be present to say a few words asking for justice."

"What happens after that?"

"It is possible that the judge will hand down a verdict. It is also possible that he will take the case back and do more research. I am hoping he will hand down the verdict."

"We will have someone there to speak for Alice."

It took me longer than I thought it would to have every piece of paper and testimony ready to present. Finally, I made an appointment on a Tuesday to take the papers to the judge.

This was an informal meeting. He greeted me cordially. "Ah, this is the

Fortenac case?"

"Yes sir."

"You have a big stack of papers there."

"The case is important sir. A child lost her life. An important man could go to prison. I wanted to do my best."

He snorted. "Well let's see what you have."

I explained the order of pages. "Mr. Fortenac requested that you view his defense first. I agreed to give you those papers first." I spent twenty minutes with the judge.

He dismissed me. "I will call you sometime next week to set a date for court."

"Thank you sir." I was almost ill by the time I left the judge's office. I decided to walk until time for my train. I walked for an hour before I calmed down enough to look around me. I found myself in the park that ran from The Compound where the emperor lived to the huge cathedral at the far end. I could not help but admire the beauty of the place. I stood and stared at The Compound. It looked so impressive and secure. I thought about the corruption it held. I went home.

My reception at the M'TK station was everything I could want. Mama fussed and fretted over me. "Yes, Mama you are right. I have been working too hard. Ah that tea smells wonderful. What is in it?"

Mama had brewed up a tea with leaves and flowers from her gardens. It smelled of lemon and tasted like flowers.

"Ah, this is good. It is what I needed." Mama fussed about giving me a good home-cooked dinner.

Papa looked at me and didn't tease Mama for making me into a mama's boy. Dinner was excellent. I began to feel better.

The judge called me on Friday. "Jake, I've had a chance to look over your paperwork. Both you and the defense attorney have done an excellent job of following procedures. Everything looks clean and in order. Let's set a court date and get this over."

After I got off of the phone, I called the defense attorney immediately. I told him the trial date and promised to send him written notice.

The older man sounded mellow. "The judge will notify me."

"Oh, I know. I will be so glad when this is over."

He chuckled, "Jake, you worry too much."

"That is what my mama says. I guess I need to go home and let her fuss over me."

"You need a wife to fuss over you."

"Um…how is that pretty blond woman who works in the court recorder's office? Her mama had just died last time I was there."

"Oh she is a stunner, isn't she?" We chatted for a few more minutes and hung up.

I spent a few minutes thinking about Leah. I wonder now why nobody could tell me anything specific about Leah. It never occurred to me that they knew no more about her than I did.

I spent as much time as I could spare with Mama and Papa. Micki came south to start university while I waited for the court date. I prepared to go up to the capital a day early.

"Jake?"

"Yes, Mama."

"Can you take Micki to court with you?"

"I suppose. Why?"

"He is still upset over the girl. Maybe it will help him to see the man who did it get convicted."

"And if he does not get convicted?"

"He will. When my Jake sets his mind to something he makes it happen. That man will be convicted and I want Micki there to see it. Papa and I will come up to the capital and take him sightseeing before you go to court."

Chapter 22 Trial

At last, the day I was to appear in court as the prosecutor in Leon Fortenac's trial for rape and murder arrived.

Micki and I arrived early for court. "Micki, I want you to act somewhat official. You will sit on this side of the room with Alice's family. Help the women with their wraps and generally act polite."

Together Micki and I greeted the family members who came. I asked Woody to sit with me. He introduced another family attorney, Ricardo. "He is speaking for the D'SnG family."

They joined me at the prosecutor's table and we talked strategy.

I was too nervous to fully take in the elegance of our courtroom. All furnishings were made from a highly polished mahogany. The judge was to sit at an elaborate table set on a raised platform. I spread my copy of the case out on a long table in front of the bench seat I shared with the Uzara attorneys. Behind us was a meter tall rail. The families sat behind us on long benches. The floor slanted upward toward the back so those at the back of the room could see over the heads in front of them.

I suddenly realized that court started in five minutes and the defense side of the room remained empty. I tried not to panic. What if they didn't show, then blamed me for not informing them of the time and place?

I looked at all the people quietly waiting for the court to open. They looked pale and tearful. Micki sat with Alice's sisters.

The court clerk entered the room. The clock told me that we were all due to be here in one minute. Woody squeezed my shoulder. He leaned forward and whispered in my ear, "Move for conviction if they don't show." I nodded. The doors in the back opened and the defense attorney hurried to his place. We waited another minute.

The court clerk asked. "Are all parties to the case present?"

The defense attorney stood. "I apologize to the court and the prosecution. The defendant is in the lavatory. He will join us shortly."

Another five minutes passed. Leon Fortenac entered escorted by two men.

The oldest man was tall and thin with the same beaked nose I noticed on Leon. I assumed he was the head of the Fortenac family. The other was possibly Leon's father. He was shorter than the older man and fleshier. He also had the beaked nose of the Fortenac family.

The older man looked around him with an expression of distain. I saw shock on his face as he looked at the people on the prosecution side of the court. His eyes grew wide as he recognized some of the Uzaras. I hoped he could figure out that the other two men in the prosecutor's box were attorneys representing the victim's family. His lip twitched showing a hint of alarm.

The court clerk asked again, "Are all parties to the case present?

I could barely speak. "All parties to the prosecution are present."

The defense attorney sounded confident. "All parties to the defense are present."

"Please rise in the presence of the judge."

We stood.

It had begun. I was terrified that I would lose my voice. Out of some memory from my distant past came I voice I had not heard for years instructing his students, *"First, you must learn to master your anger and your fear, then you can learn to fight."* I knew the exercise. I relaxed. I focused all my attention on being quick and clear in my thinking.

A deathly still settled over the room.

The judge took his place. He ran his hand over his short dark black hair. His hooded eyes appeared sleepy except that the eyes under the lids seemed to look straight into the soul. The court recorder took his place. The clerk said, "You may be seated."

We sat.

The judge cleared his throat. "I have a few comments before we get started. First, the case that was presented to me was the best prepared, and best presented case I have seen in many, many years of serving as a judge. Both the prosecution and the defense attorney have done an outstanding job of preparation. Whichever way I decide this case, the representatives of the other side may know that my decision was not due to any fault of theirs. At this time I call for motions. Does the prosecution have any motions?"

"Not at his time your honor."

"Does the defense have any motions?"

The defense attorney stood. "Yes, your honor. Our first motion is to have the depositions from those people who are not members of the southern families expunged from the case."

"Is this acceptable to the prosecution?"

I stood. "No, your honor it is not acceptable." I'd heard a gasp behind me, and the sound of people shifting in their seats.

The judge raised his eyebrows. "Can you tell the court why?"

"Your honor the preparation for this case that you have praised took months of tedious work. I deemed all witnesses who made a deposition competent to do so. If I need to go back and trace their connection to a recognized southern family, it will take me more months to determine who is qualified and who is not. The defense attorney has met and talked to each person who made a deposition. Each person appeared sober, capable and lucid. It is my opinion that tracing the family connection of every person is a waste of the court's time."

"In other words, Mr. Prosecutor, if we expunge any depositions on the grounds of family connection, you will request a stay in order to qualify each person."

"Do I have any alternative?"

"No you do not. Motion denied. Is there another motion?"

The defense attorney looked from the judge to me. He recovered his obvious discomfort and continued. "I move to have the court cleared of all persons not connected to a recognized southern family."

"Mr. Prosecutor?"

"Every person here was invited as a concerned party or member to their recorded Statement of Outrage. They have legal representation."

"Motion denied."

I studied the other side of the room. The defense attorney still looked cool. The defendant looked hung over. His father looked worried. The oldest Fortenac looked shrewd. I suspected he did not like the direction the case had gone in the first few minutes. He pulled at his lower lip. I noticed him turn and stare at Violet D'SnG.

"Is there another motion?"

Leon's attorney still sounded assured. "I move to have the courtroom cleared of all persons under the age of eighteen."

"Is that acceptable to the prosecution?"

I sighed, "If I had my way the children would be running and playing in the sunshine." I paused. "They are parties to this case. Their parents want them here. Some of them made depositions. I will not attempt to over-rule their parents. The motion is not acceptable."

"Motion denied." The judge looked at the defense attorney.

The defense moved again. "I move to have the children's depositions expunged."

The judge turned to me.

"That is not acceptable."

"Why?"

"On lines thirteen, twenty-seven, forty-one, seventy-seven, ninety-six, and one-hundred thirty-three of his statement, the defendant refers to Alice D'SnG as a whore. The depositions from the children refute that allegation." The judge sat and looked at me for a full minute before he made his ruling.

"Motion denied."

The defendant growled and shifted in his seat. His attorney touched his arm. I looked at the children behind me. Micki had an arm around each of the D'SnG girls. I was thankful he was present.

"Is there another motion?"

The defense was being thorough. "I move to have Alice D'SnG's school records expunged."

The judge looked at me.

"That is not acceptable to the prosecution."

The judge said, "I am curious as to why you felt Alice's school records were necessary."

"It goes back to the allegations that the child was a whore. I can furnish the court with ample evidence that whores do not stay in school. They do not get excellent scores. I process dozens of prostitution cases every week. I know how they live. I included this information to show that Alice was not a member of the sisterhood."

The judge cocked an eyebrow. "Motion denied."

The defense presented more motions to dismiss more depositions. They were denied. The defense attorney got a little frustrated. Finally, he lost his composure. "Oh hell, your honor the only reason this case has so many depositions was that the young prosecutor wanted to look at the pretty secretary in the recorder's office."

I scratched my nose and tried not to grin.

The judge turned to me. "Mr. Prosecutor, do you have any motions to expunge any of the depositions?"

"No sir I do not."

The judge continued. "I take it that if we do expunge any of the depositions you will go back and research the cause and we will just have to reinstate it when you finish your research. The secretary may figure in here or not."

"The secretary is very elegant, Sir. You are correct that before I allow any piece of the case to be expunged I will research it again to make certain it does indeed fall outside the limits of acceptable documentation."

The judge sat back in his chair and paused before he spoke. "As I have already mentioned, this case appears exceptionally well prepared. The court is not inclined to expunge any piece of the documentation."

The oldest Mr. Fortenac looked at Leon though narrowed eyes.

The judge continued, "I am curious as to why each piece of paper relating to this case was included. I am confident that the prosecution can give me a clear and cogent reason for each piece of paper in this case."

"I can sir."

"Counsel for the defense, I respect your thoroughness in handling the case. Your presentation so far has been flawless and serves the best interest of your client. The prosecution has convinced me that all the evidence presented is relevant to the case. I will not entertain any more motions to expunge."

I wanted to breathe a sigh of relief. I did not. I did sit down.

"I will now ask the defendant some questions." The judge turned to face the defendant. I noticed Leon's attorney poking him to sit up straighter.

"Mr. Fortenac, it says on your statement that the girl, Alice D'SnG came to your office in the Fortenac Cannery building at five-thirty PM. Do you agree that is correct?"

"Yeah." His attorney poked him. "Yes, that was her name."

"She came to your office about five-thirty."

"I guess. I wasn't watching the clock." Leon had slouched back down in his chair.

"Why were you in your office at that time?"

"I was working."

The judge continued, "The man Alice worked for said he asked her to deliver some stationary to you at that time. Did she come with the stationary?"

"I don't remember." Leon's attorney poked him again.

The judge pursed his lips before his next question. "I have a deposition from the local police that lists an unopened box of stationary with an invoice dated that day as one of the items found in your office. Is there some reason I should not believe that this was the stationary she was supposed to deliver to you?"

Leon bristled. "The local police had no business in my office."

I spared a look to see how Leon's family responded to his testimony. The old man sat stiff and erect, but his eyes darted between Leon and Violet D'SnG. Leon's father slouched on his seat and looked bored.

The judge sounded severe. "Did Alice D'SnG bring that box of stationary to your office?"

"How should I know? What difference does it make?"

"I will ask the questions. Did she bring the box of stationary to your office?"

"Yes, No, I don't know…maybe."

"Well that about covers your possible answers to my question. Pick one answer."

"I don't know. I don't remember."

The judge summarized. "Your testimony is that you do not remember if Alice D'SnG was at your office to deliver a box of stationary."

"Yes."

"Let the record so show."

The judge asked another question. "I have here a deposition from her employer stating that you asked for her to deliver the stationary. Is it correct that you specifically asked that she be the one to make the delivery?"

"I don't remember."

"That is your testimony that you do not remember if you specifically asked that Miss. D'SnG be the one to deliver the stationary."

"I don't remember."

"Let the record so read."

"It says on your statement, that you did in fact use a knife to threaten Alice D'SnG and force her to submit to forced sex with you."

Leon smirked. "It also says on my statement that she wanted me to have sex with her."

"In what way did she indicate her desire to have sex?"

Leon leaned closer to his attorney. "What is he talking about? I don't know what he is asking. What am I supposed to say?" His counsel shook his head.

The judge's eyebrow went up again. "I will make this as easy for you as I can. What did Alice say or do that gave you the idea that she wanted to have sex with you."

"Uh...well...of course she did. I know when a woman wants me. She wanted me."

The judge breathed in deeply through his nostrils and leaned forward. "If I under stand you correctly, your testimony is that you believe Alice D'SnG wanted to have sex with you because of some inner sense you had."

Leon smirked. "Yeah, I just knew."

"**Let the record show** that the defendant states he just knew--independent of Miss. D'SnG's behavior--that she wanted to have sex." The judge's nostrils flared. "Mr. Fortenac, in your statement you admit that you stabbed Alice D'SnG with your knife. Why did you stab her?"

"Because she scratched me."

"Did she do anything else to cause you harm?"

"Yes, she bit me. I still have a mark here. Um... she kicked me. And... she tried to run away." Leon finally sat up straight. He'd summoned the energy to sound outraged.

The judge clarified, "So you stabbed her with your knife."

"Yes." He still sounded indignant over Alice fighting him.

"**Let the record so read.**" The judge turned a page in his notes. "Mr. Fortenac, while this girl was trying to run away, and kicking, and biting, did it never occur to you that she might not want to have sex with you?"

"No." Leon looked at his attorney and turned to look at his father. Something in his eyes spoke of his bewilderment over the proceedings.

The judge still sounded firm and in control. "Despite the kicking, biting, and scratching, you thought she wanted to have sex with you."

"Yes."

"**Let the record so read.**"

I was sweating inside my suit. This was the heart of the case. Would the judge believe that this little girl wanted to have sex with a grown man? Leon Fortenac sounded so certain, so sure that the child wanted to have sex with him.

The judge asked, "Mr. Fortenac in your statement you state that you believed Alice D'SnG wanted to have sex with you because you are the son of an important family, that you are rich, and she wanted your favor. Is this still your belief?"

"Yes."

"Let the record so read."

"Mr. Fortenac you stated that you knew Alice D'SnG to be, in your terms, a whore. The reasons you gave for this belief are as follows. Her name was D'SnG. Her father is a fisherman. Her family connections are low. You had seen her walking on the street in the late afternoon. Were those your reasons for believing that Alice D'SnG was a prostitute?"

"Yeah." The defense attorney poked him again. He straightened with a sigh. "Yes, those are my reasons for believing she was a whore." He smirked and even winked at the judge.

I spared a glance behind me. Micki was holding the head of each of Alice's sisters with one ear against his shoulder and covering their other ear with his hands. Alice's grandmother was looking like the grande dame that she is. I felt a little afraid of her.

"Let the record so show." The judge looked grim and turned another page in his notes.

The judge went through the rest of Leon Fortenac's statement, confirming each part of the statement and entering it into the formal record. He finally finished asking questions.

"Mr. Prosecutor do you have any motions."

I stood. "Yes your honor. I would like to present a motion to correct and clarify the record."

"Proceed."

"Mr. Fortenac stated his belief that Mr. D'SnG is a fisherman. Mr. D'SnG is in fact an importer. I want this noted in the record."

The judge turned to the defense attorney. "Is this acceptable?"

"No it is not."

"State your reason."

"My client was stating his belief not a matter of his knowledge. He was correct in saying he believed."

"Mr. Prosecutor?"

"I am asking only to clarify the record as to Mr. D'SnG's occupation. Mr. Fortenac's testimony as to his beliefs may stand."

"Let the motion to clarify the matter of Mr. D'SnG's occupation stand. **Let the record so read.**" Mr. Fortenac shifted in his chair and scowled at the judge. He pulled at his attorney's sleeve. His attorney sat straight, staring straight ahead and shook his head ever so slightly.

"Do you have any other motions?"

"I move to clarify the record regarding his belief that Alice D'SnG's family connections are low. I have furnished records showing that she is the granddaughter of Violet Uzara. The Uzara family is not considered to be a low connection." I saw the oldest Mr. Fortenac turn quickly to look at Mrs. D'SnG. He turned red then paled.

"Is that acceptable to the defense?"

Leon Fortenac was tugging and poking at his attorney who remained rigid and still. The defense attorney stated, "Yes, that is acceptable."

The judge turned to me. "Do you have any other motions?"

"Yes, I would like to clarify the record regarding Mr. Fortenac's statement that he believed Alice D'SnG to be a whore because he saw her walking down the street. She was a schoolgirl and did walk home from school. I have presented depositions from her peers stating that they walked home with her. I have presented depositions stating that she occasionally ran errands for her family and the print shop. Let the record state that she had legitimate reasons to be out in public."

"Is that acceptable to the defense?"

"Yes, that is acceptable."

Again Leon poked and pulled at his attorney who ignored him.

The judge asked, "Does the prosecution have any more motions?"

I had none. I asked, "Does the court seek clarification on any questions from the prosecution at this time?"

The judge answered, "The court does not seek further clarification at this time."

"I have no further motions."

The judge addressed the other side of the room. "Does the defense have any motions?"

The defense attorney asked, "Does the court seek clarification on any questions from the defense?"

"The court does not seek further clarification."

"I have no further motions."

The judge turned over several pages in the case before him. "The court will now hear from the Parties of Interest to this case. Does the prosecution have a Party of Interest to present to the court?"

I said, "Yes, may I present to the court Woodrow Uzara, attorney for the Uzara family."

"You may proceed Mr. Uzara."

My knees nearly buckled under me as I sat down.

Woody stood. "Thank you your honor. I am here to express the outrage of the Uzara family at the death of my cousin Alice D'SnG"

The eldest Mr. Fortenac shifted in his seat again.

"Mr. Fortenac admits he not only brutally raped and murdered my young cousin, he mutilated her body either before or after she was dead. However, his actions go beyond dishonoring her body. By calling my cousin a whore, he has slandered our whole family. This in itself is an outrage committed against a respectable family with an honorable name. However, my complaint goes beyond his contempt for the Uzara family. His blatant disrespect for a young girl, a member of a prominent family in this country threatens the whole fabric of our society. If the leaders in business, government and industry do not treat one another with respect, is there any hope for the less educated, the less well off. We are to set the standard. Mr. Fortenac has set the standard unacceptably low. The Uzara family will have justice." Woody sat down.

"**Let the record note** Mr. Uzara's Statement of Outrage. Mr. Prosecutor do you have another Party of Interest to present?"

I stood again and motioned to Ricardo. "Yes Sir. May I present to the court Mr. Ricardo Uzara attorney for the D'SnG family."

"You may proceed Mr. Uzara."

"Thank you your honor. I am here to express the outrage of the D'SnG, Spinoza and Rouseff families at the death of our young cousin Alice D'SnG. Words that are acceptable in court do not express our outrage. This child was raped, murdered and her body mutilated by a man who shows no remorse. Our thoughts at this time go beyond outrage. Does the Fortenac family want to declare war on every other prominent family in this country? If they do, they have made a good start. They may think they are bigger and richer, but as this case shows we are all interconnected. Yes Alice's last name was D'SnG. Who are the D'SnGs? They are a wealthy family composed of members from the finest families in this country. They even have a Fortenac or two among their numbers, but we will overlook that. You have listened to the testimony from that...the defendant. You have seen his contempt. He admits that he killed the girl. He admits that he raped the girl. He admits that she fought him to her death. This man saw our cousin coming home from school. He made arrangements for her and only her to deliver a package to his office. He attacked her and murdered her. We demand that this court return a verdict of guilty. If you fail in your judgment, I fear that our cousin's combined families will have to seek justice and the restoration of our honor elsewhere." Ricardo sat down.

"**Let the record note** Mr. Ricardo Uzara's Statement of Outrage. Does the defense have a Party of Interest to present to the court?"

"Your honor, I...." The defense attorney turned to look behind him. The old man shook his head. Leon's father had turned purple. He shook his head as well. "The defense does not have a Party of Interest to present to the court."

"Does the defense have any other motions?"

"No we do not."

The judge turned to me. "Does the prosecution have any other motions?

"Does the court have any questions or require any further clarification?"

The judge's tone was firm. "No, it does not."

"We have no further motions." We were close to the end. Now we would hear the judge's statements.

The judge sat at his desk and turned pages in the case. He made a note. The room became absolutely silent. I could feel the sweat trickling down my side and the center of my back. I heard a sniff behind me and turned to catch a glimpse of Alice's mother wiping her eyes.

The judge turned some more pages in the case. I watched as he picked up a handful of perhaps seven to ten depositions. He shuffled through them, snorted and set them aside. He glanced up at me as he did so.

I sat up straight, but allowed my eyes to shift to the right to take in what was happening on the defense side of the room. Leon sat sprawled in his seat. His father behind him was slumped over and his complexion had turned a sick shade of purple. The old man chewed on his lower lip. His eyes slid repeatedly to Violet Uzara D'SnG. When his eyes rested on Leon the elder man's mouth compressed into a thin line and his eyes squinted.

The judge turned some more pages in the case. Finally, he started writing. From the way his hand moved down the page, I thought he might be making a list. The quiet of the room rang in my ears. Finally the judge looked up. His expression was grim. He spoke.

"**Let the record show**: There are no further motions. We will now proceed to the handing down of judgments."

"**Let the record show**: The court has reviewed all testimony and documentation presented on the case of the State vs. Leon Fortenac. The court finds the documentation to be without flaw and acceptable."

"**Let the record show**: Correct procedure has been followed for presenting all documentation and that the court, the prosecution and the defense are in agreement for allowing all the documentation received to be entered into the record."

"**Let the record show**: The court, the prosecution and the defense agree that the evidence and documentation for this case is complete--no further documentation may be added, nothing may be subtracted."

I was numb with the shock that this event was almost over. The judge would give his verdict.

"**Let the record show**: All parties are in agreement on the documentation presented. I therefore declare that the verdict of this court will be legal and binding without appeal."

I remembered to breathe slowly.

"Let the record show: This court has reached a verdict. Leon Fortenac is guilty of the rape and murder of Alice D'SnG."

I heard a gasp from behind me.

"**Let the record show**: Leon Fortenac shall be taken into custody and confined to prison for the next twenty years, without parole, appeal or pardon. This court is dismissed."

Leon stood. His face contorted with rage. I saw spittle forming at the corner of his mouth. He opened his mouth to speak.

A firm voice from behind Leon silenced him with one word. "Quiet!" The oldest Fortenac spoke only one word but that one word conveyed a world of contempt and disdain. There was no doubt in my mind that the one word was full of rejection. That one word from the leader of the family meant that Leon was no longer to be considered a Fortenac.

Leon sat down stunned. His face turned white. He shook his head in shock and disbelief. He looked around. His father and his attorney refused to look at him. His uncle vibrated with his outrage.

The court clerk spoke. "Will the court please rise?"

My legs shook when I stood.

The judge stepped down from his desk and approached the defense attorney. "Thank you for your excellent representation of your client. You are an asset to the profession."

Two police officers entered the court from the side and approached Leon.

The judge proceeded to the prosecutor's table. "Mr. Jaconovich, thank you for your excellent representation for the state. You are an asset to the profession. This case should be in every law book on how a legal case should be presented. You've made something very important happen here today."

"Thank you sir."

Police officers led Leon away. He looked back before he went through the door. His face was still drained of all color and a sheen of sweat reflected light on his upper lip and forehead. I would say that his biggest emotion was bewilderment.

The judge left the courtroom by a different door. It was over. The room was still silent with shock. I heard the sound of footsteps. We silently watched as the two elder Fortenacs left the room.

The defense attorney approached me to shake hands. "Jake, you have earned me more credit for this case than I deserve. You were the one who drove me to do everything according to the highest standard. I think I will now be able to sleep at night."

"You have earned my respect, sir."

I felt Woody's hand on my shoulder. I was thankful for the touch. Everybody averted their eyes when the defense attorney left the room. He'd earned their respect. They would not stare at his defeat. I sighed and wanted nothing more than to sit down.

Woody shook my hand. "Jake, it is an honor to know you. Thank you."

His cousin Ricardo also waited to shake hands. "Mr. Jaconovich, thank you. Something important happened here today. You do realize that don't you."

"I am too numb to recognize much of anything. I am profoundly thankful to have gotten justice for Alice."

It was my turn to leave the room. Micki joined me at the door. We left the room together.

"I knew you could do it."

"Hush."

Mama and Papa were waiting for me just inside the courthouse doors. Micki grinned his feelings of triumph at them. I allowed him to lead me toward the door. Mama hugged me and kissed me.

Papa held me for a minute. "This is the proudest moment of my life son. I am the richest, most powerful man in this country because you are my son."

I pounded Papa on the back. "Thank you. Can we get out of here?" A crowd waited outside the door. It took me a moment to realize they were there because of the trial.

Micki, Mama and Papa led me through the crowd toward a waiting taxi. Several people seemed to be shouting from a long way away. "Mr. Prosecutor tell us what happened?"

I made a statement. "He was convicted."

The reporters pounded me with questions.

"Are you excited to have won the case?"

"Do you think this changed the law in such cases?"

"Where are you going to celebrate?"

The control I'd maintained to get through the trial had drained me. I felt a deep grief washing over me. I stopped and turned to face the crowd. "A young girl was brutally raped and murdered. There is nothing to celebrate in this conviction. Will the law change? I hope to God that it does." I got in the waiting taxi.

I collapsed back against the seat. "Papa, thank you for getting us a car. I don't think I could have walked much farther."

Micki bounced on the seat. "Jake was magnificent. You should have seen him. He was so calm. He treated everybody with respect. It was so obvious that he was all over the case, in every detail."

Mama held one of my hands in both of hers. "It is over son."

I nodded.

"Jake, you were so great. Your voice was perfect. Every word you said was clear and full of command."

My hands were shaking. "I have never been that terrified in my whole life."

Mama patted my hand. What I wanted most was for my mama to pat my hand and tell me everything was okay. "It is over Jake. You did your best and it was good enough. I knew you would win."

I swallowed. "I didn't. I didn't fully realize it until the judge was handing down the sentence. It was an un-winnable case. Nobody has ever been convicted in such a case before."

Papa asked, "What does that teach you son?"

"Huh? Papa…what?"

"What does that teach you?"

Papa and his questions, I was supposed to learn something? "Um…are you trying to tell me something about no case being unwinnable?"

"Jake, I am trying to tell you that you made today happen. You can make a difference in this world. You have made a difference."

At the train station, I wanted to hide in the stationmaster's office. People turned to stare when we walked into the station. A woman about mama's age came up to me.

"Are you the man who just got Leon Fortenac sent to prison for rape and murder?"

I nodded.

She lifted my hand to her lips and kissed it. I felt her tears falling on my hand as she clasped it in both of hers. "Thank you. I had a younger sister who…" She choked. "I had a younger sister. Thank you." She turned into the arms of the man standing behind her and sobbed. The man looked sad when he met my eyes and nodded. He reached out his hand and placed it on a young girl's head. His eyes traveled from his daughter's head and back to my face. He nodded again.

The D'SnGs and Uzaras arrived at the station before I could hide in the office. They passed me from person to person, hugging me and pounding me on the back. Their faces were a haze of mingled smiles and tears. I was thankful that the D'SnGs train left almost immediately.

Violet D'SnG gave me a hug. "Now young man when you come north, I don't want you spending your nights stealing boats. You come visit me if you want some action." I stared. She laughed at me. "You don't think I know what you young men get up to, but I know most everything that happens in town."

We finally headed home on the same train as most of the Uzaras. Woody and Ricardo came to our compartment excited by the victory. They seemed to agree with Micki.

Woody said, "You should have seen him. He acted so cool and confident.

He obviously knew every word on every document. The judge was so impressed with his case."

I moaned, "Guys."

"No you did a fantastic job."

My parents sat quiet. They satisfied themselves with looking at me and smiling a great deal. Mama patted my hand.

I decided to spread credit around. "I was pleased with the judge's professionalism. I'm not sure another judge would have returned the same verdict. Of course, with you threatening to kill every Fortenac in the country, perhaps another judge might have seen things your way."

Woody sounded almost indignant. "I did not threaten to kill every Fortenac in the country."

Ricardo whined, "No you left that job to me. I am thankful we will not have to do so." He fell back in his seat. "Oh God am I thankful this turned out the way it did. Someone would have gone after Fortenac." He ran his hands over his face. "They probably--well might have--started a civil war."

A crowd turned out to meet us at the M'TK station. I just wanted my dinner and to spend a quiet evening with my family. When I got off of the train Mr. Apkouta waited to hand me down. He caught me up in a hug, then slung me over his shoulder and carried me to a bench in the open air waiting area. He propped me up on the bench. "Jake stand here. They want to see you." The people cheered. I held up my hands for silence. I looked and saw mostly the faces of the people who fled the M'TK fire on the train.

My heart filled with love for these people. "Friends, it is good to be home. As you know, today, for the first time in this country a man, from a prominent, powerful family was convicted of the rape and murder of a young girl. Today did not happen because of one man. Today happened because all of you worked together to teach a young boy about community, justice and honor." I took a breath. "To me this is the most repugnant of all crimes. It must stop. Every citizen of this country must act to keep our children, especially our young girls, safe. Today, the courts have proven that they are willing to take the leadership in protecting our children. Thank you for your love and support." The crowd cheered some more. I stepped down and was allowed to slip through the crowd and into the station office.

Mrs. Apkouta had dinner ready for us. I kissed her on top of her head before I eased into a chair. "This is what I have wanted most—to sit down with my family and have a good, home-cooked dinner."

Micki filled everyone in on the details of the trial. I sat and ate. I concentrated more on the taste of the food than the conversation. Mrs. Apkouta is a good cook. It was an excellent dinner. The food stands out in my memory as one of the best dinners I've eaten. I knew she'd taken extra care. This tribute touched me more than the cheering crowds. Finally, the crowd at the station had gone home. I could go to my own apartment and go to sleep.

Papa still acted solicitous. "Should I call you a taxi?"

"No, I'll catch the trolley or walk."

"It's late. The trolley won't be by for a half hour."

"I'll walk."

Mama dithered, "Sweetheart, I worry about you walking alone in the dark. You are a big hero to most people, but the Fortenacs will be angry."

I had to laugh. "Mama, are you suggesting that The M'TK Sewer Rat cannot walk through M'TK? I will be fine. I am careful. I can still read the street. I think I need the exercise of walking as much as I need sleep." I kissed Mama on her forehead.

Mama worried for nothing. M'TK, and the rest of the city slept in peace. I walked three blocks before I changed direction and went to the cathedral.

It was well after eleven at night when I entered the cathedral. I moved silently to the table in the front where the prayer candles are kept. I took one, lit it and set it in a holder. I noticed that my hand shook as I took the second candle, lit it and set it beside the first. I was vaguely aware of a tear running down my face. I knelt at the alter rail and began the prayer that I prayed for Kaylee. I couldn't pray. I broke down and cried. I sobbed.

I don't know how long I knelt at that rail allowing the little boy in me to cry for Kaylee. "She is avenged." I told myself. "You gave all the little girls justice today." I still sobbed.

I jumped when I felt a hand on my shoulder. I turned and found the priest beside me. His wrinkled old face looked peaceful in the candlelight. His eyes looked sad but his lips smiled slightly. "I heard the verdict. I have been praying for you, for all of us."

I turned and sat on the kneeling bench with my back resting on the communion rail. "These things should not happen to defenseless little girls."

The priest sighed. "I am about to say the midnight mass. Will you stay? We can dedicate this mass to Alice. That was her name wasn't it?"

"Yes, Alice." I swallowed and look at my old friend. "Would you dedicate it to Kaylee?"

Chapter 23 Constitutional Committee

About two weeks after the trial, I began to notice the world around me again. I saw a newspaper report of another bombing in the north. I worried about backlash and violence in the villages, but Micki's Mama wrote often assuring him that all was peaceful. She thought the bombings were the work of *"somebody's brat kid who needs to do some hard work."* She told us that every so often they get a crime wave that turns out to be the work of one young adult. He gets caught and life settles into a peaceful routine again.

I got an invitation to a student/faculty meeting at Professor Ingleman's house. I'd only seen these men twice since I graduated. I was curious about what the group was doing, so I went. I knew this meeting was different when I entered the room. In the past we'd met in a sitting room. Today we met in a room with a large table in the middle. The professors and some students sat around the table. I nodded to my martial arts professor and took the chair saved for me. Professor Ingleman introduced the students. I nodded at them and looked down at the packet of papers in front of me. It was titled, "The Constitution of..." I flipped through a few pages of the document then I looked up at the excited men around me. They looked back at me, grinning.

Stunned, I almost whispered. "You have got to be kidding me."

Professor Ingleman replied, "No, we are not kidding."

"How on earth do you intend to enact such a thing? A civil war is unthinkable!"

My old English teacher looked at me with tears in his eyes. "No Jake. No war."

One of the physics professors explained. "We think we can get the people to pass this. We want you to look at it. Tell us what you think. We do not want war. That would defeat our whole purpose."

I glanced at the introduction to the proposed constitution. *"The case of The State vs. Leon Fortenac has fundamentally changed the way we must look at the citizens of our country."*

"What?" I looked up with my mouth hanging open.

Professor Stodola smiled. "That's right Jake. You gave us the opening we needed."

"What opening?"

Professor Ingleman started to lecture. "Fortenac claimed he was innocent because his victim had the last name of D'SnG. You showed the court that her last name was not enough. When you looked into her background, you found her to be related to several of the old families."

My legal history professor interrupted Professor Ingleman. "Jake that information was entered into the record. The same family history is true for most people in this country."

Professor Ingleman interrupted his friend. "How many degrees of separation are there between one of the old families, as they are called, and the northern families?"

My English professor jumped into the excited discussion. "Perhaps there is still separation in some of the isolated areas. But, in the cities and villages—anywhere we have any industry the families have intermarried."

Professor Ingleman summed up triumphantly, "If a Fortenac cannot win a case in court based on the separation, we have to extend equal rights to all those people."

"I think you are stretching the case a bit." I scratched my nose. "The lines are very blurry." I thought for a few more minutes. "I wonder, how would this play out as a court case?"

Now it was the other men's turn to stare with open mouths. Professor Stodola spoke. "What?"

I was thinking out loud more than stating a fully formed idea. "To get your new constitution accepted, can you sue the state on the grounds that the current *Letters of Federation* do not reflect the composition of our population?"

Professor Ingleman almost gloated. "This is why I brought him here the first time. He's a little rough around the edges sometimes, but he can think through a problem."

I complained. "What me? Rough around the edges? I was such an innocent when I was in school."

Professor Ingleman waved his hand at my protest and chuckled. "You were an innocent who would stand up to your teachers and classmates and tell them in no uncertain terms that they were wrong."

I corrected him. "The exact word was, *mistaken*."

Professor History of Law chuckled. "I've seen you when you are telling someone they are mistaken. It is frightening."

"I don't intend to be intimidating. I do get angry at people, who should know better."

The men chuckled.

We spent two hours going over the details of the new constitution. It did not vary from the old *Letters of Federation* except in allowing for elected government and extending more rights to people from the north. I tapped one page. "I like this part about university enrollment"

Professor Ingleman asked. "So Jake, what do you think?"

"I need to read the whole thing again and think on it. The changes are needed. People in power will not like this. Are they likely to go on purges? Starting with this university? I am not popular in some circles."

Our oldest professor spoke up. "We don't think the Vanderholms have enough power right now to go on a purge. They are more likely to withhold grain."

"People in this country need to eat something other than grain." I started thinking out loud again. "I suppose we can encourage farmers to grow more potatoes. Mama has been growing potatoes ever since she returned from the US. She said they bake them and fry them and they are delicious." I unhooked my brain from thoughts of food. "What I mean here is that before we anger the Vanderholms can we build some infrastructure to substitute for the grain?"

"Wouldn't that take too long?" One of the Spencer family students asked.

I shook my head. "About three to four months for the potatoes. You need to spend more time in groundwork before this goes to court anyway. I think you need to find a judge in every province who will hear your case and make a ruling."

I rubbed the back of my neck. I think the hairs were standing on end as I calmly discussed the legal procedure for the overthrow of the current government. "You need to set a goal for when you want this to go to court. I suggest taking depositions from thousands of people, asking them about their family connections."

A law student spoke up. "Uh...yeah...we heard that you had an unheard of number of depositions."

"Yes, I went through every line of Fortenac's statement. I then found three people to refute each point and deposed them. You might look at the constitution in that light." I laughed. "By the time you have your case ready for court. We may have time to harvest those potatoes. I will talk to Mama about them."

We sat silent thinking for several minutes. One of my law professors spoke up. "I think we can do this. Let's explore Jake's suggestion of taking the problem to the courts."

I warned them. "You may get thrown out on the grounds that our current *Letters of Federation* already allow for the process of proving one's connection to an old family. I did it within the laws of the existing structure."

The conversation became general. "Can we present this as streamlining the process?"

The physics professor impressed me with his thinking on a legal matter. "Do we need to get people willing to go to court to get the right to stand for office?"

I liked the direction of the conversation. "He's onto a viable possibility there. We might want to start with a few people applying for appointment as mayor of their village, or a public commissioner of water rights, or commissioner of transportation. Put them through the court process of proving their eligibility in order to build a bigger base of evidence for your constitutional case."

The man next to me slapped me on the back. "Ten years ago when we first started meeting to talk about social justice, I never would have thought the day would come when we would be discussing a viable strategy for introducing a new constitution through civil proceedings. This is amazing." The others mumbled their amazement that they had come so far.

I snorted. "The problem with our government and our *Letters of Federation* is that they are based on a system of lies. Why are you amazed that when the system of lies starts to break down, we can see how to change? We will have change."

Professor Stodola proclaimed, "And, Jake will be our first president under a new constitution."

I rocked back in my chair. "You are beginning to sound like my Mama. I am a lawyer. I am not a politician."

Professor Stodola asked, "How long did it take you to prepare the speech you gave the other night at the M'TK station?"

"What speech?"

"You stood on a bench at the station and gave a speech."

"Did I?" I thought back. I remembered Apkouta standing me up on a bench. "That was not a speech. I was just talking to my friends who came to the station to welcome me home. How did you hear about that?"

Professor Ingleman answered. "It was printed in the paper along with speculations about you entering politics."

I snorted. "They probably got it wrong."

The men laughed at me.

The physics professor said, "Jake, you might think seriously about politics. You are equipped to run this country."

I shook my head.

The oldest professor spoke up. "Think about it. You have been here less than three hours. You grasped what we are doing. You've seen how we can accomplish our goal peacefully. You saw the legal side, but you also immediately grasped the social problem. Vanderholm may withhold grain. You suggested potatoes as an alternative. I think you have at least half a plan for shifting more farmers to growing potatoes to substitute for the lost grain. You will do very well at running this country. But don't worry. You are too young. You need a wife."

"Yes, I would like to have some time to work on the wife project."

Chapter 24 Dating

I was lonely. Andy got married. I dated his wife's sister for a few months. She was pretty enough with a cloud of dark very curly hair around her face. She seemed smart enough until I realized that I was so bored I wanted to scream.

I dated a lively, funny Chinese girl from the laundry where I took my shirts. I liked her, but her family would never let her marry a man who wasn't Chinese.

Johan introduced me to a violinist from the symphony. I enjoyed having her for a date. She was very intelligent, she was interested in nothing but music. My world seemed too mundane and real to her.

I had to visit the north a couple times. I visited Violet Uzara D'SnG. Over tea and cake in her sitting room, she told me that Leah had been to visit and expressed her condolences to the family and thankfulness that the court decided to convict.

The old lady smiled and raised an eyebrow. "She is certainly impressed with you. She talked about how you acted so polite to everybody when you brought them in for depositions. She says she had never met someone who could be so gentle and kind and still be able to pull off what you did." The old woman chuckled. "I was impressed with her courtesy and grace. She showed just the right amount of compassion and discretion in not wanting to intrude on the family. She said that she felt like part of the case and wanted the family to know that she supported your efforts."

I tried to sound casual, I knew my words came out a bit faster and more intense than I intended, "Um, do you know anything about her, other than what she told you? Is she seeing someone?"

"I think she wants to see someone." The old woman gave me a significant look.

"Both she and the court recorder worked hard on that case with all the people I deposed. She was always polite even though her mother was ill at home and I was making tons of work for her at work." I held in a sigh.

"Perhaps I should take the court recorder a huge bouquet for her role in the case. I think the secretary who put up with us should have a nice gift too, perhaps chocolates?"

The next time I went north, I carried specialty chocolates from a shop in the capital and a bouquet of pink roses. Leah accepted my offerings with a delightful blush. I felt self-conscious and didn't want to seem pushy. "I feel a bit like a brute making you work so hard at the office when your mama was so ill."

"I didn't mind. The case was important. Working on that case was the first important thing I've ever done outside of taking care of Mama. Actually the case took my mind off of Mama and made me feel like I was making a difference."

"You did make a difference."

"Thank you for telling me. I felt so helpless watching Mama die." Leah looked up at me through her beautiful lashes as if I was one of her chocolates.

The prosecutor came out of the back office with a client. "Leah can you copy…Oh Jake! I wasn't expecting you. I am glad you're here. I need to pick your brain. We've endured a series of small bombings. Any thoughts?"

I forced my eyes away from Leah as she excused herself to go run the photocopies. I replied, "Yeah, we've been getting letters about the problem. Could be a gang but I think it's just one punk kid."

He growled. "You're probably right. That is the pattern of crime here. Most of the time nothing happens other than fights between the canneries, the company fishermen and the independent fishermen. Every so often we get a bad apple. That is what we have now, but we can't figure out who it is. Usually, everybody knows or has a good idea who the perpetrator is, but this time, we have no idea."

I gave the prosecutor a ride up the coast to Midville in the Ona Elsee. Nicki served as my captain for the day. I told him I hoped he didn't get tired of carting me up and down the coast.

"I don't mind. It gets me out of The Cove. I can run some errands in the village.

The prosecutor winked at Nicki. "Would those errands involve a school teacher?"

Nicki grinned. "Everything I do involves a school teacher."

I slapped him on the back. "Is this serious?"

"Yeah, as soon as we work out some details. She doesn't want to live at The Cove. I don't blame her. I'd like to work at something other than fishing but I don't know what."

"Let me think. I can look over the situation at the railroad and see if there is something there."

The prosecutor asked, "Could he run that trolley between the villages? That was a lifesaver when we were working on the Fortenac case."

"I'm not certain there would be enough traffic to make it financially viable unless he could also be carrying supplies."

Nicki grinned. "Jake, can I see if I can drum up enough business to make the trolley-line bring in enough money to give me a job?"

"Research away. You could also supplement the trolley work with other work at the station. I wonder if you could get tax money to run a library trolley. None of these villages has a library."

Nicki sounded skeptical. "Do we need one?"

I tried to explain. "Yes, the library is…was…I don't know how to explain this."

The prosecutor helped me out. "Libraries are essential to an educated populace, which is why we do not have them. I am for the library plan. God knows I go crazy for something to read."

I nodded. "Yeah, I had that problem when I worked for Uncle John. There isn't much to do on a boat while waiting for the fish to find your nets."

The prosecutor sounded surprised. "You are related to John D'NO?"

"My grandmother on Mama's side was his sister."

My attorney friend stared at me. "The dastardly D'NOs are related to the Rouseffs?"

"This surprises you? We are on a D'NO boat. Rouseff opened the railroad dock to the independent fishermen and supplies fuel for the independent fishermen. The railroad ships their catch south."

"A D'NO woman married a Rouseff?"

"She is a well respected member of the family. She traveled to the United States with Mr. Rouseff and his wife. She has been instrumental in diversifying railroad interests. She is the connection for the independent fishermen that brought fresh fish to the markets in the capital and to the M'TK market. Mama is talked about as being beautiful, gracious and intelligent. She attends society parties in our city."

The prosecutor looked from me to Nicki and back again. "Jake, do you have any idea of the implications of all this intermarrying?"

"Yes. Yes I do. Many of the beliefs that run this country and dictate who has rights and who does not are based on lies. As the lies become revealed, our society will change." I didn't mention that I had a copy of a proposed constitution sitting in my apartment.

During lunch we discussed the case of the bomber. I didn't have much insight for my friend. "I'm sorry I am not more help. In the city we round up large batches of perpetrators every week. I process them. Mostly, we release them and round them up again the next week." I chuckled. "I am in trouble with my boss for telling the prostitutes to move their business outside the city. They have built a ramshackle maze of tents and shacks in the woods. They call this the pleasure palace. They don't end up as files on my desk, so I am happy. My boss complained about the loss of income from the fines we used to charge them. I finally called him a pimp, and he stopped complaining."

Mr. Prosecutor gave a deep belly laugh. "After the Fortenac win, I imagine that you really can call your boss a pimp and he won't do anything to you."

"Yeah, he has started giving me a few real cases lately. I have one where the person being charged is most likely innocent. The case is arson. Someone set fire to a laundry and ended up burning a whole block of businesses. I think they also tried to frame the person charged."

"You have more interesting work than I do. Maybe I should move to the city. My wife likes it here. She is related to the M'TGs. Which brings up the topic of the Ona Elsee. Her family thinks you are a great hero for getting the boats released."

"What the hell was that anyway? Those fishermen each got a letter from Fortenac saying he had a legal claim against the boats. The letter was done in legal form but had not been presented to court. Who wrote that damn thing up?"

His eyes narrowed. "I didn't hear about the letter."

"It was pure extortion."

The prosecutor looked grim. "I think I will look into this. Does M'TG still have his letter?"

"I told him to save it."

"I'd rather like prosecuting an extortion case. I am getting nowhere on the bombing. Now you have neatly side stepped the discussion at hand and distracted me with a shiny gem. Were you, or were you not, on the dock the night the boats were mysteriously unlocked and the locks were dropped into the water?"

I grinned. "Are you going to depose me?"

"Not unless I can prosecute the extortion case. I take it you want to be deposed."

I grinned and complained. "I only see The Elegant Leah when I need a deposition. She lives miles away from me. How does a man court a woman when he has to ride a train all day, then hope the sea is calm enough to take the boat out, then take a couple hour boat ride?"

I'd mentioned courting Leah. Someone who saw her regularly acted as if this was a good idea. He gave me no warnings that Leah was not a good choice for me. We went on to discuss the extortion case and the possibility of a permanent trolley between the villages.

Back in the city, I was not making any progress on the wife project. Micki introduced me to a woman when I took him out to lunch. I asked her out. She was smart. I enjoyed our conversations. After about six weeks I learned that she was not interested in men as sexual partners. I moved on.

Chapter 25 Twenty Minutes in Hell

I had agreed to go with Micki and some of his friends to their first-year receptions.

I briefed them in a park across the road from where the reception was to be held. "Okay, what you are about to experience will not be pleasant or fun. The hostesses will break up any conversation that looks interesting. Have all of you girls been to poise school so you can help the guys out?"

The girls wrinkled their noses and declared poise school to be old fashioned.

"Okay then, here is your crash course. We must stay twenty minutes." I quickly taught them what Candice had taught us. I thought Candice could earn some extra money teaching these kids what they needed to know to get through formal situations.

My hostess was the comptroller's wife, a member of the Gannon family, I think. She smiled at me and treated me cordially. She explained, "We are always so happy when our alumni support these events."

"I remember my first reception. I was terrified."

She smiled. I thought it looked like a triumphal smirk. "You were always perfectly well behaved."

"I was too terrified to misbehave. You'll find Micki an altogether different person. He's afraid of nothing."

"Perhaps he has more experience with formal events."

I wanted to sweat. "Micki has always been ready for any adventure. No, if anything, he has less experience at formal events. Perhaps it is ignorance that makes him bold."

When she let me attend to my charges, I whispered instructions. "Right, now, this is the part where you divide into groups of two and walk very slowly the length of the room with a pleasant expression on your face." I tried to demonstrate as Candice had done. The girls giggled, but they tried to look appropriately serious and pleasant as they strolled the room.

Professor Stodola intercepted me enthusiastically. "Jake! Jake, glad to see you here." He grabbed me in a sparring hold. I countered. He made another move. I countered.

Micki slapped both hands to his cheeks and hissed. "Cousin Jake please, do not disgrace me by throwing a professor across the room. I'm sure that is frowned upon."

"Micki," I grunted back not wanting to break my concentration and end up tossed down myself. "I do not intend to throw him, but he attacked first, and I never allow myself to be thrown." We both laughed and broke off our sparring. I introduced Micki.

Micki shook Professor Stodola's hand eagerly. "Sir, I intend to take your class next term. The family insists. I hope you won't expect me to be anywhere near as good as Jake."

"Do you have training too?"

"No."

The professor turned to me with one of his carnivorous smiles. "Bring your cousin down to my gym and get him started training. I wouldn't mind having your help with some of my private students when you are free."

I thought for a minute. "You know sir. I think I'd like to take you up on that. I need to exercise. I miss the discipline. I might have to bail out on you if I get another big case. Right now I am back to processing petty criminals."

"I heard you were prosecuting the laundry fire case."

"They arrested the wrong man. I let him go."

Professor Ingleman interrupted us. "Jake when are you going to come in and talk to my class about the Fortenac case?"

"Why would you want me to?"

"The judge says it should be in every text book. Can you explain to the students how doing things correctly and working the details led you to win an impossible case?"

"I can talk about the importance of proper procedure."

"Good. Good, I'll call you to set up a date."

I saw my former history teacher headed my direction and nearly panicked. Excuse me Professor, "I am in charge of my cousin and his friends. I see one of the boys being a pig at the refreshment table and the girls are starting to giggle. I better get them in hand before one of the hostesses eats them."

Professor Stodola chuckled, "By all means, it is hard on the faculty when the grande dames decimate our classrooms by dining on all the most promising students."

We both laughed and I went off to get the boy away from the refreshments and subdue the girls.

After twenty minutes, I had greeted some other faculty, and been irritated by my history professor. "That cousin of yours is certainly cheeky."

I tried to sound innocent. "Who Micki?"

"When I commented that he certainly had a northern name, he told me that his grandmother laughs about running off with a D'NO and declaring it the best decision she ever made."

I nodded judiciously. "It was a very good decision on her part. The D'NOs are some of the wealthiest, wisest and most educated people I have ever met. They do not make a big noise about their business like some do, but they are one of the most influential families in this country. I think grandmamma's family was pleased enough with the alliance."

"Well perhaps they have intermarried with southern families sufficiently to dilute the northern blood."

I remembered not to throw the professor across the room. "Excuse me I see a hostesses terrorizing one of the young girls I am chaperoning."

The minute I stepped up beside Shayla and placed my hand in the middle of her back, the grand dame who was interrogating her changed from scowls to smiles and declared that if Shayla was with me, she was okay.

The poor girl turned to me looking pale and on the verge of tears. "Can we leave now? What do these old women mean by being so rude to us?"

I remembered to breathe deeply and refrain from growling. "They mean to maintain control over society. They mean to control who will be appointed to political offices. They mean to control who will get the good jobs. They mean to feed on power and control. Until this system changes, young people will need to be very careful. Our twenty minutes in hell are almost over. Let's get the others and start moving toward the doors with our chins up pleasant smiles fixed on our faces."

"I don't feel like smiling pleasantly."

I was afraid any sympathy would cause poor Shayla to break down and sob. "Tough, do it anyway."

As soon as I was outside with my charges, I drew in my first easy breath of the evening. "I am not sure if I feel as sick after this event as I did after my first one, but that was hellish."

Shayla started to regain her color in the fresh air. "Jake just called that twenty minutes in hell." The name caught on among the students. As the year progressed, I heard some of the faculty using the title too.

I started giving a few lectures in some of the law classes. I found I liked teaching. I also started teaching martial arts. I really wanted to work with the youngest children. The Master wanted me to work with the older students who were getting cocky. I didn't like throwing them, but I would not let them throw me.

I was working on construction contracts for Mr. Rouseff. He couldn't find enough workers. He scoured mountain villages looking for men or women who were willing to work. We turned some organizational work over to Nicki, which gave him enough income to plan his wedding. I was honored when he asked me to be his best man.

Nicki's wedding became the event of the year in Oceana province. His bride was one of Violet Uzara's granddaughters. The D'SnG/Uzara family seemed relieved to have something to celebrate and welcomed an alliance with the D'NO family. Our family was just happy for Nicki. Uncle John acted a little grumpy about Nicki's bride, Lucinda, not wanting to live in The Cove.

Mama spoke severely to him. "Uncle John, that family has had enough grief this year to last them a lifetime. You cannot seriously be thinking of taking another of their girls away from them by insisting she live in The Cove."

He looked at Mama and winced. "No. No you are right. I am becoming a fretful old man. Let her live close to her family. We will still see Nicki almost every day. He is taking over the job of the shipping clerk too. He will still work with us, shipping our fish south."

We shipped my trolley north for the wedding to help us travel between the villages for all the parties. As soon as we arrived in the north, Violet D'SnG held a big dinner for the wedding party. The next night, the men held a party for Nicki on a small island just south of The Cove. Most of the men got drunk. They hired a couple exotic dancers for entertainment.

One of the women seemed eager for a little more than dancing. The woman who called herself Desdemona was a buxom blond. I figured she was in her early thirties although she insisted that she was only twenty-one. Perhaps her life was so hard she only looked older. She acted excited to meet me and gushed over the Fortenac case. I soon became convinced that she was more interested in my body than in the finer points of legal procedure. I took the opportunity to lose my virginity.

Desdemona seemed to get more enjoyment out of the experience than I did. Her ample bosom was lush and soft. I buried my face between her breasts only to have my brain bring up an image of Leah with her braid hanging down to the soft swell of her breasts. I immediately redirected my thoughts to someone else. I latched onto my memories of Fiona and how she jiggled in her red dress the night we met. I remembered Fiona's endearments. I think I really made love to Fiona while keeping thoughts of Leah just below the surface of my conscious mind.

Poor Desdemona may have been happy to have sex with Prosecutor Jaconovich, but Jake made love to the woman in his memory.

Of course there was a bride's party. Mama wore high heels and one of her tea dresses. She looked smashing. Everybody commented on her beauty. I noticed tears in Papa's eyes when he saw Mama dressed up and looking so elegant. I put my arm around him. "Papa you picked a stunner. That's for certain."

He gave me a hug. I smiled and felt profoundly thankful for having two parents who loved each other. I once again acknowledged their love as my greatest treasure.

I made a brief visit to the prosecutor, while I was there. He was excited to be prosecuting some of the parties to the extortion. "I don't care if these people were acting under orders from Leon. They could have come to me. I had no idea that Leon did not have any right to lock up those boats. He told me he had loaned the men money. Anyway, Leon is officially not a member of the family anymore. The old man declares that he was never so humiliated in his life as when he learned that Leon had raped and murdered a member of the Uzara family."

I didn't like talking about the trial. "He did look grim at the trial."

"I don't think Leon's father has been sober since before the trial. The autopsy report could not have made pleasant reading for them. I told them to read it. I wanted them to know what he had done. I want to get things for the family sorted out here. The Fortenac cannery is about to go under. They have trouble getting people to work for them. They had to tie up one fishing boat. The cannery is nowhere near capacity. Leon made a mess of things."

I changed the topic. "Have you made any progress on your bomber?"

"No, it was probably some punk kid as we thought. His papa probably caught him and…um…settled his behind. We haven't had any trouble there for months."

"That is best if the family puts a stop to foolish behavior." I forgot about this topic for many years.

After Nicki's wedding I went back to the routine of my life. I had enough money saved to hire an architect for the house I wanted to build on my property. We drove out in the architect's car to look the site over. He started on the drawings. I was building a house and I still didn't have a wife.

The professors working on the constitution disappointed me. I would have gone farther in extending rights to all citizens. I would have made stricter laws on child labor. Still, the constitution represented an improvement. I advised them on court proceedings. We finally decided to present our case to our judges as a procedural case.

Micki turned out to be an excellent student. I never saw him study, but he must have written his papers at some time. He received perfect grades. For his internship project in engineering class, he built a car, a little roadster style thing.

He asked me if he could store it in the garage at my apartment. He didn't know how to drive a car. I sent Candice to help him move it from the engineering lab to my apartment. I was horrified to see them pull up with Micki behind the wheel. Everybody loved Micki's little roadster. It was heavily powered for its weight.

He confessed. "Yeah, I may have over done it a bit on the size of the engine. How do you like my continuous transmission? I wanted the car to feel more like driving a speed boat without all the constant shifting of a car." Micki built the first locally manufactured automatic transmission car in our country.

Mr. Rouseff loved Micki's car so much he set up a small factory to produce them. His wife bought one of the first cars from the factory. Mama could not be left behind on something so new. My parents surprised me by buying a little Miki. Micki had not yet graduated when he became the CEO of the first car factory in the country. He engaged other students who were doing internships in helping him set up the factory. University interns designed the whole operation.

Micki went everywhere with a nice Spinoza girl, but they waited until after graduation to announce their engagement. I didn't have a date for the engagement party. Then I got a phone call at work.

Chapter 26 Leah

The phone rang and I picked it up, "Jaconovich."

A soft, cultured, woman's voice with just a hint of a northern lilt asked, "Is this Jake Jaconovich?"

My heart rate jumped. "Yes."

"This is Leah Fillon."

I felt my face break into a grin. "Yes. Yes, of course. How are you?"

"Jake, I hate to admit this, but I need help." Her voice trembled.

I wondered if the elegant Leah needed a lawyer. I almost leapt from my chair ready to rush to her side.

"I have to move to the city. I need a job and a place to stay."

I wanted to bounce up and down in my chair. My chest swelled. I wanted to draw my sword and rush forth on a white horse. In a calm voice I drawled, "I can arrange both for you. Tell me, what has prompted this move?"

Her voice sounded small and watery. "I…I…um…have a brother. He…um…he…um broke the law. He…is going to prison. I…I…was told that I…I can't work in a law office because my brother is a felon." She gulped and sobbed on the other end of the phone.

I knew she was talking about basic ethical standards. I had never stopped to consider the effect on the innocent of the ruling about relatives of a felon working for the court. "Does your brother need an attorney?"

"No." Her voice grew stronger, it began to shake with rage and anger. "He is guilty. He can go to jail." Her voice turned small and sad again. "Um… Jake…um it is really worse than not taking care of me. It is the shame." She gulped. "I am so embarrassed. He was so senseless and stupid. I…I just want to go away and start over."

I was determined to bring her to the city. "Can you do bookkeeping, typing, filing, billing, what?"

"I did all the office support work here. I can operate copy and duplicating machines. I type. I can do bookkeeping and billing."

"Don't worry. I'll find you something with good pay and working conditions. I can ask at the city offices, the university and the railroad."

"I am embarrassed to be asking for help." Her voice trembled.

I could almost see the tears in her beautiful eyes. "Please don't feel that way. We all need help from time to time. When I first moved out of my parent's home it took three other guys just to help me stay fed and clothed. I didn't know how to do anything for myself. I think finding you a job and a place to stay will be much easier than what my roommates had to endure."

She laughed weakly. "You make me feel better."

"What is your phone number? I'll call you when I have something set up."

"I don't have a phone. I am going to the south to stay with a friend until I get a job. I will call you from there and give you that phone number."

"Will your friends be looking for a job for you too?"

"No! I do not...their connections are not...I do not trust the legality of their business associates. My friend married a Vanderholm. I love her dearly, but I will not have anything to do with their business."

I thought she showed good sense. When we hung up, I wanted to dance and kiss everybody in the office. The beautiful Leah was coming to my city. She had friends. She could have gone to them, but she came to me. Every time I thought about her moving to the city, I grinned.

It did not take me long to find three possible jobs for Leah. It took more time to find three possible boarding houses. She could not stay in a home without a female chaperone. Mama and Papa said she could stay with them in their spare room. Mr. Rouseff found the most appropriate housing. She could have her choice of housing for university women near the university, or for women who worked for the railroad near the railroad offices. Cousin Philippe liked to tease me that he really thought he would put her to work in an office in the capital.

About five days after the first phone call, she called from her friend's house. "I am calling to give you my number here so you can call me when you find a job."

"I have three possible jobs for you and three places to stay. You can take your pick." I thought she started to cry again.

"Jake, how on earth did you do that so fast?"

"We don't have enough workers in the city. Everybody is eager to hire someone with experience. I advised them that you worked in a small office doing everything from bookkeeping, greeting guests, even making coffee and tea, and billing the clients."

"Jake I promise you, I am a good worker. I will work hard. I can't believe you did this so quickly. You must have worked on this for hours."

"This is my home, Leah. Everybody knows me. I know everybody. I made three five-minute phone calls to find job possibilities. I have three places where you might live. They are all respectable, clean and appropriate for... someone in your position." I'd almost said, "...for my future wife."

"How can I ever thank you?"

Prosecutor Jaconovich, the man who got Leon Fortenac convicted, took over my tongue and said what I might have been too shy to say. "You can save me from going to my Cousin Micki's engagement party alone. If you would not mind too much."

"Are you sure you want me to come to such a family party? They do not know me."

I remembered Violet D'SnG admiring Leah's sensibilities about not wanting to intrude. I admired Leah too. "Leah, I've been so busy with work, I don't know any women who will go with me. My friends are all old and settled with children and have given up finding me dates. Micki is marrying a very proper Spinoza girl. The party will be full of Rouseffs and Spinozas, but that can't be helped. My parents will be there to take care of you when I am doing my best-man duties."

"Jake I don't know what to say." I think she started to cry again. "My life has been so hard with Mama dying and then Buddy being so irresponsible."

"Say you will come with me."

"Of course I will be honored to come with you and I will behave very properly."

"Good, now when will you be arriving? I will meet you at the train station."

"Oh! Oh, I don't know. Let me talk to Isolde. She tells me that I do not have the right clothes to work in the city. I have a dress, but she does not think it is the right sort of thing." I remembered Leah's dress, while modest, it was not quite what I saw at the office.

"You know, your friend may be right. I think the women in my office wear suit jackets over their dresses."

She laughed. "Thank you. Isolde is eager take me shopping. Her husband has been eager to help me by telling me how worthless my brother is. While I agree, I don't like to hear it. For that reason, I am eager to leave here.

"You can always shop when you get here. My mama likes to take the train to the capital and shop at Sherif's up there."

"Thank you. I think I will allow Isolde to buy me one good dress with a suit jacket. Then I will call you." I think she started crying again. We hung up.

Leah called the next morning. "Jake, I have my new suit dress. If I catch the morning train, I can be there by four."

"Today?"

"Yes, today if that is okay."

"I will be at the M'TK station to meet you. If for some unforeseeable reason I am delayed, just tell anybody who works there your name. They will take care of you."

"Are you sure?"

"This is my city. In my city, you will be cared for. I have spoken that is final." The moment I rung off with Leah, I called the M'TK station. Mama answered the phone.

"Mama what are you doing in the office."

"Talking to your papa. I like him you know."

I laughed. "I have a friend coming in on the train from the south. This… this is Leah, the woman I mentioned.

"Yes, I think I have heard of her a few times." I could hear the amusement in Mama's voice.

"She is taking the train from the south this morning."

"We will be ready for her."

"I plan to be there to meet her so that my friends do not overwhelm her with questions about whether she wants to be rich and live in a big house or does she call me Jakey."

"We won't embarrass you."

"I know you won't."

Leah arrived on the train as expected. I was on hand to meet her. Wow, she looked good. She wore a dark blue dress that looked fantastic with her blond hair. She wore her hair braided and wrapped over the top of her head. The style was a little old fashioned, but it suited her and added to her elegance.

The poor woman did not quite set foot on the platform before Mr. Apkouta took her bags and ushered her into the station.

Mrs. Apkouta held the door for her.

My mouth went dry. I blurted out the first thing that ran through my head. "I like your hairstyle."

She smiled and blushed. Her eyelashes fluttered down. "I thought a big knot of hair on the back of my head would give me a headache by the time I got here."

"The braid thing is good." I impressed myself with my eloquence. "Come this way. You can stay here until we get your job and housing sorted out."

"At the train station?"

I laughed. "Come upstairs."

Leah was surprised when I opened the door at the top of the stairs. "Oh! Oh what a beautiful room."

The apartment had come a long way from the stark, smoky apartment Mama called a palace when we moved in. The wood floors gleamed with wax. The walls had been painted fresh shades of green, yellow and cream depending on the room. Fresh flowers sat in vases and pots everywhere. The rugs were a warm burgundy color with flower patterns woven into the nap.

"Mama, Papa may I present Leah Fillon. Leah, my parents."

Mama showed Leah the spare bedroom. Mama had decorated it in shades of green and white. Lace curtains hung at the window and a matching lace coverlet draped the bed.

Leah sounded like a little girl. "This is for me? I've never stayed in such a beautiful room."

Normally I would have praised Mama for how she cared for her home. Instead, I said, "You should have seen it when it was my room. There was nothing fancy about it then." I was aware that I was trying to get Leah to pay attention to me rather than her surroundings, but I couldn't stop myself.

The dinner went extremely well. Mrs. Apkouta insisted on serving us. I outlined the jobs I had lined up for Leah. "The railroad job has the added benefit of free rail travel. The university job comes with the opportunity for free university classes. The city job is a job. I don't know. You might like the work there best. Tomorrow I will take you to your interviews and you can decide which you like best."

"Could I really take classes at the university?" Her lovely eyes sparkled and I saw a hint of a smile grace her lips.

"Yes."

Papa said. "You can do that if you work for the railroad. The railroad job pays the best."

Mama patted Leah's hand. "You pick a job based on the type of work you most want to do and the people you think you would most enjoy working with."

Leah leaned back in her chair and placed both hands palm down on the table. "I can hardly believe that there is anyplace on earth where a woman like me can have her choice of three jobs and the luxury of picking what suits me best." Leah's tone turned playful as she said the last three words.

Papa nodded. "That is why Mama and I moved to the city years ago. In the north I could fish or work in a cannery. Here I've had my pick of jobs."

"Are you from the north?"

Mama answered. "I am a D'NO. My mama was John D'NOs sister."

"Have you always lived above the train station?"

Papa answered her question. "Officially I am the stationmaster here. I am the head stationmaster over all the others. Cousin Philippe keeps urging us to move into a separate house, but I need to know on a day to day basis what happens here so I can keep the other stations running more efficiently."

Leah still looked confused. I explained. "Cousin Philippe is Philippe Rouseff. The only reason he did not join us for dinner tonight is that I sent him home with the promise that we would have dinner with him on Sunday. He does live in a proper house." My parents laughed at my talk of proper houses.

I would have stayed and visited longer but Mama kicked me out. "Don't you have some work or a meeting or something? This poor girl is tired. I think she would like a hot bath with scented bubbles and then to go to bed. Go away." I left. Mama seemed happy to have someone to fuss over.

The next day, I took Leah to her appointments and to look over her housing options. "You are welcome to stay with my parents."

"I could not impose on them."

"They travel a great deal and would like to have someone to watch the apartment."

"Where do they travel?"

"Mostly around the country. They visit the other stations. Papa explores the possibility of developing new rail lines. They've been out of the country a few times. Their trip to the United States was the farthest they've gone."

Leah gave me a strange look.

"What? Why are you looking at me like that?"

"The way you talk about traveling to different places. I've never heard such talk in the northern villages."

I shrugged. "My relatives in the north have visited neighboring countries." I omitted that those visits were not strictly legal. "Our relatives certainly know that Mama and Papa travel. Most of my cousins have visited me in the city. My cousin Micki who is getting married, grew up in The Cove."

"I have never heard someone talk so casually about traveling before. Even the Fortenacs puff themselves up and say, 'when I was in the capital…' as if this is a rare and marvelous thing."

I laughed at her imitation of the Fortenacs. "I will take you up to the capital some day soon. We can tour The Compound. Then you can write to your friends and say, 'when I was at The Compound…' and you will sound as if you went there specifically to tell the emperor how to run the country."

"Well, someone needs to tell him how to run the country."

I didn't tell Leah that I knew people who intended to do a great deal more than tell the emperor how to run things.

Leah accepted the job at the university. She intended to take classes. She liked the housing near the campus.

I told her. "When you apply to take classes, you will need a letter from a graduate in order to be accepted. I will write your letter."

Leah seemed a little shy when we went to dinner at the Rouseff's. Her grace and manners pleased everyone.

Mama confided, "Leah and I went shopping yesterday morning to buy a dress for this evening."

"Where did you go?"

"Sherif's," Mama giggled.

"Mama! I was going to take her to the capital to impress her."

"You have done enough to impress her. That poor girl doesn't know downside from up when anyone mentions you."

"Good. It is about time a girl acted a little impressed with me. All my friends have kids."

Mama patted my arm and sighed. "Grandbabys would be wonderful."

I finally learned to drive Micki's car. I took Leah out to my property in the roadster and showed her where I intended to build my house. We stood on top of the ridge and watched the sun go down.

She leaned against me and I put my arms around her. "Jake I think I've forgotten how to be happy. Or, maybe I've never known how to be happy as a woman. I was happy as a child, but ever since I was seventeen I've had too much responsibility. I think I forgot how to be happy. I'll tell you now, I've never been rich, not like your family."

I laughed. "We've had tough times. When I was small, my parents were not rich by any stretch of the imagination. We had everything we needed." I did not tell her about the rats in M'TK then. I thought that could wait until she seemed more comfortable in our relationship. Later, I did not tell her about how poor we were because I recognized that her self-image was very fragile. She would never be able to admire the little boy with his rat-trap. That level of poverty was too frightening to her.

I remember how happy I felt when I was with Leah. She was quiet and refined. She was obviously smart. We talked about books we read. We talked about her college classes. She was excited about her art history class. She told me everything about her classes. This felt like sitting at our table with Mama and Papa and talking about the books we read.

On one date, we attended the symphony. The music moved her to tears. "It is so beautiful. I never knew that such beauty existed. Your world is so much more beautiful than mine."

"There has always been great beauty in your world. You have only to look in a mirror."

Her lashes dropped. "That kind of talk will get you in trouble. I just might follow you home."

I snuggled closer to her and kissed her forehead before I became serious. "Sweetheart, you have had a rough time. You've been abandoned and alone. I want to be with you. I think we have something special going here."

She lifted her eyes to mine and smiled at me.

I remembered what I'd started to say. "I would love nothing more than to take you to bed. I don't want to rush things between us. I want you to feel like you could take care of yourself. I want us to be together as equals."

She rubbed against me and rested her head on my shoulder. "You are so sweet and wise. I will wait. I admit that I still have times when I am frightened. I want to feel independent. I want our relationship to be one of equals, like your parents." She'd said the magic words. She wanted a relationship like Mama and Papa had. We waited three more months before we became lovers.

Leah had lived in the city for ten months when we decided to get married.

I wanted a big wedding. I wanted to see her in a beautiful wedding gown. I wanted my friends to stand up with me.

She burst into tears. "Oh Jake, what you are talking about is every little girl's dream. You have no idea how many times I imagined myself in so many different wedding dresses walking down the long aisle of a cathedral. It is what I want more than anything except to be with you."

"I hear the word 'but' somewhere in your speech."

"You are so amazing. Yes, there is a 'but' in what I want. But, my papa died. He cannot walk me down the aisle. But, my mama died. She would not be there to fuss over me and plan the details. But, my brother is in prison. But, most of my childhood friends married and moved away. I lost track of them. But, we would not be marrying as equals. You are bringing me a large respected family and excellent connections. I have a friend who is married to a Vanderholm. Her husband will not let her come to my wedding." Leah started crying. I held her in my arms.

"Sweetheart, this is not worth crying over. I see your point. I am not a selfish brute. We can have a quiet wedding." She smiled at me with wet lashes. I would have liked to at least have the wedding in my cathedral with my priest. We went to the courthouse.

We had a grand reception at the Rouseff's house. I think about two hundred people attended. I don't remember much about the reception. It was rather noisy. Leah looked beautiful and elegant. Everyone looked at her and declared that they now knew what I had been looking for. They declared her to be perfect.

Chapter 27 Corruption

The construction was due to start on my house. Leah and I had gone over the plans. She made a few changes that seemed sensible. She was still working at the university and taking a few classes, mostly in the arts. We went out to the building site almost every evening. We would admire the progress then watch the sun go down.

She enjoyed teasing me about how many bedrooms I wanted in the house. "Do you need new places to make love to me every night?"

"No, my wife. I expect the love making to produce children to sleep in those bedrooms."

"Are all of our children to have their own rooms to sleep in?" She sounded surprised.

"Of course. I did. After Mama's illness, when we moved back to the city, I had my own bedroom. I had my own room at The Cove although I was still a baby and wanted to be near my mama or my cousins."

We bought a Miki car. I loved the ease of being able to get somewhere without waiting for the trolley then walking two blocks. When I realized that I put on five kilos. I decided the car was for trips outside the city. I took Leah out and taught her to drive the thing. She used it to get back and forth to work.

I was extremely proud of myself when Leah said she was pregnant. Our house was being built, but progress seemed way too slow to suit me. On Saturdays, I would go out to the site and help the men and encourage them along by telling them that my wife was pregnant and we needed a roof over our heads before the baby came. I hauled lumber and learned to pound nails. Leah laughed at me for working on the house. I kissed her and insisted that our child was going to come home to our own house.

At the same time, I was advising on the legal background for the constitution. The men working on the constitution were making progress toward getting more court documentation that people with northern names were still members of the ruling families.

I still worked for Rouseff and also in the prosecutor's office. I suddenly got a breakthrough in a case I had set aside for months.

I was working in the prosecutor's office and had just taken a client to my desk. He was a small, wiry man. I guessed him to be about Papa's age. "Mr. Jake you know me, don cha?"

"Of course, Mr. S'PnG, you are in here regularly." He was a repeat offender for drunk and disorderly charges. We'd fine him and let him go. Two weeks later, we would repeat the procedure. I'd not processed him for several months, but I saw him when he was in.

"Well, da ding is, I seen somfing."

I raised my eyebrows.

"I nivver said anyfing 'cause I don wan ta get killed."

I leaned forward in my seat.

"I never said nofing ta nobody else 'cause dey'd betray me like."

I wondered what this old drunk could have seen that made him fear for his life. "I figure you are an hones man. I heerd how your papa saved all dose people when M'TK burned. I heerd how you got dat Fortenac. I remember da M'TK Sewer Rat."

I smiled.

"I figure I cin trust you."

I nodded.

"I seen some men. Da night da laundry caught fire, I seen dem and I heerd dem."

I looked around to see if anybody noticed us or could overhear us. I didn't ask him why he had not come forward sooner. I knew the city. I understood why he had not said anything sooner. I pulled out a legal pad. I wrote the case number for the fire on the top of the page and labeled it Source: Q. "Mr. S'PnG this is very important. It will help me a great deal."

"Well, I saw dat cop."

I felt like a bucket of ice water had been dumped over me. "Which police officer was that?"

"Da one what said dat other fella did it…um…skinny guy, Stash, dey calls him on da street. Yeah, Stash, says Mantega on his badge."

"I know the man." This was the man who was responsible for the arrest of the first man I processed for the fire.

"I figgered you'd know him. Know everyone, doncha. Ya, I see dat little sewer rat in your eyes. You look all growed up an fancy, but you still da kid who ran trew M'TK screaming his head off 'bout da fire."

I looked the man in the eye and smiled at the memory.

"You ant one oh dem, so I tell ya."

I tried not to be impatient.

"It were Stash, an anoder fella dey named Boney cause he's French, an anodder one dey called Munk. Now I sees them, Stash he tells dem where ta dump the fuel. It weren't gasoline like da paper said. I smelled it. It were more like kerosene. I dink it were de cleaning fluid from da laundry."

We'd told the papers, the arsonist used gasoline, but the accelerant had actually been cleaning fluid. I knew I had an eye-witness in front of me. I shivered.

"Stash, he tells dem ta spread some fluid on da next buildings. They trew da stuff on da roof ta da shed by da restaurant. Then Stash says fo da odder fellas to leave. He lit da cigar. I saw da end of it light up and I smelled da smoke. It smelled like a real good cigar. When it were goin good he trew it in da dead grass by da laundry and ran ta da end of da street. I ran inta da alley across da street and followed it ta da main road ta see what Stash would do. He goes about his bisness jus as if nofink is happenin. I sees the fire, but he don do nofink."

I felt like more ice water was dumped over me. I wondered where I could hide this old man. "Mr. S'PnG Can you must leave the city. Do you have any family here that will need to go with you?"

"I got nobody. You tink maybe I drink if I had a woman in my bed? I had a woman. I had babies. Fever got em all. Now I got da bottle."

"Can you tell me more about the men involved? Who is Munk?"

"I don know him. Dat is his name. His last name is Munk. De one dey call Boney is French. I tink his real name is Jouyet."

I felt like more ice water was dumped over me. I rubbed my hands over my face.

"Da odder day, I saw Munk and Jouyet go inta a restaurant. Dey was dressed all fancy."

"How can you be certain it was the same men?"

"By da voices. I know da voices. I have da good ear. I used ta play da violin. I got da good ear. I know da voices."

"Where is your family from?"

"Da eastern border. Da mountains are rough. Dere is no work. It is cold in da winter."

"Do you have cousins there?"

"Dere was da purge when I was jus a young man. Da mines were not safe. Da men refused ta work in the mines. Da bosses, dey come trew wid da machine guns and dey shoot all da people. My mama was at da market. Dey shot da school children. I was home alone. My family din come home dat day. Dey neber came home."

"Can you go home and get whatever belongings are important to you and meet me at the M'TK station by three?"

"Yeah, I kin do dis. I don wan dem ta come for me."

"Good, remember that."

I sent Mr. S'PnG on his way. I continued to sit at my desk pretending to process files. After a half hour, I got up and got the file on the fire from the file room. I looked around me wondering who was safe and who was corrupt. Corruption was common in the city. I wondered if I should just ignore this case. Where could I send S'PnG? I thought about The Cove. I did not want to endanger my family. I did not want to burden them with a man with a drinking problem. Who did I know who lived outside of the city? My mind turned over names. As pictures drifted through my mind, I remembered Mr. Pickett. I looked at my phone. Was it tapped? I decided to walk to the M'TK station and make the call from there.

I was successful in reaching Mr. Picket's daughter from the phone at the station. I explained that I needed to keep a witness safe.

She promised. "Mr. Jake, you just have to ask."

"I'm asking. It won't be easy. The man drinks. Maybe he has reasons to drink. I don't want him getting drunk and bragging about what he knows. I don't want him dying of drink either."

"I understand. Don't worry. He won't talk and he won't die. My husband will pick him up from the train about five-forty five."

"While waiting for Mr. S'PnG to show up, I made another phone call. I learned that Judge Gannon in the capital was in court. His secretary did not know when he would be free. I left a message that my wife and I would be visiting the capital and I would like to see him. I left my home phone number.

Mr. S'PnG arrived with a pitifully small sack of belongings. I gave him a lecture on how he was supposed to help out Mr. Picket who was in a wheel chair. "Picket is a clever man and a dead shot. He'll keep you safe." I loaded my witness on the train.

Then I called home. "Leah, I am running around town doing errands. If you haven't started dinner, I will bring you Chinese food."

"Where are you calling from?" She sounded tired.

"The station."

"Why are you there?"

"Business for the railroad. Well, do you want me to bring something?"

"Are your parents there?"

"No. I'm sorry honey. Papa took Mama out to a restaurant in Mercid. He is a better husband than I am. All I am offering is take-out Chinese food. Perhaps I can make it up by taking you to the capital." She laughed. I was relieved. She'd been subject to mood swings ever since she got pregnant.

"I will let you bring me Chinese Food then. Don't bring anything too spicy." I hung up and headed to the Chinese restaurant.

The same family who took care of my laundry owned this restaurant. At the front desk, I met one of the women who worked in the laundry. She ducked her head in the slightest of bows. "Ah it is the man with the new wife. I thought maybe you would not bring your clothes to us when you have a wife."

"You see, not only do I still bring you my shirts, now I bring my wife's dresses."

She scolded me. "Your wife does not do your laundry. Now, you are here to take home dinner. I think you spoil this woman."

I grinned. "I like what happens when I spoil my woman. She makes me very happy."

"Ah ha, do you hear that, Kim Su?" She called over her shoulder. "The man says his wife knows how to make him happy, so he brings her the dinner."

I added. "I do not like for her to be so tired." My comment led to a ft of giggling and steered the conversation to where I wanted it to go. "But what about you? You work all day at the laundry and then all evening at the restaurant. Your husband must be very lonely."

She ducked her head and looked away. "I do not work so hard."

"I think you do. I always see you working. The laundry must be very busy after the other laundry burned." I saw the fear in her eyes. She looked to see who might overhear. There was nobody about except Kim Su. There were a few people in the restaurant. I doubted they spoke Chinese.

She leaned toward me and whispered. "The laundry is not so busy." She would not lift her face to mine.

I said rather louder than necessary. "Good, I want you to make that husband of yours a happy man."

"He has no reason to complain."

"I'll bet." I paid for my meal and left. So where were people getting their laundry washed? My plumber had been very impressed and slightly intimidated about my request for a washing machine. I looked at the old buildings of the city. No, people did not have washing machines. Where did they take their laundry? I took the trolley home.

Leah sat on the sofa looking cross when I came in. "Jake, what took you so long to get home?"

I kissed her on the top of her head. "What? I love you. I walked and I picked up our dinner."

"You really should take the car."

"I'm not the one who is pregnant. I want you to take the car. I can walk or take the trolley." Leah's little spell of fretfulness passed with my display of protectiveness. She talked about her work and about her latest school assignment. After dinner, I helped clear away the dishes. We sat down to read. The phone rang. Judge Gannon returned my call.

"Sir, thank you for calling me back."

"We're not in the courtroom. You don't have to call me sir."

"It is a habit I learned when very young. I will probably insult younger men by calling them sir when I am old and gray." We laughed.

"It is a good habit to have. Now what is so important that you wanted me to call you at home?"

"Something that I do not talk about at the office."

"Oh?" The tone of his voice told me that he suspected some of my meaning.

"Yes. I have promised to bring my wife up to the capital. I would like to see you and get your opinion on a case."

He groaned. "Oh Lord, how many depositions are you going to take?"

"Oh about three times as many as the last case. This one is way more challenging."

"Well, I think I want to hear about this case of yours. Bring your wife and come to dinner on Saturday night."

"Thank you. We will be looking forward to that. Um…she is pregnant and not eating spicy foods just now."

"Jake! How could you?" I didn't realize that Leah was listening to my side of the conversation. I heard laughter from the other end of the phone.

"Congratulations."

"Yeah, I'm pretty proud. She thinks I'm a little crazy." We were still laughing when we hung up.

Leah sounded cross again. "How could you just call someone and invite us over to their house for dinner? I will be so embarrassed."

"He invited us, Darling." I said soothingly. "I think he is curious to meet you. I do need his opinion on a case. I need to discuss it privately."

Leah still pouted when she went back to her book.

"Sweetheart, I know you get tired easily, but we need to go out to parties more often."

She looked up and smiled.

"I need to socialize with other prominent men my age."

She smiled happily and set down her book. "Of course we can go out." She came and snuggled up to me. "I know I get tired and cross, but I want to help your career. As soon as we finish our new house we should have a party."

I kissed her forehead. "Of course we will have a party. We will invite our friends, but there some people I meet professionally who will not be welcome in our home."

"I understand." She smiled up at me. "We shouldn't socialize with people below us."

"I don't care about how much money someone has, or how they talk, or even how clean they are. I do care about whether or not they are honest."

Leah kissed me on my chin. "I don't want anything to do with people who commit crimes."

I settled back enjoying Leah's warmth beside me. "There is crime and then there is serious crime. Most of the people I process don't do much harm. There are others, what we call organized crime. These people look much more respectable, but they are far, far worse." Leah kissed me and we went to bed. I went to sleep a happy man.

I enjoyed visiting the capital with my elegant wife. We arrived in time for lunch. We visited some shops. I took her to the cathedral at the far end of the park from The Compound. She oohed and ahhed over the building and talked about the columns and reliefs and other architectural features that I knew nothing about.

She acted reserved when we went to dinner at the judge's house. After dinner, the judge's wife took Leah off to visit her greenhouse. The judge took me to his study. "Now, Jake what is it that you need my opinion on."

"I think we have an extortion ring in the city. The problem is that it involves at least one policeman."

"They always do involve several policemen. What do you intend to do."

"Well, I have a witness. I've stashed him someplace safe, out of town."

The judge nodded.

"I've done a little casual chatting with some potential victims. There is definitely something wrong. People are afraid when they have no real reason other than someone pressuring them. We had a major case of arson. Someone attempted to frame an innocent man. That is as far as I've gotten."

"You intend to prosecute this then?"

"I don't know enough to prosecute."

"You have a beautiful wife and a baby on the way. It might be better to let this one slide."

I leaned back in my chair and thought about letting this one slide. I wondered if my family could become targets. I thought about my friends in the city. "I couldn't leave my eyewitness in the city. I may not be able to do anything about this. I know there is a problem. I know the names of three of the men involved. I have no idea about how to build a case when I don't know how far through our system the corruption spreads."

"Very carefully Jake, you build your case very carefully. Trust nobody."

I nodded. "I think the best I can do is listen to what is happening. Meet people. I told Leah that I want her to meet more people and that we would be going to more society parties. I don't want her to be too close to the criminals, but I think I can get an idea of who is friends with whom by the parties they attend."

He paled. "This will run deep if you think you will find perpetrators at society parties."

"It runs deep. I know my city. It runs deep."

"Can you get them into court?"

"I don't know. That would be my first choice. If that doesn't work, I may have to resort to cutting off their vital services."

He almost barked at me. "Jake don't destroy your career by resorting to crime."

I laughed. "That is part of the beauty of the law. If you are determined to behave with honor and honesty, you can crush you enemies without them ever knowing what hit them."

"Be careful."

"I know how to be patient. Do you have any idea whom I can trust? Where can I go for warrants? How do I arrest a cop?"

"Those are good questions. I will think about this. I may be able to come up with some names you can trust."

"That is what I need most."

"Now let's go rescue your lovely wife before my wife bores her to death with her talk about plants." We found our wives just returned from the greenhouse.

"Oh Jake. She has the most wonderful glass house for growing plants. Your mama would love it. When we are settled in our new house, we should consider such a thing so our children will have fresh fruits and vegetables all year."

I was happy to see that Leah had not been bored. Her reference to Mama pleased me also. I thought she might be a little uncomfortable with Mama. Leah continued to talk about plants all the way home. I thought she and Mama might have a common interest to build their relationship on.

Chapter 28 Rouseff

Early Tuesday morning I arrived for work at Rouseff's offices. He and I had developed a habit of having our morning tea early on Tuesday while we ran over the railroad business. He had a list of enthusiastic ideas this morning, but I couldn't concentrate.

Finally he said. "Jake what is bothering you?"

"What?"

"You have something big on your mind. What is it?"

I stammered and wondered how he knew I was preoccupied. "What? What do…I mean…how…why do you think?"

"The aqueduct idea was a bad idea. You didn't say anything about it."

I rummaged through my memories of the past few minutes. "Oh I knew it was a bad idea. The fish farms were almost as bad. I wasn't going to let you do any of those things. Sometimes it is good to imagine the possibilities."

"You are not imagining out. You are looking in. Why?"

I knew I could trust Rouseff and I needed help. I rubbed the back of my neck. "The laundry fire that burned a whole block just off of Doh Creek Road was set by a policeman named Mantega. He was instrumental in framing the man we arrested for the fire. Two other men were with him. One was named Munk. The other was a Jouyet."

Rouseff swiveled in his chair a couple times. "Hm, that's big enough."

"I think they are running some sort of extortion/protection racket. The laundry where I take my shirts should have more work with one less laundry in town. They have less, and they are afraid of something."

Mr. Rouseff sat and swiveled in his chair while he thought. "No Jake. I don't think it is extortion—not with Jouyet involved. He usually wants land. He does not sully his hands with petty schemes like extortion. Where is a map?" He dug through papers in his desk drawer and pulled out an old, stained and tattered map of the city showing all the trolley lines. "Okay here is where the block of buildings burned. Do you think they intended to burn the whole block?"

"Yes. That is what my informant said."

"Where is your friend's laundry?"

"Here." I tapped the map. I could see no relationship.

Mr. Rouseff, accustomed to thinking about trolley lines and shopping centers, rubbed the side of his face. "My guess is that the city is proposing some new, big expenditure. If it is a road, it might follow this route to connect with the new highway to the capital. If it is a building, it will occupy roughly this area here." He pulled out a pencil and made lines and circles on his map. "So you need to know which businesses are under pressure. If you find problems here and here…" He indicated two points on his map. "…it is a road. If the problems occur here or here, you have a new building. What rumors do you hear about roads and buildings?"

I shook my head. "I don't hear anything. Knowing what I'm looking for will help me know whom to trust."

Mr. Rouseff chuckled. "Don't trust anybody." He chuckled and swiveled in his chair. "I am most eager to know if it is a road or a building. I could position myself quite nicely with this knowledge." He was still plotting and laughing when I left to go to the prosecutor's office.

I arrived earlier than expected. I hadn't been assigned any cases yet. I decided to look for signs of the corruption in my office. I got a cup of coffee and wandered past desks. I looked at the people waiting in the holding room to be processed. I greeted several I knew.

Mr. M'TL, an older man, who came in regularly for brawling called out to me. "Are you going to process my case?"

"I don't have your paperwork. Do you want me to handle your case?"

"Yes sir. I do."

"Why? I am just going to fine you again."

"I know that sir, but you are respectful. You know that a guy has trouble and cannot help himself sometimes."

"I am more inclined to think that you choose to be out of control. Are you in here for brawling again?"

"Yes, sir."

I sighed, "Fighting is stupid. Can't you just walk away?"

He grinned, "I don think the M'TK Sewer Rat ever just walked away from a fight."

I tried to sound stern. "No, you are right. It is much better to run. I can promise you the M'TK Sewer Rat ran from most fights he couldn't talk his way out of. If he couldn't talk or run, he made certain the fight did not last long enough for the police to pick him up."

Several people laughed. I didn't know them, but they all seemed to know me.

"I will have to start fining you enough that you might learn not to get caught next time."

The sound of laughter followed me to the file secretary's desk. I picked up the big stack of unsorted files and thumbed through looking for addresses that might give me a clue about the road or building. Many people lived in buildings--sheds or garages--that did not have an address. They listed their trolley instead. Ah but, I found one address that I found very interesting. I looked for the name of the arresting officer and smiled. I thought I had the information Rouseff needed.

The secretary took the file from me. "I'll take that case Jaconovich. You can go make jokes for your gutter buddies."

I was having a very productive morning. I could hardly believe how much I learned when I knew to look for it. I took a couple cases and headed for my desk.

I called Rouseff first."I was thinking about that road we talked about earlier this morning. I think we need to be certain to get a good foundation under it."

Rouseff was quick to pick up on my cautious tone. "I'll make some phone calls and see if I can get some estimates on the cost per mile of rock."

Yes, I was having a very productive morning. We might be able to derail the Jouyet problem without going to court. I sat in my chair and swiveled. We could trade the businesses along the route for shops in one of our malls. They could still own their business and Rouseff would own their land.

Delighted with my progress, I let my first case off lighter than I should. I heard the perpetrator saying on his way out, "marriage must have softened him up a bit."

I watched as my supervisor led the client from the targeted area into his office and closed the door.

I resolved to be more severe with my next client, a woman picked up for shoplifting. I lectured her. "You cannot steal chickens. I know you don't have money to pay your fine. I want you to report to the priest at the cathedral. He will assign you community service. Next, go the market in M'TK, find Mrs.

Jaconovich and tell her what you have done. She will help you get enough food that you do not have to steal." Maybe I was not being more severe, but I did use a very stern tone of voice when I told the woman she couldn't steal.

The door to my supervisor's office opened. His client looked pale and ill as he dragged himself out of the office.

Next, I processed a man who beat his wife in public. He could not pay his fine. "Then you can go to jail until you fine is paid."

He whined. "An how am I to pay the stupid fine if I'm in jail?"

I felt my lip curl into a snarl. "That is a problem isn't it? I hate men who beat women. I don't care if you spend the rest of your life rotting in jail." My voice rose enough on the last sentence that everybody stopped their work and looked at me.

My supervisor approached my desk. "Jake, take a break for lunch."

"Yes sir. Sorry about disrupting everybody." I sighed.

"Oh it won't hurt some of the others to hear you, but I have to discipline you for that, so I'm sending you out of the office until you cool down."

"Yes sir. Thank you." I smiled. I also wondered if I was being kicked out of the office for yelling or to get me out of the way for other reasons. My suspicion of corruption in my office overwhelmed my anger at my client.

I left to take a walk, but I didn't go far. I found a street vendor who was selling fish pies. I bought a pie and I chatted with him while I watched the office. Within minutes, a car pulled up at the curb. The chauffeur let his passenger out at our building then parked half a block away and started polishing the car. I wandered in his direction. I stopped and spoke to the chauffeur as I wandered past. "That is a US car isn't it?"

"Yes."

"What kind is it?" I tried to sound naïve.

"Cadillac, says so right on the front." He sounded proud of the car as he lovingly polished its gleaming door.

I walked around the car. "What? Where? Oh it does. Do all cars have their names on them?" I looked through the front window. Nothing.

"Most do."

"I don't think the Miki has a name on it." I wandered around the side of the car and saw on the back seat a child's football uniform with a name on it, Jouyet.

He sneered, "I wouldn't call the Miki a car."

"Have you driven one?"

"No, tiny little thing like that. I wouldn't be caught driving one of those little things. They're made here. You'd think we could make a *real* car."

"Perhaps someday we will." The hairs on the back of my neck told me that something major was about to happen. I caught a trolley and rode down the M'TK station and called Rouseff.

"I'm sorry to interrupt you again. I'm at the station. I think something is about to happen. Jouyet is visiting the prosecutor's office. I was kicked out of the building for yelling at a piece of scum who beat his wife."

"You are having a busy day." Rouseff observed.

"I wonder why everything seems to be happening so fast right now?" I started pacing the length of the phone cable. I'd take two steps and turn and walk back. My stomach felt tight.

"They have probably been working on this for months and you didn't notice."

I sat on the edge of Papa's desk. "I wonder why I was given the arson case when they knew the man they arrested was innocent?" They must have known I would investigate it.

Rouseff grunted. "You are young and inexperienced. Let's hope they think you are incompetent."

Such a thought offended me. "They have no reason to think that."

"If you got kicked out of the office, then they are probably going to start being real careful around you."

On Saturday night, Leah and I accepted an invitation to a dinner party. I listened for talk about city plans, but I heard nothing.

Leah did a better job than I did. She'd cut back to working half time because I thought she was getting too tired. One day shortly after the dinner party, she went to a lunch meeting for a young women's charity group. She told me about it over dinner. "I had the most wonderful time. I actually got to use some of what I am learning in classes."

"Oh? How was that?"

"Well, the Young Women's Community Campaign is planning projects to beautify the city. There is to be a new boulevard to run from the city hall to the new highway with businesses all along the route. We want to put in long strips of flowers and grass. I pointed out that the grass and flowers are nice, but not tall enough. I suggested several kinds of trees along the street. If they put their power lines underground and lined the streets with trees, it would not take so much work to keep up. The trees would shield the businesses from the noise on the street. Everybody acted very impressed."

I kissed her fingertips. "I am more than impressed. I'm thrilled that you got to use your education this way." I smiled at her. "Who was at your meeting?"

Leah, rattled off a list of names. Some I didn't know. Some I expected to hear. Leah continued with her news. "Julie and Anne were so curious about you that I was almost jealous."

I snorted. "I can't imagine why anybody would be curious. Every bit of my business has been known by everybody in this city since I was six."

"They were though. They wanted to know if you had any big cases, if you worried about your work. I told them that you like working for Mr. Rouseff but the prosecutor's office is boring."

"The prosecutor's office *is* boring. I am still upset about yelling at an offender. I wonder if I would be better off going full time with Rouseff?"

She pouted. "I think you should quit the prosecutor's office. I don't blame you for yelling at those people."

I kissed her on the forehead.

She continued to complain. "Your talents are wasted there. They don't give you any cases that will help you make a reputation. They don't pay you enough."

I nodded. "I need to stay there a little longer to get my certification for criminal law. Then, I might work full time for Rouseff to earn my certification in contract law. The advantage with staying in criminal law is the possibility of becoming a judge. I'd like that."

"But, you don't get the kind of cases to promote your career."

"This city does not *produce* the kinds of cases to promote my career. We have petty crime. We haven't had a murder for a long time. When I was a child, murder was common."

I didn't want to let on to Leah that the piece of information she gave me was important. I didn't want her associating the women who were using her to get information about me. I also didn't want to tell my wife how to live her life when she had just done something important to her. I sat quiet for a few minutes.

Finally, I hit on and idea. "You know sweetheart, I'm thinking about you seeing how to beautify the street. Perhaps you need to be part of the team of people who work on landscaping Rouseff properties. Can you do drawings?"

She smiled and blushed. "I want to take landscape drawing next quarter. I am taking basic drawing now. "

I raised my eyebrows at her. "You'll be quite pregnant by then. Will you even get through the end of the term?"

"Of course. I still want to take classes after the baby comes. I don't know how we will manage. Can we hire someone to take care of him while I go to school."

"Of course, we can hire someone, if we can get him--or her--away from my mama."

"Do you think your parents will be interested in the baby? They are so busy going here and there."

I patted Leah's hand. "They are interested. They would like to come over and talk to your tummy, but they flit here and there to keep themselves busy until they can get their hands on the baby."

Leah sounded whiny again. "I don't know. They seem so uninterested."

I looked away. "I know my parents. They are giving us space and... and...I think they are terrified for us, and the baby. They come from an older time. Mama had ten babies. Mama's last babies, twins died at birth or just before birth. I don't know. We almost lost Mama."

Leah snuggled closer. "I didn't know that. I understand about losing a child." Leah looked so sad, I reached out and touched her hand. She said, "It was so common for a woman to lose child after child in our village. My mama lost two before me."

I stopped by Rouseff's office on the way to work in the morning and told him my news. "The new road is to be a boulevard lined with grass, flowers, trees and shops on either side. The power is to be underground."

He laughed, "Grass and flowers?"

"Someone else's wife proposed the grass and flowers. Leah added the part about the trees. Leah attended a women's community improvement meeting or something, with Candice Puloski. Jouyet's wife was there."

"It sounds like a fishy group for Candice and Leah."

"It is probably innocent enough, but I don't like Leah mixing with a Jouyet just now. She was so excited talking about lining the street with trees, I suggested she work with our people on landscaping our properties."

"If she wants to look at sites and suggest trees and shrubs, I can pay her to do that. I agree with you, keep her busy and away from Jouyet's influence." He sighed.

Mr. Rouseff had information for me. "Mr. Apkouta tells me there is pressure being put on merchants down on lower ninth near the tracks. I've ordered fire-fighting equipment brought in, and I am pulling more of my men into the city."

I snarled, "Damn it, Rouseff! This is the job of the city government. They should be protecting the city. They should be investigating the first fire. Instead, I think they are in it up to their necks. It is disgusting."

"But profitable for all around."

"Not for the people who live on Doh Creek Road or lower Ninth."

He nodded grimly, "I'll see about that. Jake, I'm warning you, this fight is too big for you alone."

I grinned. "I won't do anything until I can move swiftly and completely."

After work, I stopped by to see Professor Ingleman who led the constitutional committee, as they called themselves now.

"Jake! Jake come in what a surprise."

"I hope I am not interrupting your dinner or something."

"No. No…not at all. What brings you by?"

"The project you have been working on." He led me into his study and closed the door securely behind us."

I said, "I think I may have an opportunity for you. How close are you with that constitution?"

His eyes shone with excitement. "It is ready. We have been slowly building the cases. We have people with northern names applying for public jobs. When they are told they are ineligible because of their family background we take the case before a judge. We've processed one hundred-fifty so far. What do you have?"

"Graft and corruption going back to the laundry fire earlier this year." I told him about the boulevard.

I took a deep breath. "People high up are forcing the businesses along the route to sell cheap. If they don't sell they risk getting burned out. I've watched a prosecutor in my office harassing an innocent citizen who owns property on the route of the highway." I also explained what Rouseff had in place to protect the city. "We could have a small war on our hands in the city."

The professor leaned back in his chair and swiveled back and forth. "Can you give us more details as this goes down?"

"If I have them. I was asked to leave the office the last time Jouyet visited the office. My usual informants are reporting directly to Rouseff. I'm getting information second or third hand. You will have to keep your eyes open for any opportunity to act. If this thing goes all the way to the emperor, as I think it does, you may have a brief window of opportunity while people in power are looking elsewhere."

All remained quiet in the city. I continued to process the usual repeat offenders. I kept note of anyone arrested, who lived along the route of the new road. I noted those cases were always assigned to the supervisors, or one senior prosecutor. The file secretary would reassign one of those cases if I took it off her desk. When this happened I'd whine and wail about not getting any interesting cases. I made a joke about labeling my cases by A, B or C, with set fines and lecture for the offense.

"Just don't yell at them." My supervisor surprised me by coming up behind me.

"If I can't yell at them, can I take them into the alley and beat the crap out of them?"

Christian, an attorney a year older than me snorted. "Jake, you can't fool me. I went to school with you."

I had a moment of horror.

"You're the kid who grew up so pampered you couldn't wipe your own nose when you got to university. It might be amusing to send you out to the alley with one of the drunks, but I don't think you could beat the crap out of him with a big stick and three men to hold them down."

I stared at Christian, stunned. I blinked a few times, tried to wrinkle my nose, shrugged, and sighed dramatically. "You're right. I'd probably get a bloody nose for my efforts." Everybody laughed. For the next week or so, I played the fool, encouraging the laughter while I kept track of the arrests from the targeted area and passed their names on to Rouseff.

Rouseff and I slowly built a body of evidence for our first guesses. He was keeping track of who was being harassed. I watched who was doing the harassing. Once, while looking through files in our file room for the arresting officers involved in the legal harassment, I almost got caught.

"Jake, what are you doing in here?" the file secretary asked in a voice loud enough to attract the attention of the supervisors and clerks. She scowled at me.

The lessons learned in my first year receptions saved me. If I could withstand the withering looks of the grande dames of society, I could handle our file secretary without flinching. "Where in the hell do you keep the files of the assault offenders?" I glared back at the woman.

Our head supervisor stuck his head in the door of the file room. "Jake what are you doing?"

"I'm looking for the files on the assault offenders." I snarled my answer.

Mr. Supervisor snarled back, "Tell the clerks which files you want and let them find them for you."

I whined, "I would if I could remember which ones I want."

"Go back to your desk and think about it and let the clerks fetch the files."

I'd just been kicked out of the file room for the first time, ever. As an intern and junior prosecutor, I'd fetched my own files for years. This was interesting. Of course, I knew, I was in there looking for what others didn't want found. I sat at my desk and swiveled in my chair thinking. I rubbed the back of my neck. I suspected things were coming to a head, but I had no idea what that might be.

Chapter 29 Heros

When the attack came, I knew nothing about it. Leah and I had just moved into our new house. I was snug and warm in bed with my pregnant wife when Papa got a call at the station. Fire! On lower Ninth.

Papa told me, he sounded the newly-installed fire siren, before he even pulled his pants on. By the time he started the gerry Mr. Apkouta arrived. The two men hooked the gerry to the fire fighting and water tank cars that stood waiting ready to roll.

The fire fighting car had a large water tank, hoses and a monster pump that would spray a heavy stream of water for twenty-five feet. After Micki finished playing with it, the hoses could shoot water at least fifty feet. It took four big men to control each hose. The car came equipped with two hoses.

Papa and Mr. Apkouta switched tracks and in record time had the gerry with the fire-cars behind, running along the connecting track to the trolley system. With the fire siren from the station screaming, Papa and Mr. Apkouta ran the fire fighting car to the bottom of Ninth Street. Several people told me how the crowds, who had evacuated the buildings at the sound of the fire siren, stood on the sidewalks and cheered and called Papa and Mr. Apkouta by name as if this was a grand parade.

Seven minutes after the call came in, Papa and Mr. Apkouta arrived at the bottom of Ninth Street to find the fire consuming a restaurant. Mr. Rouseff's men arrived before them. They had good training and knew what to do. Amid the shouts and cheers from the crowd, they ran the hoses out toward the burning restaurant.

At this moment, the police arrived to find the fire fighting car, volunteer firefighters and two hundred other people helping residents evacuate and cheering on the firefighters.

Much to Papa's horror, when the police arrived, they yelled over the din of the roaring fire and cheering crowds at the firefighters to leave. They yelled at Papa to get the equipment out of there. They yelled at the people to get off of the street. I learned that it was Mantega who pulled his gun while his companions brandished night sticks. Mr. Rouseff's security was better trained and better equipped than the underfunded city police. They formed a phalanx to protect their men and the fire fighting car long enough for the volunteers to take position.

Mr. Apkouta blew on his whistle to signal the hose men. He then opened up the water valve and those overpowered pumps let loose a stream of water that knocked the police to the ground and left them dazed. Once the more serious threat was subdued they could turn their attention to the fire.

The fire roared and leapt into the night sky, but it could not withstand the streams of water from the supercharged fire fighting car. The people on the street cheered and shouted some more as the flames were drowned in a billow of steam within just a few minutes. I was told there was a great deal of laughing and cheering. Again people shouted, "Jaconovich! Apkouta! Rouseff!"

Amid a carnival atmosphere, the people filed back to their homes. A few of Rouseff's men made certain the fire remained out. When the hoses were rolled back up and packed away, the street was almost empty.

I did not hear until I reached Rouseff Properties the next day that the police who had shown up at the scene were missing.

I stormed into Rouseff's office. "What the hell do you think you are doing? You cannot abduct twelve policemen."

He appeared calm. I noticed a small smile at the corners of his mouth. "Seven, there were only seven. They are being treated for injuries sustained while fighting the fire."

"You. Cannot. Abduct. Policemen."

He tried to control his little smile. "As far as they know, they are in the hospital for their injuries and shock. The doctor will release them today. They will arrive home to a hero's welcome. I have dozens of witnesses who will swear up and down that those brave, brave heroes fought the fire and rescued scores of helpless victims."

I ran my fingers through my hair. "You are evil. You know that? You are evil. I don't want to know anything about this."

Rouseff laughed. "Don't call me evil. Your papa thought up hero story."

I stood frozen and whispered. "He must have been furious."

Rouseff shrugged eloquently. "He doesn't like fire." He grinned when he said, "Vanderholm should learn not to mess me."

"You are certain that the emperor is behind the coercion then?"

"Yes, my purchasing team has been watching the sales on the properties we haven't been able to buy. They are purchased by a partnership and he is one of the partners. The highway is just an excuse to move tax money into his own pocket. He will not succeed in my city."

I ran my hands over my face. "It is the same story over and over."

Rouseff revealed his deep loathing for the emperor and his family. "And Vanderholm always loses when he faces me. He may have burned M'TK, but I learned who to trust then. He will not succeed."

I stood feeling slightly ill over the idea that we fight the same battles over and over. "I better go see Papa. If he is mad enough to do something like this, he is way too upset." I turned to leave.

Rouseff cheerfully called after me, "Now mind you, he took no part in putting those brave lads in the hospital. He just wanted them to have a proper welcome when they got home. I believe they were overcome with smoke or fell while rescuing someone. I don't know the full story."

I went straight to the station.

Mama came to the head of the stairs when she heard me. She held her finger to her lips. I whispered. "Where's Papa?"

"Sleeping." Mama wrung her apron and fretted. "Jake, he is getting too old for this. He has been fighting since he was sixteen years old. Fighting to get ahead, fighting to protect our community, fighting for us to be treated as equals. He is too old to be jumping on a gerry in the middle of the night and riding off to fight fire."

I smiled at Mama as she gave me a biscuit with some of the sausage I like. "I heard something about calling the policemen heroes."

Mama hissed. "Jake, I've never seen Papa so angry. He was cursing, and calling them oath breakers, and a scourge on the community. I was afraid for his heart he was so angry."

"Did he have anything to do with them being taken away."

She shook her head. "He let the guards take them away. They were dazed and disoriented from what I hear. He was angry, but he kept his head. He told everyone to call the policemen heroes and tell how they put out the fire."

I chuckled. "Their bosses will either eat them alive, or be confused, or know that Rouseff is up to something." I stood and I kissed Mama on the top of the head. "Thanks for the breakfast. Don't worry about Papa." As I left to go to the office I didn't follow my own advice. I worried about Papa.

The minute I stepped through the door at the prosecutor's office, news of the fire greeted me. I watched the eyes of my office mates as they asked me what I knew.

"I don't know much. Rouseff told me about the fire when I arrived for work at his office. I left and went down to see my parents. Papa was still sleeping. Mama was worrying that Papa is getting too old to be getting called out of his bed at night. Mama didn't know anything but that Papa is too old to go out at night. I think I will see about buying them a nice place in Mercid. It is time they retired." I made a mental note as to who got quickly bored with my worries about my parents and who wanted to ask me more about what I knew.

The head supervisor failed to hide his interest when he asked. "Why was there fire fighting equipment in M'TK?"

I shrugged. "The railroad keeps the same equipment in one of the eastern provinces. They have smaller rigs that they keep at some other stations. They started keeping equipment nearby after the M'TK fire. Rouseff is talking about keeping equipment in all the villages."

My boss pressed me for more information. "How did they get it onto the trolley line."

I smiled happily. "Oh, you can blame me for that. When I was young, maybe seventeen, Rouseff gave me a trolley for my own use. I could run it about town, but it was more fun to take it on the rail lines into the countryside. We built a cross-connecting track so I didn't have to get the station hands to lift the it off the trolley tracks and onto the train tracks." I launched into a story of my college camping trip and bored my audience until even the head supervisor got disgusted and walked away.

I got a stack of case files and went to work. I found it difficult to get my clients to concentrate on the seriousness of their offenses. More than one person leaned close and whispered, "You tell your Papa thank you." Or, "I never seen a more beautiful sight than your Papa on that gerry with that big tanker behind him." Or, "your Papa is a fine man." I was very proud of my papa.

Shortly before lunch, I heard my boss's supervisor swearing up a storm. I heard, "They what?" before he slammed the door shut with his foot. I tried not to smile. I suspected the policemen got home from the hospital.

"Hey Jaconovich, wanna go out and catch a few beers for lunch." Christian Van Gelen the man who claimed to have known me in college almost shouted the invitation across the room. If he actually did know me, the invitation to catch a few beers would be very strange.

"Sure. Let me clean my desk." I carefully locked up everything and left with my companion.

On the street in front of the office, Christian informed me, "I feel like taking a long walk."

"Suits me. Where are we going?"

"Oh nowhere in particular, perhaps some residential areas." He smiled angelically and looked at the sky.

We chatted about inconsequential things. I asked, "Where did your brother's wife find clothes when she was pregnant? Leah is getting so big she can't find anything to wear."

Christian didn't answer my question. He focused his attention on a group of people outside a house half-way up the block. They held signs. I got closer and wanted to hold my head. I tried very hard to show no reaction. The signs they carried read *Officer Manuel, Hero.* Eight people stood in the group telling everyone who passed by, what Officer Manuel had done. The people blocked the sidewalk. Christian stopped. He smiled angelically at the people before us.

One old woman winked at me as she showed me a framed photo of a little girl. "Look, look; Officer Manuel saved this picture of my little girl. She died just after this was taken. I didn't want to leave my house without it. I couldn't get it down off of the wall. He was so big and strong he just reached up and grabbed it off of the wall and handed it to me so gently. He is a saint." She dabbed at her eyes and sniffed.

An ancient gentleman rasped. "He carried me over his shoulder, he did, just like the firemen on the telly at the bar. He just picked me up over his shoulder and carried me away, cause I don't walk so fast since the arthritis set in." He shuffled slowly to demonstrate how slow he walked. I wanted to hold my head again.

I nodded. "I guess that is what we pay them for." We walked on our way.

Christian didn't say anything about the demonstration, and I tried to pretend I hadn't given it any thought. We passed a flower shop. My companion stopped and bought some flowers. He grinned at me. I hoped he intended to visit a woman. We rounded the corner of another street and saw another small crowd. We approached the house silently. Christian solemnly walked to the stoop and placed a single lily on the step. The crowd sighed. I turned my back.

The crowd eagerly told us their heartrending stories of heroic rescues. The story, I liked best, was told by a boy with his dog. "He saved my dog, Tip. He did. Ol' Tip was afraid to come out, but the officer whistled and…and Tip just *knew* he was safe, and he came right out." I felt tears of laughter forming in the corners of my eyes. I looked into the eyes of that deceitful little punk and saw a wisdom and glee that surprised me. I guess I was inclined to agree with the child. The officer deserved what he got.

We left the street. I suggested. "I don't think two prosecutors should be seen visiting these homes."

Christian's round eyes looked as innocent as a nun. "We may have to prosecute the dastardly arsonists. We should hear the full witness to how these brave men foiled their evil plot." He sounded as innocent as a naïve choirboy.

"We are more likely to be asked what the hell we were doing."

"Why Jake, we are paying humble tribute to our fellow crime fighters. These are the men who lay their lives on the line so that people like us can sleep at night."

I shook my head and followed my companion. I tried to hide my laughter over the outrageous stories the people told about the rescuers.

A plumb young girl told me a long tale. "…and then when my feet touched the sidewalk, I knew that I would love him forever. He kissed me and told me to wait for him. He would come to marry me when the danger was over." The young woman sighed dramatically. Her ample bosom heaved and jiggled.

With a herculean effort I kept a straight face. "My dear, you are magnificent. If I were not married, I would fight for the honor of rescuing you." I gave the young woman a slight bow.

The girl sighed and giggled.

Christian lifted his chin in an aristocratic gesture. "See Jake, you are getting the hang of this thing."

I started to laugh. "That young woman reads altogether too many trashy novels."

I thought we'd run out of luck when we reached the next house. There were more officers on the scene. They had their clubs out apparently trying to dislodge the demonstrators. I slowed down. Christian grabbed my sleeve and steered me directly toward the conflict. "Ah, Officer Rodrigues, Officer Cordova, how are you gentlemen today?"

Cordova turned on us and snarled. "What are you doing here?"

Christian's aristocratic bearing didn't waver. He spoke just above a whisper. "How is the patient? I just want to leave some flowers. They wouldn't let me do more than peak in the door of his room early this morning."

Cordova relaxed a little. "You saw him at the hospital?"

"Just from the doorway."

Officer Rodrigues growled. "We can't get any information out of the hospital."

Christian assumed lawyerly tones. "Um...that is correct. It would be against privacy laws for them to give you any information. Did you hear how these men spent half the night evacuating people and fighting fire? Of course the hospital would not want the type of scene that we have here. I'll just leave my flower like this." He paced slowly to the stoop, placed his flower on the top step and stood with a bowed head for the slightest moment.

I wanted to shake my head. I settled for trying to look solemn.

When Christian rejoined us on the sidewalk, Cordova whispered. "We have been called out to clear the street."

"But why?" Christian sounded totally innocent.

The officer nodded toward the house. "He doesn't like this."

Christian grew expansive. "Oh he is just being modest. You know that your good deeds are so often overlooked. It is about time the people express their admiration for their heroes."

I poked my companion to keep him from overplaying his part. "Perhaps if we moved the demonstrators over behind the hedge just there. He could not see them from his windows. I would find such attention embarrassing myself." We moved the crowd over behind the hedge, shook hands with the officers, encouraged the demonstrators to thank these men too and went on our way.

Christian sounded expansive as he breathed in deeply. "You know Jake, I find it so refreshing to get out of the office and get in touch with the people of the city."

"What the hell do you think is going on here?"

"Don't you know?"

"I want you to tell me." I used a firm tone with Christian.

He shrugged and dropped his aristocratic tone. "I first got an idea of something wrong in the office when they assigned you the Fortenac case. I was on my way to the back offices to ask a question when I overheard Mr. Supervisor on the phone. He said, *Well if they want Jaconovich we can give them Jaconovich. No, he won't win the case. He is almost fresh out of school. Nobody could win this case. Jaconovich doesn't stand a chance.*"

Christian glanced at me. "Then you went out and won the case. I looked around the office. I noticed both supervisors and one senior prosecutor where not happy. They were very bad tempered for weeks. They walked through the office scowling and snapping at everybody."

Christian paused while we maneuvered around some old women visiting on the sidewalk. "Then they gave you the arson case. You proved their suspect was innocent. That was not a happy day at the office. That was a very bad day at the office." He cleared his throat. "Next, I noticed they demoted you to the most obvious mundane cases in the office. I also noticed that a certain type of cases always go to the supervisors and one senior attorney. I noticed when you tried to take one of those cases, the file secretary took it away from you."

I scratched my nose. "You see way too much that should never ever be mentioned."

"Since then, I have been doing my best to make our supervisors think you are an incompetent fool who is totally wrapped up in his lovely new wife."

"That may be closer to the truth than you know."

"Jake you know something big is going on."

"Something big is always going on. I'm almost certain that whatever this is, it comes down from Emperor Vanderholm."

"Wow."

"Yeah, wow. I'm staying as far away from this as I can. As soon as I get my certificate in criminal law, I'm out of here and working on my certificate in contract law for Rouseff."

"You really think you can walk away from this?"

"When I was thirteen I watched M'TK burn from the ridge out where I live."

"The city didn't burn last night."

"That may have been more dumb luck than anything. If the army had been behind this, the whole area might have burned."

"Jake, I think I know you well enough that you will not do or say anything until you know every step to take, until you have more depositions than anyone will know what to do with. If you need help, I will help you. I want to practice real law."

I nodded. I hoped he was trustworthy. I wondered how many other people noticed the things he saw. I wondered how many others would follow their leaders. Who would follow justice?

That evening we dined with the Rouseff's. Everybody was in a good mood. Mr. Rouseff had thwarted the attempt to burn part of the city. The people knew who their protector was, and they would trust him. The people idolized Papa. Papa and Cousin Philippe were happy.

Mama and Mrs. Rouseff giggled like schoolgirls all through dinner. After dinner, the men went off to the study. I heard Mama and Mrs. Rouseff giggling and begging Leah to come see what they had. I hoped they kept Leah entertained.

Sometimes I thought that Leah did not have much in common with other women. She had not read many books. She had lived so isolated that she had not seen many books. She learned quickly and talked about the new things she was seeing but sometimes I noticed that she did not have the depth of understanding that was common among my family and friends. I was certain that would come with time.

I went off to the study with the men and relaxed into a big leather chair. A servant brought in our dark coffee. Papa told us about what happened at the scene of the fire. Mr. Rouseff filled me in on the details from his men. I told them about Christian. "I don't know if I can trust him or not."

I settled deeper into my chair and sipped my coffee. "Oh and speaking of my office," I snorted. "today one man picked up for shoplifting bragged to the others as he left. '*I got Mr. Jaconovich's son. I got to talk to Mr. Jaconovich's son. He says his Papa was tired and slept late this morning.*' His news created a stir." I smiled at Papa. "I got numerous comments asking about you and a few who told me to say thank you, they knew someone, or had family living in the area."

Mr. Rouseff chuckled, "They are not hanging out at the station with signs saying what a hero he is though."

I sat up straighter in my chair. "I couldn't believe that. How long do you intend to torment those officers?"

Mr. Rouseff's eyes narrowed and his mouth formed a thin hard line. "Until they talk to me, or their bosses get to them, or I find some other use for them."

Papa sighed and looked sad. "Jake they were armed. They tried to keep us from fighting the fire. We took them by surprise, or they would have caused some serious trouble. This is a mild punishment for them."

"Have you seen the demonstrations?" They had not. I spent the next twenty minutes or so telling them about the highlights of the demonstrations. They laughed until tears ran down their faces. "I really think some of those folks need to form a street theater. They were so good. Something has to be done about the little boy with his dog. That gleeful little liar will be in my office soon if his talents are not steered in a more constructive direction."

Cousin Philippe pounced on the idea. "Street theater sounds like a worthy project. I might be willing to fund a project if they gave short performances at the malls and stations. I wonder if they would attract more business."

Papa said. "They might attract tourists." This turned the topic back to business until Leah interrupted us.

"Jake. Jake, you have to come see this right now!" Leah spun in a circle. She sounded just like a little girl. Papa and Cousin Philippe grinned and chuckled.

Cousin Philippe said, "The women do like to have their fun."

Papa grumbled. "My wife is so excited about the grandbaby, I just about have to tie her down to keep her from following Leah around and staring at her tummy."

Grinning over Papa's words, I followed Leah into the sitting room. Tissue paper and boxes littered the sitting room. I noticed a large box and heavy shipping paper.

"Jake, look what your mama and Mrs. Rouseff have done." She held up a dark blue dress that looked rather large in front. "Jake they bought me more and more clothes for pregnant women." Leah's eyes shone bright with tears. She looked overwhelmed. I admired everything while Mama and Mrs. Rouseff took turns explaining.

"We knew she couldn't find anything here." Mama's eyes danced.

Mrs. Rouseff explained. "When we were in the states, we signed up for catalogs. Every four months, or sometimes once a month, we get all these wonderful catalogs."

Mama almost interrupted. "Some of them have *maternity clothes*." She sounded as if she was referring to a fancy boat or car when she said the words *maternity clothes.*

Mrs. Rouseff acted almost as excited as Mama. "I helped my great-niece buy clothes from the catalog last year."

"I invited Candice and Adele over to look at my catalogs when they were pregnant so I knew what young women might find attractive. They really liked the jeans and tops. They helped us by translating the descriptions from the English."

I was touched that Mama reached out to the younger women. "Thank you." I sighed. "I've been concerned because she wants to take a drawing course next quarter. She needs clothes if she is to leave the house."

Leah kissed both my parents and the Rouseff's. Her eyes sparkled with tears and she sniffed. "I have never had someone do something this nice for me"

Mama shook her head. "I remember being pregnant and trying to find clothes to cover me up. I had a large man's shirt I wore on my back and a dress to cover my front. I left it open in back."

Mrs. Philippe wailed. "I lived in my nightgown and didn't leave the house for four months."

Leah's voice caught. "You make me feel very modern to be dressed so fashionably."

That was one of the happiest evenings of my life. We were all in agreement in our joy over the baby. We had thwarted whomever wanted to burn the city. We hoped they would not try again.

Chapter 30 Tension

About a week after the attempted fire, I came to work and looked over the files from the weekend's arrests. We had twenty cases. I looked around the file-secretary's desk and glanced at the receptionist's desk. "Where are the rest of the cases?"

The file secretary assured me. "This is all we have."

"Do you mean to tell me that for the first time since I've been a prosecutor only twenty people were picked up over the weekend?"

Allison told me. "Our case load was way down during the week."

"How is that possible?"

She shrugged. "We have a staff meeting this afternoon."

"Hmph, I'll get on these cases." I picked up a couple files.

"One at a time Jake or we will all die of boredom." I noted the file-secretary took away an extremely thin file--not from a repeat offender. I wanted to know the address. I decided to trust my new office buddy.

I walked past Christian's desk and knocked some papers on the floor. "Oh, excuse me. I was daydreaming. Let me help you." We both bent down to pick up papers. I whispered, "Skinny file, want address."

"Geez, Jake, watch what you're doing will you. I had these all in order." He ambled off to the secretary's desk calling for paper clips, "because Jake is bumbling into things again."

I interviewed my first offender, Mr. Sun. He bowed when Darlene escorted him to my desk. I returned his bow and I motioned for him to sit.

He sat on the very edge of the chair and grinned toothlessly at me. "Mr. Jake Jaconovich, it is an honor to meet you sir."

I tried for a severe tone. "You are in here for public indecency. I wouldn't call that honorable."

He whined, "I had to take a piss. I didn't know it were against no law for a man to take a piss."

I wanted to hold my head.

Mr. Sun leaned closer to me and continued. "God made piss. Can't see why pissing would be against the law."

I chuckled. "Well, you are right in that God made us the way we are."

He sat up straighter and smiled at me.

"The problem was not so much the pissing." I shifted in my chair and poked at his file. "It was where you were pissing. It says here you were standing on the street corner. You are not supposed to piss where others can see you, smell you, or step in what you have done. That is what makes it against the law."

"Well, where do I piss then?" He whined.

It was a slow day. My desk sat in the middle of the room. I was well aware of the staff and other prosecutors listening in on this conversation. I tried to explain. "Some stores have public restrooms. You can go there. The bar, where you most likely drank the beer you were pissing, has a restroom. You can go there. You could try to wait until you get home. There are public toilets behind the cathedral. You can go there. If you really can't find a toilet, find a deserted alley where nobody can see you." I filled out the man's papers, giving him a small fine to help him remember his offense. Public urination was a significant health problem on the streets. I admonished him. "I don't want to see you back in this office."

He grinned and bowed some more as he got up to leave. "No sir. No sir, Mr. Jake Jaconovich. It was an honor to meet you. The missus will be real impressed that I met you."

I thought my lecture was lost on him, but the clerk at the accounts desk assured me that he repeated the lecture over and over as he stood in line to pay his fine. "Mr. Jake Jaconovich says I can piss at home, and in the toilet in the bar, and the toilet behind the cathedral, and in a dark alley where nobody can see me. Mr. Jake Jaconovich says I can piss at home, and in the toilet in the bar, and the toilet behind the cathedral and in a dark alley where nobody can see me."

I envisioned him repeating the lecture to his awestruck wife and a rapt audience in the bar.

For the rest of the day, every time someone looked at me they would say something like, "…and behind the cathedral, and in a dark alley…." They would then laugh until tears ran down their cheeks.

On our way to the staff meeting, Christian passed me a small piece of paper with numbers on it. While everybody was busy finding their seats, I glanced at the piece of paper, *1016-9ᵗʰ*, the targeted area. I would call Rouseff.

Our supervisor opened the meeting. "The crime rate is way down. We are not bringing in much revenue from fines."

I heard whispering behind me. "...and behind the cathedral." Everybody else was trying not to laugh.

Leroy blurted out. "It's Jake's fault for telling people where they can piss." This produced outright laughter."

Christian suggested, "Perhaps we will have time to work on some older, unsolved cases." I knew my friend wanted another look at the earlier fire. I was not eager for him to look too closely at Officer Mantega. The case frightened me. If we were not very, very careful the army would come through with another purge.

Mr. Supervisor bellowed. "Jaconovich!"

"Huh? What? I was startled out of my own thoughts."

Mr. Supervisor asked, "What are your thoughts on why the crime rate is so low?"

I thought quickly. "I think the people were deeply moved by witnessing those officers risking their lives and getting injured trying to save them. I think we can thank those brave officers, who fought the fire on lower Ninth for our lower crime rate. People respect the law, if they respect the men who enforce it."

Christian looked very wise and nodded. "Yes, I saw the demonstrations. I think Jake is right."

We did pull out old unresolved cases. Christian and I were not allowed near the fire case, but I was given something better.

A young man named Peter DeNough was charged with trespass for entering a private gentleman's club. The club was exclusive for southern residents. Young Peter was there as a guest of a member. He and his host protested the exclusion. The police were called. Peter and his friend left peaceably. Charges were filed at the request of the club. The case was still on the books. I went looking for Peter DeNough. I thought this might be an easy case to resolve if DeNough was a politically discrete spelling of D'NO. Many families tried spelling their names with numerous vowels to disguise their origins.

Peter was the controller for a company owned by a combination of Fortenacs and Jouyets. I shivered at the thought of a Jouyet and a Fortenac in business together. I finally met Peter, as he came off from work. His appearance surprised me. He was thin, about my height with dark hair and blue eyes. His clothing appeared very expensive.

"Peter DeNough? I am Jake Jaconovich. I need to serve you with these papers on your trespass case from six months ago."

He paled and shrunk slightly into himself. "Why are you just getting around to this now?"

"We've had a heavy backlog of cases." Along with his papers, I handed him the card of one of the men who was working on the constitutional case. "I recommend that you contact this attorney who specializes in cases just like yours.

He looked at me through narrowed eyes. His mouth twisted. "Why would you want to suggest an attorney for me? Why should I trust you? You are a prosecutor." He had a point.

"I said my name is Jake Jaconovich..." I intended to mention our family connection.

He glanced around us. He whispered, "Wait are you the one...who... Leon...?" Again he glanced right and left as if to see who might recognize us.

I smiled.

He shifted from one foot to another. "Trespassing is a small crime. Why would you...um...this isn't important enough for you."

"Ah...but, the rest of the D'NO family may not like the implication that they have low connections."

He caught his breath when he heard the slight accent in how I said the name. He turned red.

In prosecurial tones I said. "Consult with the attorney I suggested. I expect to see you and your attorney in my office at ten on Friday. Good day."

I worried about being late getting home. Leah wasn't working so she spent too much time alone. She tended to worry and work herself into tears.

Today when I came through the door, she gave me a hug and a radiant smile.

I nuzzled her neck. "Mm, my love." I kissed her. "It is good to see you are looking well."

"Oh I am fine."

I asked, "What did you do today?"

Leah giggled and almost skipped as she drug me to the sofa to sit beside her. "Your mama and I went to the capital looking for baby furniture. I just now got home." She pulled a crib mobile and a picture of a teddy bear out of a sack and handed them to me.

I smiled as I looked at the picture and mobile. "Did you find furniture for the baby?"

"Yes, we have a crib for the nursery and a cradle to keep in our bedroom. We found the cutest high chair with bears dancing on it." I kissed Leah again. "The store will ship it down to us for free. They were going to charge us shipping. I would have paid it, but your mama insisted that they were to deliver it to the train station with our name on it. It will be here in a day or so."

"I hope Mama did not make you uncomfortable by staring at your tummy."

Leah giggled and snuggled closer to my arm. "No. She was very good. We talked about landscaping for the stations when I could get her to stop talking about the baby and immunizations."

I nodded. "Our children will be immunized. I think that may be the difference between having babies that live long enough to grow up and having ten babies and only one grows up." Leah hugged me and held me. Life was good.

Peter DeNough and his attorney Mr. Gannon showed up in my office at ten on Friday. I opened the conversation. I tried to sound professional and aloof. "Well gentlemen, what do you have for me."

Mr. Gannon answered equally aloof and professional, "Mr. Prosecutor, the charges of trespassing are false. Mr. DeNough acted in good faith when he entered the club."

I tilted my head back and looked down my nose. "Do you have documentation that he was in fact eligible to enter the club?"

"I do sir." Mr. Gannon handed me a stack of papers. He had done his work well. He had five depositions stating that Peter was a member of the Fortenac and Spinoza families. He had included birth and marriage records to support the depositions.

I studied the documents then grumbled and growled. "Your papa would have done better to leave the spelling of his name alone. The D'NOs are a respected family. My mama travels everywhere and attends the best parties with the best people."

Cousin Peter had looked slightly belligerent through most of this exchange. Now he looked lost. "Who is your Mama?"

"Mrs. Jacob Jaconovich."

He was still confused. "Yes, but what does she have to do with the D'NOs."

I laughed. "She is your papa's first cousin. She grew up at The Cove. Of course we have our financial ties with the Rouseff, Spinoza, and Uzara families."

My cousin's eyes were growing huge. "Oh! Oh, now I understand why you wanted me to have an attorney and all. You wanted to clear the name."

I nodded.

His attorney patted him on the shoulder.

I continued. "Since you appear to be family, perhaps you and your wife would like to come to dinner on Sunday? Be at the M'TK station at three and Mama and Papa will bring you out by private trolley."

"Thank you. Thank you sir." Cousin Peter still sounded confused.

I stood. "I am relieved to have the matter cleared up. It must have been embarrassing for you."

My cousin and his attorney left with my signature dismissing charges against him. I wondered how many more identity cases we could collect.

My new cousin came to dinner with Mama, Papa, the Rouseffs, and Andrew with his wife, Adele. Mama looked as sophisticated as always in her dinner gown. I noticed Peter, turning to look at her often. Finally he could contain himself no longer, "My sister looks just like you. "

"She must be very lovely then." Papa looked besotted and smiled at his wife.

"Your sister is very fortunate. Tell her that her cousin gets more lovely with age."

"Everybody talks about whether she looks more like a Jouyet or a Fortenac. I am going to enjoy telling them that she looks just like a D'NO."

Leah seemed to enjoy having people over for dinner. She used a great number of spoons and forks. I smiled that she was trying so hard to fit into the role of a sophisticated lady. She didn't need to try so hard. Her natural elegance overshadowed any superficial error in protocol. She totally charmed Cousin Peter and his wife.

Mama smoothed over every awkward moment with questions about her cousin and the rest of the family. She remembered Peter's grandfather well. She also remembered meeting Peter's papa.

Over the next few months, I didn't know what to make of Cousin Peter. He was more Fortenac than D'NO. It was the Fortenac part I didn't trust.

Leah received frequent invitations from his wife who was a Jouyet. We all figured that the Fortenacs and Jouyets were trying to get information from Leah about my work or Mama and Papa's work or Mr. Rouseff. I never talked about anything sensitive around Leah.

I had very little to do in the prosecutor's office. I searched old files for possible cases. We saw a little increase in petty crime. We laughed and made jokes about the people of the city refraining from crime for three weeks in a row before they went back to the drinking and brawling. I made no effort to look for the odd cases that might be coercion and harassment. I didn't have to. Christian faithfully dropped on my desk the addresses of every case that fit the profile we were looking for. I would call Rouseff and he would be delighted with our progress. I knew he would send his agents out to talk to the victims immediately.

One morning when I stopped by his office, he was scowling at a big map that covered his desk and hug off the ends. He glanced up at me briefly before speaking. "Jake, tell me what is happening on the street."

I shrugged. "I don't know. Nobody tells me anything."

"Then go for a walk. You used to tell me you could read the street. I want you to go read these two blocks." He drew a circle on the map with his finger.

"Shall I go now?" I was surprised.

"Does the time of day make a difference?"

"I'll go now." I took the next trolley in the right direction planning to get off above the area we were concerned about and walk toward the Cathedral. I got off the trolley and walked slowly speaking to street vendors as I passed. I searched the faces around me, those that didn't turn away. I watched the school children. I listened. I debated what to do with the man who had been following me since I started walking.

He hadn't followed me from Rouseff's office. I didn't remember seeing him on the trolley. I stopped at a street vendor and bought some flowers. I chatted with the vendor while I paid for the flowers and surreptitiously studied my shadow. He'd stopped and was staring intently into the window of a shoe repair. He was dressed in the brown pants and loose shirt of a laborer. He was too thin for his shabby clothes. I wondered if he was watching for anything unusual on the street or me. I walked on my way. The man followed me all the way into the cathedral. He stood by an arch near the entrance while I approached the communion rail.

I'd entered just in time to light a candle before eight o'clock Mass. I gave the flowers to a volunteer. She placed them on the communion table. I stayed for Mass. After mass, I caught another trolley and went to the prosecutor's office rather than let anyone see me return to Rouseff's. I would see Rouseff later in the day.

I had a couple routine cases to process. Christian dropped another address from the targeted area on my desk. I called Rouseff. For the benefit of potential listeners, I opened, "You wanted me to call you sir?"

He was clever enough to follow my lead. "How is your wife?"

"Big, uncomfortable, and weepy."

He asked a question dear to my heart. "Are you getting decent food at home?"

"Only if Mama brings some over. Leah isn't up to cooking."

He chuckled. "Would it be cheating for you to have lunch with me?"

"I'll cheat to get a good meal."

We went to Rouseff's home for lunch. We ate in his study. When we were settled in his big leather chairs he asked, "Well, what do you think?"

"The man who tailed me from the trolley was not a professional. He is not acquainted with our Mass. He had no idea when to stand or kneel."

Rouseff chuckled.

I continued. "There is heavy pressure on the street there. Even the school children are aware of trouble. We had another case in today of someone unlikely charged with assault or maybe possession. Here is his address. What I think. The pressure has reached a point where something will happen within the week."

"What do you think will happen?"

"They used fire in the past. This area is not so convenient to the trolley line. We can get the fire fighting car to the top of the street, but I think the police would block us before we could get it there."

He rubbed at his jaw. "Is it time for my men to go in?"

I was still focused on the basic facts. "They know I've been there. It is not unreasonable for me to take that trolley to go to Mass, but they know I've been there. They may underestimate what I know and who my connections are."

"Surely they know that you are a Rouseff."

"Of course, they know that. Do they know you will move against them? Do they know that you know what they are planning and why?"

Rouseff shifted in his chair. "Possibly not."

I added. "The street is watched. I'd like to take out the watchers before your men go in."

"What do you suggest?"

"Chloroform."

Mr. Rouseff raised his eyebrows. "Jake where do you get these ideas?"

I tried to sound innocent. "Mr. Wu used to chloroform the rats before they dressed them out. I submit it is the proper way to deal with rats. Only perhaps these rats can wake up in the hospital? No? Okay, our other option is a diversion of some sorts."

Mr. Rouseff started to chuckle.

Now it was my turn to raise my eyebrows. "You are frightening me sir."

"Remember our street players?"

I was cautious. "They are amateurs Civilians. I wouldn't want anybody to get hurt."

Rouseff was looking into his mind rather than at me. "They can make enough of a diversion to get our people in, dance and sing and advertise some street performance. I really do need to start more organized theater groups. Do you know anybody who majored in theater?"

"Chloroform would be easier and safer."

"I'll save that idea for later. I better get my actors onto the street."

I used the phone in his office to call Professor Ingleman to tell him I was concerned. He invited me to come by about eight o'clock. I hated to leave Leah home alone in the evening, but I made the appointment.

Mr. Rouseff dropped me back at the office. I found about five regulars in the holding area. One man waved cheerfully when he saw me. I shook my head and fetched his file.

As he followed me to my office, he said in a loud rowdy voice. "Aw, I'm glad to see you sir."

I motioned for him to sit. "It says drunk and disorderly. That is not your usual crime."

He leaned toward me and whispered. "No, I needs to see you."

"Ah," I wondered if I could get some more privacy in the open room. I picked up the phone and dialed Christian's extension. "I won't need that coffee now. I am busy with a client." I hoped Christian would figure out what I needed. "Now, lets get this routine stuff out of the way." I asked routine questions for about two minutes.

A loud crash from the other side of the room interrupted us. Christian yelped. "Ow! Damn it all to hell! Who the hell made the coffee so damn hot?"

I glanced toward my friend in the corner of the room then leaned toward my client. "Now what did you want to tell me about?"

He leaned toward me and whispered barely loud enough for me to hear. "It's them men who are trying to buy out everybody and threatening people. They kidnapped Mr. Chang's daughter."

My mouth went instantly dry. "Does anybody know where they are holding her?"

"No. They say they will bring her back when Chang signs over the deed to his property. They says he is to take the signed deed in an envelope with his own name on it to the mayors office and give it to the mayors secretary."

I nodded. "I'll pass the word. Get me all the information you can. Take it to Rouseff, Mr. Apkouta, or Papa. Wait, if you see people in costumes dancing and singing in the street, you can tell them to tell Rouseff. I fined the man ten dollars and dug in my pocket to give him money to pay the fine."

"You don't have to do that."

"We have a fund to pay our informants. I'll bill the city when this is over." The man left. The coffee mess in the back was getting cleaned up. I needed to talk to Rouseff.

Chapter 31 False Alarm

Just as I was reaching for my phone to call Rouseff about the kidnapping, it rang.

"Jake?" Leah's voice sounded small and weepy.

"What is it Honey?" My heart crawled up into my throat. Leah never called me at work.

"I'm home alone and I don't feel well." She sounded anxious and fearful.

I broke into a sweat. "Do you think you are in labor?" How fast could I get to her? She had the roadster. She could…no what an idiot I was, she couldn't drive now. It would be fastest to send Mama to her.

She still sounded frail and scared. "No, I just don't feel well. I don't think I should be alone. I'm not in labor now, but this smolt may be here sooner than we think."

My heart started pounding. "Honey, I am on my way home." I reassured her some more and got off of the phone.

I called the station. "Mama, it's Leah. She says she is not feeling well and doesn't want to be alone. Can you come pick me up at work and drive me out there?"

"Is it the baby? I'll go out from here. I'll call Rosalie Rouseff to give you a ride." Mama had no intention of missing anything exciting.

"Have Philippe pick me up if he can. I don't want to ride with Mrs. Rouseff."

"I'll have her call you right away if she can give you a ride. I'll come get you if she or he can't." I hung up then paced back and forth by the phone. I gnawed on my knuckles.

"What is it Jake?" Jeffrey's desk sat close enough to mine that I thought for sure he heard the whole conversation. He sounded genuinely concerned.

"Leah."

"She is? Is she in…ah…labor?" I thought Jeffrey blushed slightly.

"She says she is not having pains, but she…she doesn't feel right." I tried to remember to relax. "Mama will go right out if she doesn't have to come get me." I paced some more while everybody in the office discussed Leah.

Darlene a clerk announced authoritatively. "The first one can come early or late."

One of the paralegals, a father of five assured me, "It will take a long time to get here."

Leroy clapped me on the shoulder and made no attempt to be comforting. "Believe me Jake, this will take a long time. You are going to be a wreck when it is over."

My supervisor came out of his office and added his opinion. "Two ounces of whisky will fix you up Jake." He returned to his own office possibly to take his own advice.

The phone rang. Rouseff assured me he was on his way. I almost wept with relief.

I ran for the door babbling nonsense. "Hey guys, I don't know when I'll be back. It is early. This may pass. It may be nothing." I left to wait for Rouseff at the curb. He pulled up and I slid in beside him almost before the car came to a stop.

As soon as I saw Rouseff I remembered why I wanted to call him. I blurted out. "Chang's ten year old daughter was abducted." I filled him in on everything I knew. "I also have a meeting at eight tonight with one of my professors. I don't like this abduction coming right at this time. Too many things are happening all at once."

Mr. Rouseff remained calm. "Your first born child is a once in a lifetime event. You stay with Leah first. I'll take care of Chang's girl."

I writhed in my seat, caught between the conflicting needs of others. "I speak fluent Chinese."

"So do other people." Rouseff continued, "I assume Leah really does need you and this wasn't just an excuse to take off from work."

I nodded and changed to worrying about Leah.

Cousin Philippe's calm voice was reassuring. "She goes to that fancy baby doctor doesn't she?"

I nodded. "I will check with his office and maybe take her in."

Rouseff snorted. "He's expensive enough that you should be able to call him anytime."

We arrived at my house a few minutes after my parents. Mama was sitting beside Leah.

Leah told Mama what happened. "It was just such a horrible sinking feeling. I was afraid."

Mama stayed calm and comforting. She smiled at me as she held Leah's hand. "She is not in labor now. I think her body is getting ready. It looks like the baby has moved into position."

I was still worried. I kissed Leah on top of her head. "Did anybody call your doctor?"

Leah sounded anxious. "I didn't want to bother him."

I strode manfully off to the phone. "I'm paying him so we can bother him. I'll call."

Mr. Rouseff slapped Papa on the back. "Jacob, why don't I give you a lift back to the station. I doubt the women want us men around. He practically dragged Papa out to the car. I hoped the two of them could handle the Chang problem.

The nurse came on the line. I identified myself. "Leah called me at work. She says she suddenly did not feel well. She said it was more emotional--fear. My mama is here. She thinks the baby changed position." I started shaking again.

"Let me talk to the doctor."

I paced and waited for the nurse to get back to me.

The nurse came back on the line. "The doctor wants you to take Leah into the hospital. He will see her there. He doesn't think the baby will be here any time soon, but the sudden change and the sense of fear are something to check out."

Mama and I loaded Leah in the car and took her to the hospital. Leah sat beside me saying how foolish she felt for calling everybody out because she felt peculiar.

We eventually got Leah as comfortable as possible in an examination room. Mama stayed beside Leah and held her hand. The nurse kicked me out of the room for pacing and making Leah nervous. Finally the he doctor arrived and checked her over. He let me back into the room and explained to Leah, "I think you experienced a little toxemia. I'd like to see if we can move some of that excess water weight without distressing you or the baby."

Mama comforted me by pacing the floor and wringing her hands. She told the doctor. "I think the baby has shifted position."

"Yes, he is getting ready to come out and explore the world, but he won't be here for a couple days yet. We will do some more tests and keep an eye on things."

Leah sounded ready to cry. "Can I go home tonight?"

"No, I want to keep you here overnight."

Mama squeaked and ran out of the room.

I tried not to panic. "Is the baby in any danger?"

"No, it has a good strong steady heartbeat. Sounds like a happy smolt in there." He turned to Leah. "I am concerned about your water retention. If we get some of the water off, you can go home in the morning. If we don't get it off we will induce labor."

I wanted to run in circles and pull my hair and yell at the doctor. I remembered my martial arts training. I stood and tried to relax. The doctor prepared to leave the room.

"Um, doctor, my mother is out in the hall. This is her first grandchild. She lost a few babies. Can you speak to her? Explain that Leah is in a good place getting good care."

He gave me a sad smile and nodded. "I see a lot of cases like this. Twenty or thirty years ago, babies in this country didn't have much of a chance." He patted Leah on the foot. "You are going to be just fine Leah. You have good sense. I'm glad you called for help." He squeezed my shoulder before he left the room.

Leah still sounded weepy. "Oh Jake, I feel so awful for disturbing everybody."

I snuggled as close to Leah as I could from my chair beside her bed. "Why? I didn't have much to do at work. The petty criminals have gotten tired of paying fines so they are obeying the law. The biggest excitement in the office was when the coffee pot overheated the coffee."

Mama put her head in the room. "Jake, Leah, I will go back to the station now. Call me if you need anything."

I got up and pulled a coin out of my pocket, "Thanks, Mama, you were a comfort." I pressed the coin into her hand. "Light a candle for me too." I kissed her cheek.

When we were alone, I sat down beside Leah. She continued to fret and fuss over everything.

The nurse brought some tea in for her to drink. She explained that it contained a gentle diuretic. As soon as the first cup was gone the nurse refilled it.

I stayed beside Leah the rest of the afternoon and tried to speak soothing thoughts. "Leah, I know you are not feeling well. You really did need to call me. We really did need to call the doctor. You really do need to be here. You are not being a burden or silly. You are my greatest joy. You are carrying my hope. Your only job is to take care of my joy and my hope. You are doing a good job with that." She smiled at me then.

Late in the day the nurse came in again. I reminded her, "Um Leah, didn't get any dinner." I remembered not to talk about Leah in front of her." I asked her, "Do you want me to get you something?"

The nurse sounded cheery. "Oh, she hasn't had dinner? We will feed her. We want to be careful how much salt she eats."

My stomach rumbled. "Ah, if you are going to take care of her then, could I slip out and beg a dinner from a friend?"

The evil nurse still acted cheery. "You can go home. We were about to kick you out anyway. We don't allow visitors in after eight."

"What? I just wanted to leave the room for a few minutes to get food." I took Leah's hand. "I can't leave her. She's been upset. She needs me with her. I can sleep right here in this chair."

The nurse snorted. "Mr. Jaconovich, get out of here."

"No."

The nurse tried to look fierce. "We will call security."

"I'm not afraid of them."

Leah started to laugh. "Jake, you are the one being silly now. They will take care of me. I think I am feeling a little better. You can go on home."

"Can I sleep in the waiting room?"

The heartless nurse stood firm. "No, we are onto all the tricks you young husbands have for sneaking into their wives rooms."

I was shocked. "Look at her! I don't intend to do anything personal. I just want to be near her."

"No."

Leah smiled at me. "Jake, it's okay."

"Are you certain, my love? You won't be afraid if I leave."

"I won't be afraid. I promise."

Finally, I was reassured that Leah was in reasonably good hands. I left, bought a fish pie from and street vender, and was only fifteen minutes late for my appointment with Professor Ingleman. He assured me that they had the judges lined up to hear our request for a procedural ruling calling for a constitution.

I tried to explain what was happening in the city. "I am not certain that now is the time for our rulings, but something big is going down. The emperor is involved. I am afraid of a major purge here in the city. Rouseff is watching rail traffic for any sign of an increase in activity, but the government has roads and the military railroad. I am not sure when they plan to move. The pattern of coercion I see in my office and the fear on the street makes me think the army will march through the city, possibly burning as they go, in a path from the city hall down Ninth Street and Doh Creek Road to connect with the new highway."

Professor Ingleman moaned. His eyes reflected his horror. "They can bring an army down the new highway."

I ran my hands through my hair. "When they get done, they will expect to buy the land cheap from any owners who survive. Rouseff is prepared to counter both their military and financial plans. I hope that when their plan fails we will have a brief moment when the prosecutor's office can charge government officials with everything we can think of from murder, arson and extortion to assembling without a permit. While the prosecutor's office is charging people, you need to have your cases calling for an election to vote on a constitution before the judges. Everybody official will be looking at the purge and trying to figure out what happened. They won't be looking at a bunch of court rulings. I figure our window of opportunity from the first attack to the time of the rulings is about seventy-two hours."

"So short?" He sounded dismayed.

"We don't dare count on more. We want the election calling for the adoption of the constitution within six weeks after the ruling."

He nodded. "We are ahead of you. We can get our job done, if you can get us that window."

I ran my hands through my hair pulling it to help me think. "I don't know. I know the attack is coming soon. I don't know if it will be enough. I have been making a list of names and their crimes. I will file charges as soon as they move, but I don't have the solid link to the emperor. I need someone to talk. I'm not sure if we can arrest enough people to keep the government from ignoring the elections and continuing with business as usual."

He bowed his head. "Jake we are ready, if the opportunity we need doesn't materialize we will wait. Some of us have been waiting for thirty or forty years. We can wait longer."

"For what? More purges?"

"You evacuate those people at the first sign of trouble. There will be no purge this time. The Southern families are growing more and more bold. They will overreach their hand, you can bank on it." He walked me out the door.

Back in my car, I debated what to do next. I really wanted to be at the hospital with Leah. I snarled that the idea of separating a man and wife at a time like this was barbaric. Home seemed too far away from Leah. I remembered just running out of the office this afternoon. I decided to go back and clean my desk.

I let myself into the empty prosecutor's office and I smiled at the prospect of getting caught up on paperwork with no interruptions.

In the first hour, I finished my reports on the cases I'd processed so far today. During the second hour I reorganized my desk. I thought about needing to prosecute dozens of high-level cases. I made a flow chart for how I would handle the work. During the third hour I restocked my desk with all the proper forms and started reading case law. My phone rang.

Papa admonished me. "I heard that your car was parked at the office. Don't stay up all night."

"I won't."

"You come here if you don't want to drive out to your house."

"I want to be closer. Maybe I'll go to midnight Mass then let myself in at your place."

"Good night son." Hearing Papa say those words made me instantly sleepy. I went back to reading case law.

I think I must have dozed off for about an hour. Something woke me. I looked at the page in front of me. My eyes rested on a line I remembered just reading. I heard something soft bump something hard. I heard an intake of breath. Someone was in the building. I listened. I could hear an occasional shuffle and ragged breathing. A shoe squeaked--Shuffle Foot didn't have squeaky shoes. I thought I picked up a third heavier step. I looked at my light on my desk. They would find me soon enough. I briefly debated trying to hide, but decided that if I could hear them move, they could hear me.

I called out, "There is no point in pretending that you are being quiet.

You are making so much noise, a man can't think straight." I heard surprised sounds.

A deep male voice asked, "Is there someone here?"

I laughed. "Use your head man. I'm talking to you so there must be someone here." I slowly braced my chair against the half-wall beside my desk. I heard footsteps, grunts, and whispers growing closer. I soon saw their shadows on the wall at the end of the room. I guessed at least one of the men to be huge.

One of the smaller men questioned me. He was still four meters away when he asked, "What are you doing here?"

I closed my law book and set it on my desk. "I work here." I moved my right foot against the sturdy leg of my heavy desk.

"It is the middle of the night." The spokesman was the smallest of the three.

"I noticed that. My wife is in the hospital having our baby. I left in the middle of the day to take care of her. I came in to clean up my desk."

I watched the men approach my desk. They halted outside the halo of my desk lamp. I couldn't see their faces, but they looked physically fit.

I continued casually. "That answers the question of why I am here. I belong here. It doesn't answer the question of why you are here? You don't work here. I doubt that you have keys. Why are three men wandering around the prosecutors office in the middle of the night?"

The spokesman said, "Look we'll ask the questions."

I snorted.

He asked again. "What are you doing here?"

I pulled to the front of my brain my memories of martial arts classes, and being accosted on the streets. I laughed. "I already answered that question. I belong here. You do not. I will leave you alone if you can explain why you are here. Perhaps you are the janitors? No? I thought not. Alas, my wastebasket is full."

"You are pretty cocky for a man alone in a building in the middle of the night."

"This is my office. You are the intruder. Why are you here?" I watched their movements. They were not street punks. They seemed more bewildered than aggressive. "Perhaps I can help you if you would tell me what you are looking for."

"Shut up." The leader turned and addressed his companions. "This presents a problem. What should we do with him?"

The big man answered, "Yes, he has seen us. We should leave immediately."

"What about him?" The littlelest one asked.

"Leave him." I revised my idea of who was the leader. The big man gave the command to leave me.

"No, let's take him with us and question him. We can't just leave him. He's seen us." The little man argued.

"Leave him."

Little Man irritated me. "No, We are taking him with us for questioning."

Big man drawled. "I doubt that he knows anything."

Little Man was bigger than me, but compared to his companion, he was small enough. "He knows we were here. He could ruin everything."

I began to suspect that this trio knew something about what was happening in the city. "I don't think you will find what you are looking for here. I've been keeping my eyes open, but nothing is kept here. Nothing is happening in the office."

Little guy sounded eager. "He knows something."

The big man sighed. "We better take him with us."

I settled back in my chair. "I think you missed the part about my wife having a baby. Under other circumstances I would love to visit with you. I am very curious as to why three men broke into the prosecutor's office."

The big man sounded almost apologetic. "Sorry about this, but you are coming with us."

"No, I am going to walk out that door, get in my car, and go stay with friends so I will be as close to my wife as possible."

The little guy actually begged. "Come on man."

"I do not want to go with you. I refuse to go with you. Any attempt to force me at this point will be prosecuted as abducting an officer of the court."

Little guy was losing patience. "Yeah, yeah, yeah, we're not worried about that."

These men were big and in extremely good physical condition. My advantage was the hope that they had no idea that I had training. "I am not going anywhere." I hoped they did not pull out guns. I strongly suspected they were armed. I tried to look non-threatening.

Little guy ordered. "Stand up."

"No."

The third man spoke for the first time. "Oh, grab him and let's get out of here."

The little man was closest to me. He stepped forward, grabbed my arm, and gave a mighty heave. I launched into the pull, pushing off from my desk and chair. I kneed my first attacker in the ribs as I flew over him. The second man tried to grab me from behind as I flew over the first. I reached behind me and grabbed him at the back of his neck. His momentum carried him down as I rolled over the top of him, knocking the wind out of him. I rolled to the side and came up under the big man. He'd made the mistake of bending over me. I knew I broke his nose. The first two men tried to get up off of the floor. They would have made it up, if their huge companion had not landed on top of them. I danced out the door, locking it behind me.

I felt like I was flying as I leapt for the roadster. I drove off as silently as I could. I remembered to breathe when I got halfway to the M'TK station. I wondered where was the safest place to spend the night. Nobody appeared to be following me. I drove home without turning on my headlights. The sky was clear. I had starlight and about a quarter moon.

When I got home, the first thing I did was call the hospital. I knew the extension for Leah's nurses' station. The phone rang. I heard it pick up on the other end.

"Mr. Jaconovich, she is fine. She is still asleep." The nurse assured me. "The baby is fine. Go to bed and stop calling us every hour." I decided I might have called too often. I went to bed. I thought about Leah. I realized that I was rather thankful for the three men who broke into the office. After all my anxiety about Leah, I felt much better for having tossed three men about.

I called the hospital again when I woke up. The day shift was much nicer...well somewhat nicer. "Oh Mr. Jaconovich, we heard about you. She is still asleep. The baby is fine. She is fine and you can see her after ten AM." That was the only information I could get out of the nurse.

When I walked into my office, I expected to see my desk lamp burning and my chair overturned. Everything looked just as it should. My wastebasket was empty. The janitor had been through. I wondered if he had to sort out the bodies on the floor.

I studied morning stack of files, but I didn't see any skinny files. We had another batch of repeat offenders. I started with another drunk and disorderly case. I let him off easy. The second case was for shoplifting a head of cabbage. I sent the old woman to the priest for community service and to Mama's market for food.

I was finishing my paperwork for the shoplifting case when a huge, familiar presence loomed over my desk. A big hand set a large, grey, rubber rat on my desk.

I looked a long way up to see a broad face with a hint of two black eyes and bandages across a swollen nose. "Sorry, about that." I indicated his nose. I picked up the rubber rat and stroked it feeling the structure of the thing. I motioned for him to sit. I suspected he'd done a little research since last night. "I've been a little crazy with the wife in the hospital and all."

He chuckled and pulled out his identification, holding it below the level of the desk as if he didn't want anyone other than me to see it. He worked for the Central Government Investigative Service (CGIS). "We need to talk."

"I am about to go down to the hospital. You may walk with me."

"Sounds good."

I wondered why this man from one of the most powerful and feared offices in the country was being so polite to me. The rubber rat told me he had spent some time investigating me on the street. I called to my boss through his open door that I was caught up on everything and was heading to the hospital.

My supervisor stopped me. "Just a minute Jake. I want your opinion on this case."

I nodded to my guest and he wandered toward the door. I stood in my supervisor's doorway.

He sounded jovial. "Come in. Close the door." I did as requested.

My supervisor hissed. "That man is from the CGIS. What does he want with you?"

"I have no idea."

His hiss took on more of a commanding tone. "You are not to tell him anything that happens in this office."

I stiffened and tried to look offended. "I would never violate client confidentiality."

Mr. Supervisor started getting huffy. "It is more than that. He may be asking about big cases."

I shrugged. "We don't have any. He is more likely sounding me out on prosecuting something they've turned up."

Mr. Supervisor switched from aligning folders on his dest to pulling at his lower lip. "He should come to me. You tell him to come to me."

"Certainly sir. You are right. He should go to you to discuss cases." I shrugged. "I need to go now. I'm caught up on my work. I came in late last night. I want to see Leah now." I left.

The big man met me on the sidewalk and matched his pace to mine.

I opened the conversation. "Major Yablonski, I should warn you that I know very little. What do you want?"

"I want to know what the hell is going on. I've been able to get hints and pieces of serious trouble on the street. Mostly, people laughed at me for tangling with you."

"Oh." Actually, I was thinking *"Oh Shit!"*

"When I finally collected my men and helped them out of the building, I found a welcoming committee in the alley all but falling over themselves laughing at us. They were the second hint we'd tangled with someone notorious."

I turned and looked at him. "People gathered in the alley to wait for you to come out? And, they laughed?"

He nodded once and looked grim, "It seems they saw you leave the building, hop in your car, and drive off without lights. They were a little disappointed that there were only three of us and that we could all walk."

I looked away, "I hate fighting. Well, except that I was upset over Leah last night and a little exercise was just the thing to take my mind off of her for a few minutes."

He grunted. "I heard about you calling the hospital once every fifteen minutes."

I looked at him.

He explained. "The nurses gossiped."

I noted. "You've been busy."

"I had to get the nose put back on straight."

"Ah, yes, sorry."

He laughed.

I asked. "What else did you learn?"

"They call you the M'TK Sewer Rat. You have mystical powers and are undefeated in battle. You were a complete mama's boy. You killed a man when you were seven. You may or may not be related to any of the big families. You grew up in M'TK, in one of the tenements. Your papa is a great hero for saving the lives of many people in M'TK when it burned. He also fought the fire on lower ninth. You are considered to be honest and fair. You got a conviction for Leon Fortenac."

I looked at the sky. "That is a reasonable list but not completely accurate. Like most street knowledge you need to sort out the myth and wishful thinking. I do not have mystical powers. The man, when I was seven, did not die from my actions. I was damn lucky with the Fortenac case."

"Ah, but I am more interested in the level of respect you generate. People on the street do not respect anybody, but they respect you. I'm told that they are policing themselves to cut down on crime out of respect for your papa. I hear they don't want him to know they weren't worth saving."

I stared at the man beside me and shook my head. "I don't know where to start with that."

He looked me in the eye. "I am going to start by trusting you. It may get me killed." He looked around us.

I told him, "The man in the black turtleneck and grey pants is following us."

"He is with me."

"Was it one of yours who went to Mass with me the other morning?"

"No, I was unaware of your existence until last night."

"Ah."

"Jake, I am in internal affairs. This government is corrupt from start to finish. I was in the prosecutors office looking for evidence of how far the corruption runs through that office."

I snorted. "You could have asked last night and saved yourself a great deal of pain and trouble. I don't trust anybody in the office. The leaders of our current little outbreak of extortion and thievery certainly control my boss and his supervisor. They will do as they are told. If you need a prosecutor to help you, try asking the judge in the Fortenac case. He is an honest man."

"I think I might have found a prosecutor."

"Oh shit."

"Shit." He agreed. One thing I've always appreciated about my relationship with Peter Yablonski was our ability to communicate a great deal with very few words.

I asked, "Do you have some idea when my services will be required?"

"Within the next two weeks. That is why we were so desperate as to break into the prosecutor's office."

"Why don't you find someone in the capital?"

"We have someone in the capital."

"Ah," I was immensely relieved that I was not the poor prosecutor chosen to charge the emperor with capital crimes. I might enjoy charging my boss.

I realized I hadn't seen any children on the street. The older children were in school, but the younger ones should be on the sidewalks, or in the shops and stalls with their parents.

I thought for a few seconds. "We do have a troublesome problem that may well be outside your jurisdiction, but it is related to the big picture. We are missing a ten year-old girl. Her last name is Chang. Her family owns shops on upper ninth. If you can find that girl, you might find someone with more answers than I can give you. People are looking. I've enquired about any new brothels, but she hasn't turned up."

Yablonski stared. "Jake! How does a nice university man with the reputation for being a mama's boy even know about such things?"

"I grew up on the streets of M'TK."

"Oh."

"Yeah."

Yablonski stopped when we reached the hospital. "I'll leave you here. You've given me a new direction. I will get my men looking for that child and the people who are holding her." He strode off back up the way we'd come.

The nurses glared at me when I reached Leah's floor. I complained. "Well, if you would let a fellow stay with his wife, that wouldn't happen."

"You are the worst we've encountered."

I laughed and hurried on to Leah's room.

"Leah." I bent over her bed and kissed her eagerly. "How are my precious wife and baby this morning?"

She pouted at me adorably. "Jake, I am embarrassed that my husband called the hospital every fifteen minutes since eight o'clock last night.

"I did not call every fifteen minutes. Sometimes I went a full thirty minutes before I couldn't stand it anymore. If they would let a fellow stay beside his wife that wouldn't happen." Leah looked more flattered than concerned.

Leah picked at her blanket. "I am bored. The doctor thinks I can go home this afternoon. They are not letting me eat any salt or foods containing salt." She showed me the list of foods she would not be able to eat.

"Well certainly this is only for a few days." I looked at the list. "If you are not supposed to eat fish, it is no wonder you are holding water. I will see about getting some chicken or lamb."

"They gave me an egg for breakfast. It was delicious. Perhaps we should have chickens and raise our own eggs."

"I'd rather raise babies." I snuggled closer to Leah and settled down for some serious kissing. My wife liked kissing.

A nurse came in. "Mr. Jaconovich what are you doing?"

I snorted. "If I have to answer that question, it is no wonder you don't have a husband."

Leah swatted my arm. "Jake! That was horrid."

The nurse shook her head over me as she took Leah's blood pressure and checked her arms and ankles for swelling. Leah looked better. She felt better. At one in the afternoon, the doctor let me take her home with instructions to eat fresh fruit, eggs, chicken and nothing with salt. I spent the rest of the day at home.

I put Leah to bed about eight PM. She was sleepy. We'd hiked to the top of the ridge and watched the sun go down earlier. I thought the exercise helped her relax.

As soon as I was free, I called Rouseff. He'd already heard half of what I had to report.

"Who was the man you walked with this morning?"

I gave Mr. Rouseff the high points of my two meetings with Major Yablonski. "He finally told me he is from CGIS. I asked him to find the Chang girl."

Mr. Rouseff sounded as fretful as Leah. "Was that wise? He could uncover our counter-measures."

"I want that child found. I think Major Yablonski is honorable enough. He will try to find the child for his own reasons. I suspect he operates outside the world of business. He did say that if a purge comes, it will come up the new highway and we won't be able to stop it."

"Does he expect a purge?"

"I think he was looking for a prosecutor to charge whomever commits such a crime against the people."

"Shit."

"Yeah." I communicated well with Rouseff too.

Chapter 32 Jacob

One full week after Leah had been in the hospital the first time, she went into labor. Luckily, she was visiting Mrs. Rouseff at the time.

By the time I got to Rouseffs', Mama and Mrs. Rouseff had Leah bundled up and ready for me to drive her the short distance to the hospital. We had to cut across Ninth Street. I realized that if a purge came, the hospital would be cut off from much of the rest of the city for hours maybe even days. I was frantic. I needed to talk to Rouseff. Thankfully he arrived not long after we did. I immediately told him my worry. He nodded.

I stayed with Leah until the nurse explained exactly how they intended to examine her. I bounded out of my chair feeling slightly queasy. "I'll give you privacy. Call me when you are done here."

The nurse snickered, "The fathers are such cowards.

Leah managed a fleeting smile through the pain of another contraction.

I started sweating. "Yeah, I am a coward. I hate pain." Witnessing the delicate, elegant Leah struggling to bring our child into the world while I could do nothing to help, was almost more than I could stand. I longed to toss the massive Major Yablonski around some more just to relieve my anxiety.

My Leah was a champ when it came to giving birth. We settled in for a long wait. I was just beginning to pace when a nurse came and got me. "Mr. Jaconovich, you have a son." Are there any words more beautiful in any language than, "You have a son?" The nurse wrapped me up in a sterile gown and took me to see my family.

Leah looked tired but peaceful with a tiny bundle tucked in the nook of her arm. I reached for the bundle as nurse hovered over me, explaining how to hold my son for the first time. He grabbed onto my finger when I stroked his hand.

"Jake, what is it?" Leah sounded alarmed. "You are crying. Didn't you want a boy?"

I did have tears running down my cheeks. "I am about the happiest, proudest man on the face of this earth." I kissed Leah. "Thank you for giving me a son. He's so tiny, the tiniest thing I have ever seen.

"You wouldn't think he is so tiny if you'd been the one to push that husky little boy out of your body."

"Compared to everyone else in the world he is tiny. I have a great deal to teach him." I looked into his tiny perfect face. My heart melted. I struggled between my desire to stare only at him and my desire to stare only at my lovely wife. "Leah you are perfect. Thank you again and again for this gift."

"You gave him to me first."

I forgot about the outside world for hours. I was completely content there in that quiet room sitting beside my exhausted wife while she slept.

At eight PM, a young nurse came into our room. "Mr. Jaconovich, visiting hours are over--you need to...."

I looked at the nurse.

"Oh!" She squeaked and ran out of the room.

I snuggled back down with my head on the bed near my wife. I was afraid to walk down to the nursery to see my son for fear I'd get thrown out of the hospital. Hospitals were barbaric back then. I should have been holding my baby boy instead of leaving him alone in a nursery. Papas should hold their babies. They did bring Jacob in to be fed after a couple hours. This time an older nurse admonished me, "Mr. Jaconovich, I really am going to have to ask you to leave."

"Go ahead." I smiled at her

"What?"

"Go ahead and ask me to leave."

She blinked. "Will you please leave?"

"No." I smiled pleasantly at the woman. She didn't know it yet, but my son was not going back to any nursery either. I stayed while Leah fed our son. He was a healthy baby and knew what dinner was all about. When he finished eating, I picked him up and held him. Occasionally, somebody would come to the door and ask me to leave. Once, they sent security up. I motioned for them to be quiet.

The nursing supervisor hid behind the security and ventured, "Mr. Jaconovich, it is long past visiting hours. Give us the baby and go on home."

"No."

She argued. "The baby needs to sleep."

I remained firm. "My son needs his papa to hold him so he knows he is loved and all is right in his world."

Leah stirred. "Jake are you still here?"

"Hush darling, everything is fine. Go back to sleep."

Leah woke all the way up. "Jake. You are still here?"

"Jacob and I are right beside you."

"Oh, You are being naughty to stay here."

"I may be naughty, but my place is with my wife and son." Leah smiled, rolled over and went back to sleep.

The younger of the guards must have thought he was big enough to make me leave. "Mr. Jaconovich, we're from security. We are going to drag you out of here if you don't come quietly."

"Oh I'm being real quiet."

"Good, now come along sir."

"I shifted in my chair beside Leah and settled Jacob against my shoulder. He made little baby sounds and burped."

I casually drawled. "I should mention this to you. This baby's grandfather is Jacob Jaconovich. They call him a hero in M'TK. He helped put out the fire on lower ninth a few weeks ago. Yes, I see you know who his grandfather is. You should now be able to figure out that I am the one they call the M'TK Sewer Rat. If that name has no meaning to you, ask anyone on the street. I am staying beside my wife and son. That is final."

The younger guard didn't seem impressed, but his older partner took hold of his elbow. "Excuse me Mr. Jaconovich. We didn't know it was you." He backed out of the room pushing the nurse behind him and dragging his partner by the elbow. After that, nobody tried to make me leave. Occasionally a nurse came in to check on Leah or Jacob. They were both happy and healthy. Leah and Jacob were happy, the nurses not so much.

In the morning the doctor checked Leah over. He listened to Jacob's heart and lungs. He chuckled. "I am going to let all of you go home early. Leah is healthy. The delivery went well. Jacob is strong and healthy, and Jake, you have scared the staff half to death."

Leah giggled. "I told him he was being bad."

I was still firm. "I want my wife and son to have all the best care possible, but I want to stay with them. It is wrong to separate a family at such a time. You need to change your policies. I stayed with my family and no harm was done."

I didn't think the doctor had really heard me. "Most fathers are happy enough to go home."

I persisted. "If there are other children at home, the father may need to leave. Otherwise, his place is with his wife and new baby."

The doctor and nurses tended to look at Leah and smile. I wondered if they felt sorry for her because I was being stubborn. I think they all breathed a sigh of relief when we were gone. I relaxed a little too. I wanted my wife and baby outside of town if a purge was coming.

I stayed home with Leah and Jacob for the rest of the week. Leah got up and about and started to complain about me being under foot. My parents came out and brought dinner. Papa looked happy to hold his grandson.

Leah watched Papa for a half-minute then exclaimed, "Now I know where Jake gets his love for babies from. Papa has the same besotted expression Jake gets when he holds that baby."

"Daughter you have given us a precious gift." Papa crossed the room to place a gentle kiss on her forehead. "Thank you for the gift of a grandson. Doesn't he look like his papa?"

Mama stood close to Papa and stared at my son. "I think he will have Leah's eyes."

I watched my family gathered around my tiny son and commented, "I am a very wealthy man."

Chapter 33 Purge

My family stayed safely tucked away in our home in the woods. Each day that passed increased the probability that today would be the day the purge would come. I'd warned my friends to leave town. I seriously considered taking Leah, Jacob, Papa and Mama and going to The Cove until the whole thing blew over. Mr. Rouseff assured me dozens of times that he was ready. I returned to my work routine.

Mr. Rouseff was happy with his purchases of property on Doh Creek Rd and Ninth. "The people liked my terms. Some have started moving into my buildings already. Let the government come. We can evacuate those who still remain."

Mr. Rouseff called me at the prosecutor's office at ten-fifteen, on the day Jacob was ten days old. "This is it." He said grimly.

I hung up and stood up and stretched. Christian across the room raised his eyebrows at me. I nodded once and wandered toward the door leaving everything just where it lay on my desk. I could work from home if the need arose. I'd brought the roadster to work. I walked out the door to the parking lot. I tried not to speed as I eased the car through town. I'd just reached the back road past the old dump when the fire sirens went off at the M'TK station. Once clear of the congested area, I let the roadster perform the way Micki had promised me that it could. Once, I looked in the rear view mirror and saw two identical roadsters behind me--my parents and the Rouseffs.

I arrived home before ten-thirty. I scooped Leah into my arms with our son between us.

Leah became instantly alarmed. "Jake! Jake what is it? What is wrong?"

Papa sounded grim as he came in behind me. "It is another purge, Leah." Mama looked sad and clung to Papa's arm.

Leah wailed, "Oh surely not. We are beyond that. We are a modern and civilized country."

I held Leah close and assured her. "We've known for weeks that it was coming." My phone rang. Keeping one arm around Leah, I answered the phone. "Hello?"

"Jaconovich?" I recognized Yablonski's voice.

"Yeah."

"Good." Major Yablonski hung up. I assumed he was checking my whereabouts.

I let my parents take Leah and the baby while I made a phone call of my own. "Professor, it is time to move on the constitution. I think we can go all the way."

"Thanks Jake." He gasped with excitement. "This is a great day."

"I'll wait to see how many lives we lose before I decide what kind of day it is."

Leah still seemed confused when my parents and the Rouseffs made themselves comfortable in our house. About an hour later, the Apkoutas arrived. "We got both trains off sir. I think almost all of our people are accounted for. Do you think they will attack our mall? We have hundreds more people there."

We discussed the possibility that the government had changed its plans. We knew absolutely nothing. We had our own Rouseff security people, really our own army, who intended to confine the government army to the two block wide swath we knew they were targeting. We wanted communication with the street but suspected that our people on the street were too busy to be calling with updates.

Jacob woke up wanting his dinner. We were all so nervous that he got indigestion and fussed. Mama took him and walked the floor for a few minutes. He settled right down. Mama seemed more calm than the rest of us.

My phone rang again.

"Jake?" Christian called to check in.

"Yeah."

"I am at my parents house about an hour south of town. What do you want me to do now?"

"I hope you didn't attempt the highway."

"No, I know a back country trail and I had my motorcycle with me. I saw the army on the highway though."

"Right now, stay put. We may need to process a great many charges with no staff. How many soldiers do you think there were?"

"Not more than five hundred. They had three tanks and a half-dozen smaller armored vehicles. The trucks all have machine guns on the front.

Listen, I figured something like this was up. I am ready to work from home."

"I'll let you know what we need, as soon as I know something."

"Right, I will get myself set up to file charges from home. What are we charging people with?" Christian sounded almost gleeful.

"Murder, kidnapping, conspiracy to commit murder, that category will be big. Basically, anything you think will stick for a purge."

"Conspiracy to violate the safety of the court." Christian added eagerly. I suspected he had something going on the side with this charge. I hoped he was thinking about our supervisors.

I agreed. "That is an excellent charge."

"What about treason?" He asked.

I paused and thought a few seconds. "No, we don't want any suggestion of that charge since the emperor ordered this purge or at least is condoning it."

"Holy shit Jake. What have you gotten me into?"

"I haven't gotten you into anything. You keep butting your nose in."

"I think I might go get drunk until this is over."

"Stay sober enough to process charges."

When I got off of the phone, I saw Leah looking at me wide-eyed. "You've known this was coming?" Leah looked around the room. "You've all known this was coming." Papa and Rouseff nodded. Mrs. Rouseff sat crying softly.

Mama's behavior caught my horrified attention. She sang and cooed to Jacob, "Your papa is going to be president some day. He'll set this country right. You'll see."

Leah snapped at Mama. "We don't have a president in this country. We have an emperor."

I spoke two words. "This week."

The room grew silent with tension. Everybody looked at me.

Papa sounded almost sharp with me. "Jake is there something you haven't told us? This is not going to be a civil war is it?"

I took a couple deep breaths. "No. No civil war. Who would fight whom? The old families against the peasants?" I started to pace as I talked. "That was the beauty of the Fortenac case. I demonstrated for the court record that the old families have intermarried with the northerners so that the distinction is no longer meaningful.

I ran my hands through my hair and continued, more for my own comfort and thinking process than for my family. "We are planning a procedural case requesting that selected judges make a ruling calling for a constitution that extends voting rights to most people based on this new reality. We will have a parliament and an elected president. That is if all goes as planned."

Mama broke the shocked silence. "I knew my son would set things straight. You have a papa you can be proud of young Jacob." Mama sounded calm and detached from the horror of a purge happening in our city.

Leah started pounding her fists into a pillow while big tears ran down her face. "Or this whole thing can collapse and you will be arrested and executed then Jacob will not have a papa and I don't know what I will do." She started to cry and wailed, "I feel like a fool."

"What is it Sweetheart?" I asked.

Leah picked at the upholstery on the sofa. "Oh everybody keeps asking me what you do at work and I tell them that you process petty criminals and that you want to do contracts for Mr. Rouseff. I had no idea you wanted to be president."

I sat down beside Leah. "I don't want to be president. I want to lead a quiet life with you and my children. I want my children to grow up and go to university without having to say they are members of this family or that. You have been telling the truth."

Mr. Rouseff sounded pensive. "Jake how can we write a constitution? That could take years."

I answered. "It is already written. It was started the day Leon Fortenac was pronounced guilty. The procedural cases calling for an election are being presented to judges in the provinces, now. By starting a purge the government, the emperor has set the courts in motion."

"Surely, you can't do this. Surely you can't." Leah sounded almost frantic.

I tried to keep my voice calm. "I am not doing anything. The men who are filing the suits are not doing anything. The judges who rule on those suits might be doing something, but we have chosen honest men. Our government, any government rules by the permission of the people. Let's hope the emperor is wise enough to know that."

We sat silent for several minutes before Mr. Rouseff's curiosity prompted him to move. "Let's see what we can see from the top of the ridge."

Mama and Papa stayed with Jacob while the rest of us climbed to the top of the ridge. From this point we could hear shelling and explosions. We didn't see much sign of fire. At several points, we thought we could see huge arcs of water shooting up in the air.

Rouseff laughed, "It is that super-powered firefighting engine. They are running it on trolley tracks. If it stays behind buildings, the army won't be able to shell it."

"It is a good piece of equipment." I said. "I'd hate to lose it." We watched for about a half-hour then went back to the house.

The phone started ringing about one.

"Yablonski here, give me blanket charges for five hundred for assault with the intent to kill."

I relayed the message to Christian.

I got another call from Professor Ingleman. "Jake, I just got word that the suits are all filed."

"What about our province?" I asked.

"We have a judge in Mercid."

"Who?"

"Stimson"

"Hmm, I wouldn't have thought of him. He is competent enough but pretty old."

Christian called back. "Jake, I just got a call from a friend. There are about a thousand troops headed south on the new highway."

"Thanks. How long do we have?" I felt my body descending into numb shock.

"At least forty-five minutes."

I hung up and made a general announcement to the others. I couldn't keep the horror out of my voice. "Okay folks, this last call says about a thousand more troops are coming toward the city from the north. "

Rosalie Rouseff sounded as shocked as I was. "Fifteen hundred troops? What do they intend to do? Level the whole city?"

I stared at the wall, not really seeing anything except the army marching on my city. "Apparently, so. We have about forty-five minutes."

Papa looked weary as he got up and moved to the phone. He called the M'TK station. "Sound the general evacuation alarm. We have forty minutes to evacuate the city." Papa sadly called each station. He came back and sat down next to Mama.

Leah still acted anxious. "Do they know about the plan to have elections? Why are they doing this?" She picked at the upholstery on the pillow she occasionally punched or threw on the floor.

I shook my head. "It is possible that they know about the lawsuits and the move to have elections. Sending fifteen hundred troops to crush one city isn't going to solve their problem. It is only going to demonstrate the need for elections. This started with a plan to grab the land for a proposed highway. I don't understand the additional troops, unless." I'd shaken off my initial shock and began to think again. It was too much to hope for. I smiled. Yablonski. He was a major. I grinned.

Leah reached out to me. "Jake, what is it?"

"This is getting bigger and more fantastic as we go. We need to evacuate as many as possible. I have a wild hope that the new troops are coming to arrest the attackers. I need to start filling out charges." I ran off to my office to do paperwork.

I kept getting interrupted with phone calls. The first call came from Professor Ingleman. "The judge in Mercid has ruled. We need to hold an election to consider adopting a constitution that reflects the true number of people in the old families."

"That didn't take him long."

"There is a purge happening on his doorstep."

I got another call. "Yablonski here, do I have my charges?"

"I am almost ready. Before I bring them into the city, are the troops coming in from the north friends or part of the purge."

"They're mine."

"I can deliver these to the M'TK station."

Yablonski sounded distracted. "I will be at your office at four-thirty. I want to pick them up there."

I wanted to be cautious. "I am not a soldier. I have a wife and child."

"Oh you'll be safe enough. Be prepared to work late."

"Shit."

"Yeah,"

I called Christian. "The new troops are friendly. We are being called back to work. We need to be in our office by four-thirty with our paperwork."

Christian-the-ghoul chuckled. "I have some creative ideas for some of the people involved. I'll be there."

I took a break to update my family. "One of my calls was Major Yablonski. The newest troops are here to arrest the attackers. I am to meet Yablonski at the prosecutor's office. I don't know if we have a judge in the city, or if everything will have to go out to Mercid. Anyway, I will be late."

My audience looked at me with various emotions on their faces. Leah looked weepy. Mama smiled vaguely. Mr. Rouseff appeared excited. His wife narrowed her eyes and looked thoughtful. Papa…Papa looked as proud as he had when I won the Fortenac case.

Shortly after four, I kissed my wife and baby, told them I loved them and left for the city.

I found the office deserted and unlocked. Most desks appeared relatively tidy. The few where someone had tried to grab papers before they left were obvious. I wondered if my boss and his supervisor knew they were in trouble. I went to my own desk and tidied up.

I had a briefcase full of papers to complete. I went to the copy room. I planned to unlock the copy machine with Mr. Picket's lock picks to unlock the copier. I didn't want to leave a paper trail that would reveal how many copies had been made and who made them. I crouched down beside the machine and started to work.

"Jake?" A quiet and feminine voice almost whispered behind me.

"Aaagh." I nearly jumped out of my skin. "Allison! You scared me!"

Allison was petite young woman with a halo of dark hair around her face. She had a slight overbite giving her an elfin look. She sounded curious. "What are you doing?"

"Making copies."

"I can do that. It is my job."

I asked, "Why are you still here?"

"I was afraid to try to get through the streets. It's a purge isn't it?"

"Yeah, we need to run a lot of copies tonight. Can you unlock this so we don't have to run a code for each copy?" She took her keys out of her pocket and unlocked the machine. I tried to get my copies organized to run. She took them away from me. The pages were suddenly obedient to her touch.

"What is happening?" She asked.

"Either the worst of it is over, or someone who hates me is about to kill me. This could go either way. If someone wants to file charges against the attackers, I'll be here to do so."

Christian came in carrying his briefcase.

Yablonski showed up about four-forty. "What have you got for me?"

I nodded to a stack of papers on my desk.

"Good. I also want five for kidnapping."

I raised my eyebrows.

He grunted. "We found the girl late last night. She's scared, but otherwise unharmed. Someone named Munk had her stashed in his basement. My men went in and out through the back of the house while your street players put on a show out front."

I nodded and wrote a note for what he wanted.

He passed off the paperwork I'd completed to one of his men. "Looks like somebody was looking for something." He nodded at one of the untidy desks.

"They didn't find it though." Christian introduced himself. "I didn't let Jake do all the work. Are you in charge of arresting people?"

"For now, yeah."

"Oh good, I have some really fun stuff for you." The two men went off to my friend's desk. I heard them talking.

Yablonski, "Holy shit!"

Christian, "Yeah,"

"Good work."

"Thanks"

I smiled that they were becoming fast friends. I wondered if Christian had noticed the one employee who had not left her post, and who was helping us. I hoped he'd notice her before the night was over.

I gave Yablonski the papers for the kidnapping. He grunted. "I'll call when I think up more charges."

"Thinking up charges is my job. You just give me a general description. I heard them firing the tank. I'll translate that to discharging a firearm within city limits. Arson is good. Collusion and conspiracy are good. Are you going to pick up the corrupt cops?"

The major just looked at me.

"I'll prepare their papers."

Yablonski left. I still had a list of chores to complete including reports for all the charges filed and lists for additional possible charges for each person.

I checked in with Leah several times. She said my parents had returned to their home. The Rouseff's were staying with her.

Major Yablonski came through the office at intervals. When he complained about not having enough places to put prisoners, I took him over to the overflow facility where we normally put drunks and prostitutes. He grunted.

The last time, Peter Yablonski came in he handed me some papers. "What do you think of this?"

I looked at the documentation for conspiracy to commit murder, collusion, embezzlement, graft and a long list of other things I could add. "Shit, the emperor is not making it difficult for us. I don't want to charge him."

Yablonski leaned on the desk across from mine. "Why not, he's just a man like any other."

I hedged. "Charging him might complicate a bigger situation."

"How does a situation get any bigger?"

I sat and swiveled in my chair. There was nobody I could call on this. I thought about the judge in the capital. I didn't want to compromise the legal proceedings. "Okay, I want you to negotiate. Get the emperor to stand aside for the next three months and let his deputy assume control."

"Why? I am going to arrest him, if you don't give me a good reason why not. I've given you cause to issue the charges."

I pulled my hair and decided to trust Yablonski. I gave him a brief history of the Constitutional Committee and concluded with my concerns about arresting the emperor. "If we throw the blighter in jail, all the injustice of the past five years can be thrown in with him and we will not get our new government. From the standpoint of the law, it is very important that we still have an emperor and uninterrupted court system when the judges make their ruling calling for an election to adopt the constitution. We can make a peaceful transition away from dictatorship. People have been working on this for years."

Yablonski shifted his weight on the desk. "Shit"

"Yeah." I grinned.

"How did you manage to do this without my office discovering what you were doing?"

"Nobody pays attention to the law and the courts."

He narrowed his eyes and studied me. "You know what Jaconovich? I'm going to trust you. We will negotiate with the emperor."

I smiled and nodded. "You can arrest everyone around him. Get him to stand aside for ninety days while the courts handle the legal questions. Is it safe for me to drive to the station?"

"Yeah."

Yablonski left. I told my co-workers that I needed to run out to make a phone call. Christian raised his eyebrows. I pointed to the phone and said, "Tapped."

I drove down to the station. Papa came downstairs when he heard me come in.

"I just need to use the phone." He came to stand with his hand on my shoulder. In that touch I felt that Papa's age beginning to sit heavy on his shoulders. He didn't have energy for this fight.

I reached the professor. "Sir, I trust I didn't wake you. We've had a slight change of plans, I hope. I'm concerned that if the emperor is arrested, our court rulings may not be valid."

"Shit."

"I've talked the CGIS representative into negotiating to get him to stand aside for ninety days. For this thing to work in the courts, we need continuous valid government."

"Yes, I see where you are coming from. I'll pass the word."

I hung up. I turned and held my papa in my arms for a minute. He had seen his own family killed in a purge. He'd watched his home burn in a purge. This time, it was going to be different. This time, we were going to change the world.

Chapter 34 After The Storm

Our first realization that Christian, Allison and I had worked through the night occurred when some of the other staff started to show up for work in the morning. "What is going on here? How early did you get here?" The office manager asked. She irritated me by looking fresh and well rested.

I blinked and rubbed at my stiff neck. "Uh, what? Um…what time is it?"

The office manager asked again. Her narrowed eyes and sharp tone told me she didn't like the idea of us in the office unsupervised. "How long have you been here?"

I looked around. I pointed to Allison. "Um…she never left yesterday. She was still at her post when I got back in the afternoon."

I noticed Allison's red puffy eyes and messy hair. I smiled and told her, "As a matter of fact, I think the worst of it is over. You can go home, get some decent food and sleep."

Christian scrubbed his palms over his face and rubbed his eyes. "Um, Jake, I'll give her a ride. I want to get cleaned up, eat, maybe sleep then I'll be back."

"Yeah sure, thanks both of you." The office manager disappeared as we discussed a few items about schedules and unfinished cases.

I heard a screech from the back room. "Who unlocked the photocopier?"

"I did." I shouted back at our office manager.

She came storming out of the back room. "Well, it is supposed to be kept locked and each case and prosecutor is to have its own code."

I tried to remain professional. "We processed over seven hundred people after the rest of you left yesterday. We've done a few things a little different just to save time."

She screeched at me, "You will get fired."

I was exhausted and grumpy. I snarled back. "I don't care. We are not locking up that machine until this whole mess is over."

The poor woman's eyebrows flew up and she recoiled at my tone. I tried to be more professional. "Let's wait to see who else shows up, then we'll have a short staff meeting to bring everybody up to speed."

Jeffrey Farley, a senior prosecutor, showed up right at eight. I glanced briefly at how he'd left his desk. He'd put everything away neatly. I thought about trusting him. I judged him to be in his late thirties maybe early forties. He didn't have much authority in the office. He hadn't been arrested so perhaps he was trustworthy.

When Jeffrey learned I'd been there all night, he put his hand on my shoulder and said, "Jake, you should have called me. That was an impossible number of people to process."

"You will probably end up cleaning up my mistakes for the next three days."

"Why did you arrest so many people?" One of the paralegals sounded genuinely confused as he stopped by my desk.

"It was the CGIS who did the actual arresting. Well, I guess the army military police arrested the most people. They are debating whether they will be tried in army court or civilian court. We issued the charges." A couple more of the support staff came in and gathered around my desk. We still didn't have another prosecutor. I looked around at the empty desks trying to judge who might be trustworthy at this stage of the game.

My eyes felt gritty with fatigue. I turned to Mr. Farley. "Sir, I haven't slept since the night before last. We have the baby who thinks nighttime is time to play with Mama and Papa and I was here all last night."

Jeffrey squeezed my shoulder. "Go home and get some sleep. I'll say I sent you if anybody asks."

I rubbed the back of my neck. "Can you call…um…say…uh…Leroy and Frank, to see if they will come in?"

He hesitated. "That isn't my job. It would look strange. If they don't show up in a few minutes, I am sure their boss will call them."

I tried to keep the fatigue and frustration out of my voice. I failed. "Look, I don't know all who can come in, and who can't. The three of us were alone all night. If there is another rash of arrests, one person cannot process papers fast enough to get charges out. I'm sure people were arrested during the night who are not charged."

The office manager spoke up. "The supervisors will assign jobs when they get here."

I growled. "If they get here." I rubbed my aching neck.

I looked at the faces around me. The confusion I saw on the faces of my office mates reminded me of a child who wakes up from a nap disoriented and still half asleep. I sighed. They needed to hear the truth spelled out for them. "We had a purge. We have more people to process than we know what to do with. The jail is full. Overflow is full. A whole line of boxcars at the station is full. Most of the soldiers involved have been hauled off to military jails."

Jeffrey stood up straighter and sounded crisp and professional when he asked, "Who was getting arrested? Why?"

I rubbed my neck again. "The purge was an unauthorized military action. The soldiers who participated were arrested by the military police. Um… some of the local police were in on it and they have been arrested by the CGIS. There was a kidnapping mixed up in the whole thing. I processed those papers. Both Christian and I were presented with just cause for every charge we wrote up last night. For Gods sake, don't let any of them go. I really need to get to bed. Get some help in here." I started preparing to leave.

"I think we should wait for the supervisor." The office manager repeated adamantly. I could see this situation was coming down to a show of wills between the office manager and the prosecutor. She had a strong will. He had none.

I sighed. "I don't think any of the supervisory staff will be in. They were working with the sect that was to carry out the purge. They were charged with graft corruption, conspiracy to commit murder, abuse of office, conspiracy to defraud, violation of the security of the court, extortion and who knows what all else."

"You lie," she spat.

She saw the rage forming on my face and made a satisfying squeak.

I turned back to Jeffrey, "Sir, I think you are in charge of this office. Some of our people may be hurt or killed. If Peter Yablonski comes in, you can trust him. The phones in this office are bugged. Do what you think best in a case where we have suffered a major breach in integrity. And if anybody locks up the copy machine, I'll wring their neck." I left. I looked back to see the only prosecutor on the phone. I hoped he was calling for help.

I went home and slept. Leah crawled into bed beside me. I slept with one hand in the cradle. Life was good.

I woke up, showered and went back to the office by three-thirty. Everybody appeared quietly subdued as if at a funeral when I entered. I felt the urge to walk quietly. A few people refused to look at me when I walked in.

Leroy had come in. He came to my desk to shake my hand. "I don't know how you managed to fill out all those papers last night. I wish you had known that you could call me." He looked at the vacant desks and supervisors' offices. "I can see why you wouldn't know who to trust."

Jeffrey Farley came over to my desk. "Okay men, let's have a strategy session. We have a great deal of work to do with a very short staff. To the best of my knowledge we have four prosecutors left in this office. Without further notice from the government, I will assume the supervisor's position, if that is okay with you."

Leroy sounded cheerful when he responded. "No man, be decisive. You had it right when you yelled at The Queen to do as she was told or she could pack up and leave."

"Did he really?" I pounded my new supervisor on the back. "Good job man."

Jeffrey blushed. "The paperwork that we've reviewed from last night looks clean. I found a few more cases where we can add charges. We have a whole nest of worms here murder, kidnapping extortion, you name it. Some of us have never prosecuted some of these crimes. Jake as the only one of our staff who has prosecuted a murder case, I'm putting you in charge of the murder cases. I think many of those will be reduced down to conspiracy to commit murder, attempted murder, and discharging a firearm within city limits. We need to know how many people were killed, how they were killed and if possible, who did the killing. I called the police department. They are as short staffed as we are."

I nodded, "I'll get onto the body count. I am hoping it will be low. We were able to evacuate Ninth Street and Doh Creek Road. We hope the second evacuation kept most people away from cross fire between the marauders and the army that arrived to contain them."

Leroy sounded curious. "How did anyone know who to evacuate?"

I told him, "Look at the extortion cases. Which brings up the question of our office manager and file secretary. They were the people behind seeing that I was never assigned the cases involving false charges against people in the targeted area."

Jeffrey nodded. "As soon as Allison returns, I'll offer her the job. She stayed at her post and worked through the night. I know I can trust her."

I was really beginning to like my new supervisor. I learned that he was a good organizer. We had a flurry of activity late in the afternoon. My cousin, DeNough was one of the people brought in. We charged him with extortion and attempt to defraud.

I asked, "Can I take him out to the alley and deal with him?"

Leroy grumped at me. "No Jake, suck it up. Every family in this country has a bad apple involved in this. I think it is almost nationwide. Nobody can spare us a prosecutor."

DeNough whined. "Jake you wouldn't really charge a cousin with a crime? Think of the family name."

I grinned. "Fortunately, you changed the spelling."

"My papa did that. I am proud of being a D'NO."

I snapped. "I am not proud of you. Here are your papers. You may have to wait a while for your court date. We arrested several judges and the rest of them are overburdened." I sent him off with a military policeman to wait in jail.

I took a walk about five o'clock to check out the street and see if I could get a body count. Ninth Street was deserted except for a cat. I stopped at the hospital. They had not been as busy as I expected. They had a few injuries from people trying to carry too much as they evacuated their homes. They had not received any bodies that had died a violent death. They thought the evacuation might have killed an old woman who had heart failure. I returned to my office via the trolley and M'TK. I didn't learn of any more deaths there. Some people thought some soldiers and policemen might have been killed. When I got back to the office I called the morgue. They had the old woman with heart failure. Officer Mantega had been shot at close range with his own revolver. I didn't know what to make of that.

I did more paperwork until ten. Jeffrey stopped at my desk. "Jake, go home to your wife and baby."

I went home and slept as much as anybody does with a new baby who wakes up in the middle of the night and wants to be held and hear his papa sing. It was definitely my voice my son wanted to hear.

I was so tired and busy at work that I forgot about our seventy-two hour window for the procedural ruling calling for a constitution.

Mr. Farley called a staff meeting early in the morning of the second day after the purge. "I have just heard some peculiar news. It seems the people of this country are tired of the gang warfare. This last attempted purge was the last straw." Jeffrey's eyes shifted to me. "The courts have unanimously decided to call for an election to establish a constitution."

I grinned and felt my eyes fill with tears. I was too tired to let out a whoop.

One of the paralegals asked. "What does it mean to hold an election to establish a constitution? Why isn't that treason?"

I answered, "It is not treason because we are working within the government-supported system, the courts, to give people a chance to say whether or not they want to change the system. We still have our accepted government. Had the emperor been arrested, we would have possibly crossed the line into treason, even if the emperor was guilty, or it is possible the court rulings would not be valid because we would not have a government."

Leroy narrowed his eyes. "Jake, how long have you known this was coming?"

"I've known since the day I talked to Violet Uzara about the death of her granddaughter."

"I don't like all this talk of change." One of the paralegals whined.

I had slipped into teaching mode. "I don't think that much will actually change. The big change is in telling the truth about who we are. This is necessary for social stability." I looked at those who seemed hostile and wondered how far they would go to make trouble. "At this point it is not the people who are presenting the petitions who are against the law. The people who do not accept the rulings of our court system are in violation of the law. They oppose the government. They are the ones who are…are…um…well… um."

Christian laughed, slapped me on the back, and finished my sentence. "Committing treason. I have no idea who masterminded this whole thing but it is beautiful."

I went home at a regular hour that night. I hugged and kissed my wife, and held my baby. Life was good.

Chapter 35 Voter Registration

W e finally got prosecutors from other provinces to come and help a couple days a week. This made a tolerable sacrifice on their part and helped us immensely. It also helped that we did not have enough of a police force to go out and round up petty criminals.

At home, Leah was tired most of the time. She kept constantly busy bathing, changing and feeding Jacob. I came home one evening, kissed my wife and asked what I hoped was a pleasing question. "How would you like to spend about four days in a hotel in the capital?'

"What would we do with Jacob?"

"Take him with us of course." I nuzzled Leah's ear.

She pulled away. "What would we do there?"

"You could buy some new clothes, visit the shops and see some new things. In the evening we can go out. I'd like to visit Johan and Candice. We would eat in restaurants."

Leah sounded fretful. "Can we just lock up the house and go?"

"Of course." I looked around me. When my parents visited the capital, they had the Apkoutas to take care of their house. I thought seriously about my household. Leah was tired all the time. She had been too tired to cook. She couldn't leave the baby and visit friends unless my mother or Mrs. Rouseff was free to baby sit.

"Jake, what is it? Why are you scowling like that? What is wrong?" Poor Leah sounded alarmed.

"Would you like me to hire someone to help with the cooking and the house?"

"You mean, have servants?" Her eyes grew huge.

"I am not sure I would call them servants. We can put our own food on our plates and dress ourselves."

Leah giggled.

"I think we could use a couple to do the chores I can't get to, and to keep you company, and do the cooking."

Leah hugged and kissed me. Her eyes opened wide. She sounded like a little girl when she said, "Who would have thought that the daughter of a fisherman and a cannery worker would have servants?"

I laughed, "It happens all the time. That is what I am talking about with this new constitution. Once, people like us were very poor. They were uneducated, and would never contemplate having hired help because they did not have anything to take care of. We can hire help. The country has changed." Leah laughed and kissed me.

All in all, our little trip to the capital was a success. I assisted Judge Gannon from the Fortenac case for a week. His schedule included reviewing the proposed constitution, hearing cases from the people we arrested, and preparing to validate an election. He pulled prosecutors from other provinces.

I liked the work. I reviewed some cases. I yelled at prosecutors and defenders who did not prepare cases as they should. I tried to teach them how they should have done their jobs. I thought the prosecutors who graduated from my university did a better job of detail work than those who graduated from the university in the capital. The prosecutors from the capital university had more verbal skills. I wished they would shut up and give me more depositions. I may have said that to prosecutors more than once.

One day, during lunch in his study, I complained to Judge Gannon about the sloppy work presented by a Papadakos attorney.

Judge Gannon actually smirked. "Why do you think I saved that case for you? The man is lazy and thinks he can argue his way out of sloppy workmanship."

I grinned. "I did not accept his sloppy work. I told him what other work he needed to do and sent him back to get more depositions. I lectured him on the importance of proper presentation. You will get to see him when he comes back, but maybe his work will be better."

"Well, perhaps he will listen to you. I am just that crabby old judge. You are the man who got a conviction for Leon Fortenac, and set the whole country on its tail in the process."

I ran my hand through my hair and tried to put a thought into words. "In a sense I feel sorry for people like the Fortenacs. Part of the problem is a system that tells people who live in the southern provinces that they are greater and better than those who live in the north. This is the same system that sends family members to live in the north to operate the factories, or canneries, or whatever. Then, they intermarry causing more confusion. It is no wonder there is trouble."

The judge changed the subject. "What do you think of the new constitution?"

I scowled. "It is good in some ways. It gives us an elected government. It gives most people the right to vote. Getting my D'NO relatives registered might be a problem because Uncle John insists that being a D'NO should be enough, but the court order wants him to list his connections to a southern family."

He grunted. "Jake, the process of registering voters is cumbersome. Can we qualify large sections of voters by deposition?"

"I'm not seeing how that would work.'

"Depose Mr Rouseff to name the family names of everyone connected to his family. Get Violet Uzara to make a deposition stating the names of everyone in her family. Depose old Mr. Fortenac."

"I wouldn't want to be the one to take that deposition." I thought for a couple minutes. "I like your idea sir. It is in the best interests of the old families to be as thorough as possible to create as many loyal voters as possible. Some people will get left out, but that is the problem inherent in this constitution." I wondered in a matter this important if Mr. Rouseff would include the Jaconovichs. I wondered if I could bluff my way through on my own credentials.

Our stay in the capital felt like a vacation. Leah enjoyed dining out. Jacob went with us to the restaurants and smiled at all the women. He was still eating at home.

Johan had been accepted into the symphony in the capital. I was thrilled to spend two evenings with him and Constance. Their children were fascinated with the baby. Johan had some news that upset me. "Adele went home to her parents and took their daughter. She said it was because of the danger of a purge. Andy says he doesn't expect her to return."

"Damn." I moaned.

"Hellish." Johan communicated well.

"Yeah." I was almost crushed by the news. "We will make it a point to invite him over for dinner."

Leah surprised me. "I am not surprised really. When just the women got together for lunch or something, she was always complaining."

Candice agreed. "She used to make me mad because she complained about everything in the city, the shops, the smells, the parks. I grew up in the south. I love it here. We eat much better here than my parents do in the south. I love being able to get fresh food. We have many more shops. There are shops in the south that carry very expensive imported goods. I don't care about those. I buy things made in this country, often by my family. I've always had clothes and furniture made in our factories. Her family imports so perhaps she is accustomed to imports."

Leah continued. "If she wants imports, she can have anything shipped on the train. We had all our baby furniture shipped from here to the M'TK station. Andy is a good man. She was lucky to get him. She should look around at our friends whose husbands went to jail."

I think I puffed up three sizes at this endorsement of my friend and implied appreciation for me.

Candice looked at Johan and smiled. "Adele is a fool. Maybe she will come to her senses and return."

Leah sniffed, "Maybe her parents will do their duty, tell her where hers lies, and kick her out the door."

Before Leah and I returned to our own home, Judge Gannon issued a ruling declaring that heads of families, or other prominent family members could list eligible voters in their family by deposition.

I prepared a deposition for the D'NO family showing their link to the Fortenacs through Peter DeNough. Violet Uzara adopted the whole D'NO family along with the D'SnGs and the M'TGs. She also included the Jaconovichs. The Spinozas claimed the Jaconovichs as did the Rouseffs. A small family named Spencer included the Jaconovichs as did Andy's family, the Corbains. I was touched that Andy's family wanted to include me. Old Mr. Fortenac surprised me. He claimed Peter DeNough with the note that the name was originally spelled D'NO.

I didn't have much time to worry about the election. My week in the capital meant that I was behind at the office. I was behind on contracts for Rouseff. He was still buying up property on Ninth Street and Doh Creek Road. I finally found someone I thought might be a good choice for help at home.

I was getting caught up on paperwork when Allison approached my desk. "Mr. Jaconovich there is someone here to see you but he doesn't have an appointment."

I recognized young Mr. Chang whose daughter had been abducted before the purge. He bowed. I remembered the correct return bow. He said, "I hear you want workers at your house in the country."

I'd mentioned to several acquaintances that I wanted to hire help for Leah, but had not really looked. "Yes, I need someone to cook, do laundry, do outside work and stay with the house when my wife and I are out of town."

He bowed again. "I will serve you. I will bring my wife and my little girl."

"Why do you want to serve me?"

"I owe you the life of my child." He looked away from me. "You understand Chinese. You know that I must save face. It is hard for me to say. The child is afraid now. Maybe in the country she is not afraid. It is an honor to serve you. My wife is a very good cook. She is good with the laundry."

I did understand the value of saving face to the Chinese. I bowed my gratitude. "We have a modern washing machine. I hope the laundry is not so hard. My son is not yet two months old. He takes all of my wife's time. Also, I do not like for her to be home alone. "

"You are the big important man. It is my honor to serve you. I know the martial arts. I will protect your family."

I brightened. "Ah good. We will make a gym and you can spar with me. I do not keep in practice."

Mr. Chang grinned. "I hear you threw the big man and two others."

I looked away. "They wanted me to go where I did not want to go."

My new man laughed.

I'd used a common saying in martial arts training in my country. Every eight year old in training knows the saying. We discussed times and places to meet. We bowed to each other and Mr. Chang left.

As soon as he was out the door everyone left their desks to come stare at me.

Darlene asked, "Was that Chinese you were speaking?"

"Yes."

Leroy rolled his eyes. "You just happen to speak fluent Chinese?"

"I read it too." I laughed. "Do any of you remember a crime boss named Mr. Wu?"

Our oldest paralegal remembered him. "Don't tell me you knew him. He was the bane of this office when I first started here. We could never get anything on him. I think our supervisors were afraid to prosecute him really. His enemies tended to get broken necks."

I explained, "I was just a child when I met him. He liked me. I learned Chinese from him and his cook. He was the one who warned Rouseff about the burning of M'TK." I sighed.

Mr. Farley said, "I take it you learned martial arts from him." Finally, he asked something that must have bothered him for weeks. "We've heard rumors of a thwarted break-in here. Why didn't you file charges against the men who broke in?"

I grinned. "They had enough identification to convince me that they had reason to be here. I didn't let them search the office, and I refused to go with them. What did you hear?"

Jeffrey chuckled. "The street people saw you leave the office in a hurry. They were still laughing about it when I arrived in the morning." He recounted a comic and wildly exaggerated account of my flight and the subsequent emergence of the three stunned intelligence agents.

At the end of the story I laughed. "They underestimated the size of the big one. I've met him a couple times since then. He is huge." I demonstrated with my hands a fairly accurate estimate of Major Yablonski's dimensions.

I called Leah and told her I'd found her some help. "Their name is Chang. They have a ten year-old daughter. Most importantly, I can trust his loyalty."

"Chang? That sounds Chinese."

"They are Chinese. I know his wife is fluent in our language. I suspect he speaks it too, and of course the child must speak it for school."

"I've never met someone Chinese. Won't they smell peculiar?"

I laughed. "I suppose, their diet is different from what we normally eat. They use different soaps, perfumes, hair care and cosmetics." I suddenly thought of how to sidetrack Leah from her concerns. "Their art, architecture and landscaping are different from ours, but it is very artistic. Perhaps you should get some books from the library on Chinese art forms."

"My teachers never said anything about Chinese architecture." She sounded dubious.

"They probably don't know anything about it. You can become the only authority on the subject in the country."

She brightened. "I'll know something my teachers don't."

"Sweetheart, you know many things they don't. Would you like me to stop by the library for you on my way home?"

"Oh yes, I need new books. All my friends have moved out of the city."

Papa and Mama brought the Changs out to our house after dinner. While Leah and I showed them which rooms they would use, Mama found Jacob and cuddled him. I noticed when Mama held Jacob, her whole being changed. She seemed to turn soft around the edges. She smiled with her lips, but her eyes grew deeply sorrowful. She held Jacob on her shoulder and turned her head often to kiss his hair or his cheek. Papa hovered over her protectively and smiled with the same sad look in his eyes as he looked at his wife. Jacob gazed at his grandparents, smiled and tried to stick his fingers in their mouths. I resolved to give them more grandchildren. I smiled at my wife and caressed her butt when nobody was looking. Leah jumped and slapped at my hand.

I made my gym and started exercising and sparring with Mr. Chang. We had fun. He used to whine and cry at me to not hurt him. I would laugh and tell him that was my line. We shared jokes related to our craft. While we sparred, I got him to talking about his family and how they came to be in our country.

"It was over three hundred years ago when my people came here." He lunged. I sidestepped.

"The Chinese built the first ports."

I countermoved. He neatly evaded me.

"The last dynasty had fallen in China. Poverty was growing. Early explorers to China offered to help our fathers find work."

We circled each other.

"They traded the Chinese workers to the southern sailors and contractors for gold. My people got work, but we were treated little better than slaves."

I feigned to the right. He didn't fall for my trick and threw me off balance.

"We have made the best possible lives for ourselves, but we are never allowed to forget that we are different."

I recovered my balance and grinned. I was excited. "I have a crazy idea. I need to get back to work." Laughing and singing, I wandered off to my study in my kimono. I reviewed the court ruling. I sat up late at my desk studying the constitution. I reread the same line over and over. "The old families shall be defined as those families who were residents of the southern provinces before the country was united. The old families shall be defined as those families who were residents...." I chuckled and looked at the clock. It was too late to get my history teacher out bed.

It took me two days to haul my history teacher in to depose him. I'd never liked the man, but if he gave me the information I expected, he would be an unimpeachable witness to support the point I hoped to make. We went over some general questions about his qualifications to be an expert witness on the history of this country especially on the southern provinces.

"Approximately what year did the Chinese come to this country?"

"Scholars are not sure of the exact year because they came over a period of time. We have one document saying one-hundred fifty people came from the orient the land discovered by Marco Polo."

"What year was that?"

"Sixteen-fifty three."

"Did they list any information about these people?"

"I am not sure what you mean."

"Did they list any job skills, education, social class?"

"Oh no. I think it did call one man a contractor.

"Did this document list any names?"

"Yes, it did."

"Can you tell me any of those names?"

"Yes, Kim, Chang, Jong, Wu and Liu are the most common."

"By common do you mean that we still hear those names today?"

"Yes."

"Which provinces did they come to first?"

"Jake Jaconovich weren't you listening in class?"

I smiled. "Answer the question please."

"You should know this. They came to the southern provinces. Nobody from the outside came to the northern provinces until the advent of steam ships."

"Thank you. What did they do when they arrived in the southern provinces?"

"They built the ports and some of the buildings."

"Is some of their work still standing?"

"Yes, the agent's house at the Portlandia Port was built back then. We also have a mausoleum or crematorium. We are not sure now what it was used for."

"Is it correct to say then that they were builders?"

"Yes."

"Is it possible that they served in the armies when the south..." Here I knew I needed to be careful. My interpretation of this event was very different from my professor's. "…uh…the south annexed the north."

"Yes, there was a whole regiment of Chinese under Colonel Liu. I think that may have been an honorary title, but he did seem to have command of a group of men."

"Is there documentation of this Colonel Liu?"

"Of course. It is in the military record. He is mentioned several times in several places. His troops were given land in this city and the capital as their reward."

"Ah, thank you. Have there been any other notable Chinese immigrations since the mid-sixteen hundreds?"

"In the early seventeen hundreds there was a shortage of Chinese women. Some Chinese men married local girls but that was not their custom. They sent a ship to China for brides for the young men."

"Is there documentation for that?"

"Yes, they came on a ship named Good Hope. There were celebrations and fireworks."

"They also arrived in the southern ports is that correct?"

"Yes."

"Is there documentation of the land that was given to the Chinese soldiers?"

"Yes, those grants are still kept in city hall. If you go up the hall to the land record office and ask for the records of the original land grants, you can find them."

"Thank you sir. That will be all. You may be called for further expert witness, but I hope the information here will be enough. I will look up the documents you mention if necessary." I was almost dancing as I escorted this man I'd always resented to the door, slapped him on the back and thanked him for his help.

Back at my desk, I called the judge in Mercid. "Sir, my research has turned up another group of people who appear to be eligible to vote under the definition presented to the court. Will you have time to look at my depositions and evidence? I know time is getting short to qualify people."

"Mr. Jake I will look at anything you bring me as soon as humanly possible."

'Thank you sir, I will be up about seven or seven thirty this evening if that is okay?"

"Can you make it closer to eight?"

My heart was racing. "Of course, whatever is most convenient for you."

I think I almost danced to Allison's desk. I knew I felt much the same exhilaration I did after wining a fight against three bigger men.

"Allison, assign someone to do your chores. I want you to look up and photocopy these documents. If you have to call another courthouse, do so. If they do not respond immediately let me know and I will yell at them."

Our youngest paralegal interrupted me. "Why are you giving her this case? That is paralegal work. One of us should do it."

"I trust Allison. This is sensitive. If one of you can maintain confidentiality, by all means assist her to get this information as soon as possible. I need it before we leave tonight." The paralegal smirked at me. I looked at him.

"Yes sir."

I went to the supervisor and growled. "We need to do something about the attitude around here. Some of the secretaries and both paralegals do not treat me with respect. I don't trust their confidentiality. I don't trust them to follow through on an important case.

"I've noticed the problem. I will meet with them. It is time to depose our insolent staff. I will make certain that everyone knows Allison is above reproach." He smiled and I thought he was going to enjoy his task.

He swiveled in his chair and changed the subject. "I am hoping for relief on the shortage of staff problem. I have asked for interns from the university. I have begged for interns. I went to the university and addressed the upper level classes. I told them they would be learning from the best prosecutor in the country. I promised that they would be working on the most exciting legal action this country has seen. I promised them that we did not have enough police to arrest petty criminals so they would get to do real legal work. I have high hopes for help."

I laughed. "I hope they will not be disappointed."

"What are you working on this afternoon?"

I explained about the Chinese being elibible to vote.

Jeffrey was instantly energized. "This sounds like fun. What needs to be done?"

I went over the details of what I had, showing him my documentation. I hoped he was trustworthy.

He rubbed his hands together. "Okay, lets get this done. This needs to be out the door by five." He got up and left his office cubical and stood in the middle of the room. "Folks, I want your attention." I noticed he got the attention of most of the staff immediately. "Jake has picked up the most important case in the office. It is time sensitive. As usual, it is confidential. I want you prosecutors to drop what you are doing and get on the phone. The rest of you be prepared to stop what you are doing and support the prosecution team. We will get this out the door by five." This was the first time I'd had a case where I had a supervisor to support me and help to do the research. I intended to tell the powers that be that Jeffrey Farley was the best I'd ever seen.

We did get the records I wanted. The last item came in by FAX. I didn't know what a FAX was. I was thrilled when I discovered that by running up to the mayor's office, a clerk from my office could receive a document sent by a clerk in an office in the south.

I ordered the presentation of my documents as best I could. This case was a first, so I did not have a set protocol for the order of documents, so I followed general guidelines. By five o'clock I had my documents ready to present. I carefully carried them home with me.

I had expected to walk home from the trolley station with the precious papers in my briefcase, but when I got off of the trolley and there was my beautiful wife beside the Miki. She waved. I felt warmed all over. Other men may have to walk, but my darling wife came to pick me up. I knew that I was beyond wealthy.

I kissed Leah on the cheek when we got in the car. "This is nice. I like having you to myself for a few minutes. How are things at home?"

Leah looked much less drawn and tired. "I am still showing Mrs. Chang how to use all our machines."

"I hope she knows how to use the stove."

"Yes, dinner smells very good and I had time to change clothes before meeting you."

"Ah good. How is my son?"

"Happy, Mrs. Chang wants to tie him to her back with his blankets and carry him around the house. I put him in his cradle and she comes and steals him to carry with her. I told her I thought she needed baby of her own. She says that now that they have a private room without her husband's brothers keeping him up until all hours, she thinks maybe they will get a nice son like mine."

"Good, I want them to be happy." I leaned over and kissed Leah on the cheek again as she was driving. The car swerved and almost went in the ditch before she got it back on the road. I laughed. "I don't think Mrs. Chang is the only one who wants some action. I think Mrs. Jaconovich would like some too."

"If you are good."

"I am always good. Unfortunately, I am going out tonight."

"Out! Why?"

"I need to deliver a case to the judge tonight. It might take a while because I hope he will rule on it in the morning, as soon as he can get a court recorder."

"I don't like you being so busy."

"I don't like being this busy. My wonderful new supervisor hopes to get us some interns after exams are over next week."

We chatted about the household and my work during dinner. I ate with one hand while I held Jacob with the other arm. He seemed to know his papa and was content when I held him.

Shortly after seven I drove the Miki into Mercid. Judge Stimson was waiting for me when I arrived at his house. In his study, I presented the papers and went over them. The judge was old, closer to ninety than eighty, but his eyes, almost lost in folds of papery skin, scanned each page quickly as he nodded in quick, sharp movements. His voice was firm. "I think I can make a ruling on this in the morning. I'll have the court recorder at the courthouse at eight AM. I want you there as well."

"Yes sir."

He started to laugh. "To think I've lived long enough to see this day. This has been long overdue. Jake let me tell you something. I very much doubt that the Stimsons have one drop of southern blood in their veins. I am very proud of that fact."

I nodded. "I understand sir. I appreciate that you are willing to hear our case without class prejudice. A clear-sighted judge is hard to find."

"I think you'll find the most honest ones are more northern than southern."

"Our case has been about abolishing the difference."

He grunted. "It's about the damned time the courts began to operate on evidence rather than who is who. Up until now, I've thought that the day the Fortenac case was decided was the greatest day for the courts of this country. Now, I see a greater day before us. I plan to live long enough to see this through." Despite his thin frail-looking body he sounded strong-- almost like a young man spoiling for a fight.

It was after ten when I got home. Mr. Chang was waiting for me with a list of phone calls. I returned phone calls until mid-night. Mostly people were checking in to see what more needed to be done.

The last call of the night was to Andy. "What is happening with Adele?"

"She says she is not coming back. She does not want to live in the north."

"What about you moving south? I will miss you, but your marriage and daughter are more important than me or your job." Andy sat silent for at least two minutes. I could hear him breathing. I could almost hear him thinking.

"Thank you for putting things in perspective. I can't imagine why I didn't think of that. She has not invited me to join her. I have family there. I am not sure what a physicist will do there."

"I'm not sure what a physicist does anywhere."

He laughed. "I didn't call you to talk about my marital problem. From the talk at the club, I think you are having fun without me. I want in on the action."

I explained as much as I thought I should to Andy. "The problem we've discovered is that we have no idea how to hold an honest election."

He grunted. "First, each judicial district needs an accurate list of their eligible voters. People need to arrive at the voting place with identification. What are you going to use for ballots?"

I hadn't thought about that detail. "We will want to print ballots I guess."

"You will want them to be readable by a computer."

I wondered if anybody else had thought about the mechanics of having an election. "I don't know how to do that."

"How long do we have?"

I rubbed my hand over my face. "Just a little over two weeks." I was horrified that we hadn't thought about this sooner.

"Okay that is plenty of time." Andy sounded confident and happy. "I'll quit my job, move in with my wife, and have your voting machines ready in two weeks. How many judicial districts do we have?"

I was slightly dizzy from the speed at which Andy operated. "I'll look into that. In the city there are too many voters to have everybody vote in the same place. We will need multiple places or at least multiple machines."

"That is good to know. I'll call you from Adele's parents'. Jake, why didn't I think of moving in with her before this?"

"Perhaps your pride and your feelings were too hurt for you to think. I know something like that would completely overwhelm me. I cannot begin to contemplate being separated from Jacob and Leah."

I went to bed and slept between Jacob and Leah. The little rascal was letting us sleep until about four in the morning, which meant I got four hours of sleep before it was time to hold him on my chest and sing.

Leah rescued me. "Jake, I'll take him and feed him. You came in so late."

I got to sleep for another two hours. I returned to Mercid by seven-thirty in the morning. I met Judge Stimson in the courtroom. We went over each piece of paper I'd presented him. He paid particular attention to the deposition from my history professor. "Mr. Jaconovich, did you personally take this deposition from Professor Holland?"

"Yes,"

"Do you deem him to be competent and honest?"

"Yes to the best of my knowledge I deem him to be competent and honest. The university also deems him to be competent and honest." I also deemed him to be a bigoted suckerfish but that was not relevant to this case.

Judge Stimson nodded, turned to the court recorder, and in a strong clear voice handed down his rulings.

"Let the record show: that the university and the prosecution deem Professor Holland to be competent and honest.

Let the record show: that the court accepts Professor Holland's deposition." So it went with each piece of paper as it was entered into the court record.

"Let the record show: the court rules that the evidence is complete and sufficient to reach a verdict.

"Let the record show: that under the definition of Southern Residents stated in case ruling AC 10002. The Chinese immigrants meet the requirements for length of time in the country and physical contributions. They immigrated to the Southern Provinces. They participated in the war of acquisition against the north. They were awarded rewards from the existing government at that time.

"Let the record show: that this court rules that the Chinese families who came to this country in the sixteen hundreds are eligible to vote."

"Let the record show: This ruling includes, but is not limited to, those who bear these names Chang, Liu, Wu, Wang, Huang, Chao, Chou, Sun, Hu, Kuo, Liang, Lo, Sung, Hsieh, Tsao, Hsu, Teng, Hsiao, Feng, Tsai, Peng, Yuan, Su, Chiang, Tien, Tu, and Han.

"Let the record show: This case is closed. No lower authority has the power to set aside or revoke this ruling. No administrative authority has the right without court permission to set aside or revoke this ruling.

I left the court happy for my success. I called the office from the train station and gave them my news. "The problem now is in communicating who is eligible to vote. We have Chinese families in all our provinces and we need to get them to the polls."

By the time I got back to the office, Mr. Farley had determined that the problem was not as big as I first imagined. I called home. "Mrs. Chang, I need to talk to your husband."

She explained that he and Leah were down at the lake.

"Well, go down to the lake and get him for me please? Have him call me immediately." I wondered what Leah and Chang were doing down by the lake. I did own a small section of lake front. Leah seemed to like the view in that direction. I preferred the wilderness of the ridge behind the house.

Andy called and interrupted my thoughts. He sounded jubilant. "Hi. I'm at my in-laws. Adele was surprised to see me. She was appropriately overwhelmed that I changed jobs so I could be with her and make her happy. I was a fool not to listen to her sooner. She just needed to be closer to her mama and sisters. "

"Oh God, I'm thankful that went well. What about our voting problem? Do you have any ideas?"

"I've made notes on how to program the computers. I am debating on the best ballot materials. I have a call into the United Nations for any information and support they can give us."

I got off the phone and made a huge whoop, mostly because Andy and Adele were okay again. "Hey folks, my friend Andy just called the United Nations to ask them how to hold an election. They promised to call him back." I sobered, "I hope they have the good sense to call him and not the emperor."

Jeffrey chuckled. "I don't think the UN, will be telling our dictator how to hold an election. I think they will assume the person who called is official and talk to them."

"Do you think they will realize that we are just making this up as we go?"

Jeffrey answered, "That is how elected governments get started everywhere. People make stuff up as they go. If an idea doesn't work, it gets thrown out. Then, people make up something else that might work."

Darlene asked, "Is that what is going to happen? We won't have an emperor. We will have an elected government? Isn't that subject to corruption?"

Jeffrey sounded patient. "Look around this office. Have you noticed we are short of staff? It is because of corruption."

"But surely the emperor is not corrupt." Poor Darlene looked as if she was going to cry.

I sighed. "The emperor has not been charged with crimes, but the head of state is ultimately responsible for any corruption under him. In this case there was so much and it goes so high, that he is at least guilty of massive incompetence." When I finished speaking the other prosecutors were looking at me in a peculiar manner. It didn't occur to me that I was telling everybody something they had not figured out for themselves. We were interrupted by my call from Mr. Chang.

"I apologize Mr. Jake that it took me so long to get to the phone. Mrs. Jake wants me to make a garden down by the lake. I did not want to leave her alone by the lake with the baby so I walked back slowly with her."

"You were right to stay with her. Now, I need you to come to my office. Oh, and congratulations. Judge Stimson just ruled that all the Chinese in this country are eligible to vote."

"I don't know what that means."

"It means that in this upcoming election Mr. Chang and Mr. Liu have as much influence as Mr. Fortenac and Mr. Vanderholm." I heard silence on the other end of the phone.

Finally, Mr. Chang responded in an eager tone. "Mr. Jaconovich, I will be in your office as soon as I can get there."

I spent several hours with Mr. Chang helping him understand the issues. He said he would take responsibility for seeing that every person of Chinese descent learned that they could vote.

Andy called. "The UN is not much help because we have not had a rebellion, or civil war, or killed the emperor. I tried explaining that we've had a demographic change that makes our old system of doing business obsolete so we are doing something different. They promised to call me back." He added dryly.

Brilliant, little Allison came up with the best solution we could find for constructing voter lists. "The only thing I can think of is to use the census rolls to make a catalogue of who in the city might be eligible to vote. We could put a notice in the paper for people to contact our office if they do not find their name on the list."

Jeffrey blew out his cheeks in a heavy sigh. "That is a huge amount of data entry, why we would need…" here he paused and calculated. "We would need at least four operators working round the clock for four days."

Allison nodded thoughtfully. "Sir, we have five terminals we can use. If the server doesn't crash, we can do it. We need more people because the rest of us need to sleep sometime."

I nodded. "Okay we can use people who can do data entry. Leah can work at least part of a shift. Can we get students from the university?"

Jeffrey grumbled, "Hell, we're more likely to get them from the secondary schools. I'll call." I'd never heard my mild mannered supervisor swear before. I credit this experience with developing my habit of swearing, too. It works.

I thought to call Rouseff to see what he could do about computers and staff. About four, a computer technician arrived from Rouseff's office. "The boss told me to set some terminals up and see what I can do to connect to your server." He looked the system over and asked questions.

I ignored the technician while he and Allison set up equipment and taped cords to the floor. By five, he had another five terminals set up. Jeffrey swore and grumbled about getting help.

I noticed six nervous youth in the holding room. They ranged from the youngest a pudgy boy with acne to a blond, young man about eighteen who had learned to wash and dress himself respectably. The group included a skinny boy who looked to be about sixteen, another boy who was expertly dribbling his football between his feet and a tall girl with the bone structure to be a striking beauty when she matured, the other girl was obviously the striking girl's best friend, small and plain with frizzy hair.

I poked my head into the room. "You don't look like criminals. Can I help you?"

The skinny boy explained. "Our computer teacher told us we can have extra credit if we came over here and helped you."

I replied, "I don't know about extra credit, but we are prepared to pay you."

The pudgy boy wailed, "I really need the extra credit."

"We will furnish you with a statement of how many hours you worked." I took them to Allison. She got them set up with the names of eligible voters highlighted on census sheets. They chatted a bit about formats and fields before settling down to work. We now had six operators for at least six hours.

Mr. Chang came to pick me up. I went home to my wife and son.

Leah showed me a picture she found in a Chinese landscape book. Before I could eat my dinner, she insisted I walk down to the lake and look at the area where she planned to build her Chinese garden. I tried to sound enthusiastic when all I could see was a swampy patch of ground and weeds. I pointed to some interesting seed heads. "Keep those. They look interesting. I think they will go well with your little bridge thing." Leah almost danced back to the house. I remembered Andy's troubles and felt grateful that my wife liked livening in my home.

Chapter 36 Bankrupt

All of a sudden my case load at work dropped to almost nothing. Everyone involved in the purge had been jailed or processed and with the police force fired or in jail nobody was picking up the usual petty criminals. I called Rouseff. "I am going to have time to work on your purchase contracts for the new road after all. I can take a couple days off here. I need to do several hours of research on those purchases before we complete the contracts."

"I'll see you later." Mr. Rouseff sounded grumpy. I found my photocopies of the Chinese land grants and went back to the records department. One of the clerks seemed a little flustered when I told him what I wanted. "Are you looking for more voters?"

"No, I am working on some land purchases for Mr. Rouseff. I want to make certain that squatters are not trying to profit off of land grant property." The clerk though flustered acted competent about helping me. The whole office promised to help do the research.

"Mr. Prosecutor, we can do the research and give you a detailed report on the recorded purchases for each section and lot of property. I promise we will be thorough." I left them to do their job and went over to Rouseff's office.

Rouseff still seemed grumpy when I entered his office. I explained my problem. "The problem that I discovered sir, is that a huge swath of land encompassing what we call Chinatown was ceded to the Chinese by the government when the invasion was successful. I need to trace the transactions to make certain that the sellers have the legal right to sell the land. Some of it may belong to the decedents of the Chinese who fought in the war."

He growled. "Fine, I want these contracts completed as soon as possible before the road right of way ends up in somebody else's hands. I need to own enough that the government will have to give me the price I want."

"Let's start with the Doh Creek properties and work inward. I am not so worried about clear title on those properties. I think we will have to research those too. The land grants are a more challenging problem."

"I want your opinion on this damn road." I looked at Rouseff hoping he was about to tell me what made him so grumpy. "It is foolish to run the road all the way to city hall. I am almost certain that is what they intend to do." He grunted as he pulled out a map and rolled it out across his desk. "I run my trolley lines based on two concentric circles intersected by cross city trolleys. I can't imagine why they would run the highway straight through here." He traced a line with his finger from the north side of town to the south, through the center of the city. "Eventually, what is needed is an inner circle that connects with city streets and an outer circle to bypass the city so that through traffic is not causing congestion." He gestured on the map.

"Where would you run the inner highway?"

"I'd bring it up Doh Creek and lower Ninth. I might stop before I hit China town and circle the city center here on Gannon, Eclipse, University and Sunset Street." I looked at his map. It made sense.

"Sir you are the master here. If you think the road should run this way, you are most probably right." I leaned back in my chair. "You know, you are a genius. Look at how you have created the innermost circle as lower density. You have the university, the city buildings, a park and some apartment buildings here. I'd like to see something done differently here with any parts of Chinatown occupied by squatters, which I suspect is the case, here and here." I tapped two places in the map that were close to the land grant property. "What do we need to do to develop these areas? I indicated two rundown blocks inhabited mostly by squatters." I sat back in my chair, and thought.

I grinned. "My thought is that we can secure as much of Doh Creek as we can then move to working on lower ninth. When it comes time to place the highway, we can come up with the best plan for moving traffic through the city."

I was not certain Rouseff heard me. He was staring at his map and pulling on his ear. It was clearly time for me to leave the genius to his thoughts. "I'll go get to work processing those purchase contracts and leave you to solve the problem of the road going in the wrong direction." I left him and hoped this problem was the source of his grumpiness.

I went down to the Rouseff real estate offices and started looking over the purchase contracts. I discovered that I'd learned something the night we processed nearly seven hundred sets of charges. I'd learned to work very efficiently. I made up a master list of all the properties on our list that needed title searches, which I finally decided to be all of them. I looked over the legal wording of the contracts. Most of the contracts followed the legal from I'd used earlier. I went to the office manager and outlined what jobs needed to be done. "The biggest delay, is the title searches. I want to be certain that all our sellers have the right to sell the land. I have the records department fairly busy with the China Town land grants. Can some of your staff do the actual research for Doh Creek and lower Ninth?"

"Yes, sir, Mr. Prosecutor, we will get right on that."

"Good. Rouseff is grumpy. I'm hoping that he will cheer up if we make some progress on this." I left to talk to the financing department. I took them the numbers for the costs on the pending sales. I called each seller and talked to them about their contract making certain they agreed with each pertinent part of the sale. I thought we could start closing on about twenty-five properties in five days. That would give us a majority ownership of the property along Doh Creek Rd. I sorted through our communications on the rest of the properties. I called the man in charge of purchasing.

"Mr. Prosecutor, what can I do for you?" I was surprised that my title was being used so frequently here. I was also surprised at the level of cooperation and respect I was receiving. Perhaps they were learning to trust me. I was pleased by the respect.

"I think we need to go back and approach the remaining land holders on Doh Creek Rd. Let's be honest with them about why they were being harassed. Assure them that they were the targets of the purge. Tell them that the problem is far from being solved. Make them a respectable offer on their land."

I thought about the road and the displaced businesses. "Those businesses sitting on the actual proposed street, will have to sell sooner or later. The government could condemn their land."

"Yes sir, how soon do you want this done?"

"Rouseff is getting grumpy. Can you start contacting people today? Have them talk to their neighbors. I will write up a notice explaining the legal complications of this project. I'll get my notice to you in a half hour or so." I borrowed a desk and wrote up a notice and asked a secretary to type it up.

The secretary brought my note back in five minutes. "Can you shorten this up and use regular people language? Let's just put this whole paragraph into a bar under the title so the court cases you used are easy for their attorney's to find."

We went over my whole notice translating it into street language. I instantly saw my mistake and rewrote the thing easily enough. I was tempted to sign this copy, "From the desk of The M'TK Sewer Rat," instead of "…desk of Jake Jaconovich."

I spent six hours in Rouseff's office before I went back to the prosecutor's office. I noticed the Miki parked at the curb. I smiled. The presence of the Miki meant that Leah had come in to help with data entry. One more person, even for four hours a day, was a great help.

Leah was very good at proof reading the other people's entries. She could spot differences that the rest of us missed. She was happy to do data entry. Most of the time she proofed the other's work. I entered to find my son in his infant seat on Allison's desk. He turned toward me the second he heard my voice. He reached his tiny baby arms out to be picked up. The other women in the office cooed and smiled at me. Leah just laughed. I picked Jacob up out of his baby seat and took him off to my desk.

Mr. Farley was waiting for me. "We have a suspect under arrest in the Mantega murder case. Look the evidence over and we will have a staff meeting to go over your thoughts and recommendations at four-thirty." I sat down to work while holding my son on my shoulder. Jacob fell asleep and drooled on my shoulder while I went over the case. I made notes and had a rough plan of action for the case. At four-thirty, I was ready.

I gave my report. "I am not sure what to think of this case. If the judge is lazy, we could get a conviction. I think I want more evidence. We will start with deposing the eye-witness. The police have not given us anything scientific to work with. They did not test the gun for fingerprints. They have not fingerprinted the accused. The autopsy report indicates that Officer Montega was shot with his own gun from a distance of about seven feet. He is implicated in the fire on Doh Creek Road. To the best of my knowledge he was deep into the extortion and corruption involved with the new highway project. We need to examine the alleged perpetrator's story for means, motive and opportunity. I don't see anything like that covered in the report I have. One person claims to have heard the shot and seen the accused run away from Officer Montega's house." Privately I debated whether the accused, if guilty, should be awarded an honor for ridding the city of that piece of vermin. I did not voice this opinion because my baby was asleep on my shoulder.

The rest of the staff jumped to help out. Christian volunteered first. "I will get onto the police about giving us some hard evidence from the gun. They should know enough to fingerprint it."

Mr. Farley commented, "They should know enough, but they have very little staff due to the rest of the staff being arrested." Mr. Farley divided up the rest of the work. I would depose the witness first thing in the morning.

I hesitated to bring up a side issue, but I decided this staff had earned my respect enough that I would warn them of impending trouble. "I am going to mention something that puzzles me. It may not have anything to do with our office. I have a gut feeling that it does. Rouseff is grumpy. He is working on some expansions in his own business, but he is grumpy. I have a gut feeling that there is something else out there that is huge and he senses it."

Mr. Farley replied, "Talk to him. So much has been undermined over the past few years that I expect to catch more fallout." He addressed the rest of the group. "I've interviewed four possible interns. I think I will hire two of them. I confess that I have been going over our budget with Connie. We should have enough money to pay everybody, but our account seems to be short."

We sat in numb silence. Allison was the first to recover and suggested. "An audit might be in order."

Mr. Farley asked, "Do any of you know an auditor?"

Allison shrugged. "Not, really. Don't we have one in the system?"

Leroy almost crowed. "No, he's in jail."

Our accounts manager sounded huffy. "Really there is no need for an audit. Everything is perfectly in order. I think you are over reacting. We operate on a calendar basis instead of a fiscal basis so of course the account is low." Her eyes darted around the room and she spit her words out rapidly. If she were a client I'd think she was guilty.

Leah came up behind me and stroked Jacob's head where it rested on my shoulder. "Jake, didn't your mama do that type of work. She told me she made enough money auditing some books for Mr. Wu to pay for your first year of college and your books."

Mr. Farley turned to me. "Ask your mama to come in."

"It has been years since she's done anything like that, but I will ask."

Mama came in the next morning. It did not take her more that a few hours to determine that someone, probably more than one someone had been withdrawing large sums of money from the prosecutor's budget and not using it to pay the office's bills. The former accounts manager had not come to work that morning. Further investigation revealed that the petty cash had been emptied. We filed a report with the police, but we held no hope of tracking the woman down.

We prepared to tighten our budget until we could get funds from the central government at the beginning of the quarter. Within a matter of days we discovered we'd underestimated the scope of the problem. The country was bankrupt. The government defaulted on all payments. There was no money in the treasury and no banks to borrow money from. In our office, the employees were grim.

Mr. Farley called another staff meeting. He appeared pale and shaken. His eyes were red rimmed and watery. I wondered if he had been crying. "Okay staff, I want complete honesty here. We are not going to get paid. None of us. We still need your help. It is imperative that we maintain a legal infrastructure in order to prevent gang warfare or civil war. Who can continue to work and how much of a hardship is this going to be for you?"

Everybody stared at Mr. Farley out of pale pinched faces. We looked at each other with varying degrees of fear on our faces.

The bile rose in the back of my throat. My stomach knotted and I felt my hands shake. I thrust them behind me. I volunteered. "I still have my work for Rouseff, which will pay my basic bills if he does not experience difficulties. I have some savings."

In the back of my mind, I worried about Papa and Mama. They needed to retire. Mama had not worked long for us, but after just a few hours, she was very tired. She almost reminded me of how she looked when papa carried her across the city from Wulfton to M'TK.

Darlene almost cried. "I must have an income. I have no savings and nobody I can move in with."

Our oldest paralegal whispered. "I can get by without a paycheck for two months. Then I will not have a cent of money.'

Leroy sounded secure enough. "Don't worry about me. I have a family trust that will keep me going as long as necessary."

"Same here." Christian reported. "And Allison will marry me and move in with me so she will be okay." This statement from my friend was news to Allison. He dragged her off to the copy room to negotiate. They both looked happy and well kissed when they returned to the meeting.

At the end of the meeting, I went to see Rouseff. "How long have you suspected the scope of the country's financial problems?"

He looked up at me. His mouth set in a firm grim line. He looked as if he'd lost weight in the last week. "Is it bad?"

"You are asking me?" I eased myself into the leather chair across from him. "I am guessing we will come close to complete monetary collapse."

He grunted.

"How are you going to hold up?" I really wanted to ask if I would still have a job with him.

"I am not sure." He leaned back in his chair and placed his hands face down on the desk as if to push the problem away. "I can lose fifty percent of my rents and rail fees before I am in serious trouble. If I lose sixty-five, I will flat line. I am not sure how long I can operate below that level." I thought about the enormity of what he was saying.

"Hell and damnation." I confessed some of my worries to Mr. Rouseff. "Everybody in the country needs to make a plan. At the prosecutor's office, we discussed ways to economize with the staff. I worry about Mama and Papa."

"Your Papa is very worried about your Mama. She gets tired too easily. When she does get tired she gets very confused. I've seen that happen once. It worried me. I will keep them at the station, but it would be better if they retired."

"How long can you continue to pay me?"

"At your current income I can pay you for a couple years, but I am not sure I will have enough work to keep you busy for more than a few months."

"I understand." I ran my hands along the back of my neck. Mr. Rouseff was one of the richest and most fiscally secure persons in the country. He was in trouble. The rest of the country was going under and we couldn't do anything about it.

We were days away from the election. Corrupt ownership had left the newspapers as bankrupt as the rest of the nation. A handful of honest journalists got together and managed to publish an expose on how corruption from the emperor's government had undermined our institutions while lining the pockets of the emperor's corrupt friends. The graft, mismanagement, and embezzlement had bankrupted the country. Our little band of reporters made an impassioned plea to the voters that our only choice was to form a new representative government.

Two nights before the election, the official collapse was announced. Our currency was not worth anything abroad. Banks shut down. Stock prices dropped to all time lows. People went to the polls in shock, not really understanding the depth of the problem. They voted to accept the constitution and establish a representative government. We'd made provisions for an interim government with representatives from the judiciary, the military, business, and the former government to lead the country until we elected a parliament and president.

We did not celebrate as I once dreamed we would. Mr. Rouseff invited several people over for a dinner party. When we arrived he came into the entry hall and greeted me with a hug. "Son, thank you for your diligence and hard work. The outlook is grim but at least the source of evil has been removed from office." Rosalie Rouseff interrupted this exchange to claim Jacob for herself.

Chapter 37 Depression

The day after the interim government was installed I got a phone call at the office.

"Sewer Rat?" I recognized Yablonski's voice. "Are you ready to process those papers for the emperor now?"

"Gladly." I wondered what kind of punishment we could apply to an ex-dictator for massive corruption. I was happy to see Yablonski when he arrived despite the seriousness of our meeting. He went over his papers with me. "Can you work with this?" He asked.

I grunted my approval. "Yes, I will need more documentation for some of my charges. That is my job to come up with that."

"If you need us, don't hesitate to call, the office is almost deserted because most of our staff is in jail which we cannot afford to keep up. Nobody else is getting paid so most people stay home."

"Yeah, we have the same damn thing happening here."

"Hellish."

I had another question for Yablonski. "Sir, something worries me. What is to stop the southern families from regrouping and overturning the Constitutional government?"

The major leaned back in his chair and studied me for a moment. Finally, he came to a decision and leaned forward again. "During the purge the provincial generals overruled the Emperor's order to carry out the purge. We were close to a military coup. The military was in position to seize the emperor's compound and certain transportation hubs when we learned of the court rulings. We waited to see how this would play out. The Southern families know the constitution is their escape from military rule or civil war. They will accept the constitution for now."

I felt marginally reassured when he left with his charges for the emperor.

To save money, Rouseff cut rail and trolley service down during the slow mid-day. We discussed endlessly the best ways to maintain vital services. We began to see how long people could live without an income. Most people survived a month. The oldest and poorest didn't last much beyond six weeks unless they had family to take them in. The morgue was another place that was overworked, understaffed and had no money to operate.

Much to our delight, Mama seemed to improve. She understood poverty. I sometimes worried that she forgot that she was financially secure. For days, she would live as if she was very poor. Mama was still essentially Mama. She went to the market. She went through the trash and found the discarded food that normally was too blemished to sell. She set up an open-air kitchen. At all hours of the day the poor huddled around the wood fired stoves to keep warm and make soup and bread. It was the only food some people had to eat.

Our mayor was in jail. We did not have a method of replacing him because he was appointed by the central government. His wife was a decent person. She organized more open-air kitchens and temporary shelters. Mama and Papa started traveling around the country, begging farmers not to destroy their crops--to give the extra to the people who were hungry.

The Vanderholms refused to sell their grain crop inside the country. They exported it to get foreign money to support their lifestyle. I suspected that many of the fishermen who already had markets outside of the country sold their fish to those markets for foreign currency.

With nobody to buy cars, Micki closed his factory and took his wife and baby home to live in The Cove.

The night before Micki left us, we invited the whole family over for dinner. Leah invited cousin DeNough's wife over too. Without her husband to support her she was struggling financially. Still she managed to take her husband food to supplement the ration he received in jail. She seemed more distraught over his circumstances than her own. "He has a big infected sore on his side. He needs medical care."

Much as the man irritated and shamed me. He was still family. Out of a sense of basic decency I said, "I will see what I can do. Lord knows we don't have any money to keep people in jail."

I thought Micki might be distressed about going home to The Cove, but I'd underestimated his energy and ingenuity. He'd always seen what The Cove needed to thrive, but he lacked the education to apply his ideas. "I can install electricity. We'll generate our own using the wind on Cove Ridge. I'm thinking of turning The Cove into an inn for luxury boaters who want to spend a few days on shore and go hiking in the mountains. The M'NO uses too much fuel. I want to make it more efficient and powerful. We need more efficient ways to bring in the shrimp nets."

"Micki don't forget the people in the city are starving. You can still put fish on the train although I don't know how we will pay for it."

Mr. Rouseff had aged five years in the past two months. He wheezed when he talked and declared that he had gout in one foot. Suddenly he sat up straighter. A year or two fell from his face and shoulders. "I have wire and everything he could possibly need in my warehouses. Perhaps we can trade him wire and materials he needs for his projects for some fish."

Mr. Rouseff's voice grew stronger. "I want you all to remember that this is a good time to make money. It will be slow going, but when this is over, you will be richer if you manage well now. Our currency is worthless now, but it will gain value again. I think the D'NOs will prosper even if times are hard."

In the morning, I went back to the prosecutor's office and requested that Peter DeNough be brought to me. He arrived with his wife and his papers with his charges. I looked the papers over again. "This is ridiculous for you to sit in jail until we find time for someone to hear your case. If you will plead guilty to these charges, I will let you out and you can do something about supporting your wife. If you can't find help anywhere else, go home to The Cove. Micki will put you to work. You won't be rich, but you will be well fed, safe, warm and dry."

Cousin Peter whined, "What happens if I plead guilty?"

"I fine you and let you go."

"What if I don't plead guilty?"

I wanted to slap his pasty, whiny face. "I will take the case to Judge Stimson. He will declare you guilty, fine you twice as much and let you go."

"Is this some sort of extortion?"

"Don't use that word with me! You deserve to be in jail." Fury bubbled up from deep inside me. My voice rose. I knew I should control my anger. Why? Why shouldn't I yell at this miserable little disgrace to the family? "You deserve to be in jail! It is only out of compassion for your wife, who needs someone to protect her that I am giving you this opportunity. You cannot begin to comprehend my disgust at your disgracing the name of an honorable family!" I was standing and leaning over my cousin at this point. "You will act with honor! You will take care of your wife! You will plead guilty, and you will pay your fine! Do you have any questions before I take you out to the alley and let you experience my full fury?"

"No." He shrunk into his chair.

"No what?" I was told later that the people two floors up could hear me by this time.

"No sir."

"Here is your fine for each charge. These are serious charges and I am letting you walk out of here for the sake of your wife. This will cost you. I want you to be certain in every cell of your body that thievery in any form does not pay."

"Yes sir." The little weasel had learned at least that much. He took the papers and blanched at the amount of his fine. I let him go home to get the money. He was back within the hour. He paid his fine. His charges were marked redressed and he was free to go.

At four-thirty, Mr. Farley called a staff meeting. "I think I see a solution to a number of problems. First, the clerks and secretaries will get paid this week. Jake will receive ten percent of the money he brought in today as compensation. Let's see if we can empty the jail by treating these offenders the same way as we do the petty criminals. The big difference will be in setting fines commensurate with the seriousness of the crime."

We were back in business getting the embezzlers and government thieves out of jail. It became an office joke--and a threat--that anybody who did not agree to plead guilty in a case we knew to be sound, would be sent to me to be yelled at. I yelled at a few, venting all the rage and frustration that seethed in me every time I saw another child or elderly woman starving to death on the sidewalk. Some of the more timid cases simply looked at me and decided to pay. I made them do community service by working in the soup kitchens feeding the people who suffered the consequences of others' greed and corruption.

While our office had stabilized, conditions in the city grew worse. With increasing poverty came increasing crime and alcoholism. Our police force could not begin to keep up with the crime. I now had more murder cases to process. We had gotten nowhere on the Mantega murder. We did get some prints off of the gun, but they didn't match either Mantega or the accused. I was not impressed with the supposed eye-witness's testimony. We let the accused man go for lack of evidence.

I doubted I would be able to get a conviction on any of the murders I had on my case load, but this was not M'TK. The people had not yet reached the stage of half-human/half-rat existence that repulsed me as a child. I did get a conviction for murder in one case. The perpetrator had killed his victim for the sum of twenty-eight dollars. He planned to use the money to stay drunk for as long as it lasted. We didn't know what to do with the man. The judge sent him back to jail until he came up with a sentencing program. We were all at a loss.

Mama solved the dilemma. Leah and I had invited Mama and Papa out to dinner when they got home from one of their trips. I unburdened all my frustrations onto Papa. "We are picking up people who can't pay a fine and we have no money to feed them in jail."

Mama sat through dinner and picked at her food. A strand of hair hung in her face, but she didn't push it aside. She poked at one of the red skinned potatoes from our garden and blurted into the middle of my fruitless diatribe. "The potatoes need to be dug. We can feed the people if we can get the potatoes dug."

Papa stroked the hair out of Mama's face and explained to me. "The potato farmers can't afford to pay workers to dig the potatoes. The crop is going to rot in the fields while people starve in the cities."

The two trains of thought ran together in my head. For the first time in weeks I felt energized. "Do you know the names of the most desperate potato farmers?"

Papa pulled papers from his jacket pocket. "We wrote all their information down."

I jumped out of my chair to take the papers. I kissed Mama and Papa. I couldn't read the names on the papers through the mist in my eyes. "I will contact these men. Perhaps they will accept some of our embezzlers and extortionists. The crooks may run away after a day in the fields, but I'm willing to try anything. We will get at least one days harvest out of the slime"

I started calling the farmers the next day. Yes, they would take any help I could send them. "I don't know how you will keep them from running away."

The answer was usually the same. "They can try. There is nothing out here in any direction for twenty kilometers. I'll see that they stay and harvest this crop."

The interim government refused to take responsibility for solving our problems. They argued among themselves. They insisted they were only placeholders until the representative government could be installed. They were horrified at the size of the fines we levied against people convicted of racketeering, embezzlement, extortion, fraud and plain old theft. A representative of the old government actually came down to our office to protest. "These are civil crimes. You should not be fining these people more than you do for real crimes."

Mr. Farley snorted. "I notice that everyone of the people we fine is able to pay their fines within a few hours with money they had stashed under the bed. Obviously we are not fining them enough. We need to raise the fines." He looked speculatively at the representative as if sizing him up for charges and a hefty fine.

"Obstructing justice, sir." Leroy piped up from his desk in answer to Mr. Farley's unasked question as to what to charge the representative with.

I grinned and Christian came prancing over from his desk on the far side of the room. The representative from the interim government looked around, made a satisfying grunt and hastily left. The government left us alone after that.

We tried to keep in touch with prosecutors in the capital and the villages. We were the only people processing the big cases. I thought the southern port cities must have some of the perpetrators in their population. They did nothing to prosecute the wealthy perpetrators.

I was taking home a regular paycheck. It was almost worthless. We spent most of it on food. I paid some to the Changs.

One evening Leah snuggled up to me. "Jake, I need to talk to you about the Changs."

"Is there some problem with them?"

"Not really. I am recovered from having the baby. We hardly have enough money to feed ourselves. We do not need household help. I really want to say we cannot afford household help at this time."

"Are you sure you are willing to cut back this much?"

"I can manage around the house. I got so tired after Jacob was born."

"I will see if I can find him another job." I talked to Mr. Chang. "You are free to find another job. Leah does not need so much help now. What would you like to do?"

He bowed. When he straightened up, he smiled, looked me full in the eye and announced with a voice full of pride, "I want to run for parliament as a candidate from my district."

I grinned at him. "Congratulations. What can I do to help?"

"If you tell people that I am honest and that I work hard, they will vote for me."

He set up a campaign headquarters in an empty storefront on Ninth. He and his wife, who was pregnant and very proud of herself, moved back in with family. Leah and I had our house to ourselves.

We had a big birthday party for Jacob's first birthday. Mama and Papa and the Rouseffs came. The young couples from the office came. Jacob was not particularly interested in his party. The adults had fun. We needed to think about something other than the desperation that surrounded us.

Jacob had graduated to a crib in his own room. After our guests left, I took Leah to our bedroom and created a sister for him. He was about twenty-three when he finally did the math and figured out that his younger sister must have been a birthday present.

Chapter 38 Interim Government

The first job of the interim government was to set a date for an election. They dithered. They argued and the country continued to flounder.

The process for running for an office caused more arguments. It seemed to me, the dissension most often came from the former government representatives in the interim government.

Our currency was so worthless, that Mr. Farley started charging fines to be paid in foreign currencies. Offenders had the option of paying in British Pounds, Swiss Francs, or US dollars. I couldn't believe that would work, but we began bringing in some stable currencies. I noticed that, from the start, offenders could pay a fine of fifty-thousand dollars US by going home and getting the money out from under the bed. I developed a deep outraged anger against the people who had swindled, embezzled and extorted those sums of money out of our country leaving the poor in the cities to die of hunger and exposure. It disgusted me that they had prepared for this collapse by hoarding foreign currencies.

The poverty we endured for the duration of the interim government was different from the poverty of M'TK. We could get food then. We lived off of the produce from the dump. The city had restaurants. Now the restaurants closed down. I could not pick up dinner on the way home from work. Leah and I had enough to eat from our garden. I had trouble finding food in the stores. The farmers could not pay people to harvest. Fishermen like Uncle John could make more money selling fish where they could get paid in a decent currency. I sent letters begging them to send a regular supply of fish. I got enough to feed myself, and my parents.

Men began to leave the city looking for work on the farms. They left behind wives and children who had no income and nobody to take care of them. Many of them died before their men could return with food and money.

The death toll rose the quickest in the pleasure palace outside the city limits. The prostitutes managed to earn enough to buy food, but a fourteen-year old girl turned up in a ditch stabbed and mutilated. Two weeks later, two children found their mother--who prostituted herself to keep them fed— dead and mutilated like the first. The murders continued. When we found two corpses murdered a day apart we knew we must take desperate action.

We still did not have enough police to make an effective force. The few police we had refused to go outside the city limits. The business community refused to help hire police to investigate. They blamed the women for being promiscuous. I could not make them understand that these women had children to feed and parents to support. Often they had whole extended families dependant on their income. The death of one prostitute might mean death by starvation for six or eight other people.

The chief of police did understand the economics. He finally recruited law students to work investigating crimes. His intent was for the students to pass him information and for seasoned officers to make the arrests. The students had no police training and were essentially training themselves on the job. I hated for the naïve young law students to have to face the reality of the pleasure palace but the students did a good job.

The students were smart. They had an experience the police did not. They'd watched foreign detective movies, and read books. They attacked the problem with passion. Enough students infiltrated the pleasure palace posing as both clients and professional women to watch who came and went. The working women identified who their regular customers were. The students watched the rest.

After twelve nights of watching, a student, eighteen year-old Sophia Uzara, encountered a client who for no discernible reason caused the hair on her neck stand on end. Instead of passing the man off to another woman with the excuse of expecting a regular customer, she signaled another student for backup and agreed to take the man to her tent. She later told me that in order to control her fear she repeated her cousin Alice's name over and over inside her head. She led the man into an ambush set up by seven of the male law students. Outnumbered the pervert fought like a cornered animal. He had the knife he used on his victims and turned it against the men who would capture him. One young man was seriously wounded and two others received minor cuts before the police arrived to formally arrest the perpetrator.

We worried about getting solid evidence linking the man to all the murders. He solved that problem for us by keeping pictures of his dead victims in his apartment in the city. He kept some of their body parts in a drawer in his kitchen. I was supposed to prosecute him. I did. Judge Stimson gave him the death sentence. A police task force executed him by firing squad.

Everything about that case made me sick. I found no satisfaction in his execution. A human being had somehow descended to something less than an animal, so for the safety of the entire community, we had no choice but to put him down. The men assigned to the firing squad looked grey and grim when they went out to do their duty in the early morning. As the prosecutor I was there to verify that they did their duty. Together with a medical examiner my job was to inspect the corpse. Only three of the seven bullets fired hit their mark, but it was enough to do the job. I left the courtyard behind the police station after my task was complete.

I walked to the cathedral knowing that the eight o'clock mass would not be held for a couple hours yet. I lit seven candles, one for each of the men on the firing squad. Next I lit a candle for each of the man's victims. My hand shook and I almost sobbed as I lit a candle for Sophia Uzara and all of her family. I lit candles for each of the other students who helped then one each for the public defender and Judge Stimson. There were two candles left in the box. I lit one for the killer and set it far from the others. One candle remained in the box and I was going to leave it there. My heart ached. I took the last candle from the box, lit it for myself and set it among the others. I knelt down to pray, but I found no words. I knelt in silence until one side of my face grew warm. I was aware of a bright light. I turned and looked at the glow of the candles I'd lit. They lit up the whole front of the dark cathedral. I found courage to face another day in that light.

Finally, the interim government publicized the process for filing for office. Mr. Farley was livid when he approached me. "Jake, look at this list of instructions for filing to run for office." He handed me a stapled stack of papers. "See here on page five." He pointed.

I read, "Each person to be eligible to file, must list a valid address in either Portlandia or Sylvania province."

I wanted to throw the papers or the idiot who made up that rule across the room. "Hell and damnation! How many times do we have to go through this? The court rulings and new constitution specifically forbid this." I was beyond furious.

"Ah, I feel better seeing you get so angry." Mr. Farley took his papers back. "This is not acceptable with our new constitution then."

"No it is not. Damn! I'd take this out to Judge Stimson right now, but I have to take Jacob to his doctor for his immunizations and check-up. I suppose I can put his appointment off until tomorrow."

"You take your son to his doctor. I will enjoy running this out to Mercid." He turned and called to the other prosecutors. "Leroy, Christian, I want you to get on the phone. We have more work to do."

When Mr. Farley explained the problem, Christian ripped the offending page from the bundle. "Allison, run this upstairs and FAX it off to the other prosecutor's offices. Let's see if we can get the judges to rule before five tonight."

Allison took the offending piece of paper, grabbed her list of phone numbers and ran for the door. Leroy and Christian consulted briefly while dialing the other prosecutor's offices. Mr. Farley buttoned his coat and headed out the door. I stood in the middle of the room and looked around me. "Right. I'll just go take Jacob to the doctor."

I returned from the doctor's office at four-thirty. The office was quiet. Everybody sat at their desks doing paperwork. I approached Mr. Farley's desk. "Well, what is happening?"

"The provincial judges have ruled that the address requirement was unconstitutional. They added a provision that any further attempts to thwart the intent of the constitution and the related court rulings will be treated as contempt of court. Members of the interim government will be fined accordingly."

"That was fast."

"Apparently it was a slow day everywhere and people were happy to have something to do." Mr. Farley winked and chuckled.

When the filing was complete, we had at least one person running for each seat in parliament. Seven people ran for the office of president. One person was Professor Uzara from Capital University. He had worked on the constitution and knew it forward and backward. The other candidates represented other old families. The list included a Gannon, a Spencer, a Papadakos, a Fortenac, and two Vanderholms. I was disgusted to learn that Hab Vanderholm, my former classmate, who had thought we should punish laborers for the crimes of the elite chose to run. I considered him the worst of the lot.

Chapter 39 Hiring Help

I divided my time between Rouseff Industries, the prosecutor's office and doing what I could to help Chang and Professor Uzara run for office. Rouseff was a big supporter of my efforts and met with other business-men to warn them away from voting for a Vanderholm.

I worried that we did not have enough rich offenders to keep us in business much longer and it was time for another potato harvest. This year there would be no free labor to send to the farms. It is a hell of a situation when an entire food supply depends on finding enough corrupt officials to form a good chain gang.

I finally called some farmers and set up an arrangement where a worker would get paid five kilos of potatoes plus room and board for a week to work in the fields. I arranged with the railroad to buy round trip tickets on the train for the workers so the men could bring food home to their families each weekend.

Leah, was getting bigger and bigger. One night I came home and looked around our house. My beautiful home looked shabby. "Leah this is ridiculous. You need help. You had a little trouble with Jacob. I don't like you staying home alone. Tomorrow I will enquire at the soup kitchen for someone to stay with you."

Leah got tears in her eyes. "I do get lonely and I can't do anything but chase after Jacob all day. Why were we so excited when he learned to walk? Today I caught him climbing the stairs on the outside of the railing. He could have fallen and broken his neck." She sat down and started to sob. I held her in my arms, made soothing noises and tried not to think about my son getting hurt.

When we sat down to a dinner the two of us had managed to throw together, Leah looked up from her plate. "You are right that I need help, but you are gone all the time as it is. I don't want you taking time to find someone. I'll go to M'TK in the morning and find someone. I can leave Jacob with Mama."

"Hire one of the women who comes to the soup kitchen. If she has children, that is fine with me."

Leah picked me up after work the next day almost bouncing with enthusiasm. She'd found a woman to come and help around the house. "She has two children. I would have liked someone with fewer children to feed, but this woman is a nurse. She used to work at the hospital. She was the most qualified of anybody.

Shirley, our new nurse and housekeeper, proved to be more than competent. She found safe activities to keep Jacob entertained. When Leah worried and fretted, Shirley seemed to have an instinct for knowing exactly whether Leah needed tea, or a nap, or more pillows, or a walk.

Leah craved eggs. She talked about them almost passionately and dreamt about them, and begged me to look for them, but there were no eggs at the market. I finally found a farmer with hens. On the weekend I drove seventy miles to his farm and bought two hens and a small pen to keep them in. He told me how to build them a bigger pen and what to feed them. I had turned into a chicken farmer. One hen refused to lay eggs, instead it woke us up with loud crowing in the morning, which I consoled myself, at least saved us the expense of an alarm clock.

We grew much of our own food. Shortly after Jacob was born Mama started a vegetable garden for us. I would come home from work and weed. I found myself putting my weeds in little piles and counting them.

One evening when our housekeeper had been with us for close to two months, I went out to weed the garden.

"What are you doing?" The young boy beside me surprised me.

"Weeding."

"Why are you putting the weeds in piles."

"So I can count them."

"Why do you want to count them?"

I wondered where the little boy came from. "Ah, it is important to know that I am getting them all. You can help me. Can you pick ten weeds out of the garden and put them in a pile?"

"I can't count."

"Do you have fingers?"

The little boy held up both hands and showed me his fingers.

I'd started a lesson on counting when his aunt, Shirley, came and got him. "I am sorry sir. I'm watching him for my sister. I didn't mean for him to bother you."

I rolled my eyes. "I'd much rather teach a child to count than weed this damn garden."

She led the child away anyway. I didn't think much about it. The next night little boy appeared out of nowhere and followed me out to the garden.

I asked, "Are you ready to count some weeds for me tonight?"

"No."

"Why not?"

"I want my mama."

"Where is your mama?"

"I don't know."

I felt like a bucket of ice water had been dumped over me. "Did you see her this morning?"

The boy shook his head.

"Yesterday?"

He shook his head.

"Did you see her the day before yesterday?"

"No."

I got a knot in my belly. "Lets go talk to Aunt Shirley." I took the child into the house. It took me a few minutes to find Shirley. She was busy trying to give five children their dinner and she looked as she might be on the verge of tears. I watched a moment silently trying to hold the horrors in my imagination at bay. Shirley did not realize I was there.

The little boy dropped my hand and shuffled to the table. Shirley gave him a watery smile. "There you are sweetie. Come get your dinner and remember to be quiet. You don't want to upset Mrs. Jake."

She appeared to be feeding them some sort of stew. It didn't have much meat. I thought longingly of rats. The children began to look at me and stare. She turned around and saw me and started to cry.

I couldn't face it, not in my own home. Whatever had Shirley upset, my imagination told me I didn't want it in my own home. I soothed. "It's all right. Let the children get their dinner. As soon as they have their baths, I will read them a story. Then they can go to bed. We will talk after." I tried to be kind, but the children distressed me.

Shirley presented herself in my study well after ten o'clock. Putting the children to bed had been a challenge. Her two shared a bed. She intended to put her sister's children in her own bed and to sleep, I didn't want to think where. I would not permit this kind of overcrowding in my home. Finding proper beds and bedding had drained my energy far more than the task required.

I wearily asked. "Where is your sister?"

Shirley tried not to cry, but big tears rolled down her cheeks. "I don't know."

"Sit. What happened?"

Shirley sat and explained. "She dropped the children off and told me she would pick them up before dinner the next evening. She was going to apply for a job in the capital. I haven't heard from her."

"How many days has it been?"

"Six sir."

I looked at Shirley and wanted to cry with her. I remembered to breathe deeply. I remembered Mr. Wu's calm voice teaching us to master our fear. I took another breath. "Don't panic yet. It may be nothing more serious than not having enough money to get home. I will call the other rail stations. Give me her name and description."

It took me ten days to find Shirley's sister. She was in our own morgue. The children's father had been gone for over a year. She had no work and no money to feed her family. She'd finally left her children with Shirley, returned to the city, and bought or stole a bottle of rat poisoning, which she drank. Her body was found in the alley by the dumpster behind Jouyet's bank. The irony of her dying so close to such wealth sickened me. I comforted Shirley as best I could, setting aside my own grief and horror and prepared my household to feed three more children.

I called north to my cousins. "I need fish. I'll pay in British or US currency."

On a Monday morning, five days after calling my cousins, I went through the M'TK station. Mama and Papa were away on one of their trips but the substitute stationmaster came out to greet me. "Mr. Jaconovich, something arrived for you and I didn't know what to do with it." He took me around the side of the station.

I found a small rowboat upturned on the platform. I turned it over and found the oars and a fish net.

Packed in the net was a note. *Catch your own damn fish.—Micki.*

I wondered where I was supposed to catch fish in the city. I bundled the oars, net and note back in the boat to take home with me in the evening. I'd walked half-way to work before it occurred to me that fish didn't have to come from the sea. I had an entire lake in front of my house. We'd seen fish jumping in the evening. I wondered if I could possibly find enough fish to feed my family in the lake. Lord knew I couldn't find any in the stores.

I think this may have been the depth of the depression. I still had a job and an income of sorts. That morning I processed a man for beating up another man and stealing five dollars. He admitted what he'd done. "I'm trying to feed my wife, two children and my parents. We haven't had anything to eat for two days." I sat and looked at him too numb with grief and impotent fury at the whole world to have any emotion left for another starving man.

"Have you been to the soup kitchen?"

He shrugged and spread his empty hands. "Last time I went there, they ran out before we got anything."

"What have you done to earn food?"

"I worked in the potato harvest."

The harvest had been over for weeks. "Can you go to family in the country?"

"They sent me here to look for work. There are too many to feed and the catch is down."

Hope that I thought was long dead burned up in my heart. "Ah, you are a fisherman then."

"Yes."

I may have been a little hysterical at that moment. I had a vision of the fates tormenting us mortals like a cat with a mouse, giving us just enough hope to keep us running before it pounced on us again. "Meet me at the M'TK station tonight at five. We will see what kind of a fisherman you are."

I sat at my desk for a few more minutes before I got up and walked down Ninth Street to the cathedral. I lit five candles, one for all the hungry in each of the boroughs in the city. I knelt at the rail and tried to pray the prayer I'd learned as a child, but the words stuck in my heart.

It took my new employee about two hours to bring us in more fish than we could eat. When they were all cooked up on a platter, I took a picture to send back to Micki.

They were not the best fish in the world. I thought they were a little too mushy and tasted slightly of mud. Still, the fish from my lake became a currency more valuable than the local paper. I could buy most anything with a fish. When Leah had the baby, I intended to pay the medical bills with US dollars. The hospital administrator, doctors and nurses begged for fish instead.

Years later, when the pain and horror of those years had healed so the memories ceased to hurt when touched, we told Elizabeth the story of how we paid for her birth with fish. We still tell the story every year on her birthday. It is good to remember where we come from.

Chapter 40 Elizabeth

We finally settled on a name for the baby only a few days before the due date. Leah and I were in bed. She was on her side facing me so her large belly with the baby slept between us. I was just drifting off when she said, "Jake?"

"Mm hm?"

"I've decided. If the baby is a girl, I want to name her after my mama, Elizabeth."

I rolled over and kissed Leah. "That is one of the most beautiful names in the world. Why haven't we thought of that before?"

"Everybody called Mama, Elle. I won't call our daughter Elle. That name makes me remember the bad things about Mama, her drinking and smoking. But, the name Elizabeth reminds me of the good things, how she sang, how she was always ready to drop everything and play with me. She made me a doll and we dressed her in fantastic clothes using scraps from the dressmaker's shop. Elizabeth reminds me of the good things about Mama."

"Elizabeth it will be then." I kissed Leah and thought the name was beautiful. I slept.

Two days later, I was interviewing an offender, a small time extortionist, when Shirley called to say that Leah had gone into labor and she was taking her to the hospital.

I got off of the phone and said to the client. "My wife is having a baby. How do you plead?"

"Not guilty." The man grinned at me. Despite being in for extortion, he did not look like he had a cent to his name. His clothes were old, slightly dirty and ill-fitting.

"Extortion is a serious crime. I will take your case before Judge Stimson. I see no reason why he will not find you guilty and fine you ten-thousand US dollars. Now, because it is faster for me to fine you and get out of here, I am willing to fine you only five thousand US dollars. Do you still want to plead not-guilty?"

The man squirmed and shuffled his feet. A muscle at his hairline twitched. His eyes squinted as if he perhaps found something amusing in this interview. I noticed his eyes darting from side to side.

I also realized he was not screaming that he didn't have that much money. "Okay, case is referred to Judge Stimson. You will return to jail until your court date is set." I wrote on the man's record, got up, and threw the file on Allison's desk as I went out the door. Everyone called blessings after me.

When I got off the trolley a block from the hospital, I saw our Miki pull up to the emergency entrance of the hospital. Medics came out with a gurney. My heart started to race and I broke into a sweat. This did not look like calmly walking into admittance as I'd expected. I broke into a run. I hit the emergency entrance door at a full run. It slammed into the wall.

Someone commented dryly, "He's here."

They remembered me all too clearly from when Jacob was born. Nobody said anything. They squeezed out of my path and pointed me in the right direction.

I saw Shirley in the waiting room outside obstetrics. "Where's Leah? I don't see her. Where is she?" I looked around expecting to find my wife filling out forms or something.

Shirley chuckled a little when she answered. "She's in the delivery room."

"What is she doing in there?"

"Having a baby." Shirley seemed to think this was funny. She kept chuckling and smiling.

"But she just got here. Shouldn't she be just having contractions for a couple hours?"

Shirley chuckled again. "That is usually how it goes."

"So what is happening?"

Shirley remained remarkably patient with me—almost as if I was one of the children instead of her employer "Mr. Jaconovich, I know as much as you do. The admitting nurse checked her briefly when we arrived then they brought her in here saying that baby was on its way out whether we were ready or not."

Shirley decided to return straight home since I was at the hospital. "The neighbor is there with the children, but I don't want to leave her long."

"Oh, okay… Um... I see."

I heard a soft voice. "Mr. Jaconovich?"

"Yes." I turned, certain this nurse was going to tell me something was wrong.

"You have a beautiful baby girl."

I was stunned. My poor brain was so set for a long anxious wait or some disaster that I stood with my mouth hanging open for a full thirty-seconds. Finally I found my tongue. "When can I see them?"

"Give them just a few minutes."

By this time, all of heaven had opened up and showered all the joy of eternity down on me. I felt it raining down and bubbling up inside me. "Well, that wasn't too bad." I turned and grinned at Shirley as she prepared to leave while shaking her head.

Within fifteen minutes I entered Leah's room.

Leah smiled at me. "Jake I think you are glowing."

"I am completely content." I found the tiny bundle tucked in beside Leah. I kissed Leah, picked up my baby girl and peeked into the folds of the blanket at a perfect miniature of Leah. The tiny face scrunched as the pink mouth yawned and made sucking motions. I smiled over the top of Elizabeth's head at my wife who looked elegant even when tired and tousled from the labor. "I love you. You are a wonderful wife."

I called my parents while the nurses fussed over Elizabeth. Mama and Papa promised to come see us when they found someone to watch the station.

While I was on the phone, a nurse took Elizabeth to the nursery and put her in an incubator. When I tracked down my baby, I was alarmed. "What? What is wrong with her? Why did you put her in there? She is big enough."

"Mr. Jaconovich, settle down. She is fine. Most babies get a little chilled after being born. She's fine. Let her get warmed up."

I stood and leaned my forehead against the glass of the nursery window staring at that sleeping angel for several minutes. I went back to Leah's room and talked to her. "Leah you are so beautiful. I'm so thankful the delivery went so quickly. I hate to see you in pain." Leah smiled wearily at me and drifted off to sleep. Leah was sleeping. My baby was locked up in a nursery. I debated what to do next.

I thought about where I left off at work. The last scene in my office played through my memory. , Mr. Kirby, the man charged with extortion, looked shabby, yet he didn't flinch when I started talking about fines of five and ten thousand US dollars. Something was off with that one. Why didn't he pay his fine and go? Why didn't he complain about being too poor to pay a fine? I might risk returning to the office for an hour or two to make sure that case didn't go anywhere. I kissed Leah and pushed her sweaty hair away from her face. I went back to the nursery window. Elizabeth showed no sign of waking up and needing her papa. I dragged myself away from the window where everything peaceful and beautiful lay sleeping and strode down to the street feeling lighter than I could remember feeling in…I couldn't remember--a very long time. I managed to catch a trolley in the right direction and then walked the other four blocks to my office.

"What are you doing back here so soon?" Allison's comment alerted the rest of my co-workers.

I grinned. "It's a girl. Her name is Elizabeth. I think she is the most beautiful baby girl in the world."

Christian asked. "Why did you come back here?"

"Something about the case that I had when Shirley called disturbed me." I stopped and melted into what was surely a foolish grin. "Well…no… actually Leah was sleeping and they put Elizabeth in an incubator to warm her up."

Mr. Farley said, "Let's take a look at that case. Allison still has it on her desk." Jeffrey, Christian and I went over the details.

I realized that half of me was still standing at the nursery window staring at my perfect daughter. I netted my thoughts back to the present and explained, "One thing that bothers me is that the man was dressed shabby. Yet he acted cocky. Either he is taking the blame for someone else or he has way more money stashed under his bed than I think. Do we have fingerprints for this case?'"

"No. It is an extortion case."

I said. "Get some."

Allison started dividing up jobs for people to do some more investigating.

"I'm going to make a phone call." I shifted through papers in my desk drawer until I found Peter Yablonski's phone number.

He answered. "Yablonski."

"Jaconovich here. I have a case that needs more investigation. I've ordered prints. Can I FAX the file to you?"

He paused then said cautiously, "I don't handle petty criminals."

"I know that, sir."

"Sir, is it?" He chuckled. I imagined his eyebrows climbing his forehead in astonishment.

"Yes, sir."

"I'll come down to look at the file."

"I may not be here. My wife just had a baby."

"Boy or girl?"

"Girl."

"Good, you worry more with girls." He chuckled. "I'll come down on the first morning train and be at your office at seven in the morning."

"Right." We hung up.

I returned to Leah's room just as she woke up. She was hungry. Her late lunch didn't look particularly appetizing.

The poor aide who brought the lunch tray in explained, "This is all we have, sir. We cannot find enough food to buy to feed the patients."

I snorted, "I have fish in my lake perhaps I should pay my bill in fish."

The poor aide's face lit up. "Oh yes, sir. I will run and tell Mr. Administrator. We've all been told to look for food for the patients."

My parents came in to visit shortly after Leah finished her lunch. Mama looked good. Her eyes were soft and shining as she and Papa examined the tiny fingers and tiny toes of their granddaughter. They admired her perfect tiny ears. Mama and Papa kissed Leah and told her that Elizabeth was a beautiful name.

Leah said firmly. "We will not call her Elle. We will call her the full Elizabeth. I don't want to hear *Lizzy* either."

"Oh no, she is such a glorious baby we will be certain to call her Elizabeth. It is such a beautiful name. Mama looked a little dreamy as those tiny pink fingers curled around one of hers.

Leah laughed at Papa, "I can't believe how much you and Jake are alike when you look at a baby. You both absolutely melt and get tears in your eyes."

Mama put her arm around Papa and snuggled close like she did when they were younger. "I have been blessed to have married such a wonderful man." They finally said they would go out to our house and stay with Jacob. They each had to hold Elizabeth a moment longer and stroke her cheek and kiss her on the top of her blond head.

I took my daughter from my parents and remembered I had an equally precious son at home. I felt torn. "I haven't seen Jacob since morning. I'd like to assure him that all is well. I also need to be here."

Papa squeezed my shoulder. "We will go out to the house and stay with Jacob. He'll be fine." They left. I sat down next to Leah and sighed.

I settled into a chair next to my wife with my baby in my arms. Leah smiled at me and her eyes drifted closed.

Shortly before eight a nurse came in. "Mr. Jaconovich it is time for you to leave and for the baby to go back to the nursery."

I whispered, "Keep that door closed. You are making it cold in here." I got up and went to close the door. "I am concerned about Leah. She was in labor only an hour at most. She slept most of the afternoon. She drifted off to sleep again just a few minutes ago."

"Well she just had a baby. She needs to sleep. I'll take the baby back to the nursery now."

"You were not here when my son was born."

"No."

"Did the nurses who know me send you down here? I bet they are up at their nurses station laughing up their sleeves over your troubles." Poor woman, I tried to smile a sympathetic smile. "Now, I'll tell you how this works when *my* babies are born. First, you are going to go find a doctor to come check my wife because I think there is something not quite right here. She is too pale. We'll discuss the rest of the plan when the doctor is finished."

"I'll take the baby with me."

"No." I settled back into my chair.

"What?"

"Go find the doctor for my wife."

"You give me that baby or I'll call security."

I continued to rock my daughter in my arms while raising a single eyebrow at the nurse. "Excellent. While you are out calling security, find the doctor. I'll deal with security when they get here." I glared at the woman. She was tough. She didn't flinch, squeak or cry. Perhaps the effect was ruined by the way I cradled my precious daughter in my arms. "And, don't leave the door open more than a second on your way out. I don't want my wife and daughter getting chilled."

I sincerely hoped that nasty little nurse would call the doctor. Leah's face, which was normally creamy almost like a china doll, had begun to look very faintly blue.

Bless the belligerent nurse, she did send the doctor. I explained my concerns. He decided to examine Leah just to placate me. She barely woke up when he uncovered her. "Everything looks fine down here Jake."

Leah rolled over and sat half-way up. "Jake do you have Elizabeth?"

"Yes, my love. I'm taking good care of both of you."

The doctor's look of amused indulgence abruptly sobered. He tried to sound calm, but his voice held a note of urgency. "Leah, Jake, I want to take Leah into surgery. She is losing more blood than I like."

The sudden flurry of activity around Leah suggested that if anything, I had under-estimated the severity of Leah's condition. As the nurses wheeled Leah away a huge monster of guilt and fear crawled out from under her bed and clutched at my heart. Elizabeth stirred in my arms. I would not let the monster harm my baby. I took a deep breath and pulled to mind Mr. Wu's teaching. *"The foolish man argues with fear and thereby calls into being the thing he fears. The wise man tells his fear to be gone and thus insures the thing he fears cannot be."* I turned my head away from the fear and said, "I will not argue with you."

I sat back in my chair and sang to Elizabeth the song my mama had sung to my sister. I hadn't known I remembered that song, but the words came back effortlessly from the past, spilled out and circled my Tiny Elizabeth in my own remembered love for my almost forgotten sister.

"Mr. Jaconovich?" The nurse came back.

I startled back to consciousness of my surroundings. "How is Leah?"

"I don't know. I've come to take the baby back to the nursery."

"This baby is going to stay right here with her papa. She is going to know that she is safe and loved."

"She will get cold."

"She won't if you stop opening the damn door." I grumped. "I'll hold her against me and keep her warm. Now go make yourself useful and find out how my wife is doing." This time the nurse did *squeak*.

I held Elizabeth and sang to her and waited for Leah to come back. I kept at bay the memory of how sick Mama had been when she lost the twins. Finally, an orderly wheeled Leah back to our room. She looked much better.

The doctor sounded irritatingly jovial when he explained the problem that I had been the one to recognize. "We found a bleeder and closed it off. We gave her two units of blood. She should feel much better now."

I suggested, "Perhaps we could use some heated blankets for her."

The doctor responded appropriately. "Yes, Jake."

I added, "You might tell that nurse who keeps coming in here to keep the door closed to keep the room warmer." Another nurse came in with the warm blankets, smiled at me and instructed me in the use of the call button.

Sometime in the middle of the night Leah woke up and held her hand out to me. "Jake, thank you for noticing that something was wrong. They said they couldn't tell that I was bleeding because the blood was pooling inside and not flowing out."

I tucked Elizabeth in beside her mama and held Leah's hand. "Leah, my love, I will always do my very best to take the best care of you. Can we make a pact that I will take care of you, and you will not tell me the details of female problems?"

Leah laughed and stroked my hair. "You are a good man." She looked a little sad. "Many men do not take care of their families."

A different nurse came in to help Leah with Elizabeth's first feeding. She cheerfully explained that feeding the baby would help close off any additional bleeding that Leah might experience. Elizabeth was a healthy enough eater, but she was not as focused on eating as Jacob had been. She stopped from time to time to look around at her mama, me, and her whole new world. That was pretty much the pattern for Elizabeth's babyhood. She was a pleasant happy child. She ate what we gave her. She seemed content in whatever we did.

I left the hospital about six in the morning. I took the first trolley out to the house, showered, shaved, dressed, kissed Jacob and assured him Mama and Elizabeth were fine and ran out the door to meet Peter at seven. I got there a minute or two before him.

"How is your wife?"

"She had a little trouble yesterday evening, but seemed fine this morning."

"Good, you get cranky when you are worried about your wife having babies."

I laughed. "That may be the problem with this case. The call from our housekeeper came while I was interviewing the man."

"Did you break his nose?"

"No, but for some reason that seems like a really good idea. There is something off about him." We sat down and went over the file.

Peter had a briefcase full of papers. "It seems unlikely that your man could be one of the people we are still looking for. I'd think he would want to avoid the extra attention of going to court."

"I offered him a fine of five thousand US dollars. He didn't whine and complain about not being able to pay the fine. I don't see how he could be innocent. He didn't act innocent either. Maybe he wants to go to jail, but we are fining people and letting them go."

Peter grunted.

I went on to explain the other investigations we'd started. I gave Peter his own set of all our records.

"It looks like you are doing a good job. Keep this investigation secret. We are still looking for a few key people. We know they exist. We don't know who or where they are. Report directly to me if you find anything more incriminating." He took his files and prepared to leave. "Congratulations on the baby. You are a lucky man. Take care of that family first. They are more important than this." He indicated his briefcase.

"Thanks."

He had left again by seven-twenty. I sat down and waited for Jeffrey Farley to get in. I pondered our protocol for a case that might turn out to be a key case.

He arrived a few minutes before eight. "Jake what are you doing here?"

"I had a meeting with the CGIS. It is possible that we have one of the major missing pieces of the whole corruption scheme locked up in our jail."

He raised his eyebrows at me. "What are we supposed to do about that?"

"Keep him safe and keep him secret."

"This is the guy, Kerby, who plead not-guilty, yesterday?"

"Yeah."

"Everyone in the office knows we have the case pending. I will tell them that they are to report anything they haul in directly to me or you, but that he has had a change of venue."

"That is close enough. Yablonski took a copy of Kerby's file."

My supervisor rubbed the back of his neck.

I gave Mr. Farley a sheepish smile. "This may turn out to be nothing more than my anxiety over Leah." Distracted with thoughts of my baby, I might have sighed. "Elizabeth is so beautiful."

"Jake you go on back to your family. If I get any hint of trouble, I will move the case to deep security and let you know immediately."

Back at the hospital, Leah looked better than she had the night before, but

I didn't even think of taking her home yet. She needed to be waited on hand and foot. Elizabeth was gone so I kissed Leah and went down to the nursery to stare through a window at my beautiful daughter.

Elizabeth was alone. I couldn't believe it. Nobody was sitting beside her. There were no other babies in the nursery. Again an ugly monster of fear reared up to snatch my helpless daughter from the nursery. I was angry enough that I wasn't having anything to do with fear. I tried the door. It wasn't locked. I bundled up my baby, carried her back to her mama's room and prepared to spend the day.

A half hour later, I heard a voices and running feet in the hall. A nurse came running into Leah's room. She looked around and almost pounced on me. She pulled back Elizabeth's blanket and said, "There she is. Do you have any idea what a fright you gave us?" She tried to sound angry and menacing.

She learned what angry and menacing really sound like when I snarled, "Do you have any idea what I thought when I found my daughter alone where any deranged person could come in off of the street take her?"

The nurse left the room.

When the doctor arrived he checked Leah over. "I want you to stay another day Mrs. Jaconovich. I'm not very happy with your blood work." He looked at me. "Your wife really does need some extra care here."

"I know."

"Can you cooperate with our staff?"

I wanted to say a great deal to the doctor. I looked at him instead. "I do not want my daughter left alone in the nursery."

The doctor scratched his nose. "Sir, I see your point. It won't happen again, but we are short of staff."

"Our housekeeper is a nurse. If you are short of staff, she can come stay with Elizabeth and Leah when I am not here."

Leah pushed herself up on her elbows. "How will you manage at home? Who will take care of Jacob?" Leah wailed.

"Mama and Papa are staying with Jacob. They can take care of the house."

The doctor patted Leah's hand, "No, you need your hired help at home. We will staff the nursery."

I spent the rest of the day with Leah. When she fell asleep, I went home to have dinner with Jacob.

My home was a joyful place. Mama looked tired possibly because

Shirley's children eat dinner with Jacob in the dining room. Shirley told me Mama and Papa had spent the day entertaining all the children.

After feeding the whole pod of rascals, Mama eased down in a chair and moaned to me. "Poverty is hardest on the children. Those babies lost their Mama and Papa. They need to be loved." I felt guilty that I had not done more than feed them and read a few stories.

After the children had eaten, Papa suggested I take Jacob to the top of the ridge to watch the sun go down. It was good to hold my son and watch the sky turn from orange and red to apricot with turquoise edges. We stayed on the ridge until the first stars came out. He was beginning to learn to talk enough so we could carry on a conversation.

"When Mama home?"

"Tomorrow, I think"

"'lizabeth?"

"Yes, we will bring Elizabeth too." I smiled. "You have a wonderful sister." I thought to myself that I intended to get immunizations for her so that my son could grow up knowing his sister.

"Play wid 'lizabeth?"

"Yes." I had no idea what chaos I unleashed on the world with that one word. I had some idea that when they were four and six they would play together.

"Stevie plays wid Suzie." Stevie and Suzie were Shirley's children.

"What dat?" Jacob pointed to a fungus on a tree.

I explained about the fungus. Jacob asked about everything he saw. I named everything for him. Life was good.

Mama and Papa went home to their own house as soon as all the children were in bed. Mama returned about dawn with a sleepy Papa in tow. She bustled off to the kitchen to cook breakfast. Papa stretched out on the sofa to finish sleeping.

I stopped by the office about eight on my way to see Leah. Mr. Farley waited until I'd given everybody reports on my wife and baby before he motioned to me to sit down close to his desk. "Uh…Jake…that case we discussed…"

I looked at him, my attention suddenly riveted on my job.

Mr. Farley almost whispered. "His fingerprints match those on the gun that killed Mantega."

I nodded, thankful that my instincts had been on target when my mind was wrapped up in my family. "Right. I'll let Yablonski know. I think we need to move this case to restricted access."

"If I get one more hint of complications on this, I will make it so top secret it will cease to exist outside of you and me."

When I arrived at the hospital I found Leah sitting up in bed talking to Elizabeth. The nurse whined, "We don't like new mothers to get tired out taking care of their babies, but doctor insisted that she was not to be in the nursery without an attendant."

I scowled. The nurse looked at me and ran out of the room.

Leah laid back down and held Elizabeth on her tummy. "Jake, you are frightening all my nurses."

"Your nurses have nothing to be afraid of as long as they give you and Elizabeth the care you need." I picked up my daughter and sat down in a chair beside Leah.

She complained. "I'm bored."

"You look like you feel better. I might let the doctor let you come home today."

"The food will be better at home."

The doctor did, much to the relief of the staff, let me take Leah and Elizabeth home, right after I promised to deliver fifty kilos of fish to the hospital to cover Elizabeth's bill.

Chapter 41 Mercid

E lizabeth was just a few days old and the economic situation was still getting worse when we held our parliamentary elections. This ballot was more complicated than the first one because different districts voted for people from their own district. They needed a district ballot and a ballot for the presidency. Andrew solved every problem in his systematic way. He upgraded the scanners to make counting faster at the polls. Thanks to Andrew this election went much smoother than the first election when we had no idea what would happen or even how to make ballots.

The outcome of the election disappointed me. My former classmate, Hab Vanderholm won the presidency. I hoped rather than believed that he would carry out his duties with justice and honor.

One of Vanderholm's campaign promises had been that he would pardon those in prison for civil crimes. This didn't make sense. He could not pardon his friends who had not been tried. We were processing them the same as we did petty criminals, fining them and letting them go. After the fines were paid, there was no point in pardoning them. We still worried that he would interfere with the process. I needed to work extra hours the few weeks before the inauguration to clear as many cases as possible.

One afternoon, a few days before Vanderholm was to be inaugurated, Papa called me at work. "Jake something has to be done. It is the poor people. They are upsetting Mama."

I had no idea what I was supposed to do about the poor people. Papa sounded close to tears himself. He never called me at work. I decided this was serious.

I arrived at the M'TK station to find Mama crying and rocking. Papa looked about ready to cry because she was crying. I had no idea what to do. I looked out the window for inspiration. I saw the soup kitchen that Mama started, crowded with people. I knew we didn't have much food to put in the soup. I knelt down in front of Mama and asked, "Mama? Is this what is upsetting you? The poor who have nothing to eat?"

Mama rocked and sobbed and gulped for breath. "The women and the babies are dying. They're dying. There is nothing to feed them. I tried. Jake, I've tried. I can't buy enough food to feed them. The market does not have enough food to feed them. There is not enough food in the whole country to feed them all."

My stomach knotted. "Papa I think it is time for you and Mama to either go to The Cove or move to Mercid. What do you think?"

Mama almost cried, "Not The Cove. I am a beggar in The Cove. I want to be near the babies. Leah needs time away. You will need us to stay with Jacob and Elizabeth. It is just that I can't stand seeing those poor people. I've never been that poor."

This statement from a woman who had lived in M'TK stunned me to the point that I forgot my surroundings. I remembered our rat-infested apartment. We always had enough to eat. Sometimes, I brought home Chinese food and we ate rat. I had my library card. We had our apartment. Mama had Papa. I looked out the window. Those women did not have anything.

While Mr. Farley, Leroy and Christian prepared to go to the capital for the inauguration, I set out to find my parents a house in Mercid. I was thankful to have an additional excuse not to attend the ceremonies. I'd all ready declined an invitation to stay with Johan for the festivities on the excuse that Elizabeth was too young to travel. In my mind I tried to tell myself that perhaps Hab Vanderholm had grown some wisdom, but I could not get past the ignorant, arrogant, amoral bigot he had been in my college law classes.

I took off from work and found an agent to show us several little houses. Mama liked the yards, but the houses didn't have close neighbors. We went home again. We would look another day.

I insisted that Mama and Papa come to my house for dinner with Leah and I. Leah had been cranky since the pregnancy. Little things upset her. "What have you been doing?" She demanded in a pout.

I answered. "We went house hunting in Mercid."

Leah sat up straighter and her pout disappeared. "Oh. Oh, I'd like to help with that. I've taken design courses and architecture. I know what will be comfortable and what may be fancy, but not practical. I'd like to help with the house hunting." Leah sat up and almost bubbled with energy. "Tomorrow morning I will drive into M'TK so we can take the train to Mercid and look for houses. Jake can go do his work. He has so much to do before the inauguration.

I want to help, and if Grandpapa can keep an eye on Jacob while we look, perhaps I will not get so tired."

Leah flitted off to find property listings while Papa and Mama chuckled at her sudden enthusiasm. I wanted Mama and Papa to spend the night with us, but they took the trolley back to the station. With Leah still absorbed in maps and addresses and bedrooms and baths, I managed to get a load of laundry washed and hung to dry. I ran the dishwasher, read all the children a story and put Jacob to bed. I barely had energy to get my own clothes off before I dropped into my own bed and put my hand into Elizabeth's cradle. I think part of my fatigue stemmed from the burden of my anxiety over the idea of Hab Vanderholm as president.

When I came home from work the next day, Leah met me at the trolley stop. She looked and sounded almost like her old self. I looked forward to having her to myself for the short ride out to the house. She chattered excitedly about her day. "I took Grandpapa and Grandmama to Mercid and we found an apartment to purchase. I thought Mama would like a house with a little garden, but the agent wanted to show us some apartments for older people. Your Mama seemed comfortable when we saw it. Papa liked it well enough. They talked about geraniums on the little deck. They have a choice of a ground level unit or a second floor unit."

I managed to slip a word into Leah's stream of chatter, "I would think they might want a place with families nearby."

Leah explained, "I thought so too, but Papa liked the idea of having other retired couples to do things with."

I grunted. "There is that. I suppose they might want to do things together. I have no idea what Papa will do with himself if he retires. He has worked all his life. What will he do without a job? Perhaps he and Mama will want to do things together."

On Saturday while Hab Vanderholm was being inaugurated as the first elected president of our country, my family drove up to Mercid along with one of the purchasing agents from Rouseff to look at the apartment in the retirement complex. Lawns and gardens surrounded an attractive brick building. The building agent showed us around and Leah pointed out features here and there. The complex had a small dining room, a game room with card tables, a pool table and several games I didn't recognize. Leah read to me from the brochure. "*The social coordinator plans card games on Tuesday and Thursday. Monday night features travel movies in the TV room. On the last Saturday of the month a formal dance is held in the common room. Folk dancing is on Fridays."* I thought it all sounded quite impressive.

The apartments had one bedroom, a full kitchen with a dining nook and a sitting room. The sitting room had sliding doors out to a patio or small deck. The view from the upper floor apartment my parents were interested in looked over the gardens. In the distance I could see the silver sweep of the river. I knew Mama would love the view.

While our purchasing agent negotiated with the building owner, Mama struck up a conversation with some women who were playing cards. The women chatted amiably. Suddenly, the years seemed to drop away. Mama looked so young I could almost imagine myself as a young child selling rats and saving my pennies to buy my beautiful Mama a dress with flowers on it. I listened to her conversation. "Oh yes, my husband and I have always said that we wanted to move to Mercid when we retire. He is retiring from the railroad any day now and I am looking forward to a little peace and quiet with my husband. We will be out of the city but still close enough to see the grandchildren."

The women looked behind Mama and smiled at Leah. They told Mama about their grandchildren.

I looked closer at Mama. No wonder she looked younger to me. She smiled and the strain and anxiety melted from her face. She stood straight as if the weight of a starving city slipped from her shoulders.

Our agent and the building owner couldn't come to terms on the price of the apartment. I asked, "What is the problem?"

The building owner shrugged and spread his hands in a helpless gesture. "You are the first people to ask to buy since the collapse. Um…we don't know how much a unit is worth in today's dollars."

I said. "I can pay you either US dollars or British pounds."

Papa put his hand on my arm. "I have money Jake. I can buy my own home."

I shook my head. "Your money is in the local currency. Save that for now. I will pay for this in something people can use. You can pay me back when your money is worth something again."

On Sunday, while the inauguration celebrations continued in the capital, Papa hired people from the soup kitchen to come help them box up their belongings and move them to their new house.

I worked in the prosecutor's office on Monday. The other prosecutors had not yet returned from the capital so I gave the interns a lesson on processing a large number of offenders with little staff. I left for home at my usual time. I came though the station to catch my trolley home and I received the shock of my life. There was a new stationmaster at M'TK!

Birth of Nation

Chapter 1 Hired Assassin

What kind of man kills his fellow man for money? I still can't answer that question. Perhaps, if I'd had my mind on my job instead of my new baby girl, I would have learned the answer. Then again maybe this is not a question an honest man can answer.

After my office mates returned from inauguration ceremonies, I decided to stay home with Leah and the children for two days. With a new baby in the house and Shirley's five children, I thought the women needed some extra help.

Actually Jacob consumed the whale's share of my energy. If I turned my back, he climbed into bed with Leah and Elizabeth to show the baby a toy or a book or tell her the names of all his body parts. He loved holding Elizabeth. We took her with us wherever we went or Jacob would be in her room showing her his toys and trying to hold her.

When Leah and Shirley insisted that Elizabeth simply *had* to sleep, Jacob would lie down on the bed beside her and wait for her to wake up or, even better, sometimes he fell asleep himself.

Elizabeth accepted the brotherly attention with wide-eyed calm. I expected her to cry when he plopped a teddy bear or a toy train on top of her, but she looked at her brother and his offerings with pleasant complacency.

Shirley did an excellent job of teaching Jacob how to behave around his sister. She taught him how to hold the baby and how to be gentle and that babies need their blankets to keep warm.

Leah congratulated herself repeatedly for her success in hiring Shirley. I agreed that I appreciated our help. It seemed to be taking the combined efforts of three adults to manage my household.

Still, after two days, I needed to return to work. Rouseff needed me to finish up some contracts, and I wanted to check on our case against Kerby. I still joked about being torn between rewarding the offender for ridding the city of a piece of corrupt scum or following legal protocol. I wondered which course of action served justice the best.

At eight in the morning, I walked into the prosecutor's office where Jeffrey Farley immediately accosted me. "Um...Jake?" He motioned me to the chair closest to his desk.

I immediately thought of the Kerby case, since normally Mr. Farley talked to me across the aisle that separated our desks. He looked as close to scowling as I'd ever seen him.

"What?" I asked.

"We got this yesterday."

I read the letter that he handed me. My stomach lurched, and I found myself actually growling at the injustice. The letter came from the office of President Vanderholm advising us to expect a new office supervisor to arrive today.

"I...I...I'm sorry sir." I stammered crushed by the injustice. "You deserve the job. You have done a fantastic job running this office under extremely poor conditions." My voice betrayed some of my anger. He'd held the office together during the chaos of our government transition. He deserved the highest honor in our office.

He sounded shaken. "I had no idea that anybody even intended to send us replacements. I find it amazing that the first thing the new president does is send us a new supervisor."

I scowled at the implication of his words as I squeezed his shoulder. "If it means anything to you, you have earned my respect and my trust many times over. Perhaps this new person will be of some use."

Mr. Farley swallowed a couple of times before he spoke. "Thank you, coming from you that is a high compliment. You don't trust until you know the other person is trustworthy."

This estimation of my character surprised me.

He pulled himself together resolutely and leaned in closer to me. "We need to make a decision now about the Kerby case."

"As you say, I don't trust until I am certain that the other person is trustworthy."

He almost whispered. "It is time then to move the case to officially non-existent?"

I nodded. "Yablonski would not want just anyone to know that this case involves his office."

Mr. Farley sighed. "Right. I'll call a staff meeting."

During the staff meeting we covered some of the general rules of making a transition of power. The staff expressed their loyalty to their friend. By this time, Mr. Farley had regained more control over his emotions than when he first talked to me. "Thank you for your confidence. Your approval means more to me than appointments from the president. The important part of this transition will be treating the new supervisor with the respect due his position. As Jake says, we might find him useful."

Mr. Farley met with the staff, who had worked on the Kerby case, in private and directed them that the case no longer existed in our office. "If you uncover any more information pass it to Jake or myself. This case is really under the jurisdiction of the CGIS, so rules of confidentiality state that we will not discuss this case in this office. The new supervisor is not to know of its existence."

Leroy snorted, "Yeah, I wondered about the timing of this. We uncover a case that CGIS finds interesting, and suddenly, the very first thing the new president thinks to do is assign us a new supervisor when there is no money to pay such a person."

Leroy's evaluation sounded reasonable to my brain, which still tended to hover over my baby's cradle clouding my reaction to the outer world. "It is possible that he is a plant."

Christian sounded almost gleeful. "We all have enough experience working with those who we dare not trust. We'll be careful, sir. If this person turns out to be helpful, then all is well and good. If he is not trustworthy, we know how to write up charges against our supervisors."

We went back to our desks. I noticed Christian talking to Allison. His tone held an undercurrent of anger. I tried not to eavesdrop but I did catch the word "injustice" in his rant. Later, I noticed Allison slamming drawers and snapping at one of the paralegals.

Later while processing a client who had been brawling, I felt a presence in the office. I ignored the presence to talk to the client. He plead guilty.

I admonished the man. "Look at you. Your face is cut and your ear is swollen. That has got to hurt."

He shrugged.

"What I'm trying to tell you is that you are no good at fighting. Give it up. Stay home with your wife and children in the evening. I'm going to have to fine you."

He said in a dull monotone, "Don't know where my wife and smolts are."

"Why not?"

"I left to find work. When I came back, they were gone."

"What have you done to locate them?"

He shrugged.

"Have you contacted her parents? Your parents? Cousins? Friends?" I started growing frantic with the fear of being separated from Leah and my children.

He shrugged.

Here sat one more casualty of the economic collapse. For my own comfort, I would do what I could for the man. I pulled out a legal pad. "Listen you better give me all the information you can about your wife and children. We can check to see if the children are in school."

He raised his head and for the first time looked me in the eye. I saw wonder and hope growing across his features. "Thank you. Thank you sir. I didn't know what to do."

"I suggest that you get in touch with all of your family and friends. Talk to everybody in the neighborhood." I got the information, gave the man a modest fine and directed him across the hall to pay it.

Nobody said anything to me about the new person in the office. I wondered if this could be the new supervisor. His suit looked expensive. Jeffrey spoke with him and walked with him toward the back offices. I decided he must be the new supervisor.

I took the time to call the schools about Mr. Krugal's missing children. The results of my phone calls were depressing. None of the school directors could assure me the boys were at school. They promised to search their records suggesting that the children might turn up later.

The new supervisor had gone into his office and shut the door. I looked at the man I still considered to be my boss.

Jeffrey shrugged.

Next, I picked up the file of a young woman picked up for prostitution. "How do you plead?" I asked gently.

The poor girl looked terrified. She sat twisting her dress in her fingers while tears made dirty tracks down her cheeks. Snot spread across a face that could be pretty if it were clean. "What? I don't know what I am supposed to say."

"Were you working as a prostitute when you got picked up?"

Her mouth curled down at the corners, and her eyes filled with tears. "No! I am a good girl!"

I leaned back in my chair. "It says here that you were picked up in the middle of the alley off of third." I remembered to translate the police talk into common words. "The policeman saw you speaking to several who passed by. What were you doing?"

"My mama fell, and I wanted somebody to help me pick her up. I tried and tried to get someone to help. The police wouldn't help me." Miss. P'NA's voice became more hysterical as she told me her story.

I resisted the urge to look at the file to find the names of the stupid fools who arrested this poor girl. I did think about making a list of future *sparring partners* containing people who were so senseless they were a hazard to the community. "Where is your mama now?"

"Still on the floor!" The poor girl wailed.

That hadn't been exactly what I meant, so I checked the address where the girl was picked up. "Come, let's go get your mama off of the floor." I bounded out of my chair and bustled the woman out to the street. Fortunately, we caught a trolley that took us to within a block of her home. I followed her to her apartment.

We found her mother, more dead than alive, still on the floor. The frail older woman appeared to be chilled through. She'd pulled part of a thin towel down to the floor and wrapped it over her shoulders. I instructed Miss P'NA to bring all the blankets in the apartment. I wrapped the old woman up and told her daughter to lie on the floor and hold her mama close to warm her. I ran to a plumbing shop a few doors away to phone for help. I stayed until the paramedics arrived to take the frail woman to the hospital. I worried about the daughter, who did not seem to be bright enough to take care of herself.

The incident left me feeling slightly ill as I returned to the office. Our country didn't have anyone trained in social services or social work. Cases such as Mr. Krugal's and Miss. P'NA were ignored. I tried to help wherever I could.

When I came through the door Allison's sympathetic expression mixed with alarm alerted me to a new crisis.

Before I got half-way to my desk, the new supervisor strode out of his office and approached me. He was tall and thin with graying hair at his temples. His suit fit his athletic body perfectly. I estimated that his suit cost at least half of what was my annual salary before the crash. "Where have you been?" The new man snarled loudly enough for everybody in the office to hear.

I didn't like attracting his attention in this manner, but I remained professional. "I left to investigate the case I was working on."

He sniffed, looked down his long beaked nose at me and declared, "It is not the job of the prosecution to investigate. That is the job of the police."

I think I must have blinked before I had the presence of mind to conceal my astonishment. "I was unaware of this change in policy. It will not happen again sir." My internal alarms clamored warnings so loud they made my head ache. "By the way sir, my name is Jake Jaconovich. I am a certified prosecutor."

He ignored my introduction. "Get back to work." He contemptuously turned his back on me and returned to his office shutting the door forcefully behind him.

I returned to my desk more astonished than not. I'd just started my paperwork for my last case when my phone rang.

"Jaconovich."

"What was he onto you about?" I wondered what had prompted Christian to call me from the corner of the office. I looked over the partition behind me. Christian had his back to my side of the room and appeared to be writing on a legal pad.

I lowered my voice to match his whisper. "Investigating a case."

"What?"

"Yeah, he asked where I'd been. I said I'd gone to investigate a case."

There was a long pause on the other end of the phone then Christian asked, "Is that what you'd done?"

"Yeah, it was a sad case. That isn't the important part. The important part was that he said we were not supposed to investigate cases."

"Surely he didn't mean that the way it sounds." Christian's tone conveyed disbelief.

"Perhaps in the law school in the capital they use different terminology than we do. I don't know, maybe I should have said I was verifying the alibi of the accused."

Christian repeated in a whisper. "He actually said we were not supposed to investigate cases?"

"He said that was the job of the police." I lowered my voice more. The office seemed unusually quiet. I suspected that the others were trying to hear our conversation. I wished they would make enough noise to mask our voices.

Christian paused a long time. "Is that something that has changed under the new constitution?"

"No."

"Well, that is very interesting. I think that I just might need to start a new case file." Christian sounded quite happy.

I asked, "Which university did he go to? Do you know his name?"

"Nobody has mentioned his name." Christian paused to think again then decided, "You try to find his name and university. I'll check on some other things." We hung up.

I made a quick phone call to Professor Ingleman and another to Judge Gannon in the capital. Neither man could explain why I was told not to investigate a case. They had not heard anything about an appointment to our office and promised to look into it. I thought about the possible reasons for our new supervisor's strange behavior while I continued to work on my paperwork. The office remained quiet except for the occasional phone ringing as we called each other.

I called Mr. Farley. "Why are we calling each other instead of walking to the other person's desk or talking across the aisle?"

"Mr. Supervisor threatened to fire Leroy for talking to Christian."

Bewildered, I asked, "Well then, how are we supposed to consult on a case?"

"We are supposed to do our own work. I hear we are not to investigate cases either."

"That's what he told me." We hung up when Allison slammed a file drawer shut noisily.

Mr. Supervisor strode out of his office and approached Allison. "Send the staff a memo stating that we are having a staff meeting at four o'clock." He stomped off to his office muttering about the lack of an intercom and the indignity of having to walk out to fetch someone.

At four, we gathered for a staff meeting. Our new supervisor read out a long list of instructions, including when we could take breaks, how long we could stay on the phone, no talking to other staff, and a half dozen other control directives that better suited a lower form classroom than a professional office. I thought of Kerby and wanted to sweat. I wondered if the new supervisor was actually looking for Kerby or if the man just liked control. I was entertaining a fantasy of taking the man out to the alley when his next comment caught my attention.

"And I was told that one prosecutor left the office to investigate…" He made a false chuckle. "To investigate a case. That is the job of the police. I cannot believe he really did that."

I noticed that a few people were shifting in their seats.

One of our interns raised his hand. "I don't understand your exact meaning sir. The police write up the report that says this person was arrested for… um…brawling. Our job is to ask that person how they plead. If they say they plead, not guilty, what are we supposed to do?"

"If the police arrest them, they are guilty. It is not your job to be asking them their opinion." I noticed the astonishment on the others' faces. The supervisor explained, "You've been being too lax on these slum scum. I'm here to put a stop to that. If you don't take a hard line with these low people, the crime will continue to escalate until the streets are not safe."

The intern gasped like a fish out of water.

I asked for further clarification. "I think we all grasp the need for law and order. We are, after all, prosecutors. The confusion seems to be over a point of law. All of us were trained at the university here. Several of us have prosecuted cases …"

"I know you are lawyers. Do you have a point?"

"My point is that what you have just suggested does not follow legal protocol. If we do not ask the client how they plead, we are violating the law. We must take certain steps to insure that our decisions will stand up in a court and will stand up under an appeal."

The supervisor looked down his nose at me and answered in his cold, hard voice. "Well we already know that the people the police bring in are guilty."

Christian raised his hand. "Mr. Supervisor, you have not told us your name. Please sir, how are we to address you?"

"You may call me Mr. Supervisor."

Leroy spoke up. His blunt tone assured me he had developed some self-confidence since we prosecuted and fined our last supervisors. "Sir, you have instructed four prosecutors to violate the law. This is not a good start to our relationship. To change the direction of this discussion, it would help if you gave us a little of your background."

"I don't intend to socialize with my staff." Mr. Supervisor stood up and abruptly returned to his office.

I immediately volunteered, "I'll call Mr. Apkouta and put the word out on the street for people to keep it down."

"Jake, before you go…" I knew what my boss wanted.

Alexander, one of our interns whispered. "What are we supposed to do to process clients?"

Leroy answered the intern's question, firmly. "You will continue to follow the law and watch what happens when someone does not."

Char the other intern squeaked, "I don't think I want to work here anymore."

"What?" Christian chuckled. "This is just getting interesting. I'll show you how I built the case against our last supervisors."

The meeting ended just before five. We returned to our desks and prepared to go home. The women started pulling on jackets and sweaters and finding their handbags while they chatted about after-work plans. Mr. Supervisor emerged from his office and snarled at the women. "What do you think you are doing?"

Allison displayed the same common sense and courage I'd witnessed the night the army came through the city on a purge. She curtly answered, "We're going home."

"It's not six o'clock yet."

Mr. Farley made a polite *ahem* sound. "This is a city office sir. All city offices close at five."

Mr. Supervisor looked down his nose at Mr. Farley and sneered, "Well I want this office to stay open until six."

I tried not to sigh. "That is not really possible sir. This building will be locked by security. Security doesn't want people coming and going outside of business hours. If you want to change the time that this building is locked and unlocked, you will need to take the matter up with the city council."

Mr. Supervisor glared at me. "I am the supervisor here now. Who exactly do you think your are?"

I remained calm. "Jake Jaconovich, sir."

He sneered. "Never heard of you."

I wondered if he had really never heard of me or if he was insisting on going out of his way to be rude.

Christian pulled out a notebook and made a note while Char looked over his shoulder and nodded.

I rowed on. "Whether you have heard of me or not does not change the fact that this building must remain locked between five PM and seven-forty-five AM."

"Oh go then." He growled.

I wished that I had the Miki with me. I wanted to get home in a hurry. I sighed and decided to walk and put the word out on the street for the local drunks to keep it down and police each other. I called Yablonski's office from the M'TK station.

He came on the line. "Yablonski."

I reported, "We got a letter that the president appointed a new supervisor to our office. He arrived today. He is not certified in criminal law. He doesn't know procedure." I paused as I thought about the supervisor's controlling rules and arrogant tone. "He...I don't know...it is like he doesn't know how professional offices operate. He made a school of silly rules as if we were first form children. He won't tell us his name—although we are researching that and should have it soon. We are to address him as Mr. Supervisor. He is very class conscious. Um..."

"Shit," Yablonski agreed. The situation sounded suspicious.

"Yeah," Gratitude for his insight flooded over me.

"Where is the prisoner?"

"Um...well...if you want a prisoner we have a pickpocket who is in a basement cell in the city jail." It had been Allison's idea to give Kerby a fake name and file with charges against him for being a pickpocket. This replaced his former file at the jail.

Yablonski grunted, "That'll do for now. Find some place to move the pickpocket at a moment's notice."

All the way home, I pondered the problem of where to hide my prisoner. I couldn't send him to Pickett, or to The Cove because he was too dangerous. I mentally inventoried Rouseff's properties knowing my mentor would allow us to use his properties if it meant thwarting a Vanderholm.

I arrived home to my cheerful, warm household. I hugged my son and tossed him in the air, kissed my wife and ate dinner surrounded by the housekeeper's children while holding my daughter in one arm. When all the children were ready for bed, I prepared to read them a story.

Leah snapped at me. "Jake, isn't it enough that you feed that brood? You don't have to read to them every night as well."

"Honey, it's the least I can do. When I was a child, I knew that I was rich simply because I had a mama and a papa. Shirley's nephews are orphaned. They really are poor." I kissed Leah. "Get some rest, Dearest. You had more trouble with this delivery than you should."

I read to the children and helped tuck them into bed.

Chapter 2 Kerby

With Leah asleep and the pod of resident, pre-schoolers in their beds, I looked forward to a few quiet minutes in my study.

At eleven, as I was about to go to bed the phone interrupted me. I grabbed it before it woke the whole household. "Jaconovich."

"Yablonski. Is this new supervisor a tall thin man, grey at the temples thin on top, long beaked nose?"

"Yeah that could be him, long thin hands, blue eyes, front teeth are crooked."

"Shit."

"That bad?"

He answered, "Meet me at your jail at...oh...um...three-thirty AM."

I napped fully clothed until about three. Then I drove into the city. Peter arrived outside the jail in a Volvo sedan about three-twenty.

We found it easy enough to get into the jail. Peter showed his ID at the door. The guard looked sleepily at the ID then suddenly sprang to attention. Peter said, "Let me in and forget that either of us were here. If word of this visit leaks out, I'll authorize the sewer rat to deal with you."

The poor guard turned pale and shook his head violently, reconsidered and nodded equally violently.

I grumbled. "The *correct* title is *The M'TK Sewer Rat*. I'm fond of the title." I smiled at the night officer. I figured that he was trustworthy enough.

Yablonski repeated his warning to the guards outside the cells. The skinny one's eyes grew round at the sight of the CGIS major towering over him. He bobbed and nodded.

The second guard looked a bit pudgy. His eyes swiveled to mine, "The M'TK Sewer...Jake! Jake! Good to see you." He held out his hand to shake mine.

I recognized him as the friend who had told me where to buy the required school uniform when we were in the seventh form. I grinned, "Kato! It's good to see you, but it is best if you do not see us. We need the prisoner, Kerby...

um we called him Adams. His file says he is a pickpocket."

Kato nodded as he hit me playfully on the shoulder and dragged his partner off to fetch our prisoner. I heard him instructing his pal. "That really is the M'TK…" I could hear the end of the story as the guards returned. "…left the three bullies in the dust, and we were only ten. I saw the whole thing."

The sleepy prisoner protested every step of the way, "I don't want to go anywhere. Why are you getting me up in the middle of the night? I don't want to go with you."

Yablonski growled, "LaBarge is here to kill you."

Kerby, turned pale and stopped whining. He licked his lips, and his eyes darted back and forth.

Peter continued, "Now, I'm real interested in why LaBarge wants to kill such a worthless piece of scum, but we won't talk here. Come."

On the way out Peter repeated his admonition for everybody to forget that we were here.

I added helpfully and rather creatively, "The man who is after the prisoner will eat you alive or at least cut off your cock if he finds out we were here. He specializes in cutting off cocks."

Peter rolled his eyes. As we put the prisoner into the car he asked, "Jake where did a well-brought-up prosecutor learn to talk like that?"

"M'TK tenements."

Peter shook his head in wonderment. "What is the legal system coming to? Leave your car at the M'TK station then come with me."

Peter followed me to the station. I parked the Miki where it could not be seen from the street. I got in the front of Peter's Volvo and Peter took off heading north. We made the four-hour trip to the capital in less than three. Peter gassed the car outside of the capital, and we headed north again.

I asked, "Where are we going?"

"You tell me. You have family up this way don't you?"

"Yes, on the coast. You can't reach their house except by boat."

"Good."

"I will not put a prisoner in The Cove. Women and children live there. I cannot put someone this vile near children."

The prisoner in the back made some sort of protest.

"What else is up here?"

I thought about my summer conducting unauthorized trade along the coast with Uncle John then I remembered Nicki's wedding. "There is a small island that has adequate shelter. It is isolated so I suppose we could put him there. People would need to be warned to stay away from the island, but it might work."

We drove on into the night. Our prisoner finally sat up and looked out a window. "Where are we?"

I answered. "Those hillsides outside the window are called mountains."

Yablonski spoke up. "I have an idea. Why don't you tell us why LaBarge is looking for you?"

"I don't know what you're talking about."

Peter had been watching the man in the rearview mirror. I turned so I could watch Kerby too. I looked at Peter and rolled my eyes back and forth as I'd seen Kerby do. Peter moved his tongue from side to side inside his mouth in an excellent imitation of our prisoner. We burst out laughing. We giggled and belly laughed until our sides ached. I knew I felt giddy from lack of sleep. I suspected that Peter had not been sleeping any better than I had. I think he might have had more practice at going without sleep than I had.

Our laughing made the prisoner nervous. "Will you two cut it out? Okay, I know the name LaBarge, but I don't know why he's after me. I mean what makes you think he's after me?"

To help our prisoner figure out how serious the problem was I suggested, "Perhaps to do the same thing to you that you did to Mantega."

Peter commented dryly, "Our friend has an expressive face doesn't he."

I snorted. "Have you noticed the twitch at his hairline? I am particularly impressed with how much his eyes give away."

"Oh no, it's the tongue that amuses me." Peter laughed, and I experienced a moment of fear that we were going to go off laughing again. We manfully controlled ourselves.

Kerby snarled, "Will you two cut it out! You have no right to move me. I think I've decided to pay my fine."

I shook my head sadly, "Bit to late for that."

Peter growled, "LaBarge is only a step or two behind us, and we won't be able to keep ahead of him for long. It would help if we knew who put him on your trail.

Kerby silently sank down in his seat and looked out the windows.

Peter drove most of the way at speeds well over a hundred and fifty kilometers an hour. Finally, we rolled into the village of Norville shortly before nine. I had a cramp in my right hand from clutching the roll grip and another in my left leg from pumping an invisible brake pedal all night. I resolved not to ride with Peter again.

I ran into the train station and called the prosecutor's office. I got my real boss. "I got called out of town on classified business. I probably won't make it in today."

Mr. Farley assured me, "I've already told Mr. Supervisor that today is your day to work for Mr. Rouseff. He's not expecting you, but he's not happy about it either."

"Well good or as good as it can be. Tell everybody especially Christian and Allison not to get creative around him unless they absolutely have to. I'll call when I can."

My phone call to Leah didn't go as well. She gave me a detailed report on how uncomfortable she was—tired and sore all over, and this morning Elizabeth had tried to chew her food. Foolishly, I made the mistake of offering to kiss Leah's injury when I returned home. She hung up on me.

Cousin Nicki covered the station duty this morning. He looked bewildered to see me arrive in a car. I explained the problem as Peter forcibly pulled the protesting, handcuffed prisoner from the back of the Volvo.

Nicki brightened. "Oh, yeah, he can stay at the island. I'll call The Cove." He picked up the phone and dialed.

I didn't understand what my eyes saw. "What? They have a phone in The Cove?"

Nicki nodded, "Cousin Micki has been busy."

I suddenly longed to see The Cove and my family again. I hadn't been there since before I got married, and I missed them. Of course Micki was still up for any adventure and volunteered to bring the Ona Elsee to move our prisoner. Nicki eagerly abandoned the station to help Micki.

Giddy from lack of sleep and the wild drive, I told Kerby that my cousins where desperate criminals—pirates and smugglers—the meaner more lawless cousins of the M'TK Sewer Rat. Nicki grinned evilly and fingered a fish-gutting knife. Micki exuded an aura of sociopathic cheer.

With the prisoner chained securely to the winch for the shrimp nets, the boys turned the Ona Elsee out to sea leaving Peter and me free to head back to the city.

While we had been waiting for the Ona Elsee, Peter had phoned his supervisor. He also talked to the stationmaster when he came in to greet the next train, admonishing him to forget we had been here. I grinned at the stationmaster, and he winked back at me. He would never betray the private dealings of one of the D'NOs. We loaded the Volvo on the train—thank God. I couldn't have faced another drive with Peter behind the wheel.

We settled into a compartment. I reclined my seat and prepared to ride home like a civilized person. I woke up when Peter poked me. I hadn't slept very long. Looking out, I saw that the train sat in a high mountain meadow in the middle of nowhere. On my side of the train a reed-choked swamp spread across the flats from the tracks to the foot of a waterfall in the distance. On the other side of the tracks the ground rose toward the mountain, I could make out a little meadow. Peter dragged me off of the train, and I finally woke up enough to notice a helicopter in the meadow. Peter pulled me toward it.

I'd never flown before and became excited to take my first helicopter ride. I scrambled into the backseat and followed the instructions for donning the headphones that would protect my ears from the noise of the machine. My seat belt distracted me until the machine lurched and tilted forward. We were airborne. I avidly watched the ground flowing away below us. Peter was no fun. He went to sleep and refused to answer my questions about how high we were and how fast we could fly. In my excitement, I didn't think I felt tired, but I dozed off.

When I woke up, I felt solid ground under us. The engines idled while Peter unbuckled his seat belt and removed his headphones. I looked out the window to see a uniformed crew coming out to refuel the helicopter. A plethora of flags and a few concrete block buildings told me we'd arrived at a military base. I started to unbuckle.

Peter put his hand out to stop me. "No he'll take you all the way home."

I resolved to stay awake and enjoy my trip. Once airborne again, I watched my country flow below me. I recognized a huddle of roofs below me as a mountain village. I couldn't see any roads connecting the village with the outside world. The hills gave way to flat farmland. I remembered my first train trip as a child and all the times I'd fallen in love with my country as I traveled north to bring fresh fish home to sell at the M'TK market. Once again, I fell in love with my country. Peace flowed over me, and I drifted off to sleep.

I woke up when the helicopter tilted sideways with it's nose down. A voice in my earphones asked, "Is this the right place sir?" I looked out the window, disoriented. I finally got my bearings and recognized the lake and my ridge. The pilot set me down on the road about a hundred--fifty meters from my house. By the time I got out, and the pilot had lifted off, the whole household had poured out to the front lawn to watch the commotion. The children jumped up and down in excitement when they saw me. I laughed when I saw that Mama and Papa had a firm grip on the housekeeper's nephew, Davy, who called to everyone to see the *dragonfly*.

Leah took a couple running steps to greet me. I got a good hug being mindful of her tender parts. "Jake, what on earth was that thing? It flies." Excitement replaced her whiny tone of our earlier phone call.

Mama answered everybody's questions. "It is called a helicopter. In the United States they are everywhere, but this is the first one that I've seen in this country, and to think, it was delivering my son to his house."

Papa asked, "Is everything okay?"

"Yeah, sure." I avoided Papa's eyes.

Papa looked at me like he did when I was a small boy caught sneaking across the train tracks to visit the dump. I realized that I had some explaining to do. He asked, "What was that all about?"

I shrugged, "A friend from work needed me in the capital last night for an urgent case. He sent me home in that machine."

Papa gave me another look that told me my careless answer did not come close to satisfying him.

While excited over my adventure, I controlled my excitement to avoid becoming careless and saying more than I should. I avoided Papa by keeping one arm around Leah. I carried her up the stairs to our room. I showered and shaved while Leah danced around the room questioning me.

I watched her in my mirror. She sounded just like a little girl in her excitement over my adventure. "To think, my husband is important enough to ride in a hel-i-cop-ter." She pronounced the word carefully, getting her tongue accustomed to the unfamiliar word. Suddenly, her tone changed to a whine. "But, I was worried when I woke up and you were gone. Elizabeth fussed, and I was too tired to change her." Leah pouted.

"It wasn't really that big a deal. The man needed my advice and expertise. He asked me to come up to the capital. When I told him I worried about leaving you so long, so he sent me home in the helicopter. I didn't want to be so far away while you were awake so I left really early in the morning." Leah finally became satisfied that I had scheduled everything to account for her comfort. She smiled happily. I went downstairs.

"Jake, may I have a word with you in your study." Papa didn't sound happy.

I nodded and meekly followed him into my study. As he eased into one of my leather chairs, Papa looked me in the eye and asked, "What was that all about?"

I looked at my papa. I knew I could trust Papa so I took a deep breath and explained. "We've had a top secret prisoner in the city. A man from the CGIS became convinced that an assassin is in the city to kill the prisoner. The case is really connected to the whole corruption problem going back to Emperor Vanderholm. We still haven't caught all of the highest-level offenders. I'm not sure why Peter needed me to go with him, but he seems to think I need to know where the prisoner is. We returned in the helicopter so that I can be seen in the city. We needed to disguise how far we drove last night."

Papa turned a little grey and slumped in his chair. "Son, take care of yourself. You have a wife and two children, and you are supporting your housekeeper and her five children." He sighed, "Half of this city depends on you one way or another." He paused and looked away for a moment. "I think it would kill your mama to lose you."

"Yes, Papa. I'll be careful." That was the most serious reprimand I'd ever had from my papa. "Other than riding in a car with Peter, we didn't do anything dangerous."

"Anything to do with the CGIS is dangerous."

"Well, there is that. That's why I was willing to move the prisoner. I called Peter in on the case. I wanted to get their case out of this city." I didn't tell Papa I put the prisoner on an island near The Cove. "I've always been careful Papa." I smiled at him and considered reminding him of some of his own exploits with firefighting cars and police.

He must have seen the look in my eye because he laughed a little sheepishly.

I smiled ruefully back at him. "Papa, I need to get into the city and be seen. I'll try to be home early. I need to sleep."

He nodded and prepared to get out of his chair. "I'll drive you into the station. You know, the Miki wasn't visible from the street, but anybody who popped into the station to say hello would see that you parked somewhere you didn't want to be noticed."

"I did my best." I sighed. "You know, you think my activities were much more dangerous than they really were."

I popped into the prosecutor's office shortly after eleven. I'd picked up sweet rolls as an excuse to make the rounds of the office. As I came through the door, Allison rolled her eyes at me. The room behind her was dead quiet, and the holding room sat empty of offenders.

Christian sat at his desk, reading law. Under the guise of offering him a sweet roll, I bent down and whispered, "Assassin named LaBarge, sent to kill Classified."

Until I'd uttered these words, I hadn't realized that my own office was the most dangerous place I'd been in the past twenty-four hours. I moved on as Christian picked up his phone. Allison's phone rang as I moved around to Leroy's desk. "Be careful." Then, I moved on to Mr. Farley.

He took his time selecting a treat. He whispered. "He wants all the names of all the prisoners in the city. He wants the names of every case that is open." I set my box of sweet rolls down on my boss's desk just as I heard my name being snarled.

"Jaconovich, what are you doing in here?"

I turned toward the assassin. "Taking a break from contracts before a lunch meeting." I walked toward him, moving away from Mr. Farley's desk. "I wanted to make certain you were not too busy before I continued my other work." I looked around the silent office.

I felt Allison approach from behind me, keeping me between herself and LaBarge. "I just got a phone call. My mama is sick and needs to go to the doctor. I need to leave now."

LaBarges's voice sent chills down my spine. He looked down his nose at Allison and snarled, "I did not give you permission. Do you want to get fired?"

I edged to my left to gain a better position for defending Allison and myself. This move also forced LaBarge to turn further away from Mr. Farley's desk where my friend busily stashed papers into the sweet roll box.

Once again, Allison proved her courage and dedication to our office. She edged further to the left and stood up straight. "Um…you do realize that we haven't been paid in months, right? "

I nodded vigorously in agreement.

Allison took another step to the left forcing LaBarge to turn his back completely on Mr. Farley and continued. "Do you realize that we don't get paid? We keep working at our jobs because we believe in our work. We are needed. " Allison's eyes met the assassin's without flinching.

Mr. Supervisor's face paled, and his muscles went slack. He glanced around the office, but could not see Mr. Farley's desk. Then he turned his attention back to Allison as if she was some sort of an alien creature. Perhaps in his world she was. She had courage enough to stand up to him.

Allison continued, "Right now my mama needs me to take her to the doctor. If you have a plan for paying us for our work, then you can boss us around."

I looked across the office at Christian. The idea of his wife standing up to a professional assassin turned his lips blue. I met his eye, trying to assure him that LaBarge would have to deal with me before he could touch Allison. Christian looked from me to LaBarge, crossed his arms and settled back in his chair with a smirk.

The sneer left LaBarge's voice. "Surely, you get paid." He must now realize that he really had no leverage over us. Would he lash out at the person who delivered the message of his powerlessness?

I didn't wait to find out. I plunged into the explanation. "Sir, the city is bankrupt. Sometimes we get some potatoes. Sometimes I bring in fish. Today I brought in sweet rolls. It helps the others get by and it helps the bakery stay in business. These prosecutors are certified attorneys. We don't get paid, but we work other jobs and have family money to draw on. Most of the women here are barely getting by. Well, the interns are just students so you wouldn't…"

LaBarge turned on his heel and stormed off to his office, slamming the door so hard the windows in the building shook and a law book tumbled off the shelf in the library. Through the window in his door, I saw him violently dialing his phone. I left the office quickly carrying my sweet roll box filled with every paper in the office regarding our delicate case.

I stopped at Rouseff's office. I planned to spend a great deal of time with him. He acted happy enough to have me there. I considered us to be well organized with our plans for the new highway, but we'd fouled the propeller as it were. Now that Rouseff owned the property along the right of way for the new road connecting us to the capital, the government didn't have enough money to build it.

One morning as we sat poring over maps of the city, I voiced a conundrum.

"If the government could build the damned road, people would have jobs and goods and services would start flowing, rebuilding our economy, which would give the government enough money to build the damn road."

Rouseff leaned back and tapped his fingers on the arm of his chair while thinking. "I'm thinking of negotiating with the government to build their road for them, then they can pay me back over the next twenty years, or perhaps I will allow them to purchase the road with a nice piece of property that I can develop elsewhere."

I thought about this last option. "You can have your people build the road the way you want it, and the government keeps its commitment to link the south with the capital. If we can work out a deal that is agreeable, I think that would be an excellent idea. Do you have numbers for how much it would cost?

"It will cost them a great deal of money." Rouseff snickered at me.

"Ah, but perhaps less than it would have under the old system. I wouldn't be surprised if some of the money budgeted for the road is still sitting in a suitcase under someone's bed." I chuckled. "I'd love to know who's bed it is under and relieve them of the burden of their crimes."

A thought filtered through my brain. I grabbed it and considered for a few seconds. "I think I might have a source for some government funding. You name your price. I'll think about how this city can come up with some money." In my mind I started calculating charges and fines for poor Mr. LaBarge.

Chapter 3 Counter Measures

I developed a routine that included hiding out at Rouseff Industries most of the time, which made Mr. Rouseff happy.

By the end of my second week in hiding, I had my work in Rouseff's office caught up. I identified who and where the squatters were along the right of way for the road. I'd researched their claims to be where they were and outlined the best approach to legalizing their continued occupation of the property. We started researching options for building the road. I told Leah that Rouseff had promised to put power and phone lines underground. "He has promised to plant your trees."

Leah's eyes lit up at the news that her education would help beautify our city. She pulled out her drawing paper to make changes to her drawings of the inner circle at the city center that Rouseff had designed.

I felt slightly bored.

I checked into the prosecutor's office almost every day. I didn't really need to. My office at Rouseff Industries became the unofficial prosecutor's office. If others needed to confer on a case, they came to my office. Christian still worked on preparing his case to arrest Mr. Supervisor. He regularly stopped by my office where we went over the details of the case. He asked me at least a dozen times, "Can you get any information out of that CGIS officer?"

"I'm working on it. He's certain the man is LaBarge. We are certain that the fellow is not an attorney so by accepting this job, he is practicing law with out a license. Actually, I've gotten more information out of our street people, who are certain the man is LaBarge. He's been asking questions around town. Apparently, he is offering rewards for information leading to the whereabouts of Kerby."

Christian nodded. "That sounds incriminating enough." Christian sighed, "He could also be an innocent paralegal investigating a case." He shifted in his seat and changed the subject. "I'm not getting any news from our usual informants. They haven't been in the office. The street people are policing themselves so our load is down. Interns do most of the work now. I'm not comfortable having students in the office under such serious conditions."

"Okay, I'll harass Yablonski more about our desire to arrest the man. I really want enough evidence to charge him with murder. If he is who Yablonski thinks he is, the judge could fine him all of his assets then sentence him to the firing squad. Is Allison still out of the office?"

"I let her come in for a few hours to straighten out a mess that Darlene made. LaBarge didn't bother her, other than snarling at her for giving Darlene a job she wasn't trained to do then making her cry. I pretended to know what I was doing with computers so I could keep myself between Allison and that monster." Christian ran his hands through his hair. This was the first time I'd seen him lose his air of jovial glee over the world around him.

I worried about my friends' safety and grunted. "We need to move on this."

"The thing is…um…Jake…I'm not one hundred percent certain that this guy is the assassin."

I sighed, "I'll come over and evaluate him again. I can at least determine if he is armed." I gave Christian a half-hour head start then I gathered up some maps of the city. On my walk over to the prosecutor's office I picked up some small bits of litter off of the street—advertisements, bits of paper, broken glass, cigarette butts and bottle caps.

I arrived at the office and announced to the receptionist, Tsulu, "Tell Mr. Supervisor that I'd like to present some ideas for processing cases."

She looked up from the fashion magazine in her lap and shrugged. "Why? We don't have any cases."

I chuckled, "Oh we will. The people will cycle back into drinking and brawling. I want to have our plan in place."

Mr. Supervisor agreed to see me. My arms were filled with the maps and a small bag containing the litter, but I still managed to step around his desk and slap him jovially on the back near his shoulder. I decided he most likely wore a shoulder holster. I dumped my maps on his desk and stood across the desk from him. "I've been thinking about our cases."

In a cold tone he growled. "We don't appear to have any cases."

I smiled innocently not knowing how he intended me to take his comments. "Oh don't worry. We will. When the moon gets full, the people come out and commit mayhem in the streets. The problem then is what to do with them. We used to fine them. Now, even if they pay their fine, the money is worthless.

They know this. It's the repeat offenders I am thinking about. Now, have a look at this map." I placed the map close to my side of the desk to get him to lean toward me. "We are here. Our trolley stop is here. I picked up this litter," I emptied the litter on the desk. A ball of paper rolled toward him.

He caught it deftly in his left hand and tossed it neatly into the trash. "Do you have a point?"

He's definitely left handed, I noted. I laughed, "Allow me to build my case." I watched his eyes. I knew I was irritating him, but he had excellent self-control. "Anyway, I wasn't really trying to find litter, but it is there. Now, part of the problem with our repeat offenders is that they don't have jobs. They don't have enough to do with their time, and they don't have money to pay fines."

He nodded. A muscle in his jaw twitched, and his cold eyes searched my face.

I ducked my head hoping he would take it as a submissive gesture. "I think, instead of jail, where they just get free food at the city's expense, we should make them do more community service. Now this is what I propose. See here on the map how University, Eclipse, Sunset… and…um…uh…" I turned my head sideways as if trying to read the street names.

He leaned forward with his hands on the desk to read the map. "Gannon." The hair on the back of my neck rose at his proximity. I remembered Wu's voice instructing his students on mastering our fear. Remembering Wu's gym allowed me to relax.

I chuckled sheepishly. "Oh yeah, Gannon. Now, see how these streets form an inner square? Almost all of this is public property. My proposal is that we start with this square…" I thought about how he talked that first day in our office. "Let's start with this square and have those nasty repeating scum pick up every gum wrapper and loose advertisement on the ground." I was making this up as I went along. "Instead of having the lazy bastards living like parasites off of the city, make them bring us five large garbage bags of litter picked up from this area. Once that square is cleaned, we can move the scum over here to the hospital area."

He shifted his weight onto his right arm to follow my pointing finger—I watched the play of his muscles on his arms shoulder and chest.

"We have another park." I pulled out another map and rolled it out as far to his left as possible. "See, we have another park over here."

LaBarge leaned to the left to follow my pointing finger, but he did not rest his weight on his left arm.

"What do you think sir? I'm hoping cleaning these three areas…" I pointed again and watched again as he shifted his weight onto his right-arm but not the left. "…will punish the scum while cleaning up the city. Maybe that'll teach them to work for a living instead of angling for free food and a bed in our jail."

He grunted, "Who'll keep them from running away?"

I started rolling up my maps. "I think we can hire some people to watch them." I was still making this up. "Um…what if we paid the guards with fish to watch the scum pick up the trash?"

He reared his head back, and his lip curled. "Why fish?"

"It is better than money. I paid for my baby with fish."

He narrowed his eyes and looked at me as if I might be making fun of him.

"No really." I hastened to assure him. "When my wife was in the hospital with our baby, they told me that they would rather have fresh fish than our currency." I tried my best to look naïve, non-threatening, and somewhat stupid. I'll confess that I know I have my mama's dimple. On her it's charming, but on a man…well…it causes other men to underestimate me. I gave him a broad smile.

He averted his eyes from mine. "Fine, I'll bring this up at our next staff meeting. Where will you get the fish?"

I flashed my dimple at him again. "Rouseff ships fish from the north. We can't always sell all of it. Some is not real good for eating, but it is food. I think I can find something to trade for the fish. Perhaps Rouseff would like some of his property cleaned. Yeah, the scum can clean the trolley stands too. That'll save Rouseff money, while making the bastards wash their own piss off of the stands." I smiled.

Assassin Supervisor smiled, a thin straight line that didn't reach his eyes. "Good. I like the way you think a problem through. We'll put the scum to work and pay people to guard them by giving them fish that Rouseff can't sell."

I wanted to sweat by the time I left the man's office. I knew better than to sweat just now. I returned to my desk trying to look like the harmless puppy I wanted LaBarge to see.

"Jake you dropped something." Mr. Farley picked up one of my maps and handed it back to me.

I bent down to take the map from him and whispered, "Seven, my house."

I sat down and stared at an open law book for twenty minutes before my heart stopped racing. I wondered what on earth I had been doing. Taking a prisoner to the north coast during the night with Peter was nothing to what I had done the past fifteen minutes. I tried to think through our problem. I finally collected my wits enough to leave. I went straight home and held my wife, my son and my daughter. I was a wealthy man.

I asked Shirley to prepare a light snack and dessert for guests. Leah still felt moody from having the baby, but she excitedly went through her wardrobe looking for something suitable to wear for company. She couldn't find anything to wear that fit. Finally, she became overtired, started to cry and went to bed. I felt sorry she was still too tired to greet guests. I kissed her tears and told her that she had done something more important than greet my guests. She'd given me a beautiful daughter. "When you are stronger, we'll go out and visit the capital. The most important thing right now is for you to regain your strength. I soothed and cajoled until almost seven."

Christian, Allison, Leroy, and Jeffrey Farley arrived shortly after seven. We went into my study and closed the door.

I opened with my assessment. "Mr. Supervisor carries a gun and wears a knife sheath on his left forearm. In an unarmed fight, he could most likely do me some serious damage. I have no idea how the police can manage to arrest the man if he decides to put up a fight or—God forbid—take hostages."

Christian turned white and took Allison's hand. "What is Yablonski thinking leaving him in an office full of women?"

Mr. Farley gave us a little reality check. "He probably thinks the man is harmless enough. LaBarge is here to kill one man. He's not going to go on a rampage and kill a bunch of office workers unless someone tries to arrest him." He took a bite of cake then continued. "This brings up another problem. I've been researching this case. President Vanderholm sent LaBarge to our office. LaBarge may not know that he is breaking the law. He has settled down since he first arrived and mostly keeps to himself. How was he when you talked to him?"

I shifted in my chair. "Aside from being armed to the teeth, he was okay, not very vocal. He actually praised the stupid plan I made up just to get a chance to evaluate him."

The others laughed, so I had to explain the plan. They agreed it wasn't half bad.

I stared at the wood grain pattern on my floor. Finally, I had to agree with Mr. Farley. "You have a good point that if he is under orders from someone else, he may have no idea that he is breaking the law."

Christian sounded discouraged and somewhat alarmed. "In which case, we will have just arrested a professional assassin, and we won't be able to convict him."

Mr. Farley finished swallowing a piece of fruit. "I'm afraid so. You've said something else for us to consider. Mr. LaBarge is a *professional* assassin. I suspect he is a successful professional. He spends more on clothes than I do." He paused to sip his coffee. "I think to a certain extent we can count on him to exercise a professional level of self-control in the office."

I thought about my observations and nodded my agreement.

Mr. Farley continued, "Frankly, it gives me the creeps to talk to him. He's a cold, hard man. On the other hand, there is nothing in my conversations with him that is out of the ordinary." He chuckled. "He seemed quite horrified by Allison's disclosure that we don't get paid. He asked Darlene for the payroll ledgers and spent some time studying them. Later, I heard him on the phone complaining coldly to somebody about being sent to do a job when he has no leverage over the people he needs to work with."

I shuddered knowing that his job was to kill Kerby, but another possibility occurred to me. "We are assuming his job is to kill Kerby. Um…what if Hab Vanderholm sent him to supervise our office to keep us from interfering with the government."

Mr. Farley sighed and nodded, "That same thought crossed my mind. If President Vanderhom remembers you from university, it may well be that he sent someone to watch us, but why not choose an attorney? No, I really think he is after Kerby."

Leroy squirmed in his chair. "It is possible that he's here to do both. That interpretation makes sense in light of all his control issues like keeping us from talking to each other so that we won't make trouble. This is really a case for the CGIS. Where is Yablonski?"

I spread my hands indicating that I had no idea. "I've called, but he hasn't called back. The best we can do is try to keep the women out of the office and out of his way"

Mr. Farley sat quiet as the other attorneys and I discussed the legal issues. Finally he leaned forward in his chair. "LaBarge is probably harmless enough unless he thinks one of us knows where the prisoner is kept."

I felt like another bucket of ice water was being dumped over my head.

Christian slumped in his chair. "So you think we may not be able to get a conviction?"

Mr. Farley looked into middle space. "I think the conviction could be overturned on an appeal."

Leroy began to grasp the problems with the case. "The other problem is, if he was sent by the president, the president could pardon him if we put him in jail."

Christian shifted in his chair and snarled. "This is ridiculous. We have a professional assassin in our office, and we can't do anything about it."

"Who says we can't do anything about it?" The slightest little smile twitched at the corner of Mr. Farley's mouth.

"Do you have an idea sir?" Allison spoke up for the first time.

"Yes, since the work load is rather slow, I want you, Allison, to reorganize the filing system." He smiled at her. "I don't much care how you do it, but I do want a special section set up for cases that got moved to another jurisdiction." He smiled again. "I think I can make up a file that will look convincing enough to make it appear that the prisoner was moved to another jurisdiction, fined and released."

Leroy sounded hopeful. "Will that get him to leave?"

Christian sounded petulant. "But, I wanted to arrest him."

I felt discouraged. "I wanted to fine him."

Mr. Farley's voice sounded firm. "I want him out of our office."

Once again Jeffrey Farley impressed me greatly. His primary goal seemed to be to protect his staff. Well, the security of the court is always a primary goal.

I gave up my ideas for financing the new road and manfully agreed with Mr. Farley's plan. "You're the supervisor sir. We haven't heard from Yablonski. We may not get a conviction since the appointment comes from the president so perhaps we can divert him. If he doesn't take our bait and leave, we'll be able to assume the president is keeping us under surveillance."

Leroy grumbled. "Which brings up the problem of our president."

I sighed, "I suspect we may run through a few presidents before they learn that they cannot abuse the office. I can talk to someone else about that." We discussed the situation in circles. We finally had a plan. Mr. Farley would prepare a file showing the transfer of jurisdiction.

After thinking, I came up with a supplemental idea. "I think I want to talk to the prisoner. Let's make certain that our location for change of venue will be plausible from LaBarge's perspective. I told LaBarge that I'd get fish to pay people for guarding our offenders while they pick up trash. I think I will go get some fish." We ended our meeting.

Leah cried when I told her about my plan to go get some fish to feed the poor.

I tried to comfort her. "I know sweetheart. I don't like being separated from you and the children, but I promised that I'd get fish to pay people to guard our offenders. When I get back, I think I'll take a couple days off and just stay here with you and the children."

I caught the night train north. Cousin John and Petral met me at the station with the M'NO. They laughed about Micki supercharging the boat's engines. The boat did have noticeably more power. They took me out to the island. When I got there I found the prisoner, Kerby, looking healthy.

He sounded surly. "You. What are you doing here?"

"I need to talk to you about LaBarge."

He pouted. "I don't know anything about LaBarge."

"I do. He's perched in my office waiting for some indication of where you are. He sits about glaring at the office help and making everybody miserable. We thought about arresting him for practicing law without a license and impersonating an officer of the court."

"Bad idea."

"Yeah, we figured that out. Our current plan is to let him find a file that shows we moved you to another jurisdiction."

The prisoner's eyebrows shot up and his expressive tongue rolled around in his mouth.

I continued. "What I need to know from you is if you think there is a jurisdiction that would be plausible."

"I don't understand."

I leaned forward. "Well...um...let me put it this way. You are in our jail because you committed extortion in our city. Um...is there some other place we can claim you committed a crime, say embezzlement, or assault, or conspiracy to commit murder."

"Why should I help you?"

I looked around me. "You appear to have enough to eat. You are still alive. We are doing everything in our power to take good care of you. The only thing you are charged with is extortion. You could pay a fine and go free."

"I'm happy here. The guys come by and bring food. They've given me new clothes. I'm happy and comfortable."

"Good. All I'm asking is that you suggest someplace to send LaBarge. What about the capital? Have you been to the capital?"

His eyes shifted and his tongue twitched inside his mouth. "Yeah, I've been to the capital."

"Um…I know this sounds like a delicate question, but did you…um…uh stay there several hours…um perhaps long enough to commit a little crime?"

He laughed. "Yeah, I suppose I was there long enough to commit a very little crime. Not that I'm confessing to anything."

"Um…right…you don't have to confess, but um…just to make our deception more realistic, supposing you did commit a crime in the capital, what would we call it?"

He folded his arms across his chest. "I'm not confessing to anything."

"Oh no! I just want to get some idea of what LaBarge might believe you have done. Any little thing, conspiracy is always good. We could use conspiracy to commit murder, or embezzlement is a gentlemanly crime. Would you prefer conspiracy or embezzlement?"

He snorted but seemed to understand. "LaBarge might believe that I conspired to commit murder."

"Ah good, there's been a great deal of that going around. It is plausible."

Kerby looked up at Nicki standing by the door then he looked back at me and asked. "What happened to your big friend?"

"Yablonski? I don't know. He seems to have disappeared. I tried to reach him to help us get rid of LaBarge, but I haven't heard from him."

Kerby snorted. "Wouldn't hurt my feelings if he were dead."

"Ah,"

Kerby shifted his weight and the muscle at his hairline twitched. He continued. "Yablonski caused enough people trouble. I wouldn't be surprised if LaBarge were in your office to look for Yablonski."

This was interesting. I leaned back in my chair and crossed one ankle over my other knee. "Yablonski has some enemies does he?"

"Well placed enemies." Kerby sneered.

"Ah, that does explain a few things. He may have disappeared right after we moved you. That might explain why he wanted me to know where you are. I rather like the fellow. He broke into my office when my wife was having our first baby." I went on to tell the story of how good it was to toss three guys around, and breaking Yablonski's nose.

Kerby laughed at my story.

Finally, I prepared to stand. I'd gotten far more information than I thought I would. Kerby obviously knew much more than we originally suspected. "I hate to break this up." I stood and smiled down at Kerby. "You think LaBarge might believe us if we say you were charged with conspiracy to commit murder and shipped off to the capital?"

The man nodded.

"Good. We'll do that. Now I need to go get some fish to cover for this little trip up here."

We took the M'NO down to rocky bay and winched some of those ugly monster fish out of the seas. Nicki admonished me repeatedly, "Remember, it's no good if it is not boiled. It doesn't keep either."

"In the city, it will not need to keep. It will be eaten within two hours after I get home."

When we got back to the train station, I called the M'TK station and told them when I would be in. I called home and talked to Leah.

"My love, how are you feeling? Are you any stronger?"

"I'm okay. I'm bored."

"Ah good. Can you help me out?"

"What do you want?"

"Can you call Mrs. Mayor and tell her I am bringing in over a hundred kilos of fish on the morning train? Tell her the fish must be boiled. It is not good otherwise."

"Did you get some of those big, ugly, sucker fish?"

"Yeah."

"Jake, they are disgusting."

"They taste good enough boiled."

"I've eaten them. I just think they are ugly. I used to be afraid of them when I was a child."

"I think I was afraid of them the first time I saw one as a man."

"I will make certain that everybody knows enough to have boiling water ready and to have someone to meet you at the train."

"Thank you my love."

"I want to help feed the poor too. I'll talk to Mrs. Mayor." Leah sounded a little defiant.

For the second night in a row, I slept away from my family. I missed holding my wife and babies. I remembered making this trip as a student and how I thought of it as an adventure then.

When the train pulled into the M'TK station, the platform was filled with waiting people. I threw the smaller fish in its canvas bag over my shoulder and let two railroad employees carry the second larger one off of the train. The hungry crowd cheered at the sight of the fish.

Leah not only called the mayors wife, she drove into town and visited each of the soup kitchens. She taught them how to cook the fish and how to prepare a barley and vegetable dish her mama made. The cooks had the vegetables chopped and ready. Everybody praised my wife for coming into town herself so soon after having the baby. I smiled, thankful that Leah was feeling better.

The market free-kitchen held a circus atmosphere, as we divided up the huge fish so that each borough kitchen got a fair share. Everybody wanted to see the big ugly fish. They laughed when they saw how it contained almost all meat. They waited silently while the fish boiled in the big pots. The rapt, awed, expressions on the faces of these people wrung at my heart as they acted so joyful over something as simple as a fish, too poor in quality for the fishermen to sell.

I needed to run one more errand before I went home to spend a couple days with my family. I went to the prosecutor's office, still wearing my fishing clothes. I knew I smelled somewhat like a fish.

Darlene was sitting at the front desk when I arrived. She almost didn't recognize me when I came in. I admit that I hadn't shaved for a couple days so she can be somewhat forgiven. When I strode into the quiet office, Mr. Farley stood up to greet me. I shook his hand and whispered. "Conspiracy to commit murder in the capital."

"What have you been up to?"

"Oh, it's part of a new sentencing plan that Mr. Supervisor came up with. We are to pay the poor fish, if they watch offenders pick up trash. He'll explain it to you."

I kept walking toward Mr. Supervisor's door. He opened it before I got there.

"What the hell? Who? Jake? What's going on?"

"I got those fish you wanted for the new sentencing program. Well, I ended up going north and carrying them back myself."

"You look and smell like you hauled them out of the sea yourself."

"Well these guys were huge, forty and fifty kilos each. We used a winch to bring them into the boat." I went on to describe the ugly fish. "The important part is that we have kept our part of the bargain. We will need to bring in more fish of course, but we can get people to guard our offenders anytime we want by asking at the soup kitchens."

"Go home and get cleaned up."

I prayed that he would believe my only reason for going north was to catch large, ugly fish. I called the house to tell Leah I would be home in a half hour. The phone at home rang several times before someone finally picked it up. I could hear a great deal of fumbling and rustling at the other end of the line. I heard breathing.

"Hello?" The voice on the other end sounded very small.

My heart melted. "Jacob?"

"Uh huh."

"This is Papa."

"Uh huh."

"What is Mama doing?"

"Sleeping."

"What is Mrs. Shirley doing?"

"Making a cake."

"Oh that sounds good. I like cake."

"S for Davy."

"Why does Davy get a cake?"

"S birfday cake." I grinned from ear to ear talking to my son on the phone.

"Oh is it Davy's birthday?"

"Uh huh."

"Then, I better get him a present before I come home. What are you doing?"

"Watching Lisbeth."

"That is a good thing to do. Can you tell Mrs. Shirley that I am coming home before lunch? Say, Papa is on the next trolley."

"Uh huh."

"What are you supposed to say to Mrs. Shirley?"

"Papa is on the nest trolley"

"Very good. I am going to hang up now. Good bye."

"Uh huh."

I stopped at the M'TK mall planning to buy Davy a small wooden train engine, but I got him a stuffed rabbit instead.

I grinned all the way home, over my phone conversation with Jacob. I got off the trolley at our stop. I sighed a little, disappointed that nobody came to get me. I needed to walk less than a kilometer. I just liked being met. I almost ran home in my eagerness to see my family. When the house came into view, I could make out a small child standing in the corner of the yard closest to the path from the station. I knew Jacob had come out to meet his Papa. My heart melted. I grinned some more.

When I got closer, I realized Jacob was struggling to hold something wrapped in his favorite blanket. The blanket trailed along the ground. My precious son smiled and wiggled to see his Papa. He remembered the rules and didn't leave the yard as he waited anxiously to show me what he held in his blanket. Soon I came close enough to talk to my precious son.

Curious, I asked, "What do you have in your blanket?"

Jacob hoisted the slipping bundle a little higher. "Lisbeth."

"What?" I reached Jacob in two giant leaps and pushed aside the blanket. My beautiful Elizabeth blinked up at me. Jacob was holding her around the middle, as her head flopped around on her wobbly neck occasionally resting on his shoulder.

"Oh! Oh yes. You do have your sister. I will take her now." I gently wrapped the blanket around her and held her in one arm. I picked Jacob up in the other arm. "Come on son. Let's find your Mama."

"She's sleeping."

"So you were watching Elizabeth."

"Uh huh. Lisbeth want see Papa."

"Ah, she wanted to come out and meet me so you brought her along."

"Uh huh."

Carrying my children felt good. I decided there was no point in scolding Jacob for taking Elizabeth outside. She seemed to be unhurt. They both acted happy. I thought we might need to be more careful about watching the children.

This behavior became the pattern, often repeated during their childhood. Jacob would decide to do something innocent enough. Then he would decide to take Elizabeth with him. We watched, but those two would make a break for adventure the second we blinked.

Chapter 4 Rouseff Moves South

As planned, we held a birthday party for Davy, complete with a cake and gifts. Shirley had found time to sew him a pair of long pants. Leah had bought him a shirt to go with the pants. Next, Davy opened the box I'd brought home from the mall, took out the plush rabbit I'd bought and pressed it to his face. My eyes filled with tears when I saw how intently that small child hugged his soft toy.

Jacob presented his gift, a bundle of paper sewn together along one side. "From me an 'Lisbeth and Grandmama helped me." I figured my mama had done the sewing. "See, a book. I read it you." Jacob pointed to a picture that had been cut from a magazine and pasted onto the paper. He pointed to a scrawl under the picture saying, "Twain."

Leah seemed restored by her nap and chatted happily about helping with the outdoor kitchens. "I had to look and look to find enough barley to buy for the kitchens. I finally found some. We ate barley when I was a child because it can be grown in the mountains. We need more farmers to grow barley." Suddenly changing subjects Leah announced, "I'm thinking about taking another class at the university."

I hadn't said much about Jacob taking Elizabeth outside. I considered the possibility that we had too many children in the house for Shirley to keep track of. She looked worn almost to the point of exhaustion. She'd written to all of her relatives looking for someone to take her nephews. I decided to hire a nanny if Leah wanted to go back to school.

I thoroughly enjoyed my days off. In the early evenings, Jacob insisted that Elizabeth wanted to watch the sun go down with us so I carried both children to the top of the ridge to watch the sun go down. Jacob pointed to things along our path and proudly told the baby their names.

In the evenings, I read stories to all of the children. When Leah wanted to feed Elizabeth and put her to bed. Jacob argued that it was unfair to put her to bed. "Lisbeth wants hear story."

We chuckled and promised Jacob that Mama would tell Elizabeth a story while she fed her.

I left my happy household to return to work on Monday. The prosecutor's office had thirty cases. Mr. Supervisor volunteered to find us guards at the soup kitchens and left looking self-important. I grinned as he went out the door. "Well? Why is he so happy?"

Mr. Farley sounded triumphant. "He found what he was looking for late on Friday."

Christian started the story. "Allison, found mouse droppings in the file room and insisted that everybody work on cleaning it out and reorganizing."

Leroy told his part in the farce. "I suggested that we could just throw out the files of cases that changed jurisdiction without being processed here. We got in quite an argument over it. It was only about a dozen files."

Jeffery continued with his role. "I called on Mr. Supervisor to make the decision. I opened about half of them and read the charges and the reason for change of venue. He decided to look the whole batch over."

I grinned, pleased that everything was going as planned. "Well, I suppose we better process some petty criminals so they can go clean public property." I grabbed a file and went to work. I called in my first case. "It says here you were picked up for drunk and disorderly. You apparently refused to leave a club.

"Well I'd had a few. They snuck up on me."

"You plead guilty then?"

"Do I have a choice?"

"You could say that you are innocent, then we will take you before a judge. He will probably fine you twice what we do, so if you really did have a few and they snuck up on you, it is best to plead guilty. I'll give you a garbage bag. You're to go outside and fill it with litter. When it is full, you will bring it to me, or a volunteer outside who will give you a piece of paper stating you picked up litter. We will mark your charges redressed, and you will be free to go without worrying about the incident."

"Give me the garbage bag." I marked his case as guilty and fined him to pick up one bag of litter.

Mr. Supervisor came back with some volunteers. He stopped by my desk just as the first batch of offenders left the office with their guards. "Jake, I didn't see how it was going to work to get people to supervise the offenders if you gave them the fish last week. All I had to do was explain what I wanted, and more people volunteered to help than I needed. They tell me that from now on they will be waiting outside for us to assign them offenders to watch. Why do they work, if you pay them first?"

"Respect, trust, honor. Most of them are honorable people. Haven't you ever paid someone half of their salary when they take a job and the other half when they finish? I had to do that when I had my house built."

"Ah yes, I've had...um...contracts...where I get paid half first."

I tried not to shudder. The man was beginning to sound comfortable in our office. I hoped he decided to honor his...um...contract and go looking for his hit elsewhere.

We'd almost cleared our caseload by lunchtime, so I decided to go to Rouseff's to start another project. As I walked, I thought about Mr. Supervisor. I shook my head over the idea that he was starting to sound happy to be in our office. I wondered some more about what type of man earns a living by killing people and about the possibility of Hab Vanderholm sending him to keep an eye on us. I shrugged.

That afternoon, I settled myself on the first floor of Rouseff Properties to look over the property owners' contracts. Some of the businesses didn't want to organize. They didn't want to sell. They didn't want to change. They didn't want the highway to come through. I couldn't get them to tell us what they wanted. I figured that at least two of them would have their property condemned because it sat in the middle of the new road.

I was deep in thought when a clerk burst into the office looking frantic and frazzled. "Jake what is happening?"

"Huh? What?"

"Have you heard anything?"

"No."

"Mr. Rouseff is upset and demanding that everybody move quickly because he has to leave."

"Leave where?" Mr. Rouseff hadn't said anything to me about leaving.

"That's just it." The clerk wailed. "He's shouting and swearing and ordering people around, but he won't say what's happening."

I ran. I took the stairs two and three at a time. I could hear Rouseff bellowing all the way down the hall. "I need that packed. And that drawer full of stuff goes too."

He held his phone in his hand. "Rosalie, I know, pack what you can. I'll need my black suit, of course. Well, pack them all." He looked up and saw me. "Hello Jake." He spoke into his phone. "What?" He looked back at me. "Jake, Rosalie wants to talk to you."

I took the phone.

Rosalie Rouseff wailed. "Jake can you do something with him?"

"What has happened?"

She explained, "His Uncle just died."

"Oh I am so sorry. You're going south then. How soon?"

Her voice sounded more calm and firm. "We will take the next train. Can you calm him down? He is running in circles and making everything worse by giving people conflicting orders."

"I'll do my best."

Rosalie's voice returned to her normal warm tone. "That is more than enough. Thank you."

I got off of the phone. "Sir,"

Rouseff stopped giving his employees conflicting instructions.

I stood with my feet spread apart and folded my arms across my chest. "Do you find me to be incompetent? Has my family ever failed to serve you in the highest manner possible?"

Cousin Philippe turned and looked this way and that. He reach for a book then pulled back. He looked behind him. "No, no, of course not. I'd love to chat, but I need to get this taken care of."

I tried to put a tone of command into my voice. "No sir, you do not need to take care of anything right now. I will see that your office is secure and those things that you need will be where you need them." I stood and stared at this man I'd come to love.

He looked around. "The rest of you get out of here." His secretary, a clerk and two other assistants silently left looking relieved. I got more than a one look that said thank you.

"Now sir, when did your uncle pass?"

He sat down and sighed. "Just a few minutes ago. He hadn't been sick. My aunt said he had been out playing tennis. She told me that he didn't look good when he came in. He said he wanted a beer so she called a servant to bring it to him and went to get ready to go out. When the servant arrived with his beer, he was gone, just like that."

I sat beside my friend. "He was quite old."

"He would be ninety in a few weeks."

"That's not a bad way to go. He was healthy up until the last few minutes. He did not have a long suffering illness."

Cousin Philippe sighed, "I should have gone to visit him more often."

"The older generation have their lives, and we have ours. My papa often chides me for hanging on Mama's hem."

He chuckled at my comment. "No my uncle did not want me hanging on his watch chain. He was more of the old school. He did not feel the horror of the burning of M'TK as I did." Mr. Rouseff sighed. "No, I am more upset about the need to move south and take over the running of the family from there."

Now I became distressed. I'd never thought Mr. Rouseff would leave the city. I heard my voice rise. "Are you certain you must move south?"

"For a while at least. I will miss my friends here."

I tried to stifle my own sense of loss "Well, some of us will come visit. I assume there is to be a Mass. Some of us will be there for that. I think Leah would love to visit the south."

He smiled at me. "I have been running most of the business from here. It is the other business--keeping those snotty kids—all the extended family--in line." He sighed. "I sense a burden of responsibility that I don't want to assume. I don't want to become a mean old man who sits among his riches and looks down the on the rest of the beautiful world."

I smiled. "I don't think you will become such a person. You can always take a vacation among your friends."

Cousin Philippe paused, swallowed and continued almost in a whisper. "I'll miss your adventures. You and your papa have adventures. You do things that the so-called elite would never think of doing. They are boring." His tone grew more desperate. "Jake I am going to have to go live among people who bore me to tears." He did start to cry then. I looked around his office. I saw his maps and the scale models of his development projects. He was not grieving for the uncle he lost. He was grieving for the loss of his projects.

"Sir, You don't have to sit among the riches others have accumulated when you would rather sit among your maps and projects. You don't have to give up your passions just because others expect something of you. Let the brats learn to take care of themselves. Would you like me to have the things in this office shipped south to you?"

He looked at me. He knew I understood. He nodded.

"Let me take you home to your wife. I'll take care of the things here."

Mr. Rouseff stood up and squeezed my shoulder. "I shall miss seeing you several times a week and yelling at you to get things done faster when there are not enough people to do the work and no money to pay for the projects." He stopped, and tried to catch his breath. "Jake, the projects. I must have someone to represent me here. The people need these projects. Yes, they make the family rich. They make the people rich too. Take care of the people. Take care of my projects. I want you to be in charge of this office."

My jaw dropped. "Of course I'll do my best sir, but I am not a road builder."

"I have people who know how to do that. You know what I want here— the two circles. Make sure my roads get built in the right places."

I prepared to help Mr. Rouseff get home. I promised and comforted him as best I could. As we walked though the building he told people, "Listen to Jake. Jake knows what I want done. If you have questions, ask Jake. Jake is in charge of this office."

Suddenly, the end of my career with the prosecutor's office loomed over me and followed me like a shadow down the hall. I understood Mr. Rouseff's sorrow. It became my sorrow. Managing Rouseff's businesses would take a great deal of my time. I would not get to spend as much time with my friends in the prosecutor's office. I'd even come to love the repeat offenders. I would miss them.

I called Leah from Rouseff's house and told her that they were taking the next train south. "Darling, I think we will need to go south tomorrow or the next day. We'll travel with Mama and Papa so we will have help with the children."

Leah's sounded sad. The soft lilt in her voice comforted me. "Tell the Rouseff's that I will light a candle for them and their family."

"Of course dearest."

As soon as I got the Rouseffs on the train, I returned to the prosecutor's office and went directly to Mr. Supervisor's office. "Sir, Mr. Rouseff's uncle has died. Mr. Rouseff is on his way south to take care of business there. He has asked me to be in charge of his office here, which means I won't have much time for processing cases here."

"Oh the interns do most of the work now. You won't be needed." He looked down his nose and dismissed me.

I needed to make him understand how the office worked. "Should you have a murder case, you'll need me to advise the others." I scowled. "I really should be investigating some of our older murder cases."

"I'll look over the older murder cases and see if I can give you any direction."

"Thank you sir. I would appreciate that." I walked away shaking my head and wondering if Mr. Supervisor would have some insights into our unsolved murder cases. I stopped at Mr. Farley's desk and told him about the situation at Rouseff's.

Mr. Farley stood. "I'll miss you."

I whined. "I realize I'll miss our repeat offenders."

Mr. Farley sounded alarmed. His voice turned firm. "Jake. Get. Out. Of. Here. Now! If you think you will miss that sorry lot of humanity, you need a break from this place."

I had one more piece of news for my friend. "Oh, and Mr. Supervisor said he would go over the old murder cases and see if he had any insights."

I watched as astonishment covered Mr. Farley's face. Then he laughed. "I can't wait to see the results from this."

I went back to Rouseff's office and found his secretary. Together, we carefully packed all his treasures into boxes to ship to him. I made certain to photocopy all the maps. I boxed up the originals. When it was time for me to go home, we had Mr. Rouseff's treasures ready to follow him.

I stayed up late that night packing up my family to go to the funeral. Leah, Jacob, and I were easy enough to pack for, but her royal highness, Elizabeth, needed a retinue to carry her luggage.

I went into Rouseff's office early in the morning and moved his boxes to the train station. I returned home in time to load all our luggage in the Miki. It didn't fit.

Papa and Mama arrived just in time to join us in the royal procession to load Elizabeth's things in the waiting cars. They happily gave Jacob and some of our luggage a ride to the station.

Jacob eagerly suggested, "lizabeth wants ride Grandpapa and Grandmamma."

I told my son, "There is no room."

"Yes. See? She here." Jacob pointed out a small opening between suitcases that might indeed hold Elizabeth.

Papa laughed. "I need to put this little suitcase in that spot. Let Elizabeth ride with your Mama and Papa." Papa winked at Leah as he took her bag and put it into the hole where Jacob intended to stuff his sister.

My parents and my family took two compartments on the train. Jacob looked out the window and pointed out everything he saw to Elizabeth. She kicked and whimpered a bit until I stroked her soft cheek. She grabbed my finger, popped it in her mouth and went instantly to sleep while her brother continued to regale her with his vast knowledge of the outer world.

Grandmamma and Grandpapa took Jacob to the dining car for his lunch. I sat with Leah while she fed Elizabeth. Jacob felt sorry for his sister and protested that she wanted to eat in the dining car too. He had to be carried away.

I leaned closer to Leah. "Our son may think his sister is being deprived, but that looks like the better dinner to me."

"Jake behave yourself."

"What? I'm just trying to comfort you because our son seemed to think his sister would prefer the dining car."

Elizabeth stopped sucking, looked up at her mama and papa then went back to her dinner.

"He may be right. She never acts very hungry."

I growled at Leah, "I'm always hungry."

She laughed. "You have my permission to go to the dining car."

"I'll wait until Mama and Papa can watch the children then we can eat together in the dining car."

We arrived in the largest city of our most southern province, Portlandia, in the late afternoon. An army of Rouseff servants came to meet us. Between Cousin Philippe's boxes and Elizabeth's luggage we needed all the cars and servants he sent.

When we reached his house, Leah thought we were at a hotel. She stopped at the foot of the sweeping marble and gilt staircase. "I thought we were going to stay at his house."

I assisted her up the stairs toward large garishly gilded double doors. "Um, Leah, is it possible this is his house? In all of those architecture books you read, did you ever see pictures of the homes of the grand southern families?"

She looked around with round eyes. "No, I don't remember anything like that. I don't see anything here that is any particular style."

I surveyed the house. "It looks as if they started farther south and have been building north as they go."

Of course, we didn't need to use the gold knocker that hung from the mouth of something that looked like the offspring of a gargoyle and cherub. Mr. and Mrs. Rouseff met us at the door. "Jacob, tha..." Mr. Rouseff stopped mid-word and grabbed Papa in a big bear hug. Rosalie squeezed Mama, sniffed and dabbed at her eye.

The Rouseffs hugged Leah and I then stole our children. As she led us inside, Rosalie said over her shoulder, "It is a comfort for you to be here. We were so comfortable in our home for so many years. It is like we are among strangers here." Mrs. Rouseff sounded so sad.

Before dinner, the Rouseff's introduced us to the rest of the family in a drawing room big enough to hold my entire house. Rouseff's daughters arrived with their husbands and children. I'd met them only once before. I enjoyed both of these women. They had married educated, sensible men. I could not say the same for the rest of the extended family.

By the time we could excuse ourselves to go to bed, I felt almost ill. Everywhere my eyes rested I saw more gold and gilt. Each room in the house contained a jumble of fine paintings, rare pottery, lavish tapestries, and ornate woodcarving. Crystal chandeliers vied for attention with ornately woven carpets. Gold vied with silver and precious gems for the grandest place of honor. If I appeared not to notice an ornate vase or cigar case, one of the cousins would shove it under my nose and assure me in superior tones that it was genuine ivory or gold or whatever.

Leah's poise and good manners made me proud. She appeared not to notice the vulgarity of the decor. Occasionally she would say something like, "Oh what a lovely baroque vase." Or, "May I take a closer look at your Renoir?" I estimated that the gold on the doorknobs alone would put our country back on a solid economic foundation for years.

By the time we went in to dinner, I'd lost my appetite. We sat at one end of the table with Philippe and Rosalie and talked about the children and roads and shopping malls. Servants arrived with course after course of fancy food that adorned fine china plates that were decorated with an elaborate gold and silver rim.

The southern members of the family sat at the other end of the table and whispered audibly about the poor display and the lack of courses. I overheard heard a hissed whisper, "Well she just got here. Of course she doesn't know how to go on." I clenched my jaw at the implied insult of Rosalie's taste.

After we went to bed, I couldn't sleep. In my mind I saw the reality of the elderly men and women in my city dying from lack of food set against the opulent vulgarity of this house. I could almost smell those damn ugly fish and feel the weight my shoulders as I labored to provide my people one decent meal. Meanwhile, here sat these people complaining that we had only seven courses for dinner. What did anyone need with such wealth? My disgust caused the bile to rise up in the back of my throat.

The funeral and Mass occupied most of our second day in the south. The Rouseff relatives displayed their grief with a great flourishing of handkerchiefs and dry eyes. They took to fawning on Philippe and hinting that Uncle had been stingy with their allowances. Finally, Phillip growled at his cousin, "You are fifty-two years old. If you want money why don't you get a job? You can catch rats if you can't find anything else."

Nobody other than Mama and Papa caught his reference to my first job when I was six. Papa quickly moved to stand between his friend and the cloying relatives. Papa's scowls frightened the cowards away from poor Philippe.

Much to my delight, Andy and Adele came to the funeral reception at the house. The moment I saw them arrive, I headed for the entrance. Andy didn't wait for me to reach him. He waved his arm in the air, "Jake! Jake, man it is good to see you, even considering the circumstances." When I reached him, he pulled me into a hug.

I sighed, "Andy thank God you are here. I'm dying for a sensible conversation and poor Cousin Philippe is beside himself."

Adele kissed the air in Leah's direction. "Oh Leah, look at you. I can't believe you have two children and still have your figure." She turned to Andy and said in tones much louder than necessary. "She still looks elegant, doesn't she? Even with two children."

Leah murmured, "Adele, Andy, thank you for coming to the reception. It is a comfort to see familiar faces."

Adele expressed her happiness to be so close to her family. "Oh yes, it is best to be among all that is familiar. All of our old friends have moved south, I don't know how you manage to survive in the north. I was afraid to walk the streets."

Leah again murmured something appropriate about making new friends.

I turned to Andy. "How are you? It is good to see you."

He grumped back, "I miss working in physics, and I miss academia, and I really want to get my doctorate. I've been thinking that we could be treating our cancer patients if we could build the accelerators to make radioactive isotopes."

Adele clung to his arm. "Sweetheart, you don't have to work. That is the whole point. I don't understand why you want to wallow with inferior people when you can be surrounded with beauty and elegance."

Andy's voice held a sharp edge. I noticed the muscles tighten around his eyes. "I'm frustrated that our people are dying from cancers that would be easily treated if we had the right equipment. I want to learn how to build that equipment."

Adele rolled her eyes and persisted, "Darling, it is okay to read and study and look at the stars. Pure science is acceptable. You want to apply it. I think science is over-rated anyway. Applied science should not be taught in a university in my opinion."

I stood stunned by this speech. I wondered how the industrious Andrew could live with this attitude.

The soft lilt of Leah's voice beside me brought me back to my surroundings. "Leonardo de Vinci combined the artistic with the mathematical beautifully. I see no conflict between the arts and sciences. It would be most arrogant to condemn de Vinci." Leah's calm statement turned the conversation to art then it passed on to other topics. I felt more than thankful for her graceful endorsement of Andrew's interests. She made me proud to call her my wife.

Before we went to our rooms for the night, Papa and I had reason to be very proud of our wives. We had dined again with the extended family that evening. Mama and Leah both wore modest black dresses with pearl necklaces. They stood out like elegant swans among the sequins of the designer gowns and wads jewelry heaped on the half-naked Rouseff women.

Later, when we started getting ready for bed, Leah commented. "Jake, I don't understand Papa's behavior."

"Huh? What?" I turned to look at Leah.

"Yes, he keeps telling me how proud he is of me. After dinner, he told me that I was the most beautiful woman in the room after Mama. He kissed my fingers and told me I was a credit to the Jaconovich name. What does he mean by this?"

I tried to be tactful as I struggled to explain. "You have not appeared to notice the vulgarity of this house or even of the dress employed by the Rouseff women."

"Oh, I know what you mean. You're talking about the poor design principles employed and the total lack of a focal point in any room. Actually the rooms have too many focal points. The eye is drawn in every direction. It is not restful."

"Ah, you do understand what Papa is trying to say. He wants you to know that he sees and approves of your understanding of good design and taste, especially in dress and personal appearance."

"The other women told me to cut my hair because long hair is not fashionable. I tried to explain that I like it long because I can pull it back so it doesn't get in my face. I'd hate my hair around my face as they wear theirs. It irritates me. They think I should follow fashion. I see no reason to be uncomfortable for fashion."

"Do not cut your hair to gain the approval of other women. I like it long. We can play Adam and Eve. Now, let that long hair down and come to bed."

The morning after the funeral, Cousin Philippe went on a rampage. He yelled and stamped his foot. He demanded the cleaning of every room he must enter. He did not want his eye to fall on one single piece of *vulgar trash* during the course of a whole day. As he yelled and swore at his household, he reduced the women to tears. They hid in their rooms while Cousin Rosalie, Mama and Leah commanded an army of servants and reordered the household. Cousin Rosalie designated that two large rooms be used to store the extra household bric-a-brac.

I wandered in on their redecorating of the dining room as Cousin Rosalie inquired, "What do you think Leah?"

My wife rested her hands on her hips and surveyed the room with a trained eye. "The size of the room and the chandelier are so impressive in themselves I don't see that anything else is needed."

Mama added her opinion. "Once the room is cleared of so many objects, some fresh flowers on the table might be all that is needed."

Servants carried armloads of items out of the room. They removed all the pictures from the walls. Some of the ornate frames were so heavy it took two men to carry them. When I went in to dinner, I found a stunning room with a long gleaming mahogany table. I sighed.

I started forming a new plan and was eager to ask Rouseff about funding our highway. I planned to pay him back through charging a toll on the road or contracting with the government to pay him back in installments. I could find an excellent use for all the gold and silver bric-a-brac.

In the evening, the men discussed business at one end of the purged sitting room. I sat on the fringe of the group and listened-in on the women in the other end of the room.

Ulahle Rouseff whined, "That painting was priceless. It's criminal to lock it up where nobody can see it."

Young Diana wailed. "What will my friends think? They will pity me. Oh I can't stand being pitied."

Mrs. Rouseff assured them, "If there are any items that you are particularly fond of, you can take them to your own apartments." She sighed and took a deep breath. "I know you are accustomed to a large display, but this is not acceptable in other parts of the country. It is not acceptable in other countries. It is considered vulgar. It is intellectually poor design. My husband will not embarrass himself in front of people from other cultures by adhering to something that is little other than a local fad."

This speech impressed me. I knew Mrs. Rouseff must feel almost frantic from the events of the past three days. Mama patted her friend's hand.

Leah's soft voice once again turned the conversation. "Are some of your young people ready for university? Jake and I will be happy to introduce them to the faculty when they arrive. I enjoy being on the campus. I don't even mind the first-year receptions. I think I see the need for them now."

Cousin Rosalie laughed. "Does Jake still call them twenty minutes in hell?"

Leah smiled gently. "I think it will be better if I attend with our young relatives. I am not a graduate, but I have taken enough classes and I know the hostesses socially."

Cousin Bianca added to the conversation. "My daughter is not sure she wants to attend university. She'll never need a career so there is no need for her to go to university. She went to poise school that is all she needs."

Rosalie said in a tone sharper than normal, "It is a good place for young women to meet intelligent and educated men."

Again Leah rescued the conversation. "I enjoyed studying art and architecture. I don't need to work, of course, but Cousin Philippe has asked me to help with some of the art and design aspects of his projects. We do not want to build ugly roads."

One of the older aunts snorted. "How can roads not be ugly?"

Leah's serene face and tone never faltered. "It depends on what is planted beside them."

Cousin Rosalie had learned a few things from her husband's nattering on about roads and malls. "All aspects of a road project need to be in scale to their function and environment."

"A well constructed interchange is as lovely as a piece of abstract art." My mama added vaguely. She seemed to have trouble joining in the general conversation. "We saw a lot of them in the United States."

Rosalie smiled at Mama, "That trip was so much fun. Travel outside the country is so broadening."

Young Lulay's eyes grew big and round, "Do the women there really dress in nightgowns and undergarments during the day?"

Cousin Rosalie laughed. "Not that we ever saw. I assume they wear nightgowns to bed and have undergarments under their clothes."

Mama tried to support her friend in the conversation tonight. "Most of the time, they seemed to wear blue jeans with various things on top."

Leah said, "Cousin Rosalie, you must show them your catalogs." She leaned conspiratorially toward the others. "She and Mama get the most wonderful catalogs sent all the way from the states. They bought me a whole wardrobe of clothes to wear before Jacob was born."

Mama's voice sounded soft and beautiful with just the tiniest northern lilt when she spoke. "I think most of the time, people were dressed much less formally than we do here. Even at the opera, very few women wore jewelry other than a pendant. I was so thankful that I had not worn anything other than pearls the first time we went out."

Cousin Rosalie shook her head. "I confess to being shocked to see women in their blue jeans at the Opera. I thought that was carrying the fashion too far. Most women wore a long black dress, but we saw every style imaginable."

Mrs. Rouseff sent a servant to retrieve her catalogs. The women spent the evening looking at the catalogs and exclaiming over how women dressed in a country as rich as the United States.

We stayed a week in the Rouseff household. Papa finally put his foot down and told Cousin Philippe that we must leave. Cousin Philippe frowned, distraught. "I don't know how I'll survive here. Jake, my son, promise me you'll take care of my projects. Jacob you must return soon. I am afraid I will not encounter one intelligent conversation until you come visit."

I privately thought he might be right.

Chapter 5 Head of Rouseff Industries

When I set down our bags in the entry of our own home, I looked around with a new perspective. I'd always thought our main sitting room looked uninteresting. Now, it looked clean and elegant. My eyes were drawn outside the window to the lake that filled our whole view. In one corner of the view, sat Leah's little Chinese garden with its bright yellow bridge and the seedpods that I admired. I sighed. I loved the rock she had insisted I drag down from the ridge into her garden. I smiled remembering how she had fussed and cajoled until I'd placed it just so.

The first morning back home, I stopped in at the prosecutor's office first. I worried that they would be overwhelmed with petty offenders. They had given up interviewing each offender personally. Offenders who were willing to plead guilty signed their papers with a clerk in the holding room. Each was issued a trash bag and sent to their locations. Everybody seemed happy. We could clear thirty or forty petty offenders in a couple hours.

Oh Jake, I'm glad you're here." Mr. Assassin Supervisor came out of his office. "I've gone over the murder cases in our files."

Those of us who knew his true profession turned away. I remembered his demeanor his first day in our office. The change in attitude confused me. I worried again that Vanderholm had sent him to spy on us. I looked at the files in his hands.

He continued, "I can see several avenues for investigation. I talked to our police department." I spent the next hour with Mr. Supervisor going over the files for our murder cases. He had done an excellent job of organizing the cases by type. "These are your desperation or opportunistic cases." He showed me the biggest folder. "These were committed by the same person who is most likely a socio-path." He set that folder aside. "This was a professional execution with an attempt to frame an innocent party." He held up the file for the Mantega murder.

"Good, except for the Mantega case this will help. To be truthful, if I ever found the person responsible for the Mantega murder, I would be inclined to recommend him for an honor. Mantega was a piece of vermin."

"I want the man who killed Mantega found."

"Where would you start?" I tried not to sweat.

"I think I'll go to the capital for several days and see what I can turn up."

"Good. I can get the word out on the street about what we're looking for. I might also get the word out about this socio-path. Do you think he prefers a particular type of victim?"

We discussed as much as my assassin supervisor could guess about the socio-path. We finally agreed that I would pursue the socio-path and some of the opportunistic cases. He would go looking for Mantega's killer in the capital. I smiled, content with the outcome of our discussion.

When I arrived at Rouseff's office, I called a staff meeting in the conference room. "Rouseff wants to move forward on the road project. We need to research purchasing land for a bypass and getting a contract with the government to pay us back for financing the construction. Our alternative to getting a promise of a government pay-off is to install a toll on the road. I need the legal team to research using a toll." I nodded to the staff attorneys. "Right now, we can begin the demolition on the right of way through Doh Creek Road. Did Rouseff talk to those of you in design about how he wants to do the city inner circle?"

They nodded.

I asked, "Can we get some people in the capital to talk to legislators about financing this road?"

"Jake, it might help if you met with some legislators."

I agreed. "I know Mr. Chang. I suppose I can run up and meet with him later this week." We continued to divide up jobs. Mr. Rouseff had already talked to financing. We were ready to hire. By the time the meeting let out I felt like I had run a long race. I felt exhausted and decided to go home early. I walked from the office to the M'TK station. I let people know that we would be hiring soon. I also passed on the word about the socio-path.

The next morning I went to work in Rouseff's office. Everybody wanted to tell me about riots in Wulfton. I asked Rouseff's—now my—secretary, "What is that about?"

"The factories are laying off more people. Do you think that will affect the road?"

I ran my hand through my hair. "How many are they laying off?"

"I heard the total will be about thirty-thousand."

"Damn, I don't think we can hire that many. Get the word out that we'll be hiring soon." I thought about hiring people, but my mind kept circling back to where I would put the road. I sat at my desk and looked at maps. I ran my finger along the line I expected the bypass road to take. I thought about where the road could go. I didn't have Rouseff's vision. I thought again, swiveled in my chair and said out loud to the walls, "I don't have Rouseff's vision."

I got up and found Rouseff's secretary at her desk next door to my office. "I am thinking about this road project Rouseff wants us to start. Can you find a helicopter to take about four of us on a fly around the city?"

"Yes, Mr. Jaconovich." I went back to my desk and grinned.

Within five minutes the secretary came back on my intercom. "Do you want it for morning or afternoon."

"Morning."

I heard the secretary talking on the phone then she came back on the intercom. "The Rouseff pilot will have the helicopter fueled and ready for take off at eight in the morning at helipad three. Is there anything else you need?"

I tried to think of what else I might need. I hadn't known Rouseff owned helicopters. In a state of moderate shock, I could only hope the rotors on a Rouseff helicopter weren't gold plated.

I went back to brooding over my maps again. I decided to pick up a camera on my way home from work.

After a few minutes, my secretary interrupted me to take a phone call. "Mr. Jaconovich, it is the prosecutor's office."

I answered, "Jaconovich."

Mr. Farley commanded, "Jake, we need help over here. The police have been arresting rioters. We need to process them. They won't plead guilty."

"I'll be there in a couple of minutes." I told my secretary where she could reach me and walked the five blocks from Rouseff Industries to the prosecutor's office. I wondered how I would walk with the new inner road filled with traffic. I got grumpy about the idea of large amounts of traffic in the inner city. I decided we needed to build the bypass first.

I still felt grumpy when I arrived at the prosecutor's office. I tried not to snarl at Darlene when I came in. She looked particularly glum herself. I looked into the full holding room. I picked up some files and called my first case.

"It says here that you were rioting and resisted arrest." How do you plead?

The man looked clean, neatly dressed and groomed except for a scrape on his right cheek. "Not guilty."

I noticed that the man's shirt appeared to have been clean when he put it on, but the sleeve had a fresh tear and the front looked dusty. "Can you explain to me what happened that led to you being taken to jail?"

"First, I wasn't rioting." He said irately. "I was on lower second and there were no riots there. All the riots were over on fourth."

"What were you doing on second?"

"I went out for a few beers with friends. We came out of Filippe's Cantina and stood waiting for the trolley. Some police came along and told us to move along. We agreed, said we were waiting for the next trolley and would get on it as soon as it came. The next thing I knew, the policeman was trying to put handcuffs on Ruben. I put my hand out and asked him what he thought he was doing. The policeman pushed me down, and the next thing I knew I was being arrested."

I studied the man again. His lined face and rough hands told me he was a laborer. His eyes betrayed no sign of dissipation. "Thank you sir. I will have to investigate this case. I will need to talk to your friends. If I find no evidence of wrong-doing, I'll dismiss the charges. Otherwise, I will take it before a judge who will give you a notice of your court date. If things turn out to be as you said, you will have no further problems." I almost ended the discussion here. For some reason I asked another question. "What do you really think this was about?"

"Oh, it is the big bosses at the factories. They are fighting over territory. They've hired policemen to arrest everybody who works for a different company."

"Do you have any idea why they are fighting?"

He shrugged, "I heard Mr. Rouseff has moved south."

I nodded. "What does Mr. Rouseff's place of residence have to do with their behavior?"

The man shifted in his seat and spoke slowly as if talking to a child. "They're fighting for control the city now that Rouseff is gone."

I sat and stared at the man. He seemed to be sober and reasonable. I knew a flash of fear and anger. "In other words they think they can go back to gang warfare."

"Yes, sir."

"Do you have anything else to add?"

"I don't have money for an attorney. I can't afford to take time off from work, and I might get fired for being gone today."

I sat and thought. "Here's my card with my phone number. I am going to check out your story. As for an attorney, we will appoint one. If I think you are innocent, I will take your case and let an intern act as prosecutor." I felt a smile creeping across my face.

"I don't see what you find so funny."

I laughed outright. "If you are telling me the truth, I am going to have some real fun cutting off some people's balls." I grinned at the man. "Come with me I will set you up with the paralegal. He will get the names and addresses of everybody who was with you."

I got another case. "Mr. Giolante, it says here that you were picked up for being drunk and disorderly."

"That's right."

"How do you plead?"

"What do you mean?"

"Were you drunk and creating a disturbance?"

"I was certainly drunk. I would not call my performance a disturbance. I was singing *Figaro*."

Stifling my amusement I said, "Ah, you are fond of the opera."

His chest expanded and his voice filled the big room. "I used to sing in the opera. I had seven curtain calls in Paris for my Othello." He seemed to shrink again. "But that was before the drink got me." His voice wavered in a dramatic tremolo.

I looked back at the report, "It says here that you were on second-street."

"That's right." He gestured dramatically.

"Was there rioting on second?"

"No that was on fourth-street." His voice almost mesmerized me as he drew out his vowels dramatically.

I pulled out my previous file. Mr. Giolante had been arrested about a half hour before my previous case.

"Ah, what can you tell me about the officer who arrested you?"

He scowled, leaned toward me, and in a stage whisper, he confided, "He was a new officer on the street. Most of the regular guardians of justice know me." He looked to the right and the left as if looking to see if anybody was listening. He continued, "Have you not heard that Fortenac and Papdakos hired a bunch of policemen. I think it was one of the new policemen."

I leaned back in my seat and stared at the man before me. "Do you have any experience with small theater groups?"

He blinked. "I was told they would send me to pick up litter."

"Oh no, you're going to help me. Rouseff has long wanted to organize some theater groups to keep some of our more creative citizens off of the street." I grinned. The man looked scared. "We will need to get some depositions to determine if you were indeed creating a disturbance. I may ask you to sing before a professional."

"I will amaze your professional." His voice boomed across the room.

I tried not to grin too gleefully at my poor client. "Here's the phone number and address for my other office. Please contact me there tomorrow afternoon to discuss the street players. Do you have any questions?"

"Oh, I got questions all right. This is not going at all the way I was told it would."

I smiled. "Come, I want you to make a deposition if the recorder is free."

By the time I finished with the deposition, it was almost four o'clock. My paralegal had finished with my first client.

I went to show him out. "I just talked to someone who gave me an unbiased deposition on your case. I'll discuss the situation with the other attorneys. I may take your case or I may dismiss your charges."

"Why do you look so cheerful when I am about to lose my job?" I handed the man my Rouseff business card. "You'll want to contact me here. Certainly if you lose your job, Rouseff will give you one at union wages with benefits."

"I heard he's gone south."

"Not completely." I grinned again and slapped the poor client on the back.

After I escorted my client out the door, I decided we needed a staff meeting. Our assassin supervisor was not in the office so I stood in the middle of the room and bellowed, "Staff meeting at four o'clock. This might be good."

Since I called the meeting, I opened, "Okay, this is what I picked up this afternoon. Have any of the rest of you encountered this? I just had two cases that were arrested for rioting well outside the riot zone. Did any of the rest of you run into similar cases?"

Leroy raised his hand. "Yeah, I had a couple cases who were picked up for rioting blocks away from the rioting. I told them that we would…" Leroy looked toward the empty supervisor's office. "…would investigate and set a court date."

Christian nodded. "Yeah, about the same story here. One man claimed his car wouldn't start so he was working on it a bit. He got picked up for car theft. I sent him to get his registration or proof of ownership. He and his wife came back with the proper papers."

I said, "This is crazy. My cases told me Fortenac and Papadakos intend to take over the city now that Rouseff has moved south. Frankly, I'm not even certain I know what that means."

Leroy said, "It may well mean that they intend to run a protection racket."

I told the others what I knew. "Perhaps they are still thinking to get their hands on property where the proposed highway will run. Papadakos could be into protection."

Leroy sighed. "Yeah, Papadakos could be into anything. My aunt Madeline is a Papadakos. I'll visit her and see what I can learn."

"Thanks." I hadn't realized that Leroy had Papadakos relatives. I remembered that I had a Fortenac relative.

Mr. Farley looked happier than I had seen him since Mr. Supervisor arrived. He rubbed his hands together. "Well good, it looks like we are going to get to practice some real law."

We cheered and clapped.

Mr. Farley continued, "I want the names of all the officers involved in arresting people who appear to be innocent. I want as many depositions you can get."

We quickly sorted the files we had not processed. Most of them came from the targeted area. Mr. Farley told the people to go on home. We would contact them when we were ready to talk to them.

One man wrung the hat he held in his hands. "We will lose our jobs if we have to take another day off work."

I stuck my head in the holding room. "Rouseff's hiring." I looked around. These people wore the clothes of laborers and domestics. "This is crazy. You might be safer working for Rouseff."

I got home in time to help feed the children their dinner. Leah had cooked most of the meal. After dinner, she found me in my study and sat down on my lap. "Jake, I'm not sure we need household help. Elizabeth is almost weaned so I can take care of the house."

I thought about the extra children in the house. "No. You have things you want to do, taking classes and visiting friends. You will have household help from now on. I've seen how the Rouseff's live. I have a salary sufficient to keep us in hired help. I may even build real servant's quarters above a garage. I will not allow one piece of gilt bric-a-brac in this house. We will not have vulgar gold doorknobs, but we will have hired help."

"A garage with servants quarters above it is a good idea. I'll start some drawings." Leah smiled happily.

As Leah prepared to leave my study, I asked, "Why is Elizabeth being weaned so early?"

Leah rolled her eyes. "She's not hungry because Jacob stuffs half of his food into her mouth. Today, I noticed the children standing around Elizabeth's infant seat. Every few minutes they started laughing. We'd fed them noodles for lunch and Jacob had a bowl them. He'd dangle one end on Elizabeth's mouth. She'd catch it and suck it down like a little bird eating worms. I couldn't help but laugh myself when the noodle would disappear. She really was quick. When Shirley caught us she scolded us that Elizabeth could choke." Leah's tone turned sulky. "I think if she were going to choke, she would have done so immediately."

Poor Leah, Shirley really shouldn't scold Leah as if she were a child. However, I would not turn a woman supporting five children off because Leah was upset.

I took my helicopter ride the next morning together with a geologist and a surveyor to join me. I also took Papa with me. He'd called the night before to say he and mama were well. He sounded a little bored.

I asked, "Can you bring Mama out here to spend the morning? Leah could use more support watching Elizabeth. The other children fed her noodles yesterday while Leah's back was turned."

Papa chuckled.

I continued, "I want you to help me look over the area where I want to build the bypass highway."

As the helicopter circled the city, I took dozens of pictures. The geologist talked though our headphones about basalt and sandstone, while the surveyor muttered about straight lines, the meandering river and rights of way.

Papa pointed out a lush green area full of willow trees and suggested we build the road there.

The geologist countered, "That is swamp the ground is too soft."

The surveyor ruefully agreed with Papa, "That would be the best route if the ground were solid."

Papa's excitement made me smile. "Build it over the top of the swamp. That is how they do it in the states. They'll build over the top of anything." He rode along silent for a minute or two. "Um, Jake, where you put your access roads into the city you will want to build restaurants and motels…oh…and…a gas station with a convenience store. In the states, some roads have public restrooms set in pretty little parks." Papa smiled sadly, "Your mama wanted to stop at every one we passed. I think she liked them better than the opera and museums."

"Thank you. Would you and Mama write down all the things you saw that we need to remember to build?"

The surveyor interrupted, "Won't Mr. Rouseff tell us what he wants?"

Papa answered the man, "Cousin Philippe has his hands full in the south. Remember we stayed with him for a full week. Let's make the most complete plan possible in order to assure him that at least his employees are not a school of silly suckerfish."

The others snorted.

I laughed out loud. "Yes, you have voiced what I am feeling. Cousin Philippe does indeed have his hands full in the south. He may also have his hands full here too. I have heard rumors of Fortenac and Papadakos causing trouble in the city. I will deal with it as best I can, but I want something to run smoothly for him. This project is very close to his heart. He can make changes when we present our proposal."

The others nodded.

In the afternoon, I went back to the prosecutor's office and headed off to the supervisor's office. He had just returned from the capital.

"What are you doing here?" He asked in a cold tone that sounded, oddly, slightly more cordial than when he'd first come to work in our office.

I grinned. "Having a bit of fun actually. We appear to have a bid by two rival…" I remembered his class-consciousness and affiliations in time. "um… gangs to operate in the city. They appear to be under the mistaken impression that with Rouseff in the south, they can run a protection racket or whatever they're planning to do here."

"What difference does Rouseff make?"

"Well that is the interesting part, none. He makes no difference. That is why the rumor that these gangs are fighting each other or cooperating to terrorize the citizenry or whatever they are doing surprised me."

"How do you know this is really happening?"

"You are right. At this stage it's still just a rumor. It's the sort of thing we watch for in a prosecutor's office. Gang rivalries can lead to civil war. We like to nip that sort of thing as quick as we can. We can't have loose bands of marauding scum interfering with business." I'd remembered the correct catch-words just in time to make sense.

Mr. LaBarge nodded and scowled. "Right. Let's crack down on the ungrateful bastards before they hurt someone important."

"We're on it sir. Did you have any luck in the capital?"

"Not really, I think I am on the right track. I found rumors of a similar crime there. I might like to take one of our staff to help me look." We discussed a couple side issues then I left to take depositions. When Darlene brought me my first case, I thought she looked particularly nice today. I looked toward the supervisor's office and entertained a horrible suspicion.

For my first case I took a deposition from one of the men who had been arrested while waiting for the trolley. "Did you see the trolley?"

"No."

"If you were at the trolley stop, where was the guard?"

"Ol' Tossley? I don't know."

"Have you heard any rumors about Mr. Tossley's whereabouts?" I became concerned for a Rouseff employee.

"No, I just heard that Rouseff has moved south and will lay off all his people here. That is what the riots are about. The paper said that Rouseff's union people will force factory workers out of their jobs because they stick together and...and will co...co...coerce the factories into laying us off and hiring them instead."

I wanted to hold my head. I wondered if Rouseff might want to buy a newspaper. Deep in my gut I knew that this battle could turn ugly. The weight of my new responsibility as Rouseff's representative in the north sat heavily on my shoulders. I started entertaining a fantasy of striding through my city tossing private policemen into walls.

The next few days followed the same pattern. I went to work early and worked in Rouseff's office. After lunch, I spent at least an hour in the prosecutor's office examining the in coming cases.

During a staff meeting, I whined to the other attorneys. "We are running into the same problem that we have met before. Someone is hiring people to do the job of acting as police, and the perpetrator may not know he is breaking the law."

Christian considered and came up with a somewhat comforting response. "I don't think that will make a difference this time Jake. The policemen may not know they are breaking the law about impersonating an officer. The police department isn't complaining. However, most of the charges we'll press are for arresting people without just cause."

Mr. Farley had done some research. "I talked to the Chief of Police about the arrests. He told me that he doesn't intend to do anything about the problem unless we bring charges."

"Will he arrest the offenders if we bring charges?" I asked

Mr. Farley sounded grumpy. "He better."

"I'll have charges ready for him in case he doesn't." Christian sounded vicious.

"You cannot charge the chief of police with crimes." Mr. LaBarge sounded shocked.

I answered. "Sure we can, and Christian's grumpy because his wife is three days overdue with that baby. Charging someone with crimes is almost as good as breaking noses and tossing huge men about."

The others laughed while Mr. Assassin Supervisor looked bewildered.

Jeffrey explained. "Jake got a little cranky when Leah was in the hospital. He broke the nose of a CGIS officer and left three of them on the floor."

I pouted, "They didn't get into our files."

LaBarge leaned forward suddenly intent. "The CGIS was here?"

I shrugged, "Yeah, they didn't stay long, and they didn't get an opportunity to look for anything." I thought we should change the subject.

Christian came to the rescue. "Yeah, we didn't need them telling us who was crooked in this office. I wrote up the charges against the traitors in our office."

Leroy concluded. "So yeah, we can charge anybody who we have just cause to believe has broken the law. The police who are hired by Papadakos and Fortenac are not real police. The Chief of Police should not be allowing them to arrest people."

Mr. Supervisor displayed uncharacteristic interest in our procedures. "What are we doing with the people they arrest?"

Leroy shrugged. "Taking depositions about who arrested them and where."

"When can we move?" Mr. LaBarge sounded eager to arrest people.

Mr. Farley answered, "As soon as we have enough trained officers to actually arrest the men."

Alexander, one of our interns had started taking a role in thinking through a problem. "Can we hire some from the capital?"

Mr. Supervisor sounded more than curious. "Who qualifies to arrest them? Can people from this office actually do the arresting?" His eagerness amused me.

"Technically, yes." I had no desire to actually arrest anybody despite my fantasies of throwing them into walls.

"Jake you have security at Rouseff Properties. Can we borrow some of them?" Leroy's question was good. Our security had excellent training.

"No, for the same reason that we are arresting the men hired by Papadakos and Fortenac." I explained what I had done with Rouseff security. "I have put extra security at the trolley stops. Which reminds me we still have not found our missing trolley guard. I'd like to charge someone with whatever happened to him."

"Some places use dogs to look for missing people." Our Assassin Supervisor was full of ideas today.

Christian said. "We don't have any trained dogs."

Mr. LaBarge volunteered. "I'll see if I can find some."

I nodded. "Thank you. At this point this is still more of a Rouseff problem than a case for this office. Of course, I strongly suspect that our missing guard is part of the bigger picture. I have extra security on the streets. They are supposed to protect the trolley guards and pass us information." I decided to shut up. I wondered again if LaBarge would pass any information from our office on to the forces we wanted to arrest. I just couldn't get a reading on the man. Part of my brain observed that his ability to appear to fit in would be an asset in his profession. I kept secret my plan to ask Mrs. Governor to loan us provincial police.

I went back to my office at Rouseff and called a meeting with my security team. "What are you hearing on the street?"

The day team leader answered, "We know there is trouble. We suspect Papadakos is the instigator. With the Fortenacs involved we know that this can be traced all the way to President Vanderholm. We still haven't found Tossley. He is a faithful employee so it is safe to assume he is being held hostage, is dead or injured."

I felt the blood draining out of my face over the responsibility for my employees.

The night team leader commented, "Sir, with all due respect, may I suggest what Mr. Rouseff would do at a time like this when we are not finding anything concrete? Sir, Mr. Rouseff would ask you to go read the street."

I nodded. "I can do that after the meeting."

I adjourned the meeting and took the trolley across town intending to purchase some soap at the soap shop and walk to the hospital. That would give me a good idea of conditions on second, and third, plus three cross streets.

I took my walk and had security pick me up at the hospital. When I got back to the office we made our plans. "Okay, let's put our men in on second between M'SK Street and Florence. If they're trying to shake down businesses, they will stick to that area. Somebody is running numbers on M'KlA and third. See if you can get an idea who that is. It feels pretty quiet down by the hospital." I went home to my wife and children.

Chapter 6 The Businessman Prosecutor

L ate in the week, I decided I needed to talk to someone in the city about the road project. I asked my secretary to make an appointment with the mayor. After she called to set up the appointment, She came to me with surprising news, "The mayor is in jail."

"What? Why on earth is he in jail? We charged him and fined him months ago."

My secretary shrugged and added, "I made an appointment for you to see his wife."

I didn't have many choices so I went to see the mayor's wife. I met her in her husband's office. She came around the large desk to greet me, and ask after Leah.

Once seated, I tried to get down to business. "Mrs. Mayor, I am sorry your husband is still in jail."

"Don't worry about it." Her mouth compressed into a thin white line, her color changed, and the muscles around her eyes tightened.

If the mayor had turned up murdered, I'd consider her the chief suspect. I pressed a bit more on the topic. "I am a prosecutor. I expected him to pay his fine and return home."

"Someone would need to pay the fine for him since he is not free to go about his business. Don't worry about it. It is not really any of your business." She moved her penholder from one side of the desk between us to the other side. "Now, was there something else you wanted to see me about? I understand that you are talking about extending the highway through the city."

The thoughts running through my brain troubled me. I could not believe the delicate little woman in front of me was deliberately refusing to pay her husband's fine. I worried about what a man could do to make his wife that angry with him. I tried to suppress a nervous chuckle.

The woman glared at me.

I got down to business. "Right. The central government has not made any public declaration of where they intend to run the new highway."

"They intend to run it straight through the center of the city. Let me have someone get you a map of the proposal." She used the intercom to direct a clerk to bring us the map.

I wanted to ask a thousand questions about her authority to fill the mayor's job. I stuck to the task at hand. "Thank you I would like to look at the map. What do you think of the idea of running the highway through the center of the city?"

"Where else would you put it?"

"Anywhere else. The problem with the idea is that it cuts the city in half. It places unnecessary traffic through our most important areas. We could not walk from city hall to the university or to the office district because of a heavily traveled highway creating a barrier. Driving across town would be equally difficult."

She raised her eyebrow and asked her question again. "Where else would we put the highway?"

"We have several ideas based on Mr. Rouseff's experience in designing trolley and rail systems." A man appeared with the maps. I was excited to be looking at the proposal that we had only guessed at earlier. We rolled the maps out on the desk between us.

Mrs. Mayor pointed out the proposals marked in red. "As you can see, the first stage is to link our city hall with the capital. The second stage is to upgrade the road leading south."

"Yes, that was what Rouseff guessed based on the pattern of arson and harassment we were picking up from certain sectors of the city. Like I mentioned. There are some problems with that route."

She raised her eyebrows again. "What do you propose?"

I outlined Mr. Rouseff's plan for the two circles. I leaned back in my chair. "There is another problem with the proposal to bring the highway through the center of the city. It would cut through Chinese land grant property. Um…well…as a prosecutor, I'm not going to let that happen. The proposed alternative is legal and workable. What do you think? I should add that our plan includes underground phone and electrical lines and trees planted along the boulevard to suppress sound and visually protect the businesses along the route from traffic."

Mrs. Mayor leaned back in her chair. "I see you have thought about this."

"What I need from the city, is the rights to a of couple pieces of land, some sort of financial agreement about paying Rouseff for building the road and support in talking to the provincial governor about running the road through provincial land for the bypass."

"The provincial governor is in jail."

"Who would I talk to? Who has taken his place?"

"You can talk to his wife." Mrs. Mayor smiled at me. "Would you like me to set up an appointment for you to meet with Mrs. Governor?"

"Yes. Yes that is exactly the sort of help I need from you." I smiled. I still felt terribly confused, but I kept moving forward with what was in front of me. I prepared to leave.

"Mr. Jaconovich," Mrs. Mayor's voice settled me back into my chair. "I suspect that you know most everything that is happening in this city. What is happening on the street with Papadakos and Vanderholm?"

"Vanderholm? We knew about Papadakos and Fortenac, but not anything specific about Vanderholm."

"I'm fairly certain Vanderholm is supplying guns and financing Papadakos. Fortenac is an ass an will do anything to please Vanderholm."

"Ah, the best I can say is that the prosecutor's office is aware of false arrests and will prosecute when we have enough evidence. As for Rouseff industries, I must protect my employees."

Mrs. Mayor looked me in the eye, took a deep breath and blurted out, "The governor's office tells me the provincial police confiscated a case of automatic weapons."

"Shit." I think I blushed at swearing in front of that delicate woman. "Ma'am, thank you for this information. I need to alert Rouseff Security. I'll do my best from both the prosecutor's office and Rouseff Industries to contain the problem. Do you think the governor will need to call out the military?"

"She can't push too hard against President Vanderholm. I think he might deny her requests for troops. We have heard rumors that he calls this city *a hotbed of rebellion that needs to be crushed.*"

I sighed, "I thought we were through with that, but...well...I will say that I went to university with Hab Vanderholm." I looked the woman in the eye. I thought she might be trustworthy. I wondered about her sources of information. I wondered if she refused to pay her husband's fines to protect him or the people of our city. I remembered her work in the soup kitchens and thought she'd protect our people first. As I walked back to the prosecutor's office her words sunk home. If Vanderholm was behind the attacks and supplying automatic weapons, we would need to research the possibility of charging him with treason.

I brought my maps with me to my meeting with Mrs. Governor. She met me in her husband's office. I noted that she looked a great deal like her husband. Somehow, her appearance comforted me. She seemed competent and professional.

Mrs. Mayor had briefed her on my proposal, so she got right down to business. "Can we legally decide we can put the road wherever we want it?"

"The Rouseff legal department has researched that question. Yes, the road can be built on provincial land. The province would own that stretch of road. My plan is for Rouseff Properties to build the actual road. We can ask the central government to pay us for it, or we can charge a toll…here for north bound traffic…and here for southbound traffic." I spread my maps out on the governor's ebony desk and showed her the proposed roads. "We would also charge tolls here and here for people to use our interchanges."

"These tolls, who would keep the money?"

"If Rouseff finances the road, we would need some of the toll to pay us for our expenses. Since the road is being built on publicly owned land, some of the toll should go toward paying the public for the use of their land in this case it would go into the provincial treasury."

She pursed her lips and said sarcastically, "That would be a shock to actually have some money flowing in."

"You do receive tax revenue." I said puzzled.

She looked down her nose at me. "Only from those too stupid to know that we have no method of enforcing the payment of taxes."

I sat back in my chair stunned, not only at being called stupid, but over the idea that many people were not paying taxes. "We do have a method for enforcing the payment of taxes. I'll tell the prosecutor's office to look into it. Can your office get me a list of people who are behind on their taxes?" I scratched my nose. "Okay, we might then have some tax money to pay for this road."

"How do you intend to get tax money out of people like Papadakos and Jouyet?" Mrs. Governor almost sneered as she gave me a pitying look.

I tried not to squirm. "Well at least Jouyet's wife will probably pay his taxes and his fines."

The woman snorted. "Brainless suckerfish."

I felt shocked almost to tears. Some men who thought that they were above the law were in very serious trouble with their wives. Part of me agreed wholeheartedly, but I wanted to stay out of their domestic relationships.

I explained, "I am an officer of the court. I must report your allegations of tax evasion to my office."

The woman gave me one of those looks that make men feel like worms.

I ran my hands over my face and tried to explain. I told her about the hungry. I told her about our morgue that was always full. I told her about my long train trips north to get fish. I told her how heavy the fish were and how quickly the people ate them. "This has been going on for years. Most people work, but they get paid too little, and it is in our currency, which is next to worthless. Even my wife cannot always find food in the market, because farmers cannot afford to bring food to market. We will never get out of this mess unless goods and services start flowing. Our government agencies need to start paying their employees every month."

"As long as men, like my husband, are in control of this country things will never get better. We call Vanderholm a president now, but he is still the same crook he has always been."

I sighed. "Perhaps in our next election, we will get someone better."

"If, our next election happens; if, the ballots are counted; if, Vanderholm doesn't find some way to cheat."

I rubbed my hands over my face and wondered if her estimation could be right.

She returned to our former topic. "So you think that Rouseff will finance the building of this road."

I nodded.

Mrs. Governor placed both hands flat down on her desk in a gesture of agreement. "Send your attorneys to me. We will make up the contracts so that the land is leased from the people of the province. You can build your road where you want it to go."

We smiled happily at each other.

Chapter 7 Tossley

I arrived for work at Rouseff Industries at six in the morning to find our chief of security waiting for me outside my office. He looked grim. I nodded to him. "Come into my office." I motioned for the man to sit and took my seat. He remained standing. I asked, "Well?"

"Sir, we lost a trolley last night, and the driver is in the hospital."

I nodded for him to continue.

"The incident occurred shortly before ten just before the stop at Third and Florence. Someone opened fire on the trolley. They killed two of Jouyet's employees and wounded several other people including our driver. They finally shot out the engine on the trolley. Our people heard the shots and assumed a position to cover the trolley as it escaped the range of fire, but the assailants had gone by that time."

I sighed and ran my hands over my face. "What on earth do these people think they are doing?"

"They are running protection rackets. They are harassing businesses in the area. Most of Jouyet's employees live in that area. He has troops on the street. They responded to the shooting after we got there and helped move their people to the hospital." The supervisor paused. "Oh…and…one more thing, they are using automatic weapons."

I felt like a bucket of ice water had been dumped over me. "Thank you. Can you meet with your staff later in the day and give me any recommendations for further action we can take?"

"We are outgunned. It would help if we had automatic weapons too."

My gut wanted to immediately shout, "No!" Instead I sighed, "Mr. Rouseff has always made it a point that our security will be up to date with the best equipment. I will call him later today and discuss this. I also need to research if it is legal for our security to own such weapons. The constitution restricts their use in this country."

"Thank you sir."

I spent most of my week in my Rouseff office debating armament for our security. I didn't want to escalate the street war, especially since things had been quiet for several days. Mr. Rouseff wanted his people to have the best equipment possible. He promised to look into the purchase of some AK-47's.

I sighed and ignored the feeling in my gut. I told Rouseff, "Thank you for taking responsibility for this purchase. As a prosecutor, I cannot in good conscience arm our security with such weapons. I have researched the question. Professor Ingleman advised me that it is acceptable for Rouseff Security to own them as long as we use them only for defense." I did not mention to anybody that he had agreed with my earlier assessment that arming gangs to assault citizens constituted treason.

"Is the prosecutor's office making any progress?"

"Yes, the other prosecutors stop by here and keep me up to date. Actually they are coordinating much of the investigation out of here because we think LaBarge may be a spy for Vanderholm."

Rouseff grunted, and we ended the call.

I stopped sleeping. As the head of Rouseff Industries, I had my hands full working on development for our projects, advising our legal team and preparing to fight a war in the city. I think the threat of more shooting kept me in a constant state of fear.

So far, the attacks had occurred in the evening. On Sunday afternoon, I got a call at home from my chief of security. "Sir, there has been an attack on the mall."

I sat down on the floor while visions of hundreds of dead citizens flashed through my mind. "How bad?"

"Bad enough. Could have been worse. They came in from the east, which we were not prepared for, but that area is not as crowded. Actually, I spotted them from my office, which could have been their objective. I alerted our men on the ground and the door guards. The perpetrators opened fire on the guards at the door, but we had them covered. Our men followed our planned defensive procedure. One guard took a hit in the lower leg. The other is fine. Our snipers on the roof managed to take out about a dozen of their men before the rest of them ran."

I held my head. "You got about a dozen, and there were more. How many do you think participated in the attack?"

"I counted forty-five. There must have been fifty. They were dressed like shoppers, but nobody goes shopping in a group that size. We don't get much activity on that side of the mall so when I saw that many men I knew they were up to no good."

"Were they using automatic weapons?"

"Yes sir. They did some cosmetic damage to that side of the building. The poor door guards had concrete chips raining down on them from above, but their reinforced shelters protected them adequately."

"Thank you for your report. Is there anything that you need from me?"

We discussed pulling more security into the city. I noticed my stomach churning as I calmly discussed armed warfare on the streets of my city. We ended the call.

Jacob found me still sitting on the floor a half-hour later. I returned to my household activities, but still felt numb with shock.

On Thursday morning Mr. A. Supervisor surprised me by calling me at Rouseff Industries. "Jake, is that guard of yours still missing?"

"Yeah."

"I have someone here who can help you find him."

"Great. I'll round up a couple of my people and be right over."

The people in charge of looking for our lost employee were at their desks. I rousted them out, and we walked over to the prosecutor's office. When I arrived, the place was uncharacteristically chaotic. Everyone ignored the cases waiting in the holding room while they stopped work to look at the biggest, grossest, bag of slimy drool I'd ever seen. The beast appeared to be mostly folds of sagging skin. It stood with its head down uninterested in us. It seemed to be focused entirely on creating a lake of drool on the floor near the supervisor's office.

Mr. Supervisor introduced his guest to my staff and me. "This is Mr. P'RZ. He specializes in tracking lost people."

The handler of the beast nodded.

LaBarge continued. "He has agreed to see if his dog can find your missing trolley guard."

"He'll find him." I thought Mr. P'RZ looked almost as bored as his dog. I expected to see him drool at any moment.

I didn't know how to proceed. "Um…right. We know the man is not here. What do we need to do to get started?"

The handler gave us a few instructions. We decided to go to Mr. Tossley's apartment first. We had a large party for this event. I came along with the

Rouseff security. Mr. A. Supervisor came with Mr. Perez. A paralegal and a clerk joined the parade followed by a couple of interns.

Tossley's apartment was located on Perigee St. just off of first. Our security had already searched it when we first missed him. They had a key and let us inside. We stood and watched as Mr. P'RZ let his dog sniff around in the bedroom.

Finally Mr. P'RZ and his dog indicated that they were ready for the next step. "Now where was your missing man last seen?"

"At his trolley stop."

We started walking toward the trolley stop to begin the search. We reached second and started walking toward the stop. The drooling dog sniffed at the ground. He turned his head back and forth. About a half-block from the trolley stop, that bag of slobber let out a long, piercing howl that almost caused me to pee my pants. God! That was a frightening sound! It came straight out of a horror movie.

The dog strained at his leash off to the right between two buildings. We followed. The narrow passageway smelled foul. The beast let out another howl. The smell as we reached an open area between porches became overpowering. Being a very smart man, I volunteered to call the police. I ran to the nearest shop, a furniture repair and used the phone to call the chief of police and the coroner's office. I remained on the street to direct the police and the coroner to the scene. I became aware of the stench from the alley drifting onto the sidewalk to mingle with the smells of cooking cabbage, urine, and cooking spices that permeated the air. I started to sweat. Mr. Assassin Supervisor looked grim when he came out of the alley.

I choked out, "What do you think?"

"Murdered." His cold tone left no doubt. I could add prosecuting a murder case to my workload.

I knew it was time to move on arresting the policemen hired by Papadakos, Vanderholm, and Fortenac for impersonating an officer and false arrest. I wondered how many others we would end up charging with treason. Who would we charge for this murder once we netted in the whole load of rotten fish, who called themselves policemen? I stayed at the scene long enough to instruct the Rouseff employees to cooperate with the police and the coroner. I needed to get back to my office and brief our security chief.

I was so tired by the time I headed back to my office that I could barely walk. I caught a trolley and rode the three blocks that I would normally walk faster. From my office, I called Christian at the prosecutor's office.

I explained. "I stayed at the scene long enough for our men to determine that it was Tossley or at least his name was on the uniform. Mr. Supervisor was certain it was murder."

"I guess he'd know."

I chuckled at the dark humor despite feeling nauseated. "Lets move on the arrests. I think we can manage if we pull in a couple officers from Mercid. My men can protect the arresting officers and assist with locating offenders."

"I wonder how much of our regular police force we will have to arrest?"

"Don't even mention that. I suspect that we'll need to at least question the Chief of Police. I'll clean up my desk here and be over there tomorrow afternoon." I don't know why I didn't say this afternoon. I didn't. I suddenly decided that I wanted to go home.

I made certain that my secretary understood that the man with his dog was to be rewarded. "I should also do something for LaBarge for finding the man and his dog. See if we have contact information for Mr. Tossley's family. I need to go home. Can you start the process for providing a proper burial and Mass for the man? He died while working for us." I called Rouseff to tell him about losing an employee. He agreed that we should provide for a proper burial. By the time I finished with the necessary phone calls and talked to our chief of security, my back had started to hurt. All I wanted to do was go home, go to bed, and get warm.

I couldn't find a trolley so I hobbled to the M'TK station. There were no trolley's running out to my house this time of day. My little trolley was sitting on a side-track so I told the stationmaster that I needed to use it. I intended to switch it from track to track myself. Two employees rushed out to help me step onto the trolley and switch tracks for me. Instead of powering my little trolley out to my station myself, one of the employees must drive Mr. Jaconovich out to his house. I appreciated the respect. I knew I really did not feel well enough to want to mess with switches or even powering the trolley. On the other hand, I was annoyed with the help thinking it infringed on my freedom. I decided I was grumpy.

I arrived home about noon to a quiet house. As soon as I didn't hear children's voices I became very quiet. I checked my room. Elizabeth was not in her cradle so I checked Jacob's room. Both Jacob and Elizabeth were in his crib. I reached down to pull the blanket over Elizabeth and noticed blood on her dress. I investigated and found her tummy was scratched raw and bleeding. I picked up my baby girl and left Jacob alone in his crib.

I went searching for the adults. I found Shirley's younger children asleep in their room. I finally found Shirley napping in her sitting room. I woke her up.

"Oh, Mr. Jaconovich! Oh! I must have drifted off. I'm that tired."

"Where is Davy?"

"He is supposed to be sleeping."

"He wasn't in his room. Where is Leah?"

"She went to lunch with some friends."

"I'll find Davy. Can you take care of this scratch on Elizabeth's tummy?"

"Oh my how did that happen?"

I replied, "Probably from Jacob dragging her over something." Elizabeth was awake and content to have her Papa holding her. She protested when I handed her over to Shirley. I went outside and walked around the outside of the house. I didn't see Davy in the yard. I looked again, searching for anything out of place. The rowboat was missing so I ran down to the edge of the lake. Davy sat in the rowboat about fifty-meters off shore.

"Young man, bring that boat back here! Right! Now!" I used my best Jake-means-business-voice. It carried across the lake.

"I lost the oars." I could see one oar floating between the rowboat and me. I looked this situation over. Davy leaned over the edge of the boat.

"You! Sit down on the middle seat of that boat and don't you dare move so much as an inch! You are in serious trouble young man!"

I am not a strong swimmer. I could still feel the fatigue from this morning sitting on my chest, and I had a dull ache in my back. I took off my shoes, shirt and pants and waded out into the cold water up to my chest.

The lake bottom felt slimy. Reeds and water plants tickled my legs. The boat drifted farther away from me. I took one more step forward. The lake bottom dropped away, and I sunk beneath the surface. I pushed myself to the surface, shook the water out of my eyes and looked for the rowboat.

I saw two rowboats. The first one held a frightened Davy. The second boat, much farther out, came toward us at a good clip. The older woman who lived half way around the lake pulled expertly on the oars and headed for Davy. I kicked myself closer into shore and watched to be certain my neighbor really intended to rescue the boy.

I went back to shore and pulled my pants on over my wet naked body. I shook so hard I could barely pull my clothes on.

My neighbor did rescue Davy. I waded out into the water to pull the boat in. I lifted Davy out of the boat and told him, "Go to your room son."

"I think he was trying to fish." The woman sounded sympathetic.

I sighed and shook my head. "Thank you a thousand times for rescuing him. I'm not a strong swimmer. I had no idea how I would manage to get into the boat after I got to him. How on earth did you know I needed help?"

"Oh, I was napping on the porch when I heard you yelling. I could hear you clear enough. I thought I could either rescue the kid or at least get a look at Mr. Jaconovich without his clothes on."

"I suspect that I look about like other men without their clothes."

She sat in her boat and scanned me head to toes. Then she smiled. "That's worth a row across the lake."

I felt too cold to blush. "Thank you for rescuing Davy. I need to get dry and make some household rules." I didn't say anything about my urge to vomit.

I caught up to Davy and carried him back to the house. Fatigue drained my body making my muscles ache while I climbed the small hill from the lake to the house. Chilled and shivering, I gave Davy to his aunt and went to take a hot shower. I stood in the shower until we ran out of hot water. When I went back downstairs, Jacob was up. Shirley's children were up but confined to their rooms. I took Jacob and Elizabeth and went to my study to read them a story. I fell asleep on my sofa with Elizabeth in my arms. I faintly remember her wiggling off of the sofa. She and Jacob seemed to be playing some game on the floor. I could hear them laughing as they played, occasionally bumping the sofa.

After about a half hour, Mrs. Shirley awakened me. "Mr. Jake, please come. We need your help."

"Huh? What?"

"It's Mrs. Jake. Um…she needs your help." I could not imagine what Leah would be doing that needed my help. I went out to the sitting room. My back started nagging at me again.

A woman I had seen before, but didn't really know stood near the front door. "Mr. Jaconovich, this was not Leah's fault. Really it wasn't. She thought she was drinking ginger ale and grenadine the same as me and Leah's drink looked the same as mine. Some of the others were drinking champagne. After Leah said she felt funny, I thought she seemed a little drunk so I tasted her drink. It was champagne and grenadine. This really wasn't her fault."

I grunted in too much pain with my back to say much of anything.

I found Leah passed-out in the front seat of her friend's car. I wondered if I could lift her with the pain in my back. I noticed a Miki coming up the road and hoped one of Leah's friends brought her car home.

Leah's friend continued to beg. "Please don't be mad at her. She didn't know what was in the drink."

I felt my face scowling. "I'm not mad at her, but I am furious with anyone who would do this to her. She...um...she...she's a little shy and wasn't raised to have much self-confidence. This type of betrayal will hurt her deeply." I sighed and stroked Leah's cheek hoping she would wake up. She didn't. I wrapped her skirt around her legs and prepared to pick her up. My back screamed at me. I wasn't certain I could lift her. The Miki pulled up.

Lena, my friend from college, got out of the Miki. She started explaining the minute she got out of the car. "Jake, oh I'm glad you are here. This wasn't Leah's fault. They planned to get her drunk so she'd pass out, and they could cut her hair."

I knew I was more than angry.

I snapped at Lena. "What were you doing at a party like that?"

Lena's eyes filled with tears. "I didn't know some of the women. We haven't been back in the city long. Nikoli started working on his doctorate this term. I came with Susan."

I looked at the other woman assuming she was Susan.

She nodded and tried to explain. "I don't usually go to parties if Julie Jouyet will be there. I didn't know this would include her set. We were supposed to be having lunch and discussing a school lunch program so the poorer school children will get one good meal a day." Susan twisted a bracelet around and around on her wrist.

Lena snorted. "They never did get around to discussing school lunches. The big entertainment seemed to be the idea of cutting Leah's hair."

I grunted over the cruelty of some people. "Thank you, both of you, for taking care of her. She will be crushed over this. She would have been frantic to have her hair cut off."

I decided that I better get on with carrying Leah into the house. She refused to wake up. I managed to pick her up. For a minute, I thought my knees would buckle. As Lena and Susan prepared to leave in Susan's car, I concentrated on putting one foot in front of the other. My back screamed at me, but my muscles seemed to be working.

I intended to drop Leah on a sofa. I looked around the sitting room to see Mrs. Shirley and all the children staring at us. I decided to take Leah to our room. I got halfway up the stairs before I started sweating profusely and waves of nausea washed over me. Some part of my mind remembered that I carried Leah upstairs fairly frequently without thinking about it. I remembered being able to carry seventy-five kilos of fish with not much more problem. I realized, something was terribly wrong with me. I made it to our room, kicked the door closed behind us, dropped Leah on the bed and dropped down beside her. I managed to lean over the side of the bed and pull a wastebasket toward me before I vomited. I stayed on the bed beside Leah and tried to breathe and relax. Another pain shot through my back, and I vomited again. I heard a tap at the door.

"Mr. Jaconovich, would you like me to help?"

"Come in." I heaved again into the wastebasket.

Shirley stopped inside the door and looked at us. "What is it? I thought she was…"

"No, my back. It's been getting worse all day."

"Is this why you came home early?" She came to my bedside and stood over me.

"Yeah." I could barely get the word out.

Shirley pulled my shirt out of my pants and started touching parts of my back.

"Does it hurt here?"

"It hurts everywhere."

"What about here. Is this worse?"

"No."

"What about…"

"Ow." I leaned over the side of the bed and heaved into the wastebasket.

"Mr. Jaconovich, I think you may have a kidney stone. You need to go to the hospital. I'm going to call your parents to stay with the children and take you to the hospital myself."

"I'm cold." Now that someone was taking charge I felt like I could complain.

"I'll cover you with this blanket, but you'll feel chilled until this is over." Shirley went away. I wanted to reach out and touch Leah for comfort, but I hurt too much. I remembered how much I hate pain. I heaved into the wastebasket. I wanted to stop the heaving because it made the back hurt more.

I stayed on the bed suffering. The heaving did stop. I discovered if I stayed very, very still, I would not heave. Moving so much as a toe would cause me to barf again.

I thought about Leah's hair. I wanted to cry over the cruelty of some women. I suffered with pain in my back and in my heart. I knew Leah was going to be deeply upset over the behavior of her friends. I got a little angry with Leah for having such friends. Well, Susan seemed okay. Lena seemed to think Susan was okay. I hurt.

Finally, I heard heavy footsteps on the stairs. I smiled. I knew those footsteps. I recognized the lighter step. My bedroom door burst open. Mama and Papa entered the room. I cried with relief.

"Take it easy son. We are going to get you into the hospital. Should we call an ambulance?"

Mama didn't say anything more than "Jake." The pain eased. Mama touched my back.

I felt much better. I managed to turn my head without vomiting.

"I'm a little better now. Let's see if I can move without vomiting." I rolled onto the side that didn't hurt so much. I didn't vomit. "Yeah, I still hurt like hell, but I think I can sit up." I did sit up. "Yeah, it is much better. If I can stand and walk, we can take the car to the hospital."

Mama stroked my forehead. Mama's touch must be healing.

I smiled at Mama and eased myself to my feet. I started sweating and shaking with chills at the same time. Mama put her arm around me. Papa supported me from the other side. Leah was still passed-out on the bed.

Slowly, one step at a time I made it down the stairs. I was aware that Papa took about half of my weight with each step. It helped.

Papa took charge of our situation. "Mama, I'll take Jake to the hospital. You stay here and help Mrs. Shirley. I'll come back as soon as he is settled. We will decide then what is best to be done."

Mrs. Shirley followed us out to the car. "I heated this bag of rice in the oven. Keep it on that kidney and wrap up in this blanket. I warmed it in the oven too. You better turn the heat on in the car."

I concentrated on breathing until I got to the hospital. Papa drove to the emergency entrance. Medics came out.

"We think he has a kidney stone. He's in bad shape."

"Yes, Mr. Jaconovich."

They brought a gurney around to my side of the car. Papa stood there, helping me transfer from the car to the gurney. The movement caused me to start vomiting again. Once I was inside, they wrapped me heated blankets and talked about shock. Finally, someone gave me a shot that put me to sleep.

I woke up when Mama and Papa came into my room. Seeing them eased some of the pain in my heart. "How is Leah?"

"She's awake and very upset. How are you?"

"Ow…I am still in pain. Can't they do anything about this?"

"They are giving you something to try to dissolve the stone. They treated you for shock. You may have some rough hours ahead of you yet."

I snorted which hurt. "I hate pain. I've never had anything like this before."

"You've been lucky, very lucky for someone who grew up in M'TK." I held Papa's hand. Mama sat on the other side of me and stroked my forehead.

"Is everything okay at home? Are the children okay? Are they upset?"

Papa reassured me. "Jacob and Elizabeth are fine. Mama has been holding them and singing and reading stories."

"What a hellish day. When I first came home from work, I discovered Davy had taken the rowboat out. He lost both oars. He had the net out, and it caught on the bottom. I thought I'd have to swim out to get him but a neighbor came in her boat." I went on to list all my woes of the day. I told about finding Tossley's body. "Why did everything hit today?"

"Well, tomorrow will probably be better. No use spreading troubles out and ruining more than one day."

I smiled at Papa's estimation of the situation.

He continued. "One problem is that you have too many children for the number of adults."

"Seven children are not so many. Many families have more than that." I argued.

"Your children are all too young for school. Usually in a large family the older children help with chores and watching the younger children. You have seven babies in that house. You need help. I phoned The Cove and talked to Uncle John. Cousin Margaret has agreed to come down. She will be here in the morning."

Mama looked a little dreamy and sad as she remembered the past. "I will be happy to see her. She reminds me of my mama's sister, her grandmother. She was so sweet to me when I first went to live in The Cove." Mama returned her attention to the present. "We told her not to worry about bringing all her things. I will take her shopping for what she needs."

Papa and I chuckled over Mama's eagerness to take Margaret shopping.

"Now Mama, Margaret is here to help with the children, while Jake is sick."

I groaned, "I admit that right now, I am thankful for all the help we can get." I hoped that when Margaret arrived, Leah could get away to come stay with me.

The pain started growing worse again, and I started shaking with the chill. A nurse came in and gave me another shot. I woke up in the middle of the night. I was alone. I tried to move and discovered my back still hurt. Another nurse came in with another shot.

Chapter 8 New Case

When I woke up in the morning, my first thought centered on the idea that Leah would be in early. Leah did not arrive when I expected her. I did get a visitor. He surprised me so I called him by name. "Mr. LaBarge!"

He looked stunned. I decided the drugs had clouded my judgment.

"You know my name."

I winced and tried to grin. "Well, yeah, when it became obvious that you were not an attorney, we asked around on the street."

"Do you know why I am here?" His tone grew wary and cold.

"We don't want to know." I paused and considered my next words. "Well, we wanted to be certain that if we needed to file charges against a high level person, you wouldn't interfere."

My mind started working better. "By the way, I am extremely thankful for your help in finding Tossley's body."

His tone sent a chill through me greater than the pain had caused. "A representative from Rouseff's office rewarded both of us well."

"Good. Knowing what happened to Tossley may help us to keep our other guards safe. Rouseff tries to be fair."

LaBarge stared at the wall. "He may be the only one."

"No there are others."

"Jake, I need to leave the country." LaBarge looked at me briefly then looked away. "These arrests--I should not be in this job--you could arrest me anytime."

I tried to smile. "We couldn't get a conviction. Someone appointed you. We knew from the beginning that you had no idea that you were breaking the law."

"You know who I am."

"We've heard rumors. We have no evidence linking you to anything, and we can't get a conviction based on rumors."

"You could with the right judge." LaBarge sat down in the chair beside my bed.

"I don't use those judges and would file charges against them if I thought I could get a conviction. Actually, we arrested, fined, and fired dozens of judges a few years ago."

LaBarge chuckled then sobered. He fingered his lower lip. "I cannot find my current...um...client. The country is so disorganized that I may never find him. Also, I...my instructions included keeping your office from causing trouble." LaBarge leaned back in his chair. "I've failed to carry out my mission on both counts. I have no idea how you managed to interfere with the president's plans for this city, but you did. I never saw any of you look like you were working, and I had no idea the people you planned to arrest worked for Vanderholm. Do you have any idea what that means for a man like me?"

I shook my head.

"It means I will be the next mark. I don't think Vanderholm knows I've failed in everything just yet. He is getting impatient. He is very angry over the arrest of the private army he has tried to move into the city. I have a few days to get out of the country."

"Why are you telling me this?"

"I will need help. You could have arrested me but you have not. You are honest. That is a curious quality. My contacts tell me that you can put me in contact with the M'TK Sewer Rat, and he will help."

I sighed and my side hurt. I wondered about the M'TK Sewer Rat reference. Did he know? The manner in which his cold eyes met mine made me suspect that he had done his research on the street. I decided to ignore the reference. "I'm not certain how I can help you. What do you need specifically?"

"I'll need someone to cover for me for a few days. I might need papers. I could get them in the capital, but Vanderholm would know immediately. I need confidential transportation out of the country."

I nodded. I started to sweat with pain. "I can help with these things. I can get you a train pass that will not be in any records." For some reason, I didn't like for LaBarge to know that the M'TK Sewer Rat title belonged to me. "But, as you say, I am an honest man." I paused and looked out the window of my room. "I am an honest man. I personally know nothing about you that would cause me to file charges against you. On the other hand, the fact that you need to leave the country secretly presents a problem for me. There is one way, that is legal and will get you all the help you need."

LaBarge leaned forward in his chair.

I continued. "I am legally compelled to protect an informant. If you can give me leads that will help me charge Vanderholm, I will be required by the full extent of the law to do everything within my power to get you to someplace safe. I have the resources to do everything you need. Vanderholm, well nobody, will know where you have gone."

LaBarge scowled. "You want me to betray Vanderholm?"

"I want you to tell me the truth about a man who by your own words may seek to have you killed. He appointed you to the position of supervisor for our office. That was against the law. I can charge him for that. It is a minor crime. I want the bigger crimes."

I watched LaBarge thinking and debating then urged, "Vanderholm would betray you in a second. I want that kind of dishonor out of our government."

"If I give you what you want, what do I get?" LaBarge seemed to be looking inward.

"Papers, secret transportation, cash. Is there anything else you want?"

"Yeah. Darlene."

"What?" I could never have expected this answer. "That would be her choice."

"She will come with me." He sounded confident. I agreed with his opinion.

"Right. Papers and transportation for Darlene also." I thought for a few minutes. "Do you intend to marry her?"

LaBarge looked shocked.

"She has worked as a clerk in the prosecutor's office for years. She is a respectable woman. I will not be party to seeing her dishonored and discarded."

LaBarge snorted. "I will marry her, if she consents."

I smiled. "This may make things much easier."

"How much longer are you going to be in this bed?"

"Until I pee out some rocks."

"Ouch."

"This will make a good cover for our activities. You need to propose to Darlene. Um…don't do this at the office. Um…she won't be able to keep anything secret. I will find you a judge to marry you or a priest if you prefer. You can get married and leave immediately. I will contact someone to do your papers. Where do you want to go?"

"I figure a man can get lost in the Caribbean."

"Hm, that's doable."

LaBarge's eyes widened, and his nose flared. I'd surprised him.

I continued, "What I want from you is a list of names, dates, and activities for anything you know that Vanderholm has done that might be illegal. I want any information you can give me related to this nastiness in this city."

"I don't know about much other than murder."

The pain consumed me to the point I was having trouble drawing in a breath. I wheezed out my words. "Murder is always a good charge. I can work with that."

"Do you want something on Papadakos too?"

A small part of my brain that wasn't concentrating on the pain rejoiced. "Yes. It is absolutely essential that our leadership is held accountable for the crimes they commit." I started sweating harder as I tried to make this man understand justice. "We process case after case of people who are drunk and disorderly or steal food because they are starving. Meanwhile we have a group of privileged people who commit embezzlement, extortion and murder in order to gain power or worse gain wealth. Have you ever been inside one of their homes?"

He shook his head.

"I have. I have visited friends' homes in the south. The vulgarity of the way they display their possessions is nauseating. I know that some of that wealth is stolen from honest business people here in this city."

He raised one eyebrow. "You are angry."

I chuckled which hurt. "I would force the very wealthy to live in somewhat tasteful surroundings by fining them the gold they have in their doorknobs."

LaBarge laughed--a chilling sound. "I will make your list." He stood to leave.

"I will make some phone calls."

After LaBarge left, I tried to reach my phone. I hurt too much. I called the nurse to come hand me my phone. She wanted to give me a shot. I told her I needed to do some work.

First, I called Jeffrey Farley at the office. He answered, "Jake how are you?"

I wheezed, "I am miserable. I hurt something awful, and they tell me I am going to have to pee out some rocks. I have also turned up a great case."

Jeffrey sounded pained. "Ooh, ouch. We are working on the arrests of the police. We charged our chief of police with accessory to murder. The arrests are going much smoother than we thought. One of our police officers, Detective Sorros, recommended we move between five and seven o'clock this morning. We've caught our offenders with their pants off."

"Good. Those arrests may cover for our bigger case. Somebody decided to give me information. I need papers for them to leave the country. This will be covered under protecting an informant. Can you make me up papers for a married couple to…um…I don't know…I've never done this before. Um…they want to go to the Caribbean."

"I know what to do. I know what they need. Will they be leaving the country by air or train?"

"I don't know. I worry about them getting caught in an airport. I can hide their passage on the train. Um, if we had the money, they could travel by private boat." I wondered about sending them on the M'NO. I thought about M'TGs sleek speedboat. "Right now, I am leaning toward sending them on a private boat but then, I am full of medication, and my mind feels like cotton."

"Jake if you can get them out of the country by private boat, that would make the job much easier."

"Fine, I can get them easily by boat to either of our neighbors to the south or the north."

"Send them north."

"Leah is here. I have to go."

I held my hand out to Leah.

She started to cry. "Are you very angry with me?"

"No. Susan explained that you didn't know your drink was different from hers. Lena learned that Julie Jouyet planned the episode to play a trick on you."

"I'm so ashamed of myself."

"Why? Because you couldn't tell there was alcohol in your drink?"

"Because my children saw me passed-out drunk. Jake, I swore to myself a hundred times at least, that my children would never see me drunk."

"Come here. I can't move so you are going to have to sit on the bed and cuddle up to me." Leah did sit on my bed. Her weight caused the bed to shift. The movement hurt so I felt like vomiting again. I wrapped my arms around her and pulled her down beside me. I felt better holding her. "Our children are tiny. They saw their Papa carrying their Mama upstairs. Shirley told them it was our naptime. How are they taking having me gone?"

"All the children are upset. Papa talked to Shirley and learned that she does have family in the east. Papa has told her that she has too many young children to give them all the love they need. He called Shirley's papa and talked to him about the children needing more family. I think he plans to put her on the train tonight. Davy seems to be particularly upset about leaving."

"Did you hear what Davy did yesterday?" She shook her head. I told her about him taking the boat out. "He may be feeling guilty for being disobedient yesterday. He knows the rule about the lake."

"It sounds like he was trying to be helpful by fishing."

"He needs to be a baby longer. Perhaps Papa is right those children will be better off surrounded by a big family to take care of them. I think I will miss them. Who is with the children now?"

"Your Mama and Papa came early this morning with Cousin Margaret. She took the night train down. Everybody sends their love."

"Ah, that is good. I worry about Jacob and Elizabeth missing their papa, and I worry about Jacob dragging his sister around with him everywhere. Did you see the scrape on her tummy?"

"Yes, it looks worse than it is, I think. They are always happy together. They have started something new. First, they look at each other, then one of them will make a face, and they both laugh themselves silly. It took me forever to get them fed this morning because they were both being so silly."

Leah left to go get some lunch. I called my house and talked to Papa. He brought me up to date. "I talked to Shirley's papa last night. He wants her to bring the babies and come home. He assured me that they have room and enough people to take care of them."

"I'll miss the children, but after Davy took the boat out yesterday, I realize they need more adults to take care of them." I stopped talking in order to gasp for breath a couple times before I continued, "I need to pay Shirley for the past week and a half. She should have some severance pay and a bonus for taking care of me while I was sick. Can you get three-hundred dollars in US currency out of my safe and give it to her?"

"I'll take care of it son."

"While I am laying all my work woes on you, I have an informant I need to keep safe. He wants to go to the Caribbean. I wondered if someone from Norville could take him. Don't let him near the island where I keep my other prisoner. If someone could take the informant to a village somewhere north of our border it would help."

"Jake, you have your hands full don't you."

"Yeah, that is what makes being sick so annoying other than this damn pain."

"Have you passed any rocks yet?"

"No, they will do more tests this afternoon." I said goodbye to Papa and felt better knowing he would oversee some of my business.

Leah came back from lunch just before an orderly wheeled me into x-ray again. When I got back, I found her talking on the phone. She got off of the phone and fussed over me, but within a minute she started to cry.

"What is it baby?"

"I talked to Susan and thanked her for taking care of me. I assured her that I did not intend to drink. She said she knew that and told me that some of the other women had laughed about deliberately getting me drunk so I would pass out, and they could cut off my hair." Leah broke down and sobbed. I pulled her down beside me on the bed.

"Leah, I think those women are so jealous of you that they have knots in their knickers. Remember some of them are married to men who have been arrested and fined. In many cases I am the man who charges against them." This didn't seem to placate Leah. "I'm telling you the truth. You are an exceptionally beautiful woman, and you dress with style and taste. You have been to university. My love, I've met some of them. They are vulgar and ignorant and just plain mean."

She sobbed. "I thought I was going to a lunch to discuss providing lunches for the poor students in school. I didn't know there was anything wrong with that group."

"Susan and Lena didn't realize anything was wrong until you said you didn't feel well." I held Leah close and stroked her hair. I suspected part of her tendency to cry was a physical reaction to being drunk the day before, and because she was worried about me.

I had another concern. "My love, most of the time I don't do much in the prosecutor's office. I never worry about the petty criminals taking their anger out on my family. Sometimes we stumble across a big case. I've prosecuted some of the elite families. I most certainly will prosecute them in the future. I worry about the safety of my family, if any of them try to get back at me for prosecuting their families. Also, Fortenac and Papadakos seem to be on a vendetta against Rouseff, so from now on, I want you to clear social engagements with Rouseff security. Mrs. Rouseff occasionally had bodyguards with her. You may need to have a body guard."

"Jake! Do you think yesterday was that serious?"

"Yes. Yes, I do. I think we may have been lucky that this assault was so minor." The drugs were wearing off again, and the pain made if hard for me to breathe, but I needed to make Leah understand the danger. "Some of those people are going to have even more reason to try to hurt my family or me. One of our trolley guards was murdered. We've resisted attacks on a trolley and on the mall. As Mr. Rouseff's representative in the north, I will not let that pass. I cannot let it pass as a prosecutor. Our whole office is aware of Tossley's murder. We have a good idea of who did it, and who ordered the killing. We've been making arrests."

I held Leah and rubbed her back while we talked about who was safe to be friends with. I suggested she could visit Allison and see her new baby. "I trust Lena, too." I chuckled. "If you are interested in the idea of a lunch program for school children, you can talk to Mrs. Mayor and Mrs. Provincial

Governor."

Leah laughed when I told her about them refusing to pay their husbands fines. She sounded vehement. "Good! Their husbands commit crimes. They didn't take care of their wives. Those women should leave the bastards to rot in jail and make a new life for themselves."

I chuckled. "Remember Leah, I will always do my best to take care of you. I try to be an honest man." This statement earned me some nice kisses. Kissing my lovely wife aroused some tender parts, which set off the kidney pain again. I broke out in a sweat and moaned. Leah called the nurse.

In the evening, the doctor came in. We talked about my options. He recommended that I have surgery. "We've played with this thing long enough. Sometimes these things dissolve. Sometimes they move out of the way again. Your x-ray looks like you have a whole cluster of stones in one area. I want to go in and clean them all out so you can start getting better by ten tomorrow morning."

"Getting better sounds good to me."

Late in the day, Mr. Farley came in and told me about Darlene's engagement and how excited she was.

I filled him in on the details of what the couple would need.

He was a step ahead of me. "Something about this engagement when you needed papers told me that they might be the couple." We discussed the details of the papers and money.

I refused to tell him much about their transportation. "All I will say now is that they can travel on my train pass. That cannot be traced." I moaned when I tried to take a deep breath.

"Get well Jake. I can handle most of this."

My parents stopped by on their way home. They had put Shirley on the train. Papa assured me they had two compartments. He had given her the money I requested. They'd fed the children in the late afternoon and sent some cake for their dessert on the train. Mama got tears in her eyes so papa stopped talking about sending the children away. I was thankful. I wanted to cry too. I changed the subject. "How is Margaret doing?"

Papa assured me. "She is excited to be here."

Mama sounded happy to have one of her family close by. "She's angry with one of the M'TG boys. He's been courting her for years but hasn't spoken to her papa. She tells me she has given up on him, so as soon as you get out of here, I will take her shopping to cheer her up."

Mama and Papa brought with them a wonderful gift. The children had drawn pictures for me. Davy made an anatomically correct drawing of me preparing to swim out and get him. Jacob drew a picture of our whole family. He made Elizabeth as big as Leah and myself. Elizabeth's picture was a composition of cake crumbs, drool, and crayon. When I got home, I framed it along with Jacob's pictures and hung them in my study.

I went into surgery early in the morning and returned to my room about eleven. Leah was waiting for me. I noticed that my room had filled with a great many cards, flowers and balloons. I slept most of the day.

Once, I forced myself awake when I heard a familiar voice. Mr. Rouseff had come to see me. "Sir, if you and Papa could be seen about town, it might settle a few rumors."

"Go back to sleep Jake."

I forced myself awake again when I heard Mr. LaBarge's voice. He and Darlene brought me flowers. I smiled at them. I also noticed that one of Rouseff's men stood in the corner of my room. Darlene showed me her ring. It looked impressive. "Congratulations sir, I'd like to help you with your wedding trip."

"Thank you Jake. I'll give you a few days to recover before I demand you get back to work."

"I expect to be out of here tomorrow. I can work from home."

They left with Darlene clinging to him and looking besotted. I wondered about the relationship. I wondered about Darlene's judgment in men. I decided it wasn't any worse than Julie Jouyet's. I remembered Mrs. Mayor and Mrs. Governor and chuckled.

Leah came the next morning to take me home. She seemed to have recovered from her ordeal. She chatted and gave me the family news as she instructed the hospital volunteers and the Rouseff guard to package up my many gifts and cards. This had grown to an impressive number over the past three days. The cards that came from the people of the city touched my heart and made me smile. I got a big card from people at the soup kitchens. They thanked me for bringing them fish and wished me well. I had cards and small bouquets from shopkeepers. Mrs. Mayor sent flowers. Mrs. Governor sent a box of tinned meats. The woman who rescued Davy sent me a rather flirtatious card. My priest visited twice. I was surprised at how each card and each flower or balloon seemed to make me a little stronger.

My pain grew less as I looked at the pictures drawn by school children. In among the cards was an invitation to a meeting from my professor and the constitutional committee. I wasn't sure if that invitation made me feel better since I was plotting to arrest their president.

The Rouseffs confessed that they used my illness and the death of an employee to take a vacation in the north. "My tiresome relatives are still weeping over my refusal to allow them to practice their vulgarity in front of me. I am insisting that the younger family members attend university starting next term. I expect you to teach them some refinement."

"Perhaps you can recommend that they take a few art courses." I smiled at Leah's delicate manner of approaching the subject.

Mr. Rouseff laughed. "My dear it will take more than a few art courses to teach that lot, good taste. Jake, I'm foisting one nephew off onto you. He needs to learn what it takes to run the business. However, I am making it clear to all of our staff that you are still in charge of the business."

"Yeah, thanks." My tone caused Rouseff to laugh some more.

"If he gets too surly just toss him around a bit." Rouseff sparred back.

"Hopefully, he can follow directions. We are prosecuting for tax evasion now. I need to spend more time in the prosecutor's office. Oh, by the way, you are all paid up on your taxes now."

Three days after I returned home from the hospital, Mr. LaBarge visited me in my home. He had what I wanted. I looked over his remarkably thorough lists. He marked those names he thought I could use for depositions with an asterisk. I felt my eyes growing round as I read the impressive list.

I tried to maintain a strictly professional tone. "Okay here's my plan. You and Darlene will meet me at the M'TK station at three in the afternoon tomorrow. We will ride to Mercid where Judge Stimson will marry you, after which I will put you in a compartment on the north-bound train. You will be riding on my pass so there will be no record of your trip in the ticket sales ledger. The Rouseff staff will know that you are my guests as my wedding gift to you. Ride to the end of the line. Nicki D'NO will meet you and put you on a boat. Finally, you will travel by private boat all the way to Barbados or the Cayman Islands whichever you prefer. I'll have your papers with me when we leave for Mercid."

"How could you do all this while you were in the hospital?"

"It was particularly easy from there. I was certain the phones were not bugged. Oh, I probably should have warned you that they are sometimes tapped in our office. Are people in the office aware of your engagement to Darlene?"

"Um…Darlene was a bit excited. I thought that our wedding trip would cover for leaving the country. Nobody, including Darlene, knows when we are getting married. When we are missed, I expect you to say that you witnessed our marriage."

I nodded.

"I hope that so far, nobody," he nodded to the list on my desk, "knows that I failed in my final mission. I've been given a deadline one week from now. I've assured Vanderholm that I know where the miscreant is holed up. I explained that locating him was my real reason for using the dogs. I've furnished Vanderholm with my mark's usual schedule, and my estimation of the best time to make the kill. The last three times and dates on that list are the information I gave Vanderholm. He will have someone in place to kill me after I kill the target."

"Ah, I suspect that you are correct. If the information on that list is accurate, I can promise you he cannot let you live. Tell me, do you think the man you are to kill knows any of this or does Vanderholm want him for other reasons?"

"He knows stuff I don't know. Vanderholm suspects that he leaked some of the information that got the emperor arrested."

I was surprised. "Is Vanderholm trying to avenge the emperor? I don't think of Hab as having that much honor of any sort."

"No. He just needs to get rid of everyone who knows anything. You are tired. I'll see you tomorrow at the M'TK station."

My guest left, and I called Jeffrey Farley at his home. "Can you bring those papers out to the house tonight?"

"Did you get enough information to make this worthwhile?"

"Yes. Bring the money too."

Mr. Farley brought the papers by. He was chortling over the nice job he had done. Each set of papers had two sets of photo identification. Jeffrey was especially proud of himself for snapping the pictures when nobody knew he was taking them.

I liked the pictures. Darlene's hair was a mess in one picture. Mr. LaBarge was wearing his jacket in one picture and shirt-sleeves in the other.

"I had to do a little touchup to erase the shoulder holster here."

"How on earth did you get these?"

"I have a special camera. I took a couple dozen of him before I got two that were clear and different enough they could have been taken years apart."

We were a little giddy over being rid of our assassin supervisor. We laughed and agreed that getting rid of Darlene was just plain sweet.

I asked about other office business, "What about the arrests of the police and gangs? Are you very busy?"

Jeffrey chuckled, "Christian supervised the preparation of those papers. He tackled the problem as a lesson on how to process hundreds of cases with little staff. He seemed a little disappointed that we had less than a hundred people to process."

I chuckled, "Do you think you got enough of the gangs to make a difference?"

"Private army, Jake." Mr. Farley admonished. "They were a private army, and yes, we got enough to prosecute for treason." His eyes met mine then he indicated the list LaBarge made for me. "This will fill out the rest of our case."

I grunted.

Leah interrupted us to offer us some dessert and admonish me to not stay up late. "He just got out of the hospital. He was so sick. I was terrified. It has been a miserable week here."

Jeffrey shifted in his seat. "Jake, feel free to work from home for a few days after you start feeling up to working. The rest of us can run paperwork out to you to review."

Leah agreed with Jeffrey. "I want him to get some good rest. He's been working such long hours, it can't be good for him." I appreciated Leah's concern more than I could express and reached out to hold her hand.

Jeffrey started making motions to leave shortly after he finished praising Margaret for the cake we'd eaten. It took him at least fifteen minutes to stammer out his praise. I thought M'TG might have some competition.

The next day Leah drove us into the M'TK Station. We met Darlene and Mr. LaBarge. She looked radiant. He looked nervous. I presented Darlene a gift of a small suitcase full of the things a bride might want. I'd sent Leah and Margaret into town to buy this as our wedding gift to her. The gift included half the cash we paid to LaBarge for his information.

Leah and I rode with them to Mercid as witnesses for the marriage. Judge Stimson performed the ceremony. The wedding lasted all of fifteen minutes then we went for an early dinner. I put them on the northbound train from Mercid. As far as Leah knew, they were off on a wedding trip. Only, Mr. LaBarge, Mr. Farley, and I knew they had no intention of returning. Only I knew they were to catch a boat to take them north. I didn't know whose boat. I assumed they would be passed from boat to boat on their way to the Caymans or perhaps someplace else. Earlier, I'd sent a package of money to Nicki to pay their fare north.

I didn't go into either office the next day. Tossley's body had been released, so I attended the Funeral Mass. By the time Mass let out, my exhaustion had returned. Leah and I went home, thankful Mr. Rouseff had come north to represent the business.

I eventually did return to work. The case for charging the president and those around him was being handled from my house. I played the fatigued invalid for days after I returned to a full work schedule. I encountered a major problem with who would actually arrest the president and vice-president of the country. We were unsure who had the authority and the integrity to do the job. I smiled thankfully every time I remembered our constitution allowed for an orderly change of office. The chairman of the parliament would assume the president's office. I called Yablonski's office hoping he could do the job. He finally called me back late one night.

"Jaconovich here."

"Yablonski. You called?"

"I have charges to make against the president and vice president."

"Shit."

"Yeah fun stuff."

"Where is LaBarge?"

"I honestly have no idea."

"What do you mean you have no idea. You were suppose to be keeping an eye on him."

"He figured out that as soon as he killed his target, he would be killed."

"Probably."

"He didn't like the idea."

"How will I ever be able to find him?"

"You won't. I want to talk to you about arresting the president."

"Holy shit! LaBarge is missing, and you want to arrest the president. I don't think I want to know if those two things are related."

"Wise choice. Would you like to do the honors or can you assign someone else to do the deed? Oh, and be certain you have all your taxes paid up to date."

"What are you people doing?"

"Oh you know, every three to four years, the prosecutor's office goes on a rampage and arrests a couple thousand members of the power elite."

He chuckled. "When do you want this done?"

"Anytime is fine. It would be cleaner if you do it within the next six days. I can run the papers up to the capital."

"Meet me in your office at seven in the morning. We'll go over what you've got."

"I'd like to give you a photocopy of everything I have."

"Shit."

I called Mr. Farley to meet us in the office at seven in the morning. Yablonski arrived on time. We reviewed the charges for the president and vice-president. We went over our supporting documents and the depositions we had taken so far.

Peter Yablonski sounded impressed. "You got this out of LaBarge? How the hell did you get this out of LaBarge?"

"Like I said, he figured out that he was supposed to be killed as soon as he killed his man."

Yablonski ran his hands over the short hair on top of his head. "So one of the most wanted assassins in the country up and decided to trust you."

"Yeah, he thought I might keep my word."

"Jake, tell the truth." Jeffrey chuckled. "We traded one of our clerks named Darlene the information."

I winced. "I still feel bad about saddling him with Darlene."

Jeffrey gave me a disgusted look and explained to our guest. "Major Yablonski, do not lament the lack of justice for Mr. LaBarge. He married Darlene. I figure by now, justice has been served. I hope he doesn't kill her. I know I wanted to often enough." He didn't sound too distressed about the fate of Darlene.

Yablonski chuckled. "Are you going to give me some hint of where you stashed Mr. LaBarge?"

"Outside the country. Beyond that, I don't know. I made certain that I would never accidently find out where he went."

Yablonski grunted. "Fair enough. All we have to do is keep him from sneaking back in."

"These are photocopies of the information he gave me. The lists are quite detailed with dates, times, and contact people. After giving me this, I don't think he has any intention of entering this hemisphere again."

"I guess not." Yablonski avidly read the list. "Excellent work gentlemen. This is good information. It checks with some of what I know. I hope your Darlene was worth all this."

We sadly shook our heads.

Chapter 9 Cousin Margaret

Five days after my meeting with Major Yablonski we celebrated Elizabeth's first birthday. We invited my parents, Nikoli and Lena, the other prosecutors from the office and Leah's new friend Susan. My cousin Margaret was still with us, and the Rouseffs were still in the north.

We had one unexpected guest arrive on the evening train, Young Lars M'TG who had been courting Margaret for years. He acted pouty and grumpy. The evening was not designed to improve his mood. Most of our attention centered on the children.

Jeffery looked the situation over with Margaret and M'TG and decided to play a sly little game. "Oh look, Elizabeth has the same dimple as her Papa. Oh, I guess that must be a D'NO feature. She will grow up to be a stunning as the rest of the D'NO women."

Margaret blushed.

M'TG turned red.

When Margaret served the cake, he had more discrete praise. "Oh good. Are we to have another one of Miss. D'NO's wonderful cakes? I am still dreaming about the one I had the other night."

Margaret blushed again.

M'TG's neck seemed to swell up.

Margaret left to get more cake plates from the kitchen. Jeffery followed on her hem. M'TG shifted in his chair and lost track of the conversation around him.

Leroy snickered. "Jake I'm thankful your cousin is with us. I think she will be an asset to the younger population of the city."

M'TG started turning purple.

Leah sounded so innocent, I didn't think she intended to bait M'TG. "I've told her to take some classes at the university. She thinks she might take some classes at the business college, but I think a D'NO should really go to university."

"You are right Leah. She will meet a better class of young men at the university and there will be more to choose from." Leroy sounded serious, but I thought he was teasing M'TG.

Margaret reappeared carrying more napkins. Jeffery followed her burdened with more plates, forks, and a carton of ice cream. "Look everybody Jeffery brought us ice cream." Margaret sounded excited about the ice cream.

M'TG left his chair and rushed to take the napkins out of Margaret's hand.

Jeffrey continued his gentle praise of my mama, and Elizabeth, and the D'NO women in general. We were inclined to agree with him so the compliments were generally pleasing to everybody, except M'TG.

Before we finished our dessert, Jeffery asked Margaret her secret for making such an excellent cake. "I eat mostly in restaurants. I am never able to eat something so excellent, even in the capital."

M'TG reached his limit. He picked Margaret up out of her chair and carried her off to the kitchen.

I grumbled. "Damn, I hate losing good help."

Mama sounded skeptical. "I'm not sure that Uncle John will approve. The young man has been hanging around for years without making a commitment."

Papa gave Mama a besotted look and declared. "He doesn't deserve her."

I added my opinion, "I suppose it comes down to whether or not she wants him."

Jeffrey added his opinion. "She can have her pick of men in the city."

"She can certainly find a man of wealth and good family here." This surprised me coming from Leah.

Papa assured her, "M'TG is wealthy enough. I consider his family to be among the finest in the country. The problem seems to be that the young man has been slow making up his mind."

"I hope his grandfather is not pushing him into something he doesn't want." Papa kissed Mama on her temple for her worries.

I explained to the others. "His grandpapa wanted to marry Mama. When Papa came along she wouldn't look at M'TG. He almost hates me for having Mama's smile on Papa's face." We laughed.

I shifted my attention back to my daughter. She and Jacob were having one of their giggle fits. I couldn't help but laugh over the way Elizabeth would wrinkle up her nose and purse her lips. Next, they both would break into laughter. This little game kept us all laughing over the magic between siblings.

Over the sound of our laughter I heard Margaret shouting at M'TG. I worried about whether she really wanted to live in a small village on the north coast. The guests were getting ready to leave when Margaret and M'TG reappeared. He looked smug. Margaret looked like a D'NO woman who has just gotten her way. After the guests left, Margaret asked us if we would be able to come to her wedding in about six weeks. She turned to Mama, "Cousin Mary Anne, will you go shopping for a wedding dress with me? Will you come too, Leah?"

Papa chuckled. "You wouldn't expect them to stay home when there is shopping to do would you?"

I shook M'TG's hand. "Congratulations. She is a wonderful woman. Take care of her."

"I intend to. I've always intended to. I wanted to get my own boat first. She says she would rather have babies than boats."

We laughed.

Papa gave Mama a hug. "Women are like that. They have funny priorities."

I was beginning to think that I should be attending to Leah's priorities. After all, Elizabeth turned one year old today.

I had a little trouble attending to those priorities. We finally got rid of all our guests. It took some doing to round up Elizabeth and Jacob. They were excited and wanted to run and play tag. I caught Jacob and hauled him off to bed while Leah captured the birthday girl. Elizabeth had eagerly graduated to the crib in the same room with Jacob. We worried about this combination for fear he would decide to do something dangerous with his sister. Our only other option was to keep Elizabeth in the cradle in our room. I wanted the privacy of my bedroom back. We decided that if we never told Jacob about Peter Pan, he would never try to fly out the window with his sister. Peter Pan was not welcome in our home.

By about ten o'clock, I felt fairly certain the children were sleeping. I'd sent M'TG off to the guest room and told him to stay there although I think Margaret was annoyed with this plan.

I had plans for my wife when the phone rang. I debated not answering it. "Jaconovich"

"Yablonski."

My heart started to pound. I'd forgotten about work for a few hours. "Well?"

"I got them."

"Did the succession go okay?"

"Yes, I took the Chairman of the Parliament and Judge Corbain with me. As soon as we arrested the vice-president, Mr. Chairman of the Parliament was sworn in as acting president."

"Good. I've learned that having a codified succession in place is important." I told him about our mayor.

"You've got to be joking."

"Same thing happened with the provincial governor. I conduct business with his wife while he sits in jail."

"Ow"

"Yeah. We'll get on with the prosecution tomorrow. Oh, and you have paid your taxes haven't you?"

"Shit. How many are you going to arrest?"

"Well, we once processed seven hundred in one night with two prosecutors and the office manager." I knew I was telling him an old story that he knew well. "We have six prosecutors in the office now. Our office manager is out with a new baby, and we're short the clerk Darlene, which should make up for the missing office manager who spent most of her time untangling Darlene's messes."

"You have too much fun."

Chapter 10 Practicing Real Law

Mr. Rouseff returned to the south. I went back to spending my mornings in the Rouseff offices. I had taken an office right next to Mr. Rouseff's old office. His nephew thought he would take the big office.

I explained the facts of life to him. "I don't think that is a good idea for you to take your uncle's office. Cousin Philippe has made it clear that I am to be in charge of these offices. I do not take his old office out of respect for him. I have the right, but I don't take it." I remembered to breathe. "The staff respects me for that. They will think you are a spoiled, arrogant, ass, if you act as if you think you are good enough to fill his office. You will never be that good." I breathed again. "Get used to it and get a room down the hall." I later realized I'd raised my voice a bit during this lecture.

Rouseff the younger, called his uncle.

Cousin Philippe called me and praised me for yelling at the spoiled brat. "Keep up the good work. I know it is a challenging project, but if anybody can make a man out of that miserable excuse for humanity it's you."

People two floors down in the building patted me on the back and smiled as I left the building. They said things like, "good job" or "That was telling him."

I walked over to the prosecutor's office. We were having a bit of a party. I arrived in time to hear Jeffery lamenting that my cousin Margaret was too young for him and too good for M'TG, but other than that bit of melancholy, people were in high spirits. We debated how to divide up our cases. Since ex-President Vanderholm was charged with murder among his other charges, we agreed that Mr. Farley and I would take that case. We assigned the Papadakos case to Leroy and Christian.

Mr. Farley looked around the office at our two junior attorneys, Char and Alexander, and at our interns Yuri and Antoine. "The rest of you, keep working on those tax-evasion cases. What the hell is going on in the holding room?"

We all went to look. It was full of the usual repeat offenders and some new first time offenders.

Mr. Farley made short work of the caseload. "Will everybody accused of drunkenness, loitering, shoplifting, brawling, and oh whatever put your file on the desk and go home and don't come back here. We don't have time to deal with you."

One honest soul raised his hand, "I was charged with lewd behavior."

I spoke up. "Don't tell me you were pissing in public."

"No I weren't in public. I was in my own house only that busybody across the alley was looking in my windows as I was relieving myself."

Jeffery grumped, "Get the hell out of here and don't come back." Our caseload for the day was cleared. We could get down to practicing real law.

We reorganized the office. We decided that the biggest supervisor's office should be used as a conference room. We rearranged furniture until we had an efficient design for processing hundreds of cases and privacy for processing some very high-level cases.

I went over the organization for prosecuting the ex-president and vice-president. I gleefully counted up possible fines. I'd given up on five digit fines and started working on fines in the hundred thousand to ten million-dollar range. I began to think it wasn't worth my time to process someone for less than five hundred thousand. We had a good start on the paperwork for the president and vice-president. I wanted more depositions. I thought they would be hard to find. I thought about our prisoner on the island. I made a phone call.

"Yablonski"

"Jaconovich. I want to depose the prisoner you left in my keeping. Can he return to the city?"

"I don't see why not."

"You think it is safe enough to have somebody who was in the military bring him down." I was referring to Cousin Nicki's brief tour of duty after being conscripted.

"Yeah, Nicki should be able to handle him just fine. He should be grateful after all we've done to save his sorry hide."

"I doubt that he will be."

"Ungrateful bastard." Yablonski grunted.

"Yeah, bye."

I hung up and called Nicki. I explained the situation and asked him to bring the prisoner down.

I got home early enough to take my wife to bed at a decent hour. I chuckled thinking of another baby in our family. I talked to Leah about going to the capital in two days. She sounded delighted to go and stay in a hotel.

The next day all my plans for a little honeymoon in a hotel with my wife were overthrown. First, I talked to Rouseff in the morning and told him I my plans to prosecute Hab Vanderholm.

He chuckled. "You have thrown this whole province into a tizzy. They think you northerners can't understand that people from the south should be held to a different standard. Our goals are loftier."

"What enriching yourselves at the expense of everybody else is loftier?"

"Of course, because peasants will just spend money on food and clothing while we know enough to spend our money on a bunch of damned, vulgar, gold bric-a-brac."

I chuckled. "Ah, is your household still lamenting their banished objects d'art?"

"They actually go into the storerooms and stroke the things and weep over the banishment."

I had a horrible feeling he wasn't exaggerating. "The situation is that I need to be in the capital for a few days so I won't be into the office here. Is there anything you need done while I am in the capital?"

"No it sounds like you'll be busy with the shopping for the wedding, and all."

"How did you hear about that? I didn't think we would be doing any shopping. Mama and Margaret were planning to go up."

"Your plan may have grown since the last time you talked to your wife. She told Margaret about your trip to the capital. Margaret called your mama. She called Rosalie. Rosalie has instructed the servants to open our house there for your party."

I grunted and thought that I might be able to get my wife alone easier if we had babysitters.

After I got off of the phone, I looked over the progress on the highway project and approved more demolition for Doh Creek Rd. I asked a few questions about the development at the interchange. Before I knew what had happened, I was hungry and due in the prosecutor's office.

I spent my afternoon re-reading every scrap of information I had on the charges for the president. I made notes on each point and listed questions to be covered in deposition.

Mr. Farley made his lists. "Jake, I think we should divide up the people we will depose. I want you to take Vanderholm's female office staff. Listen to them intently. Make certain they are comfortable and serve them tea, yourself. Smile at them. I want them to melt in your hand and tell you everything. I'll take most of the men. I'll do my effeminate, dimwit routine and let the men show off how much smarter they are than I am."

I laughed. "Your effeminate dimwit routine? Is that what you call that? Yeah, I've seen you do it. You had me confused for the first few weeks I worked here."

"It kept me alive and employed while the office was run by crooks. I even got to practice law sometimes, unlike you and your endless processing of petty criminals." We laughed.

Late in the day, we had a meeting and agreed to call our beleaguered police department to let them know they could start arresting all the prominent citizens in the city for tax evasion. We did not expect them to be happy.

When I returned home, I discovered my house had suffered a major attack that produced luggage, clothing, paper, paper bags, and cousins. I smiled to see so many of my relatives. Margaret's mama told me, "Nicki says he and Micki will bring the prisoner down tomorrow."

"Um…good." I figured this information must be a peace offering for the state of my house. I noticed magazines scattered about.

"Papa, Papa, Papa, Cousin Margaret is getting a wedding." I picked up my excited son and kissed his baby cheek. Elizabeth was too busy looking at wedding dresses in a magazine to speak to her Papa. I scooped her up and kissed her anyway. I kissed Mama too.

"Where is Leah?"

Mama look radiant as she explained, "She went to the library to see if she could find more magazines. She was supposed to stop by the market to see if she could find tulle. Then she was going to get some Chinese food for dinner."

I had no idea what tulle was. It sounded possibly like something good to eat.

"She has been making drawings for decorating the house for the wedding." Mama showed me a drawing.

I commented, "Ah the wedding will be at The Cove then?"

Margaret sounded gleeful. "Yes, Micki has designed a tram to bring people from the village over the ridge. We can get into the village in a matter of minutes now without taking the boat out. Uncle John hates it."

The women laughed. I noticed something in their tone as they laughed over Uncle John's rules being flouted that reminded me of Mrs. Mayor and Mrs. Governor.

"I'm not certain I see the real advantage over taking the boat into the village."

"The biggest advantage is that it's a tourist attraction. Boaters come in to fuel their boats. They then pay money to ride to the top of the mountain and admire the view."

"Are they fueling at the railroad dock?"

"No. D'SnG started bringing in barges full of diesel. People can refuel at the provincial dock from the barge."

I sat down with my children in my lap and asked more questions about the village and what was happening in the neighboring villages. It felt good to hear news from this part of my world. I realized I loved the villages. They had many claims to my affections. I'd met Leah there. I'd spent hours working on the Fortenac case there. I smiled, content with family around me.

The following morning, the house erupted into chaos as the women prepared to go to the capital.

I met my cousins with their prisoner at the train. "Thanks guys. We've prepared a house for him in the city."

Kerby sounded surprised but respectful enough. "You're are not putting me back in the jail?"

"No. The jail is too busy. They don't have time and space for you."

Micki asked, curious. "What is happening that the jail is busy?"

"Oh we are arresting everybody we can get our hands on for tax evasion."

Nicki sounded awed. "I heard you arrested the president."

I grinned. "Yeah, even a Vanderholm is not above the law, slimy bastard."

Our prisoner looked shocked. "Aren't you afraid the Vanderholms will come after you?"

"Well, that is a possibility. That's why we want to act swiftly in the president's case. We need to cripple the rest of the family."

The house where we stashed our prisoner was fixed up nice. We'd found his lodgings and moved his personal belongings over to his new place. We even allowed him to keep his suitcases full of money. Well, we did count it to give me some idea of how much his fines were going to be. I sat and visited with him for about an hour.

"Why was it important to kill Mantega?"

"I don't know anything about that."

"Your fingerprints were on the gun. LaBarge told us that you killed Mantega. He told us Vanderholm wants you killed. Why?"

"LaBarge didn't tell you no such thing."

The grammar confused me, briefly. "Vanderholm made arrangements to kill LaBarge as soon as he killed you. Yablonski picked up the men set to kill LaBarge. They talked. And yeah, LaBarge talked. He didn't like getting set up by Vanderholm." I had a copy of LaBarge's information. I handed it to the prisoner. "He gave us this."

Kerby looked over the papers, and his tongue started rolling around in his mouth. "Why? Why would he do such a thing? He almost admits that he killed…um…five…no…six people at Vanderholm's orders. What happened to him?"

"I don't know. Well, he got married to a woman I can't stand and left the country."

"You let him go?"

"This information was more important than prosecuting him. We want to wipe out the source of the corruption. LaBarge doesn't admit that he killed those men. He just tells us that Vanderholm ordered the killings. He gives us the names of people who can verify his allegation. You will notice that your name is on this list a couple times."

"I can't believe you let LaBarge go."

"Learn this lesson." I leaned forward. "It would help if you could learn it a little faster than you are. Vanderholm ordered you killed. He sent LaBarge to do the job. LaBarge didn't find you. It wasn't just that we hid you well. We planted clues to send him off in the wrong direction. We made certain that LaBarge couldn't find you. His failure to find you was one more reason he was desperate to leave the country, the continent in fact. He agreed to go far, far away. We've worked damn hard to keep you alive. Your best chance for survival is to help us go after the people at the center of the crime. We don't really care all that much about prosecuting you. We will, but you most probably will get off with a fine."

Kerby shifted on his sofa.

"When you are free to go about your business, you will want to be certain none of this crowd…" I tapped the papers from LaBarge. "…can reach you."

"Can I leave the country too?"

"Certainly, after you have given us what we want and paid your fines, you will be free to go anywhere you want. Australia might be nice."

"What do you want?"

"Depositions. I want you to tell us everything you know, under oath, in front of a court recorder."

"I'll have to think about it."

"Fine"

We left on a noon train for the capital. The women seemed to have organized their raid on the shops. They appeared far more organized in their pursuit of a wedding dress than I was in prosecuting the ex-president. I thought I could learn from their methods.

After a pleasant dinner in a hotel, I went to visit Judge Gannon. He'd aged since I last saw him.

"Jake, do you intend to haul every member of the elite families into court?"

"Surely, not every member. Oh, be sure to pay your taxes."

"What do taxes have to do with it?"

I smiled happily, "We are picking up everybody for tax evasion first. We'll charge them with treason, murder or conspiracy to commit murder or accessory to murder as we go along. The tax evasion charge is easy to prosecute."

"What have you got to back up your other charges?"

"I admit that we need about a thousand more depositions. We have a good list of names, dates, and times. I intend to depose everybody I can. I'll start with Vanderholm's office staff tomorrow. I want to get them before his attorneys train them in the right answers. What do you think are the important issues in this case? The biggest charges will be for treason, murder, accessory to murder, and conspiracy to commit murder."

"How do you intend to prove he hired an assassin?"

"The assassin showed us the money trail. We have a letter from the president placing the assassin in our office as supervisor. We haven't charged him with conspiracy to commit fraud through appointing someone not qualified to practice law as a supervisor in a prosecutor's office. We will do that too."

I expected the judge to chuckle. He didn't. "Jake when is all of this going to stop?"

"When people stop committing crimes."

"Why are you going after the high level people?"

"They are the most powerful. They can reorganize and continue terrorizing the citizens of the country."

"Why can't you be satisfied with arresting the people lower down in the power chain and leave the president alone?"

"That is a good question. One answer is that he tends to kill off the people lower down before we can prosecute them. He hired an assassin to kill a prisoner, charged with extortion in our city. I guess I want to know why Vanderholm sent a professional assassin to kill the man. I am calling placing a trained assassin in a law office, violating the security of the court. Curiously, I came to trust the man somewhat. He gave us good information when he figured out that he was to be killed as soon as he killed his target. As it turned out, the CGIS arrested the men sent to kill LaBarge." This name got a response out of the judge.

Judge Gannon leaned forward with his eyes open wide. "LaBarge is mixed up in this?"

"He is the man who has been in our office the past few months."

"Are you telling me that Vanderholm placed one of the most notorious murders in the country in your prosecutor's office?" The judge's voice rose to a squeak.

"I don't know how notorious Mr. LaBarge is, but he has been in our office for months. He visited me in the hospital when I had kidney surgery. I was nervous entertaining him when I was too weak to defend myself."

"Are you sure it was LaBarge?"

I nodded. "He told me that was his name."

"Did he kill the person he was sent to kill?" The judge's eyes still bulged like fish eyes.

"No, that is why he wanted to leave the country. He couldn't find his mark." I smiled and scratched my nose. "He was afraid Vanderholm would have him killed for failing his mission. When he thought about the situation some more, he decided that Vanderholm would kill him anyway. He passed Vanderholm information stating where and when he would kill his mark. Vanderholm had his men in position at the right time. CGIS arrested them."

"Where is LaBarge now?"

"I don't know. He left the country. His intent was to go very far away."

"You let him go?"

"We didn't have any evidence for anything we could get a conviction on. Yeah, we knew who he was and what his alleged profession was, but we had nothing on him other than practicing law without a license. We couldn't convict on that because Vanderholm had sent him."

"Practicing law without a license, that was it?"

"I begged and pleaded with CGIS to give us some evidence for charging him, but they wouldn't talk to us. In the end, the best we could do was accept information from him and not ask questions about where he intended to go."

Judge Gannon paused and sipped his coffee then changed the subject. "The number of high level arrests coming out of your office disturbs me."

"I think it may bother me more. We did not intentionally go after Vanderholm. He placed a problem in our office. That problem decided to give us information so we could get Vanderholm off of his back long enough for him to escape. Sir, if these people would make the slightest attempt to follow the law, we wouldn't be prosecuting them." I paused and thought for a couple seconds. "Well, we would have gone after the tax evasion. We'll get around to everyone who hasn't paid their taxes."

The judge scowled. "Why are you prosecuting for tax evasion?"

"Our government treasuries don't have any money. Many of us have worked for months without a paycheck. Our government agencies don't have money to conduct the business of keeping the streets safe or building roads or feeding the hungry. Teachers in my city went for three months before they got a paycheck this term. That won't happen next term. We will have money to pay our teachers. We will have money to hire a proper police force and train them." I shut up. I noticed I was getting a little passionate on the subject.

The judge turned his coffee cup in a circle and asked another question. "Can you tell me why your mayor and provincial governor are still in jail?"

I laughed outright. "Sir, this is something that it pains me to talk about."

"You seem to find it humorous that two prominent men are sitting in jail." The judge scowled at me.

I tried to control my mirth. "It is why they are sitting there that amuses me. They were tried, found guilty, and fined. They were told they would stay in jail until their fines were paid." I stopped to chuckle. "Their wives refuse to pay their fines. Those two women have taken over running the city and the province. They are doing a great job. They just might kill anybody who tries to pay their husbands' fines."

"Is that legal for them to act in place of their husbands?"

"I looked it up. It is not codified that they may do so, but I can't find a law prohibiting it. I have found several instances where this has happened before when the husband is ill or out of the country on business. I have found instances where the husband was appointed, but from the beginning his wife filled the office. As near as I can tell the women do a good job in general."

"You have done your research. I am still concerned over the number of high level arrests."

"Sir, are you concerned because we're charging people in prominent positions. If we were charging laborers with the same crimes would you be concerned." I thought I'd angered him. He sat and stared at me for several minutes. His jaw worked. I felt uncomfortable, but I refused to look away or squirm.

"Jake, I am an old man. It's hard for me to accept the fact that those people I have always considered to be above reproach are far from respectable. They are nothing more than common criminals." He sighed. "You are getting a name in the papers for picking on the upper class. Perhaps it is not that you single them out."

"No, I will never process as many members of the upper classes as I have workers and street people. If I never processed another street person, I would still never be able to process as many upper class as I have lower class. Do not think I single out one group over another. I have processed a working class man for murder. He was executed. We are looking for a socio-path who has murdered two people, so far. When we find him we will prosecute him. He may well be executed." The judge studied me a long time again. Finally, he spoke. "You will prosecute Vanderholm for treason and murder."

I nodded.

"You'll have to have your case very well prepared."

"I intend to sir."

"Bring me the case when it is ready. I will hear it impartially. I am old, but I will learn to look at others as equals. I think the Vanderholms will be prepared for you. Their attorneys will study the Fortenac case. They will know that you will pick apart every statement he makes. They will pick apart every statement your witnesses make."

"Good, that is how law should be practiced. I hope they can come up with a better excuse than Fortenac did."

The judge looked at me again and shook his head. "The country is changing. It is exciting to see the changes. They needed to happen. I find it challenging to change with the times."

I spent the next day taking depositions from Vanderholm's staff. One of the Vanderholm attorneys sat in on the depositions. I'd requested they bring me any phone logs or appointment books.

Mr. Vanderholm's secretary had an amazingly organized clerk. She'd documented everything. She brought me her documentation. She had listed every phone call Vanderholm had received or placed for the past five years. She had documented every visitor, including when LaBarge visited the president and the purpose of the visit--"Eliminate Kerby." She documented the phone calls. Her tidy thoroughness produced a treasure trove of information. I photocopied everything along with her deposition describing how she kept her records.

"Your notes say, 'eliminate Kerby.' What does that mean?"

The woman didn't flinch when she answered. "It means he was to be killed."

"Why was he to be killed?'

"I'm not sure. He participated in the purge. They wanted to eliminate all evidence of the purge. See, I've noted that several places in my record." She pointed out several places in the record where she made notes about eliminating various people.

I went into shock. I began to suspect the woman was not quite right in her head. "Why did you keep such detailed records?"

"Mr. Secretary told me I was to keep a log of the phone calls and visitors. That was my job." Her affect remained flat.

"You've done a remarkable job. You can be very proud of your work. This will make a difference for the people of this country."

She smiled at my words. She sounded sane enough, but no normal person keeps the kind of detailed records that this woman kept about conspiracy to commit murder.

We went over her records for almost three hours. When I saw she started getting tired, I let her go. I held my head and wondered if anybody knew this woman had kept these records.

I talked to two more office workers. They knew about the log. They agreed that Hab Vanderholm ordered the record to be kept. I asked them if they knew about his meetings with LaBarge.

Another clerk seemed willing to cooperate. "I knew that Mr. LaBarge came to the office occasionally."

"What was Mr. LaBarge's profession?"

"He was an assassin."

I went into shock again. "Did everybody know that Mr. LaBarge kills people for money?"

"Well I suppose not everybody knew, but I did."

"How did you know?"

"I heard the president talking to the vice president about who to hire to eliminate General Johan. The vice-president wanted to hire someone named Webb. The president wanted to hire LaBarge."

"Why did he prefer LaBarge?"

"LaBarge's appearance was more refined. Mr. Vanderholm did not like working with people who did not look refined."

I didn't know where to go with this. I'd expected to have to work and tease to get the information. These women sat wide-eyed in front of me and talked about killing people as if they were talking about their laundry.

"How did you happen to overhear this conversation?"

"I was serving them lunch."

"You were serving lunch, and they argued about who to hire to kill someone in front of you?"

"Yes."

"What did you think of this conversation? Did you think it was strange?"

"Well it was peculiar enough that I remembered."

"I have never heard such a conversation. Um...why didn't you report this to the authorities?"

"Who would I report it to? Mr. Vanderholm is the president. Besides, this was a matter of national security. I have a security clearance that is why I was serving them lunch. This was not a criminal act. He was acting as the president to eliminate individuals who are a threat to our security."

"Ah, thank you for clarifying that. Did you happen to learn why Kerby was considered a threat to national security?"

"He knew too many secrets related to the purge. Mr. Vanderholm wanted that mess cleaned up and settled."

"Cleaned up and settled, what does that mean? I thought we caught and jailed everyone connected to the purge."

"No, you didn't get the most important people. That's why the president needed to punish those people."

"Ah, am I right in thinking that your understanding of the president's behavior was that he was punishing people involved in the purge. He was killing those the courts had not caught and processed."

"Yes, that is my understanding."

"Thank you, you have been a great help to us. Your testimony is very important."

The woman left. I finished making my notes and met Mr. Farley at four. We went over what we learned.

"Jake, we may have a problem."

"Yeah, one or two."

He smiled at my joke. "Vanderholm's people say he was doing this for national security."

"Yeah, I heard that too. We can refute that with the constitution. That is one of the few things that the authors of the constitution got right. They were very clear that the president does not have authority to execute people. The only legal execution must be carried out by court order. If there is no court order, any execution is deemed to be murder." I ran my fingers through my hair. "I got some good stuff. One clerk kept a record of all phone calls and visitors. She wrote down the reason for the call or visit. Some entries state, 'eliminate Kerby."

"Ah a record of phone calls and visitors with a note of who was to be killed is good. I think I got something better. I got a list of people who were to be eliminated. We will have to check to see if they are still dead or alive."

"Oh shit! What is running through these people's heads? I suspect that there was something wrong with the clerk who kept the log. It is very neat and precise. She showed no emotion when she pointed out her entries about who was to be eliminated. She smiled like an innocent child when I praised her for her work.

"Do you think she is competent enough that we can use her deposition?"

"Yeah, as long as we stick to matters of the logs and her job. I wouldn't ask her any questions involving judgment."

Mr. Farley nodded. "I'm picking up an air of naïveté among the office people. They seem competent in some ways but they just don't get it. They don't understand the gravity of the situation. They don't get that the activities of the president are illegal."

"I wonder what that's all about? Are they deliberately psychologically distancing themselves from their work because they need the job?"

"I think I will call one of my friends who still works with Scotland Yard and get his opinion on the employees. If they are all simple minded, we can't base our case on their testimony."

I chuckled. "That would be one way to provide security for your actions— hire a bunch of people who can do a job, but who have mental disorders that interfere with their reasoning and judgment so their testimony cannot be accepted in court."

"Shit! Do you think Vanderholm is that smart?"

"I think we better have documentation to get around the problem." I returned to our temporary house.

Chapter 11 Continuing Investigation

I arrived home to discover that Rouseff's house in the capital had suffered an attack far worse than the one at my house. I learned that tulle is a flimsy sort of netting. The stuff draped the furnishings everywhere. They apparently needed enough of the stuff to run from the dock in the cove to the side lawn, or to the house if the weather didn't cooperate. I think I heard, "or to the house if the weather doesn't cooperate," two dozen times before I made it through the door and down the hall to find the other men hiding in the study.

I greeted Papa and my cousins, "Oh this is where you are. Why are you all in here?"

Micki asked, "How long have you been home?"

"Less than five minutes."

Micki crowed, "Give it another five minutes, and you'll understand."

Before I got settled in my chair, my wife came and found me. "Oh Jake, come. You must see what we have done. Oh this is so exciting." She grabbed my hand and pulled me toward the door. I heard the other men chuckling behind me.

As I left the room, I heard Papa saying, "I am thankful to see them so happy and able to celebrate. This is what we've worked for and hoped for, for a long, long time."

First, Leah wanted me to look at her drawings for aisle motifs. She had drawings of the house in The Cove from various perspectives and with various decorations.

The other men joined us and admired Leah's drawings. The women exclaimed over how helpful the drawings were. They argued over which motif would be best and generally concluded that depended on which dress they decided on. I concluded that a motif was apparently not food.

I tried to be supportive of the project. "Have you planned the food yet?"

"No we will get the important stuff like the dress settled first."

"Hm, roast chicken might be nice." My stomach growled at the thought.

"We can smoke some fish." Nicki came in and tried to be helpful.

"No. Not fish." The women unanimously banned fish from the wedding menu.

"Well, they have that much definitely decided." I looked at Mama, who's eyes shown bright, and she radiated peace and contentment. Leah almost danced with excitement. The mother of the bride wrung her hands and declared that her daughter would have a proper wedding. I smiled and agreed with Papa. I enjoyed seeing the women in my family so happy.

I found their feverish excitement over a wedding a little bewildering. I looked at my wife again and remembered why we didn't have a lavish wedding. This was her chance to plan a beautiful wedding without the pain of her personal loses. I resolved to be supportive.

Being supportive was becoming a challenge. "Um…what is for dinner?"

Mama dismissed the question. "We haven't thought about that."

I tried to be specific. "Um…is the cook fixing something or are we going out?"

Margaret sounded vague. "I don't know."

Leah answered my question, somewhat. "I didn't talk to a cook.'

Mama had definitive information. "There is no cook in residence."

"Ah, then we will go out." I smiled expecting some acknowledgement of this conclusion.

Margaret's mama asked, "Do you think we can find enough fresh flowers for bouquets along the railing here?" The women all moved to study one of Leah's drawings.

I looked at the other men. "They have to eat. They'll starve if they don't eat between now and the wedding."

The others grunted their agreement. We manfully took charge of the situation.

"Right, where shall we eat?"

My papa being a real-life hero spoke up. "I know a nice place. I'll make reservations for us for close to seven."

I smiled at my papa. He could always handle any crisis. At this moment I was more proud of him than when he took the fire-fighting machine into the city. My papa was going to make certain that I got my dinner at a reasonable hour. I could sit and be pleasant while I looked at pictures of wedding gowns. I enjoyed watching a room full of exceptionally beautiful women looking so happy.

Micki whispered. "How can they take so long to make a simple decision?"

"I don't know, but I am enjoying watching the women I love looking so happy."

"They are happy, aren't they?"

We sat and watched them laughing, and debating, and playing in the tulle. I worried a little about getting them out of the house to eat, but they followed along nicely enough when we got them wrapped up in shawls, and handed them their purses.

At dinner, the women wanted to sit together leaving the men at one end of the long table.

"Jake, how was your day?"

"Confusing." I described as much of my day as I dared.

"Son, you'll do fine. Everything always turns out fine when you do your best."

"That is what I intend to do. I think we can win the case as a point of law. I am not sure what kind of sentencing we can get." I decided a restaurant was not the best place for this discussion. I changed the topic. "How did the rest of you survive?"

Micki answered. "We stayed with the women for about forty-five minutes. After we had settled the questions of what the men in the wedding party would wear, and what our shoes would look like, and where we would stay before the wedding…"

Petral added, "And promised that we would not let M'TG get drunk before the wedding…"

Cousin Seb, Margaret's papa growled, "…and promised that we would not set up chairs in our tuxedos, and that we could get dressed by ourselves…"

Micki summed up, "Well you get the picture. Your papa took us on a tour of the city."

"Where did you go?"

Petral sounded gleeful. "We wanted to look over your new moorings at The Compound."

I immediately looked around me. "I really have no interest in a political career. I would feel stupid standing up in front of people and making speeches."

Papa smiled at me. "Oh, just talk like you do when you're talking to your friends. You will do fine."

"Papa! Surely you don't think I should go into politics."

Papa thought before he answered. "I think I agree with your mama. She says she sees rivers of events that carry us in the direction we are to go. We must make good decisions or we will be shipwrecked. If we do not end up wrecked or caught in a whirlpool, the river will take us where we are to go. She insists that you will be president someday."

Grief suddenly overwhelmed me at this idea. "I don't want to lose my simple life. I love my home, and I love coming home to my wife and children."

Papa's voice held pride and approval. "You love the people of our city. You want to help them lead better lives."

"I want to keep them alive. That is for certain. Between starvation and national security, it's a challenge just to keep them alive." I thought for a few minutes. "No, I cannot do that job. I cannot get elected. I am not a member of one of the elite families. Rouseff claims us, but in a campaign we cannot prove the connection. I would not try. I cannot even contemplate campaigning. I would not know how. No."

After dinner, I entertained fantasies about getting my wife to myself. I discovered that Jacob and Elizabeth were sleeping in our bedroom. They were almost as excited over the wedding as the women. Elizabeth had two small, grubby samples of tulle that she insisted on taking to bed with her. When my wife fell asleep before the children, I wondered how anybody ever managed to have more than two children.

The next morning I went back to work deposing the office staff. A different Vanderholm attorney sat in on today's sessions. He never asked questions, but I didn't trust him. I found one more person who knew that LaBarge was a professional assassin and that President Vanderholm hired him to handle select cases of national security. I got a little ill over her attitude toward hiring someone to kill another person.

"I want you to look at the names of the people on this list. Do you recognize any of these names?"

"Yes, I recognize Kerby."

"Tell me everything you know about him."

"He was in charge of making certain that there was no resistance to the purge on Ninth Street."

"What type of resistance were you expecting?"

"We thought some of the police might try to stop us."

"Did the police interfere with your plans to purge the area?"

"No, not the police."

"Then Kerby was successful."

"No, because somebody called in the army. There was somebody else there too, putting out fires and harassing our troops. They knew we were coming and evacuated the area. Later on, they evacuated the whole city. Kerby should have known about the leak." Several odd memories merged in my mind. I decided to pretend I knew more than I really did.

"How do you think Julie Jouyet learned about the purge?"

"I assume she learned it from her husband or her father."

"Who is her father?"

"Alexander Papadakos."

"So both Julie's husband and father knew about the purge, and she could have learned about it from either of them?"

"Yes." I was learning a great deal. I didn't know where I was going with this, but I intended to have a long chat with Julie.

"Let's get back to the contract on Kerby. You stated that he was supposed to prevent resistance to the purge. Is this correct?"

"Yes,"

"I am unclear why Vanderholm ordered Kerby killed when the police did not interfere."

"The main reason he was to be killed was that he knew who ordered the purge and who would benefit from the purge."

"Who would benefit?"

"Papadakos, Jouyet and Fortenac."

"I don't understand your relationship to Vanderholm. You know his plans. Why does he trust you?"

"He doesn't. He doesn't realize that I know his plans. We all knew what was going on. He…he…he…doesn't seem to know that we exist when we're not in his presence."

"Ah," I didn't understand any of this. I took a quick look back through my notes. I saw a huge hole glaring me in the face.

"I think we need to clarify the difference between Emperor Vanderholm and President Vanderholm. What is their relationship to each other?"

"The emperor is the president's uncle."

I smiled. "I didn't know that."

The witness puffed up and gave me a superior look.

I asked, "Why is President Vanderholm ordering an execution of someone hired by his uncle?"

The woman looked at me as if I was as stupid as I felt. "The men may be different, but it is still a family business."

"Was President Vanderholm involved in planning the purge?"

"Of course."

"Is it possible Mr. Kerby knew President Vanderholm was involved?"

"Probably."

"Were they ever in the same meetings together when the purge was discussed. Did you ever hear them discuss the purge?" The woman looked at the silent attorney beside her.

"Yes, Mr. Kerby was in most of the meetings."

I needed to go over the copies of the visitor's log to identify the records regarding the purge. I finally let the poor clerk leave. I thanked her and expressed my concern for her fatigue. She smiled coyly at me. Privately I worried that she would be a target if the attorney told anyone what she knew. I wondered how many of my witnesses would still be alive when we went to court. I was exhausted. I checked to confirm that the court recorder had gotten all of the information down.

His lips had turned blue, and he whispered. "Mr. Jaconovich, I admire what you're doing, but I could get killed just for hearing all this stuff."

"I doubt that they'll come after you. I question how much of what that woman said is true. I suspect that the defense wants me to build a case around the testimony of the witnesses then they will rip it out from under me."

I met with Mr. Farley to compare notes before he returned home. Again, he was struck by the willingness of the witnesses to tell all, despite having a Vanderholm attorney present. Mr. Farley was not as trusting as I am. "I confess I mentioned to the attorney at the end of the day that I sincerely hoped that all the people we depose are still alive when we go to trial."

I rubbed my hands over my face. "Some of the people I talked to didn't seem to know anything. However, I had one woman who was eager to name everybody, Vanderholm, Papadakos, and Jouyet. The defense attorney didn't flinch. Do you think she is in any danger of being eliminated?"

"It occurred to me that they may be letting their people talk to see who knows what. I don't think their case will be based on whether or not the acts were committed but rather on their right to commit those acts."

"This could prove to be a challenge to our new constitution." I ran my hand through my hair.

"I think we should keep that in the back of our minds as the underlying issue." We parted. My supervisor went home to his own home and his cat, and I returned to the House of Tulle.

I walked into the house to be greeted by a beautiful sight. Margaret was standing on a low stood in the middle of the room. She wore her wedding gown. I stopped when I came through the door. "Margaret, you are magnificently beautiful. M'TG doesn't deserve to have someone so stunning for his bride."

She smiled at me but didn't move. The women of the household sat on the floor, pinning lace all around the hem of the dress.

Leah raised her head and looked at me. "Oh, there you are. We won't be ready for dinner for at least another hour." She ignored my dismay and continued to tell me about her day. "We all thought this dress looked the best on Margaret, but she liked the lace around the hem on another dress. The other dress hung all wrong for her, but the lace was lovely." Leah's voice turned dreamy as she talked about the lace. "We bought this dress and some lace. We want to get all the lace at least pinned on while we have several people to work on it."

Margaret's mother explained. "I think this lace is nicer than that on the other dress."

Margaret agreed. "Yes, that is the best part. This lace is much prettier."

My mama looked tired, "See…um…son…." She smiled. "See how this lace has these little clusters of…um… pearls?"

The women took turns instructing me. "The clusters of pearls are almost the same as one of the motif's we designed."

"We have a ribbon with pearls on it for tying up the tulle along the walkway."

"I think pearls will be a lovely design element for a wedding by the water."

I managed to get a word into the stream of chatter. "Where are my children? Where are Papa and the guys?" My head started aching from the talk of lace, and pearls, and ribbon. I tried to tell myself working all day talking about murder caused the headache. Five minutes of talking about lace and pearls caused it. As I left the room, I thought about Leah's shining face. I had a small pain of regret. I should have insisted on a big wedding for us.

Leah called after me. "The men are all in the study."

I ran for the study and hoped they had some sort of food for me.

Papa's voice radiated concern. "Jake you look exhausted. What happened?"

I found a chair as my children jumped and ran to meet me.

"See Papa, I'm a kangaroo." Jacob jumped around the room for me.

Petral explained. "We took them to the zoo."

"Rawr" Elizabeth tried to look fierce and achieved looking adorable as she climbed into my lap. "Lion."

I held and kissed my children. "Ah it is good to be home."

Papa still acted concerned. "You look beat. Rough day?"

"Huh? Oh…um…no not particularly rough. I got caught for a few minutes talking about lace and pearls and…well you get the idea."

"You missed the tears." Papa said dryly.

"What were the tears about?"

"Beats me, something about lace and which dress to buy."

I nodded. "Ah I heard something about that."

The Father of the Bride, Cousin Seb, gave me some happy news. "Thankfully Leah came up with the idea of putting lace on the dress they finally decided to buy."

"Ah, that was Leah's idea?"

Papa nodded.

I sighed. "They all seem happy with the plan." I ran my hands over my face. "I'm thankful that went so well then." I looked out the window. "Leah… well… some of the society women have been nasty to her. I disapprove of them. She would do better to find friends among working class women."

I felt slightly guilty about bringing Julie Jouyet's name into my questioning. I smiled. I hoped someone made that little wench uncomfortable.

We spent another two days in the capital. Our numbers swelled when the rest of the women and girls from The Cove arrived on the Saturday morning train. Once the important question of the wedding dress was decided, the bride's maids and flower girls needed to find dresses. Margaret asked Leah to be a bride's maid. I looked forward to seeing my wife in a lovely gown.

Once we got the women started on their shopping, the men decided we would go to a football game. I planned to take Jacob. Jacob insisted Elizabeth was tired of shopping. She wanted to go to the game too. Elizabeth didn't look like she was ready to give up on the whole wedding dress, lace and tulle project. "Elizabeth, do you want to stay with your mama and grandmama and buy dresses for the wedding." She nodded.

Jacob remained adamant. "No Elizabeth, you want to come with Papa and me and watch the game."

She gave her brother a sad look.

I tried to speak for Elizabeth. "Jacob I really think she would rather stay with the women and do girl things." Elizabeth looked back and forth between us. Finally she wrapped her arms around my neck and put her head on my shoulder. My heart melted. "I guess she wants to go to the game."

When we got home from the game, the women were there before us. The bride's maids' dress hunt had gone well. Margaret's mama had noticed something just the green of the sea when the sun has not yet risen above the hills. Leah was wearing her dress when we came through the door.

I smiled at my stunning wife. "That is perfect with your hair." I turned to my cousin. "Did you choose this just to go with her hair?"

"I chose it to go with the cove. It looks good on all the girls."

I took my children off to wash up before they touched one of the lovely dresses.

As I carried Jacob out of the room, he asked. "Was that my Mama?"

I chuckled. "Yes son, that lovely lady is your mama."

"Wow, she is beautiful." This observation produced giggles all around.

I got the children cleaned up and put them down for a nap before dinner. I was singing them a song when Nicki came and got me. "Phone. Take it in the study."

I ran downstairs and picked up the phone in the study. "Jaconovich"

"Yablonski, what the hell are you doing?"

"Um…my cousin is getting married. My wife, my daughter and my mother will all be part of the wedding party. I'm trying to hide from discussions of lace and tulle."

He laughed. "You and your little friend are creating quite a stir."

"Um…why?"

"It seems you know a great deal that others would rather keep secret."

"Uh…I'm not so certain about the secret part. Vanderholm's attorneys are sitting in on every deposition. Yes, the people we depose are talking openly about who was to eliminate whom. That does not seem to be a big concern. Oh, I do have a copy of a list of people to be eliminated. It includes our friend Kerby. Some of the people on this list I have no idea who they are and where they fit in, like, General Johan. Who is he? Where does he fit into the puzzle?"

"What? General Johan is on a hit list that you got from, where?"

"My supervisor got it from one of Vanderholm's clerks."

"I better look at this thing."

"Fine do you want me to bring it by your office?"

"No. I'll come get it."

"How does General Johan fit in?"

"He was the person who ordered out a thousand troops to arrest the troops involved in the last purge."

"He's a good guy then."

"Yes. Yes he is one of the few people I trust."

"Well shit. You better look at this list."

"Yeah."

Papa and Micki had just left to get a take-out dinner when Yablonski arrived. I took him into the study and showed him the list. He pulled out a pen and wrote dates beside five of the eleven names. He explained to me who had done what during the purge. Of the seven people on the list who were still alive, three, like Kerby, could be considered part of the conspiracy around the purge. The other four, like General Johan were honest men. Peter explained what they might have done to anger Vanderholm.

I quizzed Peter. "I suspect that Vanderholm will claim that he ordered the executions in the interest of national security. What I need to know is how do I argue that someone was not a threat to national security at the time of the purge. General Johan may well have issued orders contradicting the Emperor."

Yablonski explained, "The emperor did not have exclusive command over the military. We have seven military bases in this country. The commanders from each base form a ruling council that can over-ride any order from the emperor, if it concerns military activity. That is why General Johan's troops were three hours behind those involved in the purge. As soon as the attack started, all of the generals got on the phone and discussed the problem. They quickly reached a consensus to halt the purge. It was within their power to do so. The emperor couldn't do a damned thing about it. General Johan had his troops ready to roll by the time he got off of the phone. We knew the purge was coming. We couldn't do anything about it until after the attack began."

"I thought we had put the purge behind us. One of the clerks in Vanderholm's office told me that President Vanderholm was in on every stage of the planning."

"I'm sure he was but why would a clerk tell you such a thing?"

"That's what I can't figure out. These people seem competent enough but when I start asking questions they just spill it all out."

"How much of what they say is true?"

"I don't know. Look at this list. Five of these people are already dead. We know LaBarge intended to kill Kerby. Does that validate the rest of the list?"

"I will find out."

"Also, there is an assassin named, Webb. Papadakos likes to use him. Vanderholm preferred La Barge, but LaBarge is out of the country."

Yablonski grunted, "LaBarge is also on this list. We picked up the people intending to kill him."

I further unburdened myself. "The court recorder is frightened because he has heard all of this stuff about hiring assassins. Do you think there is any threat to the security of the court?"

Yablonski looked at me. "I don't know. Why don't you hire some security?"

"Shit."

"Yeah." Yablonski left.

I immediately called the head of security for Rouseff. "Um…this is Jake… um…well…when I was in college you had some guys protecting me? Um… well…that might be a good idea again."

"No shit! Did that big guy from CGIS tell you to get protection?"

I looked around the room wondering how someone at Rouseff knew about Yablonski less than five minutes after he left. "Yeah, how did you know about the big guy from CGIS?"

"Rouseff told us to watch your back."

I sighed. "Thanks, it is almost more important to watch my wife and children."

"We're on it."

"I guess that's all then." I hung up and smiled over the idea of Rouseff telling someone to watch my back. Papa returned with my dinner.

Elizabeth and Jacob woke up in time to eat. Jacob horrified our relatives by educating his sister on the content of our Chinese dinner. "See? Squished up beetle blood. See? Worms. See? Maggots. See? Rat meat."

Leah let out a horrified squeak. "Jacob stop this minute. Who told you such things?"

Jacob looked at me.

I looked at Papa. "Did you check the dumpster behind the restaurant and the garbage cans in the kitchen?"

"Yes, Jake. It's chicken."

"Ah Jacob, this meat does happen to be chicken." I winked at Mama. She laughed. Leah still scowled at me. The rest of the family knew the story of me selling rats to Mr. Wu.

Sunday morning, the rest of the party prepared to go home to The Cove. Mama and Papa planned to visit one of the stationmasters. I boarded the train and looked forward to a few hours of peace and quiet in my own home.

Chapter 12 Pre-Trial Motions

As soon as I got home, I tried calling Yablonski to see if he could tell me how to find General Johan. I couldn't reach him. I looked at a map to find the closest military base. I found one between my city and the capital, but I couldn't find any phone numbers. I wondered how to call the base. Finally, on Monday morning I figured out how to call General Johan. I greeted my secretary at Rouseff Properties warmly.

She inquired politely. "Did you have a nice trip?"

Sometimes my mind works flawlessly. Sometimes I appear wise and articulate. This morning was one of those mornings. "Yes. The women found a stunning wedding dress with lace around the hem for Margaret. They found bride's maids' dresses. Leah looks fantastic in her dress." I smiled.

"Oh I bet you had so much fun."

I smiled. Then I slipped in the little favor I wanted. "Can you get hold of General Johan at the military base between here and the capital? Thanks." I escaped into my office. Rouseff's nephew followed me in to get his morning pep talk.

I started off by asking casually, "How were things while we were gone?"

"The demolition is proceeding. We found a suitcase full of money in one building."

"One of our buildings?"

"Yes."

"I suppose it technically belongs to the company. What did you do with it?"

"I put the money in the safe."

"What do you think should be done with it?"

"Is this a trick question?"

I laughed. "How could that possibly be a trick question? I want your opinion."

My secretary rescued Young Rouseff. "Sir, General Johan is on the phone."

I waved Young Rouseff off. "General Johan?"

He grunted.

"Jake Jaconovich. I am prosecuting ex-president Vanderholm on a number of charges. In the course of our investigation, we came across a list of names that was described to my supervisor as a hit list. Five of the people on the list are dead."

"Yeah, Yablonski called me right after he talked to you."

"Ah, good. I am curious as to why you think you're on the list."

"Why don't you come out to the base?"

"I can do that." I smiled when I remembered that Rouseff owned a helicopter. "Do you have a place I can set down my helicopter?"

"I'll have the helipad cleared for you in say an hour?"

I got off of the phone with the General Johan just as Mr. Farley called. "Jake, what is your schedule for working on the case?"

"Right now I am leaving for a meeting with General Johan. You know the more I think about it, the more certain I am that Vanderholm does not intend to deny the murder charges."

Mr. Farley worried, "I am inclined to think he plans to expunge the testimony of his employees."

"Are we in danger of not being able to prove murder?"

"Jake, I think we have good documentation. I suspect his attorney may also try to expunge any information we got from LaBarge."

I'd thought about this problem earlier. "If we presented it in court, they might try to expunge. I had not considered the information he gave us as evidence. I'm using it only as an outline for tracing money and important people. I wonder if he will try to expunge testimony from his employees because they are simple minded or because they are his employees?"

"I will research possible causes to expunge their testimony."

I brought up another question. "I wonder if he realizes that hiring someone to kill for you is considered murder?"

"Possibly not."

We ended the call, and I left for my meeting with General Johan, who explained the process through which he became aware of the purge. He explained the law and procedures that allowed the military to overrule an order from the Emperor. "We were able to push this provision through as law after the barge purge when thousands of women and children were killed in their homes on the barges. The military threatened a military coup if the emperor denied us this right. This was the second time we used it to stop a purge. We didn't learn about the burning of M'TK in time to prevent that."

I gave him my standard answer about the burning of M'TK.

We discussed the information I had and Vanderholm's behavior. I explained, "I have an unusual amount of documentation that he ordered not only the murder of the man, Kerby but that he ordered the execution of five other people. Did Yablonski warn you about the man named Webb?"

The general leaned back in his chair looking grim. "Yeah, he warned me. We are looking for Mr. Webb. We'd like to find LaBarge too. Major Yablonski thinks you know where he is."

"Ah, the major is mistaken. I do not know where LaBarge is. I know he was afraid. I know he intended to go far away."

We went over the information from LaBarge and brought up the topic of the automatic weapons supplied to the rioters and private police.

The general swore creatively for a minute or so over the idea that the president armed private citizens better than he did the army. "You know who else you need to talk to..." General Johan gave me more names of more people to contact. He suggested I speak first to the general who ordered his troops out for the purge. After meeting with General Johan I retuned to the city in time to grab a lunch on my way to the prosecutor's office. I felt profoundly thankful for the helicopter especially since it did not have gold plated rotors.

I updated Mr. Farley on my meeting with General Johan. We agreed that the next day I would take my helicopter to the base where the purge originated. This became my routine over the next few months. I'd work in Rouseff's office for twenty to thirty hours a week then I would spend the rest of my time traveling around the country talking to people and taking depositions when I thought I needed them. We still didn't have a statement from Vanderholm.

I continued to gather bits and pieces of information. I thought I began to understand how the Vanderholms conducted their business. I started asking two questions over and over. First I asked, "The Vanderholms have tremendous resources. Their grain exports alone are enough to make them wealthy. They have their distilleries and their shipping. They do not have to operate outside the law to be obscenely wealthy. Why do you think they don't obey the law?" I heard various theories on this. Most theories centered on the theme that they were so rich and had been so powerful for so long that they did not acknowledge that the law existed for them.

My second question concerned Vanderholm's employees. "When we talked to Vanderhom's employees. They told us everything they knew about Vanderholm's illegal activities. Why do you think they are being so open about this?" The answers were more varied. Some people commented that his employees seemed to be naïve or simple-minded. Others commented that his employees were always a little drunk. Others theorized that his employees believed that Vanderholm was a god who could, by definition, do no wrong.

My travels had one added benefit. I needed to spend some time in our two provinces furthest east. It amazed me to learn that Vanderholm had holdings in these provinces. I had not known that they were grain-producing areas and that one of Vanderholms' distilleries was located in the farthest eastern province.

For this trip, I took Leah and the children with us. We were still working on the baby project. Elizabeth was fifteen months old, and we still didn't have another baby on the way. We took the train east. That evening we put the children to bed a little early because they had not taken long naps. Before I finished reading one of their favorite stories, they fell asleep. I looked at my darling wife and grinned. She smiled and giggled.

About three weeks after our trip east, I came home a little early. Jacob and Elizabeth were playing in the front yard. Jacob greeted me. "Shhh, Mama's sleeping."

I picked up my children and carried them quietly into the house where I found Leah napping on the sofa. I stood and looked down at her. I marveled over her beauty. I looked closely at her face. It appeared rounder than usual. I mentally counted days. I smiled. The trip east produced more leads, more documents, three depositions and a new baby on the way.

We finally felt ready to move forward with the prosecution, but we had a problem. Mr. Farley and I took our problem to the judge. "We feel that we have good documentation for our charges. Vanderholm pleads not-guilty, but he has not made a statement. We cannot address his plea if he doesn't make a statement."

The judge thought for a minute before he concluded, "His attorney's have learned from the Fortenac case. They know Jake will pick apart everything he says. It looks to me like they will refuse to make a statement then try to discredit everything you say in court."

Mr. Farley explained our next problem. "Um…that may be another problem. They have had an attorney present for every deposition. They know we have talked about various documents in the depositions but they are not aware of all the documentation we have. We will be presenting to the court, case law from before the new constitution and excerpts from our current constitution. Without regular meetings between both sides, we have not been able to pass them material."

I elaborated. "We are not even certain who to pass the material to. When we took depositions in the capital we would each have a different attorney with us. I've met at least eight attorneys. They still have not declared an attorney of record."

Judge Gannon shifted in his chair. "They are not making this easy for you."

I added, "At this point the best we can do is send all the other attorneys a complete set of all our documentation. We need to get an affidavit from them stating they have given us all their documentation."

The judge rubbed the back of his neck. "I think we better set a hearing to set a court date. At that time, I will ask for the attorney of record. I will set a deadline for the defendant to make his statement. Will that work for you?"

We nodded and began working out several possible dates for the hearing.

I mentioned that Leah was pregnant and was only half-joking when I commented, "I would like to avoid any work with the prosecutor's office within three months of her due date. It seems that every time my wife has a baby, all hell breaks loose in the city." I shook my head remembering breaking Yablonski's nose.

Mr. Farley chuckled then explained. "He gets cranky when his wife is about to deliver. I think he gets much more creative about thinking up charges for anyone who interferes with his concentrating on the birth."

They laughed at me. I shrugged. We prepared to leave.

Mr. Farley remembered our routine parting. "Oh, and remember to pay your taxes."

The judge chuckled. "I think you guys are turning this economic disaster around." We left happy to have a court date.

Life was good. The Rouseff offices buzzed with activity. The road grew a little longer each day. We'd started construction on the motel. We'd designed two new parks.

The Vanderholm case looked good from our perspective. We had slightly over three kilos of documentation. People I talked to continued to call us and fax in more information. I'd gotten the import receipt and the sales receipts for the automatic weapons we'd confiscated.

We finally had a date for a preliminary hearing to set a trial date. Mr. Farley wanted our interns and two youngest attorneys to go to the capital with us. They were nervous and excited.

The hearing began. We stated that we were prepared to go to trial, but we did not have a statement from the defendant.

The judge insisted on controlling of all the questions. "How does the defendant plead?"

Mr. Vanderholm answered himself. "Not guilty." His tone dripped with contempt for the judge and whole court.

"Does the defendant intend to make a statement?"

The oldest attorney replied, "No, he will not make a statement."

"Who is to act as your Attorney of Record?"

The Vanderholm attorneys conferred among themselves. Finally a man in his late forty's stood up. "This is a farce!" The man's face turned red, and the veins stood out on his neck. "We demand that the charges against Mr. Vandeholm be dropped. He is the most respected man in this country. The allegations from this rabble are an insult to the court and to the prestigious name of Vanderholm."

The judge patiently explained. "The charges have enough documentation that the case must go to trial unless Mr. Vanderholm chooses to plead guilty."

"This is ridiculous! I demand that you drop these charges." Hab Vanderholm stood and snarled at the judge. His face turned almost purple, and his tone of voice dripped contempt and venom. His whole body vibrated with his outrage.

"Order! You have not been given permission to speak."

"I don't need your permission to speak." Vanderholm spat back at the judge.

The judge turned to the court recorder, "**Let the record show** that as the presiding judge in this case I have added one charge of contempt of court to Mr. Vanderholm's case." The judged watched as the court recorder made his notes. "Now, I will try this again, and I want you to remain silent except to answer the question. Who will act as the Attorney of Record for this case?"

Vanderholm sat down and looked at his attorneys.

Finally the eldest attorney, a man I judged to be in his eighties spoke up. "I, Fritz Vanderholm Senior, will act as the Attorney of Record." He wheezed a little as he tried to make his voice heard.

"Prosecution have you presented Mr. Fritz Vanderholm with all your documentation."

"Mr. Farley answered for us. We hand delivered the documentation to Mr. Fritz Vanderholm's office. He was not present at the time we presented it. We do have a receipt."

I heard murmurs, snorts, and shuffling from the Vanderholm side of the room.

"Attorney Vanderholm, did you receive the documentation from the prosecution?"

Fritz Vanderholm's response came out somewhere between a snort and a contemptuous laugh. "Yes, if that's what all those boxes of papers were about."

"**Let the record show** that attorney for the defense Fritz Vanderholm acknowledges receipt of the documentation from the prosecution."

Judge Gannon turned toward our side of the room. "Who is to act as Prosecutor of Record for the prosecution?"

Mr. Farley stated his name and his intention to act as prosecutor of record. "As the Prosecutor of Record, I petition the court to make note that our prosecutor's office is also a teaching position. With the court's permission, I would like for our interns to participate in the court process."

"**Let the record show** that in addition to the Prosecutor of Record, interns from his office may at times represent the prosecution." The judge entered Yuri and Antoine's names into the record also.

Again, I heard murmurs and whispering from across the aisle. We hoped the defense would be unsettled by the fact that I was not the Prosecutor of Record.

The judge turned to the defense. "Mr. Vanderholm have you presented the prosecution with all of your documentation."

"Yes sir. We have."

The judge turned back to our side of the room. "Did you receive all Mr. Vanderholm's documentation?"

"We have not received anything from Mr. Vanderholm's office, your honor."

Judge Gannon sounded impatient. "Mr. Vanderholm, you heard the prosecutor. He has not received anything."

"We do not intend to present anything."

The judge appeared more annoyed than shocked. "Prosecution, when will you be ready to present the case to me?"

"If the defense has nothing more to add, we can do so now."

The judge motioned us forward. Mr. Farley and Antione carried three large boxes forward and set them on the judge's table. He scowled at the volume of papers.

"**Let the record show** that the case has been presented to this court. We will convene in one month."

The judge looked over his glasses at me. I nodded and smiled. He set a court date for one month away—well within my time limits for getting this out of the way before the birth of our baby.

On the train ride home we speculated that Vanderholm might try to cause a mistrial. Yuri insisted, "Vanderholm is so arrogant he probably thinks he will be acquitted just because he's a Vanderholm."

Mr. Farley nodded and scowled. "Jake, how confident are you that the judge will hear the case impartially?"

I squirmed in my seat. "He returned a guilty verdict in the Fortenac case. I am certain when presented with documentation he will attempt to be fair and honest. He did admit to me that he had once considered the Vanderholms above reproach. I would have asked Judge Stimson to hear the case, if I had really believed that Judge Gannon would be influenced by Vanderholm's name."

Chapter 13 Security of The Court

We returned home and waited. Leah and I saw Allison and Christian socially about once a week. I wished the two women got along better. Although they had much in common, Leah always seemed shy with Allison.

Long before Leah's pregnancy made her tired, I talked to Rouseff security about bringing a couple into my house for security. They found me an ex-military man who assured us he was trained in the type of security we needed. His wife would be happy to be our housekeeper. When I interviewed the man, I learned he was trained in martial arts, so I hired him as a sparring partner and hoped his wife knew how to cook and do laundry.

Leah had her hands full with two toddlers and another on the way. In the evenings I spent time teaching Jacob to count and learn the alphabet. Jacob insisted that Elizabeth wanted to learn too. She dutifully recited the numbers and letters along with her brother. She was learning to talk much faster than her brother had. Perhaps his constant instruction and talking to her did help her learn.

Mr. Farley asked me as a prosecutor to present a Statement of Outrage on behalf of the citizens hurt by Vanderholm's betrayal of their trust. This obligation turned out to be more challenging than I expected. First, I wrote down all my thoughts as they related to the charges. I took each charge and wrote one sentence of why this was outrageous to me. I felt dissatisfied with the result. I went over my statement first thing every time I arrived in the prosecutor's office. I read it over last thing at night. I changed the wording I worried about it.

I finally took the statement to Papa. I read what I had written.

He leaned back in his chair. "Son, what you are saying is all true. It is what your head is telling you, but it doesn't sound like you talking to the people you love. If you are not speaking from love you can't express your true outrage."

I swallowed. I thought about the people I loved I thought about my family.

I thought about Jacob and Elizabeth. I thought about the world that I wanted them to grow up in. I agreed with Papa.

While we were waiting for a court date, Jouyet announced that he intended to close his paper mill. I was distressed that more people would be without jobs. This would probably lead to rioting in the city. I knew we could hire some people. They were not trained in construction. It would take time to train them. I intended to make a second and third shift if possible to keep the road construction progressing around the clock. Our architects were planning for the gas station and convenience store. I told our development team to start planning to build a paper mill.

I still had security at home and guards following me during the day. I worried about Jeffrey's safety because he was the Prosecutor of Record for the Vanderholm case. I told him my concerns.

He smiled at me. "Jake thank you for thinking about me, but I can't imagine that Vanderholm will try to hurt me before the trial. Not even he would try something so obvious."

I still worried. The problem nagged at me. I spoke to Rouseff security about finding someone to protect my supervisor. We didn't have enough Rouseff security to spare. They had a few suggestions. Those people were not available. I talked to the police. They didn't have staff to spare. I called Major Yablonski and told him my worries.

"Shit." Yablonski understood. He agreed with me!

"Yeah." I was begging for help.

"I'll see what I can do." My supervisor would have protection.

I smiled, relieved when I noticed CGIS special agents following Mr. Farley.

Finally, the evening before we were to go up to the capital for the trial arrived. We planned to be in the capital one day early and spend that day going over the case. I arrived home from the office and hugged and kissed my children. I chased my pregnant wife around our bedroom. When I caught her, I kissed her soundly. When I got done kissing her she was giggling. The phone rang.

I picked up the phone. "Jaconvich."

"Yablonski."

"Yeah?"

"My man who was watching your supervisor just called."

I felt like I'd just been doused with ice water.

"Mr. Farley's been shot. My man hit the assailant before he fired. Your supervisor is wounded. We sent him to the hospital. The assailant got away, but he will need medical treatment. We'll find him."

"Shit."

"Yeah."

I grabbed up the car keys I'd thrown on the bed earlier. "Look, I need to head for the hospital right now."

"No."

"Why not?"

"Security. You stay put. Alert your men."

We hung up, and I sat down and held my head for thirty seconds before I called Christian. We split up the list of the office staff between us. I explained that Yablonski had told me to stay home tonight. We decided the whole office staff should follow those orders.

Christian asked, "What about tomorrow?"

"Tomorrow we are going to the capital. If I have to hire a helicopter to take us up there I will. I really think the trains are safe enough."

Christian almost whispered. "Surely the judge will allow one of us to take over. We won't have to delay the case because the Prosecutor of Record is in the hospital?"

"Oh, I'm sure he will let one of us fill in. I want to call the hospital now and find out how Jeffrey is."

I called the hospital and learned that Mr. Farley was in surgery. They wouldn't tell me any more. I'm thankful they didn't. If I'd known he had been hit in the head I would have been frantic.

The next morning, long before visiting hours, I went to the hospital. I used my status as a prosecutor to get in. I insisted that I needed to see the patient and assess his injuries to start our procedures for prosecution. They let me in. I looked at the records. The bullet had grazed his head and fractured his skull. The surgery the night before had removed small pieces of bone from his brain. The doctor didn't think the injury was life threatening, but he was very concerned about infection.

I went in to see Jeffery. I talked to him. I wasn't sure he heard me. "Sir, this is Jake."

He opened his eyes then closed them again as if opening them hurt.

I tried to sound assuring. "You're not to worry about anything. We can handle everything at the office."

He whispered. "I think I was shot. Be careful."

"Yes sir, you were shot. Everybody in the office is being careful. We are going to the capital today. Everything will be fine."

He whispered again, "I think I was shot. Be careful."

His words frightened me more than the danger. I was terrified that he might never recover.

Chapter 14 Vanderholm Trial

All the prosecutors met early to go over who would go to the capital. We decided all of us would go leaving the paralegals to handle business at home. Before we finished our meeting, about twenty-five members of a military special-forces team arrived at the prosecutor's office to escort us from our office to the capital. General Johan had ordered them out. We rode up on the train and were escorted to our hotel where our dinner was sent up to the hotel room. We had guards in the lobby and on our floor. They were very visible. I thought perhaps they were General Johan's Statement of Outrage.

We didn't have anything to do so we sat down and ran over the case again with our interns and the rest of the staff taking turns explaining why the evidence should not be expunged. I ran a couple variations of my Statement of Outrage past the others. We debated which of the other attorneys should replace our supervisor.

Christian agreed to let Leroy do the honors. I thought he would do a better job. I also suspected that he worried about Alison and the babies and didn't want to place himself in danger. We tested, Char and Alexander, our youngest attorneys on all the charges. I kept assuring them that any of them would do just fine. "I had less experience than you when I presented the Fortenac case. The important part is to know your material." We went over the material again.

In the morning the special-forces team escorted us to the courtroom. We arrived before the defense and entered while still debating who would sit where. Most of our staff would be seated directly behind those of us who were on the prosecutor's bench. Our two interns were on the record as representing the prosecution so they needed to be on the prosecutor's bench. I sat on the prosecutor's bench to make my Statement of Outrage. Leroy sat down with us since we planned for him to replace our supervisor. Leroy and I had the interns between us. One of our guards stood on the defense side of the room. One stood at the entrance in the back of the room. The other guard stood beside us, between us, and the outer wall. He stood facing the defense.

The defense attorneys arrived with Mr. Vanderholm. Vanderholm looked at our guards. I could not quite categorize his expression. He leaned toward his attorney and whispered something. The attorney nodded.

The court clerk entered the room. "Are all parties for the prosecution present?"

Leroy answered. "All parties who are capable of being here are present."

The clerk asked, "Are all parties for the defense present?"

"All parties for the defense are present as agreed upon."

I wondered what that little phrase, "as agreed upon" meant. I wondered if they were going to protest the absence of our supervisor. I suspected they knew full well why he was absent.

The court recorder entered and took his place.

The court clerk said, "All rise for the judge." It had begun. I had a sick feeling in the middle of my stomach. I had no idea how much worse this was going to get or I might not have been able to stand.

The judge entered and sat down. Hi eyes surveyed the courtroom. He frowned when he saw the guards. "Can someone tell me why we have armed soldiers in my courtroom."

I spoke up. "Yes sir. I can explain."

Vanderholm's attorney jumped to his feet and shouted. "He is not the Attorney of Record."

The judge turned toward me. I took this as a sign that I had permission to speak. "Sir, this prosecutor's office has several issues to discuss before we go to trial. First, the guards are present because General Johan ordered out a special-forces team to protect our prosecutor's office after our Prosecutor of Record was shot. The guards are here at the order of a general in the military, and since no single individual can over-ride a decision by the council of generals, clearing the courtroom of the guards may work temporarily, but they will be back. It is a waste of the court's time to attempt to clear the court."

I took a deep breath and continued. "We have another matter to bring before the court that is not related to the charges in the case before the court. As I mentioned the person serving as our Prosecutor of Record, Jeffrey Farley, was shot yesterday evening. Witnesses at the scene called this an attempted assassination. He will not be able to serve. My colleague Leroy Spinoza-Carter is prepared to serve as Prosecutor of Record in his stead."

The judge nodded. "Is this acceptable to the defense?"

"No, it is not. They have two other Prosecutors of Record. Let them serve."

The judge sighed and turned back to me. "You do have two other Prosecutors of Record. Why cannot they serve?"

"Your honor, if you will recall, my supervisor named the other two attorneys because we are a teaching office working with the local university to train attorneys. The other two individuals listed are interns. They have not passed their exams to practice law. They must have a supervisor present for all legal work they perform. I am concerned that allowing them to act as primary attorneys of record will result in a mistrial."

The judge turned back to the defense. "The defense has heard the reason that the Prosecutor of Record is absent. He was shot. The defense has heard the reasons the other attorneys mentioned cannot serve. Is it acceptable with you for them to replace their Prosecutor of Record?"

"No it is not."

The judge scowled, "Are you adamant that they cannot replace their Prosecutor of Record with a fully qualified attorney?"

"We are adamant."

"Will you accept the interns as being the same as fully qualified attorneys?"

"Yes, we will accept the interns to act as the Prosecutors of Record the same as a fully qualified attorney."

"**Let the record show** that the defense will not allow substitutions for the position of Prosecutor of Record."

"**Let the record show** that the defense will accept the interns listed as attorneys of record to act as fully qualified attorneys."

"**Let the record show** that the defense cannot later claim mistrial because the interns lack full qualification."

"**Let the record show** that the special-forces ordered to protect the prosecution may remain in the courtroom."

I sat in shock. I heard the young student, Yuri Spencer beside me making gulping sounds. I wondered what on earth the judge was thinking.

I saw Leroy writing a note. "The DEFENSE cannot claim…"

The judge opened the case. He asked the prosecution if we had any motions.

Our interns had decided between themselves who would speak. Leroy had written yes and no on a piece of paper and pointed to the correct answer. Yuri stood and squeaked, "The prosecution does not have any motions at this time." He sat down again, and I patted his shoulder.

"Does the defense have any motions at this time?"

The Attorney of Record slowly struggled to his feet. I attributed some of his awkwardness to age. Finally, he stood. "Yes, your honor, our first motion is to clear the prosecutors bench of the attorneys who are not presenting this case."

"Is this acceptable to the prosecution."

Antoine Vibe our second intern stood. "No your honor."

"Can you tell the court why?"

"They are here to present their Statements of Outrage." Antoine sat down.

"Motion denied. Does the defense have any other motions to present to the court?"

"The defense moves to expunge the documentation for the charges of defrauding the court from the record."

The judge turned to the prosecution. "Is that acceptable?"

Yuri grinned. He knew the answer. "No sir, that is not acceptable."

"Can you tell the court why?"

Again Yuri grinned. "The first piece of documentation is a letter written by the defendant. It is not opinion or hearsay. The second piece of documentation is the accounting record showing the wages paid to a person to serve as supervisor in a prosecutor's office when that person was not an attorney. It is not opinion or hearsay. The third…"

I thought I heard the judge snort. "That will be all. Motion denied." The judge glanced our direction again.

I wondered what the judge was thinking. Did he guess that we had been drilling our interns on this case? I worried they might not be so quick to know the answers when the charges became more complicated.

The interns performed professionally until we ran into a tricky motion.

"The defense moves to expunge all of the documentation for the charges of Violating the Security of the Court."

The judge asked our interns, "Is this acceptable?"

The interns conferred. They were confused. Leroy pointed to "no." He'd also written the word "mistrial" on his note pad. He pointed to the second word.

Antoine stood up. "No. That is not acceptable."

"Can you tell the court why?"

"Yes sir, the documentation following the charge of Violating the Security of the Court is a statement rescinding the charges. Expunging the statement rescinding the charges could result in a mistrial."

The judge sighed and leaned back in his chair. He looked from one side of the courtroom to the other. I thought maybe he looked at the guards.

"**Let the record show** that the defense has requested to expunge the statement rescinding the charges of Violating the Security of the Court."

"**Let the record show** that since this request comes from the defense complying with this motion cannot later be grounds for declaring a mistrial."

"**Let the record show** that the motion to expunge the statement rescinding the charges of Violating the Security of the Court is granted. The document shall be expunged." The judge had the whole case in front of him. He removed one piece of paper and put it in the trash.

Yuri started to shake so I wrote him a note. "You are doing great." I thought the last motion must be a trick question from the defense to force a mistrial. I assumed they hoped our inexperienced students would allow the motion.

The motions to expunge continued. Our interns still knew the correct answers as to why the documentation must remain. They had a copy of the case open in front of them. One of them would speak while the other looked at the charges coming up next and made notes. They took turns speaking.

Finally we came to the charge for treason. The defense moved to expunge the documentation. He added. "This is a ridiculous charge. Hab Vanderholm could not commit treason because he was the president. How could he commit treason against himself?"

The judge turned to our side of the room. "I have seen your documentation. What do you have to say to the motion to expunge?"

Yuri gulped a few times before he spoke. "The motion is not acceptable. The documentation consists of shipping receipts and sales receipts for automatic weapons. It also consists of first person depositions from those who confiscated the weapons and those who were…um…" Yuri looked down at me. "…um…those who had been given the weapons to use. It consists of their depositions stating their orders. The final piece of documentation is an excerpt from our constitution defining a private army and forbidding the formation of private armies. None of this documentation is opinion or hearsay, and it relates to the charge of treason through hiring and arming a private army." Yuri sat and gulped beside me.

Judge Gannon made his ruling. "**Let the record show** that the documentation for the charge of treason may stand as submitted."

I breathed a sigh of relief. I'd worried that the judge would agree with the defense and rule that the president could not by definition commit treason.

The final charge in the file was for murder. The judge asked if there were any other motions from the defense.

"The defense moves to expunge the documentation for the charge of murder from the record. It is irrelevant."

The judge turned to the prosecution. "Is this acceptable to the prosecution?"

Both interns shook so bad they had trouble getting to their feet. I noticed Leroy put his hand on Antoine's back as he nodded at the lad. Antoine shook the whole table in front of us when he got to his feet.

"No sir, that is not acceptable."

"Can you tell the court why?"

Antoine swallowed a couple times. "I…uh…"

We heard a snickering from the other side of the room. The Vanderholm attorneys smirked, shuffled, and poked each other. That was a huge mistake on their part.

Antoine looked at those smug faces. He stopped shaking and stood up straighter. His voice almost rang through the courtroom. "Expunging the documentation for the charge of murder is unacceptable because some of it consists of logs and written records kept by the defendants staff at his request. It is not opinion or hearsay. Some of it consists of depositions taken from people who interacted directly as an agent for Mr. Vanderholm. They are relating their own interactions with the defendant under oath. Their testimony is neither opinion nor hearsay. Some of the records are third party records including telephone and bank records. These are neither opinion nor hearsay. The final documentation is from eyewitnesses reporting under oath, events they saw with their own eyes. It is neither opinion nor hearsay." He sat down.

"**Let the record show** that the motion to expunge the documentation for the charge of murder is denied."

We all leaned back and sighed. The judge proceeded to question Mr. Vanderholm. Much to my shock, Mr. Vanderholm admitted hiring Mr. LaBarge to kill those people on our list who were dead.

"I was the president of this country. I deemed the executions necessary for national security."

I pulled out my copy of our constitution and highlighted the passage that forbids the president to carry out any executions not ordered by the court. I noticed Leroy putting a paperclip on a page of the testimony. He wrote another note to Antoine.

I listened and made another note and watched Leroy as he started doing some serious writing.

When the judge asked if the prosecution had any motions, both interns leapt to their feet. They looked at each other and giggled.

Yuri spoke first. "Yes, the prosecution has several motions to clarify the record. First, concerning Mr. Vanderholms statement that he is innocent of murder because he ordered the executions as part of his role as president. Our constitution reads…" He proceeded to read the paragraph prohibiting the president from ordering executions." He sat down.

Leroy continued to write frantically.

Next, Antoine stood up. "I move to clarify the record concerning Mr. Vanderholm's statement that he could appoint anybody he wanted to be the supervisor in the prosecutor's office. This is covered in our constitution under Chapter Four regarding courts. It is mentioned in Section Three, Part Eight, Paragraph Sixteen. Would you like me to read it aloud to the court?"

"That won't be unnecessary Mr. Prosecutor. Do you have any other motions?"

They presented three more motions to clarify. The judge accepted all three.

The judge asked if the prosecution had any statements from concerned parties. I started to get to my feet, but Leroy leapt up before me. "Yes, your honor. I would like to present a Statement of Outrage on behalf of our legal system. I apologize and ask your indulgence for not including this with the original documents. My statement of outrage pertains to this case, but is necessitated by events occurring after the case was presented to the court."

The judge glanced briefly at the defense then back to Leroy. "You may proceed."

Leroy began to read, "I Leroy Spinoza-Carter a licensed attorney in good standing wish to express outrage on behalf of the officers of the court at the actions of Mr. Hab Vanderholm. Our country has a system of laws. We regulate who may and who may not practice to uphold these laws. We have a court system to decide when someone has broken one of the laws established under our constitution or through case law. Rule of law is absolutely essential to the peace of this country. Mr. Vanderholm has flouted those laws and shows absolutely no remorse. He claims he does not have to follow the laws because his name is Vanderholm. He has shown contempt for our court system in appointing an unqualified person to supervise a prosecutor's office. He has shown contempt for our court system through the irregularities seen here today. He terrorized these two students by insisting that they present this case when they do not have their license and have not completed their schooling. He tried to trick them with his motion to expunge our Statement to Rescind Charges. His behavior in this courtroom is worthy of our outrage. My outrage is based on something far deeper and far more destructive than the lack of respect this man has shown for the courts up to this point. He has presented a case based not on his actions but on his right to ignore the laws of this country. In asking for a verdict of not-guilty this man seeks to set a court precedent condoning murder, conspiracy to commit murder, violating the security of the court, professional fraud, treason, and all of the other charges that we have presented today. His insistence that the president has the authority to order an execution challenges our constitution. He seeks to have this court overthrow our constitution that was called for by court order and voted into existence by the citizens of this country." Leroy sat down.

"Thank you Mr. Spinoza-Carter. Are there any other statements?"

I stood up.

The judge nodded at me.

I began my statement of outrage. "I Jacob Jaconovich a licensed attorney and lifelong citizen of my city wish to express my outrage over the defendant's violation of our community, and his contempt for his duties as president of this country.

"Since the fall of Adam it has been the nature of mankind to commit all manner of evil acts. For this reason, we have instituted governments to keep order, protect the weak, curb the greedy, facilitate communication between communities, and to carry out the commandment to feed the hungry, house the poor, and to clothe the naked. It is the role of the government to enforce fair trade, equal access to essential resources and something more. It is the role of the government to foster a sense of belonging and community. It is the role of the government to foster pride in who we are as a people.

"In a democratic society such as we have become, the highest honor that can be bestowed upon an individual is to be elected to the office of president. The president is entrusted with great power and with the responsibility to present a moral example to our communities. He is entrusted with the responsibility to foster pride in our country and promote the bonds of friendship within our communities.

"Mr. Vanderholm was entrusted with the honor of holding this country's highest office and with the responsibilities of carrying out the duties of building communities. What did he do instead? He scorned the honor. He entered ruthlessly into our communities ordering attacks on private citizens and sowing fear and distrust among people who should be friends.

"His behavior has set an example of contempt for rule of law in our justice community where rule of law should be our highest standard.

"Mr. Vanderholm forced his moral pollution of murder and fraud all the way into an office that processes the problems of the most vulnerable people in the city. He brought it into an office where people, who are found guilty of such petty crimes as drunkenness or urinating in public, are punished appropriate to their crime.

"Every week in that office, one of us processes a case of a woman, usually a woman, who has been caught shoplifting food to feed her children. These women are punished appropriate to their crime. In our city, even those cases of petty crimes executed in desperation are punished according to their seriousness.

"My outrage stems from the very idea that this man who has everything in the way of money, power and prestige can come into our community, our home, and commit crimes far worse than the poorest of our poor, and he expects to be called not-guilty simply because he has money, and power, and prestige. He shows no sense of guilt or remorse. He expects us to release him without punishment. I demand justice for the people of my city; for the families of the people he has murdered; for the people who lived in fear because of his actions; for the innocent people who have suffered at the hands of his friends who follow his immoral example; and for the people who have lost their sense of pride in their home because of the actions of this man.

"If the poor and powerless, are expected to be held accountable for their behavior, our only decent course of action is to hold someone of wealth and power equally accountable."

I sat down.

"Does the defense have any statements from concerned parties?"

I was aware that the door at the back of the room opened. I knew several people entered and sat down. From the posture of our guard, and the nature of the sounds, I assumed the new arrivals had reason to be in the court. I did not look around.

One of Mr. Vanderholm's attorneys stood up and introduced himself. He launched into a statement that disgusted me. "Mr. Jaconovich has finally explained why he has been persecuting the Vanderholms. He does not understand that people with power and prestige cannot by definition be called guilty because they are acting for the best interest of the country. Mr. Vanderholm has not commit crimes--far from it. He has been acting out of charity in ridding our country of undesirables. It is unfortunate that these prosecutors have been offended by Mr. Vanderholm's methods, but he acted in the manner he deemed best to protect the security of this country. The idea that Mr. Vanderholm has anything in common with the lower orders that Mr. Jaconovich processes is preposterous." The attorney sat down.

"Are there anymore statements from either the defense or the prosecution?" The judge looked toward the back of the room.

A familiar voice from the back of the room spoke. "Yes your honor. I have something to add."

"You may proceed, General."

I did turn around then and wondered what General Johan had to say.

"I am General Asa Johan commander of the Western Provincial Military Base three hundred kilometers south of this capital. I have several things to say. First I heard Mr. Vanderholm's attorney state that Mr. Vanderholm killed only undesirable people to protect the security of this country. Since I was one of the people on his list to be killed, I object to that statement. I have served this country for more than thirty years. I have earned the rank of general and the respect of my peers. Mr. Vanderholm's uncle placed me in charge of the Midland Base.

"Secondly, we have picked up a Mr. Webb who was wounded by one of my men while he was attempting to assassinate Jeffrey Farley, the Prosecutor of Record for this case. Mr. Webb has confessed to being hired by Mr. Vanderholm and has handed over to me the written instructions given to him by Mr. Vanderholm. The CGIS ran the prints on the letter ordering the execution of the prosecutor. Those fingerprints belong to the defendant, Mr. Hab Vanderholm.

"That nice little prosecutor Jeffry Farley does not strike me as a threat to national security--far from it. My interactions with his office have led me to believe that he is of the highest moral character and an asset to his community. I object to the whole idea that Mr. Vanderholm thinks matters of national security and criminal justice are under his sole judgment. We have a military to protect us from invasion and civil war. We have the Central Government Investigative Service. We have our police departments. Finally, we have our court system. I'm a blunt man. I will speak my mind bluntly. Mr. Vanderholm a liar and a murder. He should be treated as such." The general sat down.

"Are there any further statements or motions from either the prosecution or the defense?"

Fritz Vanderholm stood. "I move that the statements from General Johan not be allow into the record.

"What is your reason?"

"They do not pertain to the charges presented to the court for this proceeding."

The judge sat and looked at Fritz Vanderholm for a full minute before he spoke.

"**Let the record show** that the statements from General Asa Johan shall be entered into the record under the charges of violating the security of the court."

The attorneys on the other side of the room shuffled and murmured to each other. Vanderholm glowered at the judge, his Attorney of Record then he turned and glared at the man directly behind him.

The judge asked again, "Are there any further statements or motions from either the prosecution or the defense?"

Both sides said no so the judge proceeded to make procedural statements for the record. He asked for the letter from Vanderholm to Webb. General Johan handed it to him together with the CGIS report on the fingerprints.

The judge read both pieces of paper then meticulously filed them among the other papers in the case. He flipped through the case before him on his desk. He started writing and making notes. Finally, he looked up and began his statements for the record.

"**Let the record show** that the court has reached a verdict in the case of the

State vs. Hab Vanderholm."

He read out a long list of statements for the record. He added one more count of conspiracy to commit murder, and one count of attempted murder for the shooting of Mr. Farley. Finally, he came to the important part.

"**Let the record show** that this court finds Mr. Vanderholm guilty of all charges."

"**Let the record show** that I will defer sentencing until I have had time to research the appropriate sentencing for each count. Sentencing shall be one week from today."

The worst was over.

We stood as the judge approached our table. He shook hands with both interns. "Gentlemen that was amazing. You did an excellent job. I was prepared to appoint someone else if I thought you were jeopardizing the case. I don't think Jake could have done any better, and he is the best I've met." The judge left the room.

Yuri sank into his chair and put his head down on the table. I patted his back and confessed something I'd not told anybody else. "I broke down and sobbed after the Fortenac trial."

He picked his head up.

I handed him a handkerchief to blow his nose. "Let's get out of here."

As soon as we got outside the doors of the courtroom, General Johan invited all of the prosecutors out for dinner.

I hesitated to accept. "Let me make one phone call before we go." I found a phone booth in the hall. I called the hospital. The nurses' station told me that Mr. Farley was much better. They let me talk to him.

"Jake? Jake is that you?"

"Yes, how are you?"

"My head hurts, and I throw up if I move. When is the trial? I don't know what day it is."

"We just finished with the trial. We won. The trial is over. We won. I wish you could have been here for the verdict. The judge added the charges for shooting you to the case. Sentencing is next week."

"Ah," I thought he groaned. "Thanks, thanks for calling. I'm relieved all went well. I have to go now." He hung up.

Chapter 15 Sentencing

We sat in carriage on the evening train home from the trial. Shortly after nine, we pulled into the M'TK station to be greeted by some sort of uproar. Yuri looked out the window on the station side. "What the hell?"

"Huh? What?" Things looked normal on my side of the train. I couldn't see out the other side because our younger staff, and other passengers blocked all the windows facing the platform.

The other passengers turned and stared at us as they prepared to get off of the train. The doorman opened the door. I heard cheering.

I still couldn't see anything. "What are they cheering about?"

Alexander turned to me. "Us, I think."

We filed off the train to the sounds of cheers. I couldn't quite figure out what was going on. As I stepped off of the train I saw signs reading, "Vanderholm guilty."

I scanned the crowd looking for a way out. Something inside me melted when I saw five people huddled together. The crowd disappeared. I smiled at my wife. Her face absolutely glowed. The crowd parted as I reached for her. I picked her up and kissed her. I ignored the crowd and kissed my wife like I wanted to. I was vaguely aware of Elizabeth crawling from her mama's arms to mine.

I hugged and kissed Mama. I hugged papa while my son crawled from Papa to me. I held my children and thought about kissing my wife some more.

Mrs. Mayor surprised me when she appeared beside me. "Jake come. Join the others. The people want to see you and thank you." She led me to a small stage set up on the railroad platform.

With my children still in my arms, I climbed the stairs and stood beside my office mates. Mrs. Mayor stood with us. "Jake, say a few words to the people. They heard what you said in court. Say a few words."

I shrugged. "Friends, thank you for coming to see us and welcome us home. We do the best we can to fight crime. It helps to know that you support our efforts. I'd like to introduce two amazing students from our university. These young men are interns in our office. Because we are a teaching office, we do our best to give them practical experience. We never expected them to be manipulated into a position of presenting this case in court. They did as well as any of the rest of us could have." I then introduced Yuri and Antoine to the cheering crowd.

Yuri raised his hand, asking for silence. "Thank you for your warm welcome. Believe me it is appreciated. This case created a tremendous amount of hard work for everyone in the office. The greatest credit for today's victory goes to our supervisor Mr. Jeffrey Farley for his organization and determination to follow every lead. Secondly, credit for today's victory must go to Mr. Jake Jaconovich for insisting that everybody in the office learn and understand the importance of every piece of paper on the case."

Antoine interrupted his friend. "I confess that until today we didn't appreciate Mr. Jaconovich his persistence in explaining and questioning us repeatedly on every piece of paper in the case. We used to make jokes about Jake, and his constantly questioning the meaning of each paper. The minute the judge announced that Antoine and I would have to present the case, I silently gave thanks to Jake for preparing us so well." He then turned to me. "Mr. Jaconovich, thank you for working so hard to prepare a couple of reluctant students."

This speech drew a round of applause from the crowd.

Mrs. Mayor spoke next. "Fellow citizens of this city, today we have all won a victory for justice. We will have a city where crime is punished according to the seriousness of the offence, and we can be proud to have the best prosecutor's office in the country." The crowd cheered some more.

I was surprised to recognize among the crowd a large number of our repeat offenders. I thought they were okay if they could come and cheer for the people who fined them and made them pick up litter. I prepared to step off of the stage when I got a surprise.

"Hallelujah," I couldn't see where the singer was located.

"Hallelujah," This came from a different singer located somewhere else in the crowd.

"Hal–le–lu–jah," Now, I saw three women singers.

I grinned when we heard the next line of the song. I recognized the professional baritone of the man I sent to organize our street performers months ago. As Mrs. Mayor and the men from my office left the platform, the street performers came forward to complete their performance of the Hallelujah Chorus. They distracted the crowd sufficiently for us to leave. I took my family and went home to snuggle down in my own bed with my pregnant wife.

Early the morning following the trial I went to visit Jeffrey at the hospital. The hospital seemed to have relaxed their rules somewhat on visiting hours. I stopped first at the nurses' station. "I'm here to see how Jeffry Farley is doing."

"Yes, Mr. Jaconovich. He is doing very well. I'll call his doctor and let him know that you are here. I'll check to see if Mr. Farley is awake enough for a visitor."

This warm reception puzzled me. I followed the nurse to my supervisor's room.

He was awake. "Jake? Jake is that you. It's good to see you. Tell me about the trial. Is it really over?"

"Yes Sir, it is really over. He was found guilty on all counts. General Johan arrived during the statements of outrage. He spoke up on your behalf and presented the evidence that it was Vanderholm behind your shooting. The judge added a count of attempted murder, and a count of conspiracy to commit murder to his charges."

My supervisor sounded weak when he replied. "It is really over, and we won?"

"Yes Sir, it is over. We won."

He smiled then. "I would have liked to present the case. I am thankful it is over."

"I agree that we all wanted you to present the case. General Johan acted particularly impressed that you had included the interns in the preparation so that they were able to present the case. They were a credit to your reputation, sir."

He chuckled. "You may have had a little to do with their preparation." He chuckled and winced. I was afraid of tiring him and prepared to leave when the doctor came in.

The neurosurgeon may have been the tiniest man I've seen. He could not have been much more than one and a half meters tall. "Ah, Mr. Jaconovich, I am glad you are here. I want to send Mr. Farley home."

"He looks far too ill to be home alone. He doesn't have a wife to take care of him."

Mr. Jaconovich, I know he doesn't have someone at home. The problem is that we have several nasty infections running around the hospital. So far it has not reached this unit. I do not want him to get an infection. I want him out of the hospital. Can you find someone to take care of him?"

"How long is he going to need care?"

"Oh, I'm guessing he'll need someone with him for about six weeks. After that, we'll see."

I gulped and nodded, "I will see that he is cared for. When do you want me to pick him up?"

"I'll have the nurses prepare him to leave right now."

"Are you sure he is strong enough?"

"He will be safer away from this infection."

I'd driven the Miki to work. Within a half hour we had Jeffrey loaded in the car. "Jake I hate to ask this, but can we stop at my house?"

"Certainly." I drove him around to his apartment. I tried to drive as gently as I could, but I noticed my passenger turned a little green when we went around corners. I helped him out of the car and escorted him to the door of his apartment building.

He looked down when we reached the entrance. "I wonder if that is my blood?"

I looked at the dark stains and spatters around the entrance. "Probably. Are you okay?"

"Yeah, I don't remember anything about the incident. How did they catch the perpetrator so quickly?"

"Major Yablonski assigned someone to protect you."

He grunted. I noticed his hand shaking so badly he could hardly get his key in the lock of his door. He finally got the door open. "Isabelle? Isabelle where are you?" A long-haired cat slinked out from behind a door. Jeffrey melted into his one easy chair. Isabelle jumped into his lap and began to purr. He stroked the cat. I noticed tears in the corners of his eyes as he petted the cat.

"Can I pack up some clothes for you?"

His voice sounded ragged when he replied. "If you don't want me running around your house naked, that would be a good idea. I have a suitcase in the closet."

I left him in his chair with his cat and went into the bedroom to find his suitcase. He didn't have many clothes. I packed all of them. I noticed a pet carrier and pulled that out too. I finally got the cat food, litter box, Isabelle in her carrier, and my friend into the Miki. Jeffrey was sweating heavily by the time we got to my house. I wanted to carry him inside, but I didn't want to damage his dignity.

Our garage with servant's quarters was finished so I took Mr. Farley into the room off of the kitchen where he would have his own bathroom and be close to the housekeeper if he needed help. I settled him in a chair.

"Papa! Papa! There is a cat in our car!" Jacob squealed excitedly.

I figured rescuing the cat from my children was the most urgent chore at that moment. "Yes, the cat belongs to Mr. Farley. He and his cat will be staying with us for a few weeks because he is sick."

"Did the bad men try to kill him?" I didn't like for Jacob to be learning so much about the ugly side of life.

"Yes, but we had people protecting him. He needs quiet and rest now. He will be okay."

Jacob followed me out to the car. I spent a half hour getting Jeffrey into bed and getting his cat settled with her litter box. She jumped up on the bed and curled up next to her human. He put his fingers in her fur and fell asleep. His appearance frightened me. He looked grey with beads of sweat on his forehead.

I finally got into my office at Rouseff Properties two hours later than I intended. Young Rouseff was waiting for me. I apologized for being later than expected and explained about needing to take Mr. Farley to my house.

"Jake, I think that I am beginning to understand why my uncle sent me up here. This whole city thinks you, and those people you work with are heroes for convicting Vanderholm."

I wondered where this conversation was going.

Young Rouseff followed me into my office. As I made myself comfortable, he continued. "In the south I doubt that you are heroes. People really do believe that they can kill others because they belong to a fine family. I am beginning now to see how that is wrong." He took his customary chair.

I looked at him wondering if he had two heads. "I grew up in this city. I've always considered all murder as wrong. It doesn't matter who does it. Are you trying to tell me that more than just a few extremists think that it is okay to kill if you are rich enough?"

"In a sense yes. Now that I can see into both worlds, I can see the wrongness in Mr. Vanderholm's actions. I was brought up to believe that whatever the leaders of the elite families did was fine because of who they were."

"Are you trying to tell me that the idea that a person can commit murder or steal or embezzle is more common than not, even among the Rouseff family?"

"I would say that the concept is taken for just how things are by the Rouseffs, the Spinozas, the Uzaras, the Fortenacs, Jouyets, and of course the Vanderholms. While people were cheering at the train station here, I suspect that they were totally bewildered by the verdict in the south."

"Thank you for explaining this to me. I found Hab Vanderholm's behavior at the trial baffling. Perhaps I should check with your uncle to see if he expects repercussions."

Our week of waiting for the sentencing of Mr. Vanderholm passed while I kept busy working in both offices. Finally, the day before the sentencing arrived. We discussed who should go to the capital. The interns needed to be there. Leroy, Christian, Char, and Alexander were deep into preparing for the Papadakos trial. Finally we decided Christian and I would go with the interns. I didn't like leaving Leah and the children, but she called me a hero, kissed me, and sent me off to the capital.

This time when we entered the courtroom, I looked about me and appreciated the beauty of the polished mahogany woodwork. For the first time, I noticed the cushions on the spectator benches were deep maroon velvet. I took my place on a spectator's bench directly behind Yuri.

Fritz Vanderholm was the only person present on the defense side of the room. I wondered if Hab Vanderholm refused to attend for fear he would be arrested.

The judge entered and settled his notes before him. "Before I hand down the sentencing, I'd like to ask a few general questions. Prosecutor Jaconovich, how is Mr. Farley?"

"He is recovering sir. He was discharged from the hospital much earlier than expected due to the increased risk of infection at the hospital. He is staying with me, and we have a full time nurse attending him."

The judge shifted in his chair. "Do the doctors expect Mr. Farley to be able to practice law again?"

I realized that the judge was not just inquiring after Mr. Farley's health. I considered my answer closely. "The doctor has not yet made any statement about the possibility of Mr. Farley practicing law. From my own observations I would say that decision will not be made for perhaps six months."

"Is Mr. Farley alert and mobile?"

"He needs to sleep twelve to fourteen hours. When he gets up he can walk unassisted for about thirty feet before he must rest. He can converse about what is going on around him. Discussing matters related to our office or the practice of law fatigues him."

The judge began his statements. He listed each charge and pronounced the fine for that charge. He made a few statements that surprised me.

"**Let the record show** that on the charge of violating the security of the court, a fine of one hundred thousand US-equivalent dollars shall be paid directly to Mr. Jeffrey Farley for the injuries he sustained."

Finally we came to the sentencing for murder.

"**Let the record show** that on six counts of murder the standard sentencing is execution by firing squad." Here the judge stopped and looked at both sides of the courtroom. He steepled his fingers then continued. "I am tired of the killing. Too many lives, both among the innocent and the guilty, have ended prematurely. By the laws of this country and human decency, the defendant deserves a sentence of death. He will not get it from my courtroom. As far as I am concerned the killing stops here. I therefore fine Mr. Vanderholm the sum of four million US-equivalent dollars for each count of murder. It is my hope that in depriving him of that which he loves most, he will learn to repent and reach a state of grace with God.

"**Let the record show** that in addition to the fines paid to the court, Mr. Vanderholm will pay the sum of two-hundred fifty thousand dollars US-equivalent to each of the immediate families of his victims for the hardship his actions have caused these families."

"**Let the record show** that in addition to the fines and compensation, Mr. Vanderholm is sentenced to…" Here the judge paused and thought. "I would like to say life, but I will have mercy on those who must interact with Mr. Vanderholm. He is sentenced to three years of community service to be supervised by a probation officer appointed by the prosecutor's office in his judicial district.

When the sentencing was complete, Hab Vanderholm's fines amounted to over twenty-eight million dollars US-equivalent not counting the compensation to Mr. Farley, and the families of his victims. The property he purchased for his personal use using tax money was confiscated and assigned to the office of the president. This included two nice helicopters, a huge yacht, and a private jet.

After the sentencing, we met with the judge to determine how the monetary fine was to be divided up. We finally agreed that seven million would be paid to those other cities and provinces where his crimes were committed. Most of this went to the capital but almost a million went to an eastern province, and another million to the province south of mine.

Chapter 16 The Very Best Hot-Shot Prosecutor's Office

Every day, Mr. Farley got a little better. Finally, he started taking walks outside. Six weeks after he got hurt, he asked Leah to drive him into the office in the afternoon.

I arrived at the prosecutor's office about a half hour after Mr. Farley did. "Ah, this is how the office should feel when I come in. Sir, I'm happy to see you here." I kissed Leah for bringing him in.

Leroy stood on his desk and shouted, "Staff meeting in ten minutes."

Within ten minutes, we gathered in our conference room for a staff meeting. Mr. Farley said that he had no idea what this was about and turned the meeting over to Leroy. "Okay, the first item on my agenda concerns the position of supervisor. We do not have one. As the very best, hot-shot, prosecutor's office in the country, I think we have the right to choose our own supervisor. I nominate Mr. Jeffrey Farley."

"I second that." Christian bellowed.

Leroy still acted as the chair of the meeting. "All in favor." We all voted yes. "Good, we need someone to draft a letter to the president informing him that the position is filled and that he does not need to appoint anybody else."

Perhaps the very best, hot-shot, prosecutor's office in the country should not have done anything to bring ourselves to the attention of the president. About ten days after we arrogantly sent a letter off to the president, he wrote back.

Dear Sirs,

Thank you for your letter informing me of the recovery of Mr. Farley. He risked and ended up almost giving his life for justice in this country. I intend to nominate him for a Gold Metal of Merit. As far as I am concerned Mr. Farley can supervise any office in this country that he chooses.

As for the rest of you, I would like to see you supervise other offices. I'd like to place one of you in the Central Prosecutor's Office here in the capital. This is a prestigious position and a great step up in your career. I would like to place two more of you, one each, in the southern cities. Your

*dedication and expertise are greatly needed there. If you can just get those
people to pay taxes!*

*Talk this matter over among yourselves and decide who would like
which position.*

Sincerely,

B. R. Uzara, President

"We should have kept our big mouths shut." This letter distressed me. "I own a house here. My parents live here. I do not want to move. I'll advise Mr. President that I am in charge of the combined Rouseff family business in the north." I satisfied myself. I refused to move.

Christian spoke up next. "What do you think? We've been through a lot together. I hate to break up a winning team."

"I've come to think of you as family." Leroy rubbed his hands over his face. "If I moved south, I would be closer to my parents." He shifted his weight. "I hate to leave this office, but the idea of an advancement and being close to my parents is tempting. I don't know what to do."

I understood Leroy's dilemma. "It is good to be close to your family. I will miss you if you leave. I have another thought. You are not married. Perhaps women from this city do not appeal to you. I had to find one from a village near where Mama grew up." I got distracted thinking about seeing Leah for the first time. I netted my attention back to the point I started to make. "Anyway, I guess I'm saying that if you decide to take the career advancement and move closer to your family, I would respect your choice."

"Jake has brought up one point to consider, career advancement." Mr. Farley immediately got our attention. "There is a much bigger issue to consider. We have worked hard in this office to bring justice to our city. We even have fewer petty offenders than we used to despite the greater poverty we are seeing. I wonder if we can spread our sense of justice to other cities. The president mentions getting people to pay their taxes. What do you think?"

Leroy spoke up again. "I'd like to think it over. Finding a judge in the south who will contemplate convicting a member of the elite will be a challenge."

The rest of us looked grim. Char spoke up. "Surely he's not referring to Alexander and myself. We have what? Two years experience? I am not qualified to supervise an office."

Mr. Farley surprised me. "I don't see why you would not be qualified.

You could have presented the Vanderholm case. You have been processing tax evasion cases. You've processed hundreds of cases of petty crime. You are young, so earning the trust and respect of your subordinates will be a challenge. I think you can handle the job."

I sighed. I really did not like the idea of losing my co-workers. I also wanted to see them get the career advancement they deserved. They would make more money. Perhaps they could spread justice.

Finally, one week before Leah's due date, we lost three members of our staff. Christian took the job in the capital. Leroy and Char moved south.

I thought the office would be empty and lonely with three people I'd grown to count on gone. The first day they were gone, I think I stayed an hour longer at Rouseff Properties than I needed to. Finally, I walked from Rouseff offices to the prosecutor's office.

I walked into the prosecutor's office to find it crowded. I quickly realized that about a dozen of the occupants were university students. I wondered what they had done to get arrested. I stood and watched as Alexander picked up a file and called the offender to come to his office. I noticed one of the college students following him as he went to the file secretary's desk then to his own desk.

Mr. Farley greeted me. "Jake, we are processing our petty criminals today. Here are Carlos Spinoza and Sophia Uzara to observe how you do this."

I raised my eyebrows

Mr. Farley explained. "It is the start of a new term. We have twelve interns."

I scratched my nose and decided that twelve interns would keep us lively. "Will we have enough criminals to keep twelve interns busy?"

Mr. Farley laughed. "This is Jake Jaconovich."

Carlos's eyes grew round. He blurted out, "Wow, are you really Jake Jaconovich the father of modern law practice?"

"Last time I checked my children are named Jacob and Elizabeth. We're expecting another, but I doubt that my wife will let me name the baby *Modern Law Practice*."

The students giggled.

"Now Miss. Uzara, how are you related to my Uzara friends?"

"Both Richardo and Woody are my cousins."

"Well welcome to our office, both of you. What have you done so far?"

They explained that they had watched Mr. Supervisor process a drunk and disorderly case and do the follow-up paperwork.

I grinned and thought that before the end of the day I would not be doing my own follow-up paperwork. "Good. Miss Uzara will you go get a file and bring us an offender. Mr. Spinoza my office is right over here. Can you bring us a couple of chairs from the conference room?"

While my students were busy, I rearranged my office. My office was just a cubical with low walls. I had inherited a plastic palm tree. I removed the palm tree, so the students could fit in.

As soon as we were settled, I looked at the file in front of me. "Oh...um... Miss P'NA you were picked up for creating a disturbance." Her file told me she'd been picked up once earlier. "Wait, I remember you. You came here just before your Mama died. I went to your apartment and called for help."

She sniffed. "You were the man who called the medics?"

"Yes."

"It didn't help. She died anyway."

I tried to use a gentle voice. "I'm sorry, yes, she was very sick." I wondered what else I could say. I couldn't think of anything so I got down to business. "It says here you were arrested for creating a disturbance. What happened?"

She told us a long sad story about the man who got her pregnant and abandoned her. I sent the girl home. She hadn't done anything worse than follow the man telling him what she thought of him. He deserved worse.

After we interviewed Miss P'NA, I instructed the students on how to fill out the paper work and outlined our procedures for investigating the case. Jeffrey called a staff meeting when we ran out of offenders to process. The staff meeting turned into a classroom lecture with each of us going over our role in processing cases when we have a team. At this point, our office transformed into a satellite of the university. I started spending more time teaching than I did actually practicing law.

I got home to my family a little late. They didn't miss me. A few days earlier someone had abandoned a batch of kittens near our house. My family instantly adopted them and divided the kittens up among themselves. When I came in, Leah was sitting on the floor playing with her kitten. She had a feather on the end of a string, and her kitten was chasing it. Well, all the kittens were chasing it. Then they would chase each other. Everybody looked like they were having fun.

"Look Papa. Look. Baby wants to play with his kitty." Jacob scooped up one kitten and plopped it down on Leah's belly. He poked his mama's tummy twice. Sure enough Leah's top jumped and wiggled as the baby kicked. The kitten pounced on the wiggling dress."

"Ow, ow, that's sharp. Jacob the kitten is hurting me." Leah floundered around trying to get up off of the floor.

I rescued the kitten and helped Leah up off of the floor. Jacob's little chin began to wobble. His whole face radiated dismay. I tried to distract him. "Do we have time for a climb to the top of the ridge before dinner?"

"Yes"

"Yeth"

Leah tried to stretch her aching back. "Count me out. Oh Jake, the doctor says he wants you to come with me to my appointment tomorrow." I immediately began to worry.

Elizabeth and Jacob were eager to walk to the top of the ridge so I put my worries aside and set off to climb the ridge. We watched the sun go down. Jacob pointed, "Look a star."

I explained, "That is the planet Venus. Venus is another earth. Stars are like our sun."

Elizabeth refused to be convinced, "ftar."

When I caught myself worrying whether my not-quite-two year-old daughter had a serious lisp, I decided that I worried too much. I gave myself a stern talking to about impending purges and uncovering a major lead in a criminal case that went all the way to the president. I assured myself that Leah would have the baby just fine, and there would be no national crises.

The next day, I went to the doctor with Leah.

He assured us that she was fine. The baby was fine, but we should have a nurse move in with us since Leah delivered so fast with Elizabeth. He ran his hands through his hair. "I'm not sure what to do with this case. We have a nasty infection that has been running around the hospital for months. I am having my younger patients deliver at home to avoid the infection. Leah had trouble with that bleeder last time. She is not as young as my other patients."

Thrilled, I added, "On the other hand her husband is a terrible nuisance at the hospital. I was the one who realized something was wrong when she had the bleeder. The road between my house and the hospital has been improved. We could call an ambulance at the first hint of trouble."

"If you are willing to have a live-in nurse, I think I will plan a home birth rather than risk infection. You are a responsible man. I expect you to pick up any problems before they become serious."

We made our plan. The nurse would arrive later in the day. The hospital would send out an incubator. I asked about the possibility of the incubator carrying infections. I obsessed about the incubator carrying infection.

The only person who would listen to me about my concerns was my mama. She fussed at Papa until he took her to the library. They came to my house after dinner two nights after the nurse arrived. They had a bottle of bleach. Mama had instructions on how to wash down the incubator with bleach.

After Mama and Papa left, I sat down and did some thinking. I finally concluded that Mama's memory problems were caused by something more than fatigue. She seemed confused about where she was and sometimes when she was. I had a sense Mama was drifting away from us. We didn't have a name for the baby. We planned to call a boy John after my Uncle John. We had several girls' names. I knew what I wanted to call my baby girl. I went to bed and woke up poor Leah.

"Sweetheart?"

"Uh…I want to sleep."

"I know you want to sleep. I want to name our baby girl Mary Anne, after Mama. Mama is not well. It would be a comfort to me to name my daughter Mary Anne."

"Fine, we named Elizabeth after my mother. If it's a girl we'll name it after your mother." She went back to sleep. I smiled content.

Preparing to be gone for the birth kept me busy at both offices. At Rouseff Industries Young Rouseff was coming along nicely. He got along well with Cousin Micki, who was working for us now to design a paper mill. Young Rouseff confessed to being fascinated with Micki's ability to turn ideas into machines.

In the prosecutor's office, I thought Carlos and Sophia together could process some routine repeat offenders while I was gone.

Chapter 17 Mary Anne

One day, after sending another offender off to pick up litter, I wanted to go home. I felt tired of petty crime and of people who cheated. I was tired of dealing with the consequences of poverty. I explained to Sophia and Carlos. "I'm worried about Leah. You two can take over now. I'll find you some straight forward cases." We didn't have any cases. Mr. Farley called a staff meeting to go over some old cases, and I went home.

I got home to find my parents visiting. Mama was sitting on the sofa next to Leah reading a story to Jacob and Elizabeth. She held Elizabeth on her lap, and Jacob snuggled beside her with her arm around him. Occasionally she would lay her cheek against one or the other of the children. I knew she was reading to the baby too. Poor Leah looked exhausted. I could understand how having the whole family interacting with her tummy would be tiring. I kissed everybody and went to my study to go over reports from Rouseff Industries.

First, I read a report for the new paper factory. They had worked out a formula for making bathroom tissue. They didn't have machines to do the job but they knew how to make the product. Micky had designs for the machines. The large digesting tanks for preparing the pulp were under construction. I leaned back in my chair to think and dozed off.

"Papa, Papa wake up. Baby is coming. Baby is coming."

I woke up wide-awake.

Jacob was leaning over my chair and shouting his news into my ear.

Elizabeth jumped up and down in the doorway shouting, "Baby, baby, baby."

I don't remember getting out of my chair. I found Leah still on the sofa. "I'm sure this is it. That was a good strong contraction."

The nurse called the doctor on the phone. I scooped Leah up in my arms and carried her upstairs to our room.

Mama followed behind me and competently made up the bed. I thought about why they needed the waterproof sheet and all the other padding. I wanted to run, but I stayed manfully by my wife and helped her out of her clothes and into the gown she'd bought for this occasion.

The nurse came in to examine Leah. Mama stood nearby ready to assist. I ran.

Papa had captured both of my children at the foot of the stairs. Jacob was holding the baby's kitten. "He'll want his kitty when he comes out."

Papa laughed. "Son, getting born is tiring business. The baby will need to sleep. Babies like to sleep. Your mama will need lots of sleep. Your papa will take care of you, mama, and the baby. Grandmama and I are here to keep you company while everybody else is busy. What do you want to do?"

Jacob immediately answered. "Go rowing."

I thought Papa turned a little green at the thought of taking a boat out. He asked, "How far can you swim?

"Swim? What is swim?"

Papa went on to teach Jacob about swimming. Soon, he had Jacob down on the floor practicing swimming.

I sat on the stairs and watched Elizabeth entertaining herself by wrapping kitties in blankets made from bathroom towels. She wrapped one up and put it to bed in an easy chair. Then she captured the next and wrapped it up and put it to bed next to its sibling. By the time she had the third kitten ready for bed the first two escaped.

I heard a car in the yard and went to let the doctor in. I was beginning to worry about having two toddlers who wanted to play with the baby. I thought we needed a nursery maid or something. It didn't occur to me to wonder why I didn't think Leah could manage three young children.

This delivery did not go as fast as with Elizabeth but the doctor assured me that everything was fine. He speculated that the speed of her last delivery might have caused the bleeder. I surprised myself by nearly fainting at the word, *bleeder*. I stayed beside Leah except when they examined her to see how the baby was coming. Mama and the nurse stayed with Leah. The doctor stayed with Leah. I broke out in a sweat and escaped the room in a hurry.

Papa entertained Jacob and Elizabeth until they finally fell asleep in his arms. I offered to take them to their beds.

"No. This is just fine. They are growing up so fast. I'm happy to hold them while I can."

I smiled at my papa and remembered to be very thankful for him.

Leah got to the part of the delivery where I excused myself permanently from her room. I could not stand to watch her pain. I sat down on the top step of our stairs. I was close to Leah, and I could watch Papa with the children. He fell asleep too. I sat and waited and said the prayer I'd learned years ago.

After two and a half hours of waiting, I heard the sound of a healthy baby expressing her surprise at her arrival into the big world. I started grinning. I didn't wake Papa or the children. We didn't need their insistence on playing with their new sibling just now.

"Jake? It's a girl." Mama's gentle voice made me smile even more. Mama looked radiant.

I got up off of my stair, went to see my wife and hold Mary Anne. I kissed Leah. "My most precious wife thank you again and again for giving me another daughter." I expected to see another little blond girl like Elizabeth. Mary Anne had dark hair like Jacob and me.

Mama kissed Leah and thanked her for giving us another baby. "I'll go tell Papa and the children that it is a girl."

"We are naming her Mary Anne." I loved saying that name.

Mama kissed me as big tears rolled down her face. "Thank you. I will tell Papa." She had her joyful, sad smile on her face as she left the room. I knew she wanted to be with Papa just now.

I sat down in a chair next to Leah and held my baby. "Does she need to go into the incubator?"

The nurse seemed reasonable. "You can hold her for a few minutes more then we should make sure she gets warmed up again."

Within minutes, I heard excited children's voices drifting up from downstairs. I recognized the sound of Mama and Papa laughing. Next I heard footsteps on the stairs. Elizabeth's little voice chanted, "Baby, baby, baby."

Jacob sounded more sophisticated, "Mawy Anne, we're coming to see you. I've got your present"

I shuddered wondering what the present was. Elizabeth opened the door and shushed her brother. I had hopes that Elizabeth would have some sense about the baby. I smiled at them and let them come see their new sister. Jacob was following Elizabeth. I didn't see his present until he got right up to me.

Jacob held the kitten out in both hands and put it close to Mary Anne's face. "See! You have a kitty."

Mary Anne kicked and wiggled. I was so surprised I might have dropped her had I not been seated with the arm that held her resting on the arm of the chair.

"Jacob!" Leah sounded cross.

I smiled at Jacob. "Here, give me her kitty and I will hold both of them. Give your Mama a hug and kiss and thank her for giving us this wonderful baby." Both children turned their attention to their Mama and thanked her in their own way for their sister.

After a few minutes, we sent the children back downstairs, with the kitten because Mary Anne needed to go into her incubator.

Leah was excited and wanted to tell me all the details of her labor. I practiced my breathing and mind control exercises from my martial arts classes. I breathed, nodded to my wife and made comforting noises. When her words penetrated into my brain I broke out in a sweat. Leah laughed at me then. "Jake you're sweating. Are you really so squeamish that you are uncomfortable talking about what a miracle this is?"

"Honey, it is not the miracle part. I like the miracle part. I hate pain. I can't stand to think of my precious wife in pain."

"Jake you are a sissy."

"Yes. Yes I am. I've always been this way. The first time I got hurt I was six. Some bigger boys broke my nose. I've hated pain ever since then."

"I don't mind the pain so much after it is over."

"You're braver than I am. I still hate the pain from when I was six." I kissed Leah again. "I love you."

She smiled. Leah never told me that she loved me. She married me. She gave me three children. That was proof enough of love for me.

Mama seemed to feel particularly well so she and Papa stayed with us until after we put the children to bed. They promised to return in the morning to help with Jacob and Elizabeth.

Jacob and Elizabeth were so excited I wasn't certain they could sleep. They'd worn themselves out with excitement. They fell asleep before I had finished reading the second story.

Mama and Papa returned in the morning to help dress Jacob and Elizabeth. I almost wept to see them. Both Leah and I were exhausted. Mary Anne had fussed all night. She seemed happy enough to nurse. She would fall asleep after nursing then about an hour later she would wake up and fuss. I tried sitting in the chair and holding her while I sang. That helped for about another hour. Then we let her nurse. She'd fuss about that for a few minutes before she settled down. I would sleep. Then we would start all over with the fussing. I tried holding her. I tried putting her in the incubator. Nothing calmed her for long.

Mama arrived with a gift for Leah. We all trooped up to Leah's room to give her the gift. Jacob and Elizabeth went straight to the incubator. I heard them conspiring to get their sister out.

Grandpapa solved the problem for them. He picked Mary Anne up. "Now we are all going to sit in the chair. You must be sitting down when you hold a baby this new." Papa sat with all three children in the chair. Jacob talked to his sister telling her all the wonders of the outer world. Elizabeth patted her and made noises to agree with Jacob. Papa looked completely happy. Mary Anne didn't fuss. She waved her baby arms in the air and made her brother and sister laugh.

I turned my attention to the gift Leah was unwrapping. When she pulled it out of the wrapping, I couldn't figure out what it was.

Mama explained. "It's a sling for carrying the baby on your front. Papa and I figured with those other two," Mama nodded toward Jacob and Elizabeth who were poking at their sister. "Leah was going to have to carry the baby with her to protect her from her siblings. This way Leah can go about her business with her hands free and still hold Mary Anne."

"Will this fit me?" I tried to wrap the thing around me. Mama showed me how it worked. I put it on, took Mary Anne away from Papa, and put her in the sling to see how the thing worked.

Mary Ann started to fuss so I gave her back to Papa and the children. She did seem content with her brother and sister near by. All through her babyhood, Mary Anne was happiest when she could hear the normal voices of the family. When all got quiet at night, she started to fuss.

Leah and I did not get much sleep for the first six weeks after the baby was born. In my office at Rouseff, nobody noticed when I fell asleep in my chair. In the prosecutor's office I got teased for falling asleep with my head on my desk.

Chapter 18 Fish in The City

In the prosecutor's office we let interns learn to practice law by processing petty criminals. Months passed without any big cases coming in. I thought I saw a change in the type of crime in the city. By far the most common crimes were those committed out of desperation. People would do anything to feed their families when there was no food to be found. It was a relief to me to get home in the evening where the biggest problem was keeping Jacob and Elizabeth from playing with Mary Anne.

Each day, when I got home from work, I would sit down in my chair and hold Mary Anne. Jacob and Elizabeth would climb into my lap with all the kitties and tell me their adventures of the day. Elizabeth would have a series of pictures on her chalkboard to show me. Sometimes Jacob would interpret her pictures and tell me the story behind it.

Elizabeth could communicate a great deal through pictures. One day she showed me a picture of Leah with a frown and big tears on her cheeks. After I put the children to bed, I found Leah in the sitting room reading a book. "Now my love, tell me what made you so sad today."

"What? How do you know about that?"

"Elizabeth."

"She can't talk yet."

"No but her pictures tell me a great deal."

"You mean to tell me that you can make something out of all those squiggles."

"Yes, and one of those squiggles told me you were sad today and cried."

She sighed. "I don't know. I am so tired all the time. Trying to do anything upsets me. Nurse was cross because Mary Anne had a slight diaper rash this morning."

"Did that upset you? That Mary Anne had a rash?"

"No babies get rashes. Mrs. Nurse upset me by telling me to change the diaper more often. I don't like her telling me what to do." Leah sounded cross.

"Sweetheart, you get so tired. I think you need the help. Mrs. Nurse is here to change diapers not tell you to do it. I'll speak to her." I kissed Leah on the temple. She still looked grumpy. I worried about her complaining about being tired. She had Mrs. Nurse to help with Mary Anne. My parents came every morning and helped with Jacob and Elizabeth. We still had our housekeeper to do the cooking, cleaning, and laundry. I decided that when I talked to nurse about changing Mary Anne's diaper, I would mention that Leah seemed to be too tired.

I talked to the nurse. She said that she noticed that Leah was tired and over sensitive. "I didn't scold her about the rash. I think I said we *will* have to change the diaper more often. Leah doesn't change the diapers. I change the diapers. I think you change them too."

When the doctor came to check on Leah, I talked to him about her fatigue. He told me that she was getting too old to have babies easily. Her body just could not recover from pregnancy as quickly as a young woman. "Give her time. I will prescribe some iron supplements."

I went to work where I could control my world. Rouseff's profits were high despite the dismal economic conditions in the country. We kept hiring, but more people flooded the city from other parts of the country.

Getting enough food to feed the city remained a challenge. One day, I got a peculiar report from the road construction crew. There were monsters in the swamp where we were building the road. I called Micki. Together with about two-dozen department heads, we went out to the place where the monster was sighted. We didn't see anything. We asked what the monster looked like. The description sounded familiar.

I asked Micki. "Do you suppose those things can live in fresh water?"

"I don't know. I wonder if the meat would be too soft to withstand boiling."

"How would we get one out of here? My boat is too small."

Micki is amazing. He stood on the rough rock roadbed and looked around him. I wondered if he thought a boat was going to magically appear. He pointed to a huge tractor with a bucket on the front. "We'll use that. I'll get us some line and a lure. We can both get in the bucket and see what we can get."

I thought about pulling a monster out of the water. "I'll get my net. If we put the net out at the water's edge we can drag the thing into the net." We made arrangements to meet back at the site at five.

When I called home to explain why I would be late, Papa answered the phone. "This sounds like fun. I'll leave Mama here with Leah and Elizabeth and bring Jacob out to watch this."

"We're not sure the fish will be edible."

"Even if it isn't edible, it will be fun to see what you get. I can think of a few things you might want. I'll see you at five."

Papa wasn't the only person interested in our fishing adventure. Mrs. Mayor came with her husband. I greeted him warmly. I wondered about the domestic situation at the mayor's house but refrained from saying anything.

Mr. Mayor told me soon enough. "Jake," he smiled at me and shook my hand. "I can't begin to thank you enough for putting Vanderholm out of business." He looked at his wife and smiled. "The missus was afraid for my life. I thought that was all nonsense, but when that prosecutor was shot, I thought maybe she wasn't being silly. She paid my fines right after the guilty verdict came in. I hope that nasty piece of work is finished."

"I hope so too. He was a threat to everybody trying to get a job done." I wondered how much of this story was based on Mrs. Mayor having a valid concern, and how much was Mrs. Mayor taking advantage of circumstances to let her husband out of jail and end up looking like a heroine. I would miss doing business with her.

"Jake, come on. The bucket is ready." Micki climbed into the bucket.

"Papa catch sea monster. Papa, papa." Jacob jumped up and down and shouted.

My papa picked Jacob up and swung him up to sit on his shoulders just like he used to do with me so Jacob had a great view of the whole proceeding.

I climbed into the bucket with Micki. He directed the tractor operator to take us out over the swamp. We could see down into the water. Within a minute, I saw something. "There, Micki is that it? Yes, it moved. Is it really that big?"

"Where?"

"There by that clump of grass and willows. It has it's tail out in the…"

"Yeah, I see it. I wonder how to get it to take the bait? Perhaps from here we should have tried to spear the thing." Micki lowered our line over the edge of the bucket. It wasn't long enough. He signaled the operator to lower the bucket. When the bucket was almost touching the water we couldn't see our prey. Micki put the line into the water north of the fish and pulled the lure and bait south thinking to bump the fish.

The fish moved much faster than we expected. I wasn't sure the lure and bait actually bumped the fish before the water below us churned and our line went tight. Micki wrapped the line around the teeth on the bucket and signaled the operator to bring us up six inches. Next, he signaled the operator to bring us in toward the rough roadbed six inches. Micki knew what he was doing.

I'd imagined us hauling the monster to the surface using brute force. I never landed a fish so easy in my life. The tractor operator soon figured out what he needed to do. Slowly he brought us into the net, six inches forward and six inches up. I could see the head of the monster now. I figured it must be a fresh water cousin to the fish in Rocky Bay.

I heard Papa shouting. "Watch out for the bucket. Get four men on the net. Keep your heads down. That's right crawl. Okay now let's work this net a little lower into the water so we don't knock the fish off on the rocks."

I looked over the side of the bucket and saw Papa and three other men positioning the net below us. I looked back at the crowd. I didn't see Jacob. I looked to see how the tractor operator was doing. Jacob was helping him and looking excited. He waved to me.

Micki commented, "I'm glad to see your Papa on the net. He may get seasick, but he knows what he is doing."

I grunted my agreement.

The whole procedure went smoothly. We pulled the fish into the net. Papa and his helpers tossed us the ropes on the corners of the net. We tied them off to the teeth of the bucket. When all was secure, the operator and Jacob lifted the bucket with the fish underneath up to the roadbed.

By six o'clock, we'd measured and weighed the fish. We estimated its weight. Estimating the weight of the fish was not as easy as it sounded.

Micki asked, "Jake how much do you think it weights?"

"I don't know. It could be fifty kilos."

"Well pick the thing up and toss it over your shoulder."

I looked at Micki and thought I'd get back at him. I picked the fish up over my shoulder. "Hmm. I think it is not quite fifty kilos." I bent my knees a couple times as if judging the weight. The fact that I could stand up straight again told me the fish was probably under fifty kilos. "Here, you take him and walk around a bit to see what you think" I slid the fish off of my shoulder onto Micki's."

"You are right. Definitely less than fifty kilos."

"Well the surface isn't too rough here. Run with him a bit." Micki proved to be game for some fun. He ran with the fish a dozen meters or so.

"I don't know Jake. You try running."

I took the fish and ran two-dozen meters and back. "Ah yes, forty-two and a half kilos."

The tractor operator wanted to hold the fish. "It can't be that much if you two sissies can carry it." I slipped the fish onto his shoulder. His knees buckled.

Micki and I stood and watched as the tractor operator tried to stand. Micki looked the situation over. "Maybe forty-three kilos."

"Naw."

Papa took pity on the man or perhaps he didn't want him to drop the fish and bruise it. "Here." He passed Jacob to me and took the fish off of the operator's shoulder. He bounced a little. He walked a few steps. "This fish is not a kilo over thirty-nine."

The operator would not be put to shame. "That monster has to be fifty-kilos at least. Possibly closer to sixty."

Papa stood there with the fish on his shoulder looking cool. I remembered Papa's back injury. "Papa you should not be playing around at your age."

I took the fish. "Let's get this cleaned and cooked." Just at this moment a photographer arrived and started snapping pictures of me with the fish over my shoulder. After Papa took the fish to clean it, Micki and I had to get back in the bucket of the tractor for the photographer.

The fish turned out to be firm enough to boil. I took a piece home to see how it would bake. It stunk up the whole house and was impossible to eat.

Everybody grew cautiously hopeful about a source of fish nearby. I had some idea that those who were out of work could actually bring the brutes in.

Shortly after our fishing experience, my world became unbelievably busy. We had dozens of projects underway at Rouseff. The motel at the highway had one wing completed, and it was full every night. It didn't occur to me that the prostitutes might use the motel until a couple of the men snorted and giggled, saying something about a pleasure palace. I held my head. I didn't mind if they used the motel. I just hoped that people didn't try to connect me to the motel. Nobody did make the spurious connection for years.

I noticed Young Rouseff hanging out with Miki. The Young Rouseff's invited us for dinner one night. This was Leah's first social engagement since Mary Anne's birth. Our housekeeper insisted that she would keep Mary Anne safe from her siblings but I still worried about anybody being able to keep Mary Anne safe. At least three times when Mary Anne was still so new that she stayed in the incubator part-time, I went to pick her up and found her kitty asleep in the nice warm bed with her.

Despite our worries, we left the housekeeper in charge of our children and went out. As we were headed out our road, we saw Mama and Papa coming up in their Miki. I looked at Leah. "Good, reinforcements are on their way."

Leah felt well enough to tease me. "I blame you and Papa for the children's fascination with babies. You two are just about as bad only you are old enough to have sense."

I chuckled and grinned at my wife.

At dinner Micki told us about his progress on the fishing project. "I sent north for more lures and lines. I figure we can build barges out of old shipping pallets. We can find some workable engines to winch those babies out of the water. I want something stable so these city dwellers don't get dragged overboard and drown."

After dinner, the men continued to talk about the fishing project. I was thrilled that Young Rouseff sounded excited over the prospect of being able to feed more people. They figured they could start pulling fish out of the swamp in about ten days.

Within a week after our dinner at Rouseff's, I learned that some fishermen, who had come down from the north to find work, had built themselves a raft and managed to pull in a fish by hand. I admired their ability to pull one of those things in without upsetting their raft. I don't know what they did with their fish. I didn't care.

A few days later, Micki had his barge with a winch out on the swamp. Micki launched his barge off of the bypass road. The fishing operation interfered with the road building. I didn't care about that either.

I began to get an idea of how many people were coming to the city, when I arrived at the prosecutor's office and looked into the full holding room. I didn't recognize anybody. My first case was a first offender.

"It says here that you were arrested for camping in the city park. How do you plead?"

"I didn't realize it was against the law to camp there."

"Where are you from?"

"M'T of M'KF."

"Good grief, how did you end up here?"

"I heard there was jobs here."

"We can't put the whole country to work in this city. What did you do before you moved here."

"I was the local policeman, but the town didn't have money to pay me and I couldn't get another job so I came here."

"Our police department is short of men. Did you apply there?"

"No."

"I will write you a note to the police department saying you are looking for work. Um…you will have to attend police academy as soon as next session classes start. You will get paid while going to classes. This piece of paper is the address of a shelter."

I looked up. Our young mother-to-be Miss P'NA stood outside my office. I knew Sophia had befriended the poor girl who had been Sophia's first case, so I turned to Sophia and nodded. As Sophia got up I had a thought. "Find out what she needs. If she is not busy, I will have a job for her."

Sophia nodded.

I continued to ask the accused more questions about what they did before they moved. I explained where the soup kitchens were located. "Half the people in this city do not have jobs. We are struggling to feed and house so many. I hope you can get on with the police department. We just got some funding for more policemen and the academy."

"What about the other people arrested with us?"

"Are they friends or family?"

"No, but they came here looking for work too."

"We will help as many as we can. We have limited space in our shelters. If they have experience at something they might find work."

I turned to Miss P'NA. "How are you feeling?"

"Fine."

"I mean really. Are you tired?"

"No. Really, I'm fine."

"I can pay you to take these people over to building two-thirteen on upper ninth. Tell the person at the door that I sent them. If you are not too tired after that, take him to the police department so he can apply for a job. Can you do that without getting tired."

She giggled, "Yeah, I'll take them."

"Here are some tokens for the trolley. Here is two dollars for you for helping me out."

"Yes, Mr. Jaconovich." She sounded like my employees over at Rouseff. I hoped having a simple job would help her regain some pride. Sophia confided that Miss P'NA still grieved over the man who seduced her when she didn't hate him for abandoning her.

I called after them, "Oh, and when you get off at ninth, don't forget to get transfers to get to the police station."

"Yes sir."

I smiled to see her politely direct her charges to come with her.

"Thank you sir." Sophia sounded like she might cry. "She made an appointment with the adoption agency. She wants me to go with her. Giving her a job she could do just now, might help her feel better about herself."

The next day, Miss P'NA came back to help out. I didn't mind having her around. She needed to be someplace safe and warm. I didn't like for her to be alone. We had more people from outside the city getting picked up for brawling and squatting. We did our best to find shelter for families who had come looking for work. Miss P'NA escorted them to the shelters or to where they were to pick up litter for community service.

Late in the day on a Thursday, Mr. Farley and I had a meeting with the Mayor. I wondered how this would go.

The mayor greeted us warmly. "Gentlemen, come in, come in, it is an honor to meet you."

Jeffrey responded diplomatically. "Thank you for your kind invitation."

I grunted.

After more small talk than I had patience for, the mayor got down to business. "It seems the city is about to receive a windfall from the Vanderholm case. It took some balls to press charges against a Vanderholm."

I snorted impatiently. "Not really. It was a matter of survival. He put Mr. Farley on his hit list. I understand that you were somewhat aware of his illegal activities. He would have gotten around to you, and to me, and to anybody else who knew of his activities. He had developed an appetite for murder."

Mr. Mayor's oily tone set my teeth on edge. "Oh now, I don't know about that."

I may have raised my voice a little. "I saw the evidence. I drilled our staff on each piece of evidence. That man was on a murderous rampage and needed to be stopped."

I noticed Mr. Farley slipping into his effeminate-dimwit-routine again. Apparently, he didn't fully trust the mayor either. "I still suffer headaches from the head wound. I have intimate knowledge of his ruthlessness."

"Oh um…well…yes. I too am personally thankful he was stopped. I didn't believe he would go so far as to have a prosecutor killed. My wife was right. I wasn't safe." The mayor shook his head.

I quickly tired of this line of talk. "Now, about our portion of Vanderholm's fine."

The mayor smiled. "I think the prosecutor's office should be richly rewarded."

"Yes." Mr. Farley sounded almost greedy. "Yes, we need new equipment. Our poor photocopier is about to die any day, poor thing. It has done as much as any human to bring about justice. It is time to retire the poor old thing and purchase a new photocopier. We need a FAX machine. I want a computer system. I will need ten terminals. We will need a high-speed printer and a scanner to go with the computer system. I want to convert all our files to electronic files, so we can keep records farther back."

Jeffrey paused for breath so I took over. "We need a rainy day fund so if we do not have income, the office personnel will get paid. I want to increase our number of employees. We lost our office manager and one clerk in the past two years. I want to hire a graduate of a business college to manage the office. We will also need some pages so our clerks are not escorting offenders to where they will do community service."

Mr. Farley took over. "My employees have not had a pay raise in years. Some have gotten promotions without accompanying pay raises."

Mr. Mayor's hesitated. "Ah, this is getting to be quite a list." He definitely lost his jovial smiles.

I jumped into the conversation before Mr. Farley. "Oh, and I want us to have a couple auditors on staff. We've been prosecuting for tax evasion. We could do our job easier if we had a couple auditors to help us understand what we are looking at and they could help us process government employees for accepting bribes."

Mr. Farley caught the direction of my hint. "Oh yes, I think a couple auditors would more than earn their keep in fines from prosecuting people for embezzlement."

The mayor started looking grim. "Yes, you have done a good job of getting the city back on its feet with the tax evasion cases. Um…do you have other concerns?"

Jeffrey spoke up again. "Yes, perhaps our most important change…well… after the copy machine, is a proper police force. I want us to use some of the money to fully fund our new police academy here in the city."

"I'm not so sure about the police academy." Poor Mr. Mayor looked bewildered. "What do policemen need to know?"

Mr. Farley adopted his teaching tone of voice. "I learned about law enforcement at a class I took in England. Some of our teachers were from Scotland Yard. I learned that our officers need to know how to handle evidence. They need to learn proper investigative techniques. They need to know effective methods for breaking up riots." My supervisor looked at me.

I continued. "They need to learn how to listen to people on the street before they bring them in for us to process. We get too many people in who are innocent or we do not have enough evidence to convict them. Lately, I am letting more people go than I am fining because the police are picking up people they should be sending to shelters." I took a breath and changed gears. "On the other hand the police need to know enough self-defense to keep themselves safe. I can imagine our police department could use some computers. The police need to know how to use them to track trends in crime and build cases for crimes that follow the same patterns."

The mayor rubbed his hands over his face. "Ah, you two have quite a shopping list."

Mr. Farley dropped his effeminate routine. His tone turned crisp. His eyes looked deep into the mayor's soul. "Yes. Yes we do. We have been thinking about this ever since President Vanderholm placed a trained assassin in our office as a supervisor." I'd seldom heard Mr. Farley so angry.

I tried to express our frustration. "We see the consequences of much that is wrong in our country. Right now we are seeing thousands of people flocking to this city because we have been able to open up a few jobs. I am working hard at Rouseff to house people and find them jobs, but I have a fiduciary responsibility to the family to make a profit. I think to some extent I can do both. It would help if the city could shoulder more of the burden for putting people to work. Your wife and I discussed a parks department."

Mr. Mayor shifted his weight and looked at some papers on his desk. "Yes,

I have looked over the new Park Director's plans for the city and some private land. He has suggested several more community gardens such as your mama started in M'TK."

I softened at the mayor's recognition that my mama started the community gardens in M'TK.

The Mayor continued. "I've given the director the go ahead to design community gardens where he sees fit. I have forbid him to dig up lawns around the city hall or to cut down old specimen trees."

We nodded. This sounded reasonable.

I volunteered, "When you are ready to hire, call the main number for Rouseff's offices. We are printing a newsletter to display at the trolley stops. We can advertise the jobs."

The mayor looked at me warily.

I wondered what he thought he was going to do with the money from the fines. I brought up some concerns that I knew were important to my parents. "Of course, if we have a bit of money in the city treasury, we need to make certain all of our teachers are paid up to date. I think a reward of a small bonus is in order for those who stayed at their posts when they did not get paid for months."

"Speaking of children's issues..." Mr. Farley almost interrupted me. "... another problem my office has become aware of, is abandoned children." This topic surprised me coming from Mr. Farley. I was impressed that he thought of other people's children. "We've had many people die. We have no idea how to return their children to the extended family. I processed a case of a boy about seven, stealing food to feed his younger sisters."

I nearly cried on the spot over the thought of such a small boy needing to find food for his sisters.

Mr. Farley had a plan. "We need adequate food and shelter for these children. They have had enough trouble with losing their parents. They need to be in school. We need to open an orphanage for those children we cannot place in private homes."

The mayor nodded. He looked serious. I suspected we were seeing a political face rather than something inspired by true compassion. He spread his hands. "I agree with all you have said. I think an orphanage will be another place we can put people back to work. Um...perhaps we can hire someone to be certain that the soup kitchens receive equal food distribution."

We both nodded. I thought the person in charge of the food distribution would get regular visits from our auditors. "Um…for all these new positions of responsibility, we need to be certain that adequate records are kept. We will need to hire good bookkeepers to be certain that the money is spent on projects that benefit the city."

When we left, I suspected that the mayor was not feeling so honored by our visit. I had the strong feeling that he had intended to buy us off with big bonuses then pocket a goodly amount and share the rest with his friends. I started making a list of people for our auditors to visit regularly.

I'd hoped that the settlement from Vanderholm would ease the suffering in my city. We had so many people pouring into the city nothing eased the suffering. Micki found a crew of fishermen to haul fish out of the swamp. They would bring in one fish for each soup kitchen every day. The fish were boiled and made into stew. The whole meal would be gone in a half hour at the most and people were turned away hungry.

We formed a whole department out of the mayor's office dedicated to feeding and housing the hungry and dislocated. I started eyeing the streets for signs of rats for the people to eat. I didn't see any so perhaps the people had already started eating them. Once again, I found someone to fish my lake for food for the hungry. Micki and Young Rouseff went north to get fish out of Rocky Bay. With the help of Cousin John and Petral, they brought back ten of the monsters. The people ate them all the first day then they came back hungry the next day.

About three weeks after our meeting with Mr. Mayor, he asked to come over and talk to our employees. He had an odd request. "I'd like people in your office to take a look at our inventory of property confiscated in lieu of cash for taxes. We've been selling items at an auction, but some things haven't sold. I'm asking city employees if they would be willing to accept some of the items instead of a cash salary. We will try to give you a fair price, but we have a fiscal responsibility too.

I thought the idea sounded odd, but I did go look at the items that had been at auction for three months without selling. I noticed a white, diesel Mercedes. It looked like a beautiful, well cared for car. I asked why it hadn't sold.

The clerk on duty at the auction yard explained the problem. "Oh that car is worthless. We don't have diesel stations in the city. You can't fuel it up."

I knew I could buy diesel fuel at the M'TK station.

I called Micki and asked him to go over the car for me. He told me that the car had never been underwater, a common problem with imported cars. He thought the problem with getting fuel was the reason nobody wanted it. He urged me to buy it.

I got an image of my beautiful wife sitting behind the wheel of this beautiful car. "The Miki is too small for our family. Jacob doesn't fit in the car seats and he is getting too big to sit on our laps. If you think this is a good car, I'll buy it." Micki agreed that it would be good for my family.

While I was completing the transaction, I noticed Micki eyeing a diesel Volvo. Now I encouraged him. "You are a Rouseff employee. You could fuel up at the M'TK station. You know, when the new gas station goes in at the interchange, we should be sure to put in a pump for diesel fuel."

Micki grinned, "This is a great buy. I'll take it. I feel slightly guilty since we have the control to put in a station to serve our needs."

"I wouldn't have thought about putting a diesel pump at the interchange, if I hadn't been thinking about the car. I will still buy at M'TK as long as I can. It is convenient to my house."

I didn't tell Leah about my purchase. I drove the car home and put it in the garage. I went into the house and found Leah. "Honey, there is something curious out here that I want you to see."

"Can it wait? I am setting the table."

"No, the table can wait. This is extraordinary. I can't wait for you to see it."

She followed me out to the garage. Her response was all I could hope for. She looked at the huge white car. "What is that?" She walked part way around the car and peered through the window. "Where did it come from?"

I grinned ear to ear.

"Jake, you didn't."

I grinned more.

"It must have cost a fortune. Only the very rich drive these."

I held out the keys to her. "The very rich, and my wife. The Miki is too small for our family. Come on, I'll show you how to drive it. Starting it is a little different than the Miki."

We took the car into the M'TK station and back out to the house with Leah behind the wheel. She was thrilled with the car. I went to sleep a very satisfied man that night.

Chapter 19 Homeless in the City

The city continued to struggle. Once again, I paid the round trip train fare for people to go work in the potato harvest. We harvested more potatoes than the year before. They sold out of the stores soon after they came in. The soup kitchens could not get enough to last more than a few days. I wished my parents were well enough to travel the country looking for more food.

One afternoon, I stayed at Rouseff offices longer than usual to look over some purchase agreements. Young Rouseff came to my office. "Mr. Jake, I want your opinion on something."

I nodded and leaned back in my chair.

"Well it is so easy for you and Micki to be able to see what needs to be done. I would like to be able to see what needs to be done and how to do it." He licked his lips. "I think I want to go to university. I have my first year out of the way."

I grinned. "I think that is an excellent idea."

"Can you tell Uncle Philippe?"

"Why would you want me to? He will be thrilled."

Poor Young Rouseff picked at his cuff. "I'm not sure."

"I am sure. I'll tell him if you want, but I think you need to hear his initial response."

"If you think it is okay, I'll call him then."

I smiled and nodded.

He left my office. I didn't expect him to call his uncle immediately. He was more excited over the idea of going back to school than I thought. He came back to my office in about ten minutes. "Uncle Philippe is happy. He thinks it is a great idea. He says he may send some of my cousins up here too."

I grinned. "I will help out wherever I am needed."

I felt so much happier over Young Rouseff's show of responsibility that I decided I could leave him in charge and check in at the prosecutor's office. I found a long line of offenders who were new to the city. They'd been arrested for various minor offenses. I knew the interns were capable of processing the accused, but they didn't have my sense of authority for dealing with problems. I decided to help out.

I started to interview my first client. "It says here...Oh for crap sakes...I can't make out the officer's writing. What were you doing?"

"We was cooking some fish on a charcoal burner."

"Where were you?"

"In that big grassy area with all the trees, and the big brick buildings."

I had to think a minute before I put together grass, trees, and big brick buildings. "Right. That is the University Campus. It is private property. If you want to cook, go down to the parking lot by the M'TK Mall. Stay away from the cars. In fact there is a nice area on the north side of the mall away from the road. That is private property so the police will not bother you there. Don't get drunk. Don't get into fights. Don't practice prostitution, and most of all don't get sent back here. You may go."

My second client was arrested for camping outside the city buildings. I sent him to the back of the parking lot at the mall. I added an extra admonition. "Help the people in the soup kitchen."

The third client got a different admonition. "Get a trash bag and pick up any bits of paper and litter you find on the ground down there, and put your trash bag in the dumpster under the big green R on the side of the building."

The fourth person was also told to pick up litter. I started processing people in less than five minutes each. I marked their files innocent and went on to the next. Alexander came to watch me process the next person hauled in for sleeping on the sidewalk.

After the client left to pick up his trash bag he asked, "Um...sir would you mind if I did the same thing.

"I don't care. They will be out of the way. They have to eat and sleep someplace. I'll send extra Rouseff guards down to keep the peace."

Alexander went back to his desk in the middle of the room, climbed on top, and shouted, "Staff meeting in ten minutes."

I took the ten minutes to call over to Rouseff security to tell them the problem. I explained that I didn't want people evicted.

"Sir, the property behind the parking lot belongs to us. It is just scrub land. The fence isn't really necessary. Mostly it is there to keep people from driving out of the parking lot. Shall I open it up to let the people into the brush?"

"Yeah, sure. Make sure you tell them not to set themselves on fire."

"I'll take care of that."

I went to the staff meeting. Alexander explained what he had observed me doing. "Jake?"

"Send your homeless down there. I've notified Rouseff security."

Mr. Farley grinned. "Thanks Jake. I'll go tell everybody else who got arrested for homeless offenses where they can go. Can I tell the police to send people down there instead of arresting them?"

I nodded, exhausted by the shear weight of problems. The city didn't seem like home anymore. It had become a giant hungry beast.

The other prosecutors started digging into old files. When I looked at the murder cases, I immediately saw a problem and took it to our senior staff.

"You know, one problem I see is that we don't get the information on every murder. We get cases where someone is charged. All the cases in our files come from murders when we couldn't convict. Mr. LaBarge thought the same person was involved in these two cases where two separate people were arrested. We need to be working with the coroner's office and the police to see if perhaps they have other murders committed by the same person."

Alexander agreed to take six interns to go talk to the coroner. I went over the details of the two cases we had that led Mr. LaBarge to think the same sociopath committed both crimes.

With the case overload in the prosecutor's office reduced to manageable levels, and Young Rouseff acting responsible, I decided to visit The Cove. I longed to see my cousins and their children.

Jacob and Elizabeth jumped up and down with excitement over visiting The Cove. They'd heard us talking about it, but had never met most of their cousins. We needed to go home. While the children danced and started packing their toys, Leah looked sad and listless. I pulled her into my arms. "My love, what makes you look so sad when we are going to take a vacation?"

"Oh, I don't know. It is going north. I guess I'm afraid I'll meet someone who'll wonder what Leah Fillon is doing with Jake Jaconovich."

"Mmm, wife, I know what Leah should be doing with Big Jake, but that's not anybody's business."

She giggled. "Jake you know what I mean."

"The answer is still the same. It is none of their business who you married."

She smiled and repeated. "It is none of their business who I married."

I kissed the end of her nose.

We stayed ten days in The Cove. I went out fishing one day. We didn't catch much. The season hadn't really started. Some of the cousins got some shrimp and picked mussels. We sent them south on the train. I wondered why the stores were always out of food, if the fishermen were shipping the same as usual. I couldn't understand why we could never find enough to feed people who were out of jobs.

Chapter 20 Opening the Road

When I returned to work at Rouseff, I heard some surprising news. My secretary was the first to tell me. "Oh Mr. Jaconovich. It is good to see you. You'll never guess what has happened here. Jouyet left the country. He took his wife and children and left declaring never to return."

"I assume *never returning* may be more like not until after the statute of limitations expires."

"Oh no, he said never. His relatives are quite upset."

Young Rouseff made it a point to come to my office to tell me about Jouyet. "It is good to have you back sir. I completed the purchase of the machinery you ordered. Our legal department went over the purchase agreements. Oh! And everything in the south is disrupted. Jouyet has left the country! The Vanderholms are talking of leaving."

"Ah, I don't think they are a great loss to our society. Does anybody expect them to return soon?"

"No. Those family members who have left insist they are not coming back. Julie Jouyet's family is very upset because one of her brothers went with them."

"Ah."

Young Rouseff continued his report. "Also Sir, I have a piece of agreeable news. We can open the new highway next week. The tollbooths are almost in place. We're planning a big ceremony with the governor, and the mayor, and you, and Uncle Rouseff."

"It will be good to see Cousin Philippe and Mrs. Rouseff. Papa and Mama will be happy to see them. How long will they be staying?"

"I don't know sir."

"I'd like to invite them out for a dinner party."

"Um, won't that be a bit much for your staff?"

"No. Why should it be?"

"Well with all your relatives staying there, and all."

I was confused. "Why are my relatives staying?"

"For the same reason several of my Rouseff cousins are staying with me. They are attending the university. I expect my cousins to arrive next week."

"Oh yeah. I remember Uncle John making some statement about the cousins attending the university. I invited them to stay with me, but that would be only two that I can think of."

Young Rouseff shook his head. "Your Uncle John may be kinder than my Uncle Philippe. Every dependent Rouseff under the age of thirty has been ordered to get a university education. I think I am to be invaded by at least six cousins."

A week later, Rouseff Construction opened the new highway. We held a grand celebration. Mr. Rouseff attended with the governor, the mayor, and the head of our construction team. I sat in a place of honor although I didn't feel like I had done much. In the evening after the road opening ceremony, we held a huge dinner and ball to raise money to feed the poor in the city.

Leah and I attended the party with Micki and Katheryn. Mama and Papa came. Mama had a new dress. Her hair had turned totally white now. She still looked beautiful. I think it was easier for the world to see how sweet and kind she was as she aged.

We sat with the Rouseff's at dinner. He told us about bringing everybody in his family between the ages of seventeen and thirty so they could start university at the beginning of the term. We laughed and explained that Uncle John had done the same thing. We confessed that we'd been surprised to see eight cousins show up at our house. We agreed that between the D'NOs and the Rouseffs we would make up a large portion of the first year class.

From the dinner-dance, we raised over twenty thousand dollars to help with the homeless problem. Mr. Rouseff donated free train fare for anybody who wanted to return to their family in other parts of the country. We decided to give anybody who wanted to leave the city one hundred dollars for one individual, and two hundred dollars cash for a family along with a one-way ticket out of town. We didn't have enough jobs for all the people pouring into the city.

We returned home from the dance to a lively family party. We began to sort the cousins out. Two of the boys intended to live with Micki their first year. "We want to get an apartment next year."

I raised their hopes. "I talked to Mr. Rouseff at dinner. He has sent some of his family up here. He suggested putting the lot of you in one of his houses that is divided into flats. Some of his nieces and nephews are in their late twenties."

I sat and thought. "I suspect that he wants you to keep an eye on his relatives and set a good example for them. He may also expect you to teach them how to live simply and tastefully."

My cousins groaned.

Margaret sounded concerned, "Since we have the baby with us, I am not sure I want to live in a house full of university students."

"You are welcome to stay here. All of you are welcome to stay here although you might find conditions crowded."

Margaret had already looked the situation over. "I have put our things in the room I used when I was here before."

Lars scowled at the memory.

I asked, "Lars, will you be looking for work in the city?"

"No, Grandpapa decided that if John D'NO could send all his children to university, he could send his children. I will be taking classes with Margaret."

"Good. I'm thrilled to hear this. I know the fishermen are feeding this country, but as Uncle John says the catch is getting less. I think we need to find different ways to feed our people and different careers for the families in the north."

Lars's tone struck me as outspoken, "The people who lived in the villages and worked for the canneries will continue to fish. Those of us who lived in the coves and have always been independent will find new careers."

I wondered how Lars was going to get along in school. I trusted the others to do well.

I asked Margaret her intentions. She explained, "I plan to study law. After school, Lars and I will return to the north. The northern people need lawyers, and we will need a new prosecutor soon. I can start in the prosecutor's office as soon as I get out of school."

Chapter 21 Cousins Start University

O n the first day of classes, I managed to get home a little early. I surprised my children having a picnic in the front yard. As soon as I got close, I realized that Mary Anne was on her stomach on the ground. She was filthy. I picked her up. "Mary Anne needs to go back in her stroller."

"No. Clara's stroller." Elizabeth explained.

I looked in the stroller and found Margaret's daughter Clara who was only weeks older than Mary Anne. "Well, let's all go inside and surprise Mama that I am home so early."

Jacob and Elizabeth picked up their playthings and dumped them in the stroller on top of Clara. She protested. I picked her up out of the stroller and carried both babies into the house.

When we entered the house with Clara still loudly protesting the insult of having toys dumped on her, Leah heard the commotion and came to investigate. "Is she hurt?"

"No. Just insulted, I think. Jacob and Elizabeth put their toys in her space."

"I'll take Mary Anne. Were they outside? I was helping cook by picking greens for dinner. I told the children they could have a picnic. See I put that blanket on the floor for their picnic." Leah sounded cross and defensive as she pointed out the pristine blanket on the sitting room floor.

I looked at Leah and snorted, "Yes, I can see just how this happened. Jacob decided Mary Anne wanted to go outside and Elizabeth decided Clara wanted to go outside."

My son corrected me. "No. Mary Anne wanted Clara to play with her."

"Ah, well, I will take Mary Anne off to get her cleaned up for dinner." I looked at the other three children. They were varying degrees of filthy. "The adults will be dressed up when they get home. You children should be dressed up for guests too."

It took me an hour to get all the children dressed presentably. I put the two babies in the playpen.

"No Papa. They want to come out and play."

As a matter of desperation I told Jacob that this was going to be lesson time, not play time. I sat down with my older children and asked Jacob to read a story to me. I couldn't tell if he could read as well as he sounded or if he just had the words memorized.

The students returned on the five-thirty trolley, all thirty of them. They brought Chinese food with them and were eager to tell about their first day of school.

I thought I was taking charge of the guests as the host. "Um, first things first. I don't recognize a few of you as being either a Rouseff or a D'NO."

This simple statement sent the lot of them into wild gales of laughter. Cousin J. J. recovered first and introduced a scattering of Spinozas, Uzaras, and Gannons.

J. J. started the story of their first day of class. "Yeah, well, we got to history class."

I smiled and sat down preparing to enjoy this story very much. They took turns telling me the highlights.

"Well, some of us sat together and the teacher looked at us and asked if we were the D'NOs on his list. We nodded."

One of the Uzara girls interrupted J.J. "That was when the fun started. He asked if all of them were related to a southern family. I immediately spoke up and said that if they were not, I'd marry one of them, then they would be."

All the students broke into laughter.

"I interrupted her and complained that just because her great aunt Violet had run off with one of their family she didn't have exclusive rights to them. I said my cousin married Micki D'NO." I was still confused as to who was who, but this girl must be a Spinoza.

J. J. said, "I thought the old man was going to faint at Micki's name. He asked if we were related to Micki. We smiled and nodded. He looked horrified and agreed that he could see that we were."

I looked at my cousins smiling and agreed that the curly dark hair, blue eyes, and dimples might give them away.

J. J. continued. "Things went down hill for the teacher after that. He sorted out who were the Spinozas, Uzaras, and Gannons."

The Spinoza girl's eyes danced as she giggled. "Then he asked M'TG where his name came from."

The class went off on another round of laughter. Lars grinned and looked sheepish. Margaret had picked up her baby. She looked at her husband and her face lit up the whole room. She commented, "We had a really good history lesson."

The Uzara girl sounded awed. "I've never learned so much in a history class in my whole life."

A Gannon agreed. "Yeah, I didn't know any of that stuff."

"Well, I wouldn't put too much store by it." Lars shifted his weight and looked self-conscious. "Some of it came from old family stories. Some of it was guessing based on information I've learned other places. Some of it was made up on the spot just because that bigoted windbag irritated me."

I joined the others in their laughter. I sincerely hoped someone had gotten even with that bigoted ass. "Well what did you tell him?"

Margaret handed Clara to Lars and he bounced his baby on his knee as he told his story. "Well first, he asked me what kind of a name M'TG was. I explained that it is Danish and originally it was Torgeson. I said we adapted it to fit with the local language when the Torgeson men married native women. He asked me when the Torgesons came to this country. I explained about the Vikings, how they were great sea explorers and they had large sea going boats propelled either by sail or oars. I said we were not certain when the first Danes landed on the north coast, but speculation places the date around the thirteen hundreds. Well, he had a little trouble with that date. Well, I kinda' made that up based on when they were exploring, and all."

Everybody snickered.

One of my cousins couldn't contain himself any longer. "Then the teacher huffs and says that we may be European, but we didn't fight in the War of Acquisition."

Again all the students laughed again.

Lars continued with his story. "Yeah, well we all know that part. I assured him that we did indeed fight in the invasion. I pointed out that the southern sailors were never successful in entering any of our ports. He said that was because of the lack of wind. I agreed that it is hard to maneuver a sailing ship in a light breeze when fighting against a bigger boat with oars. I then pointed out that the southern troops did not make it over our mountain passes either."

Cousin San bounced up and down. "Oh! Oh! Oh! Then Lars says that the church yard in Norville has a section devoted to the fifty-two men and women who lost their lives defending the mountains against the southern invaders."

I held my head, then I held my sides as I laughed at the thought of my stuffy history professor hearing the other side of the story.

Lars still grinned. "I went on to remind him that the Oceana and Montsea provinces did not join the rest of the country until a little over a hundred and fifty years ago and that we joined through a mutual trade treaty."

"Lars, thank you. That man has pissed me off since my first day of class."

The students went off into another round of wild laughter.

J.J. explained. "Yeah, well, when Lars got finished with his history lesson Professor said he was going to talk to you about the behavior of some of your distant cousins. He assured us that you would not want to associate with liars and ruffians."

I shifted my weight at the idea of my family being called liars. "I think I will have to have a little chat with your history professor."

"You don't have to. We can handle him."

"Oh but I want to. This is too good an opportunity to pass up. That man has been spilling his vile poison onto impressionable students for years. I rather like besting him." I paused. "Besides when I was a student I was too afraid of getting expelled to really stand up to the man."

I didn't get to talk to the history professor until much later. The second day of history class, only those students living with us came home to dinner. They acted subdued.

At dinner I asked. "How did your classes go today? Did you have any more trouble in history?"

Lars put his fork down and leaned back in his chair. He looked at Margaret and smiled. "No we didn't have any more trouble in history. The professor tangled with Margaret."

"Oh no! What happened?" The D'NO women are not shy and retiring when they know they are right and others are wrong.

Margaret explained. "Oh, he started talking about how southerners are perfect, and wise, and can do no wrong, while northerners are little better than animals. I got mad so I stood up and told him to stop, just stop. I said that most of us from the north knew Alice D'SnG. Our fathers and uncles did business with Leon Fortenac. Then, I explained that most of the rest of the class was related to Alice D'SnG. Well...I was a bit angry. I said that I counted Violet

Uzara D'SnG as a friend and my cousin married into the family. Anyway, I told him that his line of talk is exactly the attitude that killed Alice D'SnG and destroyed Leon Fortenac's life. Mr. Fortenac believed that lie."

Margaret took a deep breath. "Well, I went on to explain that when you took the case to court you proved that the distinction doesn't exist because families have intermarried. I said that I suspected that even working class families can point to a cousin or niece or nephew who has married into a family connected to a southern family. The more I talked the angrier I got."

Margaret smiled at me. "I'm afraid I got very angry. I went on to explain that my cousin Jake was the one who prosecuted the Fortenac case. My brother Micki was in the courtroom. Micki told me he was stunned as he listened to the statements of outrage. At that moment it became apparent that this idea that large portions of people who live in the north are almost animals will lead to civil war among the families. Our whole constitution was adopted to prevent that civil war."

Margaret sat quiet for half a minute. "I think maybe I got through to him. He said that yes of course I was right for today. He had been speaking historically. One of the Uzara girls, I think she is only eighteen, spoke up and said that she lost one cousin to that kind of thinking. She conceded that it is acceptable to teach the thinking that led to her cousin's death and the imprisonment of a Fortenac, and it is important as the reason behind our change in government. She said it hurt her deeply to hear those ideas put forth as current truth."

Lars shifted in his seat. "I think all the women agreed that that type of hate speech frightened them. I explained to the teacher that when people think they are better than others, it is the women who suffer most. I could see why that type of talk would be distressing to all the women when they know it led to the death of their cousin."

Cousin Helen spoke up. "That was the point at which the teacher turned the conversation to questioning our relationship to you and Micki. We assured him that we grew up in the same household with Micki and that we are living with you now. Then the teacher turned to Margaret and informed her that even Micki was not so outspoken."

Lars grunted. "I assured him that, yeah, the D'NO men are pretty mellow. It is the women you have to watch out for. They'll set you straight every time and the damnable part is that they are right and you know it."

We sat quiet for a few minutes. I thought about the women in my family.

Lars seemed to understand them fairly well. I formed a new respect for his relationship with Margaret.

I remember the four years my cousins were in college as a happy time for me. Lars surprised me the most. He discovered a passion for history and decided he wanted to teach school. He prepared to become a teacher. They would live in one of the villages where Margaret would practice law and he would teach.

Having a house full of cousins created many changes in my household. One change was the celebration of Christmas. They insisted on celebrating Christmas in the home, with a tree, and decorations, and presents. I'd always gone to Mass at Christmas, but I'd never celebrated it at home. This was becoming a new custom in my country.

We all went outside and cut branches off of trees and brought the greens into the house for decorations. My home was turned into something vaguely foreign and elfish. I recognized that tulle was used abundantly.

Leah had never celebrated Christmas. I was surprised that she didn't know the dates of Christmas, or that it was about the birth of Jesus. She had never gone to church. I wondered if this was the reason she didn't think it was important to get married in the church.

I felt thankful that Leah seemed eager to participate in the decorating. She and I went shopping for gifts for the children. I went by myself and bought her a diamond pendant. She did not think it was necessary to buy me a gift.

During those years, we appreciated having extra eyes to watch our children because Jacob refused to start school. He was almost seven before I could convince him to attend. As it turned out, I think the only reason he went was because Elizabeth could come too. She was five and ready for the second term of the second form. Jacob entered fourth form.

They both lamented that Mary Ann would be home alone. I reminded them that Cousin Clara came to stay everyday. Mary Ann and Clara got along almost like sisters.

Chapter 22 Tonsillitis

Once I got my children separated and in school. Jacob decided he wanted to play football. He got along well with the other boys despite being smaller. He knew the fundamentals of the game. I'd been teaching him some martial arts at home especially the exercises and moves. I explained how they were used in football.

Twice a week I started sending him to Professor Stodola's school for martial arts. I didn't want my son getting beat up at school.

Elizabeth wasn't old enough for football when she entered school. She decided she wanted to take dance lessons. She insisted that Mary Anne wanted to take dance lessons too.

Mary Anne was becoming a challenge. She wanted to do everything her brother and sister did but she was younger. When the older children started school, I was certain that Mary Anne was past ready for the first form. When Elizabeth started talking about dance lessons, Mary Anne wanted to take lessons too. I talked to the teacher about letting a three year old into the class. I amended my idea to letting Cousin Clara into the class. With the promise of a little extra money for the younger girls, the teacher agreed to take them.

Leah was kept busy running the children to their activities or picking them up. She drove Jacob and Elizabeth to school because they were too young to travel into the city by themselves. She picked Elizabeth up and drove her to dance class. Sometimes if I was working too late to bring Jacob home with me, she picked Jacob up from football.

Jacob's games and the girls dance recitals became one of my greatest joys. Mary Anne did keep up in dance class. She was so tiny that everyone marveled at how well she did. I watched her dance and recognized that teaching her the exercises and moves in martial arts had paid off in dance. She could keep up with the older girls and sometimes surpassed them in leaping and jumping.

I was thankful for the distraction and joy of my family. Work once again became challenging. Rouseff Industries functioned well enough. Young Rouseff was doing most of the day to day running of the business. My challenge came when I tried working with the other family heads and business leaders to promote development in order to get people back to work. More than once I heard others, even a Uzara or Spinoza, say that one of the advantages of the purges had been to prevent the problem of having more people than jobs. I felt sickened by this attitude and went to the prosecutor's office.

I thought the police academy was producing results in our office. We had fewer days when we turned people out in mass because they were arrested for things the police could redirect on the street. We now had a full police force.

The prosecutor's office was becoming more and more of a satellite campus for the university law school. Most of the law students had to spend some time in our office. We had enough interns that I often felt slightly silly with ten or twelve students following me around.

After my family had been at the university two years, I had a special joy at the prosecutor's office. Cousin Margaret started her internship. Of course Mr. Farley knew that we were cousins. Everybody else knew she was well connected, but they called her Mrs. M'TG.

She and Lars were living in one of Rouseff's houses with the rest of the D'NO's and Rouseffs. They seemed happy there. Margaret commented on being especially happy to be with family when Lars took off on one of his research trips to the north.

Margaret quickly established a reputation as an excellent prosecutor. The other prosecutors declared her the new champion for glaring at people. "She makes tough men weep when she glares at them and primly asks them to tell her why they did something so inanely improper." They joked that once someone met up with Margaret, they didn't re-offend or they didn't get caught. I thought this was more than an idle joke.

While Margaret was in her second year of internship, our office got a case that still makes me shake my head. The accused was guilty of great evil. Out of that evil something good arose. All the prosecutor's offices in the country developed a new level of respect for each other and a willingness to cooperate, which enhanced our effectiveness in practicing law. This case also gave me a base of friends and acquaintances across the country.

Of course, if I was to be involved in something big at work, we must have a crisis at home. This has long been one of the laws of my life.

The case began when Detective Sorros came to me with more murders like the two LaBarge thought were commit by a socio-path.

We sat down and looked at everything he had on the cases. He had listed the similarities of the victims, the locations, the weapon, and the type of murder. We looked at how far apart the murders were. Our first two murders had happened three years apart. He'd found more that fit the pattern since those first two. The last two murders were three months apart.

Detective Sorros explained, "Our murderer is reaching a crisis. We needed to find him soon. He is due to kill again any day. We know the area where the murder is likely to happen. His former victims were all former Jouyet employees who lived in Wulfton."

I outlined where I could help. "This office can put out flyers at the trolley stops telling people to be careful. I am still active enough at Rouseff to authorize flyers. I will call over to have an announcement made at the paper mill."

Detective Sorros asked. "Now that so many Jouyet workers are working for you and living outside Wulfton, do you think our murderer might track down his victims in other neighborhoods?"

"I don't know. We really need to talk to former Jouyet employees to see what else these people had in common. You have my permission to have your men talk to them. I'll help where I can."

Detective Sorros surprised me with his respectful attitude toward me. "Thank you. I'm uncomfortable that the victims are both men and women. I will have my men interview people at the paper mill."

A knock on my door interrupted us. I thought it was very strange that someone would interrupt me, so I opened the door. Leah stood there holding Mary Anne. I could see tears on Mary Anne's face.

Leah sounded cross. "Take her. I am scheduled for a meeting to raise money for the school lunch program. She is cross and the housekeeper was too busy to watch her." Leah shoved my daughter into my arms.

I heard Mary Anne sniff. I sat back down in my chair and held my daughter against me. Her little body shook with the agitation of a recent tantrum. She settled her head against my shoulder and put her thumb in her mouth. I wrapped her favorite blanket around her.

The detective chuckled. "We can continue this later if you are busy."

I looked at Mary Anne. "She looks ready to sleep. I want to think this through some more. I worry that this person may be someone working for Rouseff."

He grunted then explained. "If they stand out at all at work it would be as a nice person, possibly a snitch. You would want to look for someone who is always complimenting the bosses, but is not necessarily productive."

"We have a mix of Rouseff people and former Jouyet people. I could write up this profile and give it to our people who we know are not the perpetrator and have them look for people who fit this profile." I took notes as I talked.

Mary Anne fell asleep. In the back of my mind I though her previous tantrum may have been because she was too tired to go out. I wished we still had the nanny. Leah had let her go weeks earlier because our older two were in school.

I returned my thoughts to the problem of the sociopath. "Another group of Rouseff employees who need to know about this are the trolley guards. I think I will double the number of guards at the six Wulfton stops. Can you think of any other back-up either Rouseff or the prosecutor's office can give you?"

"Other than telling your offenders in this office to avoid Wulfton. If you get an offender from Wulfton question them about the people who live near them and about strangers who come to the area."

"Of course, what am I thinking? We always have drunks from every part of town in here. I can make certain the ones picked up who have any relationship to Wulfton are questioned. They are often one of our best sources for news from the street. People don't notice the drunks, but the drunks see far more than most people realize." I thought for a couple more minutes. "Also, Rouseff employs a troop of street entertainers. They see a great deal when they are performing. We can also sneak plainclothes officers in with them. I can direct them to anyplace you want watched."

"Right now, I don't want any extra people in the area."

I stood firm on one point. "We will post extra guards at the trolley stops. This is for the protection of our guards."

"Of course, I appreciate your willingness to cooperate and extend the resources at Rouseff to the city."

I wanted to take off my jacket because Mary Anne was starting to make me over-warm, but I stayed focused on the discussion. "Rouseff needs rule of law in the streets in order to run a successful business. It's imperative that our employees be able to get back and forth to work safely and almost more importantly, go shopping safely."

The detective started to stand up. "I think we have a good outline for now.

I want to get started getting my men prepped to interview people over at the paper mill. Thank you for your help."

I started to stand with Mary Anne in my arms.

The detective waved at me to sit. "No, no stay where you are. She's an angel. We wouldn't want to wake her up."

I smiled and waved the detective out the door. When he was gone, I kissed Mary Anne on the forehead. She felt hot to me. I pulled the phone closer and called the pediatrician. I explained that Mary Anne had been unusually upset earlier and now she felt like she had a fever. They told me to bring her in whenever I could get there.

I took time to call Rouseff's offices and outline to Young Rouseff what we were looking for and why.

He grasped the situation immediately. "Jake thanks for calling. I will tell our people to cooperate with the police. I would hate to start losing our people to a madman."

"Thanks for your help. We are hoping to prevent the next murder. Listen, I will be away from the phone for a few hours. Let me give you the detective's back line so you can call him directly if you have questions." We finished our call.

I looked at Mary Anne still sleeping in my arms. I thought about trying to take her on a trolley and carry her a couple blocks. I carried her to the outer office and looked around the office for Margaret to see if she could drive me. She was out of the office. I called a taxi.

Mary Anne woke up when we got to the doctor's office. She started to cry and throw herself around in my arms. The nurse ushered us into a little examination room immediately. She took Mary Anne's temperature. It was way too high. Mary Anne needed to be in the hospital. I tried not to panic as I waited for the taxi to come back and take us to the hospital. I soothed and comforted as best I could but my daughter was miserable and let us know.

The pediatric department at the hospital asked me to stay with Mary Anne. Perhaps they didn't know that I intended to stay beside her all night if necessary. They offered to put Mary Anne on one of their little carts. I told them she was light, so I would carry her. It seemed to take forever for the staff to find her a room and a nightgown. I got her changed and ready for bed.

Finally, they started an IV and gave her medication to bring the fever down. The nurse explained that Mary Anne's tonsils were so swollen they were almost touching. We worried about her being able to breathe.

Mary Anne's fever did come down within an hour. The doctor finally arrived to examine her. He inspected her infected throat. Her tonsils were covered in nasty infection. He explained that he'd start her on antibiotics immediately. He wanted to get the infection cleared up then he would remove the tonsils.

I sat and nodded dumbly. I was thankful that right now the doctor was making decisions. I felt too terrified to think. My baby was seriously sick. I was furious at the rest of the world. Silently, I blamed everything and almost everyone for Mary Anne's illness. I wondered if the staff knew my thoughts.

Mary Anne's nurse assured me, "There was nothing anybody could have done differently. Children get sick. At her age they do get high fevers. You caught it early. She'll be fine." I sat and wanted to blame myself for talking to the detective. I thought that she had not been overly hot when I first took her from Leah. I looked at the time and wondered where Leah was.

I called the house several times before the housekeeper returned from her shopping. I told her where I was and left her a message to tell Leah what was happening. I called the prosecutor's office to see if Leah had come back to pick up Mary Anne. I told them to give Leah the message that Mary Anne was in the hospital. It was time for the older children to get out of school. I still hadn't been able to get hold of Leah and it was my day to pick Jacob up from football practice. I finally decided that I would have to leave Mary Anne for a few minutes to go pick up Jacob in a taxi if I didn't hear from Leah. I called the housekeeper again.

Mary Anne had slept most of the afternoon. The doctor wouldn't let her keep her favorite blanket. The nurse wrapped it up in a plastic bag, and the doctor told me to be certain it got washed with a little bit of bleach. I held Mary Anne's hand assuring her that I was better than a blanket, so she slept with one hand holding my finger and her other thumb in her mouth. She fussed if I moved.

Finally, I needed to pick Jacob up at school. I asked the nurses to call me a taxi. Mary Anne cried when I started to leave the room. I told her that I needed to go pick up Jacob.

"Jacob come? I want Jacob. I want Jacob."

I turned to a nurse who was passing in the hall. "Can I bring her brother to see her? I think it would comfort her."

"How old is he?"

"Eight." I rounded up by a few months

"He can come visit."

I told Mary Anne, "Okay honey, I am going to go get Jacob to come see you."

"Jacob." Mary Anne smiled and drifted back to sleep.

Jacob was surprised to see me picking him up in a taxi when he expected us to take a trolley. I told him about Mary Anne and that we were going back to the hospital.

He sounded like he might start to cry. "She is going to be okay isn't she?"

"Oh yes, she will be fine. We caught the fever right away. The doctor says she will have to have her tonsils out."

"What are tonsils? Is that serious?"

"No it is not serious. Tonsils are fleshy things at the back of the throat. I have no idea why we have them, or why some children need to have them out." Inspiration struck on how to comfort my son. "You can look at Mary Anne's tonsils when we get to the hospital. I warn you they look pretty nasty."

"But, Mary Anne will be okay won't she?"

"Yes, she will be fine." It comforted me to see my son as worried as I had been. It helped to say all the things to him that the nurses said to me.

Jacob and I got back to the hospital within fifteen minutes after I'd left. He walked ten steps in front of me, eager to see his sister. He grew very quiet when we got to her room. She was sleeping again. Her cheeks were scarlet. Jacob very quietly tiptoed up to her bed. He touched her hand then he put his head down on the bed and cried.

I rubbed his back. "There son. She'll be fine. Don't worry so."

Mary Anne's eyes fluttered open. She whispered. "Jacob! Papa brought me hospital. See tube. See bed. See nurses outside." That was all Mary Anne's sore throat would allow her to say, but it comforted her brother. He smiled.

"Jacob, can you take care of Mary Anne for a minute? I need to go to the nurses' station and call your mama to tell her where you are. All you have to do is hold Mary Anne's hand. Her throat hurts too much to talk."

Jacob nodded to me then started assuring his sister. "Papa says you will be fine and you will get to have an operation and everything. Can I see your tonsils?"

I finally got hold of Leah on the phone. "Oh Darling, I'm so glad to finally reach you. Jacob and I are fine. He is with me. Mary Anne has a bad sore throat with a high fever. We're all at the hospital. She will have to stay here overnight until her fever and the infection are under control. She's miserable so I'll stay with her. Can you come to get Jacob? He was terribly upset to learn that she was sick. You might have trouble with him crying over this."

"Jake, are you sure you are not the one upsetting him? Mary Anne has a sore throat. Children get sore throats. It's not that big a deal."

I didn't want to argue with Leah. I thought perhaps she was more upset than her words indicated. She never snapped at me that way.

"I've been very assuring with Jacob and tried to distract him with how nasty the throat looks. Still, when he saw how sick she looks, he was upset. The doctor wants her to stay here over night. The children don't like being separated. That reminds me, bring Elizabeth when you come to pick up Jacob."

"I am tired and want to change clothes. I'll be there in an hour or so."

I felt sick when I got off of the phone. I refrained from throwing the phone across the room. I didn't like Leah's attitude. I grumbled to myself, "What kind of mother refuses to rush to see her daughter who is in the hospital?" I was so upset that I couldn't talk myself down from being angry with Leah.

I returned to Mary Anne's room. "Your mama will be here as soon as she can get here. She needs to take care of some things at home, then she will be here."

The doctor came in before Leah arrived. He remembered Jacob's name and assured him that Mary Anne would be fine. "Her throat hurts her a great deal. That is what troubles her most. She needs to stay here so we can give her antibiotics to fight the infection and something to keep her fever from getting too high."

The doctor asked when Leah would be in to stay with her. I explained that Leah would be in soon to pick up Jacob. I said I would stay. "I have another question. The children are very close and do not like to be separated. Can Elizabeth come see her too?"

"How old is Elizabeth now?"

"Six."

The doctor rubbed his face. "I guess. She can visit for a few minutes. We usually don't let children that young visit, but we'll make an exception for this time."

Leah eventually arrived to pick up Jacob and see Mary Anne. She'd left Elizabeth at home with the housekeeper.

I explained, "I'd made arrangements for Elizabeth to visit Mary Anne."

"Jake, I don't want all three children down with this."

"If the others are going to get it, they will get it whether they visit or not. They are always together at home." I felt like I was arguing with my wife, so I shut up.

Jacob crawled up on Mary Anne's bed and kissed her goodnight. "You'll be able to come home tomorrow."

I glared at Leah. She kissed Mary Anne on the forehead and promised to see her tomorrow. My head knew that she would have kissed her daughter goodnight if I had not been glaring, but my heart believed that she intended to go home without a goodnight kiss for her daughter. She didn't kiss me. I would have liked a kiss and to be reassured, or thanked for taking care of Mary Anne.

I sat down by Mary Anne's bed and tried to remember if Leah usually kissed the children goodnight. No. She didn't always kiss them goodnight. I did. I remembered Mama's kisses and Papa saying, "Goodnight son." I grew instantly tired. I fell asleep with my head on Mary Anne's bed while I held her hand.

In the morning, I expected Leah to arrive as soon as she dropped the children off at school. I watched my watch. Leah was late.

I had to leave Mary Anne for a few minutes to call into both offices and say I wouldn't be in today. Both secretaries I talked to tried to comfort me.

I got grumpy with Leah again. She was late. I wanted to go home, and shower, and change clothes, and eat. I'd missed my dinner so I wanted a breakfast. I felt instantly relieved when I saw Jacob's head peaking around the door.

"Come on in." I smiled at Jacob.

He came in holding Elizabeth's hand. All my children looked happy to see each other.

The change that came over Mary Anne made me smile. She smiled and wanted to sit up. She instantly looked much healthier. "Hi, I'm in the hospital. I have tonsili…something. I have to get better then I get an operation."

"Show Elizabeth your throat." Jacob sounded gleeful over sharing the nastiness of Mary Anne's throat with Elizabeth. The children crawled up on the bed to look down Mary Anne's throat.

"I think it looks much better. The tonsil things are not so big." Jacob sounded a little disappointed in his beloved sister's improvement. His interest in looking at her throat and his ability to recognize that it was better made me wonder if he would like to be a doctor someday. I would like a doctor in the family.

I finally began to wonder where Leah was. When she didn't come in with Jacob and Elizabeth, I thought she had stopped at the washroom. "Where is your mother?"

"She went home I think." Jacob cast this information off as if it was not important enough to warrant his full attention.

"Did she just drop you off here and go home?" This didn't sound likely. It didn't look likely.

Elizabeth shook her head in response to my question. Jacob picked up a book that one of the nurses had brought up for me to read to Mary Anne. Elizabeth looked at her brother and took a deep breath before confessing. "We took the trolley. We didn't have any money, but we told the station guard that we are your children, and we wanted to go see you and Mary Anne at the hospital, and he helped us get on the right trolley, and told the captain where to let us off, and that you are our papa."

I sat down stunned. My first thought was that it wasn't safe for my children to be traveling around town by themselves. They'd arrived here so maybe it was safe enough. I thought about myself traveling around the worst parts of the city when I was Jacob's age. I thought perhaps the difference was that I was the son of a laborer. My children were the children of a well-known man. I had enemies in the city. I had many friends. I didn't know if my friends would take care of my children.

While I tried to figure out whether my children could safely travel through the city, the nurse brought in a big bouquet of flowers and a bunch of balloons.

Mary Anne's face lit up. "Flowers for me?"

The nurse smiled at her. "Yes, someone sent you a big bouquet and someone else sent you these balloons."

Mary Anne's eyes grew huge. She smiled and looked a little less sick. I was thankful and found the cards for the gifts. The cards only said, "Get well soon." The flowers came from the prosecutor's office. My secretary from Rouseff Industries send the balloons. Mary Anne's eyes sparkled with delight.

The flowers and balloons reminded Jacob. "We made you cards too." He dug in his backpack for two handmade cards and gave them to Mary Anne. "Oh and we brought you this magazine too."

Mary Anne hugged her gifts from her siblings and smiled some more. I watched as the love of other people seemed to be healing my daughter. I suspected that the penicillin had a great deal to do with her improved health, but the love was an important healer too. Mary Anne sat up in bed and talked to Jacob and Elizabeth. She looked almost like her usual self.

After a half hour, I saw Mary Anne looking sleepy again. I thought she was fighting sleep. "Okay kids. Mary Anne needs to sleep some more. You need to go back to school. I'll call a taxi for you. You will need notes for your teachers explaining why you are late"

Jacob used the crank to lower Mary Anne's bed while Elizabeth tucked the blankets around her sister and made soothing noises.

I put my children into the cab and walked back upstairs. Something inside me was breaking. I was deeply thankful for the love my children displayed for each other. I was also deeply aware of the one person who had not visited. My eyes stung, but I refused to cry where someone could see me.

Twenty-four hours after I first realized that Mary Anne had a fever, she was ready to go home. She could swallow water and gelatin. I was instructed to give her fruit and foods that would slide down easily for two days. She would need lots of water and moist foods.

I called home to tell the housekeeper that we needed someone to pick us up. She said she would come as soon as possible. I finally asked the question that had been uppermost in my mind all morning. "Where is Leah?"

"Oh, Mr. Jake, she is in bed with a terrible sick headache. She vomits every time she moves and cannot tolerate light. She was vomiting terrible when she got home from taking the children to school."

I grunted. "We will be ready for you when you get here. I expect that having her daughter get home will help Leah feel much better." I walked back to Mary Anne's room while scolding myself for being mad at Leah. The poor woman had worried herself sick over Mary Anne. Another part of me knew that Leah could have handled the situation better.

When I got home I carried Mary Anne to her room and told her she could have her toys in bed with her. I helped her into pajamas and into bed. "Now honey I'm going to have to leave you alone for a few minutes while I check on your mama. She got so worried and sad about you being sick that she got sick herself. I need to check on her."

Mary Anne nodded bravely. "She can have my balloons. They will make her better."

"You keep your balloons. Just knowing you are home will make her better."

Leah was sleeping when I got to our room so I kissed her lightly on the top of her head and went to take a shower. I spent the rest of the day taking care of my family. We still wanted to wait on Mary Anne, but by the time Jacob and Elizabeth came home, Mary Anne had dressed herself in jeans with a dress on top and was running up and down the stairs.

Leah managed to get up in time for dinner. She kissed me on the cheek and thanked me for taking care of everything. "I feel so guilty for not being more help. I've been fighting this headache since yesterday. I can get up to do something like drive the children to school, but by the time I get there, I know I'm going to be sick and I can hardly get home again before I'm sick again."

"If you are not much better by tomorrow, I am calling the Chinese doctor for you."

"Why him? I don't like him because he speaks Chinese."

"I speak Chinese. I think he is the proper person for a headache that gets worse when you do something like drive a car."

I did call the Chinese doctor the next morning. He examined Leah and told me that Leah had blockage in her neck that caused the headaches. He poked at her. He stuck some needles in her. Finally, he gave me some oil to rub on her neck. Leah complained about the poking, the needles, and the smell of the oil. Within hours she felt well and confessed that I was right about whom to call.

Chapter 23 Trouble at the Paper Mill

I had been gone from work for a day and a half when I got back to Rouseff Industries. Sometimes, I thought I wasn't needed at work—that Young Rouseff could run the whole business. I came in to find a gratifying about of work had piled up in one day. I had contracts to look over for the sale of some houses in the development. Young Rouseff had identified another piece of property to buy. We still had one person refusing to sell in the right of way for the new boulevard. I had a busy morning ahead of me. My secretary came in. "Oh Detective Sorros wants you to call immediately."

I called. "What is happening?"

"Several people at the paper mill identified the same person as a possible suspect."

"Good, I think. Don't tell me he works here."

"Um…yes. He is one of the former Jouyet employees you hired."

I scratched my nose. "Um…uh…is there anything you want me to do?"

"Yes. Talk to the people we talked to, then talk to the suspect and tell us what you think."

"I'm not a psychiatrist."

"No. You are the most respected prosecutor in the country. You know people. Talk to the man and tell us if you think he is straight."

"Um…right…uh…do you have the names of the people you want me to talk to?"

"I've all ready Faxed the list to your secretary."

"Uh…thanks."

Detective Sorros laughed at my tone of voice and ended the call.

I went to find my secretary and tell her I wanted to talk to the people on the list. She had all ready set up appointments with each person. I had only to wait for them to come to me. I went back to my office and typed up the questions I wanted to ask each person. For my suspected sociopath, I typed up a list of behaviors that would lead to a promotion to management. The list was impossible. I figured a person in touch with reality would recognize the impossibility of the list and complain.

The first employee came in. He hesitated in the doorway. I invited him in and told him to sit. He turned his wedding ring around and around on his finger and adjusted his clothing as he took his seat. He didn't speak until I asked him a direct question. "I understand that Detective Sorros told you that we are looking for a specific type of person and you identified someone."

"I did sir, it was easy enough to do. Brokerhoff is a slimy bastard, excuse the language."

I waved my hand to dismiss the language.

He continued, "Anyways, Brokerhoff is always over-polite to me. He asks me about my wife and children every time he sees me. It slimes me, but otherwise I don't have anything bad I can say about him. He does his job well enough. He likes to tell me about little problems he's solved, or how he could make things better if he could talk to the engineer. The person who follows him on the next shift complains that he leaves little things undone."

I nodded. "Frankly, I know nothing about what we are working with here. You've mentioned that this man is a boot licker. There is nothing particular in that. What else caused you to name this person?"

"Things are always going wrong when he is around. People get into fights or equipment gets fouled. He is never identified as the person behind the incidents. I think I may be the only person who noticed that when he was out sick for four days we didn't have any little problems."

"When was he out sick?"

"Oh, let me think. Um…I had a cold. The whole family was sick…um… it was Jonathon's birthday…Oh yes…"

I felt a bucket of ice water dump over me when he named the date of the last murder. "Listen, if he doesn't show up for work on time, call me immediately or call Detective Sorros."

"You are watching this guy?"

I nodded. "For your safety don't say anything about this to anyone. The man may be nothing more than an innocent boot licker or he may be related to a serious criminal problem." I didn't tell my informant that I intended to send security to protect him. "I have one more question for you. I've typed up a list of goals an employee must meet to get a promotion. Tell me what you think of it." I took the list out of my printer and handed it to the employee.

The man read the whole list. He set it down on my desk. His manner became slightly cold but still polite. His eyes narrowed and his tone turned brisk. "It is impossible sir. We cannot expect an employee to do half of that to get a promotion."

I smiled happily at him. "Thank you. Thank you for your honesty and reaction. That is the response I hoped to get."

"You aren't really going to use this as a standard for getting a promotion?" He still sounded wary.

"No. No, I am not. We have a contract with the union that sets that standard. I want to see how normal people respond to unrealistic demands. Again don't mention anything we've talked about in here."

The man relaxed again. The anger dissipated. He still did not respond to my remarks dismissing him with the same level of trust as when he entered.

I ran through basically the same interview with three more people before I saw the suspect. I met him at the door, invited him in and offered him a chair. He sat before I got back to my chair. This was not serious, but it seldom happens. One of my bigger frustrations was trying to get people to sit down-- especially if I wanted to stand.

He opened the conversation. "Sir, I am honored to be asked to your office. Be assured that I am willing to help you any way I can. Others may not respect the efforts you have made to treat people fairly, but I do recognize your fairness, and I respect that sir."

I wanted to laugh.

He'd looked at a point off of my left shoulder and started talking before I gave him permission. He didn't appear to be nervous. Everyone before him had displayed differing levels of discomfort at being in my office. I recognized their respect, but they were uncomfortable. This man appeared very comfortable as he settled into his chair.

I laughed a little. "Thank you for your offer of help. I don't have anything too difficult for you to do. We are reviewing our policies for promotion. I want to talk to several employees at several levels to get their opinion." I thought about a potential danger to my other employees. "Your supervisor gave me your name as someone who is interested in making the paper mill a better place for everyone."

My interviewee puffed-up and interrupted me. "That is true. I am always seeing little ways to make things better. The machinery could be improved. It could run faster. The other employees are lazy and don't want to work faster, but they could. The machines are too slow. I could work much faster than I do."

I wrote what he said down on a note pad. "Good. Yes the machines are designed to work faster. We could consider speeding them up. Thank you for the suggestion."

He beamed upon me and took breath to tell the object over my left shoulder more.

I interrupted him. "What position in the company would you most like to have?"

His eyes darted greedily around my office. I thought I should warn my bodyguards about him. He sounded confident when he answered, "I am willing to work wherever the company needs me, but to be honest, I am wasted on the production line. I would be an asset to production planning."

"Ah then you are interested in staying in production rather than sales or research."

"I think I would excel in either sales or research, but my passion is for production."

"I see." I didn't see. This ignorant man had a high opinion of himself but did that make him a murder? "Um…do you know of other employees like yourself who want to get ahead in the company?" I was fishing and watching for his emotions.

"No. Well, maybe Sharon. She is a hard worker and tries to get along with others." I wonder if this assessment made Sharon a target. "She sees my potential and encourages me to succeed."

"Thank you. I will make an appointment to talk to Sharon. Is there anybody else you can name?"

"No. Most of the people on the production line are lazy. They don't want to work hard." He pulled at his lower lip and rolled his eyes toward the ceiling. "Jake, I'll be honest with you." He leaned confidentially forward in his chair.

I wanted to lean back away from him.

He lowered his voice. "I know you are a fair man. I know you want what is best for your employees. The others…well most of the others…they…um… well they don't like you. They call you names." He leaned back. "I try to tell them that they are lucky you are their boss and that they should respect you, but they don't listen to me. Some don't like me because I see how things could be better and others don't like me because they do not want to work harder."

I started practicing my lessons on not showing the opponent my feelings. This man was as senseless as a suckerfish. Still, I questioned whether that made him a murderer.

I decided to end the interview. I brought out my notes on getting a promotion. "Here is a proposed list of goals or steps an employee must meet in order to get a promotion. What do you think of it?"

He glanced at the list. "It is very good. You have done an excellent job. Why I have done half of this list all ready. Oh this is easy." He read. "Gets along well with peers and supports their efforts to succeed." He looked over my left shoulder. "Oh yes, I like everybody. I am always giving them little hints as to how to get along better. I like to make peace when they have little spats. Not many employees can do all this, but I can do it easy. How soon do you think you will be making promotions?"

I wondered if we could make him director of production at a plant in the middle of nowhere with no equipment, and no employees. "This list has not been approved by Mr. Rouseff. He is in the south. I will visit him in a couple months. We will be making promotions as employees come up for annual review. That is the annual review after this is approved. Believe me, I am trying to think of the best place for you." I stood to indicate an end to the interview.

He stood. "You can trust me to do a good job wherever you decide to put me. You won't be sorry sir."

The way he assured me that I wouldn't be sorry sent chills down my spine. The words sounded innocent enough. They were appropriate to the occasion. They were spoken in the right tone of voice. The inflection told me that while I might not have reason to be sorry, other people might.

I immediately called Detective Sorros. "I talked to all the people you recommended and to the suspect."

"What is your impression of the man?"

"He's as senseless as a suckerfish. I'm not certain he is a murderer. I advised security at Rouseff to keep an eye on him and his boss. His targets seem to be coworkers. I gave him an opportunity to name people who displeased him. The only name I got out of him was Sharon, but he mentioned her as a friend. He didn't tell me her last name. Rouseff staff is working on that."

"Good, Do you think he is capable of killing?"

"He is the right height for our suspect and right handed. His build and physical abilities are capable of doing the deed. Mentally...I...I...can't say for certain. He is out of touch with...well...he has no idea how the real world works. At one point, I got the impression that he thinks he can do my job without a degree in law. He thinks he can do a mechanical engineer's job without an education in engineering." I got off of the phone with the detective.

I packed my briefcase with work to do at home after I put the children to bed and headed over to the prosecutor's office.

My first project at the prosecutor's office was to set one of the new clerks to the task of tracking down every known relative of Mr. Jouyet to tell them that we had uncovered someone who possibly intended to kill Mr. Jouyet. I told the secretary to advise those people to notify their security of a problem and be careful in case the suspect decided to strike out at the rest of the family. I left her to her job with no idea how successful she would be.

Next, I processed a couple squatters and sent them to the encampment by the mall. I sighed because people who lived in the apartments above the mall were starting to complain about the squatters begging. I'd hired more security to send the beggars to the proper service centers. We'd identified more places they could do small errands for change.

We had a staff meeting to go over some cases. This was basically classroom time for the interns. We tried to get the second year interns to teach the first year interns. Antoine and Yuri kept emphasizing the need for the interns to be ready to try a big case. "Don't think you have plenty of time to learn. You may get something dropped in your lap long before you think you are ready."

I frequently added to this admonition. "I was a junior prosecutor without my certificate in criminal law when I got the Fortenac case. To make matters worse, I knew the supervisors in this office were corrupt. I was afraid to ask anybody for help for fear they would sabotage my case. You need to be prepared, now, to handle anything. Pay close attention in Professor Ingleman's class."

At the end of the day, I got a phone call. "Jaconovich?"

"Yes."

"What do you mean by terrorizing my whole family and telling them someone is out to kill them?"

"Jouyet?"

"Yes, and I'm pissed at you."

"I don't care if you are pissed. I'm damned thankful you called. Tell your family to be careful. We are close to arresting a serial killer. Our chief suspect is one of your former employees. You fired him about four years ago."

"I had no interaction with my employees."

"If it is the man I interviewed today, that may be part of his motivation. He certainly believed that he could run Rouseff Industries. He probably thought he could run Jouyet Paper."

"I know nothing of this. I don't want to talk to you. I will inform the rest of the family that you think the threat is real and not just an attempt to locate me."

"I don't care where you are. The statute of limitations has run out on the laundry arson and I didn't have evidence to prove you dumped cleaning fluid on the surrounding buildings. I am concerned about who this killer targets next."

"I had nothing to do with the laundry."

"I don't care. All I care about is this slimy little suspect named Cecile Brokerhoff."

"Wait. Wait. I do remember something about a Cecile. A bootlicker?"

"That's him."

"I think he was fired for sabotaging the machinery. Um…."

"Yeah, that's him."

"Uh…yeah…I'm trying to remember the supervisor who fired him."

"Ruben Mendoza."

"Yeah, a Mendoza fired him. The man appealed, blaming everyone around him and said he was framed. He was crazier than a blowfish."

"About two weeks after the appeal, according to my records, someone killed Mendoza."

"That was years ago. Why are you just getting around to this now."

"Oh, lets see, a corrupt police department, no money, lack of communication between the prosecutor's office, the police, and the coroner for starters."

Jouyet laughed. "Yeah, the place is a mess. I am well out of it."

His statement had touched something inside me. I thought we were talking honestly. My voice turned softer when I said, "It is a mess. I get tired. Did you get any threatening letters or phone calls? Is there something that could be related to this case that caused you to leave?"

"Not that I know of. Look Jake. Yeah, I knew about the new highway. I planned to buy land cheap and sell high. I did some stupid things to convince people to sell. I knew nothing about the purge. When the whole thing started to unravel, I started thinking. Then the whole economic thing hit. I wondered why I was living among such squalor when I could be living among equals. Yeah I noticed the murders of people who had done business with Vanderholm. After his trial, I took another long hard look at my surroundings. I tried living in the south. I nearly suffocated from a sense of gilded rot. The family sits in their fancy home with their fine possessions and dies. It didn't help that Mama died. It was her death that really caused me to move."

"Ah, thank you. I admit that Vanderholm's hit list was so extensive that I worried that I missed something about you."

"I don't think so. I started disconnecting myself from Vanderholm and Papadakos right after the purge. I have no stomach for murder."

"Neither do I. I will do my best to catch this man. I do want your family here to be safe."

Jouyet said something that I'd heard before but it surprised me coming from him. "If you are doing your best, the man will be caught and punished." We disconnected the call.

Chapter 24 Brokerhoff

M ary Anne's sore throat cleared up quickly enough. I took her into the pediatrician. He still wanted to take her tonsils out. He was concerned because they had swollen and closed off her throat so she couldn't swallow. He worried about her breathing. The tonsils must come out. We set a date for the surgery. The doctor thought she could come home shortly after the surgery and that we should be able to take care of her.

I explained my concern. "When she got sick last time, my wife got so upset she made herself sick. I want a nurse to care for Mary Anne, so I can call in Leah's doctor if necessary."

"If you are concerned, I will give you our list of home duty nurses. You should be able to reserve someone if you call now."

I called immediately and explained the circumstances. The nurse grumbled about booking for only two days, but we set a date.

I had a good routine operating at Rouseff. We were watching Brokerhoff at work, and the police department watched him after hours. He seemed to be innocently going about his business. Our security noted that he acted excessively polite to everyone he encountered. The sole exception to the polite behavior was a drunk at the trolley stop. He insisted the drunk stand on the outside of the stop because he didn't want to smell him. Our guard knew we were watching Brokerhoff, so he gently removed the drunk from the shelter by paying the man a dollar to run a short errand.

We located the woman he called Sharon, and I made an appointment for her to come to my office. When she entered, she appeared apprehensive, but very respectful. I asked her about her work. I told her the same story I told Brokerhoff. "Anyway, Mr. Brokerhoff suggested that you might be interested in a promotion. What do you think?"

"I think Brokerhoff is full of shit. Yeah I'd like a promotion. Who wouldn't? Don't listen to what he says. He talks big, but he is always making more trouble for us. He rushes about tattling to the boss and doesn't get his own work done."

"Ah, thank you for your assessment." I smiled. "Why do you think he named you out of all the other people?"

"Because I am a widow. He is always saying little suggestive things to me. He told me he recommended me for a promotion, and that you are going to give him a big promotion and put him in charge of production. He hinted that when he is in charge of production I can work directly under him." She stopped and looked out the window. "I've said too much. I don't want to get him in trouble. He got fired at Jouyet for the same behaviors we see here. He fouled the machinery there. He has tried some things here. Your machines are more suckerfish-proof."

I chuckled. "My cousin will be happy to know that. He designed them." I took a more serious stance. "Sharon, since you are aware of Brokerhoff's behavior at Jouyet, I will say more than I normally would. We don't like to fire employees. In fact our union will not let us fire an employee without just cause. Proving just cause in the case of Mr. Brokerhoff may be a problem." I looked around my office for the right words. They were not on the book-lined walls. No words appeared outside my window. I searched my brain. "When you get back to work, Brokerhoff may ask you about this interview. Lie. Lie your head off. I am afraid this man has a temper. Be nice. Thank him for referring you. Tell him we talked about how you could get a promotion. Make him believe that you are supportive of his efforts."

I swiveled in my chair and ran my hands through my hair. I wondered how to keep this woman safe. "I have half a notion to send you on a tour of our other facilities. Do you have children?"

"Yes, I have three."

"Um…what is your living situation? Do you have a close male relative to protect you?"

"My brother in-law lives close by. I lived with him and helped him and his wife pay back taxes for a year. Now I live with my grandfather. He is old and crippled."

"Oh, I think I know the rest of your family. Is your grandfather a member of the street players?"

"Yes,"

"Ah." I swiveled in my chair and thought some more. "Okay for your safety, and the safety of your children, do not repeat what we have talked about.

I frankly do not trust Brokerhoff. I think he may see you in a romantic light and have unrealistic fantasies--that you are in love with him. I also fear that he may be violent if he is forced to face reality. I will assign security to keep an eye on you. I will see that the street players perform in your neighborhood when you are off work. Do you understand?"

She nodded. "Do you think he is the M'TK Sewer Rat?" Her eyes grew wide with fear.

I pinched the bridge of my nose. "No. He is not the M'TK Sewer Rat." I wanted to elaborate about the sewer rat being a child, but I left my answer where it was.

After she left my office, I called Detective Sorros and told him Sharon's address. I told him that Brokerhoff had taken particular interest in her. "I think that if he realizes that she describes him as a suckerfish, he will turn on her."

"You are becoming more certain that Brokerhoff is our sociopath, aren't you?"

"Yeah…well…not in my head, but something in my gut seems to know he is our man." I got off the phone and returned to reviewing purchase agreements for Rouseff.

Several days, then a week went by, without any trouble from our sociopath. The day for Mary Anne to have her tonsils out grew closer. I constantly congratulated myself for hiring the nurse. I might end up being very busy at work just when she needed extra care. I joked at work that the killer would strike either just before, or after, Mary Anne had her surgery.

He struck the night before her surgery. I was reading a story to the children when Detective Sorros called and said, "This is it."

"How do you know?"

"Your men have been watching Brokerhoff and reporting his movements to us. He went into a clothing store and bought a pair of cheap gloves. Another one of your men followed him from the clothing store to a dry goods store. That man observed the clerk wrapping a long knife in paper for him. Brokerhoff was wearing the gloves when he made the purchase."

"Shit."

"Yeah, my men are following him now. Your men are in touch with the trolley guards to track which trolley he takes and where he gets off."

"I hope we don't lose him."

"I'll keep you posted. What charges are you going to write up for him?"

"The papers are drawn up on my desk at the prosecutor's office. Tonight we will charge him with attempted murder, harassment, carrying a weapon with intent to kill. I have a long list of charges that will hold us long enough to get the rest of the case together."

"I am working on the rest of the case. We have knives from the other scenes. Do you think you can get him for the other murders?"

"I intend to. Give me every bit of evidence you can. I will want a complete history on this man back to when he started school or earlier." I hung up the phone. Privately, I worried that Brokerhoff might not be in touch enough with reality to make a plea. We would see in the morning. I went back to reading the story.

I waited almost thirty minutes before the phone rang again. "Jaconovich here."

"This is Sorros. We got him. His supervisor escaped with a slashed jacket. Our men wanted to let Brokerhoff get close enough to speak to his victim. He walked right up to his supervisor. We weren't sure he intended to act. He said something about it being a nice evening then he lunged. Fortunately, the supervisor was wary of him and jumped clear without anything more serious happening than getting his suit jacket slashed."

"Where is the supervisor?"

"He is coming in here to make a statement."

"I'll be there in..." I looked at the big clock in the hall. "I'll be there in twenty minutes." I got off of the phone and ran my fingers through my hair.

I picked up Mary Anne and kissed her then I kissed Elizabeth and Jacob. "I have to go out again."

I stepped over to where Leah sat in her favorite chair reading a magazine. "Sweetheart, I'm sorry about leaving you to get the kids into bed. Believe me I would rather put my babies to bed than chase after crooks." I tipped Leah's face up to mine and kissed her soundly. I thought she must be angry at me for going out. She didn't respond to the kiss.

Leah sighed, "I am perfectly capable of putting the children to bed. You can go chase your crooks and stop hanging on my hem."

I pouted. "I like hanging on your hem. I married you so I could hang on your hem. That is my right."

I'd made Leah laugh. The children laughed at my silliness with their mama.

Leah swatted my hand. "Jake get out of here and take care of business."

"Papa, is this a very bad crook." Jacob sounded very grown up when he asked this question.

"Yes. Yes Jacob, he is one of the worst crooks I've ever encountered. I want to be certain he never hurts anyone again. That is why I have to go out tonight, to talk to a witness."

Elizabeth and Mary Anne gave me hugs. Jacob tried to look manly. He clearly looked proud of his papa.

I arrived at the police station while Brokerhoff was being processed. I found the supervisor waiting to make his statement. I surprised him when I put my hand on his shoulder. He had good reason to be jumpy.

He acted surprised to see me. "Mr. Jaconovich what are you doing here?"

"Well several things. The first thing I want to do is make certain you are okay."

"Other than a hole in my good jacket I'm okay."

"I think Rouseff Paper can replace your jacket. I didn't really believe he would go after you."

"Yeah, well…"

Detective Sorros interrupted. "Don't say anything until we are set up to take the formal statement." He fussed over getting paper into the court recorder's machine properly.

I thought I'd clarify my position. "The second reason I'm here is that I want to prosecute this case, if the judge doesn't think I am too close to the case as a Rouseff employee. I've been trying to find this guy since before we charged Vanderholm.

"It's that serious then?"

Sorros admonished, "Gentlemen! We're almost ready, wait please."

I sat down, leaned back in my chair and tried to smile reassuringly at our witness.

Finally, the recorder was ready. The detective started with simple questions like name and address. In a few minutes he got to the part about, "tell us what happened."

Our witness was on the way home from his weekly men's Bible meeting. "I'm a Methodist you know."

This surprised me. I knew he was talking about a church, but I didn't know we had Methodists in the country.

The detective continued his questions. "Do you attend this meeting every week at this time?"

"Yes."

I wondered if we would charge the perpetrator with stalking, too.

"Have you ever seen Mr. Brokerhoff when you were coming home from your meeting before?"

"Yes. Last week he approached me and spoke to me the same as he did tonight. The week before…uh…I'm…I'm not one hundred percent certain, but I thought I saw Mr. Brokerhoff at the corner near the trolley stop."

"Was he waiting for the trolley?"

"No. He was standing in the shadows under the awning at the grocer's. I got the impression he might be watching the street."

"What in his behavior made you think he was watching the street?"

The detective questioned the witness for a half hour then turned him over to me. "Thank you for helping us. I will try to make this as easy as possible. So far, you have told the detective that Brokerhoff had the opportunity—made the opportunity to strike at you. Next we need to determine why he chose you."

"I don't know why he chose me."

"Did you criticize him at work? Or ignore one of his plans for improvement."

The witness snorted. "Oh you know about his grand plans for improvement."

I smiled.

"No. I've tolerated him pretty well. He's a boot licker, but I put up with him."

I wasn't getting anywhere. "It could be something small."

"Well how long ago would it have to be?"

"I don't know. Have you thought of something?"

"The only thing I can think of occurred just before you called me into your office. He'd been hanging around Sharon, pestering her. She complained about it to me, so I promised I'd do something. I had no idea how to handle the situation. One day he made a move to pat her rear end. I called him on it and told him to keep his hands to himself at work. I saw that I made him angry, but that was weeks ago."

I still wasn't certain where this was going. "Has he treated you differently since then?"

The witness thought for several minutes. He finally shifted in his chair and answered the question. "Yeah. Yes he has. Usually he would come to me at least once a day with gossip and tattling. He almost stopped doing that. Then, he went in and talked to you. He started telling everyone how you were going to give him my job. He said you gave him a list of things he would have to do then you would give him the promotion. He bragged that he had done almost everything on the list. I saw that list you made, so I just shook my head and walked away. He called after me that he was telling the truth. He was getting a promotion. After that, he hasn't said anything to me except the other night when he greeted me on the street just like he did tonight."

I leaned back in my chair. "I think we have enough to get a warrant to search Brokerhoff's apartment. Let's do it now or about six in the morning."

Detective Sorros looked at me.

I explained, "I want to be in on the search. My schedule is so full I have to do it at odd times."

We searched the apartment at six in the morning. Most of the place looked ordinary—perhaps a little formal for a laborer. A picture sat on the dresser in his bedroom. It looked like a bad composite of Brokerhoff and Sharon. Her head appeared pasted onto the body of a woman in a wedding dress. In a drawer beside his bed we found more pictures of her. One picture appeared to be taken on the street with her grandfather. The old man's eyes had been punched out of the picture leaving two holes.

We found pictures of other people, some I assumed to be victims. I found a picture of a children's school class. Brokerhoff had circled one head and labeled it, "me." The teacher's eyes had been punched out. As we lifted the pictures out to put in the evidence bag, they began to make me ill. Many of the pictures were torn with the head of a person missing or an arm or leg. We found more pictures of people with their eyes punched out. I wondered what a psychologist or psychiatrist would think of the pictures. I planned to ask someone at the university to take a look them.

I studied the pictures on the wall. At first, they just looked like prints of famous tourist places. I recognized Paris. I thought one might be of New York. I would have left them in the apartment, but I noticed he'd pasted pictures of himself into the prints. I thought the psychologist should look at those pictures, too. When I left to pick up Mary Anne for her tonsillectomy, the evidence team was still searching the place.

The surgery went well. She was done in just a few minutes. Leah and I waited another two and a half hours before Mary Anne was well enough to go home. While we waited, Leah told me about her charity projects. She talked about taking more of her mama's recipes to the outdoor kitchens. She told me how the school lunch program was having trouble feeding all the children whose parents were homeless and living behind the mall. She told me that she had ideas to help. She wanted to help the poor.

I realized that I still felt super-alert from the arrest of Brokerhoff. I got the feeling that Leah was starting to sound like Brokerhoff. I scolded myself, then stood up and bent down to kiss Leah on the forehead. "Honey, anything you want to do to help feed those people, I am behind you. I need a cup of coffee. I got up too early. Would you like one too?"

I went down to the cafeteria and got two cups of coffee. I decided the difference between Brokerhoff and Leah was that Leah's ideas were realistic, and she was following through. There was nothing grandiose about writing out recipes made by one poor woman and giving them to other poor women. I sighed and decided I was tired and worried.

After Mary Anne came home, Leah showed no signs of developing a headache. I decided having the nurse present helped her. I kissed Leah and thanked the nurse for staying and assured the nurse that just having her present kept Leah from worrying herself sick. I went to the prosecutor's office and called Detective Sorros for an update.

When Mr. Farley called a staff meeting, we crowded into our conference room. Someone grumbled about being too crowded. Jeffrey took command of the meeting. "Jake, tell us what you have turned up so far."

I outlined the history that led to Brokerhoff's arrest last night.

A student interrupted me. "Wow! From the little bit of information you had, you knew who to follow, and you caught him in the act? I'd never be able to do that."

I chuckled. "Remember I became aware of such a person years ago. It wasn't until the police started communicating with the coroner's office and us that we could get enough information to know that one person was killing Jouyet employees. It wasn't until Detective Sorros had some more training that he could begin to figure out how to investigate the case. In this case, he needed the cooperation of Rouseff Paper. Everybody there was willing to cooperate."

Another student snorted. "Yeah, well the boss was on the case."

I chuckled and explained. "No. Security went farther in carrying this through than I expected."

I got back on track. "I'm not sure what the final charges for this man will include. We have one good charge of premeditated, assault with the attempt to kill. His weapon matches that of two others found in other murdered Jouyet employees. I think we can convict on two counts of murder. There are other murders that we may not find solid evidence to link to him. Last night I wrote up the assault with intent to kill charges. I added stalking." I added my information from searching the apartment

Mr. Farley took over. "Do any of you have questions for Jake?"

"Can you tell us more about these pictures you mentioned?"

I described the pictures of Sharon and those with the eyes punched out. "They may be of no more significance than that he had a crush on the woman."

Margaret asked, "Was she young?"

"No. She has three children. She's close enough to his age to make a relationship unremarkable."

Sophia sounded shocked. "She's married?"

I replied, "No. She's…um…uh…I think the next thing we will need to do is find out how her husband died."

Mr. Farley divided up chores, outlining what needed to be done. He sent three interns and a junior prosecutor off to the police department and the coroner's office to see what they could learn. "See if the police will let you into his apartment. I want pictures. Leave the place untouched otherwise."

My secretary from Rouseff called to say, "The union is calling a meeting with the day shift at seven o'clock tonight to go over what happened."

"I wonder if they cleared that with Detective Sorros. Okay, I will check with the union and the detective. I may decide to be there too."

As soon as I got off the phone with my secretary, I called the union leaders and asked them what they were planning for tonight's meeting.

"Well, people want to know the truth. They want to know why a dangerous man was working for Rouseff."

"Ugh. I've answered that question a dozen times or so all ready. Will you go over the union policy of not firing someone without just cause? As for the rest of the questions, let me clear things with Detective Sorros. The last thing we want in a case like this is for something to get out that will compromise getting a conviction. If Detective Sorros agrees, I might come to the meeting and be prepared to answer questions."

"Thank you Mr. Jaconovich. That's real helpful. I can talk to the employees about not firing someone without just cause. As far as any of us knew, the man was a boot licker. We don't fire people for being boot lickers."

"I'll talk to Detective Sorros, and to my supervisor to discuss how much information we can give out."

When I called Detective Sorros, he answered, "Oh Jaconovich. I have an office full of your people."

"Good. After the problem with the Vanderholm trial, every prosecutor in the office will know enough about the case to take it to court." I got back to business. "I have a couple issues." I told him about the union meeting.

"What time?"

I gave him the time and place.

Detective Sorros grunted, "I'll be there."

I added, "Now, can you put Miss. Uzara on the phone? I want to send the women over to talk to Sharon. Do you know how Sharon's husband died?"

"Shit and damn!" Detective Sorros was learning to communicate effectively.

"Yeah."

"I better go with them."

I cautioned, "I thought I'd let the women do girl talk. Believe me, those two can worm any information out of anybody."

"Okay, we'll do girl talk first, but I want a full report." He let me talk to Sofia.

I left my office to report back to Mr. Farley about sending the women over to talk to Sharon. I found him standing outside his office scowling at the office wall across from his door. I updated him about the meeting at seven in the evening. "I'll go with you and assign some interns to come along." He still seemed distracted--apparently by the wall in front of him. He walked a slow circuit of the office while I told him about sending the women to talk to Sharon. "Jake we have to have a conference room big enough for us to work in. We need more space."

"Do you want to move to another building or remodel here?"

"We'll remodel here. We'll take out this mid-section of offices, assign attorneys to the paralegals' offices along that wall and give the paralegals new offices in the holding room."

"Where will you put offenders waiting to be processed? Do you want me to call Leah to come over and do some drawings?"

"If she doesn't mind."

I decided to call home. I got Leah on the phone. "Hi Sweetheart, how are you coping?"

"I'm just fine. I really could have managed by myself."

"Ah, but, you are forgetting that all hell breaks loose at the office if we have a problem at home. Are you planning on picking Elizabeth up from school?"

"Yes. She has dance today, so I planned to pick her up, take her to dance, go to the market and then pick up both kids and bring them home."

"Good. Send the cook to the market. Leave Mary Anne with the nurse I so fortuitously hired and come to the prosecutor's office as soon as you drop Elizabeth at dance. We have a design problem for you."

She giggled. "Jake, I don't know how I am to get all my work done and do your design work too."

I knew she would be here promptly. She was always excited to use her education.

Leah arrived as expected while I was on the phone with Detective Sorros again. Mr. Farley walked her around the office. When I got off the phone, they were measuring the hallway.

"Sweetheart do you want me to pick up Elizabeth so you can finish up here and bring Jacob home?"

She nodded and wrote numbers on her note pad.

Elizabeth and I got home earlier than I usually do. Mary Anne had just gotten up from her nap. She was fussy. I held her and read her a story. Elizabeth went to the kitchen and found some gelatin for her to eat.

When Leah arrived home with Jacob, she was excited about the remodel of our office. "We decided that you could use the hall, and the janitor closet, and bathroom across the hall, to give you more space, and another bathroom."

I went back to work shortly before seven. The meeting was to be held in the union hall--a warehouse near the industrial district that the union had bought. When I arrived at the meeting, I found most of our office staff there. Detective Sorros greeted me. I introduced him to the union bosses.

The union leader brought the meeting to order. He introduced Detective Sorros who said that yes, his men had arrested Brokerhoff for assault.

Someone in the crowd called out. "What does this mean for Rouseff?"

I took the podium. "This really doesn't mean much for Rouseff. I expect we will hire someone to replace him. That is, I am assuming the union leaders agree that assaulting your supervisor is grounds for dismissal." I turned to the union boss, Mr. T'KA.

Mr. T'KA came to the microphone. "We have looked over the information from the police department and agree that this assault is grounds for dismissal. The man is effectively fired. We will follow procedures outlined in your contract for replacing him."

Another person asked a question about Rouseff procedures. I responded somewhat confused. "We will treat this the same as any other case where an employee leaves. We will hire someone to replace him, and we will try to promote someone who works for us. This may mean some extra work for a few people while the new person is trained. Anybody who works extra hours will be paid for their time."

I stopped and scratched my nose. I wondered why they seemed so concerned about procedures at Rouseff. I continued. "I can see one other impact on the routine at Rouseff. I am also a prosecutor. I am the only senior staff prosecutor for the city. Our supervisor has his certificate in criminal law, but he spends much of his time supervising so I may need to spend more time in the prosecutors office."

The collective sigh from the crowd confused me. I couldn't believe they would be relieved that I would not be in my office.

A man called out. "You will be the one prosecuting this case then?"

"I will help prepare the case. It is really up to Mr. Farley how much time I spend on the case."

Mr. Farley stepped up beside me and whispered that he would take over this question. I introduced him. He smiled and asked the crowd, "What do you think? Mr. Jaconovich has responsibilities to Rouseff that take up his time, but his schedule is somewhat flexible. Um…uh…as people who worked alongside the accused do you want Mr. Jaconovich to take the lead in prosecuting this case?"

Great cheers and applause broke out. I was astonished. One of the workers jumped up on the speaker's platform and took the microphone from Jeffrey. "Folks, the way I see it, that slimy bastard made trouble for all of us. I want to be certain that he gets punished as he deserves. I trust Mr. Jaconivich to do the job right. What do you all think?"

The crowd applauded again and shouted yes.

Mr. Farley took back the microphone. "It is perfectly acceptable for concerned bystanders to choose the prosecutor they want to represent their interests. If you want Mr. Jaconovich, I am happy to name him as the Chief Prosecutor. I agree he will present a flawless case."

People started shuffling, and collecting their friends and family, and heading for the door. The meeting was over. The questions were over. I stood on the platform bewildered. "Is that all they wanted; to be certain I would be working on the case?"

Mr. T'KA laughed and slapped me on the shoulder. "Apparently, that was their big concern. I didn't know why they wanted this meeting, but putting you in charge of the trial was what they wanted."

I shook my head and went home to my family.

Chapter 25 Prosecutors Uzara and M'TG

I spent my next morning at Rouseff being amazed that the production workers wanted me to prosecute the case. I went over more contracts and did a lesson for the interns on why we include a title search with land purchases. Before lunch, I took the Miki out to inspect the interchanges and the construction on the new boulevard. I checked to see how the toll collections were coming. They were not as good as I hoped but they were acceptable.

Apparently, Jeffery complained to the union leader that we needed to hire someone to remodel the prosecutor's office to give us more room. The union leader was getting into the idea of organizing. He went looking for construction workers for us.

It pleased me that he looked in the camp behind the mall. Before noon the day after the meeting, he brought a construction team to our office. He negotiated their salary and how much work they would do.

After listening to the story of the success in hiring workers for the remodel, I called Detective Sorros. "Do you have any more information on the accused? Has he always lived here?"

"Oh, he gave me names and addresses for where he lived before. He's moved around a bit. He is encouraging us to talk to people who know him. He's given us names and addresses of contacts."

"That is helpful. I will need to get a statement of how he pleads."

"Oh Miss Uzara from your office has done that. Mrs. M'TG is bringing you everything she has."

"Ah, those two will have this whole case wrapped up by the time I get organized to start."

Sorros snorted, "I thought they were having fun. Brokerhoff talked to them quite eagerly. I think he liked having two pretty women writing down everything he said. That is how we got so much, I should say, they got so much. He wouldn't say anything to me other than that we got the wrong man. He told me he was just offering to shake hands with his supervisor.

"Yeah with a ten-inch filleting knife."

"He says the knife was in his left hand, and he just fumbled and dropped it. His story is that the clerk in the store didn't wrap the knife properly. It is all the clerk's fault."

"I listened to his talk in my office. I think I am glad that I didn't have to listen to it today."

I hung up the phone when the women returned to the office. They were quite excited. "Jake you are going to love everything we have."

I wasn't so sure about that, but they seemed happy. Mr. Farley called a staff meeting in our cramped little conference room. "Before we start hearing reports, I want to let everybody know that we will have construction workers in here at night. We are going to get a decent conference room. Jake, be sure to tell Leah how much I appreciate her suggestions."

I smiled and nodded.

"The important part of having workers in here is keeping our work confidential. The workers don't need to know the names of the people we process. I don't want anybody having access to the information we have on the Brokerhoff case. Jake, can you keep our documentation off site during renovations?"

I nodded.

"Now, most of you have been out and about on this case. What have you learned?"

Alexander nodded at an intern to make his report. The intern hesitated, shifted in his seat, looked at his notes and looked at Alexander before beginning his report. "The clerk at the dry goods store has sold Brokerhoff the same knife on two other occasions. He told us he asked Brokerhoff why needed so many filleting knives. He states that Brokerhoff said he gives them as gifts."

Mr. Farley included generous praise while he conducted the meeting. "Excellent gentlemen. Have the clerk come in for a deposition. Ask him if he has sales records for the other knives he sold Brokerhoff. We will want copies of those. Who is next?"

Sofia and Margaret raised their hands. Jeffrey waved at them to speak. Margaret started. "We got something we didn't get a chance to tell anybody last night. We went over to Sharon's house on a sympathy call. We assured her that everybody on her shift was upset by Brokerhoff's betrayal of the work bonds. She said then that she hated Brokerhoff and hoped he faced a firing squad. We made soothing inquisitive noises. She wanted to talk. She said she hadn't noticed him before her husband died. After he died, Brokerhoff came to her house with a huge bouquet of flowers and said he bought them for her. She said that as soon as she returned to work, she learned that everybody in the office had chipped in to buy the flowers, and the supervisor placed the order. Brokerhoff volunteered to deliver them personally."

Sofia took over the story. "I agreed with her that it was wrong for him to pretend the flowers were from him at a time when she needed assurance that all her friends thought of her, and that it must have been difficult for them to spare the money for flowers. She nodded and looked as if she might cry. I decided to steer the conversation in a slightly different direction. I asked her if her husband had been ill for a long time. She shook her head again and whispered that it was sudden."

I smiled at the seamless cooperation between Sophia and Margaret as Margaret picked up the story. "I commented on how difficult it must have been to lose her husband with three children. She told me she was pregnant with the third when he died. We had some good girl talk for a few minutes before Sofia tried for more information."

Sofia nodded, "I could see that she was still very upset about her husband's death. She seemed to be beginning to trust us. I asked if her husband had an accident at work. She shook her head. She could barely speak above a whisper when she said he was murdered. I asked if the police found the man. She nodded and told us that yes it was just a drunk. He was executed."

I think I startled Sofia, "Have the police pull their records on that case. Somebody look through our records on the case."

Mr. Farley sat back in his chair and rubbed his head. "I think I remember something about the case. The drunk plead not-guilty. He said he came upon the man…and…there was something else. One of the supervisors at the time tried the case. Yeah…I think…yeah…I think the accused said he was a medic in the army…yeah…that was it…he had been a medic, and saw an injured man, and tried to help. He was convicted."

Sofia resumed her report. "We didn't push Sharon about her husband, but we did do some calculating based on her boys' ages. The birth of her youngest fits in the time frame for this series of murders."

Mr. Farley summed up. "And our suspected sociopath knew her then. We need to go over the pictures to see when Brokerhoff became obsessed with

Sharon." I noticed our office manager writing notes. It felt good to have a team to work on a case.

Margaret picked up the report. "We spent this morning talking to the suspect. He was quite willing to talk about everything. He's outraged that he was suspected of assault. He is certain this little misunderstanding must be cleared up soon. Let's see. He told us his parents' names and that his father is dead and his mother lives with his brother. He gave us their names and last known addresses. He hasn't heard from them for several years because his brother is in the army and moves around. He told us where he went to school and who his teachers were. He has lived in five different towns, and he gave us his address for each town. He kept insisting we talk to this person or that, they would vouch for his character." Margaret paused. "I could almost believe him because he spoke with no sense of guilt. He was confident and upbeat."

The junior attorney snorted. "That is not how innocent people talk. They are usually self-conscious and terrified, and they don't want anybody to know they were accused. The guilty usually whine and have excuses or blame everybody else for their behavior."

I was anxious that Margaret's feelings might be hurt by this public correction and prepared to intervene. Margaret is a D'NO woman. I sat back in my chair again to watch. "You're right. I'm a mother. I know when a child is guilty and trying to get out of it or even confessing. I know when they are innocent. I think one danger in talking to Brokerhoff is in forgetting that this is not how a normal person talks. He can be very persuasive and innocent sounding. This may be a problem when we go to trial. I don't doubt he has a long string of acquaintances and relatives who would be convinced he is innocent if we caught him with his knife in his victim and drinking their blood."

I decided to add my observations. "I talked to him in my office. I agree that his talk might seem very ordinary in the right setting. I might not have picked up on how far off his talk was if I had not just been talking to his supervisor and some coworkers who had specific complaints about him. Then, it was easy for me to see how different he really was. I agree for a judge who sees the accused for the first time in the courtroom and who has fifteen witnesses giving him a perfect character, it might be a problem."

The other interns had talked to Brokerhoff's neighbors. The interns proved Margaret's point. The neighbors all described Brokerhoff as a nice man. They related incidences when Brokerhoff had helped his neighbors with packages, or a lost cat, or some little errand that needed to be done. He'd told them that he had a girlfriend. The neighbors hoped he hadn't had any trouble. He was such a nice man.

There was one exception to the nice man opinion. Yuri mentioned it. "I talked to a couple. They had a son about eight. He said he didn't like Mr. Brokerhoff because he's mean. The parents tried to shush the boy, but I explained that sometimes children see things adults don't. I assured them, and the son, that I was interested in his opinion. I asked why he thought Brokerhoff was mean. He explained that the girl next door couldn't talk. She was allowed to play on the stoop outside. He had been playing in the yard when Brokerhoff came in. He saw Brokerhoff take the girl's doll and put it in the incinerator. The girl couldn't tell anybody. He said he didn't tell anybody because he didn't want to make Mr. Brokerhoff mad. He also told me that he though that Mr. Brokerhoff had shut a cat in his apartment for several days before he returned it to the owners. The boy said he could hear the cat crying during the day when it was in the apartment alone."

I didn't hesitate. "Depose the child. Check his story with the little girl's parents."

One of the interns asked, "Why depose a child? We can't use his testimony in court."

Margaret raised her hand. "Can I answer this one?"

I nodded.

Margaret used an excellent teaching voice. "First, you can use the testimony of a child if it is a first person account and there is supporting evidence. In this case we have a report of a missing cat. We need to ask the girl's parents if her doll came up missing."

Another intern interrupted. "I have the answer to that one. The girl in apartment 2E had lost her doll. Mr. Brokerhoff replaced it with a much nicer one."

We all groaned at the thought of this man tormenting a child with a disability, and then, making himself look good to her parents by replacing the doll.

Margaret continued. "Okay so we have supporting testimony that the boy's story is true. There is another reason this office will depose any children who have anything significant to say. It was the testimony of the children in the Fortenac case that led Jake to find Mrs. D'SnG and learn that she was, in fact, a Uzara."

Sofia added. "Which is the reason I decided to study law."

Mr. Farley prepared to end the meeting. "Right, you all now know that the observations of everybody are to be treated with respect, and you will follow through. This man is too dangerous to be turned loose in society. It is up to us to build the case that will see he is convicted without question."

My stomach knotted. The use of the term "convicted without question" meant that the guilty would be executed.

I sighed and went to look over the details of the two cases that started this process and to see if I could find the casework for the murder of Sharon's husband. Most of us spent the afternoon going over paperwork. Margaret and Sofia had huge reports to type up.

Antoine and Yuri took some interns out to pick up the people we wanted to depose. I sat in on the depositions of the storeowner and the little boy.

By the time I was ready to go home, we had tomorrow's work outlined. Our team would talk to every child in the apartment building. I would talk to other people who had worked with him at Jouyet.

We followed the same schedule for two weeks. I finally decided to start questioning his contacts before he moved to the city. Detective Sorros wanted to take a couple investigators and an intern with him and talk to local police departments. I needed to take about a dozen people from our office. I decided to take a court recorder with us for depositions. I took a paralegal to help with the paperwork.

One of the advantages of my Rouseff connection was that I could charter a train car just for our party. The eastbound train hooked us on at M'TK, and we traveled with ease while talked about the case. Some of the interns from the police academy and the law interns started a noisy card game. When we needed to go farther from home, we left in the evening, slept on the train, worked all day, and came home the next evening.

Chapter 26 Brokerhoff's Mama

As we got closer to Brokerhoff's trial, the newspapers condemned me for taking so long to come to trial. They condemned me for looking into his past, and they condemned me for not treating him the same as anybody else charged with assault while a large vocal group of individuals declared him to be innocent.

We found a trail of people through his past who were willing to stand up and say he was a good man, a good youth, a good boy. We also found a trail of unsolved murders. They were all the same. We traced his connection to each person. We were successful in identifying a photo from his collection of pictures of each of the murdered people.

The number of people willing to say he was innocent and would never hurt a fly, continued to distress us. People came forward to list his numerous acts of kindness or piety. Still, in every village where he lived, we found someone he knew who had been killed with a filleting knife.

When we questioned his former coworkers, we found a group of people who hated Brokerhoff and told us tales of how he lied about them to supervisors and how he blamed them when he didn't get his work done. People who worked with him complained that he made them look bad to their employers, because he didn't give them the information they needed. He also took credit for successes when he played no role in making the success happen.

We traced his past all the way back to his mother and brother living in the eastern province. I took a staff of twenty people including Detective Sorros and called on the Brokerhoff family. Brokerhoff's brother was a career army sergeant. He lived on the base with his wife, his mother and three children. They looked like a prosperous family. His wife worked in the local hospital as a nurse. His mother took care of the children after school hours.

We talked to Brokerhoff's mother first. "Mrs. Brokerhoff, I hope you won't…

"It's D'YG. I remarried."

I thought I should perhaps turn the interview over to Sofia and Margaret. I decided I would later. "Thank you Mrs. D'YG for seeing us. I know it might be hard for you to talk about your son."

She sighed and shook her head. "I've come to accept that he is not right. I don't know what went wrong with him." I took a chair, and I sat back to listen. I made quick eye contact with Sofia to indicate that I wanted her to keep this woman talking. Sofia took a chair next to Mrs. D'YG.

I don't think we could have shut Mrs. D'YG up once she started talking. She started her tale. "I've thought and thought about Cecil's problems. The only thing I can think of is that he was four when his papa died. He took it hard. I tried to give him extra attention. I moved into a house next door to my brother so he would have a man around. My older son was seven. He was obviously sad about losing his father, but he was different about it somehow. Anyway, I don't know when I first began to think there was something wrong with my darling. I loved that boy. Really, I did. I just don't know."

She sighed and took up her story. "I got him a puppy. I think that is when I first suspected something wrong. He stayed with my sister in-law while I was at work. He could run home to our house if he wanted something. He told my sister in-law that he was running home to let the puppy out." Mrs. D'YG shook her head. "My sister in-law said she was impressed with his responsibility in caring for the puppy. She said he loved that puppy. He went back to her house after walking the puppy and went back to playing. When I got home, I found the puppy dead on the kitchen floor."

She reached for her handkerchief. "Anyway...where was I? Oh yes, the house was locked but the puppy was dead on the floor. Cecil acted upset at the death of his puppy. Everybody was very nice and gave him hugs and candy. I was his mother. I thought he was not as upset as he pretended. I thought I saw something excited under his act. I found a man, a child psychologist who worked at the army base to talk to my son."

She looked at her lap and smoothed the wrinkles out in her skirt. "I sent him to the psychologist for over a year. The psychologist told me he worked exclusively with children whose fathers are away or injured or dead. He told me that my son was not processing his grief properly and that he was so disconnected the doctor couldn't reach his emotions. The doctor continued to see him for another six months then he got relocated to the capital."

Anyway, things went along fine for years. I thought maybe the doctor had helped Cecil. He did well in school. His grades were excellent. He was often the teacher's pet. The only thing I worried about was his inability to make friends. I enrolled him into sports at school. He didn't make friends there. He didn't make friends at boys club."

She gulped and looked at a painting of Jesus on the wall. "He had another tragedy at Boys Club Camp his second year. One of the smaller boys decided to go skinny-dipping in the middle of the night. He drowned. I was called to come get Cecil immediately. The other parents were picking up their children. Cecil told me that several of the boys dared the little boy to swim out to the dock. The camp director told me that Cecil had given him their names. I asked the director point blank if he thought Cecil was involved in the bullying. He assured me that no, Cecil was a good kid, and I could be proud of him. I wanted to believe that so I did."

She turned the rings around on her finger. "I had another reason for not wanting to believe that my son had a serious problem. I'd met Mr. D'YG. He came to town to help harvest wheat. He harvested the wheat then stayed in town to start a mechanic's shop. His business was becoming successful, so we were talking about getting married. I tried to tell myself that the boys needed a father. The truth was that I was crazy wild to marry Mr. D'YG."

She took another deep breath and ran her hands through her hair. "Both boys treated their new step-father with respect. I was pleased when my oldest started finding common interests with his new father. Cecil was always polite and even affectionate. He told me he was happy to have a father because the other boys at school said his mother was a whore because I wasn't married."

She cleared her throat. "Well as you can imagine I had something to say about that! I didn't say much to Cecil, but I had a great deal to say to his teacher and the director of the school. They both acted horrified. They knew I had a respectable job as a clerk in the mayor's office. I didn't stop there. I called the parents of half the kids in the school. They knew me. We all knew each other. They were contrite and assured me their children would soon learn how wrong their behavior was. In the middle of my anger, I became aware of a hint of triumph from Cecil. You better believe that he heard better from me for gloating over his friends' punishment."

She paused for half a minute, looking inward. Sofia appeared prepared to prompt Mrs. D'YG. No prompts were needed. "When Cecil was fourteen, my husband wanted to take me for a honeymoon to the capital. The boys were old enough to stay alone, but I decided to send them to my brother's house. I told my brother that I worried about leaving Cecil home alone for a long time. He told me to stop fussing over the boy. Cecil was fine. I went off with my husband feeling reassured that all was well."

She choked and twisted her handkerchief. "When we got back home, the whole town was abuzz. A girl, who lived about a kilometer from us, had been murdered. I was concerned that my boys would be upset. The oldest was. Cecil said all the same things his brother said. I may sound like a very bad mother for saying this. Maybe Cecil's only problem was that his mother thought there was something wrong with him."

Margaret moved to sit at the woman's feet, and Sofia moved her chair closer.

"Anyway…I thought that Cecil seemed excited more than upset by the death of someone he knew. I asked him about her. He said he didn't know her well. He told me she and her friends picked on smaller children, so he was not friends with them."

Mrs. D'YG's tone of voice turned vague. She stared at her fingers in her lap. "That was the year Cecil got a crush on his teacher. She was an acceptable young woman. I liked her. I thought that at least Cecil showed good taste in women. My husband assured me that it was normal for boys his age to get a crush on their teacher. I was thankful that my son was acting so normal."

Margaret had placed her hand on top of Mrs. D'YG's. I was thankful to have the women with me for this interview.

"Cecil got interested in sports then. He played football. He played well enough that others praised him for his game. Sometimes he complained to us how his team would have won the game if it were not for some stupid mistake made by the coach or the captain. He told us repeatedly that they would win more often if he were the captain. My husband tried to tell him about sportsmanship. He told him that the strongest players are the ones who make others look good. I thought the lecture helped. I decided that Cecil's traumas had healed, and he would be okay. Shortly after he finished the fourteenth form, the teacher he had a crush on years earlier got engaged. He was upset by the news. Again my husband lectured him about wanting our friends to be happy and to be happy ourselves because they are happy. He thanked his father. He came to me and gave me a hug for finding him such a wise man to guide him. I was pleased, but I though it was odd behavior.

She paused and stared at the wall for a full minute. Sophia leaned forward.

Mrs. D'YG gulped and resumed speaking in a whisper. "By this time, my oldest had entered the army. We talked to Cecil about what he wanted to do. One night, he came in with a catalog from a business school. He asked if he could go to business school. We told him we had enough money to send him. He smiled and said he was going to his room to work on the papers. He came out several times and asked us questions. Finally, he declared that he had a headache and was going to take a pill and go to sleep."

Mrs. D'YG looked ten years older than she had when we'd entered her home. I ventured to say something reassuring. "I know this is difficult for you."

She shook her head. "I need to tell it. I need to tell it all to someone who might see what I saw." A tear rolled down her face. "The next morning Cecil got up when my husband was getting ready to leave. I got up as he was asking more questions about his application to business school. He asked me to look it over. He told me he planned to put it in the mail. He seemed a little excited, but I thought that it was only because he was starting school."

She shook her head. I could tell her eyes were looking into the tragic past. She recovered and continued her story. "I went to work as usual. About ten in the morning, the mayor's secretary came into our office and announced that the schoolteacher had died, and the police were looking for her fiancé. When I got home I asked Cecil if he had heard the news about his teacher. He said he had been busy all day cleaning his room and thinking about what to take to school. I told him about his teacher. He sat down on the edge of the chair and looked like he might cry. He said that it was sad. She was a good teacher. He wished other children could have a teacher like her. He excused himself and went to his room. I thought he acted normal. I didn't see the little bit of excitement that I'd seen earlier. I decided his earlier reactions had been due to lack of maturity, now he was grown up, but the next day the police came to talk to me about him. I tried to be honest. Cecil came in while the police were there. They asked him if he bought a knife two days ago. He said he did. He had the store wrap it in gift paper. It was a wedding gift for his teacher. They asked if he gave her the gift. He agreed that he had taken it to her house, but she wasn't home, so he set it on a table inside the door. That was when we learned that the knife he bought was the murder weapon."

Mrs. D'YG disconnected from herself as she talked to her fingers. "I started worrying again. Cecil told the police that he had come home late in the afternoon and worked on his application to business school. He mentioned his headache and that he had slept all night."

She dabbed at a bead of sweat running down her forehead. "The police came back twice asking about where Cecil had been. I tried to be honest. I honestly could not say if he had gone out, or if he had gone to bed and slept all night as he said. I knew he was in bed when I went to bed. Finally, the police found the fiancé. He was charged with murdering the teacher. The young man acted stunned. He insisted he did not kill his fiancé. He insisted that he had left town to pick up some materials for his father's business. He had returned with the materials. The prosecutor convinced the judge that he had more than enough time to visit his fiancé and kill her before he left town. The young man declared that he did not want to live without his love. He didn't put up much of a defense."

Mrs. D'YG paused looking away. "He was convicted and executed."

We sat silent and stunned. The sounds of birds in a shrub outside the front window broke the silence of the room. Mrs. D'YG gulped and swallowed then continued her story. "By the time the conviction came in, Cecil had left home to go to school. All my earlier fears came back. I couldn't sleep at night for fear I would learn that he had killed his teacher and caused the death of a promising young man. After that, I didn't hear any rumors of trouble around Cecil. He spent three years in business school. After he got out of school, he got a job doing the books for a distillery. I worried about that, because the distillery often paid employees in whiskey. They did pay him some of his salary in whiskey. He told me that he spent his weekends taking it someplace he could sell it to a store."

I had not been taking notes as Mrs. D'YG talked. I looked at the detective. He nodded, acknowledging that we would follow up on this report.

Mrs. D'YG continued, "I didn't hear of any problems for…oh…about six or seven years. He told me he was moving to the city to take a management job for Jouyet Paper. I had convinced myself that he was doing okay. About two weeks after he announced that he had moved and would send us his address when he got settled, policemen came to the door. They wanted to ask me questions about Cecil. They wouldn't say what it was about until just before they left. I told them then and there that if they suspected my son of murder, they were probably right. I sat down and cried and cried. They went away then. They came back when my husband got home. I was still crying. I cried for weeks after that. My husband told them we didn't know where he was. He said that I had worried about him ever since he was four. He told the police that I tried everything to help him--we both did. The police tried to comfort us saying they had no real reason to believe he had killed the two people except that he apparently knew both victims and both of them had been killed the same way, stabbed. I cried harder and told them he had killed his nice teacher too, and her fiancé was executed for it."

Mrs. D'YG looked somewhat gray. I feared telling us this story might kill her. She continued, "Like I said, I cried and cried. Finally, I realized that my crying was hurting my husband. I stopped crying then and realized he had tried his best to raise Cecil up right. We talked a little about something being broken in Cecil. It was something we couldn't fix. My husband never said how he felt about Cecil. He just bottled his feelings up inside of himself. Sometimes I thought he was sad. Other times I thought he was angry. After about six months of hiding from his feelings, Mr. D'YG died of a heart attack. I told my oldest son, but I didn't write or call Cecil. I have not contacted him since the day my husband died. After my husband was gone, I moved in with my son and daughter in-law. He was stationed in the capital. I took care of the babies while she worked. I wanted to work, but I would get too tired. Something inside me broke when I admitted my son is a killer. Something broke, and I have never been strong since. I have never recovered from losing the husband I loved."

She stopped and looked at a photo on a dresser behind me. I turned and saw an attractive older man.

Before I could comment on the man, she picked up her story again. "While we were living in the capital, my son was called out on maneuvers. I was home alone with the children. I sat down to read the paper. On the third page, I saw an article about a man who worked for Jouyet Paper being murdered. I couldn't help it. I started crying. I didn't know what to do. I was home alone. When my daughter in-law came home I told her that Cecil had killed someone again. I showed her the article in the paper. She was very sweet to me. She made me hot tea and soothed and comforted. Finally, she said that since her husband wasn't home. She would take our concerns to his commanding officer at the base. She took the paper and was gone for two hours. When she got back, she told me the officer would look into what was best to be done. About two weeks later, my son got transferred to Northbase in the mountains. We moved, and I did not hear the outcome of the murder. My son forbid me to make contact with anybody who might tell Cecil where we were. We were all afraid of him now."

Mrs. D'YG seemed to recover herself and stroked Margaret's head where Margaret rested it on the arm of the chair. Margaret sat up and smiled at the woman. Mrs. D'YG looked into Margaret's eyes. "I don't know how many people he has killed. We do not get the papers. I tried to tell people years ago. I know I lied to myself for years, but I stopped lying and told what I knew. I tried to get help for him when he was young. His step-father was a wonderful man. He tried to be a good father to my boys. He was a good father. My boy will tell you that."

I leaned forward in my chair. "Mrs. D'YG, I am sorry you had to go through this. I am doing my best to see that Cecil will never hurt anyone again. I think he has spells of trying to be nice, then something makes him angry, and he lashes out. I know this was hard for you. It was the right thing for you to tell us." I moved to stand up.

Margaret started to get up off of the floor. Mrs. D'YG spoke again. "Please get him convicted. Lock him up or shoot him, I don't care. Just make him stop."

Margaret patted the woman's hand. "Mrs. D'YG you are talking to my cousin Jake Jaconovich. He is the one who got Leon Fortenac sent to jail for raping and murdering one girl. He got ex-president Vanderholm convicted on multiple charges of murder. I can promise you that my cousin Jake will stop this man."

Tears spilled out of Mrs. D'YG's eyes. "Are you telling me that a Fortenac and a Vanderholm have done these terrible things too?"

Margaret nodded. "They did. And my cousin Jake made certain they were punished for their sins."

The old woman smiled at me then and said. "Good."

We left exhausted. I didn't like leaving her alone after she had just gone through the ordeal of telling us that her son was a serial killer.

We spent several more weeks following more leads. Finally, Detective Sorros had a list of murders most of which were unsolved. They were paced about three years apart over a twenty-year period. We had an additional four murders over the past two years. Cecil Brokerhoff knew and had access to each person. Each murder had been committed with a filleting knife. Each time the victim had been stabbed from the front, under the sternum, and up into the heart. Most of our depositions were from police departments and families of the victims. The defense had deposed twenty-five people who claimed he was of excellent character. We started collecting depositions from people who knew the other side of him.

We used a local judge for the Brokerhoff trial. He seemed a little taken aback by the amount of paperwork we gave him. I told him that we were presenting documentation on eleven charges of murder, one assault with intent to kill, and two cases of perjury resulting in unfounded execution.

The judge commented. "Your suspect has been a busy boy."

"He has had a long sad career." I left to wait for the judge to set a court date.

Chapter 27 Guilty Without Question

Afull month after I presented the Brokerhoff case to the judge, he called me to come in with the defense attorney and set a court date. I couldn't get a reading from either man on what they thought of the case. I thought the defense had done a good job with what they had to work with. We set a date for ten days later to give my concerned parties time to take off from work and travel. My insistence that I would have concerned parties present did draw a surprised look from the defense attorney. I wondered if he realized that Brokerhoff's mother and brother intended to be present.

On the day of the trial, my team arrived in the courtroom with the concerned parties twenty minutes early. Our courtroom was not as elegant as the one in the capital. The judge sat at a desk facing the rest of the court. The court recorder sat at a table beside him. The attorneys sat in a row of chairs in front of a rail that separated us from the concerned parties. We had a long table for our papers in front of us. This was a ground floor room, so we could look out through large windows to a small courtyard garden. Occasionally, a secretary or janitor would walk through the garden unaware that procedures that could lead to the execution of another human being were unfolding just meters from where they walked.

We had a long row of chairs in front of the rail on our side of the room. Prosecutors from our office were representing several of the concerned parties. Three prosecutors came from other districts. The elderly prosecutor who had won the case to convict the teacher's fiancé, asked me very politely if I would allow him to speak in order to right the wrong he took part in years ago. Margaret came to represent Brokerhoff's mother and brother. We had time to position his family where he could not see them easily. Sofia sat with us to represent Sharon's family.

The defense arrived shortly after we were settled. Armed guards brought Mr. Brokerhoff into the courtroom. He looked respectable in a business suit. I expected him to show an emotion appropriate to the occasion--fear, anger, distain. He walked into the room with confidence. He seemed to preen at the implied attention. He smiled and nodded to people on both sides of the aisle. He winked at Sharon.

The judge entered, and the trial began. The judge commented on the size of the case and the complexity. He then began the motions. This time I led with motions to expunge.

"Your honor. I respect the case the defense has prepared and hesitate to expunge any of it. However, there are several cases in the depositions where the witness reports hearsay. I therefore move to expunge the following pages of testimony containing hearsay—Section two page five, Mr. Totter's testimony--Section five page ten, Mrs. Davies testimony..." I listed seven depositions containing hearsay. The judge upheld my motion to expunge.

Mr. Brokerhoff's attorney moved to expunge the deposition given by Mrs. D'YG on the grounds that it was hearsay. The judge asked if that was acceptable. I nodded to Margaret. She stood. "That is not acceptable your honor. I took that testimony from a woman who fully identified herself as Mrs. Brokerhoff-D'YG the defendant's mother. A representative for the defense attorney was present at the time, and he was satisfied that witness was who she claimed to be. Further that testimony is Mrs. D'YG's own experience and contains no hearsay."

"And who are you."

"Margaret M'TG, an intern for the prosecutor's office and the attorney representing Mrs. D'YG and Mr. Brokerhoff, the defendant's brother."

"Did you have a fully licensed attorney with you at the time you took the deposition?"

I stood. "She did your honor. I was also present during the deposition. The family has asked her to represent them. Perhaps, we should state for the record that this prosecutor's office works as a teaching office in cooperation with the local university. I will be asking other interns and junior prosecutors to speak to their part of the case as the case proceeds. I was present for every deposition they took." I sat down.

"Thank you Mr. Prosecutor. I respect the teaching activities of the prosecutor's office. When someone other than the Prosecutor of Record is speaking will you please identify yourself for the court recorder before you speak. He turned to the court recorder.

"**Let the record show** that the prosecution will be presented by various members of the prosecutor's office as agreed upon at the hearing on…"

Margaret sat down, flustered. She knew she was supposed to introduce herself. I reached across Sofia to give Margaret a pat. Poor Margaret blushed furiously.

The judge addressed us again. "Mrs. M'TG, you presented your statement very well. In a normal situation when you are the only Prosecutor of Record it would not be necessary to introduce yourself." He turned to the defense.

"**Let the record show** that the motion to expunge the depositions from Mrs. D'YG in sections ten and eleven shall be denied."

Margaret sighed.

I noticed Brokerhoff twisting in his chair trying to look at the people around him, especially on our side of the room. I didn't think he could see his family seated at the far end of the row directly behind us.

The case proceeded with very few motions to expunge and no motions to clarify.

I was interested in watching the interaction between the judge and the defendant. The judge spent almost an hour talking to the defendant. Throughout the whole interview the defendant maintained his innocence. I thought I noticed a lack of grief for the friends he had lost. I also wondered if the judge felt that he was being treated with a lack of respect from the defendant. I wrote a note to Margaret. "Your mistake was good. The judge had an example of how a normal person behaves." I thought I saw clearly that the defendant was not behaving normally. Brockerhoff acted naïve, chatty, confident, and a bit whiny when confronted with the accusations.

Finally the judge asked, "Mr. Brockerhoff, this is an astounding number of your friends who have died the same way over the years. Can you tell me your understanding of these deaths?"

"Everybody dies. Everybody has lots of people they know die." He shrugged.

I heard sniffling behind me and knew his mother was crying again. I heard her son trying to comfort her. Margaret moved her chair back closer to them and reached over the rail behind her to pat Mrs. D'YG on the hand.

The judge moved on to the statements from concerned parties. We started with an attorney from Rouseff who expressed his outrage over the disruption Mr. Brokerhoff had caused in his assault on the supervisor. Alexander, our associate prosecutor represented the families of the other two people

Brokerhoff was accused of killing. Sofia represented Sharon's family. She did a great job of describing the plight of the family when the father died. Mr. Farley represented the city, our office, and the family of the man falsely executed for the murder of Sharon's husband. We worked our way from the present back to the past.

Finally it was time for the prosecutor from the town where Cecil had grown up to speak to his outrage. "Outraged? Yes, I am outraged." He paused and breathed for about thirty seconds. "I knew the young teacher. I knew her fiancé. I thought she was a bit good for him, but he loved her. When he died, I knew he loved her, and I had misgivings. But, I knew Cecil Brokerhoff, too. I coached his football team. I knew he tried hard. I knew his papa." A tear ran down the old man's cheek. "Cecil tried hard to be a good boy. He had a temper, but I saw him hold it in check. I felt sorry for the lad. He didn't make friends easily. Your honor, I confess, I didn't look past the eager little boy who tried to be good. I didn't look past the son of a man I respected. I prosecuted the fiancé, and got a conviction based on little fact and a great deal of imagination. I didn't see the man Cecil had become. When I learned of another murder, I sat down and went over my evidence. I had twice the evidence to convict Cecil of murdering his teacher, as I had to convict an innocent man. The judge, who pronounced the verdict that sent an innocent man to the firing squad, drank himself to death years ago. I didn't fall into the bottle. I lived. I lived to take part in correcting my mistake of twenty years ago. I'm telling you, your honor. Don't make the mistake we made years ago. Don't be fooled by the man who tries so hard to make friends, who works so hard at being good. He murdered his teacher. Don't be fooled." The old attorney sat down.

The judge asked if we had any more statements? Margaret came last. She stood up. "Yes, your honor, I have a Statement of Outrage on behalf of the Brokerhoff-D'YG family. I am Margaret M'TG, a second year intern in the prosecutor's office in this city. The family has asked me to represent them with a Statement of Outrage. Perhaps some might call this a statement of grief, but it is a Statement of Outrage. When her husband, Cecil's father died, Mrs. Brokerhoff tried to get help for her son. She knew he was not taking his father's death as he should. She tried to get help. She took him to every professional she could find. They could not help her son grieve the death of his father. Sometime after the third murder that she learned of, this mother started begging the police to stop her son. She knew something was terribly wrong with her son and that he killed. When she learned through the newspaper of another murder, she took her concerns to her elder son's commanding officer. Despite the information supplied by the commanding officer, Mr. Brokerhoff, again, was not charged. His mother and brother have been hiding from him for years. Yes, this family is outraged over the events that make Mr. Brokerhoff the way he is. Their outrage over the inability of our legal system to stop this string of senseless murders goes deep and resides with their grief over the loss of the man he could have been. You have the power to free this family from their prison of hiding, grief, and anger created by someone they love. They beg you to return a verdict of guilty and stop his senseless murdering." Margaret sat down.

Brokerhoff jumped up. "What do you say? Did you talk to my Mama? You are lying. Mama doesn't know. Mama doesn't know the things. Mama mustn't know."

The judge pounded his desk with his fist and called for order.

I felt a movement behind me.

Brokerhoff fell silent. His mouth fell open. He ignored the judge telling him to sit. He stood with his mouth hanging open looking at his mama standing behind me. I felt his brother stand beside their mother. Brokerhoff spoke then. His voice sounded soft like a little boy, almost babyish and coy. "Mama you shouldn't sit there. Those people are bad. You should sit with me. You know I didn't kill anybody."

The judge started pounding his desk again, calling for silence. I felt Cecil's family sit down again. I watched to see how the man would take the knowledge that his mama knew what he had done. He showed no emotion. He sat down then turned in his seat and smiled at someone behind him.

The defense began their statements from concerned parties. I liked the statements. These were mostly testimonies to Mr. Brokerhoff's character. I thought they supported our testimony as much as they did his. One attorney representing neighbors from his previous community almost echoed the statement of the old attorney who had known Cecil as a boy and had been fooled.

The attorney presenting the Statements of Concerned Parties for the defense summed up, "I represent a dozen of this man's neighbors. You have depositions enumerating his countless acts of kindness. Do you really think that a murderer could fool all these people into thinking he was a good man?" The attorney sat down.

We went through a few more housekeeping items. The judge declared the evidence complete and binding, meaning there would be no possibility of appeal. I knew the defense had presented a good case. I wasn't certain we could get a conviction on any one case alone, but I thought the whole case together was compelling. I didn't know how the judge would view the case.

We waited while the judge made some notes and looked through the case. He didn't spend much time reviewing before he started to make his statements.

"**Let the record show** that this court has come to a verdict."

"**Let the record show** that this court finds the defendant Cecil Brokerhoff guilty without question on all counts as charged."

"**Let the record show** that this court is prepared to pass sentence."

"**Let the record show** that Cecil Brokerhoff shall be executed by firing squad no later than one week from today."

An officer entered and led Brokerhoff away. The judge and the defense left the courtroom. The concerned parties for the prosecution murmured among them selves as they gathered wraps and purses to leave. I heard Mrs. D'YG sighing, "It's over. Thank God it's over."

Nobody wept over the verdict. Nobody suggested we celebrate. I told the others to meet me back at the office to debrief. Back at the office, I thought to call home and ask my cook to prepare dinner for ten extras. I suspected we needed more time together to go over the case and how it felt to present a case where the sentencing was execution. I couldn't disagree with the sentence. I didn't like it and wished my country had a better solution.

Before the prosecutors from the other provinces left, they shook my hand and thanked me for including them in the prosecution of the case. They shook Mr. Farley's hand and asked him how they could get some interns. This is the point at which we started sending interns to prosecutor's offices all over the county.

The Brokerhoff case could never be compared to the Fortenac case in its importance as a point of law. The case came close to being as important in producing social change. The combined prosecutors' offices got more than a conviction and an agreement to share interns. A new sense of unity, community and cooperation in how law was practiced grew out of the case. We bonded over our grief from the number of senseless murders and the death sentence for a sick man in his prime. Within a few years, this bond saved more lives than Mr. Brokerhoff took. When the country was in famine, the prosecutor's offices cooperated to equitably distribute food to the starving.

Chapter 28 Children's Schooling

During the months we spent preparing for the Brokerhoff trial, several issues came up to distract me from my work on the case. We were about to have another election. I spoke for Mr. Chang again. The legislators had passed a law making the governor's and mayor's offices elected positions. I spoke for Mr. Mayor, because I knew his opponent to be worse than he was. The attorney who represented the union ran for governor from a party that supported issues benefitting mostly the middle and lower classes. They wanted to use tax money to start road and school improvements that would put more people to work.

While waiting for a court date on the Brokerhoff case, we had our election. The election came off extremely well. Andy again designed the ballots and voting machines. He kept his designs secret until the morning of the elections. Only he and a foreign printer knew about a watermark on the ballots. We did have some problem with false ballots, but the fakes were easily sorted from genuine ballots by the watermark.

The gubernatorial contest disappointed me. The incumbent won. I'd hoped the attorney for the union would win. I knew him to be an honest man. I thought working with the union had taught him to respect the needs of the working class. With the incumbent, I could only hope that his wife kept him in line.

I thought I saw the country developing a two party system. The Vanderholms and Papadakos families led the most powerful party. Some of the professors who worked on the new constitution led the second party. I supported their efforts. Mr. Chang and about half of the parliament were closer in allegiance to the independent party than the old family party. They were producing some balanced legislation. My understanding of how some sections of the new constitution would work over time was proved to be correct. The current constitution still created a class of people who could not get a full education. They were limited in which jobs they could fill, and limited in owning property.

One day in the mid-afternoon, I got caught up on my work. I couldn't proceed on the Brokerhoff case because we were waiting for more depositions. I had staff scheduling those depositions for me. Things were running in a nice routine at Rouseff. I went home early. I found Leah in our bedroom. She was lying on the bed crying. I noticed her suitcase was out.

I sat down on the bed. "Sweetheart, what has happened? Why are you crying?"

"I don't know what to do."

I lifted her up and pulled her into my arms. "Now, tell me your problem, and we will see if I can solve it." Her suitcase made me worried that she was thinking of leaving me.

"I don't know what to do."

"What has happened that you don't know about?"

"It's Isolde's son. He…he…had an accident with his father's car."

"Is he seriously injured?"

She nodded.

"Now what are you trying to decide to do?"

"Isolde has asked me to come stay with her."

"Of course, you must go. I am caught up at work. I can manage here. You can take the night train down and be there in the morning."

Leah sniffed. "I don't want to stay with them. I don't want to see her husband."

"Then you shall stay in a hotel and take a taxi to see Isolde. Is there anything else that worries you?" This would have been an excellent time for Leah to tell me her secrets, but she shook her head.

I sent the housekeeper to collect the children from school. They got home in time to have a fish-stew dinner with their mother before I took her to the train. I didn't understand Leah's mood. She acted weepy and afraid. I cursed Isolde's husband for tormenting Leah so bad that when Isolde needed help, Leah was afraid to go to their house.

I muttered to myself. "Just like a Vanderholm."

Leah was gone three days. I missed her for the first night. The second day, I took the children to school and afterschool lessons. I felt better having spent the time with my children.

When Leah came home, I took the children and met her at the evening train. Leah was smiling when she got off of the train. She greeted me with a big hug. "The boy will be fine. He regained consciousness shortly after I arrived. He could talk fine and even remembered me. Isolde's husband was nice enough. He even praised you for prosecuting Hab. He told me he hated that conniving bastard ever since the brat was born. He said you did the right thing to fine him so much." Leah hugged me again. "I am so relieved to feel like I can be friends with Isolde again."

I waited for Leah to say how good it was to be home. She hugged the children at the station, but didn't...I don't know what I felt was lacking in Leah's greeting. I was hoping for a little romance after I put the children to bed, but Leah stayed up late taking care of things left undone when she went away so suddenly. I fell asleep before she came to bed.

I scolded myself for moping over my wife and focused my attention on work.

After one trip to investigate the Brokerhoff case, we arrived back in the city in the early morning, I went straight home to shower and see my family. I kissed my wife. She didn't return the kiss. "Jake, I'm trying to get out the door. I'm going to a meeting just as soon as I drop the children off at school."

"What is your meeting for?"

Leah explained as she finished collecting her scarf and bag. "The children who live in the camp by the mall don't have anyplace to study and read. The soup-kitchen board is meeting to discuss what can be done."

"Honey, tell them that I will pay for library cards for all those children. They can study in the library."

Leah did kiss me then. "Thank you. I will tell the other women that you will do that. It will be a good place to start."

I thought about my childhood and my little bed in the converted hallway where I could read. I thought about my parents sitting at the table with me while I did my schoolwork. "I was an exceptionally fortunate child. I forget that others still are not as well off as I was."

Leah was ready to leave to take the children to school so I kissed them all and went to take a shower.

When I got out of the shower, I went looking for Mary Anne. I felt like I had not been spending enough time with her since her tonsillectomy. I couldn't find her. I asked the housekeeper, "Where is Mary Anne?"

"I saw her getting in the car with the older children. I thought Mrs. Jake was going to leave her with me, but she must have changed her mind."

I was disappointed at not getting to spend a few minutes with Mary Anne. "Perhaps she wanted to keep Mary Anne with her at the meeting. She does take her to meetings some times."

"She must have. Mary Anne is such a sweet child I'm sure she is no trouble."

"Well if my whole family is gone, I might as well go to work. I think I will be home early tonight." I went off to work at Rouseff.

Just before lunch, I was still in my office at Rouseff Industries looking over the results of an internal audit. In the back of my mind I was thinking that my country needed more auditors.

My secretary interrupted me. "Jake you have a phone call. It's Micki's boy."

I experienced a moment of panic that something was wrong in his household. "Yes, this is Uncle Jake."

"Uncle Jake, is Mary Anne supposed to be at school?"

The question confused me. "Um…no…not that I know of. Is Mary Anne at school?"

"Yes." He did not elaborate.

"Where is she?"

"In Elizabeth's classroom."

"What is she doing?" This was as challenging as taking a deposition.

"Just sitting with Elizabeth, and reading."

"Ah, I see."

Finally, Young John told me his story. "I take the daily bulletins to each classroom. I always smile and wave to Elizabeth when I go into her class. I was really surprised to see Mary Anne wave to me too."

"Yeah, I bet you were."

"Uncle Jake, will you talk to the director and tell him it was okay for me to use this phone. He is glaring at me like I've done something naughty." He passed the phone off to the director.

"Jake Jaconovich here. Listen, John D'NO is my cousin's boy. He called to tell me that my youngest went to school with her sister. My children like to be together. I will be down to pick up Mary Anne in a minute."

"Young Mr. John D'NO could have told me the problem."

"He knows my phone number and how to get past my secretary." I decided to protect my young cousin. "My secretary might not put through a call from you. Don't be harsh on the lad. He knows his cousins, so he thought he better check out the situation with me before he made accusations. Damn, I'm a prosecutor. I wish more people would do that."

The director grunted.

"I'll be there in about seven minutes."

I went down to the school thankful that I'd brought the Miki with me today. It was proving to be useful for me to have a car with me.

When I reached Elizabeth's classroom, I peeked through the window in the door. I instantly recognized Elizabeth's blond head. I saw a shorter dark curly head next to hers. Most of the other desks held two students too. I wondered if today all the children were to bring a younger sibling. I opened the door and slipped in. The teacher had just finished asking the children a question about English grammar. Both Elizabeth and Mary Anne raised their hands.

The teacher seemed startled. "Miss. Elizabeth, who is that with you?"

"This is my sister Mary Anne."

"Why is she here today?"

Nope. The other students were not bringing their siblings. The teacher noticed me standing in the back of the room. I shook my head at her. I wanted to hear Elizabeth's answer.

"Mama had to go to a meeting today to help the poor. Papa is busy chasing a very bad crook, so I decided to help by bringing Mary Anne with me."

Mary Anne spoke up to answer the English question. "Mrs. Teacher the correct verb is *saw*. The sentence is *I saw the car*."

One of the boys in the back of the room had noticed me. He said in our language. "And I see the papa."

The other children turned to look and giggled. The teacher walked to the back of the room to speak to me.

I took the offensive. "Your classroom seems to be overcrowded."

"Yes it is. We don't have enough of anything. Most students share a desk. That is why I didn't recognize that Elizabeth had her sister with her. She usually sits with one of the students who has more trouble."

"Well, as long as neither girl was disruptive, I'll take Mary Anne with me."

"Did she know the right answer, or did Elizabeth tell it to her."

"She knew the right answer. We practice English at home. The children speak it better than I do."

"I would like to talk to you about your children." She looked back at her students who were starting to get rowdy. "I'd like to talk to you away from school."

"Would you like to come to dinner some evening? Perhaps tomorrow night?"

"Thank you. I'll be there."

I walked up to Elizabeth's desk and told her to give her teacher our address and phone number. "Now, Miss Mary Anne, you best come with me."

"I want to stay with Elizabeth and go to school."

"I understand. I'll have to do something about that." I had no idea what to do with a three year old who should be in the first form, if not the second form.

I carried Mary Anne out of the classroom. Mary Anne is my mother's granddaughter. She gave me a look that made me feel lower than a worm. I kissed her cheek because she reminded me of my whole family of women, but most of all because she reminded me of Mama.

I decided to take Mary Anne and go visit Papa and Mama. Mama was having a good day. She recognized me right away. She remembered Mary Anne's name after just a short search through her memory. She wanted to rush around to feed us.

Papa reminded her that he is a rich man now. "We will order something from the cafeteria when it is lunch time. You just sit and enjoy this visit from our son and granddaughter."

I told them about Mary Anne going to school with Elizabeth. "She is really too young, but she certainly knows enough to get through first form. She knew an answer in Elizabeth's English class."

Mama took Mary Anne from my lap and held her. "You know Miss. Mary Anne, you are just like your papa. You are just like him. He wanted to go to school when he was just your age. We were living in The Cove, and he used to get so frustrated because he was too small to go to school. He learned how to read and how to do math, but his body was too small. You are going to have to wait until your body begins to catch up to your brain just like your papa had to wait."

Mary Anne leaned against her grandmamma, put her fingers in her mouth and looked at me. Big tears filled her eyes. "But I don't like staying home with Mrs. Cook when everybody else is gone."

Papa asked. "Why is it you don't like staying with Mrs. Cook?"

"She is always busy and doesn't have time to talk to me."

Papa looked at his granddaughter and nodded his head. "Yes, that is a good reason to not want to stay alone with her. You need someone who is doing interesting things."

He looked at me. "When Leah is busy, you best bring Mary Anne to us. It is hard for us to get out, but we would like to have her visit." He leaned forward and looked at Mary Anne. "How does that sound to you sweetheart. Grandmama and I want to have you come visit more often. We will try to do things that are fun for you."

Mary Anne looked at Papa and Mama, smiled, and nodded her head. I was thrilled with this idea.

I left Mary Anne with Mama and Papa and went to the prosecutor's office. From then until she started school, Mary Anne stayed with Mama and Papa three days a week. Papa said Mama seemed to have good days when Mary Anne was there.

Elizabeth's teacher came to dinner. She praised all of my children. She talked about Elizabeth's intelligence and imagination. She spent at least twenty minutes before dinner talking to Mary Anne.

The conversation remained general during dinner. I noticed the teacher watching Jacob and listening to everything he said. After dinner, she got down to business. "Mrs. and Mr. Jaconovich. You have three remarkable, bright children. I am not certain they belong in public school."

Shocked, I wanted to protest. The children looked at each other with something like glee in their eyes. I didn't think the conversation was really going where they wanted it to go.

Mrs. Teacher continued, "I have no idea what Miss. Mary Anne will do in school. She appears ready for the second form now but she is only four. She absolutely cannot start until she is five. We can't put a five year old in third or fourth form."

We all sat silently waiting for Mrs. Teacher to solve the dilemma she spread out for us.

She went on to outline some more problems. "I understand that Mr. Jacob will be in seventh form next year. He is young for seventh form. In addition to being much younger than some of the bigger boys who will never make it past seventh form, he will have the same teacher that you had." She sat silent while these words sunk in.

I almost jumped out of my chair at this news. "No! Good God how old is that woman! I had her almost thirty years ago. I don't think my son will have that woman as a teacher. He could probably pass his eighth form exams." I turned to my son and asked him in English. "How are your English language lessons?"

His reply was halting. "I...no do...no...I do not...um ...speak...the English good."

I smiled and replied in our language. "That is just fine. I had trouble with that language until my third year of college. It is very difficult to learn. I found Chinese much easier."

I turned to Elizabeth's teacher. "Do you have some suggestions?"

"Well yes. I don't want to sound pushy or classist, but your children need something different than our overcrowded school system."

I wondered what could be done about the overcrowding.

The teacher continued. "Some teachers are working with the university to start a private school for children like yours, who are very bright, or for children like the young Rouseffs who have security issues with public school. I think that Micki D'NO's children will want to go there."

My children started bouncing up and down over the idea that their cousins would be in the same school the same as now. I shook my head at their silliness.

Mary Anne spoke up. "Could I go to this new school?"

"Well we would certainly want you to go there when you are five. Perhaps it would be acceptable for you to visit occasionally. Yes, I think it would be a good idea for you to visit once a week or so for a half day."

I asked, "How is this school different enough to solve the problems of my children being in classes with other children who are much older?"

"The classes will be grouped more by age. Within each age group, students will work at their own pace. Elizabeth will still be doing third-form work, but she will be in with other six year olds. Jacob would do his seventh form work but his classmates will be his own age."

I leaned back in my chair and thought about the situation. "I went through school with children older than me. I never noticed the difference, except when my classmates joined boys club, and I was too young." I thought about the bullies who picked on me. Jacob took martial arts classes but not everyday. I didn't think he could toss three bullies on the sidewalk and walk into class looking un-rumpled.

"Thank you for your concern about my children. I remember it was in the seventh and eighth forms that the bullies started picking on smaller kids."

The teacher tried for a compassionate tone. "Oh. Did the bullies pick on you?"

My family giggled at the teacher's question.

"No." I didn't intend to elaborate. My family giggled some more.

I addressed the teacher. "You say this is a private school. What does that term mean. I've never heard of a private school."

"Well, this will be the first private school in the northern provinces. They are all over the world in other countries. Nuns will teach some of the classes. The priest has volunteered to teach math. University interns will help teach. Classes will be held in the auxiliary building at the cathedral. The church will pay part of the costs. The parents will pay the rest."

I liked the idea of my children attending a smaller school. I knew many of the nuns had completed graduate level degrees. I liked the idea of classes at the cathedral. "At this time, I am favorably disposed to the private school idea. Removing students whose parents can afford to pay for their schooling will help with your crowding and financial problems. I am concerned that my children will be exposed to the idea that they are better because they are richer. I don't like that. My children do well in school because we started reading to them when they were tiny. They have owned books since they were tiny. They grew up with material goods that many poor students will never see. This has helped them get ahead in school. I got ahead because my mama taught me to read early. I got a library card when I was six, and I used it regularly. Some families don't have those advantages. I want my children to understand that."

"Mr. Jaconovich, I don't think your children could miss that lesson if it wasn't taught at school. Remember the teachers are nuns. The priest does not believe in the classism we have in this country."

I looked at my children. "What do you think? Do you want to try this different school where your classmates will be your age?"

"The children looked at each other, silently communicating." Mary Anne looked eager.

Finally, Jacob nodded his head and announced, "We will try this new school."

When their first term started, I was happy to have my children in a school where the classroom building and the cloisters made up two sides of their play yard, and a strong fence, and the cathedral itself made up the other two sides.

The public could not just walk in.

A year and a half later, the day after Mary Anne turned five, she got up at the same time as her siblings and presented herself at the front door ready to go to school. It was my turn to drive the children. "Mary Anne what are you doing?"

"I'm going to school."

"Ah, I see." I pinched the bridge my nose, while I tried to figure out how to handle this problem. I looked down into that little face that looked so much like my mama. I had a moment of epiphany. I was dealing with a D'NO woman who had made up her mind. My path stretched clear before me. I opened the door. "Yes, you are five now. I will talk to the director. Are you sure you don't want to stay with Grandmama and Grandpapa?"

Mary Anne nodded. She went out and got into the car. Jacob and Elizabeth joined us and gave Mary Anne a long list of unnecessary instructions.

When we got to the school, I took Mary Anne by the hand and went to the director, and announced that I was enrolling Mary Anne in school.

"How old are you Miss Mary Anne?"

"I am five and Papa said I could come to school when I am five."

The director, a stern looking nun, looked into Mary Anne's determined little face and said, "Ah. I see." She looked at me. "Is her information the same as for the other two?"

I nodded.

"Well, I guess we can take her to the class for five year olds."

Mary Anne sounded just as sweet and angelic as can be. "I should warn you that I am ready for the second form, so I expect to be reading and getting some help with my math. I find math hard."

The nun looked at me, grinned, and rolled her eyes. "Yes, I'm sure you will have plenty of opportunity to read." She headed out the door with Mary Anne, and called over her shoulder as I prepared to return to the car, "She'll do fine. Don't look so sad."

I looked at the nun. She was a nun. What did she know about seeing your youngest child leave for school?

I drove to Rouseff offices, and I wished we'd had more children. Leah didn't say in so many words that she didn't want more babies. She didn't discuss the subject with me until I found birth-control pills that she'd left out in the bathroom. When I asked about them she said the doctor thought she was too old to have babies. I assured Leah as best I could that I didn't like to see her go through that pain. "If your doctor thinks it is too risky, I agree that I don't want you to take any risks. You are too precious to me."

She turned away. I thought perhaps she didn't like being reminded of her age.

I had several projects where I invested my own money. I'd completed a small, clean, comfortable hotel off of Rouseff Boulevard, just before the road intersected Gannon at China town. I'd just broken ground for another hotel near the mall.

I worked with some classmates to start a bank. We'd gone over and over the problem of employee theft from the bank. We thought we had good accounting practices set up. I consulted with Andrew about the computers for the bank. He was helpful to the point of making several trips north to help us get set up.

Late at night, Andrew and I sat and talked about our marriages. Andrew voiced his dissatisfaction with Adele wanting everything her own way. He had no life. He confessed that he would leave her if he could get a divorce. We talked about taking a mistress. I found the idea impossible for me, but could not condemn Andy if he wanted some companionship.

I finally went to Papa with my concerns about my marriage. "Papa, I want to have a marriage where we share everything especially intimacy. That is not happening. What can I do differently?"

Papa sighed and thought before he spoke. "Jake everybody is different. Your situation is different from ours. Some days I wish that Fiona had possessed the brains to wait four months for you."

I chuckled. "Brains were Fiona's only deficiency."

Papa smiled then sobered. "Son, I don't know what to say. Leah is a beautiful, elegant woman. She seems to have enough brains, but she has no depth. She just doesn't get the importance of events around her. It isn't you. Leah has trouble relating on a deep level involving absolute truth. Something is missing. She may love you to the best of her ability, but she is broken in ways that may never heal."

It was many years before I fully appreciated the wisdom behind Papa's words. They comforted me. I was afraid I was doing something wrong. I went home and played with my children. I tried to be a good husband, but I felt a wall between Leah and me.

The country was still having financial troubles. Nobody was building. Much of our population lived in shacks or were homeless. We had over fifteen hundred temporary units that we build beyond the mall. The crime rate in the overcrowded slum was not as high as one might think for such an area. The residents were too poor to make stealing from each other worthwhile. Stealing in wealthier neighborhoods would require some form of transportation. The poorest residents got into fights.

We still had a high death rate in the city. Women died of starvation or commit suicide. Babies died of about everything. Men left without word of where they were going. Men tried to do work too hard for their weakened bodies. They got hurt and died.

Chapter 29 Prisoner Release

After the Brokerhoff trial my life returned to a routine of managing my investments and processing petty criminals. Young Rouseff took over most of the management at Rouseff. I still spent one day a week there, mostly as a consultant on the legal research needed for various projects. Every time I went in, I needed to remind someone that Chinatown was land grant property. They could not buy or develop land grant property.

The weather turned dry. As a city dweller, I didn't think much about the lack of rain. I finally became aware of the problem when Mr. Farley mentioned a serious problem for our office.

"Because of the drought and consequent food shortage, the president is thinking of pardoning most of our prisoners and turning them loose. His thought is that it will save the government money if they don't have to feed criminals."

"Does he have any idea of what type of people are locked up?" Alexander, our newly promoted second senior prosecutor, sounded like he was about to panic.

Mr. Farley stayed calm. "Oh, I'm certain the man does not understand the scope of the problem. I also figured-out that his mama is a Fortenac cousin. This may be partially a plan to spring Fortenac without appearing to do so."

I resolved to hire security for myself, and my family. I had long since sent the Rouseff security off to more important business. I had a couple I found at the soup kitchen helping at home. I was still thinking about security when I voiced my thoughts. "We need to go through our records to see who we might have sent to prison and assess the safety of the court issue. The judges may be in more danger than we are."

Alexander asked, "What about all those people you arrested when the government changed."

I tried to remember. I scratched my head. "We need to check our files. I think most everybody we processed was fined and released. We didn't have money to lock them up then. The prosecutors from this office were fined and debarred. They went south and crawled into their nests of like minded relatives."

I spent my afternoon looking for trained security for my family. I called Detective Sorros. Next, I called the head of security at Rouseff. Finally, I called General Johan. General Johan proved to be the most helpful.

His secretary had identified his caller before he came on line. "Jake, I'm glad to hear from you. That is unless you are calling to tell me I am on someone's hit list."

"No. I don't think you are on a hit list, but we do have a problem. This drought is causing some financial problems for the government. They are making serious noises about pardoning all the offenders in our prison system and letting them go."

"You are not serious."

"I'm afraid I am serious. Part of the motivation for this may be to get Fortenac out of prison. I am looking for someone trained in security to protect myself and my family."

"Shit"

"Yeah," I suddenly felt better. I'd found someone who understood, and knew how to communicate.

The general growled, "What are you doing about it?"

"We've petitioned the president to let the courts go over our records to determine if some prisoners present a danger to the population. The president has not been responsive. The legal community is scrambling to find some legal method of overruling the president. This is another flaw in our constitution. It flatly gives the president the power to pardon prisoners despite the fact that the judge sentenced Fortenac to be jailed without pardon. By issuing blanket pardons based on government finances, he can circumvent the Fortenac sentence. The president's authority to pardon is one reason I changed to the policy of fining offenders and letting them go."

"Shit."

"Yeah, if it is possible you have enemies in prison…well…it would be a good idea to check."

"Shit. You know Jake, I have an idea of someone who knows how to do the type of security you need. His name is Paul Duboughski. He is still technically on active duty, but he took a bad hit in the purge. I'm going to assign him to coordinate court security."

"I intended to pay for my security."

"You may have to pay for anybody he hires. I'm calling this national security. We do have the obligation to protect the court." General Johan thought for another few seconds. "I will notify the other bases that we must provide security for the court in their neighboring provinces. Colonel Duboughski will be in charge of the whole operation."

The lion that had been standing on my chest and snarling into my face disappeared. "Thank you General. This is exactly what we need."

I was finishing up an endless stack of paperwork in the prosecutor's office when the receptionist called and said I had a visitor, a Colonel Duboughski. This news surprised me. I thought it would be a few days before support arrived. I went out to the reception room to meet the colonel. He reminded me a great deal of Peter Yablonski.

After the general greetings, I asked. Do you know Major Peter Yablonski?

"Yeah, he's my half brother. He's a colonel now. He got promoted after the last election."

"Ah, you look enough alike to be twins."

"Naw, I'm prettier. He's had his nose broken more times than I have."

I snorted and choked.

"Naw, don't tell me. You couldn't possibly be the prosecutor who broke his nose a few years back."

I nodded.

Paul went off into a loud booming belly laugh. "He told me it was a great big fellow who attacked him."

I shook my head and tried to look sheepish.

Paul laughed again. His laughter had the effect of solving my problem of how to call a staff meeting. Everybody came out to see what the merriment could be. I motioned for them to sit in our conference area.

I opened the meeting. "Right, I intended to talk to Mr. Farley first then call a meeting, but our problems seem to be solved sooner that I expected. Folks, this is Colonel Paul Duboughski. General Johan has assigned him the task of providing for the security of the court in the case that the…"

The staff interrupted me with cheers. Everyone stood up to introduce them selves to the colonel.

Colonel Duboughski worked with Mr. Farley to outline the risks and what was needed. I forgot about security. I went back to working on my own projects and processing petty criminals.

Sofia asked to work exclusively on the problem of the proposed prisoner release. She got together with her cousins. What the rest of the legal community could not do, the Uzaras, Spinozas, and D'SnG's were able to ameliorate. They got the pardon conditional on obeying certain conditions including no future offenses, staying away from potential victims, and avoiding the families of the people they hurt. After they got as far as they could with the president, they went to old Mr. Fortenac.

Apparently, The Mr. Fortenac didn't want anything to do with Leon, and the Uzaras could hunt him down and kill him for all he cared. Leon's mother agreed that she and servants would pick Leon up and take him to their home in the south, and he would not leave the grounds.

Sofia admitted that she was the one who promised that if Leon was caught off of their property, he would be hunted down and shot like a dog. I learned later that the Uzara/D'SnG security watched the house where Leon was staying to make certain he did not leave the grounds.

It surprised me that Sofia seemed so vehement about this topic. She had been particularly happy around the office, practically kissing and blessing the repeat offenders as she let them off with little more than extracting a promise that they would be good.

I looked around my office and smiled as Jeffrey smiled and patted the hand of one of our little old lady shoplifters. The woman couldn't help herself, but I usually made her pick up litter for attempting to shoplift. I thought about Sofia and Jeffrey and smiled. I hoped their relationship would last.

In a matter of days after Sofia's last efforts to contain Leon Fortenac, Paul appeared in our office. He addressed the staff. "The release is due to start this afternoon or tomorrow morning. I will be stationing officers with those who appear vulnerable. Jake and his family will have round the clock security as will Mr. Farley and Miss. Uzara." He turned to Sofia. His voice dripped disapproval. "I heard that you threatened the life of Leon Fortenac."

Sofia didn't blanch. "No sir, I did not threaten. This is a fact of life. If that slimy, perverted bastard shows his face near a Uzara, he will get the punishment he deserves."

I was shocked.

Paul suddenly grinned and nodded.

Jeffrey looked at Sofia with a totally besotted smile.

Toward the end of the meeting, I looked up to see my children coming into the office. I wondered what they were doing in town so late. It must be almost five PM. The children looked a little distressed. They came directly to me and hugged me.

"What are you three doing in town so late?"

"Mama forgot to pick us up."

I looked at Paul. He nodded.

I felt like ice water had been dumped over me, but I didn't want to alarm the children. "Well, I guess we will all have to cram ourselves into the Miki."

Paul volunteered. "I have a jeep, and I am headed out to your place anyway. The children can ride with me."

The meeting ended. Paul and I took the children home. I took Mary Anne with me. At first, she acted quite willing to discuss the problem of her mother not picking her up. "Well, it wasn't so bad. Mama doesn't like driving all over town so after dance class Elizabeth and I walk back to the Cathedral and meet Jacob."

"Didn't Jacob have martial arts?"

"Yes,"

"How did he get back and forth?"

"Trolley."

I tried not to growl. "I don't like for you to be walking around town and riding trolleys."

"Papa, how old were you when you rode around town on trolleys."

"Older than you are."

"Uh uh, you were five when you moved to M'TK, and Grandpapa told us you walked to school by yourself."

"Ah but I didn't ride a trolley until I was seven. Mary Anne there is a difference between you and me. My papa was a respected laborer." I sighed. "Other people watched out for me. I walked with other children like me."

Mary Anne took breath to argue.

I continued. "I am not mad at you for doing as you did. We need to do things different. I am a prosecutor. I am also a wealthy businessman. I put people in jail. I make them pick up litter. They could get mad at me and try to get even by hurting my children." I tried to sound reassuring to Mary Anne when I was angry with Leah. "I thought your mama was meeting you at school and taking you to dance and Jacob to football and martial arts. I think I will hire someone to drive you if your mama is too busy."

When we got home, Leah wasn't there. The housekeeper didn't know anything other than, "The missus got a phone call. She grabbed a few things and told me she would be late. She said to tell you not to worry. She would be fine."

Paul and I did worry about Leah. She didn't come home all night. By morning I decided she had driven her car in a ditch somewhere. When I wasn't picturing her in a ditch, I knew she had left me. I knew our marriage had not been what it should be. She stopped responding to me in bed. She never asked how I was or anything about work.

In the early morning, Paul and I discussed what to do. He wouldn't say what he was thinking. He finally made some phone calls. I drove the children to school at the regular time. Two enlisted men met me at the school. They would watch the children all day. I would pick them up after school and take the girls to piano lessons and Jacob to football practice. I took the girls home after piano and went back to pick up Jacob from football.

I worked from home all day hoping for news from Leah. I alerted all three of my offices to the fact that I would be at home and should be contacted there.

By the time I got all the children home from their activities I was convinced that Leah had run away because she couldn't keep up with the children's schedules. We had dinner an hour later than usual because I waited for Leah. Every time the children asked where their mama was, I answered honestly. "I don't know."

Just before bedtime Mary Anne started to cry. "Do you think the bad people you make pick up litter got mama?"

I pulled Mary Ann into my lap and motioned for the other children to snuggle with me. "I don't think bad people got her. She took the car. She told Mrs. Cook she was going out. She told us not to worry. I think your mama got upset about something and drove to the capital to spend some time thinking about things. You know she spends a great deal of time helping the poor. I think she got tired. Paul has asked questions. We know she fueled the car at the interchange. We know she headed north."

If Leah thought she was going to sneak into a sleeping household at two in the morning, she forgot how noisy the Mercedes could be. She came through the door to bright lights and all four of us rushing down the stairs to meet her.

She'd come home. I felt so thankful that she'd come home that I couldn't be angry at her for going away without telling me where she was going. I picked her up and held her in a hug. "You're home."

"Mama, Mama why did you go away? Were you tired of the poor people?"

"Mama, if you are tired of driving me to sports and things, I can take the trolley."

Elizabeth sounded heartbreakingly mature. "Really, Mama, if you get too busy, or too tired to drive us, we can make other plans."

All three children nodded. I grew angry then that Leah had upset her children.

I made an announcement. "We will make other arrangements. I shall hire a chauffer."

Leah chided me. "Oh Jake, don't be silly. I like driving my children to school and things."

I ended the discussion at this point and sent the children back to their beds. I followed Leah back to our room. "Leah," I looked away. This was going to be harder than I thought. "Leah, I know that you are tired of me in bed." I gulped for air. "I assume you went away to think about whether or not you are tired of me as a husband."

"Jake don't be silly. I went away for a day because I...I...well..." Leah looked at the floor. If she were a client, I'd expect a lie. "Well, I guess Mary Anne came closest to the truth. I remember your mama looking out the window at the lines of people needing to be fed. I remember how one day she just sat, and rocked, and cried. I know how she felt. We raise money. We find food. We find jobs for people and still more keep coming needing food, and shelter, and jobs. We've placed thousands of people and more keep coming."

I held Leah and kissed her. "Sweetheart, I know you must need to get away sometimes. You don't have to work so hard to feed the poor. Please Darling, before you reach the breaking point and run away from it all, tell me. Call me at the office. I'll understand. It gets to me too. I'll help you take a vacation."

It never ever occurred to me until many years later that my wife had taken the car, and driven fifteen hundred miles round-trip, almost non-stop, to meet a convicted felon.

Chapter 30 Cousin Marianne

One of my greatest joys during this time was that my cousin Marianne started classes at the university. She lived with us and helped with the driving when she wasn't in class. I told her the same thing Papa told me when I started university. "Marianne this is your job. You are to treat school the same as any other job. You will get up in the morning and go to the campus whether you have a morning class or not. You will study when you are not in class. One other thing you will do is learn to make friends. You will participate in campus activities. You will learn how people live outside of The Cove."

I had a long list of instructions about foreign films, and games, and the right places for women to hang out. I took her to her first year receptions. I thought the standards had eased up over the years. When I entered with Marianne, the hostesses greeted me happily.

The first hostess acted gracious. "Mr. Jake it is so good to see you. You always liven up these little affairs."

I wasn't so certain about the second hostess. "Mr. Jake, are we to be honored with another D'NO student? I'm not sure the university has quite recovered from Micki."

I tried to be reassuring. "May I present my cousin Marianne D'NO?"

The hostess graciously offered her hand. "Miss. D'NO, welcome to our little university."

I couldn't help adding. "You don't need to worry about Marianne following in Cousin Micki's footsteps. She is much closer in temperament to my mother and Cousin Margaret M'TG."

I thought I saw the hostess blanche. Mama was known and respected in the city, even though she didn't get out much. I suspected Margaret had left a lasting imprint on the university.

The reception went well. My martial arts professor attacked me. I was unprepared for an attack at a reception so he was able to throw me off balance. I recovered and counter-moved.

A hostess came running in great distress. "Gentlemen! Professor! Mr. Jake! Please, please this is a polite function."

I tried to look innocent. "He was just giving me a little polite quiz to be certain I remembered what I learned in his class."

Professor Stodola and the university provost grinned.

Marianne giggled.

A group of first-year students giggled and stared wide-eyed at our uncouth behavior.

I approached several students and introduced Marianne. I tried to do the things that would have helped me with my first reception. By the time it was polite for us to leave, Marianne had found some students who would be in her classes. She met a couple professors who remembered her cousins.

I couldn't tell if the English professor was trying to be intimidating or complimentary when he addressed her in English. "Ah, Miss. D'NO, I will be delighted to have another of Jake's cousins in my class. Your cousins have all gotten perfect scores and provide such lively discussions."

Marianne replied with ease. "Thank you for the compliment. I am thankful my cousins have not disgraced the family name. I look forward to your class."

As far as I could tell Marianne sounded more like a Yankee than someone from my country."

The professor laughed. "Your English is excellent despite being slightly Americanized. What does your family do? Teach each other?"

"Of course we teach each other. I suspect that the Americanization comes from meeting people from the states at the resort my family owns."

I decided to ease out of this discussion. "I see a hostess headed this way to make certain we are bored out of our skulls. We better break this up."

"Mr. Jake, spend some more time speaking English with your cousin. Your accent is still wrong."

I knew I was certain I wanted to leave. I did not come off as will with my English professor as I did with the martial arts.

Chapter 31 Challenge to the Constitution

Before we left Marianne's reception, Professor Ingleman invited me to a meeting at his house. I hadn't kept up with his group, so the invitation aroused my curiosity.

On Sunday afternoon, I went to the meeting at Professor Ingleman's house. When I arrived, many of my old acquaintances were there along with a fresh batch of students. When I entered the room, the professors greeted me with great respect. One law student blushed furiously when he learned my name. I was forced to command him quite sternly to sit. He seemed to think he should remain standing in my presence.

I decided to open the conversation. "Well gentlemen what sort of frightening horrors prompted you to call me out on a Sunday afternoon when I would rather play with my children and snooze in my chair?"

Professor History of Law snorted, "Yes Jake, it is truly a frightening horror. Rumor has it that Vanderholm, Papadakos, and Fortenac have hired a team of lawyers to file a suit in the courts to declare our current constitution illegal."

I replied in a bored tone. "Well good. That is encouraging. Perhaps they have learned that using the courts is far more effective than sending the army in to kill off ten thousand citizens."

My comments were met with laughter. "Jake you always manage to come up with a new perspective."

Professor Ingleman seemed to puff up. "That's why I invited him to that meeting the first time."

I looked at the students. "Don't be too intimidated by this group. After my first meeting my friend and I spent hours trying to figure out if this group would get us into trouble. I still don't know the answer, but so far nothing too terrible has happened."

My friend and sparring partner, Professor Stodola, spoke up, "Yes Jake we intend to disturb your Sunday afternoon naps for months to come. Professor Ingleman wants you on the defense team."

I shrugged. "My expertise is in criminal law and contracts. I take it this is to be a civil case. I am not certain I will be a particular asset to this case."

Professor Ingleman chuckled. "Jake, I am sure that if this case can be won, you are the man to have on my team."

I felt myself walking through the library of my mind. "I hate the thought of losing such an important case. We will win. I wonder what they think they can come up with?"

We speculated on which grounds the Vanderholm coalition could name to invalidate the constitution.

Finally, I voiced my frustration. "It really does no good to speculate. Most of our procedure for adopting the constitution was flawless. They cannot overturn those court decisions. They will have to find fault with the document itself, or possibly who wrote it. That will be the easiest thing for them to do. Also, I can name a dozen faults off of the top of my head."

"Jake, can you go over that thing with a magnifying glass and identify the weakest points where they might attack? We are all aware that you don't think the document goes far enough. Can you find the points where they will attack."

I leaned back in my chair and rubbed my hands over my face. "Yeah, I can take a look at the thing. I've almost got it memorized." I paused, and a thought started clawing its way out of the depths of my brain. "Okay men, if they have a strong case, I want to turn their case on its head and get the constitution I want. I can almost see how to do this in the back of my mind. I'll want about twelve student interns. Professor Ingleman, I want to work closely with you on procedure." I smiled. "I've been to court against a Vanderholm and a Fortenac before. I hope they put up a better fight this time."

Professor Uzara sounded horrified. "Jake our constitution is at stake!"

"What I want for a constitution is at stake. The better their case, the easier it will be for me to call for the changes I want."

Professor Ingleman steepled his fingers and looked at me though narrowed eyes.

The nervous law student started whispering "Oh God. Oh God. Oh God." Finally he blurted out. "Do any of you know what shit you are talking about?"

I looked at the student. "Yeah, we've been making this shit up for years just as we go along. I want you to be one of the students who works on this. You show an appropriate understanding of the case. The rest of the men here would like to rock in their chairs and call out to God. You'll do."

The men laughed. Professor Ingleman spoke up. "Jake, I think I see what you are seeing. Depending on what they do, we could turn this on its head."

"The worst case scenario is that the voters will be given a choice of constitutions to vote on." I stopped and ran my fingers through my hair. "That could be a problem because the old families have more money for advertising the constitution they want. I'll have to think on how to get around that problem."

"Jake, I think you have access to something the opposition does not have. You have a master list of all the registered voters in the country."

I nodded and smiled. "I'll get Andy to work on the security for that right away."

We tossed around several more ideas before the meeting adjourned. Finally just before I left, the students made their exit. I made an appointment to meet with Professor Ingleman in a week and followed the students after a minute or so. I found the poor law student vomiting into the shrubbery. I went up to him and placed a hand on his back. He jumped.

I handed him my handkerchief. "Is it something you ate, or the meeting that has unsettled you?"

"The meeting."

"Yeah, that was pretty bad. Damn. I am hoping we will get a new constitution out of this."

"Do you really think you can make that happen, or will things go back to the way they were? I'm not really a member of the elite."

"We have three outcomes, well four outcomes to this possible suit. One, Vanderholm etcetera will figure out that they don't have a good enough case and drop the idea. Things will stay the same. Two, we go to court and the opposition loses. Things will stay the same. Three, we will go to court, the opposition wins with the provisions I want the judgment to have. We will get a much better constitution. Four, we go to court and lose, and the opposition gets to install a constitution of their own. Then all hell will break loose, and I will join you in vomiting into the shrubbery, just before I take my family and flee the country. Number four is not an acceptable option, so we will make certain that doesn't happen."

When I got home, I called Andy and explained about the voter registration lists.

"Jake you worry too much. I have a copy of the master list with up-to-date addresses from the last election."

"Put copies someplace safe."

"Okay, why don't I come up, and we can discuss security with that big guy who was following you around pretending you needed protection." Andy chuckled and continued, "Oh no Mrs. Jaconovich, Jake wasn't fighting. That would imply that someone else had an opportunity to hurt him."

"I am particularly fond of the part where you confessed to Mama that things got a little confusing just before everybody fell down." It felt good to laugh with Andy over shared memories.

The next day, I took some time off after I dropped the children at their lessons. I went to visit the Apkoutas. They lived in an apartment complex for railroad retirees, where Wu's restaurant used to be. I told them about the challenge to the constitution. They were sympathetic.

When I went into the prosecutor's office the morning after visiting the Apkoutas, the holding room was full of familiar faces. Many of the people were about my parents' age. Some were older.

I went to the door of the new holding room. "What are you doing here? I can't imagine the lot of you rioting."

They giggled.

One of Papa's friends explained. "I don't know about them others, but I wants to talk to you about this constitution thingy."

I looked at the others who nodded and made sounds of agreement. "Well come this way, we will meet in the conference room."

Everything I said must have been funny because everybody giggled at each statement. By the time I got my guests seated the other prosecutors had joined the group.

Mr. Farley opened the discussion. "What is this Jake?"

"I don't know for certain yet. There is a rumor that Vanderholm and a group of cronies want to start legal action to overthrow our constitution."

This news was met with a general outcry,

By this time, I was feeling more comfortable with the idea. "Well, I'm not too upset about this. This constitution has never been what I wanted. What I hope is that this action will open the door to getting the constitution that we need. I want to allow every native born resident over the age of eighteen or twenty-one to vote."

My friends from the city liked this idea.

I rubbed my hands over my face and pinched the bridge of my nose. "Of course, it wouldn't do for Vanderholm's team to learn how I plan to use this action."

Everyone shook their head.

I saw Andy wandering in past reception and waved at him. I continued with what I knew so far. "Our biggest problem will occur if this thing gets to a vote. We will need to get the message to the voters to vote for the constitution written by the law professors at our university."

Papa's friend seemed to be the spokesperson for the group. "Is there somefing you want us to be doing right now? I kin go knocking on doors and telling people to vote for the conseytution you think is right."

I glanced at Andy. He grinned. I smiled. I addressed the group, "That may be exactly what you will need to do. Until the judge makes a ruling, you won't need to do anything. Well, if you can think of laws and rights that you want in a new constitution bring them to me, and I will see if they are something the central government has jurisdiction over."

"That's fair enough. You tell us when you need us to go door to door, and we'll get to work."

"Watch for the trial if one happens. It is possible the opposition will realize they don't have a case or that taking this to court will put them in a worse position, and they will drop the whole idea."

Andy spoke up. "They won't drop the idea. They are out for blood the only way they can get it. They think the constitution is limiting their freedoms and killing their profits. They will carry this through."

"Ah Andy, you've done a little research since I talked to you Sunday night."

"I took Adele to the country club for drinks and dinner. Then we went to a party. I heard enough. Adele heard much more than I did. She told me all about it on our way home in the car. What everybody is debating is whether you will be involved in the case. Most think that since you are in criminal law, you won't get involved. They don't know about Professor Ingleman and his merry band of scholars."

I grinned some more at seeing Andy and how amazing he could be.

I called for questions. Everybody seemed happy with their understanding of the situation and told me they were behind me. We later learned that those people who came to the prosecutor's office that morning were only the tiniest tip of the iceberg of people fighting for a better way of life. I never considered that the people who ate at the soup kitchen would want to help. I never thought about the people we worked so hard to find jobs for. The city held thousands upon thousands of people who were eager to support our office.

It quickly became obvious that I had the support of the whole office. Mr. Farley took charge. "Okay do we have a timeline for this case?"

I shook my head.

Andy had better information. "They have Judge Neuton lined up. He is a Papadakos/Fortenac. He will rule in favor of the Vanderholm crowd. I think they will be ready to move in less than a month. They've done a good job of keeping this secret if I didn't hear about it."

I shocked everybody in the room. "Ah, the judge has all ready decided." I grinned. "Good, I can work with that."

Mr. Farley asked, "Jake what can this office do?"

Sophia sounded bewildered. "This sounds like a civil case not a criminal case."

Jeffrey Farley has an excellent mind despite the nervous tics he developed after getting shot. "It is a civil case against a constitution put in place by the courts. It is an attack on the courts. I wonder why our two attorneys in the south haven't notified us."

"If I didn't hear of it until Jake called me, they may not be aware." Andrew squinted his eyes. I knew he was searching his brain for any previous hints that something was afoot.

He looked at us. "No, I can't think of any time I've overheard something or people stopped talking when I entered the room."

One of the interns questioned. "I wonder how long they have been working on this?"

Another student added helpfully, "I'll call Mama tonight. If anybody has details it will be Mama. She is the one interested in law. She wanted me to study law. She practically commanded me to get a job in this office and learn everything Prosecutor Jaconovich knows."

Andy and I laughed. He explained. "Jake makes most of it up as he goes along. Don't let that fool you. He knows the law. He follows every detail. He has a fantastic memory. For the rest, he looks at what is happening and rolls with it."

Our supervisor admonished the students. "One thing you must learn in the practice of law is the practice of confidentiality. Eventually the opposition will have to tell us what they are planning. They have to give us forty-five days written notice. But, the less time they give us, the better it will be for them."

"I have a horrible or stupid question." One of our second year interns spoke up. "Who do they give notice to? How do they give notice?"

I looked around for a phone. I grabbed one off of an intern's desk and called Professor Ingleman. I kept the conversation short. I gave him all the information I had. He said he would call Judge Neuton. I asked. "Is it possible that the coalition will not know who to give notice to? Jeffrey Farley thinks they should give notice to all the prosecutor's offices, because the case challenges a court ruling."

Professor Ingleman growled, "He's right. I have no idea what that school of suckerfish you call a coalition is thinking." We hung up.

My supervisor sent a paralegal to get rid of all the petty offenders and make an appointment for anybody who had a serious charge to come back another day. The paralegal cleared the offender list in five minutes.

We started dividing up the case among our staff. I held a class on the constitution. I pointed out its weak points from my perspective. We invited the students to see how it could be attacked from a southern perspective. We got some good information.

Professor Ingleman called back. He was chuckling. "It seems that they are learning from us. They intend to send the case to selected judges in each province to get a ruling without letting anybody argue the other side."

I snorted, "Ah, clever little monkeys aren't they? Do you know who the judges will be?"

"They haven't selected them yet as far as I know."

"Okay Mr. Farley is calling this a challenge-to-the-court because they are challenging a court mandated constitution. We can work with the other prosecutors' offices. The whole staff here is looking at this thing. Andy doesn't think they have been preparing this for a long time."

Professor Ingleman sighed, "Good, we can use all the help we can get."

At the end of the day, Leroy called us. He'd just learned of the case. He apologized and asked what could be done. We told him that this was a challenge to the court, so his office needed to be informed of any hearings or proceedings. We gave him Judge Neuton's name.

We notified all the other prosecutor's offices that there might be a challenge to the court issued in their district. Jeffrey emphasized the need for cooperation between offices. "We have access to the law school here and to the attorneys who wrote the constitution. Professor Ingleman is on call to help with procedural questions since nobody in the country has actually done anything like this before. Stay in touch with all the judges in the area and let them know you expect forty-five days advance notice before they hear a case challenging the court."

We had our bases covered. While I was out moving my children from school to lessons and football, our intern called his mama—bless her heart. We had a meeting when I got back.

Mr. Farley called on the student.

He looked self-conscious. "Um…do you want to know what mama said?"

We nodded. I refrained from trying to shake the information out of the poor lad.

"Well, she learned about the whole thing about a week ago. She didn't know it had anything to do with our office so she didn't call me. She said that her friend told her the whole idea got started at a dinner party about a month ago. The party was at Fortenac's, and it was Leon who suggested turning the tables on the northern constitutional conspirators."

We nodded and barely breathed for fear of stopping the flow of information.

"Anyway, Mama says they have about ten attorneys preparing a statement of dissolution. I asked her what they were stating for Cause for Dissolution. She wasn't real certain. She thought perhaps it was not bringing the case for a constitution to trial."

I felt the hair standing on my head, and my eyebrows creeping upward. I wanted to punch the air and shout, "Yes! Oh thank you, God, yes!"

"She said they had a judge in Sylvania Province. She thought they might have family judges all over the country, who will rule in their favor. She asked if you want her to get a list of the judges."

Mr. Farley made the decision. "I don't want your mama to do anything illegal, or anything that would place her in danger. The list of proposed judges would be very helpful. Because the protocol for this type of civil suit is obscure, they may not know who needs to be informed of their suit and the involvement of the court in their actions."

Our student continued, "Mama said that they planned to use the same procedure that the constitutional conspirators used and present their case to the judges for a ruling without informing anybody else."

Andrew mouthed, "You conspirator you," at me.

I looked at my supervisor. He nodded so I explained the delicacies of the case. I rubbed my hands over my face and tried to pull my eyebrows back into position from where they flew a few moments earlier. "I will explain why the two cases are not the same. One, we had a basis in case law." I went on to explain the Fortenac case. "Two, the prosecutors presented the case after years of collecting cases substantiating that the Fortunac case was not unique in disclosing the true nature of our demographic make up. We had case law backing up the petition. Three, when the prosecutors took the case to court we became the entity responsible for constitutional questions, because we were representatives of the government."

I looked at the student's faces. They didn't get it. "Um...let me say this again. When we went to court to adopt the constitution we were part of the existing government. We were official officers of the court presenting a matter of procedural law to the court. We do this all the time. Um...Professor Ingleman has lectured on this in Procedural Law."

"How is the case that the coalition is presenting any different?"

"Part of our research will be to see if they have a body of case law to back up their position. They are not representatives of the existing government unless they have all the prosecutors' offices in the country presenting the case in their district. In which case one of our attorneys is hiding something from the rest of us." I looked at the others severely.

An intern squeaked.

"Jake you are frightening the children. Nobody in this office would go behind the backs of their office mates to do such a thing." Alexander glanced at Sofia. "Sofia would kill them."

We all smiled happily at Sofia.

I wasn't certain my students understood the legalities. "As far as we know this coalition consists of a group of citizens who have hired a bunch of attorneys to present a civil case. They are not representatives of the government. They are not representatives of the court. They can file a civil suit, but they must inform the defendant, in this case the prosecutor's offices who act as attorneys for the state. Their actions in filing a civil suit are legal as long as they name a defendant and give forty-five days notice."

"Who was the defendant when you filed the original case?"

"It wasn't a civil case. It was a procedural case. If it had been a civil case, the prosecutor's office would still be the defendant, because we had been prosecuting assuming a false set of demographics."

A third year intern spoke up. "So the constitutional conspiracy could do what they did, but someone else cannot."

Andrew was listening to this and broke out laughing.

I had to smile. "I don't know where you get the term constitutional conspiracy. It was one of thousands of court rulings on procedural law."

The student sounded belligerent. "I still think you are talking smoke and mirrors."

A couple students gasped at hearing another student talk to me this way.

I tried to be patient and reasonable. "You think that, because I am not explaining the case correctly. Discuss this with Professor Ingleman. He can explain it better than I can."

Andrew snorted again. "Let me put it this way. The prosecutor's office can do things other citizens cannot because they are part of the government. This is true for every prosecutor in the country. I suspect it is true for most positions of prosecutors around the world. The case calling for a constitution was done within the strict confines of the law. A civil case presented with the prosecutor's office as defendant is perfectly legal. This is reality. Get used to it."

"You're not an attorney. How do you know this?"

"Oh me?" Andrew grinned. "I was in on the whole conspiracy from start to finish. I helped write the new constitution."

The belligerent student asked, "Are you some sort of spy?"

Mr. Farley scowled and interrupted the discussion. "Students are in this office to learn. Several people have tried to describe the legal complexities of this case. If you cannot, or will not, understand the case, I will excuse you to work on our other cases, or you can request a change of internship."

The students and junior attorney's cringed. I wondered if it was because of their supervisor's words or Sofia's scowl.

Mr. Farley followed through on his threat that anyone unwilling to learn on the suit against the court would be excused from working on it. He sent the skeptical young man who didn't want anything to do with a constitutional conspiracy, to work processing repeat offenders. He wasn't happy about that either.

The student from the Sunday meeting at Professor Ingleman's, Ruben S'TO, came to see me after class the next day. I smiled, happy to see him. "I hope you are feeling better?"

"Yeah, I couldn't believe that all of you could sit around and talk so casually about all of this."

"Come with me, and I will show you how casual we are. We have confirmed the rumor. I think by now the coalition filing the suit knows we know what they are doing." I finished bringing him up to date on what had happened.

"Wow, you worked fast."

"Most of what we did was making a few phone calls. The prosecutors' offices often work together on cases. I had a serial murder case a while back where we combined cases from six provinces from here to the eastern border and north to the mountains."

Ruben sounded hesitant when he asked a question. "I am only a second year student, so I can't be an intern. Professor Ingleman said he would give me class credit if I worked on this case with you."

"Does he intend for you to work in the prosecutor's office after graduation?"

"No, he wants me to learn constitutional law. I think he wants me in the legislature or as a judge."

"Why doesn't he have you working on writing a new constitution?"

"He has some students working on that. I will be attending some of their meetings. He specifically wanted me to work with you."

"I'll be happy to have you. Well everyone in the office will be happy. We enjoy our role as teachers. It keeps us sharp. I will check with Professor Ingleman to see how many credits he wants to rate this and what jobs he expects you to do. I will be careful that you don't end up pleading the case."

Poor Ruben laughed as if this was impossible.

"Check in with the two junior prosecutors. They were the ones who actually plead the Vanderholm case when they were interns." I grinned evilly at poor Ruben.

By the time I outlined where we were, it was time for our daily staff meeting on this case. I introduced Ruben. "He is working on this case for class credit."

Mr. Farley took over the meeting. "Welcome aboard son. Right now we are doing mostly research. We are looking at the constitution from several angles to determine how someone might attack it, and what changes this office would like to see, like limiting the ability of the president to issue blanket pardons for everyone in prison."

Our intern whose mother was interested in the case started with his report first. "My mom sent me pages of information." He passed around packets of paper-clipped information.

I noticed the list of judges first.

Our student sounded nervous. "Um…uh…please keep your source confidential. I…um…I…I'm afraid the rest of this stuff is…well…this might be…um…their case."

"Holy crap!" Alexander was learning how the practice of law in this office expanded one's vocabulary.

Sofia sounded prim. "We have students present. Watch your…Oh My God!" Sofia realized the same thing that was dawning on us. Our student's mother had gotten us copies of the case as far as it went.

Mr. Farley pounced on top of the situation. "Okay, we need someone to fax this to all the other prosecutor's offices, now. I want them to have this before five tonight. Someone else get on the phone to those offices and tell them what is coming in."

Antoine snarled. "Jake stop that! You are making us nervous."

"What was I doing?"

"Humming."

"Singing."

"Rubbing you hands together."

"Chortling."

The staff was playing a game of naming all my happy little behaviors.

I explained. "They are presenting this in the form of a civil suit, which is good. That will save us a great deal of trouble. I have no idea how they could possibly document some of these charges. This case may boil down to nothing more than hearsay and opinion. Okay on charge number three, they make several statements about laborers. Lets take each statement and depose as many people as we can on each point." I thought for a minute. "You know those people who were in here the other day may help us find laborers who… lets see…," I looked at the list. "…people who are laborers who can read and write, appear to be clean, are active in charitable work, that should be easy. Well you get the idea. If they come up with a dozen depositions from people who fit their description, we will come up with fifty of people who don't."

I noticed the others looking behind me moments before Mary Anne slid her small hands around my arm. I turned and looked at my children. My mind recognized that I wasn't surprised to see my children in my office when their mother promised to drive them today. "Put your things in my office."

Jacob recognized that I was busy. "We took a taxi. Mama told us to come here after lessons."

I nodded and smiled. "That's fine son. Thank you for remembering the rule about taking a taxi."

I was angry but I didn't want my children and co-workers to know. The interruption made me forget my line of thinking.

One of the second year interns had the floor. "I see exactly what they are thinking. This is exactly how my family talks. Point two is exactly what they say, that a small group of individuals got together and wrote our current constitution."

I netted in my attention to think about the case. "That is what happened somewhat. After the courts called for an election to adopt a constitution. Nobody else brought anything forward so a group of law professors from both universities wrote the constitution we have now. I saw it and didn't like it from the beginning."

Mr. Farley pounced on this information. "Good Jake. That is excellent information. Were you working here when you saw this?"

"I smiled. I was working here."

Sofia almost bounced up and down. "University Professors receive their money from which government? Central or Provincial?"

I knew the answer, but let one of the junior attorneys answer. My children had left their bags and sweaters in my office. Mary Anne and Elizabeth wanted to sit in my lap. I pulled them into my arms and settled them in my lap. Jacob hung over the back of the chair while the conversation continued.

"Okay, we will need depositions from everybody who worked on the constitution stating that they were employed by an agency representing the government."

"Jake do you know all of those people?"

"No, but Professor Ingleman knows all of them. I will set up an appointment with Professor Ingleman."

Sofia summarized the situation. "Okay, we've got points two and three covered. What about point one? It is just so much gibberish to me."

We sat quiet for a moment while we reread point one.

Yuri snarled, "He's doing it again."

Mr. Farley asked, "Jake what are you seeing out of this?"

"Well we have to assume this is a draft. They started writing point one as a point of procedural law. I think somewhere around line twelve they changed it to be a civil case. They didn't do a very good rewrite. I assume this will be much nicer when they get to court. We can also assume they know that we are aware of their activities. Remember this is just a draft."

An intern raised his hand. "But, what does it mean."

"It means, they are having the same problems some of you have had in understanding the difference between a case of procedural law, and who can bring it before a court, and a case of civil law which any attorney can bring to court." I paused. "What that means for this office is that we can turn their muddle whichever way we want."

Another student commented, "I think that one area where we will have problems is the…uh…difference…of…of perspective…uh…between…um…like…um this office and…um the…uh parties presenting this."

Sofia's voice was way more severe than I'd ever heard her use with a student before. "It looks like we are fighting the same battle over, and over, and over. The Fortenac case should have sunk that damned southern bigotry into the deepest ocean. Still they keep coming up with this crap."

"Yes Dear." The supervisor's placating tone and use of an endearment in the office surprised all the students and too many of the staff. The staff should be more observant. "Sofia is getting under the scales of this case. In many ways it is the Fortenac case all over."

I tried for a bored tone. "Let's hope they are getting better at building a case. This looks promising. You have no idea how frustrating it is to do a ton of work and then end up prosecuting a case where the defendant says they are innocent because they say so. It gets…um…boring." Since I was holding my daughters on my lap, I refrained from swearing.

The clerks and paralegals came back to say that they had called all the other offices and Faxed off the material.

I looked at the clock. "It is almost five. We better clear the office. Listen, why don't we pick up some Chinese food and meet at my place to go over this. All the students who need to be home are free to leave. You can come to my place if you would like."

Chapter 32 Ruben

W e adjourned the meeting, and I went to my office. First, I called Professor Ingleman and invited him out to the house. Next, I called my housekeeper and told her my plan.

My housekeeper sounded ill. "Oh Mr. Jake that is good that you don't need me to cook. I think I have the influenza and just want to stay in my bed. I'll tell the missus when she gets here." We hung up.

I called the Chinese restaurant run by the family I'd known for years. The young girls from the laundry were mothers with a houseful of children running them ragged, now. I always enjoyed visiting with them. I ordered the dinner and got off of the phone.

Ruben stood in the doorway with his mouth open.

I looked at him and raised my eyebrows.

"Sir, do you speak Chinese well enough to order a dinner?"

My children giggled. Jacob explained, "Papa speaks Chinese as well as any of the Chinese people. I've learned a little in my martial arts class." My children passed a few bathroom jokes back and forth in Chinese as we headed out the door.

Of course, I had the Miki with me today. Getting the three children in the car was difficult. The girls sat on pillows on the floor behind the seat. By the time we added enough Chinese food for twenty people to the load of children and books, the Miki was completely full.

Marianne had gotten home in time to learn that I was bringing home my office mates and dinner. She'd already made Mr. Farley, Sofia, Yuri, and Antoine comfortable.

Ruben arrived with the other students. I thought the number of students looked suspiciously large. Some of the extras explained, "Professor Ingleman told us to tell you that he is getting more Chinese food and will be here shortly."

Leah had not gotten home yet, so Marianne did the hostess duties and served a light snack while we got ourselves organized. Ruben displayed pleasing manners in helping her. I learned they shared some classes.

The evening meeting went well enough. I refrained from discussing our options for changing the constitution through this. I wasn't exactly certain how I would get this done.

I found the help of the students who had grown up with the southern bigotry very helpful. I tried to explain. "I admit that I have lived in this city all my life. I've mixed with people from all backgrounds. I cannot see the southern perspective."

A young Gannon student sounded confused. "Surely you don't spend much time with the lowest orders!"

All the prosecutors laughed. Yuri explained. "I grew up in the south, so I know what you mean. We are prosecutors. Um…how do I put this? Uh… well first of all, we spend most of our day with the lowest orders as you call them."

"Why?"

Yuri smiled. "Because, they get into trouble and end up in our office. Working in the prosecutor's office, I've learned that most of our repeat offenders share a basic humanity with all of us."

A Spencer student sounded horrified by Yuri's statement. "Surely not!"

Antoine took over. "I remember when I first came to work as an intern. The offenders all wanted to get Jake as their prosecutor. I discovered that part of the reason was that Jake's papa is a big hero in this city."

My children were sitting behind my chair pretending to read books. I heard Jacob whisper to his sisters. "I didn't know that Grandpapa was someone special."

I turned to look at my children. "Someday soon, remind me, and I'll tell you stories about Grandpapa." I smiled at my children.

Antoine continued to make his point. "Well, at first I though it was because Jake would let them off with a scolding. Then I heard him scold somebody. That wasn't the reason they wanted to have him for their prosecutor. I watched. He was as tough as anybody or perhaps worse about handing out fines. He also smiled at people. He treated them with respect. He expected them to do better than they did. Those people needed to be treated with respect, perhaps more than college students do."

"So?"

"So what I am saying is that when I watched Jake, I discovered that even our repeat offenders, have lives and family. They have loved and still love the families they lost. They frequently behave with more honor than I witnessed in my own home and community."

He cleared his throat and went on. "The lowest of the low almost always know the difference between right and wrong. When I was an intern, I ended up pleading the Vanderholm case. I was so scared all I could do was focus on the papers in the case. When I recovered enough to think about what happened, I realized that the crimes Vanderholm committed were hideous, far worse than our repeat offenders. Vanderholm showed no sense of right and wrong. I cannot place anyone like him on a level with the drunks I process. The drunks are far more respectable."

"Yes, but shouldn't the rules be different for people who have more understanding?"

My response came out as more of a reflex than thought. "In a sense, yes." I noticed surprise in some eyes, triumph in others, and wry understanding among those who knew me.

I continued. "Yes, people with education should be expected to act in a manner that shows education. People who grew up with privilege should act with more generosity. People who grew up with in a position of power should behave with more responsibility. Part of the problem that I faced in both the Vanderholm and Fortenac cases was that the accused recognized their superiority in education and position and believed they could behave with less responsibility."

Sofia continued. "It wasn't just the crimes that Fortenac committed against my family that mark him as not worthy of our respect. He was given a successful business to run. He destroyed the business. It went bankrupt leaving three villages of people without jobs and the rest of the country without food. He committed other crimes against his neighbors. His problem was that he had been brought up to think any behavior was acceptable just because he was born to wealth and privilege."

Ruben was sitting and watching the debate with keen interest and a smile on his face. I asked for his opinion.

"This is fascinating. I was brought up in the countryside outside the capital. Like Prosecutor Jaconovich, I associated with all sorts of people. I find the idea that wealth and rank mean that you can do whatever you want very strange. I would have gotten in so much trouble for treating Papa's employees with disrespect! I find this struggle from a minority of people trying to maintain a position that is basically a lie, interesting."

He looked at the other students and tried to explain another way. "When I was little, I sometimes played with the neighbor boys who lived about a kilometer from us. The family had two boys. The youngest was a little simple in some ways. One summer, when the younger boy must have been about eight, he decided fairies lived under the roots of a big, old, willow tree behind the barn. He decided he wanted to find the fairies, so he started digging under the tree. His father told him there were no such things as fairies under that tree. He didn't believe his papa. His brother and I teased him and told him there were no fairies under the tree. His papa punished him for digging at the roots of the tree and made him fill in his holes. His mama hugged him and told him fairies would not live under that tree, because it was too close to the barn. He didn't believe her either. He would sneak out to the tree and dig every chance he got. His father made him fill in his holes, but he would sneak out and dig them out again."

The room grew totally quiet while we listened to Ruben tell his story. "Well instead of believing what everybody told him, the boy continued to worry at the roots of the tree. He got sneaky, and covered his holes with boards, and covered those with leaves so his father wouldn't see where he dug. He managed to crawl through some brush and piles of old wire to the side of the tree by the barn. He opened up a big old hole on that side. He kept at this all summer and into the fall. He smirked at us and told us the fairies were going to give him gold. We told him fairies would cast a spell on him so that he couldn't talk if he found their home."

Ruben took a drink and continued his story. "Finally the rainy season came. I was busy with school and forgot about the neighbor boy and his obsession with digging up fairies. One night at dinner, Papa shook his head and told us that the neighbor had suffered big losses in the wind the other night. That old willow behind the barn had fallen on the barn. The neighbor had put four pregnant cows in the barn to keep them safe. The only surviving cow had miscarried. This was a huge financial disaster for the family. They had to lay off four of the people who worked for them." Ruben paused and pulled on his lower lip. "It seems to me the southern families are like that simple-minded boy. They are convinced of a fairy tale, and they destroy everything thing around them pursuing that fairy tale."

"Is it really a fairy tale?" Our Gannon student asked.

Professor Ingleman answered, "Yes. That is all it is, a fairy tale."

Sofia explained. "The reason we needed the constitution we have is to keep this country from descending into civil war based on that fairy tale."

I grumbled. "The reason we need a better constitution is to get that damned fairy tale out of government all together, to keep it from destroying the country."

I heard my children gasp over my profanity. I looked around the edge of my chair at them. Then, I looked at the clock. It was past their bedtime.

Jacob said, "Yes, Papa." He and the girls went off upstairs. The cats followed them making the students laugh at the trail of children and kitties.

When I looked back to the group of students, I noticed Cousin Marianne looking at Ruben like a D'NO woman who has just made up her mind.

The students stayed until ten. By the time we decided to punch our pillows for the night. I had a better understanding of how the southern coalition might make their case. The tricky part would be in supplying evidence from a procedural case to a civil case. We would have to think about the best way to present our case.

Leah didn't come home for four days. When she did get home, she was reluctant to tell me where she had been and what she had been doing. I finally asked her point blank where she had been. She screeched at me. "It is none of your business where I go, or what I do. I don't ask you about every little thing you do."

"Well, you could take a little more interest in what I do. That is not the point now. The point is that I am your husband. It is my duty to see that you are safe. It is my right to know where my wife is. Good God Leah! Anything could happen to you, and I wouldn't know where to start looking for you." I was angry and heard my voice starting to get louder. I didn't want my children to hear us arguing. I hurt everyway imaginable over Leah's behavior. Most of all, I hurt because my precious children did not have the security of having a mother who loved their father.

I hissed my next statement to her. "Leah, I am your husband. I can make the rules for this household. If you want to leave without telling me, fine. But, you cannot take the Mercedes and go cruising around the country acting like a fine rich woman when you've left your family to crowd into the Miki. You can take the train."

Leah gasped and paled at the news that she couldn't take the big car.

I was so hurt and angry I couldn't look at her anymore. I went to my study and slept on the sofa. The next morning Leah tried to make peace. I tried to be amiable in front of the children. She offered to take them to school. I took the big car and my children and left for work.

The prosecutor's office was busy trying to second-guess a case we may never get. We still had our petty offenders to process. One morning I arrived at the office to find a line of people waiting to get in. As soon as I got out of the car, someone explained. "Mr. Jaconovich, we've come to see what we can do about this case on the constitution."

I decided I should listen to their concerns. "Well come on into the conference room and get comfortable." When we were settled, I asked, "What concerns do you have that brought you here?"

"We're concerned that they'll take away our constitution."

I though about this before I spoke. "Okay, if you want to help this case, tell me why you think the constitution is important."

As other staff arrived, they joined us in the conference room.

I indicated that the man on my left should start the discussion. "Well I think the constitution is important because we have a representative in the capital making sure that the rich people don't make laws that hurt us common folk."

"Good, next."

"I was impressed when we could get a new mayor who isn't such a big crook, not that our first Mrs. Mayer didn't catch a full net as mayor. Too bad she bailed her worthless husband out of jail."

Mr. Farley arrived and sat down to take notes.

"I think the constitution is important because you can take a man like Vanderholm to court and make him pay for his crimes."

I snorted. "I suspect that is exactly why Vanderholm wants to get rid of the constitution."

"Can he do that?"

I debated the best answer.

Mr. Farley spoke up. "No. We don't know what kind of havoc they intend to create. They cannot legally overturn the court mandate for a constitution."

The next person voiced her opinion. "I know times are still hard and many people don't have jobs, but things are changing. I see more children in school. I see the streets are clean. I see things are getting fixed. That is because everybody even the rich are made to pay their taxes. That wouldn't happen without the constitution."

I smiled. "Very good. You're right. The Letters of Federation didn't give the courts the power to enforce payment of taxes."

From the twenty people gathered at the table, we got at least a dozen talking points and four perspectives for addressing the case. I felt better about how we could document our position.

Some people remembered that I had asked for suggestions about what people wanted to see in a new constitution. Occasionally someone would stop by the office with a couple pages of their ideas written out. Some of the ideas were excellent and eventually were incorporated into the new constitution.

Chapter 33 Constitutional Trial

At home, Leah acted very sweet and contrite. She apologized for upsetting me and explained somewhat. "Jake, it isn't that I want to keep secrets. It is just that I…I…well…you know I don't like talking about my past. Jake you can never know how much…I didn't grow up with loving parents. Mama was a drunk. I…I…I was thankful when Papa died. I…I did have friends. I just don't want to talk about it. I am away from that." Leah looked at the floor. "I…um…I had a friend. Um…her husband… well he's gone…um she got in trouble with another man. Jake I really don't want to tell you this. I promised not to tell anybody."

"You don't have to tell me names, but your behavior hurt me deeply. I was worried about you."

"I know. I don't know why…Jake, I don't want for you to know how… how poor we were. I don't want to talk about it—those people. Anyway, she needed help. I knew I could help, but…I…I can't talk about it."

I held out my arms to her. "Come here." I pulled her up close to me. She didn't turn soft. She stood there stiff. "Leah, the thing I want most in this world is for us to love each other—to have a good marriage."

"Jake I want that too. Honestly I do. I think I am not so good at knowing how to love."

After that, we got along much better. She was still unresponsive to me physically, but she didn't run off again.

We finally got the official notice of the suit. Well, we got the notice of the suit after they delivered it to a judge who notified us, and we notified all the prosecutors in the country. They didn't present the case to the other courts, just to the Sylvania provincial court. Leroy our former prosecutor who now headed that office learned of the case from us.

We had forty-five days to get a case together on a chaotic suit. Because all the prosecutors' offices had been involved in the procedural case we wanted them involved in this case.

We had one delicate situation with the Sylvania office. Mr. Farley called and asked Leroy, "The case is in your province do you want to present the defense? What help do you want from us."

He answered, "I want Jaconovich to come down here and make my life hell drilling me on every piece of paper in the case." Mr. Farley was still chuckling when he related this answer to the rest of us.

We held meetings with all the head prosecutors in the country at our office. We finally cobbled together a case. We had depositions from over a hundred-fifty laborers testifying that they were educated, had responsible jobs and served their community in the church or though volunteering in hospitals and at civil service positions. We had the documentation for the adoption of the constitution. We had kilograms of case law. The coalition hadn't presented much documentation. They didn't have to. They owned the judge.

I wanted to go down to Sylvania about five days before the court date. Leroy sounded anxious. "Jake, I mean it, I want you to drill me on each piece of paper."

I told Leah when I was leaving. "We can leave the children with Cousin Marianne, and you can come with me. You can have a vacation and visit with Isolde while I am working."

Leah looked away from me. "I don't want to leave my projects just now. I will stay here and take care of the house and children. You don't need any distractions from your work just now. Do you think you can win this case?"

"No, as far as I can see, we'll get a mistrial. The coalition owns the judge."

"A mistrial is okay isn't it?"

"Nothing will change." I smiled at Leah thankful for her interest in my work. "I'd hoped we could use this to force the adoption of a better constitution. They've blocked us on that point as far as I can see now. Please won't you come with me? The poor can take care of themselves for five days, and Cousin Marianne is so good with the children."

"Jake, don't beg. It's unbecoming."

I kissed my children goodbye before I left on the southbound train. About half of the people from my office were on the train. Christian came from the office in the capital. Margaret and Lars surprised me by traveling so far for this case.

I gave them each a hug. "Oh it is good to see you two. Lars, congratulations on completing your dissertation. When do we get to call you Doctor M'TG?"

"I don't graduate until the end of the next term. My family already refers to me as Doctor Lars. I think papa knows more about my dissertation than I do. Oh! And I should warn you, Grandpapa is fond of commenting that none of John D'NO's children have doctorates."

I snorted. "Good, I'm glad he is proud of you."

Leroy met us at the train with hugs and servants to help with the luggage. We spent most of the next four days in the hotel room going over the case.

Leroy admitted. "I don't dare mention this around my parents. They… um…disagree with the position of the court and think things ought to go back the way they were."

Leroy had taken the precaution of naming about half of us as prosecutors of record. "The judge wasn't happy about it. I reminded him that the last time a prosecutor went up against a Vanderholm, he ordered the prosecutor shot. I admitted that I was naming everybody else as insurance against getting shot."

I looked at Leroy. "Shit."

I picked up the phone and called General Johan and explained the situation. He sent us a nice collection of special-forces troops to guard us. Colonel Paul came along too. I appreciated having his bulky body guarding my back.

When we finally got to court, we had a strategy. Leroy asked me to plead the case. "That will keep me out of trouble with my parents." He chuckled. "It will also make the plaintiff a little crazy. Their biggest fear is that you would plead the case."

"Leroy, you are as capable as I am."

"As capable? Yes." He paused. "I don't think as fast on my feet. I don't have your imagination for dancing out of a corner."

We went to court. The courtroom featured ornate marble and a painted domed ceiling. I detected naked cherubs flitting around the dome. I rather admired the elegant, plush, red velvet chairs the attorneys got to sit in. About three-dozen attorneys took our places on the defendant side of the room.

The judge seemed dismayed at the number of people in the room and questioned, "Why does the defense find it necessary to fill the courtroom with spectators?"

Leroy made the preliminary statements. "The civil suit questioned a case of procedural law presented by all the prosecutor's offices, which brings up a point, your honor. Some of the other attorneys may be speaking as persons of interest to the case. We couldn't all fit in the attorney's box so you will be hearing from people behind the rail if necessary. Everybody who has agreed to speak is a fully licensed attorney."

The case began. The judge asked for motions from the defense. It felt strange to me to be sitting on the judge's left. I stood and introduced myself. I greeted the judge and other attorney's cordially. "Now I have beside me Professor Ingleman, a fully licensed attorney and professor of procedural law. I wish to use him as a consultant if we run into complexities. This case is going to be tricky because it is a civil suit questioning a case of procedural law."

Judge Neuton snarled, "I don't see what difference that makes."

"Of course not sir. I was trying to emphasize that because of the complexities involved I intend to be extremely detailed and correct on every point. This brings up my first motion. I move to reposition all the plaintiff's depositions for points two, three, five, eight and ten."

"Is this acceptable to the plaintiff?"

A Fortenac growled from the plaintiff's side, "No. Nothing that man says is acceptable to the plaintiff. Leave the depositions where they are."

"Defense?"

I disciplined the most respectful tone I could manage into my voice. "The depositions are presented without backup documentation. They consist of opinion and hearsay. Because of the importance of the men making those statements I am reluctant to expunge. Failure to move them will result in a mistrial."

The judge sighed, "Where do you want to move them to?"

"Point fourteen just after page three will be acceptable."

"**Let the record show** that the plaintiff's depositions for points two, three, five, eight, and ten will be placed under point fourteen after page three." The judge moved the papers in his folder. "Are there any other motions?"

"Yes, on point one." I paused and looked at Professor Ingleman. I ran my hand over my face. "Point one is problematic. I move to expunge point one. It is unclear, indirect, and violates Procedural Code, Chapter One Section Two, Paragraph Twelve which states…" I picked up the book to read.

The judge snapped at me. "That won't be necessary. Defense is this acceptable?"

"No it is not."

The judge turned back to me.

I looked down at the book in my hand and read, "Failure to comply with the rules describing proper presentation of a plea will result in a mistrial."

The judge glared at me.

I stood firm, looked at the judge and kept my mouth shut.

The attorneys for the plaintiff were making noises. Finally Mr. Fortenac stood. "As the defense has stated this is a complicated case based on a basic disagreement about the events that led to this complaint."

The judge looked at me.

I stated, "The issue the attorney for the plaintiff has mentioned in point one is dealt with properly under point six. We have placed our documentation there."

The judge looked back at the other side of the room. "Is it acceptable to deal with point one as addressed properly under point six?"

Fortenac sneered, "What happens if I say no?"

I will still have to uphold the motion to expunge, or they will call for a mistrial, and I could lose my license. Do you have any point of law that will require us to keep point one as stated rather than dealing with the topic under point six."

The Fortenac attorney shrugged. "I guess."

The judge looked at him.

"Well if you put it that way, you may expunge."

A murmur of shock went through our side of the room at the insolent tone used when addressing a judge in a courtroom.

I'd known from the beginning that the judge was biased. I also knew we were putting him in a position between a mountain and the sea. I expected him to make a move that would result in a mistrial at any moment.

We continued with the case. I moved to expunge two pieces of documentation from point eleven. The judge looked at the plaintiff.

Fortenac barked. "No. Those are receipts of actual transactions they are neither opinion nor hearsay."

The judge looked at me.

"I agree that the documents are neither opinion nor hearsay. However, they are illegible. Neither document carries a date. They could be ten years old for all the court knows."

A Vanderholm attorney yelled across the courtroom, "Are you calling us liars?"

My stomach knotted at his tone. "Your honor will you read out the dates on your copy?"

The judge looked at the two receipts then turned to the court recorder.

"**Let the record show** that the two receipts under point eleven shall be expunged." The judge refused to look up.

I made two more motions to expunge. The judge upheld both of them. He had to or face mistrial. The case was almost to the point I wanted.

The defense attorney stood to make his motions. He moved to expunge all the depositions taken from laborers. The judge looked at me.

I tried to sound humble. "That is unacceptable the depositions are neither opinion nor hearsay. Point eleven describes laborers as lazy, uneducated, selfish, and filthy. Everyone of those depositions addresses exactly those issues for laborers from all over this country."

"Motion denied." The poor judge again refused to look up.

The case continued. I was aware of the attorneys on every side of me keeping track of our place and frantically researching everything the opposition said.

I spent probably twenty minutes refuting their motions on point six. I read from procedural case law and repeated the word *mistrial*.

The case moved slowly toward my goal. Now came the time to clarify. I remembered my breathing exercises from my lessons at Wu's. Now was the time to dance this case to where I wanted it.

My knees felt week. I sensed the attorney's around me barely daring to breathe. I spoke. "I would like to clarify some points. First, the plaintiff has no documentation for points two, three, five, eight, and ten. The defense has furnished documentation showing the points to be false. As a point of clarification, I want those points restated from our perspective. Point two shall read: A constitution is a necessary document for ruling this country." I heard the outcries from the other side of the room. "Point three shall read: Procedures for determining eligible voters were conducted in a legal manner." I heard someone slam something down and walk out of the room. I didn't look. "Point five shall read: Labors participate in the charitable functions of our society. Point eight shall read:"

Fortenac stood along with Vanderholm, and an attorney I didn't recognize. "Your honor. We get his point. Can't you do something about this? Our case is flawless."

I stopped. My heart pounded. The judge had the choice to stand up to his family and continue hearing the case. He could dismiss the case. He did the thing I least wanted him to do.

"Gentlemen!" The judge sweated and looked at the plaintiffs then turned to our side of the room. "Professor Ingleman, is it not within my powers to state that I have come to a verdict on this case?"

Professor Ingleman stood. "It is within your powers to so state."

Judge Neuton pronounced, "As the defense has stated, it is a complicated case. Both sides have presented well-reasoned evidence.

"**Let the record show** that the court has reached a verdict."

"**Let the record show** that full procedures have been suspended in favor of both parties."

My heart sank.

"**Let the record show** that this court upholds the decisions of the provincial courts in calling for an election to adopt a constitution."

"**Let the record show** that this court decides in favor of the plaintiff that the voters were not offered options in accepting a constitution."

"**Let the record show** that this court orders all parties concerned with this case to offer to the registered voters of this country the choice of two or more constitutions in an election to be held no later than ninety-days from now."

"Court is dismissed."

The judge left the room without speaking to anybody.

I sat shaken and stunned.

Professor Ingleman chuckled beside me. "Jake you won the lawsuit. They didn't throw out our constitution."

"Yes, but we will have to take our new constitution to the voters. They could win with a return to the old system."

"Jake, you came damned close to getting what you wanted right here. We can appeal with another judge and possibly get a ruling in our favor. I think right now, our best bet is to get that list of registered voters and start telling them the benefits of our plan. I really don't think that many people will want to go back to the way things used to be."

Everybody on the train ride home chatted happily about the result of the case so far. They debated the options if our constitution didn't get the votes we needed.

Mr. Farley pointed out, "The judge left the case wide open for an appeal."

Professor Ingleman sounded sanguine, "We have more people in the north than in the south. I think we will win."

Christian repeated vehemently at intervals. "They cannot undo the work of the case that required a constitution."

Alexander worried, "Do you think they will try to eliminate parliament?"

Jeffrey leaned back and clasped his hands behind his head, "I've thought about what would happen if this case came to this point. I think that the prosecutor's offices as the representatives of the government will need to write a booklet for the voters presenting both sides of the case. Both constitutions need to be made available to the public. We will put them in libraries and courthouses for anybody who chooses to read."

I heard murmurs around me. I looked out the window of the train into the gathering darkness and wondered what others found to laugh about. I made a plan to flee the country with my family. The Cove would be safe. We would go to The Cove.

Alexander poked me. "Jake, stop daydreaming and pay attention. Our supervisor has suggested we write a voter's booklet. You are good at these things. How do we manage to write the book so that our side looks way better?"

"Huh? Oh." I decided I better start paying attention if we were going to prevent disaster or civil war. "I think telling the absolute truth is always best. Do you really think the coalition will come up with something good for this country? We'll need to emphasize that one constitution was written by representatives of the government and professors of law from the university."

We continued to discuss strategy and timelines. Our first step would be to ask the prosecutors and judges to set a procedure for the voter's book and to set dates for when material needed to be turned in, and a deadline for getting the book out. We made excellent progress.

It saddened me a little when Margaret and Lars decided to stay on the train and continue home so she could get started on presenting our procedural case to the judge for a ruling.

I got off of the train at the dear M'TK station and went straight home. The stress of the day disoriented me. I expected to walk into a sleeping house. I got home ten minutes later than usual. My children came to greet me. They declared they missed me and wanted me to see their projects.

Cousin Marianne came running downstairs. "Jake, how did it go? You won of course. How did it go?"

"Well, I came within two or three motions of getting what I wanted. The judge saw what was about to happen and stopped the case, demanding an election to adopt a constitution. He set the date for ninety-days from now. We will hardly have time to get everything set up for an election. Andy will have to order the ballots from wherever he gets them. We have no idea what they will have on them yet."

Marianne hugged me. "I knew they couldn't defeat you."

I ran my hands through my hair. "I am afraid of the outcome of an election."

Jacob had listened to this conversation. "Will the courts have any recourse if the election goes wrong?"

"Theoretically, yes. I don't know how that will play out."

Elizabeth sounded very grown up. "Papa is there anything we can do to help you get the constitution that makes everybody equal?"

I stared stunned at Elizabeth's understanding of our government. I sat down and motioned for my children to climb into my chair. "Thank you for offering to help." My heart melted. My mind jumped to a new idea. I chuckled. "My precious children, there is something you can do to help."

I smiled and explained that we needed to write a book for voters. "Well, when a bunch of attorneys start writing they can be hard for regular folks to understand. I won't ask you to read the constitution, but would you mind terribly much reading what we say about the constitution and honestly tell me if we make sense? I might talk to your teachers about letting all your classmates help us this way."

Mary Anne wiggled with excitement.

Elizabeth hugged me. "Papa of course we can do that. If we can understand it, then regular people will be able to understand it."

Jacob looked shrewd. "Papa you said this book will have things written by the coalition in it too."

I nodded.

He grinned at me. "Papa I don't think we will have time to be reading what they say to see if it makes sense."

I grinned back at him and brushed his hair off of his forehead just like my mama used to do with me. "No, the coalition is responsible for making their own statements understandable."

I continued to talk to the children and Cousin Marianne. She thought, for several minutes then came up with a suggestion of her own. "You know Cousin

Jake, it would be a good idea for us university students to form a committee to discuss the constitution and educate voters on the best plan."

I think that falls under the category of your schooling is your career. You are in a position to influence people who are already registered to vote."

I stopped and pinched the bridge my nose. "It would be good if your committee could survey students to find our what they think are good ideas for us to put in a constitution. We have a finished constitution to present to the voters. We can change it easily now if we get some good ideas."

A few minutes before dinner was served, I ran upstairs to wash up. I hadn't asked where Leah was. I didn't want anybody else to have to tell me she had run out on her responsibilities again. I found her in bed in our darkened bedroom.

She whispered, "Jake is that you?"

"No it is Mr. Kim Liu come to steal your jewelry."

"Oh Jake don't be silly."

I sat on the bed beside Leah. "Do you have another headache Dearest?"

"Yes, and having you jiggle the bed doesn't help."

I stood up, and she moaned.

"Are you nauseated again?"

"Yes."

"What do you think triggered this?"

"Oh, three days for driving the children here and there."

"I made arrangements for them to take a taxi to their activities."

"I still had to drive them in the morning. Then I went back and picked the girls up from dance. I told Jacob to take the taxi to the M'TK station and take the trolley out here. I picked him up at the station. Do you have any idea how many times I had to take the car out just for that?"

"Yes, I know it must be hard especially if you were on the verge of one of these headaches." I spoke very soft so as not to make her head hurt worse.

"Do you want anything for dinner?"

"No."

"Was the doctor here to see you?"

"No. I forgot about calling him. I forget everything when this hits."

I washed up quickly and went down to call the doctor before dinner. By the time I sat down the others had been waiting for me for several minutes.

Chapter 34 Building a Better Future

When I went to work in the morning, I felt better about the election. I'd planned to spend the morning at Rouseff Industries. I met with Young Rouseff.

"Jake, I heard you stirred up a hornet's nest down south."

"I didn't do anything."

"I hear Vanderholm and friends lost a court case against you."

"They were suing the government. The local prosecutor could have pled the case, but he has to live among those people. He is a friend, so I agreed to plead the case. They were trying to overturn a procedural court ruling with a civil suit. I see I am boring you. They couldn't win."

"Uncle is chortling fit to soil himself. I hear you forced the court to say that laborers are educated, and do acts of charity, and what-all-else."

I chuckled. "Those people are getting better at presenting a case, but their damned arrogance gets in the way. So, people have heard about the case and are upset."

"I've gotten a number of phone calls from friends and family. They want to know if you really believe all that stuff about educated laborers. I've had to confess that you deposed a large number of my employees to prove your point. They're now quite disgusted with me."

"That is unjust. You are doing an excellent job for your family. They don't appreciate you enough."

"Thank you for the praise. Coming from you that is an honor."

Our conversation turned to business. I was a little concerned because he didn't have any ideas for expansions. I thought of my old friend and his dancing eyes, and his maps, and his head full of ideas. "Have you thought any more about a sports arena?"

"The numbers look good. I am not certain where we could put it. There is the flat area across the tracks from the M'TK station, but the city owns that."

"That is the old M'TK dump. I notice nothing grows there. It may still be poisoning the ground with methane and who knows what else. I shudder to think of how many human bodies are buried there."

"Surely not at the city dump!"

"I saw enough of them as a boy to know that the dump is the final resting place for a number of people."

"Jake, sometimes your stories horrify me. See, the problem with the arena is there is no place to put it."

"What about between here and Mercid? Or at the one of the interchanges?"

"At the interchanges, people could arrive by car rather than train. I thought to increase rail usage by placing it near a station."

"You could place it on the far side of the mall. I have no idea where to put the homeless people camping there, but that is not your problem."

After spending the morning and part of the afternoon at Rouseff, I went over to my office at the bank. I went over more papers there. Late in the day, I withdrew five hundred thousand dollars. I intended to put it in my safe at home in case we needed to flee the country.

The next day when I went to the prosecutor's office, I found more people lined up outside wanting to help us with our new constitution. I invited them into the conference room. About half of the staff busily processed the offenders who had been picked up the night before. I growled, annoyed that there seemed to be so many when we had important work to do.

I asked Mr. Farley to join me. When he was seated with his notebook, I opened the meeting by explaining where we were in the process of adopting a new constitution. "Now, I want you to tell me what we are going to put in the booklet we put out for the voters. What do you want to know about the constitution?"

It took almost three hours to listen to the people gathered around the table. More people came as the meeting progressed. Some people left after telling us what concerned them. Our legal staff started lumping the questions into themes and specific questions under those themes. By the time the meeting was over, the staff was looking happy.

Yuri gave the list of about twenty questions to a secretary to type up along with our answers. "I want that as soon as you can get it to me. We can FAX this to all the other prosecutors' offices with an explanation of where we got the questions. We can ask them what they have."

The list of questions went out right after lunch. Ruben arrived after his classes let out. "What do you want me to do sir?"

I handed him the list of questions we had. "Here, we got these questions from a group of people this morning. Look them over and see what you think. Um…did you have a chance to talk to Marianne about organizing the students this morning."

He blushed and nodded. "She has some students with notebooks out inventorying students about what they want in a constitution now. She is scheduling a meeting in the big lecture hall on Friday. She has asked Professor Ingleman to speak."

"Good. Help her out where she needs it. Can you discuss the constitution in your law classes?"

"We haven't talked about anything other than the lawsuit for days. I got a big laugh when some of the students sounded shocked that you came close to forcing the court to admit that laborers are equal to the ruling class."

I chuckled. "Actually, I'm still smarting over my failure to run that case to its logical end."

"That is another point that is being discussed. It looks to us as if you can appeal the case if the constitution you present fails. Some students argue hotly that you cannot appeal."

"The judge left the case wide open to appeal. We may manipulate that position to our advantage." I sighed. "The problem with this lawsuit as with everything else those folks have done is that it is based on a lie. They cannot find evidence to substantiate that lie."

I sent my student off to gather the questions the students asked about the new constitution.

When I got home, I discovered Leah had not picked up Jacob. I had time to run back to the city, so I went and got him to save on taxi fare. We got home just in time to get cleaned up for dinner.

After dinner, I went to my study for an hour and worked on wording the questions and answers so that my children could read and understand them.

Leah was listening to music and knitting when I came back with the questions for my children to proof read. I handed them the questions.

Jacob remembered something. "Oh yeah, I told the teacher about this, and she would like our class to help.

Mary Anne added her part. "I talked to my teacher, and she said I could make a report to our class about the constitution, but she didn't think the class could read well enough to help you."

Elizabeth looked guilty. "I forgot."

I smiled and hugged Elizabeth. "That's okay. We're not ready for our readers just yet. These questions were something a group of people came by the office to ask. I think they will go into the book."

Leah put down her knitting. "Jake, what in the name of Neptune, are you having the children do?"

"They wanted to help with the election for the constitution. We are putting out a book of information on both choices for the voters. Well, some voters do not read any better than our children, if they read as well. I want them to understand what the book says. The children are reading the stuff we will put in the book to see if they can understand it."

"Oh. Well I would like to help too. What can I do?"

"Thank you Darling. This is important. Can you invite a number of your friends and people on your committees over sometime very soon and ask them what they think is important to include in a new constitution. Write down what they say. Write down any questions they have."

Leah did have her lunch. The women had some good ideas. The former Mrs. Mayor took notes and brought them by my office. "Jake, some of these ideas are a bit silly. The importance of equal rights for women isn't silly. The child labor prohibition isn't silly."

"You are right. These are things we want in the new constitution. Just a minute while I look at those provisions." We went over the two most important measures. I made it a point that those would read as the women intended. We also included their request that domestic violence be treated as any other assault if the wife wanted to press charges.

I added the women's questions about the new constitution to our list of questions. Late in the day, I took the information from the women over to Professor Ingleman's committee. We discussed the wording for their questions and additions.

The union held a meeting to ask people what they wanted in a new constitution. We sent interns to write down what the people wanted and any questions they had.

Every prosecutor's office in the country held public meetings to discuss the new constitution. They asked people what they wanted in a constitution and what questions they wanted answered before they voted.

Margaret hand-carried a section for the new constitution down to our office. Her contribution regarded the integration of the northern provinces into the country. She'd found the original trade treaties in the courthouse. She wrote up a section affirming the citizenship of the northern provinces. I liked the way she subtly made everybody living in the northern provinces citizens. She also included a paragraph about acknowledging the trade treaties that the independent northern provinces made with other countries. She'd found the treaties and included them by name and title number. She'd done a fantastic job. We included the whole body of her work as she submitted it.

Early in the third week, we were able to send the coalition a list of questions the voters wanted answered about their proposal for a constitution. We sent them the procedural rulings mandating the booklet. We were ready to roll.

The coalition said they would hire someone to do the ballots. I protested. They said they didn't want the government cheating. Since they were the ones using the word *cheat*, I figured they hoped to do just that. I argued that the person who had done the job in the past had done a great deal of research, and worked with the United Nations.

Before I panicked and called the other prosecutors, I called Andy. I told him my whole story and worries about the elections.

"Jake, you worry too much. Let me do some research. You cannot believe how much fun I am having these days. I love taking Adele out to dinner, so I can catch pieces of conversations of the lazy, ruling families wringing their hands about this election. They are absolutely livid about the poor judge who wouldn't rule in the coalitions favor. These people cannot get it through their heads that there are other people in this world who are more capable, and educated, and cleaner than they are."

"Andy, yes I worry. How long do you think the coalition will allow me to live if their idea of a constitution passes?"

"Why would they blame you?"

"Because I won the Fortenac case that started this all. Leroy was afraid to plead this case, which is why I did it. They saw where I was going with it."

"Yes, they saw where you were going. Half of the people think it was a good trick and very funny. I'll admit the other half are horrified. You were just practicing law."

"Well the thing to do is win this election. I know I worry too much, but I don't trust anybody else to do technical end of the election."

"I'll talk to some people and find out what is happening."

I believed Andy could straighten out this mess. I'd been relying on Andy to straighten out my messes ever since college. I thought about him. He was smart and more than wealthy. He was a handsome man. Things just seemed to come easy for him. He could talk to a few people and solve the problem of keeping the election honest. I thought about his relationship with Adele. I reprimanded myself for being jealous of Andy because everything was easy for him. His marriage caused him great grief. I remembered my own marriage.

It didn't take me more than a few minutes to come out of my funk and start thinking about how to win this election. The election and its possible outcomes started taking up all my thoughts day and night. I started having nightmares of a new constitution that mandated a purge every eighteen years. I didn't sleep well for the next month. Even after the election, I had nightmares. Truthfully, I had them for years--until after Celia came to live with me.

The coalition sent us their material for the voters' booklet. When I saw it, I laughed and danced to Mr. Farley. "Look, this is what they sent us to put in the booklet." I grinned.

He grinned back before looking at the material I handed him. "Well it is good to see you looking animated. You've slunk around here pinched with worry." He flipped through the pages and snorted as he read several items. "I think I will call the coalition attorneys and go over each part of this with each of them."

"That is a big job. Just to cover our backs, why don't you have Christian call half of the attorneys to see if you both get the same response."

"Good idea. I think maybe I'll have Leroy call them and ask for a copy. He is closer to them. Maybe he can shed some light on whether or not they think this is adequate."

I shook my head. "I think they do. They think because they have done it, it is right."

The booklet came out with our presentation of our proposal. We included a picture of a potential sample ballot. The coalition explanation of their proposal was a tangled line compared to ours. The coalition had demanded to be placed first in the booklet.

We used a gray border on the coalition pages. We used a blue and gold border on ours. A women's group from the capital had wanted to put the colors of our new flag into our constitution. They wanted blue to represent the shipping and fishing industries, and gold to represent agriculture.

Our proposed constitution was a huge document. We included as many suggestions from the discussion groups as were reasonable to put in a constitution. Most of the suggestions were well thought out and presented in a plausible manner. We adapted sections from the US bill of rights that were applicable to our country. We had a section from the eastern province that, like Margaret's section, dealt with border issues. Unfortunately, we left many internal issues to a clause reading "established rule of the land." Water rights fell under this heading. We were forced to untangle that later, but the constitution allowed us to do so.

As soon as the booklets were finished, we mailed them to everybody on the voters list. This is where the people of the country came together to do the most amazing thing. The people in the city contacted their families in the country and told them that they would get full rights as citizens if this election went well. They all decided to buy blue sweaters and pin a gold ribbon on it in order to look official.

They got the list of registered voters from their local prosecutor. Thousands of people all over the country went out and knocked on the door of each registered voter.

They had a little speech. First, they asked if the voter had received their booklet. They carried extras with them in case the voter had not. They pointed out the two sections. They called the gray pages the coalition proposal and explained it was written by a group of attorneys. They showed them the court proposal and explained that government officials and officers of the court had written it. They pointed out the question and answer section. They pointed out several sections that had been included from citizen input. Most importantly they emphasized what it would be called on the ballot.

The coalition owned the media. The TV and newspapers advertised heavily for the voters to choose the only proposal written by the true government. They called it the only fair option. They had a couple judges talk about it as mandated by the court. I saw some of the ads. I wondered how we would ever get our point across.

I knew about the door-knocker campaign as the participants called it, I had no idea how many were going door to door and setting up booths on street corners. I also underestimated the power of the personal, helpful interview over the TV ads. I knew people in the office were speculating that people would think the TV ads were for our proposal because the coalition kept claiming their proposal was the one written by the true government.

Three weeks before the election, Andrew called me back. He was chuckling. "Well you can stop worrying about cheating. I found out who was doing the ballots and had a little chat with him. It was a Vanderholm/Jouyet brat. He intended to have the local printer make them up. I knew him to be a lazy sort so I explained that if we hold an election with homemade ballots the United Nations would invade to support the previous constitution. He didn't believe me. I told him whom to call. I knew he wouldn't research anything beyond the one call."

Andy had to stop and gasp for air he was laughing so hard. "Well you know I had been talking on the phone to this guy and communicating with him by e-mail. I'd told him our concerns about election fraud to force through a constitution to force a dictator on us. He was ready when the brat called. He threatened to send election inspectors down. He asked if the UN needed to send in troops to protect the polling places. He gave the brat the name of the same company I use to order ballots."

Andy paused so I grunted my approval.

"So I kept calling him asking if everything was okay. Did he need my help? Did he have any questions? He told me when the coalition approved the ballot design. I asked if he needed help with ordering. I gave him a phone number for the back-line and a name of someone to talk to. Well about two days ago, the company called me for my approval because I am the person on their records. I'd also alerted my contact there about the possibility of fraud. We talked about security and how to detect fake ballots. They told me how to download a new program for the voting computers, and we worked out a security code that would cause the computer to reject invalid ballots. I need help loading the program onto the computers in each district."

"Ah help. Ask at the local secondary school. Kids should get extra credit in computer class or civics for helping you."

The day before the election Andy called to verify that the ballots had arrived on time, and the machines were ready. The military was delivering everything to the polling places. "The coalition acted a little distressed that they couldn't open the boxes of ballots, and that they had been turned over to the military so quickly. Still they know the basic design, but not that the ballots contain security coding."

Chapter 35 Fleeing the Country

The night before the election, I told my family we were going for a vacation to The Cove as soon as we voted. I'd had a long hard talk with Micki, and he agreed to go to The Cove as soon as they voted. I would take the car and pick up my parents after they voted. I knew that if I couldn't catch up to the train, I could reach The Cove by driving straight through. I loaded our luggage in the car the night before.

Leah was suspicious. "Jake, what is the sudden trip to The Cove. I can't leave just now."

I was tired and terrified for my family. I snapped at my wife. "Well I need to get away. I've been working long hours on this constitution to make it the best it can be. I need a break. You run away every time you get a little stressed. Now, I am going, and you, and the children are coming with me." Perhaps I raised my voice to something more than snapping.

Leah turned meek, "Yes Jake. I was only asking."

"Well put your things in the car."

Early in the morning on election-day, I loaded my wife and children in the Mercedes. I fueled it at the train station. Leah and I arrived before the polls opened. Several people had come early. While we waited, I fidgeted and worried, and Leah chatted about some art project, and the possibility of establishing an art museum in the city.

Finally, I got my ballot. The right side had a grey and pale pink stripe down the margin. The right was for the coalition constitution. The left side had a blue and gold stripe down the side. I shook my head over Andy. I hoped the coalition never learned about the use of blue and gold in the campaign. The left side stood out.

I signed-in right after Leah. I decided a little last minute campaigning wouldn't hurt. I kissed Leah on the cheek. "Sweetheart thank you for helping write this." I indicated the left side. "I am proud of you."

I voted, then fed my ballot into the scanner.

I took the Mercedes to pick up my parents to vote. I'd called Papa about being prepared to come to The Cove with me. He hadn't wanted to make Mama travel. "Papa, I don't want to do anything to upset Mama either. Frankly, I am terrified. If we lose this election, you will not be safe in the city. I won't be safe in this country. I want all of us out of town before the results come in."

Papa sighed. "I am old and tired. Mama is sick. You are right. If the evil people have a chance at power, they will come after us. I will be ready. I'd go vote before you can get here, but Mama might need help."

I picked up my parents and their luggage at their apartment. Mama was quite animated. "I wanted to vote sooner, but Papa said I must wait for you. Jake I am so proud of you for doing this."

"Mama many people helped write this constitution, that is what makes it so good. Professor Ingleman and his friends deserve far more credit than I do. They have worked toward this constitution for over twenty years."

Mama turned dreamy. "So long."

They didn't have to wait to vote. They finished and came back to the car within minutes. We could catch the train. We'd arrive in The Cove before the polls closed. We were a little later than I liked, but the stationmaster knew Papa and me so he didn't grump at making the train wait a few minutes for my family to board.

When we arrived in The Cove, Mama started to weep. She talked about losing her parents. "I remember sitting in the upstairs window of the house. Nanna was with me. I saw Papa and Mama coming home. They were walking beside the street. I knew they were happy." Mama stopped as Papa wiped her nose and told her to blow. "A truck came. It made a loud noise. Papa and Mama fell down right there on the ground. They were all dressed up and lying in the dirt. They didn't get up and come home. Why don't they get up out of the dirt and come home?"

Papa knew the words to comfort her. "They were happy when they died. Neither of them knew the pain of losing the other, and now we are together."

I was too sick and worried about the election to eat.

My cousins tried to tease me out of my worry. "Jake this is ridiculous. You are more danger to yourself than any laws or elections. Now stop insulting the women by refusing their cooking."

I smiled and tried to eat. Mama patted my hand. "Don't worry son. You'll be president soon, and you'll set things right. You'll see."

I went to bed and pretended to sleep until about two AM. Finally, I got up and went downstairs to sit by the phone waiting for Andy to call. We'd insisted on having representatives of both sides present as the districts called their results in to the president's office. Andrew, Leroy, and Christian were present to represent the court.

Andy would call me at The Cove as soon as the results came in. If we lost, my family would be ten miles out to sea before anyone knew we were missing. I paced the floor and debated putting our luggage in the M'NO for a faster start. I tried to be rational and calm. I would leave Mama and Papa at The Cove. Mama acted uncomfortable at The Cove. I wondered if they could possibly be safe in their apartment. I worried about how Leah would take the need to flee.

I paced and decided Leah was right to be upset with me. My insistence on pursuing the law had placed our family in danger. I paced and wondered what I could have done differently.

About four, Micki came down to the sitting room. "Jake, sit down. You are making so much noise crashing around down here that you are likely to wake up the whole household."

I dropped to the sofa. I knew I was exhausted. "Micki, what could I have done differently? How could I have avoided reaching this point?"

"When your Papa called and asked me to bring the family up here after we voted...,"

I looked at Micki. "My papa called you?"

"Yes, he thinks we'll get the court approved constitution, but he said that you would worry yourself to death if you thought we were in danger."

"Uh...he's right." I sighed. "Thanks for coming. It is better to have you here."

Micki continued, "What I was going to say was that he's certain the new constitution will pass. He told me about your mama seeing rivers of events and that the rivers have to continue to flow. She sees how everything that is happening is flowing together. The time is right for the river to bring us the new constitution."

"Micki, that is just the mumbling of a sick woman who has lived with too much grief."

"No Jake, that is the wisdom of a D'NO woman. She may be sick, but she is still a genius in how she sees events flow together. Trust your mama."

"Do you really think Papa believes that all will be well? He brought Mama up here. He called you to come up here."

"Yeah, he's humoring you for many reasons. One reason is that you are absolutely sick with worry. The other reason is that it isn't only this election that bothers you. Jake, everybody sees that there is trouble between you and Leah."

I started to say something. I don't know what.

Micki put out his hand. "No we all see it. It isn't you. Really, it isn't you. Kathryn says she sees it when she and Leah are together at meetings. Something is wrong with Leah. She doesn't really talk or think. She repeats phrases that she has learned elsewhere. It sounds good until you've heard the same phrases five or six times. If a question comes up on art or design, she can talk about it quite a bit. She has had insight on the lives of the poor. I suspect that may be from her past." Micki looked at me.

I nodded my confirmation.

"You know, Kathryn tries to be friends with Leah. She thinks that Leah likes her. She says when Leah sees her, she smiles like a child who sees their mama or nanny coming to help them."

"Thanks, it does help to know that it isn't just me. I see the little girl vulnerability about her. I think when we first got married, she...she felt more secure. We didn't have so much money. She worked at the university. Working was familiar to her." I thought some more. "You know, years ago, Julie Jouyet played a nasty trick on Leah, got her drunk, intended to cut off her hair. That was when I first noticed her acting more insecure. Damnit Micki we are wealthy. How can she feel insecure when we are wealthy?"

"Being wealthy is strange to her. She knows about being poor, but wealthy is strange, and so she feels insecure."

I looked at Micki. "Thanks. Talking about the bigger problem has helped me forget the smaller problem for a while. How long do you think it will take for the results to come in?"

"I'm guessing that getting printouts from the machines won't take long. It may take longer to compare the number of votes counted against the number of people who voted."

I wondered if I worried about the election in order to stop worrying about my marriage. "Micki, do you think I will need to leave the country if we lose this election?"

"Yes. Have you thought about where you would like to go?"

"Who takes in refugees?"

We sat and thought in a half-stupor for another half hour or so. The phone rang. I lunged and landed on the floor with the phone in my hand.

I answered, "Jaconovich."

"It's me, Andy."

"Well?"

Andy chuckled, "Well, you've been a fool running away from your lovely home for nothing."

"Huh? What does that mean? Did we get our constitution?"

I could hear Andy's grin. "We got our constitution. Everybody born in this country is now a citizen."

This is when tears started flowing down my face. I've never been too proud to call myself a coward or a mama's boy. When I became aware of the tears, I wasn't embarrassed.

Uncle John came in while I was still on the phone getting details from Andy. How big is our percentage?"

"Sixty-eight."

"Ah that's good."

"Is there any sign of voter fraud?"

"The machines won't count counterfeit ballots."

I sat cross-legged on the floor. I looked at Uncle John and tried to smile triumphantly. Micki told me my smile was exhausted.

I decided to get off of the phone and talk to my family when I saw Jacob peeking around the edge of the door.

I held out my arms to my son and all three of my children came to huddle around me. "Papa what happened? Do we have to leave the country?"

I shook my head. "No. No we can go home and all will be well." I sniffed. "We got the constitution I wanted. It is good."

"Son, I'm proud of you." Papa followed my children into the room.

I looked at my family. "Wasn't anybody asleep in this house?"

Micki said, "I told you. Your thrashing about down here was keeping everybody awake."

Papa grinned at Micki. "Oh, I slept some, but the sound of the phone woke me."

"Papa you have excellent hearing if you could hear this phone in your room."

Papa chuckled. "Well I admit Jacob shouting at his sisters to 'wake up the phone rang' might have had something to do with waking me up."

"I'm sorry if my worrying has distressed all of you."

Uncle John sighed as he eased himself into his chair. "Jake, you were more than worried. And I don't think anybody blames you for a second. You were taking the responsibility for setting things right. Maybe some of the rest of us have lived with wrong so long we ceased to care about others, or to think that the wrong could be made right. I'm proud of you. Today changes the way things have been in this country for over three hundred and fifty years."

I was beginning to feel better. "Oh! And Cousin Margaret got the ancient fishing and trade agreements into the constitution so you can sell your fish wherever you need without worrying about duties and excise tax."

Uncle John chuckled, "Margaret is a smart woman. It is easier to sell our fish to the railroad. The catch might be getting better with the big cannery boats out of service."

My cousins came into the sitting room about five-thirty. "Well?"

I think I was up to grinning.

My son answered for me. "We won. Some of the children at school told me that the south would never let laborers be citizens, but we won."

Papa said, "Well, Young Jacob, that should teach you to not believe everything you hear."

Chapter 36 Leah's Vacation

The transition from the old constitution to the new went extremely smoothly. We joked that the transition went smooth because people could continue doing the same as they always did. The difference was that they were not breaking the law.

My workload was easy enough now. I bought two more houses that Rouseff built and sold them on contract. The weather remained pleasant. I took Jacob out on the lake and taught him to fish using a line and hook. I hired workers to built a dock with a float on the end so we could get out on the lake without launching the rowboat.

My bank started making some mortgage loans so Rouseff Properties was able to sell all their houses in their second development.

A couple weeks after the constitutional election, I stopped at the school to take the girls to dance class. They got in the car. I headed toward their dance studio.

Elizabeth sounded distressed. "Um…Papa?"

"Mmm?"

"We can go straight home. We aren't taking dance anymore."

"What? What happened? Did your teacher retire?"

"I don't know."

Mary Anne spoke up. "Mama can't drive us to lessons anymore. It makes her too tired, and she gets a headache."

"Ah. What about piano?"

Elizabeth sighed. "She says she won't drive us to anything." My baby girl sounded like she was about to cry. She loved playing the piano.

"Ah, well, I know your mama gets headaches. I'll see what I can work out."

I dropped the girls at home and went back to the city. At five I dropped by the dance studio and went inside as the students were leaving. The teacher saw me and came to greet me immediately. "Oh, Mr. Jaconovich your girls are not here. They are not taking class anymore."

Her tone set me on alert. "Yes, my wife has been having sick headaches and can't drive them. I would like for them to start up again, and I will hire someone to drive them."

"I'm sorry Mr. Jaconovich. I respect you more than about anybody else. Your daughters are perfect little girls, but I will not take them as students. I hate to hurt your feelings, but I won't deal with Mrs. Jaconovich ever again."

"I see." I didn't see at all. "She won't be driving the girls. I'll have a chauffer bring them."

"No. Mrs. Jaconovich likes to say things that hurt my feelings. I adore your girls, but nothing is worth the risk of experiencing her tongue. My decision is final."

"Um… what if I offer you combat pay…say twenty percent extra for my girls just in case Leah shows up here."

"No."

I left. I got home just as Jacob was getting off of the trolley. I stopped to give him a ride.

"Thanks. I'm glad you came along. My books were heavy."

"Jacob, why didn't your mother pick you up from your game?"

"Oh she says she doesn't like driving, and I am to find my own rides. She said I can take the trolley, or the taxi."

I sighed. "I think I will need to hire a chauffer."

"I can take the taxi or a trolley."

"Oh I know that you are capable of getting back and forth. I worry about your safety."

"Papa, I am perfectly safe in public. The streets are full of people who adore you and would never let anything happen to me."

"I know that I have many friends. I don't worry about my friends. I do worry about a few enemies, and people that would try to profit from you."

Jacob snorted. "Papa nobody can throw me in my martial arts class. I figure I'm pretty safe on the street."

I smiled at my son. He was getting to be quite good at martial arts.

"Papa? What is wrong with mama? She has headaches all the time. She doesn't want to drive us. She hasn't been to a game for months. She even missed the girls last dance recital."

"I'm not sure. I'm worried about her. I'll talk to the Chinese doctor again. Son, when women get to be your mama's age their bodies change. They get too old to have babies. Some women have more trouble with this change than others do. Your mama is also extremely shy. She may have other problems making this change more difficult for her."

This conversation seemed to help Jacob. I talked to the girls about their piano lessons. I talked to their teacher explaining that Leah was ill with headaches. I finally made arrangements for the teacher to come to our house. She didn't seem to have any trouble with Leah.

I made arrangements for Leah to see the Chinese doctor. He said that he thought Leah's headaches came from always keeping her muscles ready for attack. I took her to her "women's" doctor. He told me the headaches could be symptoms of the change. We discussed her mood issues. He said he noticed the mood change from when Jacob was born. He wasn't much help.

I made an effort to spend more time with the children. I took them hiking. The weather stayed unseasonably dry.

I made an effort to be supportive of Leah. I suggested she might want to go the capital and go shopping.

She replied stridently, "I don't want to buy clothes here. I want to buy them in Paris. The other women shop in Paris. You have money. Why should I go around dressed like a frump?"

"We can go to Paris, and you can shop."

Leah smiled then. "Oh yes, I want to go to Paris to buy clothes. I will go with Isolde."

"I can take you."

"No. You are a man. I don't want to shop with a man. I want to go shopping with my girlfriend."

"Leah, I worry about you being so close to a Vanderholm. The family doesn't like me."

"Oh Isolde's husband doesn't mind you. He says one form of government is as bad as the next. He'd like to get rid of all government."

"Leah, your happiness is very important to me. If you want to go shopping in Paris with Isolde then you can go."

I didn't admit to myself that I was rather looking forward to having Leah out of the house. I told the children that they could each have a party at our house with their friends. Football season was over. The children needed something to keep themselves busy.

Jacob invited his football team for games outside. The weather was so warm, they all went swimming in the lake.

Elizabeth invited all the girls in her class, and they made cookies and decorated them. They laughed, and talked, and looked at magazines.

Mary Anne invited all the children in her class at school. They played games outside and wanted their lunch on the dock by the lake.

Our poor cook/housekeeper was exhausted when the last child went home from last party. I offered her a bonus for all her work.

"Mr. Jaconovich, what I want more than a bonus is a healthy girl to help me clean up the house."

The next day I sent a couple girls from the soup kitchen out to help her return the house to the way Leah liked it. I was thankful I had hired more help. When I got home, I found the party was still flowing in and out of our house. Each of the children had friends over. They were swimming in the lake and sitting on the grass to get dry. Mary Anne had a noisy tape player they took outside to listen to music. I was thankful that Cousin Marianne was out on the dock, acting lifeguard. Ruben had appointed himself Marianne's official assistant.

Chapter 37 Rouseffs Move North

Before Leah returned from Paris, I had added the two young women to our permanent staff. I decided I needed another man too. Our house had become the official party house for our children's friends. We had young people over almost every day. As the weather grew hotter, our lake became a popular spot to keep cool. I appreciated the parents who came to help watch their children.

Leah seemed relaxed when she returned from Paris. She acted delighted that our children had friends over. I breathed a sigh of relief. She was so cheerful, I hoped for a romantic evening.

"Oh Jake, we're too old for all that stuff."

"No we're not."

"Well, I'm not in the mood."

Soon the hot dry weather caused tempers to flare in the city. The prosecutor's office did a brisk business processing people for rioting and brawling.

One afternoon, Young Rouseff called me at my office in the bank. "Jake, Uncle Rouseff had an heart attack this morning."

"How bad?"

"He'll live. They think the heat caused it. The house has been too hot for days."

"Are you going down there?"

"I have to."

"Would anybody be offended if I came too?'

"Aunt Rosalie would appreciate your support. She asked me to call you."

"Okay, is she at home? Can I reach her? I'll go down on the evening train."

"She's at the hospital."

After I got off of the phone with Young Rouseff, I called the hospital and talked to Rosalie. "Oh Jake, thank you for calling."

"I can be down on the evening train."

"No. I don't want you here, just yet."

Bewildered, I tried to sound supportive, "Anything."

"Jake can you go out to that place where your parents are living and see if you can find us a nice apartment? It is too hot for us here, and Philippe can't stand living among these ignorant snobs. It's killing him."

"My parents and I will be delighted to have you close by. I think some of the units have air conditioning. I will go out right now and see what I can find."

We made arrangements for me to call her later. I called my house and left a message for Leah telling her that Mr. Rouseff was sick. She could reach me through my parents.

I called and made an appointment to look at units in the retirement complex. I called papa and told him I was coming out and why. I gave him the information to call Rosalie.

I found two possible units for the Rouseffs. Papa called Rosalie and described them to her. She instructed him to take the one facing east in hopes it would be coolest. Papa explained about the air conditioning.

Papa got off of the phone. "The poor woman is frantic." He looked at Mama. "If she felt better, I'd take her down there to comfort Rosalie."

"Let's get things set up here then I will go down and help her pack-up to move."

Five days after Mr. Rouseff got sick, Leah and I went down to direct the packing. I took a hotel room. It was hellishly hot, but it was away from the Rouseff women. They were already bringing their vulgar possessions out of the storeroom and setting them out where they could worship them.

Young Rouseff said he would take care of the family in the south and sent a cousin who had completed a business course up north to handle the business.

I shipped the Rouseff's personal belongings north on a train the day after we arrived. I went back north the next day to buy furnishings for the Rouseff's new apartment. Rosalie gave Leah and I a fist-full of money before she sent us back north. "Leah, I know you will find us things that are simple, elegant and tasteful."

Mr. Rouseff went directly from the hospital to the train. They got off at Mercid. I picked them up in the Mercedes and took them to their new home. Papa and Mama were there to welcome them.

I thought Mama sounded happy to see her old friend. She hugged Rosalie. "Dear, it will be good to have you near. Papa and I have missed you. See, we got a print of this picture for a housewarming gift." Mama gave Rosalie a picture of the four of them at a mall in the United States.

I left right after my parents. As I walked down the hall behind my parents, I heard Mama asking, "Who were those people again? How do we know them?"

Papa answered, "They are our best friends outside of the family. We used to travel with them. You and Rosalie were the most fashionable and respected women in the city."

I smiled and went home to chaperone a lake full of youth.

The rioting in the city became perpetual. It moved from block to block. We encouraged people to go to the parks where the shade under the trees was cooler. We lost electricity in parts of the city because so many people were running air conditioning units in their apartments. The morgue was extremely busy. We had more old people dying from the heat. We lost some babies and toddlers to the heat.

Finally, the hottest summer on record gave way to the hottest fall on record. Then the rains started like I had never seen rain before. I noticed the Chinese people out in the fields apparently planting. Chinatown was deserted as everyone went out to plant. I thought their fields would soon be flooded.

I learned that flooding was the idea behind the planting. They leased fields from all the farmers they could find. I talked to the women at the Chinese restaurant. They explained that everybody was planting rice because their records showed that after a very hot summer the rains would be heavy in this area.

The rains continued to fall. Our lake started to fill up again. The party of children and youth moved inside to play card games and board games. Boys club met at our house. One other girl took her piano lessons with my girls at our house.

The rain put a stop to the rioting and deaths. My routine at the prosecutor's office returned to normal. I went to the Rouseff offices on my usual day to be there. Cousin Rouseff invited me into the office that had once belonged to his uncle.

I asked. "What can I do for you?"

"Well, that is the point Jake. What can you do for me?"

I knew his tone meant trouble.

He continued. "As far as I can see, Jake Jaconovich you are more trouble than an asset."

I interrupted him. "Ah, I understand. That time comes sometimes. I will clean out my desk. I don't keep many personal items here." I stood and left the room without another word. I checked my desk drawers and removed the litter that collects in a desk. I left the pencils and pens neatly in their drawer. Cousin Rouseff stood over me watching me pack up. I picked up a picture, shook hands with Cousin Rouseff, and left. I wished I could have said goodbye to my secretary. Really, I wanted to hire her to work at the bank.

I went to my office at the bank. I sat in my chair and swiveled for a half hour before I took out a notepad to write down what I planned to do with the time I would not spend working for Rouseff. Finally, after thinking, I wrote on my paper, "I can spend the time with my parents. I can spend the time with my children. I have no idea how I will spend my time." It was still early when I headed for home. I decided to go out to Mercid and see my parents and check in of the Rouseff's.

Mama was napping. I talked to Papa for a few minutes until he sent me downstairs to see the Rouseffs. Mr. Rouseff smiled, delighted to see me.

"Jake. Jake come in. Tell me how is everything at the office?"

I would not tell this man that I got fired. I thought it would upset him. "Oh everything in the city is slow. Sending Young Rouseff south and replacing him actually went smoothly. We are discussing the best place for a sports arena. Young Rouseff tried to place it near the railroad. I foolishly suggested near an interchange. The river is over its banks and my location is under water."

Cousin Philippe wheezed. "See if you can buy the old Halspen Cannery property. It is convenient to Mercid, the railroad, the city and the freeway."

"It never occurred to me that they would sell. It wouldn't hurt to ask."

He wheezed some more. "I'm thinking that we need to build a whole entertainment complex in the area. We'll put in the sports arena, then a concert hall and perhaps something for live theater."

"Oh that reminds me, your street theater group is very self-supporting. When they all get together they have an impressive chorus. Some members are teaching their skills. They work with the arts department at the University."

"Ah good. I still want them on the streets, but I want a performing arts center too."

"I'll have our staff start researching that." I left wondering about everything I said to Rouseff.

The next day was slower than the day before. I called Micki. I mentioned my release from Rouseff and feeling at loose ends. "I tacked about a bit when Cousin Philippe asked about the business. Micki, I don't have the heart to tell that old man that his relatives have failed him again."

Micki started laughing. "Jake, you may have gotten fired from Rouseff Industries. That brilliant old man still considers you family. I think we are going to build a sports arena."

"We don't have the people."

"You leave that to me. I still work for Rouseff Industries. I can sound out people who might work for us."

"I don't have that kind of money."

"You and I together are closer to having that kind of money. Call some of your friends. Andy has money. I bet if you mention it to him, that bored specimen of brilliant humanity will be up here shoving money into this project. Let's do this." I think Micki knew the magic words to get to me. "Think of all the jobs this will create."

"I guess it won't hurt to see how much land we can get."

I left the bank and drove out to the Halspen property. The cannery buildings took up enough land for a football stadium. I wandered until the caretaker came to run me off.

"Hello, I am Jake Jaconovich." I handed the man my card.

The man's mouth dropped open. His eyes got round. I surreptitiously looked behind me for attackers. He glanced at the card then turned and ran toward his house yelling for someone to come look.

I turned in a full circle looking for something that could have set the man off like that. I followed him toward a cabin on the edge of the property.

A woman with a toddler on her hip came out of the house. The man continued to call to her to "come see." She looked as bewildered as I was.

I caught up to the man and his wife. He introduced me after a fashion. "See here honey, this here man is Jake Jaconovich. I got his card and everything."

I decided that I would behave correctly despite being disoriented by the strange behavior. "How do you do ma'am. And who is this pretty baby?" I shook hands with one finger with the toddler."

His mama almost whispered. "His name is Joshua."

I smiled. "A good name. I came out here to look at the property and find out how to contact the owner."

The caretaker said, "That would be Jouyet properties. I don't know how to contact Mr. Jouyet."

"Ah, I do. Thank you folks. Take care of little Joshua." I walked back to my car.

I overheard the excitable couple instructing their child. "See that man. He is going to be our next president. Joshua, say president." I winced.

I went back to my office at the bank and called Andy. I told him the whole story about the entertainment complex, and getting fired, and not telling Mr. Rouseff what happened.

"Jake, what a great idea. If you have the old man guiding you, I'm in." Andy laughed. "His family doesn't respect him or what he has done for them. I'd like to rub their noses in it a bit. Let's go with it."

"First I need to talk to Jouyet Properties."

"No. Let me talk to Jouyet Properties. Let's not let them know that either you or Rouseff are involved in this."

"Micki is going to see if we can get some Rouseff employees to help research this."

"I'll get back to you on what I learn from Jouyet."

While I was making phone calls, the skies opened up and poured down sheets of water on the city. When I left the bank to go to the prosecutor's office, I needed to slosh through the rain for six blocks. I went back inside and called a cab. It seldom rains during the day in the central part of my country. This much rain was unusual.

The streets started running with water. I thought I should call the school and tell them to have the children take cabs. I didn't want Leah driving in this weather. The prosecutor's office had an air of holiday when I got there.

"What is happening here?"

The receptionist Tsulu giggled, "Mr. Farley took Sofia shopping for a ring."

"They are out in this weather?"

Tsulu giggled some more. "I don't think they are aware that it is raining."

I chuckled. "Is Alexander in?"

"No. He called in with a cold."

I grunted, "That leaves us a little short. What is the situation?"

"We have a couple people in the holding area. The file secretary went home early. I have the files."

I held out my hand for their files. The file on top was fat. I took it and went looking for my drunk and disorderly offender. I found an intern to help.

"Where are the other interns?"

"They are flooded in, sir. University Street is impassable."

We processed the old man who had been picked up while sleeping off a drunk on the sidewalk. I dismissed the disorderly charges since the report clearly stated that he was unconscious.

I asked him, "Do you have a dry place to sleep?"

The toothless old man wheezed, "No dry places in this weather."

"I am serious. Do you have a place to sleep that is up off of the ground, and has a solid roof, and no rain blowing through windows or doors?"

"No sir, I don't."

I sighed, "Okay I am going to sentence you to staying in the holding area for drunks until this rain lets up."

"Thank you sir. That's real kind of you sir. I want you to know that I got all signed up to vote, sir. I'm going to vote for you when you run for office."

I tried to deflect some of the admiration. "You know my supervisor Mr. Farley worked on the constitution as hard as I did, so did some of the professors from the university."

The old man continued to stare at me and smile inanely. "But they ain't one of our own. I used to work for your papa in the warehouse. He were always a real kind man, just like you."

My heart melted. "Thank you it's a compliment to be compared to my papa." I sent the man on his way. I checked in with our junior prosecutors and told them to send the homeless to the holding area for drunks.

The mayor called. "Jake that area below the mall where the shanties are is turning into a muddy mess. We need to move those people out of there. Do you have any ideas where we can put them?"

I was stumped. I didn't work for Rouseff. I couldn't just "tail and fin" move people onto Rouseff property. "Shit, this is getting impossible. I am telling the homeless to stay in the drunk holding area." I thought for another minute. "Okay, I'm not working for Rouseff anymore so I can't order in box cars. Um…I don't know. Can we put them in the armory and school gymnasiums?"

"I don't like the school idea. I've never heard of us having this much rain—especially during the day--before."

"Perhaps one of us should call General Johan. Maybe he can move those people into barracks until this is over."

"Will you call him? I don't know him at all."

"Yeah, I can call."

It took me a while to get hold of General Johan. He finally came on the phone. "Johan."

"Jaconovich here. We have about seven thousand people living in shanties that are getting flooded out."

"Shit."

"Yeah."

"Get them to the train station, and I'll have military trains there for them."

"Thanks."

That part of the problem was solved.

I called the Mayor back and told him about the military trains. "Jake will you go talk to those people? They trust you."

I went to look out the door of the office. I really didn't like the condition of the streets. I wanted my children at home. I called a taxi for them. I learned that the taxis wouldn't run the children out to my house. I made arrangements for the taxi to bring them to my office. I called the school and told them to send my children to me in the taxi.

"Yes sir. Do you think we should send the other children home?"

"Not unless their parents have made some arrangements. The streets are awash. I don't think they would be safe for unaccompanied children.

While waiting for my children to arrive, I called a staff meeting. We had emptied the holding room. I sent the last person home without charges. I decided to close the office and send people home. "A cab is bringing my children here. You can take it home if you like."

When the children arrived, I faced the challenge of fitting them into the Miki. Jacob was almost as tall as I am. The girls were slender, but tall enough that it was a tight fit to get into the tiny car. By the time I got the girls in behind the seats and I got in front, a puddle of water had formed in my seat. I sat in it. We discovered the convertible roof leaked.

"Jacob how old are you?"

"Twelve."

"So this car is fifteen. It is in good shape for its age. I think I'll talk to Miki about a new roof."

I took my favorite back-route home. I didn't see many cars on the road. A few people were out in trucks. At one point, I drove on the sidewalk to void a deep puddle. At another intersection, the water came up under the floor of the car and soaked the girls. I took it slow and easy. We made it home. We were wet when we got there. I intended to take the Mercedes back into the city. It was gone.

The housekeeper told me the Mercedes was at the train station. Leah had declared that she was going someplace where it wasn't raining and left on the noon train.

I changed into dry older clothes and found our ratty umbrella to walk to the trolley station to go talk to the people below the mall about evacuating.

I was chilled through by the time I reached the M'TK station. I wanted to go upstairs and get some warm soup. I didn't know the people who lived here. I didn't work for Rouseff. I couldn't even go into the office to talk to the stationmaster. I stood at the little window and explained about refugees from the city getting on the military train.

"Yes sir. We got a call from the base. The train will be here in two hours. You will have about forty-five minutes to load your people before the evening train comes in."

I scowled over the short time allowed to load thousands of people on trains. They couldn't do it. I got in the Mercedes anyway and turned the blessed heater up high. I drove slowly through a shallow river of surging water to the mall parking lot. When I started talking to people about evacuating, they were happy enough to roll their few possessions into blankets and slosh through the rain to the train station.

The local police and fire departments came to help with the evacuation. They sent me home.

It rained the next day, so I called Mr. Farley and said I was staying home with my children until the flooding was over. I'd caught a cold and felt generally miserable and sorry for myself.

The mid-section of the country had a major flood. It covered two and a half provinces. In places, the river backed up over the freeway. One underpass into the city was flooded. My lake rose so high it was over the end of the dock that usually rested on the ground.

I called General Johan to ask about the refugees. He sounded cheerful. "Yes, we got all your people on the trains. They were happy enough to get out of the wet. We've got families in barracks. Single men get military tents, but they are happy enough for the dry tents."

"You sound cheerful."

"We don't do much here. This is giving my people a chance to get out and do something useful. They are sandbagging everything vital. We have rescued people trapped in their farmhouses. Some people we have had to take out by helicopter." The general sounded totally happy.

The worst part of the whole flood was that the violence of the waters washed away the rice crop. The Chinese always kept good supplies of rice, but this was a blow.

The country finally got through our devastating wet season. I hadn't worked much. We didn't have many offenders to process. Everybody was too busy staying dry to get into trouble. Then again we evacuated most of the regular troublemakers to the military base.

Chapter 38 Famine

When the sun came out again, my group of business partners had a good plan for building the sports arena. We had more Rouseff employees than I expected. Cousin Rouseff started shutting down all new development so we hired the development crew. They expressed their eagerness to work for Mr. Rouseff again. I told them to visit him, and talk about their projects, and show him their designs. We had a silent pact not to tell him the true state of affairs at Rouseff Development.

Once we got the contracts for the arena project in place, there was little for me to do. I spent more time at home chaperoning the youth who came to swim in the lake.

With more leisure time on my hands, I had time to think about my marriage. I realized that I never knew if my wife would be home or not. I made another effort to reconnect with Leah. After three months of asking for dates and buying gifts, I gave up again and started thinking about my business.

One day, the ex-Mrs. Mayor called the house looking for Leah. I answered the phone. "I'm sorry, this is Jake. May I help you with something?"

"Oh, this is even better. Jake the people have nothing to eat. The grain crops dried up in the heat. The rice crop got washed away and now I'm told the potato crop doesn't have enough water."

I ran one hand over my face. "What would be the best thing that we can buy in bulk to feed the people?"

"Wheat. They can always eat bread. I'd buy rice next."

"I'll see what I can do. This might take me a while. Do you have any idea how many boxcars of wheat we need? Do we need wheat or flour?"

"Well, we need flour, but Vanderholm can mill the wheat here."

"Okay I'll do some research and see what I can do."

Doing research involved calling my friends and asking them where to buy flour. I got a good answer when I called the prosecutor's office in the capital. Christian sounded happy to hear from me. "Let me get this straight. You are on a mission to buy tons of flour to feed the country."

I felt as helpless as when I didn't know how to get my shirts washed. "Yes, but I have no idea which countries grow wheat."

"Most countries grow wheat. You need a country that we have relations with."

"Oh. Okay." I had no idea what-so-ever what I was doing.

Christian had the answer I needed. "Allison is friends with someone who works in the Canadian embassy here. They grow wheat."

I asked, "Are they selling it here? Why do they have an embassy here?"

"I have no idea."

I decided to blunder forward. "I'll talk to them."

I'd hired my wonderful secretary away from Rouseff Industries. I gave her the job of getting me an appointment with the appropriate person from Canada.

I met with the Canadian ambassador and told him I wanted to buy milled flour. He said he hadn't heard anything about buying flour from the president or government channels.

I gave the man the most expedient explanation I could think of. "Well this is outside his duties. He probably doesn't know about this."

"Well, I'm not sure of the legalities."

I relaxed. "Oh, that's okay. I am an attorney. I am well aware of the legalities. Thanks to my cousin Margaret I can import most anything I want without paying duties." I chuckled and shook my head.

"Are you sure? I am not completely familiar with your new constitution."

"I am. I helped write it. We kinda forgot about who does what for imports except for people from my mother's province. We can do most anything we want. I want to buy flour."

The ambassador said he would do some research.

About a month after Mrs. Mayor called me I started preparing for a trip to Canada. Cousin Marianne was eager to come with me. I decided if she was coming I would bring my children. Leah claims I didn't invite her. At first, I assumed she was coming. When I was checking our passports, she said she wasn't coming "because you didn't invite me."

"Leah, you are my wife. I said I was taking my family to Canada. That includes you. Now get your things together. I hear it is cold there."

"I don't want to come if I'm not welcome."

"Leah get this straight, I am the one who has been making an ass of himself trying to make this marriage work. You are my wife. You are coming with me."

She pouted for days, but she came with me.

The trip was successful. I knew nothing about buying flour. My friends knew nothing about buying flour. I went. I talked to a grain cooperative or some such thing. I didn't know what I was doing the whole trip. All I knew was that I obligated myself for one million dollars worth of flour. That was my whole savings. I had nothing left to invest in the arena.

I made arrangements for the shipment to come into the D'SnG/Uzara dock in the southern port.

A million dollars of flour turned out to be a great deal of flour. The flour arrived in a timely manner. The D'SnG/Uzaras got it off of the ship and onto trucks headed north. They kept one pallet of flour for themselves as payment for the use of their dock. I tried to pay them money instead. Woody was finally commissioned to reason with me.

Woody tracked me down by phone in my office at the bank. "Jake about the flour deal. We don't want your money. We can't eat that."

"Are you sure?"

"Jake have you tried eating money?"

I laughed at his joke. "No. I've never eaten money. Is the food problem getting bad in the south?"

"Yeah, it's bad. We have some farms that usually supply the family needs. They didn't get enough rain. We are trying to buy food and there is none to be had."

"Ah, if I could get a fishing boat in there with a load of fish, would you assure me that the valuable boat would be allowed to leave the harbor without being harassed or confiscated on some fool charge."

Woody remained silent for almost a minute, "Jake, I don't know what to say. My first reaction is...I don't know...um...uh...is that what fishermen think of southerners?"

"Yes. I can get you some fish, but I am not going to go way out on a limb with the fishermen by promising that fishing boats won't be harassed."

Woody thought silently again. "Jake, wait before you send us fish. I think people will need to be hungrier."

I asked, "I know Rouseff never shipped fresh fish that far south by rail. What do you normally eat?"

"Chicken, canned fish, a little pork, lamb, and some beef. The problem is the weather has been so dry the farmers can't water stock so they've butchered before the animals were mature." He was silent again. "Things can get ugly here."

"I won't send an expensive fishing boat into an ugly situation."

"Yeah, I am going to have to think on that."

"Should I get the fishing boats a military escort?"

Woody's voice rose to a squeak. "Jake can you do that?"

"I don't see why not."

"Shit! Jake, what do you do up there that you can call out the military?" I whined. "I don't do anything."

"I can't call out the military."

I was confident. "Sure you can. It's easy. You tell your secretary that you want to talk to the general in charge of the nearest base. When she locates the correct person for you, you just tell him what you need."

Woody started laughing. "I can believe that you would do that. I can almost hear you telling your secretary to find the general in charge of the nearest base. Somehow that reminds me of how your friends had to take care of you when you first moved into an apartment." Woody laughed some more. "I'll tell you what, when I think the time is right, I'll call you about those fish and the military." He laughed some more and hung up.

I wasn't a Rouseff employee anymore. I would have to pay for a stall to sell my flour at a market. All of my money was riding on this flour. I didn't want to pay someone to sell it.

Finally, I called the prosecutors in every district and told them the flour was on its way north. "My main goal is to get this into the hands of people who will eat it. Do you know who in your district would be honest enough to help me sell it?"

The usual answer was, "Send us the flour. We'll see it is sold honestly."

We worked out how much flour each district could have out of the whole shipment. My housekeeper told me how much money to charge for a pound of flour. My mayor let me sell the flour from outside the courthouse, because I was solving a huge problem for the city.

I encountered a problem when the truck drivers wanted to be paid in flour. I wanted to give them money. "We can't eat money." If I heard that phrase once, I heard it a hundred times.

Two weeks after the flour arrived, it was gone. My payments came in as the flour was sold. By the end of the two weeks, I had somewhat over two million dollars back in my bank account. I slept sound for a few nights.

I met with Mr. Rouseff at least twice a week. I told him the problems with Jouyet wanting more for the land than it was worth. "Wait a month. Keep working on your plans for the arena. In a month, I will call Jouyet, and we will get the price we want for the arena.

While waiting for Jouyet to think about our offer for the land, I called my contacts in Canada and ordered another shipment of flour.

Shortly after I ordered the second shipment of flour, I got a call from Vanderholm at my prosecutor's office. "What is this I hear about you importing wheat?"

"Not wheat, flour."

"You can't do that."

"Actually, I can."

"We have a pact among the families that I am to be the only one to sell wheat."

"Sir, I respect that. You are free to sell all the wheat you want."

"You know damned well the sun dried out the crop in the field."

"I am at work. Do you have a point?"

"Yes, do you have a permit to import wheat? And why are you buying it milled? You should at least let us mill it."

"Yes, I have the permit. I buy it milled because I don't trust your family. Do you have any other questions?"

He hung up the phone.

The second million I spent on flour did not buy as much flour. The price had gone up. I'd instructed my contact to find me more wheat. The second shipment sold out faster than the first. The third shipment was smaller yet, and sold out faster than the first two.

Woody called. "I decided to see if I really could call out the military to protect a shipment of fish. The answer was no. We need the fish. Can you see if you can get the military to protect the boats in the harbor?"

"How soon do you need the fish, and how much are you willing to pay per pound?"

Woody huffed a couple times before he answered. "What is this going to cost us?"

"Because of the price of fuel and the risk to the northern fishermen, I think five dollars a pound is a fair price. The fishermen will have to be away from home for several days."

Woody grunted. "Jake, I'll be honest. Charge ten dollars a pound. People are hungry. They'll pay the price and be thankful."

"I'll tell the fishermen what you need. They can set the price."

Fortunately, I talked to one of my cousins instead of Uncle John. Petral grumbled. "You know what Uncle John would say about taking the M'NO into any ports in the south."

"I know what he would say. I happen to agree with him. You would use the D'SnG dock. I think they will be fair with you. Also, I am thinking of asking for military protection for your boats while they are in harbor."

"The price makes the deal attractive enough. Why don't we just ship what is needed south by train?"

"Because I don't trust Cousin Rouseff who is in charge now. I don't like the way the family treated Cousin Philippe."

Petral dryly commented, "Nest of snakes. Tell me again why we are trying to feed them?"

"Um…uh…I don't know…uh…well."

My cousin laughed. "We will feed them because we think we can make a great deal of money from them."

I liked Petral's explanation. "I suppose that is an adequate answer. I'll call General Johan and see if he'll get you some support."

When the fishing boats arrived in the harbor, they were escorted by both of our Coast Guard ships. A unit of soldiers guarded the land end of the dock. The fish were unloaded, weighed and paid for. The fishing boats left harbor full of richer, happy fishermen.

After the fish were delivered, I got a call from a Fortenac. "What the hell was that display about delivering a few fish?"

"What display?"

"The armed soldiers and the Coast Guard."

"Ah well, in case you've never noticed, independent fishermen never come into your port. It isn't considered safe. Oh…and…you can thank Cousin Leon for that bit of distrust. He stole a bunch of boats up north and locked them up. I really didn't want to be crawling around a strange dock in the middle of the night to unlock a bunch of boats again, so I asked for protection. Food is a vital resource. The military was willing to protect the shipment."

"You people up there are crazy." He hung up. I looked at the phone and thought he was the irrational one in that conversation.

My interference in the food chain produced some positive results. The Fortenacs opened their canneries and started sending one ship out to fish. They even started buying from fishermen with small boats who lived in the villages. The D'SnGs found rice to feed our people.

It had started to rain again. It was raining too hard for people to grow anything, but we had fish and rice to eat. It wasn't enough.

Once again our morgue became the busiest place in the city. Once again, the very young, and the very old died first, then the women. Our suicide rate soared. The river flooded. People drowned in the floods. Other people were murdered and dumped into the flooding waters. We didn't know how to begin to find out whom the bodies belonged to.

Once again, I had people fishing my lake to supply the food kitchens. The new highway connecting the north and the south was flooded in several places preventing the flow of goods between the north and south. Mr. Rouseff called the head of the railroad and yelled at him until he agreed to add more trains, and more cars to get goods and people moving again. His wife worried that getting upset would make him sick. When I arrived to visit, he confessed. "It felt good to yell at someone. It should have been those ignorant relatives of mine. They don't think."

"I thought Young Rouseff was getting the hang of the business. He was no good at development, but he was capable with what we had. Cousin Rouseff has a great deal to learn."

At the end of the month, Mr. Rouseff called Jouyet about selling the property. I didn't hear the call. Mr. Rouseff assured me that I didn't want to know what he said. "It wasn't all completely honest. We got the price we wanted. Do you have the buy/sell contracts ready?"

"Yes sir. The contracts are ready. We can close any day."

The old man gave me a shrewd look then smiled. "Good." His eyes drifted closed. He was ready for his nap.

I went back to the bank to prepare to buy a piece of property under the name of Consolidated Investments. I wondered if Cousin Philippe had an idea that we were no longer operating as Rouseff Industries. His look told me he knew I was hiding something. I would tell him the truth if he brought the subject up. I didn't want to distress him about his relatives.

Chapter 39 Consolidated Investments

It energized me to be working for Mr. Rouseff again. Most of the old development team now worked for Consolidated. In addition to the football arena, we decided we needed to build an office building. Some staff was still hiding out in their offices at Rouseff. A couple people had offices near mine at the bank. Others were working out of their homes or cars. We had tents for offices at the construction site until they were stolen.

My house regularly filled with youth and various people I brought home from work with me. Andy visited frequently. I missed Cousin Marianne when she finished school and moved north to live near Margaret. I wasn't surprised when I got an invitation to her wedding. I approved of her choice of Ruben S'TO.

Andy stayed often. He invested the most in the sports arena complex. He decided to do research on sports facilities. He spent six weeks touring other countries with Adele and his daughter. He came home with hundreds of pictures and ideas. Adele wasn't speaking to him by the time they got home.

Andy and I stayed up late one night discussing the problem. "Do you have any idea what set her off?"

"No...well...maybe. I think she got tired of visiting sporting coliseums. I don't really know. We were in New York. I sent the women shopping while I visited Yankee Stadium. We'd already taken a ferryboat out to see the statue of liberty. I noticed she wasn't speaking to me when we went to a play in the evening. Christiana wouldn't tell me what was bothering her mother."

"Andy you know what scares me about these women? Not knowing what they are thinking and what has upset them. I'm sure it is something like that with Leah. Everything was fine. Then after Mary Anne was born she couldn't have any more children. I don't know if she's upset about not being able to have more babies, or whether I did something. If she could just tell me what is troubling her, I'm sure we could work it out."

"That's the thing though, they don't say what is troubling them. I don't know if Adele got mad because I didn't take her to Yankee Stadium, or because

I didn't go shopping with her, or because she thinks I am engaging in business, or working, or doing something vulgar." Andy shook his head. He looked as sad and frustrated as I felt.

We stayed up until two for several nights trying to figure out what went wrong in our marriages. This was the point at which I became certain that there was something important Leah hadn't told me. I was equally certain that if she told me we could make our marriage happy again. I was half right in my guess. Perhaps if she'd told me her problems, we could have worked something out that would have made her happier, and I would have been free to approach another woman with honor. She kept her secrets, and I was as confused as Andy.

The foundation for the arena was progressing nicely. The land proved to be excellent for building. First, we built a four-story office complex with an elevator between floors. The elevator became a tourist attraction.

One day, I arrived at the site of the arena to find a shiny Miki parked in the spot closest to the office. I grinned and hurried into the building. I expected to find both of the Rouseffs. Instead, I found Papa and Mr. Rouseff.

Papa chuckled, "Rosalie and your mother were busy with some women's thing so we snuck out for the day."

I smiled to see that Papa got out. He seldom left Mama's side. I guess that was where he was happiest. "I'm happy to see both of you. How much of the complex have you seen so far?"

Cousin Philippe gave me his sharp look. "Oh, we toured the development offices on the third floor. The construction on the first two floors looks good. We have been admiring the offices on this floor. We haven't seen your office yet."

I knew the time had come. I was going to have to explain to this precious old man that his relatives were a bunch of disrespectful skunkfish. "Ah certainly, from my office you can see the whole complex and the river beyond. Um...we did reserve an office for you if you would like us to finish it up." I led both men to my office, motioned for them to be seated and closed the door.

Cousin Philippe waited until I took my seat before he started asking questions. "We might as well start with why all the signs say Consolidated Industries instead of Rouseff."

I hoped the old man would catch the compliment in my explanation. "Well sir, Cousin Rouseff told me my services were no longer needed at Rouseff.

In fact, he told most of the development people that they were not needed. Well…um…this was just about the time you started feeling better. I…uh… well when you asked about the business I thought I might as well bring up a problem that had frustrated me earlier."

Mr. Rouseff nodded.

I grinned. "Young Rouseff and I had puzzled and puzzled over where to put the sports complex." I chuckled at the memory. "You didn't have to think more than a few seconds before you came up with this idea. Well, I had a little time on my hands. I talked to some of my friends about building this complex. They agreed to finance the thing. So, we hired the development staff and went to work following your instructions."

I watched Mr. Rouseff thinking. He sat and took several seconds to process this information. He scowled. The first sign of a response came out as half a cough and half a laugh. Then he got into the idea of laughing. He opened his mouth and laughed from his belly. Finally, he clapped Papa on the back. "Jacob, he's your son all right. When my own family let me down, he stepped in and did the right thing. You have a son to be proud of."

"I am proud of him." Papa's eyes said more than his words. I felt ten feet tall.

I had to walk back through the whole office building with Cousin Philippe. He stopped and thanked every, former employee for their loyalty. I thought he looked almost twenty years younger as he walked briskly back to the Miki with Papa. His old man's shuffle disappeared. He up stood straight and looked around him. I knew he was seeing the finished complex.

Chapter 40 Andrew Corbain

T he afternoon when my world collapsed, I was in a staff meeting at the prosecutor's office. I took charge of the office while Jeffrey and Sophia were on an extended honeymoon. They had promised to return when their new house out on my lake was finished. I was conducting the staff meetings and spending more time than usual in the office.

We were hashing out more streamlined methods for getting offenders who plead not-guilty through the court system without compromising justice. The secretary on phone-duty looked distressed when she interrupted the meeting. "Please sir, the phone is for you."

I remained focused on the topic of our discussion. "Tell them I'll call back."

She shook her head. "Please, the caller said it is urgent. You might want to take this in your office."

I looked closer at the anxious, secretary twisting her wedding ring on her finger. Her sympathetic look told me something terrible had happened. Without pausing longer, I ran into my office and grabbed the phone. "Jaconovich."

"Jake? Woody Uzara here."

Woody? What could Woody have to tell me that could be so urgent I needed to interrupt a staff meeting? "Yeah, what's happened?"

"You're still friends with Andrew Corbain, right?"

"Andy? Yes." I slid into my chair wondering what could have happened to Andy.

"Well, I just learned a few minutes ago that he was over at the school, helping one of the science teachers with a demonstration."

Relief washed over me. This couldn't be serious if it happened at a school.

Woody continued, "Well...uh...apparently there was some sort of...uh... malfunction somewhere. Uh...anyway...there was an explosion."

"Andy, how is he?"

"Jake, he's burned real bad. He is in the hospital. I don't know much more than that. The teacher died."

My brain froze. "Woody thanks for calling me. Uh…" I wondered if Adele was with Andy. I thought it best not to ask Woody. "oh…what hospital is he in? What is the address? Uh…do you have a phone number for them?"

I called the hospital as soon as I got off of the phone with Woody. I identified myself. After getting transferred to several different people, I finally found someone who knew something. "Oh, Mr. Corbain? Uh his condition is serious. We don't expect him to live through the night. He was burned very badly over one side of his body."

"Is his wife with him?"

"No, his father and brother are here. Would you like to talk to them?"

I talked to Andy's papa for a few minutes. Finally, I could think enough to make some decisions. "Okay, I will take a helicopter down there. You tell that son of yours that he is not going to die because I said so, and tell him I'm on my way down there myself to tell him so."

I finally remembered the staff meeting. I went out to the silently waiting staff. "My best friend has been critically injured in an explosion and fire. I'm leaving almost immediately to head south." I placed Alexander in charge of the office and went back to my office to make some phone calls. After I arranged for the helicopter to pick me up near my house, I called home to tell Leah what happened and see if she would pack for me. Leah wasn't home. The housekeeper agreed to pack.

My children were waiting for me in the corner of the yard when I arrived home. I guessed the housekeeper had told them the problem. The girls looked ready to cry. Jacob spoke up. "He's going to be okay isn't he?"

I pulled all three children into a hug. "Will you three do me a favor? Get someone to drive you into the cathedral and light a candle for Andy. He is going to need all the help he can get."

My children told me that they had helped pack for me as we walked into the house. By the time I finished washing-up, I heard the helicopter coming . I ran out to wait in my front yard for it to land in the road. An hour after I got the call from Woody, the helicopter rose up over the lake to take me south.

When I arrived at the hospital, I hadn't heard any news since I talked to Andy's papa. I felt relieved to hear that Andy was still with us. A volunteer escorted me to his room. I looked around me as I followed the volunteer. I noted dust and grit on the floor. I saw places where the paint was peeling on the walls. Occasionally, the walls had been spattered. Attempts to clean up the spatters met with varying degrees of success.

Andy's father and brother waited in his small room. The room smelled of urine and antiseptic. The one window looked filthy. Andy lay on his back. The left side of his face and body were covered in bandages. His right hand rested free on top of the covers. I wondered if his father had been holding it.

Andy made a noise in his throat when I spoke. His father looked surprised at the noise. I took two steps to the side of the bed and took hold of the hand resting on the covers. The fingers tightened around mine.

I spoke. "Okay Andy, I've got your backside, you are going to have to take the rest of this fight yourself. There is no way out, except through, and you are going through this. Got that?"

He squeezed my hand.

"Good. I'll do what I can for you, but you're not spilling out on this one."

He tugged on my hand.

I thought he wanted me to come close enough to hear him whisper. I bent down toward the bed.

Andy moved his hand up my arm and up my face.

I bent closer.

His fingers moved into my hair. I felt them tense. He was weak. I tried to follow the pressure of those fingers in my hair.

My head almost touched the bed. I pulled a chair under me with my foot, sat down and rested my head on the bed so close to Andy that I could feel his body touching my hair.

I wasn't sure what Andy really wanted. His hand relaxed resting on my head. I thought I heard him sigh. He relaxed and went to sleep.

I heard Andy's brother whisper, "No wonder Adele won't have anything to do with him."

From my awkward position I tried to explain. "You are mistaken. This is his way of saying he wants me close. I know it is, because he knows I will fight to get him the best services in this country."

I felt the fingers twitch in my hair.

I continued. "He wants to live. I'm sure of that. He knows I won't give up on him."

The hand in my hair relaxed.

Andy's brother left about ten. His father stayed, and we talked. "Jake I'm sorry about that comment earlier. It was uncalled for. The problems with

Adele." I heard the older man sigh. "I never thought Adele was right for him. She is beautiful. She's smart enough in some ways…but Andy…well…he's always been curious about everything on heaven and earth. Adele could never see that part of Andy—the curious part, that drives him to always be busy trying new things."

From my awkward position on the bed, I replied. "Andy is an exceptional human being. Perhaps Adele would have been happier with average." I chuckled. "That may be what got to her with the sports stadium, she wanted someone content to sit and watch the occasional game. Andy was wild to research how to build a stadium. He sees how this country can be better. He isn't content with our current poverty."

Mr. Corbain agreed somewhat. "She was angry with him for spending money on a stadium so a few people could have jobs."

"She was mad for the wrong reasons then. The stadium isn't about jobs. It's about cultural richness." I sighed and thought for a few moments. I tried to explain. "I talked to Young Jouyet after he left the country. He'd been living in the south. He said something about living among the dying, and gilded rot when he lived in the south. He wanted to move someplace where he wasn't surrounded by poverty. He wasn't talking just about money. His family is very rich. I think he was talking about cultural poverty. Even in the south, people don't see movies, or plays or the opera or attend sporting events. They don't play games. They don't attend car races, or garden shows. They don't grow flowers. They don't read novels. They don't do anything. They don't take vacations to see mountains. They don't travel. It was a huge and curious thing when the Rouseff's went to the United States."

"I remember that. Yes, it was a curiosity. I never knew why they did that." The older man sounded truly mystified over Rouseff's bizarre behavior.

"My parents went with them. They went to see how other people live, to see how other people solve problems." I chuckled. "Mama and Rosalie Rouseff brought home catalogs from the states. They have more fun when they get a new catalog. Those catalogs aren't about money. The things in them aren't expensive. They are about novelty and trying something new and different."

The older man sounded somewhat stubborn. "I don't understand what you mean about this cultural poverty. Perhaps you and Andy see something I am too old to see."

"I don't think age has anything to do with it. Rouseff sees it. That is why he wanted to build the arena…well actually a whole entertainment complex." We fell silent again. I wondered if Mr. Corbain was trying to understand Andy.

I stayed with my head on the bed until the pain in my neck grew beyond endurance. I took Andy's hand in both of mine as I sat up. A nurse had just come into the room with a needle.

"What is in the syringe?"

"Morphine."

"You be careful with that stuff. He needs something for the pain but don't overdo it."

The nurse gave me a pitying look as she inserted the needle into the IV tube.

I glared at her.

I noticed some painkiller still in the syringe when she hurriedly left the room.

Both Andy's papa and I stayed all night in his room. We napped a little and talked a little. Sometimes, if Andy seemed restless, I put my head down in the bed, and he put his fingers in my hair.

The doctor came in about seven in the morning. I disliked him from the moment he opened his mouth. "Don't tell me this patient is still here."

"Where would he go?" I glared at the doctor.

The doctor looked startled by my question. "Who are you?"

Mr. Corbain answered. "He's Andrew's best friend. He's been here all night. He's also forbidden Andy to leave us."

"Mr.?" The doctor raised his eyebrows.

"Jaconovich, Prosecutor Jaconovich"

"Mr. Jaconovich, you must understand. His burns are extensive. If he survives the actual burns, infections will set in, and that will kill him."

In the back of my mind I wondered if this doctor was capable of putting someone down because he didn't know how to treat them. I smiled anyway. "Ah, I think I understand. Mr. Corbain is still alive this morning so the burns have not killed him. The next problem is the possibility of infection."

The doctor nodded.

I smiled again. "I understand that problem. It was a problem when Vanderholm shot my supervisor."

The doctor coughed and flinched as if startled. "Who are you?"

"I am Prosecutor Jake Jaconovich."

The man looked at me through narrow eyes then snarled. "I don't think I want you in this hospital."

I tried for a humble tone, but my thoughts were swinging more toward the idea that he would put down a troublesome patient. "I understand sir. I will be leaving in a little while. I must get back to my family and business." I tried for a sad smile. "Now, as I was saying, the problem of infection is something I've dealt with in the past. I am thinking that I want to fly Andy north to the city where he will have access to doctors from the university. They may be more equipped to deal with infections."

"Fly! That man cannot sit in an airplane. That would kill him faster than an infection." The doctor clearly thought I was crazy. He hadn't watched as many foreign films as I had.

I remembered to act patient. "Of course he wouldn't sit up. I will take him on a stretcher with a medic or two to take care of him. We will take a helicopter. People do this all the time in other countries when someone needs to go to a special hospital. Our hospital is connected to the university. It would not be unusual for them to receive a patient like this."

I watched the doctor while he thought about my plan. It didn't take him long to decide to get rid of the responsibility of Andy. "I will call the hospital there and see if they can take him."

I debated telling him to tell the hospital that I would be with Andy. On one hand, they knew me, at least by reputation. It was my reputation for staying with my wife when they wanted to send me home that worried me.

I decided I would make a few discrete phone calls too. "Excellent. I will make arrangements for the helicopter to pick us up." I started making this up as I went along. I didn't even know where I could get a helicopter that could carry a man on a stretcher. First, I called the hospital emergency room and told them that I would be arriving by helicopter in a couple hours with a burn patient."

"Yes, Mr. Jaconovich. We will have everything ready. Do you want to set the helicopter down here?"

"Yes, if I can."

Now, I faced the problem of finding a helicopter to transport Andy. I knew of only one place to get such a helicopter. I called General Johan and told him what I wanted.

"Jake, I can't send a military helicopter out to transport your friends just because you ask."

"Oh! Oh yes sir!" I coughed and finally the magic words came to me. "I should have explained. Um…this is another security-of-the-court case. Mr. Corbain is the person who has been assuring the security of our elections. He has been fantastic at finding methods to prevent cheating."

The general questioned, "Do you think this attack has anything to do with our electoral process?"

I hedged. "That is a distinct possibility. There are a large number of people, particularly in the south, who would be happier if he were not the person in charge of our balloting process."

"I see."

I didn't say anything more.

General Johan became brisk. "Well, it will take us about forty-five minutes to get something off of the ground. Where are you?"

"I told him the name of the hospital again."

"Okay, I don't think they have a helipad. Have them clear the parking lot or a large lawn and spread a white sheet in the middle of it. I'll call the Southern district base to send someone to pick you up."

"Right. Thank you sir."

I went back to Andy's room. While I was on the phone, his brother had come back with Christina, Andy's daughter. I gave her a hug. "Christina, I've made arrangements to take your papa north so he can have the doctors from the university hospital help him. You and your mama can come stay with me."

She sniffed and looked at me in wide-eyed wonder. "I thought he was going to die."

"No your papa is too important to die, and he's too brave to leave us now. The army is sending a helicopter to transport him in about an hour."

I spoke to Mr. Corbain and Andy's brother while I kept an arm around Christina. "Any of the family who would like to stay near him is welcome to come stay at my house. I also own a decent hotel that is closer to the hospital if you would prefer."

Young Corbain looked at me and scowled. "Why is the army sending a helicopter? Our family doesn't have anything to do with the army."

"I called them. Oh! I better let the nurses know how soon they have to have him ready to transport." I returned to the nurses' station to send nurses scurrying in every direction to figure out how to prepare a patient for transport by helicopter.

The doctor returned to Andy's room just after I got back. He looked a little bemused. "They told me the emergency room will be ready for him."

The process of preparing Andy to be transported turned gruesome. He had been bleeding and losing fluids from his burns. The whole mess stuck to his bandages, and they stuck to the sheets. When they tried to move him off of the sheets the skin started coming away from his body rather than his body off of the sheets. Andy let out a yelp of pain. Christina screamed and started to cry. Mr. Corbain nodded to Young Corbain to remove Christina from the room.

I took charge. "Cut the sheets! Cut the sheets away from the bed!" I used a firm voice.

The nurse turned to me and whined, "We don't have enough sheets to be cutting them up."

Andy's Papa turned slightly purple. "Good God woman. I am The Mr. Corbain. Cut the sheets, and I will pay for them!" He used a firm tone too.

I looked at him and grinned. "You know sir, you might really be his father."

The hint that Mr. Corbain's wife might have cheated on him nearly fifty-years earlier made everybody giggle. I thought the giggling was a better attitude to have around Andy than the insisting on his death had been.

I never let the possibility that Andy could die enter my head. Perhaps my heart feared for his life, but my head refused to admit the possibility. We got him onto a stretcher while Mr. Corbain kept assuring the hospital staff that he would pay for every bit of equipment his son used.

The helicopter was waiting by the time we had Andy ready to leave his room.

On the way out Christina hugged me. "Thanks for yelling at them. Take care of my papa. I'll come when I can…but…Mama…Mama…might not let me come."

"You talk to your Grandpapa Corbain about that."

She smiled at me.

I rode in the helicopter with Andy and the medics back to the city. They gave him enough morphine that he slept during the whole trip. When we reached the hospital, the emergency room staff was waiting for us.

Andy spent six hours in surgery having his burns treated. The doctor was reassuring when he came out. "He made it this long, he has a good chance of survival. He will be badly scarred. One eardrum is broken. We'll have to wait to see how the eye on that side recovers."

While Andy was in recovery, I decided to go home and get cleaned up. I remembered I hadn't seen Leah before I left home. She was home when I came in shortly before I usually got home. She was surprised to get a big hug and kiss. For a few seconds I thought maybe our marriage would be better if she got more big hugs and kisses.

"Jake stop that. I have to go get the children. I'll be late. I'm mad at you for taking off like that and not telling me where you went."

"We'll discuss that on our way to get the children." I turned and headed for the door. "Is Jacob at the gym? Where are the girls?" I let Leah drive.

As soon as we were on the road, Leah told me through gritted teeth that yes Jacob was at the gym, and the girls had stayed after school for Mass. "They've been insisting on lighting candles for Andrew. Nothing would calm them down last evening except for me driving them in to the cathedral to light candles."

"Ah, so as soon as you got home, I assume they told you where I went."

Leah's silence told me that she had known where I was.

"Now, for the mad-at-me-for-taking-off part of your complaint. I suppose that could be valid. Leah, I stand by my friends. I was certain before I left that the children were cared for. Leah, would you really want a man who abandons his friends when they need help?"

She looked away from me.

"I thought not. I stayed by you when the babies were born. I made certain you had the best care possible. I've taken very good care of you. You have no reason to complain when I take a day to take care of a friend."

She looked pouty.

"Now, do you have any further complaints?"

She didn't answer.

"Ah. Well, I liked that hug I gave you and think we ought to do that more often. The kiss was rather fine also." I was trying to give this discussion a slightly silly tone, but it was hitting close to the center of what I imagined to be our troubles.

"Jake, don't be silly."

"Leah, I'm dead serious."

"We're too old for that."

"For what? For love? People are never too old to love."

She pouted. "You know what I mean."

"No. I have no idea what you mean. Do you think we are too old for sex? I'm not too old for sex, and you are a very sexy woman." I smiled at her hoping the compliment would make her smile. It didn't.

When we picked up the girls from Mass, we discovered that Jacob had left the gym early to attend Mass with his sisters. The second the children were in the car, Elizabeth demanded. What happened? How is he?"

"He is still alive." I went on to explain about Andy's injuries and what I had done.

Jacob asked, "Did you bring him up by helicopter?"

Leah was still driving so I could turn and look at Jacob in the back seat. "How did you know that?"

"I didn't know. At break-time today, we all saw the military helicopter come from the south and sit down at our hospital. We all wondered. I suspected that was you bringing Uncle Andy up here."

Mary Anne spoke up. "Some of the children had never seen a helicopter before. We all stood and watched. Some didn't believe that you had ridden in one before. I told them that you had just gone south in one."

Her tone told me a great deal about how she felt when the others had doubted her.

She continued. "We all thought the helicopter might be you bringing Uncle Andy back because our hospital has university doctors."

Now I looked at Mary Anne. The mixture of schoolgirl resentment over her peers doubting her word, mixed with her understanding of why Andy would get better treatment here confused me slightly.

I smiled at her. "I am thankful that at least somebody grasps the need to transport him without a long explanation about the university."

Jacob took a stern, admonishing tone with me. "Papa have you been looking at people again so that they pee their pants?"

"It sounds like he may have raised his voice a few times." Elizabeth seemed to know me fairly well, and giggled as if this was funny.

"Well, I may have scowled a few times, and Christina thanked me for yelling."

Elizabeth sounded doubtful. "Should I call Christina?"

Leah surprised me with one of her rare moments of insightful advice. "Yes, it would be a good idea for you to call her before dinner. She may need to talk to someone closer to her age. Invite her to come stay while her father is here."

Chapter 41 Andy and Adele

Andy healed faster than the doctors expected. I thought that might have something to do with the salve and leaves the Chinese doctor, I hired, used to treat his burns. The salve and leaves horrified the hospital staff. I got a lecture about superstitions, and barbaric, unscientific treatments.

I looked at the staff, who had formed a small committee to confront me about the Chinese medicine. I sighed. "You know, you may be right. What if you are wrong? Is Andy comfortable enough?"

"Yes, he does seem as comfortable as possible under the circumstances."

"Well let's not interfere just yet." I was glad that we hadn't interfered.

The Chinese doctor told me the minor burns hurt the most so he treated them before he started on the bigger burns. He agreed that some areas were beyond his skill. "Let the western doctors do their skin grafts. I will make certain the grafts take."

The combination of treatments together with Andy's sheer stubborn will helped him live. He didn't get an infection. Eight weeks after the explosion, I brought Andy home to stay with me and hired a nurse to take care of him. He was by no means well. He no longer needed IV fluids.

Christiana was staying with us when he came home. I noticed she was particularly weepy. Elizabeth finally confided the problem to me. "Christiana has told me that her Mama filed for a divorce."

I hugged Elizabeth. "Sweetheart, I don't believe in divorce. I believe that people should live as my mama and papa have." I looked out the window. "Sometimes people were never meant for each other in the first place. I think that is the problem with Andy and Adele. She is a nice enough person. Andy is someone special. He is a seeker of knowledge. She never understood that in him. I'm sorry for Christiana's hurt." I sighed. "I am not surprised. I don't think Andy will be surprised. Is there anything I can do to help?"

Elizabeth whispered, "Will you talk to Christiana?"

"Of course."

After dinner while the others were busy with schoolwork, I took Christiana to my study. "Elizabeth told me about the divorce. I am sorry for you. Is there anything I can do to help?"

Poor Christiana bust into tears and nodded.

I waited while she cried then netted herself in.

She sniffed and gulped. "Mama wants me to...me to...." She gulped and blew her nose. "...she wants me to give Papa the papers. That is why she let me come up."

I was beyond angry. "No wonder you are upset. You should not be a go-between for your parents." I paused and breathed trying not to raise my voice in front of poor Christiana. "You may bring the papers to me. I will discuss this with your papa and make the proper arrangements."

Christiana sniffed again. "Mama doesn't want you to be Papa's attorney."

"I am not a divorce attorney. I will be acting only as a friend. I will find him a proper attorney since he is too injured to find someone himself. Assure your mama that I will not be representing Andy in this matter."

"She doesn't even want you to know."

I sighed. "Christiana, I've known for years that things are not right between your parents. Andy and I have talked half the night away several times trying to figure out what went wrong, and what he could do to make things better."

"You mean he doesn't even know why she wants a divorce?"

"No."

The poor young woman before me looked unbelievably sad. "He never figured it out?"

I shook my head. "He has no idea."

Christiana sighed. "Mama has a cousin, Stiles. They are very close. They're cousins so they can't marry, yet they want to be together. She wants to be with Uncle Stiles." She looked away. "I see how happy she is when she is with him. I want her to be happy. She would never admit this, but I think she was often cross with Papa because she blamed him for separating her from Stiles."

I sat silent for a full minute, stunned. "No. No, Andy never guessed that she loved someone else." I sighed and looked at the ceiling. I shook my head. "We had no idea."

I searched the ceiling for some clue that would have told us that Adele loved someone else. While I sat in the silent room, I remembered to breathe in and out. Finally, I was able to speak. "Thank you for explaining this to me. Believe me when I say your papa had no idea. I think this knowledge will help him." I looked out the window, still in shock. "I'm sorry you had to be the one to bring this news. Your Mama, or Stiles, or someone other than you should have been the one to share this knowledge."

"I'm not certain how many people know. They are not often together outside our rooms."

I asked, "That is the real reason she wanted to live in her family home?"

"Yes, I suspected as much before we moved south. Uncle Stiles called several times a day. Once he came to visit. When Papa was gone, they went into the bedroom and locked the door. I was alone in the house for a long time. I remember Mama didn't put me in my bed for my nap. I decided to sleep in my doll's cradle, so I did. While I was sleeping, it broke, and I fell on the floor. I woke up afraid. I went to Mama's room and tried the knob, but the door was locked." Christiana looked at the wall as she talked.

I watched her and ached for the little girl who grew up knowing her mama did not love her papa. I kept my mouth shut and listened. I knew Christiana needed to tell her story to someone who would listen.

"One day when there was talk of a purge in the city, I heard Mama on the phone with Uncle Stiles. She was crying and saying how she hated being separated from him. They talked for a long time. The next morning she took me, and my favorite toys, and boarded a train south. She promised me that papa knew we were leaving. She said he needed to stay in the north." She paused.

I told Christiana. "He didn't know you were leaving. He was horrified to come home and find you gone. He was afraid to be alone that night. He took the train to the capital and stayed with Candice and Johan."

Christiana nodded, "When Papa came south just a few days in our wake, I thought then that Mama hadn't been honest. I saw how Uncle Stiles hovered over her. I saw how Mama smiled at him. I heard her laugh." Christiana paused and thought for a minutes. Her last words were wistful. "She hadn't laughed for a long time." Christiana ended her story there.

"Honey, I'm sorry you had to grow up with these secrets all around you. You don't have to keep those secrets. Nobody should have to keep those kind of secrets."

She smiled at me. "I'm glad I told you. I assumed Papa knew, but loved

Mama anyway." She looked away and repeated, "He never knew."

I tried to sound comforting. "When he is feeling like talking about the subject, I will tell him. It will be soon. I think knowing the truth will give him more energy to heal. His guilt from thinking that he did something wrong has troubled him deeply."

When Christiana left my study, I hoped she felt as if she had a friend who didn't expect her to keep secrets.

The day after my interview with Christiana, I found a divorce attorney for Andy. I still hadn't talked to him. He was much weaker than I had realized. It was taking all his strength to get well. I thought I would let the subject rest. I could talk to his attorney.

Two weeks after Christiana shared her mama's secrets, I finally talked to Andy about Adele. The doctor told him that he needed to start walking short distances. This was a challenge because the burns had damaged the nerves to his left leg. In the morning before I left for work I helped Andy stand and walk twice across his room. I did the same thing after I got home from work.

Late in the evening before I went to bed, I checked on Andy again. One night I found him sitting up in bed reading.

"Why aren't you ready to sleep? Did you take your sleeping medicine?"

"Yes, it didn't help. My skull is spinning and spinning. It runs from one subject to another."

I sat down beside the bed. "Well what subject is it running on right now?"

"The explosion. There was no need to have anything in that room that would explode."

"Ah, yes. The explosion. We're working on that. Several people suspected that there was something wrong with that explosion, and several people know that you are the person who has been in charge of the balloting process for our elections. Colonel Paul is in charge of the investigations."

"Ah. It is in capable hands. What have they learned?"

"It was in fact a bomb. The thing had been stored in the janitor's closet earlier. Someone moved it to the classroom."

"It seems unlikely that anyone would know that I would be there on that day. Is it possible the teacher was the target?"

"The current theory was that it was a student with a grudge against that teacher."

Andy shook his head.

I said, "Next."

"Did I really ride in a military helicopter to get up here? Or more importantly, how did the man who didn't know how to take his clothes to the laundry manage to get the military to transport me?"

"First of all, I didn't know of the existence of laundries. I did know of the existence of helicopters. I've seen enough foreign films to know they can be used to transport wounded people."

Half of Andy's face grinned at me.

I told him the story of how I got the army to furnish him with a helicopter. "Next."

Andy sighed, and his face sagged. "Christiana was upset over something more than my injuries when she was here."

"Yes, I suspect you will want to call her soon. I promised her I would talk to you about Adele." Again I told Andy everything I knew.

"Another man? She has been making me feel like shit because of another man? She has been cheating with another man since Christiana was a baby?"

I nodded to all his questions.

"Is this attorney you got me any good?"

"He's the best I could find. He has made the preliminary responses."

"Thanks for taking care of this. Another man?'

"Yeah, apparently this started before she married you."

"She couldn't marry him, so she married me and kept him." I couldn't blame Andy for the anger I heard in his voice. "She shamed me in front of my family, friends, and acquaintances." He paused. "Jake I may not be thinking rationally. No…Jake…that first night in the hospital, I knew you would protect me. I wanted you close to protect me. I was afraid the doctors would give me too much painkiller and kill me. I knew you wouldn't let them. When I was totally defenseless, I heard what my brother said. Jake, I want my family and friends to know what Adele did." He paused and thought for several minutes.

"Jake you know the truth. She pursued me. You saw how she was. I was flattered that such a beautiful girl was so wild about me. She was beautiful. She was everything a man could want, and she was wild about me."

"I remember. That is something that always puzzled me, how a girl so much in love could change her mind so suddenly."

"She wasn't in love with me then. She saw I was gullible, and she pursued me. Jake I have a big enough fight just to get well. Can you make certain everybody knows the truth?"

"Is the truth that important?"

He nodded.

"Do you think it will hurt Christiana?"

Andy paused and thought some more. "Christiana has been living with the truth all her life. I don't want my daughter to think that it is okay to use a man as Adele used me. Let her see what others think of the truth."

I nodded.

"Promise?"

"I promise."

Andy's eyes drifted closed.

Chapter 42 Jacob's Birthday

Two months after the hospital released Andy, I got an invitation to a meeting at Professor Ingleman's house. I sent my regrets saying it was Jacob's thirteenth birthday. I got an invitation back for the following week, so I responded for both Andy and myself.

For Jacob's birthday, we gave him a party with his friends. The boys spent the afternoon playing games and swimming.

As soon as the young men left, I told the housekeeper not to wait dinner for me and took a walk to the top of the ridge. I remembered my thirteenth birthday. I looked at the growing city. I tried to remember how much smaller it was nearly thirty years ago when I stood on this ridge and watched a quarter of the city burn.

Where had the thirty years gone? I remembered scenes from my past. I realized that the country had changed. I remembered the purge when Jacob and our new democratic country were born.

In my memory I saw the flames of M'TK burning. That was the first purge I remember. I'd lived through two purges, a change of government, and two constitutions. Strange, I didn't really feel much older than when I stood on this ridge and watched my home burn.

I stood there until after the sun went down then descended the ridge in the dark. My house lit the night guiding my footsteps on the well-worn trail. The housekeeper had waited dinner for me. I thanked her. "But, that was unnecessary."

"Oh, everybody is so full of cake and picnic lunch that they weren't ready for dinner."

During dinner, the children enjoyed reliving the delights of the day. Mary Anne giggled, "I think the funniest part was when Elizabeth tossed Zini in the lake."

I repeated the rules about the lake horrified that Elizabeth had disobeyed. "Funny? I've warned you about the dangers of fooling around on the dock."

Elizabeth's cheeks flushed red. "I wasn't fooling."

Mary Anne wasn't giving up her point. "That is what made it so funny. He has been hanging on your hem for months. You served him right."

I decided the best thing to do now was eat my soup and listen to how the conversation played out.

Mary Anne continued. "He deserved it."

Jacob gave me more information. "Do I need to take him out behind the cloisters?"

Ah so the boys settle their arguments behind the cloisters do they? I was learning a great deal so I kept my mouth shut.

Elizabeth tossed her hair. "I can take care of myself. If he tries touching me again, he will find out today wasn't an accident."

"Be careful you don't get in trouble." Mary Anne warned.

Elizabeth sounded angry and whiney at the same time. "Do you really think the nuns will punish me? He has gotten me into trouble with them enough with his cornering me and trying to hold my hand. If I hear one more lecture on the Virgin Mary, I will scream."

Now, I had an idea that Zini's papa was going to get a call late this evening. I looked around the table. My children were discussing the best moves for Elizabeth to use to toss Zini. Andy's good eye twinkled as he watched the children. Leah, looked…Leah looked…well…like Mama does when she is tired.

I asked, "Leah honey, are you tired?"

"Yes, I'm afraid I feel one of my headaches coming on. The sun was so bright. I stayed by the lake too long I think."

"Do you need my help getting to bed? I think you should go lie down now."

"Perhaps you are right." I stood and helped my wife to her feet and asked again if she needed my help to go upstairs.

She left, and I sat down. We sat and silently ate our dinner until after we heard her close the bedroom door.

Jacob sighed, "Whew, I don't hear her puking so maybe she'll be okay."

"Eww, Jacob." Both girls rounded on their brother at once.

"Well, she's not."

Elizabeth scolded. "You don't have to discuss it."

"Why?"

"Because when mom starts puking it is really spectacular and ugly."

Elizabeth's answer sent Andy and I into whoops of laughter. Elizabeth looked so tiny, and delicate, and beautiful like a china doll. To hear Jacob's language coming out of her perfect mouth was so incongruous we couldn't help but to laugh.

I wanted to find out more about the nefarious Zini. "I disagree with Jacob on the use of Otter on the playground. I preferred swinging elephant. I found Ducking Bird useful too. Neither of those will get dirt on your clothes." My children giggled so I continued my lecture. "Next, if your teacher asks if you have been fighting you can ask innocently if you look like you have been fighting. Ask if you have a smudge of dirt on you somewhere."

Andy got in on the discussion. "The word fighting implies that someone had a chance to hurt you. There is usually a confusing bit where others fall down, but that is not fighting." We laughed some more.

Andy laughed so much that one of his burns broke open and bled. I instantly turned contrite and helped him change his bandages. "Oh Jake, get over it. It was good to laugh. I feel better if I laugh. Ow! Take it easy with that. What are you doing?"

"I'm getting more salve on this. I think I will use a leaf too."

"You are a good friend to take me in and share your family."

I grunted as I worked trying not to hurt my friend. "That is how the world works. Twenty some years ago, you took care of me. You took me to meet your parents. You gave me a shadow of legitimacy when I was in school under false credentials."

"You give me too much credit."

I suggested, "Um what about the weekends we went to visit your family when the professors wanted us at one of their little meetings."

Andy instantly agreed, "Okay, we're even."

I snorted, "Well, those professors are still after our hides. We've been invited to another meeting."

"Oh hell, I wonder what it is this time?"

"Something horrible. They only invite me when something horrid is happening."

Chapter 43 Food, Failure and Starvation

Getting Andy to the meeting at Professor Ingleman's challenged both of us. He was fairly mellow with morphine, which allowed me to get him all the way to the car.

He could still barely walk. He put his left hand on my shoulder, and I reached around behind him, under his coat, and held him up with his belt. He hadn't been invited to the meeting by name, but we knew he was always welcome.

When we arrived, Professor Ingleman showed his surprise at seeing Andy. "Oh my God! Andy! Come in, are you okay? Can I help you?" I noticed his eyes fill with tears as he looked at Andy. Andy was too busy getting his left foot over the door sill to notice the look of horror on Professor Ingleman's face as the older man took in the visible scope of Andy's injuries.

We managed to get seated in our usual conference room. The poor students present made little effort to conceal their horror over Andy's appearance. The gathered professors did somewhat better, and greeted both of us cordially. Once settled, Andy asked for some water. He looked at the students.

"Good afternoon, students. I am Andrew Corbain. I remember my first visit to this group. If you are not terrified at being here, get over it. This group is terrifying, and I can promise you that today's discussion will be particularly bad. They only invite Jake and I when it is particularly bad. Oh, and don't assume for one second that my face will be the most terrifying event of the day."

I scolded, "Andy, don't frighten the children. I once needed to rescue one who was vomiting in the shrubbery after one of these meetings. We don't want them to start vomiting until after they leave." I hoped to ease some of the tension in the room and be perversely reassuring.

The other older men chuckled. Professor Stodola spoke up. "Andy, Jake, it is good to see both of you. Andy, I can't tell you how thankful I am to see you up and about. Jake, I should warn you to watch out for that son of yours. He doesn't have your reluctance about throwing others. He'll be tossing you around soon enough."

"Nobody tosses me unless I let them."

"Oh, I tossed you a couple times."

"You were the professor. I was a student with sketchy connections to the elite. I didn't wish to draw attention to myself." I tried to look haughty. The professors laughed.

Professor Ingleman opened the discussion. "Mr. Corbain was correct in stating that we save our more challenging discussions for him and Prosecutor Jaconovich." I saw a law student squirm in his seat. Professor Ingleman noticed it too. "Yes, this is the same man I've been talking about in class. Now, gentlemen and ladies, we have come a long way toward creating social justice in this country. I'd hate to see our attempts fail because of temporary circumstances beyond our control, in short, this country is starving to death."

Andrew's physics professor growled, "The grumbling from the south is that we are overpopulated because we haven't had a good purge."

I growled.

Professor Ingleman nodded to me. "Yes, Mr. Prosecutor, we thought you might have some better thoughts on the subject."

I leaned back in my seat, "I have been keeping something of an eye on the problem. Yes, our weather has not been cooperating with the farmers. We haven't had wheat for two years, and we lost one year of a rice crop. We've lost two potato crops. The catch from the north is down, partly due to fewer fish in the ocean, and partly due to the fact that the Fortenacs have only one boat operating. We have villagers with smaller boats going out, which is good for stability, but they are not big enough to haul in enough fish."

Andy added his evaluation. "Both Jake and I have been rather occupied elsewhere for the past couple months, but we can turn our attention to this question." Andy shifted in his seat and smiled. "I see an opportunity for internships in civics and public service." He looked at the students. "We can send students around to survey the countryside asking what people are doing about fresh foods. We will want to know if they can expand their production. We need to know why they are not getting food to market." Andy went on to list everything the students would need to find out about our current food supply.

I noticed the older men looking at him with a mixture of pride and grief. I saw Andy's former physics teacher brush a tear from his face. I thought perhaps they were seeing their old friend and former student under the scars and blind eye.

Professor Uzara said, "I can send my economics students out to research that question."

I remembered the university in the capital and wondered if they had students who could help with this inventory. A thought flitted through my skull. "When I am president, I will have student interns working at *all stages of government*." I wondered where the thought came from. I quickly smacked it down, and told it to never enter my head again. Ever. Never.

One of the students raised his hand. Professor Ingleman gave him permission to speak. His question was a good one from the point of view of a student. "Why should we have to do all this? Why doesn't the government do this?"

Professor Ingleman nodded. "The government is so new they may not be organized enough to do the job. Hell, they may not know they should be doing this job. Also, I see another possible reason the government has not done its duty. There are many, in this country, who want to see our elected government fail. It benefits some who seek power, if it can be shown this type of government doesn't work."

I thought Professor Ingleman believed his last statement to be at the root of many of our country's problems.

Andy shifted in his chair. "Ah, so I take it Jake and I have our marching orders. We are to figure out how to feed all the people in the country. What is that one or two million?" He started to get to his feet. "Well, we better get on this. Things should be better in a week or two." He stood.

I could see Andy's pain, but he continued in his jovial tone. "Stop by Jake's place and visit. I get a bit bored. His family coddles me so much, I don't have enough to keep me busy.

Andy and I did start researching the food problem. He used my phone at home to call his friends. I called from the prosecutor's office where I served as the acting supervisor while Mr. Farley and Sophia got their new house in order.

I instructed our staff to ask our offenders where they we finding food. I asked one man what he had been eating. "I has me route. I check the dumpsters behind the restaurants and bakeries. I killed a rat the other night, but there weren't much meat on it, and it was tough."

"Rat is okay. How did you cook it?"

"Over an open fire."

"Ah. First you clean the rat, then you boil it until the meat is loose on the bones. Now this is important, don't boil it too long or you will be forever trying to pick the bits of bone out of the meat. It should still be fairly firmly attached and come away from the bone in large chunks."

"How does a fancy man like you know this."

I chuckled. "You don't want to know."

When I arrived home from work, the children were waiting for me with their usual hugs. "Mama has a headache so Uncle Andy picked us up. He went to lie down."

I kissed Mary Anne on the head to thank her for her report. "I should call Dr. Liu for your Mama."

Elizabeth reported next. "I just called him. He will be here in about an hour. I told him that Andy seemed to be in pain after driving the car.

The last report came from Jacob. "Oh. And Uncle Andy said that he has a report for you on the food situation. It is on your desk."

"I suspect that what your Uncle Andy needs more than the doctor is a pair of handcuffs to hold him to his bed so he doesn't overwork."

Mary Anne sighed, "No, he would just drag his bed around the house, and look very white, and claim that the added exercise was good for him."

We all nodded and laughed. Jacob piped up in a fairly good imitation of Andy, "You all do so much for me."

"Miss. Elizabeth let me help you with your homework." Elizabeth didn't quite catch Andy's inflection.

Mary Anne had another revelation with her imitation. "Oh no, Mrs. Jake I can't let you carry water to those chickens when I like eggs as well as you do."

"That settles it, I'm tying him to the bed before I go to work." I tried to sound fierce which made my children laugh.

I read the report. In addition to the information Andy gained from friends inside the country, he'd printed-out an e-mail from the UN concerning emergency food shipments. They could ship us standard boxes containing basic foods. I looked at the list of foods in each box, and decided I would mention this to the men at our meeting next Sunday.

I called General Johan about the food situation. He listened to my whole story before he said anything, then he took charge. "I'll get my people working on the problem of getting food to market."

"Thank you general, that will help us all."

The army was able to buy some food from isolated locations and get it to market, or use it to feed themselves.

The weather remained hot and dry. The morgue remained constantly full. My parents were the oldest people living in their complex. Many of their friends and neighbors had died, mostly from the heat. Mama's and Papa's apartment was hot, but not dangerously so. I worried about Mr. Rouseff. He sat in his air-conditioned apartment and did not get enough exercise.

The number of women who couldn't carry a baby to term rose to a sickening number. All too often the mother died when she lost the baby. That year, at the depth of the famine, we had a small fraction of the live births normal in our country. The huge dip in the number of live births that year, has challenged our social planning and budgets ever since.

We faced another, thankfully small, source of business for the morgue. Vanderholm distilled the grain from Montangna Province. As usual, he paid his workers part of their wage in whisky. The prosecutor's office learned of the problem almost immediately. Mr. Farley called a staff meeting just after lunch break one day.

"We have a report of twelve people dying and another dozen or so getting sick from tainted whisky. We don't know how far the shipment has traveled."

"Has the Ministry of Health been notified?" I was beginning to wish our new government could get something right.

"Yes, I think so. The local prosecutor wasn't quite certain who should know, but he thought there was something about the Ministry of Health in the constitution."

"I will call them right after the meeting." I sighed. As far as I was concerned nothing was working right in my country. I was also grumpy, because Leah had taken off on one of her trips again without telling me where she was going.

"Thank you, Jake. I know this isn't really our business, but the prosecutors may be the only people who have read the constitution." Jeffrey ran his fingers through his hair. "Now that the weather seems to be cooperating, we may be facing more difficulties." He sighed. "I got a call from a friend in England. He says that he is certain our currency will be devalued again. I'm afraid the local currency is going to be worthless, once again. The importance of this for this office is that whenever possible, we need to be collecting fines in foreign currency."

This last statement produced moans, grumbles, and protests that our offenders didn't have currency from any country. "They might not be getting picked up for mugging people for money if they had any of their own."

Mr. Farley grunted. "Ah, the local poverty keeps us in business. The problem will be whether or not we will get paid in any form that is valuable. We may have an excellent source of foreign currency if the tainted whisky produces an excuse to take the Vanderholms to court again." He hastily added, "Don't ever tell anybody I said that! We are not supposed to be thinking about collecting money. We must think only of justice."

The whole country was unsettled. Gangs of marauding thugs roamed the country stealing food, destroying homes and killing those who could not escape them. The army would round up one gang only to have another spring up someplace else.

We had some problems with people rioting. The hunger made them angry. The heat made them mean. Much of the time they were too lethargic from lack of food to riot. Finally, the potato harvest came in. A rice harvest followed the potatoes. The fish run was good. Fresh fish came south on the train. The famine was over.

By this time, Andy felt well enough to live on his own. He went south to visit his parents and make certain everybody knew that Adele had married him when she was in love with her cousin. He finally returned north and settled into an apartment near the university. He intended to work on his doctorate.

Chapter 44 Constitutional Party

Andy was not to be allowed to work on his doctorate. He enrolled in classes. The first day of class he got an invitation to a meeting at Professor Ingleman's house. He called to invite me. "Jake, I don't know what new horrors this country is facing, but you and I have been invited to another student-faculty meeting."

"Shit."

"Yeah, that is what I said right out in economics class when I heard about the meeting."

"What? You disturbed the decorum of economics class by swearing?"

"Yeah, the professor didn't bother to look at me. He just laughed. He's evil."

"Well damn. I'd rather stay home and play with my children and work in the garden."

"And sleep in your chair in your study."

I sighed for my lost pleasures of the day. "I guess we better go."

"I think it's mandatory."

"Don't tell me you are afraid of getting kicked out of class for insulting a professor."

"I don't think I could insult him. He fawns on me and is suspiciously ingratiating."

"Damn."

"Yeah, damn." He hung up to go do his homework.

On Sunday, I picked Andy up, and we went to Professor Ingleman's together. When the professor opened the door, he acted overly delighted to invite us in. Andy and I looked at each other. He raised his good eyebrow. I nodded. This was going to be bad.

We greeted the new batch of students. The students who had met us before groaned when they saw us. Andy sounded grumpy. "What are you groaning about? It is Jake and I who bear the brunt of their insane ideas."

The professors laughed nervously.

"I notice we have some new students." I smiled at the unfamiliar faces. "Don't be too frightened. You won't be asked to do too much." I tried to be reassuring.

A student protested, "Except travel from one end of the country to another counting eggs under sitting hens." The student's companions looked miserable and nodded.

One boy whined, "Chickens are mean. I'm glad we get to eat them." The students nodded some more and looked pouty.

I looked at the students. "It's Andy and I who bear the brunt of their schemes."

Andy fingered the scar on his face, and a couple of new students looked ill.

The oldest professor cleared his throat. He voice was thin and frail. I knew his mind was sharp. Right now, his sharp eyes boring into me caused the hair on the back of my neck to rise. The elderly professor wheezed. "Jake, I wasn't so sure about you when you came to that first meeting. You didn't look much like a Rouseff. You had a reputation for disrespect. I later learned that your connections to the elite are sketchy to non-existent. I underestimated you. Forgive me. You have earned my respect many times over."

"Thank you sir, I am honored by your praise." Out of the corner of my eye I could see Andy looking smug and a bit uncomfortable. We both realized that I was being dressed and primped for something.

The other professors muttered their words of praise and assured me of their respect.

I decided to get to the heart of this discussion. "Ah, so I am so greatly respected that you disturb my Sunday afternoon to discuss some momentous topic."

They nodded and smiled.

The professors seemed to be reluctant to get to the point. This wasn't their usual style. I pulled out my skills for examining a hesitant witness. "I really don't think you invited me here to express your respect."

They shook their heads.

I slogged on. "Um, actually, the invitation was handed to Andy. Is he the object of your latest scheme?"

They looked fondly at Andy and smiled. I could tell they had no particular plans for him.

Professor Ingleman finally confessed, vaguely. "Jake, you have done more than any single person to bring about this new constitution and to keep enough people alive to support it."

"Others have done as much or more." I looked at Andy.

"Others have helped from time to time. You have worked constantly in the prosecutor's office and in your developments to bring justice and prosperity to this country. It is time for you to reap your reward." Professor Ingleman smiled and seemed to puff up with pride.

I still harbored uneasy suspicions. "Um…yeah…uh…just what might that reward be?"

Andy had started to smile and smirk. He was leaning back in his chair watching me. I wondered if he had figured out what they were talking about.

My martial arts teacher continued the dance around the topic as he addressed the other professors. "Well, we need to give him some background." Professor Stodola turned to me and began to lecture to the group. "I think we have formed a good foundation for a two party political system in this country. The old families have organized around what they are calling the Traditional Party. They call us the opposition, or occasionally the constitutional…." He stopped to cough.

Andy finished for him. "…Constitutional Conspiracy."

My old sparing partner clarified. "Um…uh…well…yes. I think Constitutional Party sounds better."

I looked at the speaker and chuckled. "Aw, Andy and I have been having more fun with being members of the constitutional conspiracy." I relaxed and settled back into my chair. We were just discussing political parties.

Professor Stodola chuckled and took up the discussion again. "We can hardly call it a conspiracy party. By calling it the Constitutional Party, we gain identity as the people who support the constitution. We are now to the point of recruiting members."

I nodded.

Professor Ingleman announced proudly. "Jake, it would mean a great deal if you would consent to endorse our new political party."

I almost laughed with relief. All they wanted was for me to support their political party. I tried to return their compliments with a gracious answer. "You have been honest men, willing to wait a long time to reach your goals and to work through legal channels to reach those goals. I will be honored to support your party."

I heard Andrew bark beside me. I looked at him.

He choked and chided the group, "You guys aren't fair. Look at that innocent baby. He has no idea what you want him to do to endorse your political party. I agree with you that there is nobody better, but he has no idea what he just agreed to."

I sat up and looked around somewhat alarmed. "What? What? I didn't agree to anything really. Did I? What is wrong with attending a few political meetings and helping plan policy?"

"Jake, my old friend, it is where they expect you to be sitting when you plan that policy--that is the problem." Andrew gave me a pitying look.

The physics professor sounded harsh when he addressed Andy. "You are staying beside him all the way, aren't you Corbain."

Andy nodded. "All the way. The only person who will give him more support is his dear mama. She's been waiting for this day for a long time."

I began to get the idea of the meaning under Andy's words. At least, I knew my mama. I looked at the men around me. They looked at me with pride, respect, and a shuttered joy. The students looked bewildered.

"Gentlemen, if you think that my support of this party includes running for president of this country you have the wrong man."

The students grew intent, as if they knew they were watching history.

Professor History of Law answered, "No Jake, we have made it clear for years that we think you are the best man we can find for this job. We know plenty of men who would like the job. They would be excellent, if they could get elected. We know you can get elected. You have the insight to stabilize this country."

At this moment, I looked into myself and recognized my isolation. I looked at the men around me. I recognized their respect. The hope I saw in their eyes humbled me. I was alone. They would be beside me, but it would be my life that would be torn apart.

I ran my hands over my face. "This is not the first time this idea has come up in this group, and my mama has talked about this for years, long before our first constitution—ever since the Fortenac case."

Professor Ingleman spoke in a soft, low, mellow voice. "Yes Jake. This has been your destiny, ever since the Fortenac case, or rather, ever since the event that caused you to attack that case with so much energy and passion."

The room fell silent while I remembered that event, while I remembered Kaylee's death. I remembered wanting to do something to help her. I remembered my impotent frustration. I remembered my grief. I remembered Papa's compassion when he took me to the Cathedral. I remembered my feelings as I lit that candle and prayed, "Thy will be done."

I realized I had bowed my head almost into my lap. I raised my head and looked at the eager faces around me. I sighed. "Mama is right. I am going to be your next president."

Delinda McCann

Delinda McCann is a social psychologist who has worked in the field of developmental disabilities for over twenty years. She has served on committees for the state of Washington and been an educational advisor to other governments. Her work has earned her the praise of doctors, government officials and families all over the world. She has published numerous articles on disability issues, education, and adoption. Her unique perspective and sense of humor have delighted her readers even when she has been writing about the reality of caring for a loved one who has a severe disability. When the world turns crazy, as it frequently does for the disability community, her friends say there is nobody they would rather laugh and cry with.

Fetal Alcohol Syndrome (FAS) is a major cause of numerous social disorders, including learning disabilities, school failure, juvenile delinquency, homelessness, unemployment, mental illness, and crime – US Senate Resolution Aug. 1 2012

Delinda lives a on a small farm near Seattle, WA where she raised her daughters and now runs a small organic flower business with the help of her husband and two giant poodles. She enjoys singing with her church choir and playing the piano-poorly. A brush with cancer made her realize that she needed to slow down, so she turned to writing fiction inspired by her behind-the-scenes experiences of advocating for and loving the people who are just a little bit different

Power and Circumstance

The last thing Jake and Celia have time for is romance. As President, Jake struggles to rein in an unruly country and Celia's farm demands every extra moment of her time. Both are caring for loved ones with dementia. Despite all the obstacles, being separated by thousands of miles, and a social gap the size of the Pacific Ocean, something begins to grow between them. Could this be real? Could they possibly find true love amidst all of the pain and responsibility?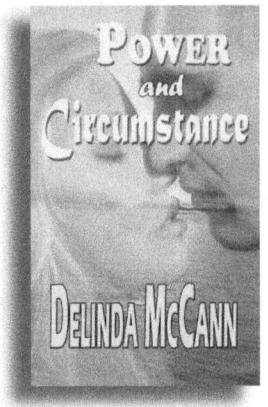

ISBN: 978-0-977723-55-3 Paperback
ISBN: 978-1-938586-73-6 eBook

"POWER AND CIRCUMSTANCE IS AN ABSORBING AND HAUNTING MUST-READ"

WILLIAM BERTRAM MACFARLAND
AUTHOR OF BACK CHANNEL - THE KENNEDY YEARS

Janette

When Janette's husband of almost twenty years tossed her out of their home so he could bring home his pregnant girlfriend, he set Janette on a path that sent ripples of change through the small desert town of Cascadia.

Life isn't all crime and detective work for Janette. As she put it, "My husband had a fertile week." She finds that she too is pregnant. Her age, exposure to farm chemicals, and the stress of being rejected by her husband combine to create a high-risk pregnancy. Her doctor tells her to avoid stress, which is easier said than done when someone convinces the regional library board to close her library.

ISBN: 978-1-938586-27-9 Paperback
ISBN: 978-1-938586-71-2 eBook

M'TK Sewer Rat - End of Empire

Jake was born the son of a common laborer and grew up on the mean streets of the Empire's worst slum, M'TK. Despite that, his father was able to instill a sense of worth and integrity within Jake that the streets could never beat out of him. M'TK did teach Jake when to fight and when to run and when he learned the army was coming to burn the city, together with his father, they saved the people of the slum.

ISBN: 978-1-938586-32-3 Paperback
ISBN: 978-1-938586-33-0 eBook

M'TK Sewer Rat - Birth of Nation

The new president's first act is to appoint a Supervisor over the Federal Attorney's office, a man loyal to him. Jake quickly discovers his new boss is one of the most notorious professional assassins in the country, an opponent worthy of extreme caution. It plunges Jake into a raging firestorm of corruption and greed among the highest levels of the fledgling democracy.

ISBN: 978-1-938586-34-7 Paperback
ISBN: 978-1-938586-35-4 eBook

Something About Maudy

Blackfish United Methodist Church was dying when Pastor Maude and her cat, John Wesley, accepted the assignment and moved into the parsonage. The elderly congregation did not want her. Pastor Maudy represented radical change with her navy-blue Porsche and actress background. Pastor Maude finds her place with the people as they all become embroiled in a tumultuous riot of assault, floods, and burglaries while the threat of closure hangs over the small congregation.

ISBN: 978-1-938586-43-9 Paperback
ISBN: 978-1-938586-44-6 eBook

Writers Cramp Publishing

http://www.WritersCramp.us

editor@writerscramp.us